Beryl Kingston was born and brought up in Tooting. After taking her degree at London University, she taught English and Drama at various London schools, as well as bringing up her three children. She now lives in Sussex with her husband.

Beryl Kingston's six previous novels, HEARTS AND FARTHINGS, KISSES AND HA'PENNIES, A TIME TO LOVE, TUPPENNY TIMES, FOUR-PENNY FLYER and SIXPENNY STALLS, are also available from Futura.

BERYL KINGSTON

London Pride

Futura

A Futura Book

First published in Great Britain in 1990 by
Macdonald & Co (Publishers) Ltd
London & Sydney

This Futura edition published in 1991

Copyright © Beryl Kingston 1990

'There'll Always Be An England' by Parker and Charles
Reproduced by permission of Dash Music Co. Ltd,
8/9 Frith Street, London W1
All Rights Reserved

'London Pride' (Noel Coward)
© Chappell Music Ltd
Reproduced by permission of Warner Chappell Music Ltd

ISBN 0 7088 4979 2

Printed and bound in Great Britain by
BPCC Hazell Books
Aylesbury, Bucks, England
Member of BPCC Ltd.

Futura Publications
A Division of
Macdonald & Co (Publishers) Ltd
165 Great Dover Street
London SE1 4YA

A member of Maxwell Macmillan Publishing Corporation

During the blitz the first plant to colonize the bombsites was a tall purple-flowered weed called rose-bay willow-herb or the fireweed, but known locally as London Pride. The irony of its rapid and perky appearance in the rubble was much enjoyed, and the plant soon became the symbol of London's resistance to the bombing. It was an excellent symbol, being everything that Londoners were at that time, boldly cheerful, resilient, cocky, undefeated, life-affirming, defiant, courageous and, like all weeds, potent and deeply-rooted.

I dedicate this book to those Londoners.

PROLOGUE

3rd August 1944

'Keep going, you bugger,' the chief warden said. 'Don't stop here. We don't want you.' He was standing outside the Wardens' Post by the council flats behind Greenwich Station, squinting up into the shimmer of the early morning sky.

'Aye, Mr Goodall, you can say that again,' his fellow warden agreed, squinting in the same direction, as he adjusted the chin strap of his tin helmet. 'Have you seen it yet?'

The two men could hear the doodle-bug's horrible tinny rattle somewhere to the south-east of them, phut-phut-phut, like a clapped out motor cycle, grossly amplified. It sounded pretty close but they couldn't see it through the huddle of roofs that hemmed them in.

It was the first flying bomb of the morning and the rescue teams had only just arrived at their post. Now they waited beside their battered rescue truck, checking last minute details and gathering strength and resolution just in case it fell in their patch.

'Did Tom get that ladder fixed, Mr MacFarlane?' the chief warden asked, not taking his eyes from the sky.

'Aye, he did.'

'Is Peggy on today?'

'This afternoon. She was there at both the incidents last night.'

1

'Ah.' Two doodle-bugs had fallen within two hundred yards of each other the previous evening and the reports showed that both rescues had been very difficult. 'She's a good girl our Peggy.'

'The best,' Mr MacFarlane said. 'I'd sooner be rescued by our Peggy than any other person I could think of. Present company excepted of course.'

The courtyards all round the flats were full of people, but none of them were moving. Factory workers sat poised on their bicycles with one foot on the ground, listening and waiting, children off to school with faces newly cleaned stood hand in hand, listening and waiting, women with shopping baskets over their arms and their hair tied up in workaday scarves, scowled at the sky listening and waiting. After two months under fire they all knew what you had to do when you heard a doodle-bug. You stayed close to the nearest cover and you didn't move away until the thing had passed over, just in case the engine suddenly cut out and you had to make a dive for it. Which God forbid! As the noise of this particular doodle-bug grew louder and closer they were all secretly saying the same prayer as the warden. Don't let it fall here. Send it somewhere else.

'Can you see it yet, Mr Goodall?'

A child's voice sang out immediately above their tin helmets. 'Over there, Mr Goodall. Look, Mr MacFarlane! There it is!'

There was a little boy actually leaning out of one of the windows on the first floor. Good God! what was he thinking of? If it comes down now he'll be cut to shreds.

'Get in out of it, you silly young fool,' Mr Goodall bellowed.

'That's young Percy,' a woman said. ''E ain't got the sense 'e was born wiv, that one. Shut the winder, Percy!'

'And go in to yer gran,' another woman ordered. 'His ma'll tan his hide for him when she hears.'

But just as the child obeyed and the window clicked shut, the sound of the doodle-bug suddenly stopped.

The courtyards cleared in less than two seconds. The two wardens shepherded half a dozen helter-skelter children before them and retreated inside the first aid post

2

which was on the ground floor of the flats behind a barrier of sandbags. But despite their speed the explosion began before they had time to crouch. They heard the first crunch quite clearly and then the appalling roar that lifted the floorboards and filled the air with dust and made their bellies shake and their ears feel as though they were swelling and splitting. Two of the children were whimpering and they all had their hands over their ears.

'That,' Mr MacFarlane said, 'was a wee bitty too close for comfort.'

'All over,' Mr Goodall said, automatically comforting the children, as the dust drifted past his eyes and all the other now familiar noises began, glass tinkling, falling debris pattering and crashing, somebody screaming. 'Anybody hurt?'

One little girl had a nose bleed, which the first aid team would soon attend to, but apart from that they were all OK.

'Come along then, Mr Mac,' he said.

Their bikes were still in the corridor and still upright. They cycled out into the beautiful warmth of the day, to the glass-strewn courtyard and the pall of dust and smoke that always marked the site of an explosion.

'It's just around the corner,' Mr MacFarlane said.

'With any luck, it'll've hit the recreation ground,' Mr Goodall hoped, pedalling towards Haddo Street.

But luck was out that morning. The flying bomb had fallen right in the middle of the line of terraced houses called Paradise Row. They set their bikes by the nearest wall and walked into the dust cloud. It was so thick that they could hardly see a thing, not even the ground under their feet.

'Is this not where Peggy ...?' Mr MacFarlane asked.

'Yes,' Mr Goodall said shortly. There wasn't time for conversation, or speculation, or compassion. They had a job to do, and difficult though it was they would have to do it.

The two men walked through the swirl of dust towards the centre of the explosion, peering to left and right, trying to assess the damage and to work out where they ought to start. There was no sign of the wood yard on the south side

3

of the street, and as there was so much shattered wood under their feet they felt fairly sure that was where the doodle-bug had fallen. The street shelter that had stood in the middle of the road all through the war had completely disappeared too. They must have walked right through the place where it had been. Now they were clambering about among piles of debris from a house, bricks, planks, plaster, shards of glass and broken furniture, and the chief warden had grown sufficiently accustomed to the dust to be able to see that two of the houses had gone too. There was an ominous fire burning in the rubble, and two other houses were shattered, their roofs gone and their bedroom floors tilted out of true and strewn with wreckage. Although, as the warden noted with his usual automatic accuracy, there was a brass bedstead still intact, covers and all, against one chimney stack.

By now several people were staggering out of the end houses, white-faced and dusty and obviously shocked. But they would have to be attended to later. First there was a message to send to Headquarters and then he had to check his list of occupants and then there would be the victims to rescue. As the dust cleared a little he could see one, a woman in carpet slippers and an apron, lying on her back in the middle of the road, streaked red and black with blood and dirt and so still she was either unconscious or dead. And not far away from her, pulling itself through the rubble by its front paws, was a small dazed tabby cat with two bleeding stumps where its back legs should have been.

'Tell 'em serious,' Mr Goodall said, giving Mr MacFarlane his message for HQ. 'Four dwellings, one fire.' Sniffing the air. 'Gas main's fractured.'

'Aye!' Mr MacFarlane said and ran off to collect his bike.

The chief warden checked his list. Then he took off his helmet and wiped the sweat out of his eyes. The rescue team were climbing over the debris towards him and there was an old man with a spade in his hand approaching from the other end of the street.

'Where d'yer want me ter start, Mr Goodall?' he called.

'Number six,' Mr Goodall said. 'Put that cat out of its misery will yer.'

'Poor little beggar,' the old man said. And he crushed its skull neatly with one heavy blow.

The woman in the road was being covered with a sheet.

'There's a Morrison shelter under this lot,' the warden said, walking carefully into the debris that had been number six. 'We'll start here.'

No, there was no time for compassion, barely time for thought. Just a job to do. But as the rescue team began to call instructions to one another, his submerged anger was thinking as it always did at such times, 'What did we ever do to deserve this?'

CHAPTER 1

4th August 1921

Peggy Furnivall was so happy when she woke up that morning she felt as though she was going to burst out of her skin.

It was the beginning of August and the beginning of the long school holidays, and the weather was so lovely you could play out every single day. But best of all – oh much the best of all – today was her seventh birthday, and seventh birthdays were special in the Furnivall family because they lived in the Casemates in the Tower of London and Dad was a Yeoman Warder, so when you were seven you were allowed to stay up late to see the Ceremony of the Keys. Imagine that! The Ceremony of the Keys. She was so excited she could have burst out singing.

She didn't of course. She didn't make a sound, for fear of waking her sisters. Big sister Joan, who shared her bed, was twelve and very nearly grown up, and although she was usually all right about most things, if you woke her before she was ready she could get a bit shirty. If you woke Baby it was worse, because she got straight out of her bed and went and told tales to Mum, and when that happened Mum got ever so shirty, and groused about it for ages afterwards. So birthday or not, Peggy got up quietly like the sensible child she was, easing herself from under the covers so as not to disturb Joan and tiptoeing about so as not to wake Baby, who was fast asleep in her truckle bed with her mouth open and most of her curl papers coming undone.

She washed ever so quietly too, pouring the water from the ewer to the basin over her fingers so as not to splash, and smoothing the soap from her face with a damp flannel so as not to make a sound. It was more difficult to empty the basin quietly into the bucket when she'd finished, but by that time Joan and Baby were beginning to stir, and Dad had gone clumping down the stairs making ever such a noise coughing to 'clear his pipes', so she didn't have to be quite so careful. She got dressed in her blue cotton frock, put on a nice clean pinafore, tied her hair back with her new blue ribbon and went downstairs to the kitchen to start her special day.

Dad was in his uniform trousers and his shirt-sleeves, sitting in his chair beside the stove, polishing his boots, and Mum was standing beside him busy with the frying pan, cooking bacon and tomatoes and thick slices of fried bread, and wafting trails of appetizing steam into the warm air of the room.

'How's my birthday girl, eh?' Dad said, beaming at her as she trotted across to kiss them. 'How's that girl who was born in the Tower?'

'I'm hunky-dory,' she said, using his favourite word and beaming back at him, as she climbed on his knee. 'Morning, Mum.'

'Born in the Tower,' he said, stroking his moustache with the remembered pleasure of it. 'If that ain't something to be proud of, I'd like to know what is. There ain't many can lay claim to an honour like that, let me tell you. And you done even better than the others, because you was born on a day of history, the day the Great War began.' He reached behind him and lifted the family Bible from its place on the dresser the way he always did on a birthday, opened it with a flourish, and showed her the familiar entry. 'Margaret Furnivall born in the Tower of London, 4 August 1914.'

The Great War meant nothing to Peggy beyond a muddled recollection of some very noisy celebration when it was over. It was the present day that was important to her. The present day and its pleasant rituals.

7

'Tell me all about it,' she said, and her voice was easy with the certainty that he would tell her at once, as he always did. She'd heard the story so many times she knew every word of it by heart, but she never tired of it. It was the start of every birthday. 'Please, Dad.'

'Well,' he said, settling her on his lap, 'when you was born – and a dear pretty little baby you was, so quiet and good – when you was born, I had to go straight off and tell the Constable of the Tower, didn't I, same as I did when your sisters was born. I had to go straight off and tell the Constable of the Tower, and the Constable of the Tower, *he* had to write straight off to tell the King. King George himself. You think a' that! And when the King heard you was born, bless me, if he didn't sit right down and write a letter to your mum, with his congratulations. And here's the very letter, bless me if it ain't.' And the letter was drawn very carefully and delicately from the envelope at the back of the Bible where it was always kept, so that they could read it together.

'So you see that makes you very special,' Dad said, finishing the story. 'A Londoner, you see. You can't get no better than that. Citizen a' the biggest town in the whole wide world. And a soldier's daughter to boot. Don't forget that. So you got to grow up strong and brave and proud a' yerself, ain'tcher?'

And she agreed with him, as she always did, nodding and smiling and feeling very strong and brave and proud of herself.

She adored her father. She knew every line of his dear old face by heart, all the lovely odd mixtures of colour and texture, his bristling hair, ('pepper and salt, that is,' he'd explain when she patted it) and the beard that was white on his chin and gingery where it curled about his mouth, and his cheeks that were covered all over with little wavery red lines like threads of cotton, and his eyes that were neither green nor brown but a sort of olive colour, striped with brown lines that radiated out from the centre like the spokes of a little toy wheel until they reached the rim, which was an extraordinary dark blue. ('God couldn't make up His mind, that's what it was, so He give me a bit of allsorts.')

8

Peggy's eyes were exactly the same colour as her father's, so God hadn't made up His mind about her either. It was nice to think that God wasn't quite sure of things, providing, of course, they were always unimportant things like the colour of your eyes or whether it would rain or not. He'd be sure about all the important things, she knew that, because Dad said so. Thanks to the things Dad told her and the things she heard in church of a Sunday, she had a very clear image of God. He lived in a palace, of course, just like the Tower, only bigger, and He was tall and bluff and kind and gentle and patient and protective, rather like Dad really, only older and with a white beard and a commanding voice.

Dad's voice was a mixture like everything else about him. He was gruff and gentle when he spoke to her or Mum or her sisters, but when it was his turn to be a guide and give a lecture to the visitors, he spoke so loudly you could hear his words right across the green as clear as though he was using a megaphone. Oh he was a lovely dad.

'Here's your sisters down,' he said, setting her feet on the kitchen floor again. 'Time for presents, eh, birthday girl? You ready?'

She scrambled onto her chair, more than ready, bright with happy anticipation, and the second birthday ceremony began. Baby first, because she was the youngest, shyly offering a card she'd made herself and signed with seven kisses. Then big sister Joan with a colouring book, which was a lovely present, or would have been if she only had some colouring pencils left. Hers were all worn down to the stubs. She kissed Joan's cheek affectionately and made private plans to buy herself some crayons bit by bit with her pocket money. And then it was Mum's turn.

Mum always made a great fuss of birthday presents, wrapping them up in tissue paper and tying them with a ribbon, but they weren't always as exciting inside the wrapper as they looked outside. In fact more often than not they were a bit of a disappointment. And this year's gift was no exception. It was a long, hand-knitted, tweed-coloured, winter scarf, beautifully pressed and carefully folded and undeniably dull.

9

When Peggy unwrapped the paper and saw what it was she was disappointed, but she didn't say so, because she knew you weren't supposed to pass comment on a present no matter what you thought of it. That would have been looking a gift horse in the mouth and Dad said you must never ever do that. Besides if she said the wrong thing she'd be bound to upset Mum, and that was something they all went out of their way to avoid, because Mum suffered with her nerves and when her nerves were playing her up she could get very shirty indeed.

It took quite a few seconds to think of something suitable to say, and they were very long seconds because Mum was standing right beside her, poised, with the newly-filled teapot in her hand, waiting, and Dad had his encouraging look on, and Baby and Joan were both watching her every move. She looked at the scarf all the time as though she was examining it carefully, and eventually she found the words among the threads.

'Thanks, Mum,' she said. 'It'll be ever so warm in the winter.'

'I should hope so,' her mother said, setting the teapot down on its trivet at last, 'the hours it's took me.' But despite the querulous tone of her voice, they all knew she was pleased by the answer, because she was patting the tea cosy, and she always patted things when she was pleased. 'You can wear it tonight,' she said, 'when you watch the Keys.'

'You got another present yet,' Dad said, handing his across the table.

It was a pencil box absolutely crammed with lovely coloured pencils.

'Oh!' she said, quite breathless with the pleasure of it. 'Oh Dad! It's just what I wanted.' And she slipped from her seat to kiss him rapturously, over and over again.

'Do you mean to eat this breakfast, Joe Furnivall, or don't you?' Mum said, quite crossly. 'You muck about any longer an' it'll all go cold on you.'

Peggy tidied her presents onto the dresser at once, and Dad looked a bit sheepish, and they all settled down to breakfast. There were meals to eat and chores to do no matter what sort of day it was.

10

The chores took quite a long time that morning, because their usual supper was going to be a birthday tea, so Mum was hard at work in the kitchen, and Joan and Peggy had to see to the bedrooms on their own, turning beds and airing bedding, emptying heavy slop buckets, polishing basins, beating rugs and sweeping into all the corners, tidying and dusting. As Joan said, rather wearily, there was no end to it.

'We shan't neither of us get out before dinner at this rate,' she complained.

'Never mind,' Peggy said, smoothing a pillow case. 'We got all the afternoon.' They were always allowed to play out in the afternoons.

'Eileen'll 'ave been waiting hours,' Joan said, tweaking the counterpane. 'If I don't look sharp she'll have something to say, I can tell you.' Eileen was her best friend and not one to wait with much patience.

Peggy's friends always waited for her without complaining at all. She had lots of friends because there weren't many children living in the Tower and they all went to the school in the Casemates so you could be friends with everyone. It was nice living in the Tower of London, like being in a village only right in the middle of the City. They had their own hospital in the Barracks and their own church on the Green and there were lots of wonderful places to play, out in the Casemates when it was dry, sitting in one of the arrow slit windows when it was wet, on the Green before the visitors arrived and even in the gun park on the Wharf overlooking the River Thames where you could strut about lording it over the visitors like anything because they were never allowed there. You weren't really supposed to be there either but that made it all the better.

That afternoon they played in the Casemates, British Bulldog and long rope skipping and 'What's the time Mr Wolf?' until heat and exertion finally slowed them down. Then they paired for gentler games like tops and dabs and hoops, and Peggy and her very best friend Megan found a quiet corner down by the archway that led to the Green where they could chalk out a game of hopscotch.

The chalking out took longer than the game because

11

both little girls were very particular about it. The squares had to be perfectly straight before they were satisfied with them, so there was much spitting on fingers and rubbing out, and they'd only just hopped the first round when Megan scrambled to her feet and put her grubby hand to her mouth in alarm.

'Oh lor'!' she said. 'Here comes the Bully boys. I'm off out of it.' And she went at once, trotting through the arch into the Casemates before Peggy had time to pick up the pebble for the next go.

The Bully boys were Fred and Sam the ten-year-old twins of Sergeant-Major Bullough, and most people ran away from them. They were rather undersize for their age, but what they lacked in inches they more than made up for in aggression. They had rough red hands and big booted feet and the fair hair that could have redeemed their faces with some softness if only it had been allowed to grow was cut back to a mere eighth of an inch of stubble so that their skulls looked misshapen and brutal. They walked like battering rams, bent forward from the waist, fists clenched and bullet heads to the fore, squat faces scowling.

Just the sight of them made Peggy feel uneasy, but she stood her ground and put on a bold face, because she was seven years old now, wasn't she, and a soldier's daughter and born in the Tower, and she had to be brave.

Even so, Fred, who was the first to reach her, looked horribly fierce. He came straight to the point. 'Stinko says you're staying up fer the Keys ternight. Is that right?'

'Yes,' she said, standing defensively, her body turned away from him as though they were fencing, and her toes flexed just in case she had to run.

'Yeh. Stinko said,' he nodded. 'That's all right then.'

She felt vaguely glad that it was all right, but she remained alert because the words were more ominous than their meaning.

'Me an' Sam are going on a ghost hunt after the Keys,' he said prowling round her so that they were face to face again. 'You game?'

'A ghost hunt?' she said, her heart quaking at the idea.

'Take you with us if yer like,' Sam said. 'Our mum's

12

cleaning the Salt Tower. We got the keys.' He had such an eager expression on his face, he looked as though he was barking.

Peggy didn't want to go on a ghost hunt at all. She knew there were lots of ghosts in the Tower, because everybody who lived there knew that, but until that moment, being a sensible child, she had managed to avoid thinking about them.

She tried to temporize, using her mother's formula. 'Don't know,' she said, staring him out. 'Depends.'

'What on?' Sam said.

She didn't know the answer to that, because nobody had ever queried her mother when she said such a thing. 'Why don't you take Stinko?' she suggested. 'He'd like it.'

'Give over!' Sam mocked. 'He'll be in bed, same as all the others. We'll be the only ones up that time a' night. Are you game?'

They had argued her into a corner. What could she say? She blinked at them in the strong sunlight. 'I don't think I want to.'

Her answer aggravated them. That wasn't what they wanted to hear. Nor what they expected, because she was renowned for being a sport and good for a dare. Look at the way she'd balanced along the wall that time. Oh no! She was to come with them, that's what. It wouldn't be half so much fun without a girl to frighten. They turned their combined powers upon her at once.

'What sort of answer d'you call that?' Sam said scornfully.

'She's scared,' Fred said, thrusting his bullet head at her. 'She's nothing but an old scaredy-cat.'

She defended herself at once. 'No I ain't.'

'You are!'

'I ain't!'

'If you don't come with us,' Sam said, 'you're a scaredy-cat. Proven.'

Faced with such crushing logic there was nothing she could do but agree to join them. She couldn't admit to being a coward, and specially not today. 'All right then,' she said. 'Only . . .'

13

But they'd taken her agreement and were already walking away with it.

'Ten o'clock sharp,' Fred called back to her. 'By the Bloody Tower.'

She stood where she was in the sunlight, turning the pebble round and round in her fingers, calm and still even though her heart was throbbing with alarm at what she'd agreed to do. A ghost hunt. She *couldn't* go on a ghost hunt. What if they actually saw one? It made her blood run cold even to think of it. Imagine being touched by a ghost. And what if it had no head? She'd heard enough about them to know that lots of ghosts were people who'd been beheaded. Imagine seeing a ghost walking towards you, ready to touch you, and *with no head*. Oh, she *couldn't* go. She just couldn't. But how was she going to get out of it, now she'd given her word?

'What did they want?' Megan said, shadowing up beside her.

'Nothing much,' Peggy said. But then as Megan continued to look curious and she felt she had to offer some sort of explanation, she added, 'Just if I was staying up for the Keys.'

'Did you tell 'em you was?'

'Yes,' Peggy said, thinking, if only I hadn't.

'Lucky you!' Megan said with some envy. 'I wish it was me.'

'Your go,' Peggy said, handing her the pebble. Their conversation was making her feel uncomfortable, keeping thoughts of the ghost hunt prickling in her mind when she would rather have been cheering herself up by thinking about something else. As Megan went hopping through the squares with her skirts and apron swinging, she looked back across the cobbles at the Green, where two ravens were strutting and a Yeoman Warder was lecturing a party of elderly ladies.

The White Tower rose confidently before her on its high green mound, its rough stonework as yellow as sand and the dressed stone at every corner a quite dazzling white in the sunshine, battlemented, solid and dependable. It made her think of her father. I'll tell Dad, she thought. I'll tell Dad at teatime. I'll drop a sort of hint and then he'll say I mustn't go. That was the answer to the Bully boys.

But it was easier planned than done.

For a start there was a ritual to a birthday tea that couldn't be interrupted, and certainly not by stories about a ghost hunt. Mum's meat pie had to be properly admired before it was eaten with the customary green salad and chips and pickles, and the pie had to be followed by the singing of 'Happy Birthday', and then there were candles to be blown out and the cake to be cut, in carefully equal sections, except for Dad's. But when the last portion had been handed across the table and they were all contentedly munching, the moment seemed to have arrived.

'When me and Megan was playing out . . .' she began.

But Baby was speaking too and her voice was a lot louder. 'I want to stay up and see the Keys with Peggy,' she said, giving her father the benefit of her wide open eyes.

Dad went on munching and didn't say anything.

'When me and Megan was playing . . .' Peggy tried again.

'Well you can't,' Joan said, scowling at Baby. 'Because it ain't your birthday.'

'Don't see why not,' Baby pouted, tossing her curls. 'I'm a big girl now.'

'So you are, darling,' her mother agreed, spearing her next mouthful of cake with a deft fork. 'I don't see why she shouldn't, Joe. She's plenty big enough and she'd love it.'

Joe Furnivall raised his great head from his double slice of cake and munched for a while, contemplating his family with the placid gentleness of all grazing beasts. 'Yes, she's big enough,' he said peaceably, 'I'll grant that, Mother. The point is, she ain't *old* enough. Seven is when you see the Keys in this house. Our Joan was seven, weren't you, Joanie? And now Peggy's seven. And in three years our Baby'll be seven and *then* it'll be her turn. But not before. Fair's fair.'

Peggy made her third attempt. 'When me and Megan . . .'

'Hush!' her mother said, flicking the word sideways at her before she turned her full attention to her husband. 'It

15

wouldn't hurt,' she said. 'She'd be ever so good. After all she's nearly old enough, and if you let her go, we could all go. All the family.'

'Seven,' Joe Furnivall said. 'Seven's old enough. And in any case it ain't a family treat. It's my treat for my daughters on the day they're seven.' And he closed the subject and ended the meal, standing up with an abruptness that showed that any further attempt at argument or conversation would be quite impossible.

'Time I was off,' he said, polishing his moustache with his napkin. 'Get to bed sharpish, you girls. You too, Peggy. Three hours, shut-eye under the coverlet, there's a good girl, same as Joanie did. I'll be back for you at twenty-five to ten. Lovely tea, Mother.' And he was walking away.

'Dad!' Peggy called after him. But he'd already reached the door.

'Twenty-five to ten,' he said, putting on his blue jacket. 'Make sure you're ready,' setting his cap on that salt and pepper hair. And then he was gone.

Oh dear, Peggy thought, now what shall I do? The lamplighter was lighting the gas in the street outside the parlour window. She could hear the pop of the gas, and then his feet clomping away along the cobbles. Then two Yeoman Warders passed in their everyday clothes on their way to the Club, chattering companionably. What was it Dad always said, when you were worried things might go wrong? 'Never trouble trouble, till trouble troubles you.' That was it. I won't think about it, she decided, for the second time that day. I'll think about the Keys. But it was the key to the Salt Tower that kept swinging into her mind, held up in the tough fingers of Sam Bullough.

16

CHAPTER 2

'This way,' Joe Furnivall said, leading his little daughter through the arch and into the Tower green. It was twenty-five to ten and the ceremony of the Keys was about to begin.

Peggy walked beside him, holding his hand for protection. She had never been out in the Tower at night before, and even though there was a full white moon in the black sky above her head, it was very dark out there beneath the White Tower and now that the visitors had all gone home the place looked enormous and strange and threatening. During the day it had been a village green surrounded by familiar houses, now it was a place of menacing shadows flickering against the walls and patches of terrifying darkness breathing in doorways and arrow slit windows squinting down at her like sharp little eyes. Oh there were certainly ghosts about tonight.

'Is it far?' she said, and her voice was no more than a whisper.

'Traitors' Gate,' he said cheerfully, bounding down Broad Walk Steps.

'When me and Megan was playing ...' she said, making yet another effort.

But he wasn't listening to her. His mind was set on the treat ahead of them and he was striding towards it so quickly that she had to trot to keep up with him. Down the steps, along the path, under the Bloody Tower. No sign of the Bully boys yet, which was a relief, but once they were

17

through the archway and into Water Lane she could see a group of toffs standing about in front of the terrible bars of Traitors' Gate. That was a surprise. Had they come to see the Keys too? She thought she'd be the only one.

They were making ever such a noise. The ladies kept giving little high-pitched laughs like rooks cawing, and flicking their fur stoles over their shoulders, and shifting about on the cobbles in their high-heeled shoes. And the gentlemen were all going 'Waw-waw-waw' like bloodhounds baying, when they weren't sucking at their cigars. Oh dear, she thought, he'll never hear me in all that row, even if I speak up as loud as I can, and in any case she couldn't do that, because it was a bit private really, not something to go shouting about in front of strangers.

'Here we are,' her father said, walking right up to the group and standing beside them. 'And here's the others, and your Uncle Charlie.'

Uncle Charlie was really called Yeoman Warder Macpherson and he wasn't her uncle at all, only her godfather. He was a very loud man who smelt of snuff and brass polish, and had a nasty habit of pulling your hair or tweaking your ears when you weren't looking, but for once Peggy was quite glad to see him, striding up Water Lane towards them with three other yeoman warders all in their ordinary clothes. If she couldn't get Dad to forbid it, then the more people she had round her tonight the better.

'Right on time,' Uncle Charlie said, rolling his R's in that Scottish way of his. 'Looking forward to it eh, girlie?'

'Oh yes,' she said, because she *was* looking forward to the ceremony.

'Been going on four hundred years,' Uncle Charlie said. 'Every evening the same. Never stops. Not for war or plague or peasants' revolts or anything. While we've ravens in the Tower and the Ceremony of the Keys every night, we've no need to worry about the safety of the nation, eh?'

Peggy tried to look impressed, but it was difficult because it wasn't the safety of the nation she was worried about.

'Here they come,' her father said. 'Not a sound now.'

There was a little procession marching towards them

18

along the lane. The toffs stopped talking and turned towards it, craning their necks, and in the sudden silence, Peggy could hear the crunch of boots and something jangling rhythmically. Then peering round her father's bulk, she saw a lighted lantern bobbing towards her and above its light two ranks of scarlet jackets and a gleam of rifles. And there was the Chief Yeoman Warder in his lovely red uniform marching along between two rows of guardsmen and looking really rather short and stout between their tight-fitting jackets and the great furry height of their bearskins.

She watched absorbed as the procession marched down Water Lane and through the gate beneath the Byward Tower and on through the darkness towards the outer gate in the Middle Tower, the lantern flickering and diminishing but the sound of boots as strong as ever. Keys rattled and clicked, an invisible sergeant-major sang orders, boots stamped, their steel tips sparking quick flashes of fire against the cobbles, and they all came marching back again, as everybody in the little watching crowd stood still, listening and waiting.

And then, when they were no more than fifty feet away, a sentry sprang out of his box by the Bloody Tower and challenged them.

'Halt! Who comes there?'

It was very dramatic. Several of the ladies jumped, as though the challenge had been directed at them.

But the Chief Yeoman Warder took it all calmly, singing back the answer. 'King George's Keys.'

Not the Keys to the Tower of London, Peggy thought, nor the Keys to the Middle Tower, but King George's Keys, no less. King George's Keys. It sounded marvellously important.

And it satisfied the sentry, because he was allowing them to march back through the Bloody Tower the way they'd come.

'Is that it?' Peggy asked her father. The rich people were following the procession through the arch. Now perhaps she could tell him about the ghost hunt.

'No,' he said happily. 'The best bit's to come.' And he took her hand and led her through the arch and through the toffs until they were standing at the foot of the steps leading up to the Green.

It was like the pantomime she'd seen in the theatre last Christmas, when the curtains opened and you saw the stage full of beautiful people in lovely bright costumes all lit up with lots and lots of bright lights. The gaslights on either side of the Broad Walk Steps had been turned right up and the steps themselves were full of guardsmen standing to attention, jackets scarlet, buttons gleaming, bearskins ruffling in the night breeze. There was a trumpeter standing on the top step just above them, and the Keys and their escort had come to a halt at the bottom of the steps and were plainly waiting for something. Now what?

The watchers stood quite still, the guardsmen were motionless, and the trumpeter raised the golden bowl of his trumpet into the night air and sounded the Last Post. As the last sad note drifted away, the Chief Yeoman doffed his Tudor bonnet and called out in a loud clear voice, 'God Preserve King George'. And all the guardsmen answered 'Amen', their mouths dark O's in the gaslit pallor of their faces. And at the very same moment the clock began to strike ten, the long notes licking the silent air as the guardsmen stood to attention. Peggy was so moved that she felt tears pricking underneath her eyelids. To live here, in the middle of the great city of London, at the heart of the British Empire, with all the brave men who guarded the king, it *was* an honour.

'There,' her father said when the clock was silent and the crowd began to disperse, 'what did you think a' that?'

'It was like magic,' she said.

'Glad I brought you?'

'Oh yes! Thanks ever so much, Dad.'

'There you are then, little Peggy. You're a real Londoner now you've seen the Ceremony of the Keys. Never forget it.'

Uncle Charlie was standing in front of them breathing snuff-sour all over them. 'Are you coming to the Club, Joe?'

'In a minute,' her father said amiably. 'When I've seen the child to the door.'

'We'll walk with you,' Uncle Charlie said. 'We'll escort

you, girlie, as though you were the Keys. How's about that?'

It was a very fast-moving escort. This time she had to run to keep up, but she was very glad of their presence. Even if the Bully boys were already waiting for her under the arch they could hardly expect her to slip away with five Yeoman Warders guarding her.

'There you are,' her father said, when they'd crossed the Green and tramped through the arch into the Casemates. 'Off you go. There's a good girl. Kiss your old Dad goodnight.'

She kissed him happily. They were in sight of her front door. Almost home. She only had to run a few steps and she'd be safe.

'Night night. Sleep tight. Pray the Lord the bugs don't bite,' Uncle Charlie said, waving as they all marched back through the archway.

Silly old thing, Peggy thought. We don't have bugs in *our* house. Just as if Mum would allow *that*. But she smiled at him politely as she waved goodbye. Then she turned to run home.

And the Bully boys were standing right in front of her.

'They gone?' Sam said, squinting in the poor light.

She was so frightened she couldn't answer.

'Still on the Green,' Fred said, peering round the corner of the archway.

'We'll go the other way,' Sam decided. 'Come on.'

And he was off along the Casemates at a loping trot, with Fred beside him.

What can I do? Peggy thought. If I made a bolt for it and ran home they might ...

'Come *on*!' Fred hissed back at her. 'D'yer wan' us to be caught?'

'No,' she said, finding her voice. But perhaps she did. If they were caught, they couldn't ...

'Well then!'

'It's just ...'

'Shut up and run,' Sam said, loping back to her and threatening her with his face.

'And look sharp about it,' Fred said, equally fierce, pulling her by the hand and dragging her along.

21

So she had to follow them. There was nothing else she could do when they were bullying her so. She knew there must be an excuse, a reason for not going, something she could say to stop them, but her heart was banging like a side-drum and she couldn't think of anything. They were running along the inner wall towards the Salt Tower before she'd recovered from the shock of their sudden appearance, and by then her mind was jammed shut and incapable of any independent thought at all.

Despite the moon it was hideously dark, and below them the space between the wall and the White Tower was completely empty except for ghostly shadows and the eerie whispering of the plane trees. Sam had the key in his hand and was thrusting it into the black void of the doorway, making a scraping, grinding noise that sounded very loud and alarming out there in the night air.

But nobody heard it except them and the door opened just a little too easily.

'Come on,' Sam whispered. And they all went in.

It was dank and smelly and horribly silent. And when the door shut behind them with a reverberating clang the darkness was total. Oh please God, Peggy prayed, speaking instinctively to her protective deity, don't let there be ghosts please, don't let anything happen. And she backed until her hands were touching the chill stones of the wall.

The twins set about their evening's enjoyment immediately, making 'ghostly' wailing noises, and lunging at anything they could sense moving in the darkness.

'Look behind yer! Ooooooh! Ooooooh!'

'You don't sound like ghosts a bit,' Peggy said into the darkness, alarmed but trying to be scornful. 'You sound like owls.'

'Look beside yer!' Sam's voice warned on a note of rising hysteria.

She turned despite herself, her skin prickling, for there was something moving and breathing right next to her. And the next minute there was suddenly light in the darkness, and there was Fred, leaning against the wall with an electric torch held underneath his chin. The odd angle of the light made his face look just like a skull, all grinning

22

teeth and huge nostrils and glinting eyes set deep in awful black sockets.

'Don't!' she said.

He grinned at her more vilely than ever, delighted by the fear in her voice.

'Wooooh!' Sam howled, his face just discernible in the mist of diffused light at his brother's shoulder.

'I'm off upstairs,' Fred said, lowering the torch. Now that he'd scored first blood, he knew he could *really* frighten her. 'There won't be any ghosts down here. Stand ter reason. Not in a doorway there won't.' He was already feeling his way up the spiral staircase.

'They walk through walls, don't forget,' his brother said, panting at his heels, 'so why not doors?'

'Up here!' Fred's voice echoed down the stairwell. 'This'll be the place.'

If it was, Peggy had no desire to see it, but she followed the ascending flicker of the torch, feeling her way along the rough stone of the walls, because it would have been even worse to be all by herself in the pitch darkness. The unseen stones were rough and cold and as tacky as slugs under her fingers. She tried not to think that ghosts were trying to ooze between them.

'Here we are!' Fred sang above her head. And she stumbled on and found herself in the upper chamber.

Downstairs in the darkness had been bad enough but this place was worse. There was a faint metallic blue light filtering in through the high window, and the silence was so profound she could hear it hissing. As her eyes grew accustomed to light again, she could make out the brooding mass of a huge stone fireplace opposite her, solid and black-shadowed, and the stones of the tower wall which were a weird unearthly grey and seemed to be flickering and shifting as she watched them. A ghost could come walking through those walls at any moment, she thought. There'd be nothing to stop it. Oh please God, don't let a ghost walk through the wall.

Sam was prowling about shining his torch at the stones. 'Over 'ere somewhere is where they used ter call up the devil,' he said. 'Here it is. Look. That's black magic that is.'

The other two went to join him, Peggy trying not to appear too reluctant, Fred with swaggering eagerness.

The torchlight was shining on a complicated carving cut into a broad stone next to another door. It consisted of a circle inside a square, with lots of criss-crossed lines inside the circle and letters and figures all round the square. Despite her apprehension Peggy examined it closely. It had been a mistake to let them see how frightened she was downstairs. From now on she was going to keep her feelings hidden.

'That's not black magic,' she said, reasonably. 'Somebody's cut his name on it, look. "Draper of Brystow". And those figures are times tables. You can see.'

'No they're not,' Sam insisted, annoyed by her calm. 'They're black magic. Everyone knows that. Because why? Because this is the very room where the ghosts walk. They used to torture people in 'ere.'

'No they never,' she said stoutly, hoping it wasn't true.

'They did,' Fred said. 'They used to stretch 'em on a great wooden rack. When they'd finished with 'em their arms was so long they used to trail on the floor when they walked. When they come back – you know, as ghosts,' making the word as hideous as he could, 'that's how they look. With their arms all long and horrible.'

'They don't,' she said, but she wasn't quite sure. It all sounded just a little too likely in a room like this.

'They had a torture mask to put women in an' all,' Fred gloated.

'Yeh!' his brother said. 'When they talked too much. It had all spikes inside and they used ter wind it up tighter and tighter until all the spikes was sticking in. When *they* come back as ghosts, they come back all covered in blood.' It was frightening him to think of it and Fred was looking quite green.

She didn't argue at that, in case somebody walked through the wall and put her in a mask. She was feeling more and more upset by everything they said.

'I'll tell you somethink else,' Fred said, ghoulishly. 'If the mask didn't work, they used ter wall 'em up alive.'

The idea of being walled up alive was so terrifying that she couldn't keep her feelings hidden any longer.

'They never,' she said, her eyes bolting with fear. Oh what a dreadful thing to be walled up alive. It was making her feel panicky just to think about it.

'Straight up. Bricked in they was an' left ter croak.'

Fear swelled in her throat until she thought she was going to croak herself. She could imagine it, boxed in, with bricks all round her and no light and no air, boxed in, struggling to breathe, waiting to die. Oh it would be a dreadful, dreadful thing to be walled up alive.

'Come on,' Sam said, seizing his advantage because he could see how frightened she was. 'They got the instruments a' torture in the room above this. I'll show yer.'

He was through the second door and blundering about in the passage behind it, before she could say anything.

Fred went leaping after him, waving the torch. He was taut with fear himself and it was making him swagger more than ever. 'There's the stairs,' his voice called out of the darkness. 'Come on, Peg. I dare yer!'

Left on her own with her imagination, Peggy was so frightened she hardly knew what to do. In the horrible half light the great stones of the Tower walls seemed to be moving towards her, inch by inch, ready to crush her. I shall be shut in for ever, she thought, and she could already feel herself being buried alive under all those awful stones with ghosts walking about everywhere, trailing their long arms and covered in blood. Oh please God don't let me be buried alive. I couldn't bear it.

'Wait for me!' she called, running through the archway towards the stairs. Her heart was beating so wildly she could feel it in her throat and her knees were so wobbly it was an effort to walk leave alone climb stairs, but she couldn't stay there on her own waiting to be crushed under those walls. She couldn't.

The second staircase was steeper and narrower than the first had been, but she stumbled up, feeling her way along the stones, peering through the dusty half-light. Then she was round the first spiral and the curve of the walls suddenly cut off the light. She was on her own in total, terrifying darkness, with the hair standing on the nape of her neck and panic crushing her chest like a vice. She turned on the sloping step and flung herself downwards again.

'I'm going back down,' she called, trying to be sensible even then.

'What?' Sam's voice answered, eerily from the darkness.

'I'm going back down.'

But she hadn't gone more than four steps before something really dreadful happened. Somebody punched her in the small of the back. *Somebody* punched her. It was such a violent blow and so terrifying when she was already trembling in panic, that she stumbled and fell forward, losing her footing and her control at the same time and screaming like a banshee. 'It's the ghost! The ghost! On the stairs! Aaaaah! Aaaaaah!'

Panic and fear were constricting her throat like a noose. She was shaking all over. Even her stomach was shaking. There was nothing in the world except that awful shattering terror. She had to get out. To get out now. To get away. Now. Now.

Somehow or other her feet carried her downwards, stumbling and slipping, and then she was in the moonlight again and there was the high window gleaming before her and she threw herself at it, scrambling onto the stone sill and beating at the glass with both fists. 'Help! Help! Dad! Oh please somebody help me!'

After that it was as if she was frozen to the glass. She went on beating and screaming, weeping incoherently, on and on, even when she was aware that there were figures on the path below her, looking up and waving their arms. She was locked in with a ghost somewhere behind her and the walls about to bury her alive and she couldn't bear it. 'Help! Help! Oh please help me!'

Doors banged, and there were heavy feet on the stairs, men's feet, not ghosts', feet with boots on, crunching, and men's voices. 'Hold on! We're coming!' and then her father was picking her up, cuddling her close, carrying her away.

'Oh Dad! Dad! Dad!' she wept, clinging to him. 'I'm *so* glad to see you.'

'Hush, my pretty,' he soothed as he carried her down the spiral staircase. 'Hush now. You're all right.'

They were out in the fresh air, with the moon bright and

clear above their heads. Bright and clear and comforting. 'Oh Dad!'

He sat down on the grass underneath the nearest gaslight and cuddled her on his lap and set her beret straight and brushed the wet hair out of her eyes and produced a clean handkerchief and told her to blow her nose like a good girl. And her sobs gradually subsided.

'Now then,' he said, when she was calmer, 'tell yer ol' Dad all about it.'

'There was a ghost on the stair,' she said, still clinging round his neck.

'Did you see it?'

'It punched me in the back.'

'Did you see it?' he insisted gently.

'No,' she said. 'It punched me in the back.'

'Ah, then it wasn't a ghost,' he said easily, patting her shoulders. 'It was that ol' trip stair. Caught a lot a' people out has that ol' trip stair.'

The twins were being marched out of the tower by their father. They looked much smaller than they'd done when they were tormenting her, smaller and crestfallen. And they were both crying.

'A trip stair?' she said, beginning to take comfort.

'Oh yes,' her father said. 'Caught a lot a' people out has that. Grown men an' all. Uneven you see. Makes you trip up and when you start ter fall, well that's like being hit in the small a' the back. See? Just a trip stair. That's all. Now blow yer nose again like a good girl. Time we was getting home. Yer Mum'll wonder where you are.'

It sounded so reasonable. A trip stair. Yes, that must be it. And yet it had felt just like somebody punching her in the back.

They began to walk towards the Casemates.

'You won't tell Mum I was . . .' she hoped, trotting along beside him.

'Not a word,' he said. 'It'll be our secret.'

'But what if the twins go saying things?' she worried.

'The twins'll have sore backsides by now,' he said, 'if I'm any judge of the Ser'nt Major. I don't think the twins'll want to tell anyone about it, and especially not your mum, or I might lam into 'em an' all.'

27

'Are we very late?' she worried. 'Mum'll be ever so cross, won't she?'

But Mum was surprisingly mild. She was sitting by the stove, darning one of Joan's black stockings. 'You been a long time,' she said as they walked into the kitchen, but the words were an observation not a rebuke.

'Got talking,' Dad said, stooping to kiss her cheek.

'You going back to the Club?' Mum asked.

'No,' Dad said. 'I'll give it the go-by tonight.'

Mum folded up the stocking and put it back into her workbox. 'Time that child was in bed,' she said. 'She's all eyes. Up you go, Peggy. We'll be along presently to tuck you in. Did you have a good day?'

By now Peggy had recovered enough to give a sensible answer. 'Yes, Mum,' she said. 'The Keys was ever so good.'

'I've left the landing light for you,' Mum said. 'Mind you don't wake the others.'

Oh the relief of being back at home, in her own nice neat bedroom, with the light on the landing for her where it always was, and Joan and Baby asleep, the same as always, and Mum and Dad downstairs, the same as always, and everything quiet and peaceful and secure. She undressed quickly and slid between the covers into the chilly space beside her sister. And as if she knew how frightened she'd been, Joan turned over in her sleep and put out an arm to cuddle her.

It was wonderful to feel so safe again, with the great outer wall of the Tower like a strong defence behind her head, and the moat another defence beyond that, and Joan's arms round her waist, and Dad downstairs to keep all harm away from all of them. As she drifted off to sleep she was warm and easy in the certainty that while she lived in the Tower and her dear lovely old dad was there to look after her, nothing could ever really go wrong.

CHAPTER 3

Flossie Furnivall was much younger than her husband. Twenty-three years younger to be exact. She had married him in a fit of youthful bravado when she was barely seventeen, to show her father and her older brother and sister that she was a cut above *them* and their dull country ways, and that *somebody* loved her even if her mother *had* died and left her.

It had been just a little too easy. All she'd had to do was stand by the kerb and look charming while the troops marched in and out of the Stoughton Barracks in Guildford. Sooner or later she invariably caught the eye of one of the handsome ones, for she was pretty in a piquant way, with her narrow foxy face and her fair hair fluffed and bushed about her temples in the very latest style, which she'd copied assiduously from the fashion plates in the drapery. She took care to accentuate her slender figure by wearing a tight leather belt and the elaborate summer blouse she'd made for herself from one of Mr Weldon's patterns, and she topped off the whole effect with her mother's beautiful floradora hat to frame her face and make everyone notice her. She knew the hat was a success from the violent way her father had reacted against it when she first put it on.

'That's your ma's,' he growled.

She placated him by sweet-talk and flirtation the way she always did, because she was afraid of his ill-temper. 'Oh Dad!' she said sweetly. 'You know she gave it to me.'

'It looks ridiculous. You ain't a duchess, gel.'

'Neither was Ma, and didn't she look the prettiest thing?'

He sighed and grimaced, temporarily defeated by her sweetness.

'Well don't think you're gadding off to Guildford 'fore your chores are done,' he said growling again.

But the chores were done. She'd been most particular about them. So there was nothing to stop her.

Company Sergeant-Major Furnivall of the Royal Fusiliers had been the fifth gallant soldier to offer to escort her that summer. He'd been in camp just outside the town and had come in one afternoon to look up some old South African comrades who were now stationed at the barracks, but he was so smitten by her pretty face that his friends never got their visit.

They were married three months later, she delighted by her new status and all the fuss and attention that went with it, he dazzled at his good fortune in finding a wife at just the right moment in his career when he was about to leave active service and take up his new post as a Yeoman Warder at the Tower.

'You done well for yourself, gel,' her father had said at the wedding, and so she had, and all by her own efforts.

It wasn't until she arrived in the Tower as the pregnant wife of a new Yeoman Warder that she began to suspect that she might have made a slight miscalculation. For a start she found his lovemaking too regular and too demanding. Once a week would have been plenty, swollen as she was, every other night was too much and too exhausting. But perhaps even worse than that was the fact that she was well and away the youngest wife in the Casemates, and she had no mother to turn to for advice. The other wives were kindly but they were all very very old, and it made her feel inadequate to stand speechless amongst them while they talked of ancient campaigns and barracks they'd shared before she was born.

And she felt even worse when baby Joan was born and turned out to be a squalling brat who never left off crying. The other wives were all so much better at mothering than she was. Their children, who were mostly over ten years old or already grown up, were all sensible and quiet and well-behaved like children ought to be, and their grand-children never cried. Sometimes she was at her wits' end with the noise the baby made, especially at night, and Joe took to sleeping in the spare room. Which was a relief in one regard, but left her coping with the racket all on her own.

Her brother and sister came up to London to see the new arrival but they weren't any help at all and she never invited them again. Her sister Maud, who wasn't married and had no right to criticize, said that none of the babies she knew had *ever* cried, ever, and brother Gideon, who *was* married and had two children of his own, said he'd put the horrid little thing in the sausage machine if she belonged to him. He was training to be a butcher and it hadn't improved him.

Flossie tried everything she could think of, slapping the baby, shaking her, shouting at her, even leaving her in an upstairs room and ignoring her, but nothing seemed to make any difference. The only time she wasn't crying was when she was sucking, and she did *that* with a horrible intensity that reminded Flossie of Joe when he was making love, which didn't help matters. And besides, as Flossie reminded herself every time she withdrew her reluctant nipple from the baby's eager mouth, you're not supposed to feed a baby all day long. So the child went on screaming. And even when she was a twelvemonth she was still prone to horrible outbursts and usually at the most inopportune moments, when one of the other wives was looking.

But four years, two miscarriages and much heartache later Peggy was born and even though she was rather an ordinary-looking baby, with a bland round face and a nose like a Napoleon cherry, at least she knew how to behave, feeding decorously and sleeping like a model child. It was a great relief to both her parents to have an infant they didn't have to worry about. By this time Joan had grown into a peaky five-year-old with a foxy face like her mother and her father's sandy hair. She was still given to outbursts of temper and needed a lot of punishment, but at least she was controllable. And thanks to the doctor who

31

attended Peggy's birth, Flossie had discovered an answer to all her difficulties as Joe Furnivall's wife.

After losing two sons, Joe had insisted on Flossie seeing a doctor when she was pregnant the fourth time, and even though it was horribly expensive and she couldn't see the need for it, she made an appointment just to placate him. Not with either of the Tower doctors, of course, because they were a rough lot and thought aperients were the answer to everything, but with a new lady doctor who had set up her brass plate a mere hundred yards away, outside the walls.

She was a lovely lady, so attentive and sympathetic that Flossie soon felt she could tell her anything. And did. After a five minute examination the pregnancy was pronounced to be 'quite perfect', and after a twenty minute conversation, the doctor told Flossie that although she was 'physically very strong, my dear,' it was obvious that she was 'suffering from nerves'.

'I will prescribe a good nerve tonic for you,' she said. 'You must take care of yourself, you know. Nerves are debilitating. And as to that other matter we were discussing, if your husband makes advances to you when you feel you can't bear it, you must tell him not to. You have a duty to yourself and the baby now.'

Flossie returned from the surgery a woman transformed. From then on she took spectacular care of her health, making sure that there were always copious stocks of nerve tonic in her bedside cabinet, besides all the most useful proprietary medicines like iron jelloids and Eno's Fruit Salts and Dr Cassell's famous tablets, which according to the advertisements were specially for nerve trouble and jolly good value at one and thruppence a box. And in addition to all that she now 'indulged' her temper whenever anyone annoyed her, and she kept Joe at arm's length whenever she 'didn't feel like it.'

It wasn't long before he grew accustomed to the fact that sex was now a Saturday night treat. And soon he and Joan were living in dread of 'Mum's nerves' and would do anything rather than provoke an outburst.

Nevertheless, three years later, like a reward for her good health care and his patience, Baby arrived and Baby was delightful, so soft and pretty with fair, curly hair and exactly the same expressions on her pretty face as her mother. Joe was secretly disappointed that she wasn't the son he wanted so much, but Flossie doted on her from the first moment, and fed her whenever she cried, and picked her up and petted her if she so much as whimpered. She was christened Barbara, but nobody ever called her anything except Baby, because she was so soft and pretty. And delicate too, of course, for she resembled her mother in everything.

Now that her life had acquired a pattern that was pleasantly dominating even if it wasn't always entirely agreeable, Flossie was often quite sorry for poor Joe. Of course it was much, much better for him not to go exhausting himself night after night. He wasn't getting any younger after all. Although there were times when he had such an awfully wistful look about him that she wished there was some way she could make amends for having to treat him so sternly. But then just as she was feeling quite well disposed towards him, he'd go and do something unkind like refusing to take poor Baby to the Ceremony of the Keys, or something stupid like dragging them all off to some ceremony or other in the pouring rain. And there was enough rain that autumn to remind her of that.

By the end of October the city was positively waterlogged and on November the first they were facing a flood. There were high spring tides that morning and by ten o'clock the Thames was lapping the walls of the Tower and threatening to overrun its banks.

The two girls came home to their midday meal full of excitement. Even Joan was animated. 'A flood!' she said. 'Think a' that. I'll bet there'll be lots of people drowned.'

'Megan says it's going to come right in over the wall,' Peggy said, her eyes as round as pennies. 'Is it, Dad?' The thought of torrents of water pouring over the walls was really rather alarming.

But the tone of her father's voice reassured her. 'Be over the embankment I shouldn't wonder,' he said. 'Eat up quick an' we'll go down and see.'

'All of us?' Baby said hopefully.

'All of you.'

33

Flossie was instantly irritated. Wasn't that just like him? Rushing off at a minute's notice. Not thinking. 'They'll be late for school,' she protested, trying to deter him.

He wasn't put off at all. 'No, they won't,' he said easily. 'We'll only go a step. We'll have plenty of time to be there an' back before the bell.'

'You'll catch cold,' she complained, trying again. 'You just see if you don't. The flu's back, I hope you realize.' Ever since that terrible flu at the end of the Great War there'd been one epidemic after another and the newspapers had taken to publishing ghoulish lists of the numbers of dead every week.

But he pushed that objection away too. 'We'll be all right, won't we girls? Put your macs on. And your Wellingtons.'

So they went to see the floods, which turned out to be marvellously exciting and not a bit frightening. The river was battleship grey and peaked all over with big white-tipped waves and wider than they'd ever seen it, and the clouds were so thick you couldn't see the sky, and the plane trees so wet that their trunks were black, and there was water simply everywhere. Down by Temple Underground Station the river was gushing through the gratings in fountains of dirty brown water so that people had to keep jumping out of the way, and on the embankment the waves were slopping over the wall. They went for a paddle where the pavements had been, and when they kicked it, the water came right up to the top of Baby's boots, and she didn't grizzle about it or even complain because they were with Dad and she knew Dad wouldn't let her make a fuss.

But the trams were the best of all. They were still running despite the floods, and they came rocking along the road one after the other like great red boats, trailing a choppy wake behind them and spinning up plumes of grey-white water on either side so that everybody got splashed. By the time the Furnivall family finally slopped back to the Tower Joan and Peggy were late for school, and they were all soaking wet.

'What did I tell you?' Flossie grumbled. 'Well don't

34

blame me, if you've all caught cold, that's all. You'll be taken ill as sure as fate. Just look at the state of your stockings. As if I haven't got enough washing to do without you making more. Go upstairs and change directly.'

'I'm off,' Dad said quickly, and slid himself out of the door, wet feet and all, before he could be scolded too.

'It's all very well for your father,' Flossie nagged as the girls escaped up the stairs. 'A great strong man like him. He never takes cold. *I'm* the one that has to do all the worrying in this house.'

But she might have saved her breath, for she was worrying needlessly and nothing would stop Dad when he'd set his heart on a procession. He took them to the opening of Parliament, to a parade at Christmas, and to the royal wedding of the Princess Mary and Viscount Lascelles in February.

And then one Friday evening in June he arrived home with a hat box, so they knew he was planning yet another expedition.

'What's that?' Mum said unnecessarily.

'Open it,' Dad said beaming at her. 'Special hat fer a special occasion.'

It was a lovely hat, red felt with a broad brim and two little pink feathers stuck in the ribbon.

'Very *à la*!' Mum said putting it on and admiring her reflection in the looking glass. 'Thank you, Joe. It's lovely. Where are we going?'

'London's got their new County Hall finished at last,' Dad said, putting a programme down on the kitchen table beside the empty hat box. It was a very grand programme with the LCC coat of arms on the cover. 'The King and Queen are going to open it. Date's all set, see? Tuesday 17 July.'

'I suppose you'll be on duty,' Mum said, still admiring herself. For an occasion like that they'd need all the Yeomen Warders.

'Course,' Dad said. 'Every man jack of us, but I've got the best job of the lot this time. I'm to be a wheelman and walk beside the State Coach. What d'yer think a' that, eh girls?'

'Right by the King and Queen?' Baby asked, much impressed.

35

'As near to 'em as I am to you.'

'Gosh!' Baby said.

'Can we help you to dress?' Peggy said. 'As it's special.'
She'd always wanted to help him into his ceremonial
uniform, but Mum always said she was too young.

'Yes you can,' Dad said confidently, 'and so can Joan
and Baby. It's about time they did, don't you think so,
Mum? I shall need all hands to the pump, bein' it's
London we're honouring an' we're all Londoners.'

Mum was still admiring herself. 'Well I suppose so,' she
said.

'And then,' Dad went on, 'you can put on your best bibs
an' tuckers, and Mum can wear her new hat, – won't she
look a swell? and you can all come down to Westminster
Bridge and see the procession. How about that?'

Mum smiled at him through the mirror. 'We could have
a special supper afterwards,' she said. 'I could make a
meat pie.'

Joan and Peggy were so excited they could hardly keep
still.

'Will there be flags?' Baby wanted to know.

'Flags an' bands an' guardsmen an' cavalry an' all
sorts,' Dad said happily. 'Not every day a' the week the
capital of the world gets a new seat a' government. You'll
be seeing hist'ry made that day I can tell you.'

'Oh,' Peggy said. 'I can't wait.'

'Twenty days,' Joan declared, having counted it up.
'That's all. Twenty days.'

Dad gave them both a grin of pure delight. 'What's for
supper?' he said.

Getting a Yeoman Warder dressed in his ceremonial
uniform is like preparing an actor for a play by Shakespeare. The costume is so complicated it is almost impossible to dress without help. Joe Furnivall could manage to
get into his shirt and breeches and to fasten the statutory
red, white and blue rosettes just below the knees of his red
stockings but the ruff was beyond him. For a start Flossie
always starched it so stiffly that it was very difficult to
fasten, and once it was round his neck he couldn't look
down or even move his head with any degree of comfort.

36

On that special day in July he stood in the middle of the kitchen while his women completed the rest of his preparations for him, lowering his heavy scarlet and gold doublet over his head, arranging the skirt so that it hung neatly, fastening his sword belt, brushing the gold embroidery on his chest before they slung the red, black and gold cross belt over his left shoulder, slipping his black shoes on the red stockinged feet he could no longer see, handing him his white gloves, and finally, while he watched them in the mirror, arranging his black velvet hat on his head, its red white and blue ribbons giving a dazzling finish to his peacock display.

'Very nice,' he said, twirling the waxed ends of his moustache. 'Many hands make light work, eh?'

'You look a treat, Dad,' Peggy told him. Oh it was lovely to look after him and help him dress. 'Don't he, Mum?'

'Very handsome,' Mum agreed, because he really did look very fine. 'If it don't rain.'

But it didn't rain. At least not when the procession was passing. It was a marvellous day.

The Furnivall family took up their positions on the south side of Westminster Bridge where they had a good view of the new County Hall and they could see the carriages arriving for the opening ceremony and driving off again for the second procession afterwards.

There was so much to see it made Peggy's head spin. It was really quite hard to realize that she was looking at the same embankment that had been under water last November. But that was what was so nice about London. It was never the same two days running. There was always something different happening. Today the Thames was like a beautiful sky-blue pond shimmering in the sunshine and full of pleasure boats and barges all neatly lined up to watch the ceremony. There were crowds and crowds of people everywhere you looked, three or four deep on either side of the bridge, and shoulder to shoulder along the embankment, all in their best hats and waving little Union Jacks made of paper, just like she was doing.

County Hall was ever so grand now that the scaffolding was off and you could see it properly. It was made of white stone with lots and lots of windows and the middle bit was curved like a shell and had white pillars all round it. The roof was covered in bright red tiles and the windows on the top floor were painted duck-egg blue to match the little tower in the middle so it was red, white and blue really, which was very appropriate. All along the terrace in front of the building there were rows and rows of empty chairs, and they'd set up an orange canopy where the King and Queen were going to sit. The capital city of the world, Peggy thought, remembering what Dad had said, and she felt herself swelling with pride to be part of it.

Presently they could hear cheering to the north of the bridge and they knew the opening procession had begun. Viscount Lascelles and Princess Mary arrived first and in a motor car, which caused quite a stir, but the King and Queen did things in the old style, driven slowly in the State coach and bowing and waving to the crowds right and left, with a troop of guardsmen following them, breastplates shining, and Dad marching beside them.

Joan said she thought the coach looked gorgeous, because the King was in a Field Marshal's scarlet uniform and the Queen was all in white, in a long white coat embroidered in gold, with a white fox stole on her shoulders, and one of her cream-coloured toques on her head with three white ostrich feathers fluttering to one side of it.

And Baby said she wished she could ride in a carriage and wear diamonds all day.

But Peggy only had eyes for her father, striding along beside the coach and winking at them as he passed. 'I think we're ever so lucky,' she said, 'to have a Dad like our Dad.'

CHAPTER 4

'There's a raven on your roof, missus,' Sam Bullough said as Peggy and her sisters followed their mum up the Casemates after the ceremony. They'd come home in a hurry because Mum suddenly said it was going to rain and it certainly looked as though it would, for the sky above their sooty row of houses was a menacing colour, like bruised plums. 'That's a bad omen, a raven on yer roof.'

'Clear off out of it,' Mum said, waving her arms indiscriminately at bird and boy.

'What's an omen?' Baby asked as Sam ran off.

'It means somebody's going to die,' Joan said heartlessly. 'When a raven croaks on the roof, somebody croaks in the house.'

'One of us?' Baby asked fearfully.

'It's a lot of superstitious nonsense,' Mum said, speaking quickly before Joan could enlighten them any further. The raven was still strutting along their roof and now it was squawking. 'Clear off,' she shouted at it. 'Go and annoy someone else.'

Peggy looked at it fearfully, hoping it wasn't an omen, or that if it was, it wouldn't turn out to be true. After that ghost on the stairs she wasn't sure whether to believe things like that or not. And they did say a raven always knew when somebody in the house was going to die. 'It must have flown up,' she said, trying to be reasonable about it. 'I thought they had their feathers cut so's they couldn't fly.'

The raven hopped to the parapet where it perched, looking down at them malevolently, its thick beak axe-blue in the afternoon sun.

'I'll give it fly,' Mum said, opening the front door. 'If it's not gone by the time I've got the kettle on I'll fetch a broom to it. Vile thing.'

'Does it mean one of us is going to die?' Baby persisted.

'No it don't,' Mum said. 'Look sharp inside all of you. We got a pie to bake.'

Fortunately they were soon very busy preparing the supper and making sandwiches for their dinner because it was too late to fry anything and they were all extremely hungry. And then the rain came torrenting down and not long after that Dad arrived home sopping wet and had to be skinned out of his finery and wrapped in two bath towels and sat by the stove with his feet in a mustard bath until he stopped shivering. So they soon forgot their unwanted visitor and none of them had any cause to remember it until three days later.

Dad had been on guard duty all afternoon, and after his supper he'd changed his clothes and gone whistling off to the Club as usual, leaving his womenfolk to a quiet evening. There was nothing remarkable about it, Mum tackled the mending, Joan darned her socks, and Peggy helped Baby to stick the latest cuttings in her album. They were making a collection of all the newspaper pictures of the opening of County Hall, especially those that showed the State Coach, with their father's diminutive figure beside it ringed in red crayon and labelled OUR DAD in letters taller than he was.

They went to bed a little later than usual because it was Friday and they didn't have to get up for school in the morning. Baby slept at once and her sisters didn't talk for long. They were sleepy and easy, listening to the familiar sounds of the house, the stairs creaking as they cooled, the tick of the tin clock on their mantelpiece, Mum downstairs lighting the gaslight beside the stove and moving her chair so that she could sit beneath it and finish her mending, sleepy and easy, oh very very sleepy. So when somebody knocked at the door the sudden, unexpected sound made them jump awake with alarm.

It was Uncle Charlie. They knew at once from the burring sound of his voice and the strong smell of snuff that was rising to them from the hall. And he was worried about something. He was speaking in such a low hesitant way and Mum's reply was like a startled bark.

Peggy was filled with a terrible sense of foreboding, as if an icy wind had blown straight into her body and locked there. 'It's Dad,' she whispered. 'There's something up with Dad.'

'Shush!' Joan said fiercely, straining her ears to hear what was being said. Uncle Charlie's voice had stopped and now his wife was speaking, not in her usual stern voice but as though she was patting somebody with her words. And Mum was wailing, 'Oh my dear good God! What shall I do? What shall I do?'

'I know it's Dad,' Peggy said again. 'Did we oughter go down?'

There was movement in the hall, doors being opened and shut, feet scuffling, a renewed smell of snuff. And then the front door was opened again and closed quietly and the house was suddenly still. Both girls skimmed from the bed to the window to see who had left. It was Mum and Uncle Charlie and they were heading towards the Green. They were both walking very quickly and Mum had one hand at her throat as if she was trying to strangle herself.

'Shall we go down?' Peggy whispered.

'No,' Joan whispered back. 'Let's wait till Mum gets back.'

It was a long vigil, hours and hours of it. They stood by the window and watched until they were shivering with cold, and they crept back to bed and cuddled together for warmth and comfort, and dozed and woke and dozed again, to hear the clock striking once, twice, three times, and the light was still on in the hall and Mum still hadn't come home.

But at last, when the sky was definitely getting lighter, they heard the scrape of a key in the lock and sat up achingly to listen. It *was* Mum. They were sure of that, because Aunty Connie was talking to her, 'Did you ...? Flossie dear ... Poor ...' But she was answering so quietly

41

they couldn't hear what she was saying and presently all three grown-ups went into the kitchen and shut the door behind them.

They talked for ever such a long time. It wasn't until the sky was quite bright that Uncle Charlie took Aunty Connie home at last and Mum came slowly up the stairs to her bedroom.

Joan and Peggy tiptoed out onto the landing to meet her, peering at her in the half light. Her face was puffy with weeping.

'What is it?' Peggy asked.

She turned on them as though they'd attacked her, her sagging face lifted into a blaze of fury. 'Go back to bed this instant!' she said. 'Don't you dare ask me! Don't you dare!'

'Is it Dad?' Joan said, made bold by fear.

But persistence only made their mother worse. 'Go back to bed!' she screamed, stamping her feet. 'Can't you see what a state I'm in? Do as you're told!' And she pushed Joan away and blundered into her bedroom slamming the door behind her.

The two girls retreated into their own high double bed, hearts pounding, shocked and afraid.

'It *is* Dad,' Joan whispered. 'He's ill, that's what it is. I'll bet she went to the hospital block.'

'Or hurt,' Peggy whispered. 'He might be hurt.'

But they couldn't believe either possibility. Dad couldn't be ill. He was *never* ill. Look how strong he was, the way he carried them all about. Even Joan and she was nearly grown up and ever so heavy. And he couldn't be hurt either. Who would want to hurt him? They couldn't think of anyone. Unless it was an accident.

'It was that raven,' Peggy said.

'Shut up!' Joan spat. 'Shut up! Shut up! I don't want to hear about ravens.'

Peggy shut up at once, because she could see that Joan was getting shirty. But it *was* the raven. It *had* warned them. Ravens always knew. But what had that one known? That was the thing. Oh what *was* the matter?

They were still whispering anxiously together when the clock struck four and the sky was quite blue, and they

42

whispered again when they woke four hours later after a ragged sleep.

Mum was up and about. They could hear her setting the table and talking to Baby. Fancy Baby being up before they were.

'Perhaps he's back,' Peggy hoped, as they rushed to wash and dress.

But when they got downstairs there was no sign of him, no boots by the hearth, no coat on the hook, no morning paper, nothing. His chair had been moved from the fire and set against the wall and, what was worse, there was no place laid for him at the table. Oh where was he? Wherever was he?

'Sit up to the table,' Mum said, speaking sternly as if they'd done something wrong. The swelling of the previous night had all gone down but her face was set as if it were made of concrete. 'We're all behind this morning and I've got to be out by ten o'clock.'

They sat down subdued and anxious, wondering whether they could ask her where she was going, as she filled the teapot and set it on the trivet. Neither of them could ever remember eating a meal at that table without their father and worry was taking away what little appetite they had.

It was Baby who said what they were all thinking. 'Where's Dad?' she piped as her mother put a plateful of eggs and bacon in front of her.

Being Baby she got an answer. 'Your Dad's ill,' Mum said flatly as she forked two rashers of bacon out of the pan for Peggy. 'He was took bad yesterday evening at the Club. He's in the hospital block.'

'What's he got?' Joan asked, her foxy face peaking with concern. 'Is it the flu?'

'No, it's not. It's pneumonia,' Mum said, still speaking flatly as though it wasn't important. 'Now eat your breakfast and don't let's hear any more about it, if you please.'

'When you go to hospital you're very ill, aren't you?' Baby said. 'Is he very ill?'

But she got no answer to that. 'Eat your breakfast,' Mum ordered. And went off into the larder.

The three girls looked at one another in alarm and warning.

New monia, Peggy was thinking. Perhaps that wasn't so bad whatever it was. New things were usually better than old ones. At least it wasn't the flu. But if it wasn't bad why had Mum cried so? And what about that raven? It *had* been on their roof and it *had* croaked. Oh if only it hadn't croaked. Perhaps Mum would tell them a bit more when she'd been to the hospital block and seen him. That must be where she's got to go at ten o'clock. I don't suppose she'd let us go and see him too.

She was right on the last count at least. The moment the breakfast things had been washed and put back on the dresser all three girls were sent out to play.

'It's lovely weather,' Mum said too briskly. 'You can play out all day. It'll do you good.'

'Me too?' Baby said, very surprised.

'Peggy'll look after you,' Mum said. 'You stay by Peggy, you'll be all right.'

Baby stayed by Peggy all morning and a horrible nuisance she was. For a start she wanted to play all the games and grizzled when she couldn't, and then she was perpetually whining for something or other, for a hanky or a drink of water or for her socks to be pulled up or to go back home because she wanted a wee-wee. Megan was ever so good about her and said the baby next door was just the same, but Peggy was too worried about Dad to see her as anything other than a burden. She hoped she wouldn't have to look after her all afternoon too.

But she did. All afternoon, and all day Sunday, until her grizzling presence in the Green was an established fact and Peggy her acknowledged keeper. And Mum went to the hospital block three more times without telling them anything about it. Joan and Peggy knew because although she walked the long way round so as to avoid coming through the Green where they'd see her, they'd kept a sharp look-out for her and spied on all her comings and goings. And Dad didn't come home.

The next day was Monday and school and the hope that he'd be home for dinner. Or supper. Or breakfast next morning. But he wasn't and the week went by with the unreality of nightmare, with life at school humdrum and normal and life at home fraught with unanswered questions.

44

Mum never mentioned their father, even though she visited him every day, and her face was always so stern when she came back they didn't dare to ask how he was, partly because they didn't want to provoke an outbreak of nerves but mostly because they were afraid of what she might tell them.

Uncle Charlie and Aunty Connie came round nearly every night and she talked to them for hours and hours but in voices too low for the listeners above them to catch more than the odd word or two. 'After the crisis ...' 'It must go one way or the other ...' 'Poor old Joe ...'

The only time they heard anything clearly was on the second Thursday night, when Dad had been in the hospital block for thirteen days. Uncle Charlie was in the hall saying goodbye. 'If there's anything we can do, Flossie,' he said, 'you've only to ask. You know that, don't you?'

And Mum's answer was clear too, clear and weary. 'There's nothing anyone can do now except wait. Oh Charlie, I don't know what will become of us.'

The cold wind blew icy into Peggy's heart again. 'I wish that raven hadn't croaked on our roof,' she said.

'Shut *up* about that raven,' Joan said furiously. 'You make me sick, always on about it. I don't want to hear about it ever again.'

'I wish she'd tell us what's going on,' Peggy mourned. 'You ask her, Joanie.'

'No, you,' Joan said. 'She wouldn't tell me.'

'She wouldn't tell me neither.'

'She's coming upstairs,' Joan warned. 'Pretend to be asleep.'

So Peggy closed her eyes obediently, resigning herself to sleep and continued ignorance.

The next day when she and Joan came home to dinner they found Mum and Baby waiting in the hall in their outdoor clothes, hats, gloves and all. And Mum had something to tell them.

'Your Dad's asked to see you,' she said. 'We'll have dinner when we get back. I shan't send you back to school this afternoon. We'll go the long way round. We don't want everyone gawping.'

45

'Is he better?' Peggy said as they followed her out of the house again.

'We'll see when we get there,' Mum said. But she looked so stern it wasn't an encouraging answer.

They walked between the great stones of the inner and outer walls, and the sun was warm on their heads and shoulders, as a fearful ice expanded in Peggy's chest. Please don't let him be worse, she prayed. He can't be worse. Not here. Not in the Tower. People are protected in the Tower. Please dear God, protect my dad. Make him be better.

The porter on duty at the hospital block that morning was an old friend. He used to throw balls back for them when they were playing on the Green and sometimes, when he wasn't too busy, he could be persuaded to take one end of the long rope for skipping. But now he looked as solemn as Mum.

'Come to see your poor Dad 'ave yer?' he said to the girls. 'Sister Turner'll be along presently.'

They stood together in the unfamiliar hall, shuffling and embarrassed and growing steadily colder now that they were out of the sunshine. Sister Turner was a long time coming and every second diminished the hope of good news. Joan and Peggy shifted from foot to foot and tried not to look at one another or their mother, and Baby sat on the bench by the wall feeling small and staring at the floor. But at last Sister Turner approached, skirts swishing. It was a surprise to all three children when she took Peggy and Baby by the hand, signalled with her eyes that Joan was to follow, and led them away, leaving Mum on her own in the hall.

But they didn't say anything because you didn't argue with doctors and nurses. They simply followed her meekly up the stairs and along a corridor smelling of disinfectant and gleaming with floor polish and full of brown doors, each with its own neat label and some open enough to allow them a glimpse of a heaped bed and a pale face against a pillow. They knew that they were foreigners in this place, interlopers who had to be on their best behaviour to survive, so when Sister Turner opened one of the closed doors, they hesitated, unsure whether they were

46

supposed to go in or not. She smiled at them quite kindly
and as they still didn't move, she ushered them round the
edge of the door with one hand placed briefly but firmly
against their necks.

They were in a white brightly-lit space with white
curtains and a table with a spittoon on it and a dish full of
cotton wool and a plain, glass jug full of water, and a white
bed with three red cylinders standing beside it like bombs.

It was a few seconds before any of them realized that
the person in the bed was their father, even though they
were expecting to see him. He'd changed so much.

He was lying limply against a triangular mound of
pillows, with his hands resting on the coverlet and his eyes
shut tight, and he looked frail and small as though he'd
shrunk. His skin was greyish-yellow, his cheeks had caved
in, his hair and moustache looked like dried grass, and
there was an angry cold sore at the corner of his mouth
oozing into the pepper and salt stubble on his chin. But
worst of all was the awful noise he was making as he
breathed. It was a sort of knocking and bubbling and
wheezing, like a kettle boiling, or as if he had pebbles in his
chest, and they could see that every breath pained him for
even though his eyes were closed they were wincing at
every rattle.

None of them knew what to say and Baby's mouth
turned down as if she was going to cry.

Sister Turner swished to the bed and stooped until her
white cap was almost touching the pillow. 'Mr Furnivall,'
she said. 'Your girls are here.'

He made a harsh muttering sound and his head rolled
to one side.

'Mr Furnivall,' Sister repeated. 'Your girls. You asked
to see them. Remember?'

To Peggy's relief, he opened his eyes and became
himself again. Oh those lovely greeny-brown eyes. Neither
one thing nor the other. 'Peggy?' he said looking at her.

'Yes, Dad,' she said, tiptoeing to the bedside. 'We're all
here.'

Joan followed her, pulling Baby by the hand.

'Good girls,' he said, but his voice was harsh and husky
as if he had a throat full of spit. 'Got somethin' ter say ...'

Then he started to cough, and Sister Turner put the spittoon deftly under his chin and supported him with her arm until he'd coughed up a long sticky strand of awful brown spit and wiped his lips with a piece of the cotton wool.

They waited full of horrified sympathy for him.

'Somethin' to tell you,' he gasped. 'Can't talk much 'cause of the ... I want you ter promise ...'

'Anything,' Peggy said as he was panting too much to be able to go on.

'Anything,' Joan echoed.

The panting went on as they waited for him, strained and afraid and yearning with pity.

'Look after yer mum,' he said. 'She's – not strong – with her nerves an' everythin'. Look after her – eh? – when I'm gone.'

The icy wind blew into every corner of Peggy's mind and body. She was cold from the hairs on her head to the tips of her fingers. Her dad was dying and there was no way she could either avoid the knowledge or take it in and make sense of it. 'We promise, Dad,' she said, passionately. 'We promise.'

'All of yer?' he said, looking at them one after the other.

Joan said yes in a voice that sounded almost as if she was angry, and Baby nodded.

'Good girls,' their father said. 'Give yer ol' Dad a kiss.'

They kissed him solemnly, one after the other, appalled by the awful smell that was rising out of his mouth and trying not to look at that spittoon, and loving him with a terrible desperation.

Then Sister Turner's hand was on Joan's shoulder and they were being suggested towards the door. Peggy followed obediently even though she was torn with the need to run back to the bed and plead with him not to die, to kiss him once more, to tell him she loved him, that she'd do anything to save him. But all she could manage was to look back at him once and briefly before the door was shut between them. And he looked back at her, once and briefly, smiling his lovely old smile even though he was keeping his eyes open with an effort.

'That's my girl,' he said.

48

* * *

Long afterwards Joan and Peggy confessed to one another
that they had no idea how they got through the rest of the
day. They supposed they must have eaten their dinner or
Mum would have got shirty and they'd have remembered
that, and after dinner they had a vague recollection that
they helped clean the parlour, because Peggy could
remember smelling the wax polish. But they were numb
with emotions too strong for them, terror and pity, revulsion and anger, and lurking most hideously behind them
all the monstrous fear of death.

All three of them slept fitfully that night, and Joan and
Peggy took Baby into the double bed because she cried so
much when she was in the truckle bed on her own. And in
the morning they came down to a house even more unreal
than the one they'd left when they went to bed.

The curtains were all still closed as though it was the
middle of the night and Aunty Connie was in the kitchen
making lumpy porridge by gaslight.

'Your Mum's gone to the hospital,' she said when they
came quietly into the room. 'They're bringing home the
coffin at ten o'clock. She's gone to see to it. Eat up quick. I
want to get clear in here before they come.'

Coffin, Peggy thought. Oh Dad. Are you in a coffin
already? But although the awful question filled her throat
she couldn't bring herself to ask it.

It was Joan who spoke. 'Then he's dead,' she said flatly.
'That's it. He's dead.'

'Yes, my dear,' Aunty Connie said, speaking quite
kindly. 'I'm sorry to have to tell you. He is. Eat what you
can a' this porridge. You'll need your strength today.'

We'll have to look after Mum now, Peggy thought,
trying to be sensible. But as she gazed down bleakly at her
bowl of porridge, she knew she didn't have the faintest
idea how they were going to do it. The world had become a
foreign place, a place where there was no one to protect
them, a place full of threats and fears and horrors.
Nothing would ever be the same again now Dad was dead.
How could she endure it? But even as the question formed
itself in her mind, she knew she would have to endure it,

because there was nothing else she could do. And she remembered Dad's voice saying, 'What can't be cured must be endured', and she missed him with a sudden rush of yearning that made the tears brim from her eyes.

'Eat what you can,' Aunty Connie said, patting her head. 'We got to go shopping before ten o'clock.'

None of the girls could eat their breakfast. They were too shocked and unhappy for food, too shocked and unhappy to know what they were doing. They simply let the rituals of mourning carry them along the treadmill of the next few days. They went shopping with Aunty Connie and bought three skirts made of 'serviceable' black bara-thea, and black ribbons for their hair and three cheap black cotton blouses 'just for the time being'. And they came home quietly and were sent upstairs with orders to change into their new clothes as quickly as they could and then wait in the bedroom until they were told to come down again.

None of them spoke much. What could they say? They stood by the bedroom window in their unfamiliar clothes and opened the curtains just a crack so that they could watch while their father's coffin was carried into the house, with their mother weeping behind it. And they came obediently downstairs when they were sent for and went into the parlour together to 'say goodbye' as though that was their normal behaviour.

The coffin was balanced on a long trestle table in the middle of the room with its lid removed and four white candles set in brass candlesticks at either end of it. But the thing inside the coffin, the thing they'd all been secretly dreading, turned out to be simply a cold waxy image of their father lying awkwardly on a soppy-looking cushion of padded white satin. It was too unreal to be upsetting.

'They've parted his hair the wrong way,' Joan said as they stood in a row beside the trestle table.

'It's not him though, is it?' Baby whispered, clinging to Peggy's hand.

'No,' Peggy assured her. 'It's not him. He's gone to Heaven. With the angels.'

'Smell the polish,' Joan said. 'I'm glad we got the room clean.'

'Why've they put candles?' Baby said.

Joan knew the answer to that. 'To save the gas,' she said.

It was only when they were out of the parlour and back in the kitchen with Mum and Aunty Connie that Peggy knew how much she missed her father. She suddenly remembered him alive and full of vigour sitting by the stove and showing her the Bible and telling her how she'd been born in the Tower. And she missed him with a raw aching pain in her stomach that made her feel as though someone had been hitting her there, and she had to go upstairs quickly so that she could cry on her own and not upset Mum, because Mum was upset enough already without her making things worse.

For the rest of the day the house was full of Yeomen Warders. They came in one after the other, with their shoulders hunched and their bonnets in their hands, to 'pay their respects'. Mum sat in the corner of the kitchen and cried and cried, and the three girls kept out of the way as well as they could, retreating into their bedroom or sitting on the stairs, because it made them feel so awful to see Mum in such a state and because there really wasn't room for so many people in such a small house. But more visitors kept arriving, all that day and all that evening and all the day after, in a never-ending procession of sorrow and mumbled admiration. And Aunty Connie and Uncle Charlie came in and out to whisper to Mum about 'arrangements' and Mrs Jonson from next door took them all in to her house every evening for supper, which was just as well because Mum seemed to have forgotten all about meals.

But after two more bewildered days Mum told them it was 'the funeral' and that they were all to be as good as gold. By mid morning the house was full of people again, only this time a lot of them were strangers, all dressed in black and most of them smelling of mothballs. Wreaths arrived and were dangled into the candlelit parlour, and then six Yeomen Warders were at the door in their black cloaks and between them they carried Dad's coffin out of the house in a waft of ferns and roses and carnations.

Peggy couldn't understand much of the funeral service

except that the chaplain said how brave Dad was, 'Valiant in war and dependable in peace' were the words he used, and they sounded lovely even though she wasn't quite sure what they meant. And then their black visitors shuffled out of the church, looking solemn, and they were all driven off to a churchyard in a parade of black cars and stood round the grave like black crows making silly remarks, and afterwards they all came home again and Aunty Connie produced cups of tea and plates and plates full of sandwiches to feed them. Which Joan said was downright unnecessary.

Peggy was most upset by them, because they were all talking such nonsense and none of them were thinking about Dad at all and some of them were laughing in a horrible high-pitched way. But she tried to be sensible. I mustn't cry, she told herself, even if they *are* horrid, because someone's got to hand round the sandwiches. But they were horrid, just the same.

There was a bad-tempered old man that Mum said was their grandfather, and a woman with hardly any teeth, who was their Aunt Maud, and a large man with a red face and sandy hair who was their Uncle Gideon. He was a very jolly man with a booming voice, but to Peggy's horror he'd lost the top joints of the two middle fingers on his left hand.

'Chopped 'em off fer sausage meat,' he said cheerfully when he saw her looking at the stumps.

'Really?' Baby said, most impressed.

'Gideon!' Aunt Maud warned. 'That's quite enough, if you please!'

What a nasty man, Peggy thought. Fancy chopping off his own fingers. And she went off at once to serve sandwiches to the people on the other side of the room.

But at last the long peculiar day was over and all the guests had gone away and Flossie and her daughters had washed the dishes and returned borrowed crockery to their neighbours and swept the house clean, and now they were alone together in a curiously empty kitchen. Peggy felt completely exhausted.

'We'll just enter it in the Bible,' Mum said, 'and then we can get to bed.' She spoke sharply as if she was cross with them. 'Lift it down if you please, Joan.'

So Joan put the family Bible on the kitchen table, and Mum got the ink stand and took up the pen and wrote: Company Sergeant-Major Joseph Furnival died Thursday 27 July 1922. 'Ah well,' she said when she'd finished. 'Off to bed all of you.'

They went to bed obediently but none of them could sleep and Peggy cried all night. Watching his death being entered in the Bible had upset her terribly. It was all so final and it made her realize that she would never see him again. Oh Dad! she mourned inside her head. How are we going to manage without you?

CHAPTER 5

The fortnight that followed was very subdued. The three girls ran errands and helped with the housework and kept out of the house as much as they could, although there wasn't anywhere particular for them to go because they'd broken up for the summer holidays. And gradually, day by miserable day, they got used to living without their father even though his absence was a perpetual numbness in their minds.

And then one day they came home at dinner time to find a travelling trunk in the kitchen.

'What's that?' Joan asked.

Mum answered her brusquely. 'We're packing,' she said.

'What for?' Joan said, scowling at her.

'We're going to live in the country with your grandpa and your Aunty Maud. It's all arranged.'

'Leave the Tower?' Peggy said. Oh they couldn't leave the Tower. They couldn't possibly.

'Don't start!' Mum said. 'If I say we're going to the country, we're going to the country.'

'But why?' Joan said.

'Your father's gone an' they'll need the house for the next Yeoman Warder,' Mum said. 'We've had a fortnight's grace. Now it's up.'

'But ...' Joan began again.

'Set the table,' Mum said. 'Can't you see my nerves are

54

in shreds? D'you want to make *me* ill next? Is that what you want, you horrible girl? You just set the table.' And she banged out of the room and up the stairs.

Joan and Peggy laid the table quickly.

'I don't want to live in the country,' Joan said.

'Nor do I,' Peggy said miserably. This sudden news was so dreadful she could hardly bear to think about it. To have no Dad to look after them and then to be told they were going to leave the Tower. It was as if the earth had been snatched away from under her feet. All safety and security was gone.

'Nor do I either,' Baby echoed.

They sat round the table unhappily and waited.

'It was your birthday,' Baby said to Peggy. 'You was eight, only you never had it.'

Peggy had forgotten all about birthdays. During the last two weeks there'd only been Dad and that awful empty feeling. 'When?' she said.

'On the Saturday,' Baby told her. 'After the funeral.'

Peggy tried to remember dates and couldn't do it, but Baby was probably right. It was certainly well into August by now. 'Perhaps you don't have birthdays when your Dad's dead,' she said reasonably.

They all thought that very likely. But it didn't solve the problem of their banishment to the country.

'We shall hate it,' Joan said. 'I don't think we ought to go.'

But young though she was, Peggy knew they would have to put up with it no matter what they might think. 'Perhaps it'll be all right,' she said, trying to look on the bright side.

But it wasn't. It was awful.

For a start, it went on and on and on for miles and miles and miles and everything about it was either green or greeny-yellow, which was dreadful after all the different colours in London. There were green fields of grass and yellow fields of something she supposed was corn, green hedges bristling, green trees as tall as houses, and hills everywhere curving one behind the other, green and yellow, on and on and on like the waves of the sea. Even the sky looked green, although that could have been the dirt on the windows of their awful racketty train. But worse than the green was the fact that everything was so empty.

Even when they finally arrived at a station labelled Gomshall, of all funny names, that was empty too.

The train went clattering off almost as soon as they climbed out of it. Peggy watched it caterpillar round the bend and disappear, and after a very few seconds she couldn't even hear it any more. They were all on their own with no Dad to protect them in a green foreign world. Even the porter had disappeared and it was so quiet they could hear birds singing.

'Come on,' Mum said, picking up her suitcase and opening a little wooden gate beside the platform. 'Look sharp or it'll be dark before we get there.'

'Where's the tram?' Baby said.

'You don't have trams in the country,' Mum said. 'You walk.'

So they walked, past a busy coal yard where the air was peppery with the smell of coal dust and colliers were at work loading scores of horse-drawn carts, and downhill along a muddy path lined with black dust, and bordered by untidy bushes and brambles with long grasping claws. It smelled like a river down there, a dank mixture of damp earth and rotting vegetation.

'Is it far?' Baby said anxiously.

But Mum didn't answer. She just went plodding on ahead of them, through the main street of a tiny village, over a bridge where there was a higgledy-piggledy house made of white planks with a river flowing right through the middle of it – what an amazing thing! – past a pond on the other side of the path full of white ducks and grubby children who stopped paddling to stare at them, and then uphill along another dusty path between even more trees. And eventually they came to a house, standing all by itself in a clearing.

It was a grey ramshackle terrace with a black pump before it and a muddle of hens and cabbages behind, and it appeared to have been put together by many hands and at many different times, for although the entire building was topped by a single green thatch, there were several front doors, windows at a variety of levels and in a variety of shapes and sizes, two non-matching gables set side by side at the further end, and a wooden outhouse more or less attached at the rear. It was obviously very very old. The thatch was growing weeds as though it was a field, the grey walls bulged and split like old flour sacks, and there was a musty, elderly smell about it.

'Is this it?' Joan said in disbelief.

'This is it,' Mum agreed, knocking on the bare wood of the nearest door. 'We're home.'

There was no answer to her knock but that didn't seem to worry her. She gave the door a push and they all trooped in.

They were in a dungeon, a dark awful room, standing awkwardly on stone flags between very dark brown walls among furniture as black as a rack, a dresser that looked as though it was frowning, a gnarled table, several ill-assorted chairs. And sitting by the sink, wiping his hands on a grimy dishcloth, was the cantankerous old man they'd met at Dad's funeral, the cantankerous old man who was their grandfather, Grandpa Potter. In the poor light his face was scored with black lines, down his cheeks, across his forehead, over his chin, and running as deep as pits between his long nose and a mouth that looked even narrower than they'd remembered it. There were two deep frown lines between his spiky eyebrows, and they deepened when he glanced up and saw them hesitating before him.

'What sort a' time d'you call this?' he said. He sounded as cross as he looked.

To Peggy's surprise Mum spoke to him in the oddest way, bridling and flirting her eyes at him and using a voice she'd never used before, a wheedling, deliberately sweet voice, like Baby when she wanted something. 'Oh come on Dad, that's not like you. We can't help the trains.'

Grandpa grunted and stared at the carrier bag she was carrying. 'Don't you go making the place untidy,' he said.

'As if I would,' Mum wheedled. 'Where's Maud?'

'Down to Tillingbourne,' Grandpa said. 'Prayer meetin'.'

'Ah yes,' Mum said.

Then there was a long pause while Grandpa finished

57

wiping his hands and his four relations stood where they were in the dungeon and watched him. Isn't he going to say 'sit down' or 'make yourselves at home' or something? Peggy wondered. But he didn't.

'I'm off to see to the 'osses,' he said, walking to the door. 'We've had our supper long since. Don't know how you'll make out, I'm sure. Serves you right for comin' so late.'

'We'll manage,' Mum placated. 'Are there eggs?'

'You can 'ave four of 'em,' Grandpa said from the doorstep. 'Don't let 'em go to waste. That's all. And remember this is a tied cottage so you mind your P's and Q's. No bad behaviour, d'you hear?'

Mum's tone changed as soon as he was out of earshot. 'Four eggs!' she snorted. 'The idea! We've not come here to starve, an' he needn't think it. Not with my pension. We're not beggars. You could eat two, couldn't you, Baby? My, this place is in a pickle. You can see Maud's out. Never mind, we'll all get set to tomorrow and give it a good scrub down once he's out the house. Now where's the lamp? We'll need to look sharp with these eggs or he'll come back an' catch us at it.'

'What's a tied cottage?' Peggy asked.

But Mum didn't enlighten her. She was already cooking.

With an oil lamp lit and Mum's nice fluffy scrambled eggs inside them the girls felt a little more cheerful. Peggy was just going to ask her mother where they were going to sleep when Aunt Maud came in through the door.

She was uglier than they remembered her too and not a bit like Mum, with that squashy looking face and hardly any forehead and those rotten teeth. And so fat, like two great bolsters tied in the middle with string. She grimaced when she saw them and bent forward to peck Mum's cheek.

'You got here then,' she said. 'Seen Dad, have yer?'

They admitted they had.

'Had supper?'

They admitted that too.

'Well that's a mercy,' their aunt said, taking off her hat and hanging it on a hook on the back of the door. 'We'll put those dishes in the sink before he can see 'em, an' then we'll get you children off to bed. Don't want 'em up when he gets back, eh?'

'No,' Mum said with feeling. 'We don't.'

Then he *is* cross, Peggy thought, instinctively under-standing that Mum and Aunt Maud were afraid of him. And she made up her mind to try and keep out of his way as much as she could.

The two women put the dishes in the sink and covered it with a red cloth. 'I don't know where you're all going to sleep, I'm sure,' Maud said, lighting a second oil lamp. 'There's only the two beds. Darn silly idea comin' here, you ask me.'

'Where else could I go, Maud?' Mum said plaintively. 'A poor widow woman. I couldn't manage on my own.'

'I'd ha' found somewhere in London,' Maud said, 'if it'ud been me. Why didn't you go to Greenwich with Gideon?'

Peggy's opinion of her aunt improved at once. She might be hideous but she had the right idea. They should have found somewhere in London.

'You don't know how difficult it is all on your own with three young children,' Mum said, wearing her most hard-done-by expression. 'You need someone to look after you then, I can tell you. Why shouldn't I come home, I should like to know?'

'That's all very well,' Aunt Maud said, picking up the second lamp. 'I can't see how we shall all make out crammed in here, and that's a fact. You never think though, do you?'

'We'll manage,' Mum said, rather grimly Peggy thought. 'If the worst comes to the worst one of us can sleep on the floor. I'm sure we're tired enough.'

'It'll be me,' Joan whispered to Peggy, when Aunt Maud turned away from them.

And of course she was right.

As the three girls rapidly discovered, Grandpa's cottage was cramped and inconvenient. It had two irregular rooms on each floor, kitchen and parlour below, two bedrooms above, and a smelly earth closet out in the garden. The staircase that divided the rooms rose as steep as a cliff and entirely unlit from behind the dark door of a cupboard in the corner of the kitchen. When Aunt Maud led them upstairs on that first evening she held the oil lamp above her head to show them the way, but even then it was horribly dark and Peggy and Baby both stumbled.

At the end of their climb they found themselves crowded into a narrow landing lit by one small attic window. Two ricketty doors led to right and left, one to Grandpa's bedroom, which faced the path at the front of the house, the other to Aunt Maud's, which was the smaller of the two and overlooked the cabbages and the hen run.

'In here,' Aunt Maud said opening the left-hand door and setting the lamp on the sconce beside the jamb. 'Mind how you go.'

It was a necessary warning, for if the kitchen was a dungeon, this room was an overcrowded draper's shop. In the flickering light it seemed to be full of linen. For a start there were two beds piled with coverlets and embroidered pillows and draped with chintz curtains, each with at least two valances decorated with huge floppy bows of cheap pink ribbon. One was a brass bedstead pushed against the wall under the eaves, the other was a high double bed set in the middle of the room, like a galleon in a pool. The ceiling bulged towards them, which was really no surprise because clothes hung from hooks all over it, ballooning dresses, petticoats like yellowing sails, stockings on strings, a mud-coloured coat as stiff as a board, turning and swaying in the breeze between the open door and the cracks under the window.

'Gosh!' Baby said.

'You can sleep on the floor,' Aunt Maud told her. 'I'll put pillows down.'

'Indeed she will not,' Mum said, bristling in defence of her darling. 'With her delicate bones. The very idea.'

'They can't all sleep in a single,' Aunt Maud said, sucking her remaining teeth. 'Even if they top and toe. I told you that. The springs wouldn't stand it.'

'Joan and Peggy can take it in turns,' Mum decided. 'A night on the floor won't hurt them. Not now an' then.'

'She seems to forget it'll be every other night,' Joan said from the pillows when the two adults had taken the lamp downstairs again and left them all in the darkness.

'It won't be for long,' Peggy said, trying to cheer them both up, ''cause we can't be going to stay here for long, can we?'

'Don't ask me,' Joan said. 'Bli this floor's hard!'

None of them got much sleep that night. Mum and Aunt Maud made ever such a row coming to bed, and then, when Mum was quietly asleep, Aunt Maud either lay on her back and snored, or bounced about so that the springs twanged like a banjo. In the middle of the night, when the room was as black as pitch, she got up and pulled a chamber pot from under her bed and made a lot of noise using it. And when it was very clearly morning she suddenly swung her legs out of the bed and flung back the curtains.

'Harvest!' she shouted. 'Ups-a-daisy! It's a beautiful day. Weather's holdin' up lovely.' She was struggling into the clothes she'd left strewn all over the foot of the bed the night before. 'Up gets Flossie!'

'What?' Mum said, sitting up among the tousled bedclothes with her hair wild about her face. 'What is it?'

'They'll be harvestin' the long field today sure as fate,' Aunt Maud said, buttoning her blouse across the straining mounds of her bosom. 'If I don't get his breakfast 'fore they come a-callin' for him, he'll have somethin' to say, I can tell you. Get up, do!'

'What's a time?' Mum groaned.

'Ha' past five.'

By then all three children were awake and yawning. 'You stay here,' Aunt Maud told them. 'Get yourselves all nicely washed an' dressed, while me an' your Mum gets breakfast. We got a busy day ahead.'

That was an understatement. It was the most exhausting day they'd ever known.

In the morning Mum and Aunt Maud rolled up their sleeves and made two fruit pies while the bread was baking. Then they gave the kitchen what they called 'a good clear out' while Baby sat in the sun and played with her dolls and Joan and Peggy shifted the furniture about and washed the windows and polished the spoons and finally cleaned the knives with pieces of cork and a harsh powder that coated their fingers with dark grey grime. And then just when they thought they were going to sit down and have a rest and something to eat, their trunk arrived on a wagon and had to be lugged indoors and unpacked and hidden away in the attic at once before Grandpa could know anything about it, and after that Aunt Maud took her new bread from the larder and packed it into a basket with a hunk of cheese and pickled onions and a flagon of cider and off they all went into the fields.

It was hot and dusty in the long field and the harvester was hard at work cutting the corn, and Grandpa and all the other men were hard at work with pitchforks gathering it into sheaves. Peggy saw that there were other women and children trudging through the stubble with their baskets, and she wondered whether they would all be allowed to stay in the fields after their dinner and play.

But harvest was no time for play. When the food had all been consumed and every last drop of cider squeezed from the flagons, the men returned to their labours and the women and children worked with them. For the rest of that long hot afternoon, they tied sheaves and carried sheaves and balanced them neatly into stooks, until their arms and legs were criss-crossed with scratches and Baby's nose was sunburnt.

'Poor Baby,' Mum commiserated, examining her reddened skin, 'You'd better stay at home tomorrow, darling.'

The farm hands laughed them both to scorn. 'Poor Baby!' they mocked. 'Hulkin' great lump. If she's a baby your Dad's the farm bull.' And that made them all raucous with laughter, which embarrassed Grandpa horribly and made him look shrivelled and unsure of himself, which Peggy thought very odd when you considered how fierce he was at home.

From that day on she and Joan worked every morning in the kitchen and every afternoon in the fields. By the end of the third day their backs ached and their shoulders were sore and their arms felt as though they'd been pulled out of their sockets. And to make matters worse whoever was sleeping on the floor had precious little sleep no matter how tired they were.

But at last the corn was cut and the fields had all been gleaned and there was a sack of flour from their gleanings sitting on a chair in Grandpa's kitchen like the honoured guest it was, and the labourers were looking out their Sunday clothes ready for the harvest supper.

'Be school soon,' Aunt Maud said to Mum, 'an' then we shall have to see about gettin' a job for your Joan. She can't go sleepin' on the floor for ever.'

'She can't take a job yet,' Mum objected. 'She's not fourteen till the end of September.'

'A few weeks,' Aunt Maud said. 'We can wink at that. I'll ask up the Manor.'

'What about the School Board man?' Mum worried. 'I don't want any argy-bargy.'

'Never you pay him no mind,' Aunt Maud said. 'He won't argy bargy with the Manor.'

'Aren't we going back to London then?' Joan hoped.

'Not yet awhile,' her mother said.

'By Christmas?' Peggy suggested. Oh if only it could be by Christmas.

'Now don't start,' her mother said. 'My nerves are ragged without that.'

Two days after the harvest supper, which had been a rough and rather drunken occasion even though there *was* plenty of food, Aunt Maud told Joan to 'dress black and white' and pack her things in a carrier bag because they were going 'up the Manor'.

'Is this the job d'you think?' Peggy asked as Joan put on her funeral skirt and her best cotton blouse.

'I 'spect so,' Joan said.

'D'you mind?' Peggy asked. It was awful to think she was being sent away like this.

'Not a matter 'a minding, is it,' Joan said, setting her belt and her mouth. 'We've all got to work. That's the way it is. It'll be your turn next.' Her resignation was stoical and total. What was the point of minding? 'We've all got to work.'

'Yes,' Peggy said, putting on her pinafore, 'I suppose so.' But it was horrid just the same.

63

There was no time for any more conversation because the kettle was whistling, and no time for farewells either. Breakfast was eaten in its usual munching silence, and the minute Grandpa was out of the house, Joan was told to put on her hat and coat.

'I'll send you a letter,' she whispered to Peggy as she buttoned her coat.

'I hope you get on all right,' Peggy whispered back.

And then her sister was gone, oh so quickly, walking quietly up the hill beside Aunt Maud's determined bulk. Nobody was surprised when two hours later Aunt Maud waddled back to the cottage on her own.

'Took on in the kitchens,' she said to Flossie. 'She's a lucky girl. Now we've only got to get these two down to Tillingbourne school and we can have this place back to rights. I never seen such clutter in all me life.'

The next day Mum walked Peggy and Baby through the fields and down into Tillingbourne where she enrolled them both at the village school. Baby was pale with apprehension at the thought of being away from her mother's protection for the first time in her life, but Peggy took it calmly. One more change among so many would hardly make any difference, and school was school, wherever it was. And her calm was rewarded because this school made her so welcome. She liked it at once.

For a start it reminded her of the Tower, because it wasn't just one school but three, infants, juniors and seniors, in three separate buildings standing side by side behind a long fence in an asphalt playground where trees and bushes grew. Two of the schools were made of sand-coloured stone and red brick like the barracks and the one she went to was exactly like the Beauchamp Tower. She felt at home straight away.

And her teacher was lovely. She was called Miss Butt and she had nice smiling eyes and smelled of lavender and wore her hair in two thick mounds piled on top of her head like a cottage loaf.

'We shan't be stayin' long,' Peggy told her, when she'd hung her coat on a peg and had her name written in the register. 'We're Londoners you see, Miss. We got to go back to London soon.'

'Yes,' Miss Butt said kindly, 'of course. However while you're here perhaps you wouldn't mind writing your name on this book.'

The autumn days grew shorter and colder and the cross-country trek to school longer and more mud spattered. Joan wrote a letter from Tillingbourne Manor to say that she was 'working hard and hoped it found them as it left her', and Grandpa started 'the ploughin'' with the result that he came home every evening chilled and mudcaked and ready to find fault with the least little thing. And Mum suffered torments with her nerves.

But Peggy could endure all these things now because she had school to look forward to. She made friends with two girls called Rose and Lily, she learned to play the local games, and her classroom was a warm, welcoming place that felt more like a home to her than her grandfather's cottage. There was a fire in every classroom in the building where wet gloves and boots were set to dry and where she and the other farm children were allowed to sit and eat their bread and cheese at dinner time. And the school was full of familiar reassuring sounds, the drone of prayers, and the sing-song chant of times tables, and the gaslight being lit in the middle of the afternoon with its lovely reassuring plop. Oh so much nicer than those smelly old oil lamps.

'School is alright,' she wrote to Joan. 'I like Miss Butt.'

'Tillingbourne Manor is alright,' Joan wrote back. 'The work is hard. Cook is alright. Food is good. There are four of us in my room but I would rather it was you. I have a bed of my own. Cook says I can have a day off Wednesday week to come and see the Carnival. See you then.'

She arrived at the cottage just as they were dishing up dinner. It was lovely to see her again. She was wearing her uniform and black stockings and black lace-up shoes that made her look ever so grown-up, and she smelled different, of carbolic soap and greasy dishes and starched cotton, and there was a long red burn not quite hidden on her right forearm, which everybody saw and nobody mentioned. But she kissed them all most lovingly and said she was getting on all right.

After dinner they all went down to Tillingbourne to

65

watch the procession, except for Grandpa who said he was too long in the tooth for that sort of caper. It was a very cold day and they got quite chilled while they waited, but the procession got going eventually. There were decorated trade carts and shire horses rattling their brasses, and floats from the Women's Institute and the pubs and all the village shops, and a fairy-tale coach painted red and gold for the Carnival Princess who sat huddled on her throne in the middle of her shivering attendants, red nosed but smiling bravely. The only trouble was it reminded Peggy and Joan of the last procession they'd seen, when Dad had walked beside the State Coach and they'd all been so happy. And that cast them both down into unhappiness again.

When the streets were empty again, and Mum and Aunt Maud and Baby and all their new neighbours went rushing back home as fast as they could, Joan and Peggy dawdled behind the rest. They walked arm in arm for comfort along the footpath from Tillingbourne and although the wind was blowing in their faces they paid no attention to it, for now at last they would have a chance to talk to one another again. Half-way up they stopped by the hawthorn hedge where there was a clear view across the valley to Tillingbourne Manor, neat as a doll's house on the opposite hillside.

'I look out for you every morning, you know,' Joan said, squeezing Peggy's arm.

'Do you?'

'Every morning.'

'Can you see us?' Peggy said, amazed by the thought.

'I can see your red beret walking along behind the hedge.' And every time she saw it she felt weak with homesickness. But she couldn't tell Peggy that because she was only little and it would upset her.

'I shall wave tomorrow,' Peggy promised. 'An' every morning after. Right here. By this big tree.'

'That's an oak,' Joan said. 'Cook's been teaching me. How are things at home?'

'All right,' Peggy said. 'Mum gets shirty sometimes.' It was cold in the cottage and uncomfortable and full of tensions she didn't like and couldn't understand, but she didn't think she ought to say so. Not now that Joan was in service because it might upset her, and that wouldn't be kind. 'What's it like working in a kitchen?'

'It's not so bad,' Joan said, but she had to change that subject quickly too in case talking about it made her cry. Now that she was home again she realized there was rather a lot she couldn't say. 'Tell me about school. I bet they don't learn you much.'

'There's a swimming-pool in the field at the back,' Peggy said, glad to find a topic that wouldn't upset either of them. 'You pay a shillin' when it opens, which is May, I think, an' they let you go swimming all through the summer. What d'you think a' that? If we're still here after Christmas I'm going to run errands with the others and save up for it. Only I don't suppose we shall still be here, shall we?' And she looked up hopefully at her big sister.

'If you ask me we shall still be here the Christmas *after* next,' Joan said. 'She don't mean to move, does she?'

That was too awful for Peggy to contemplate so she changed the subject. 'Will they let you home for Christmas?' she asked.

'Shouldn't think so,' Joan said importantly. 'The whole Bromwich family's coming down, the Captain and his wife and Miss Amelia and Master Toby and everybody. We're cooking a turkey an' a goose an' a sirloin a' beef. I 'spect they'll let us off afterwards though. In the New Year.'

It made Peggy feel sad to think that they would be apart at Christmas time, but she didn't say anything about that either, because she could see that Joan was putting on a brave face.

'I shall see you at midnight mass,' Joan promised. 'We're all coming down to the church at Tillingbourne for that.'

But it wouldn't be the same, Peggy thought sadly, because they wouldn't be in the Tower, and they wouldn't be with Dad. It would be sad like it had been at the procession. And she missed him with the same dreadful lurching sensation she'd felt so terribly when he died. Dear, dear Dad. Christmas would be awful without him. 'It's ever so cold,' she said, shivering.

'Let's make tracks,' Joan said.

CHAPTER 6

The family pig lived in a sty behind the chicken run. Actually, according to Aunt Maud he was only half theirs because they owned him jointly with Mr and Mrs Matthews next door, which seemed rather odd, but he was an amiable animal however much they owned of him. At first Peggy had been rather wary of him because he had mean little eyes like Grandpa and an enormous chomping mouth and a habit of barging the side of the sty as though he was going to knock it down, but as the days passed, she realized there was no malice in him at all and she became quite fond of him. She and Baby were sent off every day to gather buckets full of acorns for him, which he scrunched up with ridiculous pleasure, dribbling and snuffling and watching them eagerly in case there was more to come, and when they'd fed him they leaned over the side of the sty and scratched his back with a stick and talked to him.

'He's a funny sort of pet really,' Baby observed. 'I'd rather have one you could keep in the house, like a cat or a puppy.'

'It's different in the country,' Peggy said. The farm cats lived in the barn and the dog was kept in a kennel when she wasn't working the sheep. 'He's jolly useful though, aren't you, Pig? He eats up all the scraps.'

The pig snuffed the toes of her shoes, leaving a trail of white slobber across the leather.

'D'you think we could take him for a walk?' Baby asked, trying to unwind his tail with her stick.

'No. I don't,' Peggy said, sensibly. 'You don't take animals for walks in the country. Come on. Time we were off to school.'

It was half a mile from Grandpa's cottage to Tillingbourne school and the darker the days became the further it felt. The fields were full of alien creatures, tatty sheep with peculiar eyes, pale blue with a black stripe down the middle, rooks strutting aggressively or sawing the air with malevolent cries, massive cows with grey tongues and eyelashes like brushes, the great concave bones of their haunches as sharp as cleavers under their mud-caked skin.

All this was bad enough in the daytime, but it was worse when Peggy was lugging her sister back home in the lessening light of a winter dusk, for then the half-seen animals were at their most threatening and the hedges creaked and glittered with little watching eyes. She walked as quickly as she could, half trotting, half afraid, with her senses at full stretch, ready for anything.

Even so, the sudden noise she heard that evening in November was so awful it made her heart jump with fear. It was a high-pitched terrified squeal, and it went on and on, getting higher and higher and more and more terrible.

'It's Pig,' she said, grabbing Baby's hand. 'Run! It's Pig!'

They skimmed over the rough earth as quickly as they could, stumbling and panting, and now they could hear shouts and roars, and see the flicker of lanterns behind the hedge, and at that she dropped Baby's hand and ran on ahead without her, struggling through into the clearing, and there was Pig running madly from side to side as though he was being pulled between two ropes, with Mum and Aunt Maud and all their neighbours chasing him and shouting at him, their long shadows leaping beside them on the trampled grass.

'I'll get you some acorns,' Peggy shouted into the hubbub. 'You could catch him with acorns as easy as pie.'

And a strange man rose up behind the pig, tall and black as an avenging angel, and hit the frantic animal on the side of the head with a huge sledge hammer.

The sickening thud of the blow reverberated in Peggy's

69

skull as though she'd been struck down herself. She was so shocked she couldn't move. They're killing him, she thought. They're killing our pig. And she knew they wanted to kill the poor thing, that they'd planned it, because they were laughing and cheering as though they'd done something wonderful. And the butcher lifted Pig by his snout and slit his throat. The gush of bright red blood from that awful slit was too much. With a strangled cry of horror and compassion, Peggy ran from the scene into the bushes where she was violently sick.

When she came back, the poor pink corpse was lying on a trestle table surrounded by women, who were scalding him with boiling water and scraping him with long knives and as little concern as if they were scraping earth from new potatoes. Baby had joined the group and was standing beside their mother watching the proceedings with great interest.

'There you are,' Mum said happily. 'Ain't he a fine fat pig?'

'You killed him,' Peggy said, with disbelief and revulsion.

'A' course,' Aunt Maud said. 'That's what pigs are for.'

'We got to eat,' Mum said. 'No good bein' sentimental when you live on a farm. We always kill off old stock in the autumn. Old stock and young pigs. We don't breed 'em for old age. Bred for the table they are. He's had a good life.'

'We shall live off this pig all winter,' Aunt Maud said. 'Us and the Matthews. Pig's fry, trotters, chitterlins, lard, pig's head, roast pork, nice salt bacon. Won't be a thing go to waste, you'll see. He'll last till the spring. Wait till you taste the bacon he'll make.'

But Peggy was still white with shock.

'You've bred a townie,' Aunt Maud said to Flossie.

'She'll prefer the spring,' Flossie said, scraping vigorously, 'won't you, Peggy? All those pretty new lambs. An' Easter eggs. She likes Easter eggs.'

Then we're not going back to London after Christmas, Peggy thought, but she was too numb with shock to do more than register the fact. It was something she ought to have known, just as she ought to have known they were going to kill the pig. Oh Dad, she grieved, if only you were

70

still alive none of this would have happened. And she took Baby by the hand and walked miserably into the cottage away from the nightmare.

Spring was a long time coming that year. The footpaths were still slippery with mud when the first primroses appeared, pale and hesitant and vulnerable beneath the rough claws of the hedges. And the little new lambs were vulnerable too, huddled beside the dirty fleeces of the ewes, like little heaps of unmelted snow. Peggy felt sorry for them, bred for the table, and when the first balmy days stirred warm air along the hillside and they began to jump and frisk on their stiff little legs, she felt sorrier than ever.

'It's ever such a cruel world,' she said to Joan when she was home one Sunday afternoon and all three girls were walking down to evening service together.

'Yes,' Joan said easily. 'Course it is.'

'I wish it wasn't.'

'Well it is,' Joan said, 'so there's no use fretting about it is there?' She'd had a very bad week in the kitchens, with two dinner parties that hadn't gone as well as they should have done and Cook bad-tempered as a result, and on Friday she'd gashed her finger when she was chopping carrots, and had then been sent to mash spinach through a hair sieve, which was a job she really hated.

'One of the cats had kittens this morning,' Baby told them. 'They're ever so pretty.'

'We'll go an' see 'em after church,' Joan decided. 'How many's she got?'

There were four, one black, one ginger and two tabby like their mother, who was lying in the nest of straw she'd made herself at the far end of the barn, purring and contented as the little creatures squeaked and suckled, their tiny bodies trembling with pleasure.

Peggy was enraptured by them. 'They're so soft,' she said, stroking the velvety fur on the black kitten's tremulous back. Soft and defenceless with their tiny scrabbling paws and their eyes shut tight. 'I can feel his spine. All the little bones. Could we pick them up?'

'I don't see why not?' Joan said. 'She don't seem to mind.'

So they each picked up a kitten to cuddle and Peggy

71

had one of the tabby ones, which she held right up under her chin, thrilled by its tiny warmth and the way its little paws scrabbled into her neck. 'It's trying to climb,' she said. 'Oh it's lovely. D'you think Mum would let me have it for a pet?'

'I want one too if you're having one,' Baby said.

The mother cat was beginning to look anxious, her green eyes very watchful.

'She wants 'em back,' Joan said, setting her kitten gently down on the straw beside its mother's extended flank.

Baby and Peggy relinquished their kittens too, Peggy very reluctantly, and they all watched while the mother cat washed all four with her harsh pink tongue, gently holding them down with one paw and licking them, from their dear little round heads to their funny little spiky tails.

'They're the prettiest things I've ever seen,' Peggy said. 'I shall come and see them every day. An' I'll ask Mum tonight.'

'Wait till I've gone back then,' Joan said. 'If you're going to make her shirty I'd rather be out of it.'

'Will it make her shirty?' Peggy wondered. But she knew it was likely. Mum and Aunt Maud were both the same. They got shirty at the least little thing and they always seemed to be on the edge of having a row. One would start to say something unkind and then stop and make a grimace, and the other one would reply with something equally nasty, and she'd stop half-way too, and shrug her shoulders and look hateful. There wasn't any sense in it.

'Yes,' Joan said. 'Either her or Aunt Maud. You know what they're like.'

'Sometimes I wish they'd have a proper barney and have done with it,' Peggy said.

Joan had her own grimace now, which she put on when-ever a grown-up was being silly. 'I think they enjoy carping,' she said.

'The only time they agree with one another is when they're hiding something from Grandpa.'

'I've noticed,' Joan said. 'Come on, we'd better be

getting in, or it'll be time to set the table and we shan't be there and then we *shall* cop it.'

So they went in, and as the atmosphere round the supper table was rather fraught Peggy decided to wait till next day before she asked about the kitten.

It was a decision she was to regret for a very long time.

The next evening as soon as she got home from school, she left Baby sitting by the stove and rushed off to the barn.

She could hear the kittens squealing as she ran in the door. Dear little things. Then she noticed that one of the farm hands was kneeling in the straw where the mother cat had made her nest. He looked up as she came running in, shifting his body slightly in her direction, and she saw that it was Josh who lived in the end cottage, and that he had all four kittens held tightly in one hand.

'You won't hurt them, will you?' she said, walking towards him, and worried in case the mother cat was upset by having all her babies removed from the nest at once. 'They're ever so little.'

'Hurt 'em?' he said, and he laughed in a rough horrid way, showing the gaps in his teeth. 'That's rich! Hurt 'em!'

She was suddenly afraid, remembering the pig. 'What are you going to do with them?' she said.

His answer was immediate and laconic. 'Why drown 'em, gel. What else? Vermin they are.'

'Oh you can't!' she cried, her hands to her mouth in distress.

But he was half-way across the barn, with the mother cat mewing at his heels, and already thrusting the kittens into a bucket. She could hear the slop of the water as he pushed them down, and their paws scraping against the tin sides, and their frantic, tiny screams. 'Oh please!' she said. 'Don't! I'll look after them.'

'Don't be daft,' he said, prodding into the bucket with a broom handle. 'Always drown kittens we do. Tha's the way of it. We'd be overrun else. You wouldn't want that.'

But she would, she would. She couldn't bear this awful, unnecessary, lingering death. And the mother cat crying so terribly too.

It seemed hours before the little mewing cries finally

stopped and then it was so quiet in the barn that she could hear her own heart beating. The farm hand trudged out of the door swinging the bucket in his hand. 'Shove off home,' he said to her as he passed. 'You got no business in 'ere.'

But she stayed where she was. She was too shocked and miserable to do anything else, and besides somebody had to look after the poor mother cat, who had crept back to her empty nest and was licking her swollen teats. Didn't he understand how awful it was to see your babies being killed? He could at least have left her one. He didn't have to drown them all. It was too cruel. Weeping with pity, she crept into the straw beside the little cat and began to stroke her back, very very softly.

'If I was grown up,' she said passionately, 'you could be my cat. I'd take you away and keep you somewhere safe and you could have as many kittens as you wanted and I wouldn't drown *one*. Not *ever*. You poor thing.'

But she wasn't grown up. She was only eight and she had no power at all.

After that she took tit-bits out to the cat whenever she could, although she was very careful to do it when there was no one about to see her, just in case Josh came back and decided to drown the mother as well as her babies. And the kittens died again and again in the misery of her dreams.

If only we could go back to London, she thought, when she woke wet-eyed and grieving. If only Mum would make up her mind and take us all back. Joan wouldn't have to go on working in the kitchen and getting burnt and Mum wouldn't have to go on living here and arguing with Aunt Maud, and we could take the cat with us and let her keep all her kittens.

But Mum showed no signs of wanting to go back to London. She never ever mentioned the place. And that was because she very rarely thought of it.

For although none of her daughters knew anything about it, Flossie Furnivall had found an escape from her cramped existence in Grandpa's cottage and it was an escape that suited her extremely well.

* * *

Once Joan had been settled at work and Peggy and Baby were both at school, life on the farm had been undeniably dull and difficult. She and Maud spent all their time in the house, scrubbing, sweeping, washing up, feeding the chickens, feeding the pig, placating their father and cooking endless, boring meals. And they really didn't get on. There was no denying it. There was always a row hanging in the air between them, like a perpetual unspoken complaint. After three weeks of the same unvaried repetition and the same nerve-racking, half-spoken disapproval, she felt she couldn't face another day of it. Something would have to be done about it. And just at that moment a letter arrived with the Postal Order for her widow's pension. She put half of it away in Joe's old wallet for her keep and decided to spend some of the rest of it on herself. It was high time she had some pleasure in her life. She'd been dull long enough.

'I think I'll go into Guildford,' she said to Maud when the girls had left for school and they'd finished doing the washing-up. 'Buy a few bits and bobs. Candied peel, some nice dried fruit perhaps.' She took her compact out of her handbag and considered her face thoughtfully. What a very long time it had been since anyone had told her how pretty she was.

'Today?' Maud said, emptying the washing-up bowl so crossly that the dirty water splashed over the edge of the sink.

'Why not?' Flossie asked, stroking her eyebrows.

'Can't see the point,' Maud said, wiping her soapy hands on her apron. 'It's not as if you ...'

'Make a nice change,' Flossie said, starting her make-up.

'All that tittivating,' Maud mocked, as her sister powdered her nose, tilting the compact towards the window so that she could see what she was doing. 'Anyone'ud think you was royalty.'

'When I lived in the Tower a' London,' Flossie said, 'I'd never have dreamed of going out without looking my best. None of us would. We had standards to keep up. Which is more than I can say for ...'

'Standards my eye,' Maud said. 'You're in the country now, gel.'

But criticism only made Flossie more determined. She put on her brightest lipstick and her best hat and caught the very next train in to the town. Guildford had been an escape route fifteen years ago. Perhaps it would be an escape route again.

But fifteen years is a very long time, and if she had a vague hope that she might meet up with another attentive soldier to pay court to her that day it was squashed the moment she set foot outside the railway station, for although there were plenty of soldiers about, the women they were escorting were very, very young, little more than girls really, not thirty-two-year-olds with grown children.

Never mind, she comforted herself, as she crossed Town Bridge and headed uphill towards the centre of the town, there's still the shops. I've still got money to spend and it's better being out here than stuck in the cottage with Maud. The pavements were crowded and there was a brass band striding down the High Street making a proper racket. If she couldn't find something to amuse herself in a town like Guildford she'd have to be deaf and blind.

She'd walked in to North Street to buy her groceries and some more nerve tonic and treat herself to a new pair of stockings, and when her shopping basket was pleasantly full she strolled on uphill towards the market in North Street to see what the fruit and vegetables were like, and there, just around the corner in Woodbridge Street, was a queue of people patiently standing in line. They were waiting outside a new building that looked like a fairground kiosk with coloured lights all round the entrance. Intrigued, she turned aside into Woodbridge Street to see what it was. 'New Cinema' it said and plastered right across the front of it was the biggest poster she'd ever seen. It caught her eye and her imagination at once.

A beautiful girl with a mane of thick curly hair and enormous eyes were gazing adoringly at a tall impossibly handsome man who was looking straight down at her parted lips for all the world as if he were just about to kiss her. The sight of it made her go quite weak at the knees. 'Romance of Redwood' the legend said, 'starring Mary Pickford'.

Flossie had been to the pictures now and then with Joe,

76

usually to see the newsreels, which she found rather boring, or one of Charlie Chaplin's comedies, which were funny but not as funny as she expected. But this picture looked like something quite different. Does he actually kiss her? she wondered. Do you see it? And she knew *she* would like to see it, if he did, and if she could.

The queue shuffled forward several paces, excitement warming the faces of the women as they trotted to the ticket office.

Why not? Flossie thought, hugging her shopping basket. I've earned a bit of pleasure after all these weeks, and I'm sure Joe would want me to. He always said 'all work an' no play' so he wouldn't want me to stint myself. Suitably justified, she joined the end of the queue, which was moving again.

It was the happiest afternoon she'd spent in years and years. To sit at ease in the plushy darkness and be carried effortlessly away into another world was a luxury beyond her most luxurious dreams. And such a world it was, a fantasy coming true before her eyes, where a dashing hero rescued the beautiful heroine and foiled every dastardly deed just in the nick of time, as the audience sighed and caught its communal breath in longing. And when the last reel was finally running and the hero bent his handsome head to take the kiss he'd been promised all through the picture, tears of sentimental joy rose into Flossie's eyes and she let them fall in exquisite abandon. Oh it was sheer bliss, that's what it was. Sheer bliss.

She travelled home still wrapped in fantasy, reliving the romantic swooning pleasure of that kiss, fancying herself in Mary Pickford's pretty shoes, entirely and vicariously happy. From then on her dreams were full of impossibly handsome men who would do anything for her, who vowed their everlasting love for her, who begged to kiss her, but never spoiled themselves by wanting to do anything else. There was never any nasty sex with her dream lovers. They were all gentlemen to the ends of their brilliantined hair.

After that first rapturous experience she went to the pictures every Thursday afternoon. She saw *Good Women* and *Under Northern Lights* and *The Story of the Jaguar*.

77

She laughed quite a lot at Charlie Chaplin in *The Fireman* and she very nearly swooned away when she watched Douglas Fairbanks in *The Three Musketeers* because he was more handsome and dashing than anyone she'd ever seen.

Now, no matter how dark and difficult life in the cottage might be, she had her dreams to sustain her. The weeks passed quickly, the chores were soon done, Christmas came and went, it was the New Year, the spring, but none of it meant very much to her. There was only that gleaming screen and the romance of the black and white world that flickered upon it. If she could enjoy that once a week, she could endure anything.

CHAPTER 7

The Reverend Beaumont, rector of the church of St James at Tillingbourne, had just taken assembly for the elementary school. Now he was praying.

'Lord,' he said, looking down kindly at the rows of poorly-clad children fidgeting before him on that dreary December morning, 'Lord, give us the strength to endure those things that ought to be endured, and the courage to change those things that ought to be changed, and the wisdom to know the one from the other. Amen.'

'Amen,' the children grumbled, coughing and shifting their feet. It had been a long assembly and they were slummocky with boredom. Only Peggy Furnivall was really paying attention to him.

This was her third Christmas at Tillingbourne school and she was ten years old now and grown quite big. She knew all her tables and the capitals of the world and the Kings and Queens of England and how to do sums and how to write essays, and she had all her grown-up teeth and a long plait of straight brown hair to hang down her back, and she'd even learned to swim during that first hot summer.

Nowadays she kept out of the way when pigs or kittens were being killed, because it grieved her enough to know it was happening without having to witness it. She still fed the mother cat whenever she could and did her best to comfort the poor thing when her kittens were gone, and she still dreamed of her dear old Dad and London and the

79

Tower, and more than anything else in the world she wanted to go back and be a Londoner again. That was what she'd change if she only got the chance. But it would be three and a half years before she could get a job and look out for herself. So until then she just had to endure those things that had to be endured, the way the Reverend Beaumont said. But she added her own private prayer every day, after the Lord's Prayer and before 'amen', even though she really didn't have very much hope that it would be answered. It was simple and to the point. 'Please God make something happen so that we can go back to London.'

And that Christmas something was happening, and it was happening at Tillingbourne Manor.

During the two and a half years that Joan Furnivall had worked at the Manor, first as a kitchen-maid and then as a plain cook, she had changed from a gawky thirteen-year-old to a confident well-rounded sixteen. Good feeding had put flesh on her bones and given her something of her mother's foxy prettiness. Her hair, now neatly bobbed, was thicker, her eyebrows were more pronounced and her eyes were a darker brown. In fact she was beginning to fear she might be growing vain, her image in the bedroom mirror pleased her so much. She had grown skilled in the arts of the kitchen too, learning not to burn herself or cut her fingers, and discovering that she had a talent for fruit puddings, which endeared her to the rest of the staff, and that she was a dab hand at pasties, which pleased Cook, who said they were 'nothing short of a bloomin' wonder'.

Now, buoyed up by their approval, and rather to her own surprise, she had followed Cook's trenchant advice and applied for a new and more important job. Miss Amelia Bromwich, the daughter of the house, was coming home from her finishing school in Switzerland to be 'launched upon society' and according to Miss Quinn, who was the lady's maid and looked after both the ladies, she would need an extra maid whenever she was at the house, because she had asthma. So somebody would have to sleep in her dressing-room and keep an ear open in case she had an attack during the night.

80

'Try for it, gel,' the Cook said. 'Nothing venture, nothing gain, that's what I say.'

'What else would I have to do?' Joan wondered.

'Clean her clothes, do her mending, run her bath, make her breakfast,' Cook said. 'All the ordinary sort a' things. Miss Quinn'll do the tricky stuff.'

So she'd applied and since then she'd been surreptitiously studying how to be a lady's maid, offering to help Miss Quinn when she was cleaning Mrs Bromwich's fine clothes, taking over the preparation of dishes she knew Miss Amelia particularly liked, learning how to use a steam kettle and make a nitre cone for the asthma, picking up tips from conversations. She was very determined so she'd learnt quickly. She already knew how to wash lace, how to remove grease from gloves and shoes with the white of an egg, and how to reduce mildew by soft soap and powdered starch mixed with salt and lemon juice. Oh, it was hard work trying to better yourself.

It would have been easier if she'd been able to talk about it at home before she'd made her decision, but Aunt Maud wasn't interested, and Mum was so vague and distant nowadays she hardly said a word to anyone, and although Peggy would have been pleased to hear what she was doing she was too young to give advice.

So she still hadn't said a word to anyone at home when Christmas Eve arrived. She sat beside the Christmas tree in the hall that afternoon, feeling presumptuous and uncomfortable and idle, because all her friends in the kitchen were hard at work preparing for Christmas dinner and all she had to do was wait to be called into Mrs Bromwich's parlour. It was the first time she'd been above stairs and the richness and lightness of the place made her feel exposed. Grandpa's cottage was so dark and drear, and Dad's house in the Casemates had been dark too, but here the walls were white and the stairs were covered in pink carpet and the banisters were made of a lovely light-brown wood and the windows were so big they were like brightly-coloured pictures on the walls. It was like sitting inside one of the new electric lights. She twisted her handkerchief in her chapped hands and licked her lips nervously, her head bowed, because it wouldn't have done to have someone come out of the room and find her staring at things.

Which was how young Toby Bromwich saw her, as he came springing down the stairs two at a time.

Young Toby Bromwich was the only son and heir of his father's considerable fortune and as such he was spoilt, arrogant and self-centred. Although he was only sixteen he already had a portly figure and the beginnings of a double chin and jowls, but in his opinion, as he frequently told his school friends, a little rotundity was admirable and infinitely preferable to the scarecrow raggedness of all those awful smelly beggars you saw on the streets of London. Ex-servicemen and tramps and such. They oughtn't to be allowed. He couldn't think why the government didn't pass a law against them.

He liked his women plump too, as he expounded with equal frequency. 'Good tits on 'em,' he'd say, while his friends admired his boldness. 'Nice bit of flesh for a chap to get his hands on. That's what *I* like.'

Actually for all his lecherous talk he was still a virgin, which was a source of great annoyance and frustration to him. Girls were never allowed in school, that was the trouble, and at home his sister's friends poked fun at him and called him 'little brother' because he wasn't in society yet, and all the servants were old and crabby and uninteresting, like Miss Quinn.

So he was roused and delighted when he reached the hall and saw a nice plump sandy-haired *young* servant licking her lips outside his mother's parlour. Good tits too. Things *were* looking up. And standing up as well, with a rush of happy pleasure.

'Hel*lo*,' he said standing as close to her as he could. 'D'you work here?'

As she sprang to her feet, her cheeks reddened. What fun! She was actually blushing. He'd never made a girl blush before. Better and better. 'Yes, sir,' she said. 'In the kitchens.' So that was why he hadn't seen her before. They might as well be buried when they worked in the kitchens. You never saw them above stairs.

'Not in any trouble I hope,' he said.

'Oh no, sir,' she said, blushing again.

'Then what brings you here?'

She confided in him. He was being so friendly she felt it was permissible. 'It's just – well, sir – it's just I've applied to be Miss Amelia's maid.'

'Have you indeed?' he said. 'Well I wish you luck. Hope you get it.' And if you get it, he thought, and it brings you above stairs, I might get what I want too. What a turn up for the books!

The door was being opened. He could sense Miss Quinn. Better scoot. His mother would hardly approve of him chatting to a servant. He dodged into the library, beaming at the girl as he went. But she was straightening her cap and looking anxiously towards the door.

It was a very quick interview, which was just as well, for by then Joan was in a state of such nervousness she hardly knew what she was saying. She walked into Mrs Bromwich's lovely blue and yellow parlour in a dream that focused all her attention on a single object to the detriment of everything else. She saw nothing of the room although she was acutely aware of her mistress, that her bobbed hair was bound with an embroidered fillet which flashed and glittered as she spoke, that she was wearing a silk dress with a three-quarter length jacket to match, that she was haloed in rainbow light from twin lustres on the mantelpiece, that she spoke beautifully and seemed kind.

Fortunately the questions she asked could all be answered with a simple 'yes' or 'no'. Joan agreed that she was quite prepared to sit up at night with her new mistress should that be required, that she would obey Miss Quinn in every particular, that she would return to her work in the kitchen when Miss Amelia was away from the house, that she would be happy with an extra one and sixpence a week for her services. And the matter was almost settled when Miss Amelia herself breezed into the room, a strong spicy perfume wafting before her, thin as a rake in a suit like a blue and green tube and trailing a fur coat along the floor behind her as though it was a mop, a vision of careless affluence.

'You have a new maid, darling,' her mother said.

'Oh yes,' the vision said without much interest.

'Her name's Joan.'

'She may start tonight,' Amelia said. 'We're all going on

83

to Tufty's after dinner. Very swish affair. I shall wear my white satin with sequins, Quinn.'

And that, apparently, was that.

Joan had never been so busy as she was that Christmas, for her young mistress apparently required a change of clothes every two hours, for the morning, the afternoon, the evening, to hunt, to ride, to dine, to 'go on', whatever that was. There was no end to it. But she liked the work for it took her out of the kitchen into the space and ease of life above stairs.

'How the other half live!' she said to Peggy when she finally got home to see her family in the New Year. 'You should see the way they eat. Nine courses last Saturday there was. Nothink short of a bloomin' wonder they weren't all sick.'

Peggy was interested in Miss Amelia's asthma. 'What d'you have to do if she gets an attack, poor thing?' she asked. 'When Peter-at-school gets his he turns all blue an' Mr Marshall has to carry him out.'

'They all turn blue,' Joan said. 'That's part of it. We've got nitre cones for Miss Amelia. Paper, you know, soaked in saltpetre. We light one and she sort of smokes the fumes. And a spray. We got two sprays, hers an' a spare. We soon get her over it.' Which wasn't quite true but it sounded good. 'No, asthma's not a problem, leastways not when you're rich.'

The problem was Master Toby. Ever since that first day when he'd talked to her in the hall, he'd taken to lurking in Miss Amelia's bedroom when his sister wasn't there and jumping out on her as she came in through the servants' door, like some huge pink spider after a fly.

'He*llo*!' he'd say, leering at her. It was really rather embarrassing. And he stood so close to her too. She could feel his breath on her face, all hot and puffing. She would duck out of his way, with a rapid excuse, 'Just off to get this mended for Miss Amelia.' But now and then he'd put his hand on her arm and pin her to the wall, and then she didn't know what she ought to do, for there was something demanding and disturbing in the pressure of that fat hand of his, and his face looked really peculiar.

If only Peggy was just a little bit older she could confide

in her, but it wouldn't be fair to tell a ten-year-old things like that. Not things about – well – things about how boys went on. Sally would have listened all right but Sally was gone. She'd been a parlour-maid in the house until October and she'd enlightened all four of her room mates about all sorts of things, especially the monthlies when they'd first 'come on'. They wrote to one another occasionally, but writing wasn't the same as talking, and in any case she couldn't find the words to explain what it was about Mr Toby that alarmed her. When she tried, it all seemed rather silly. Perhaps it was silly and she simply ought to put it out of her mind. As Dad used to say, never trouble trouble, till trouble troubles you.

Toby Bromwich was in his sister's sitting room, trying to smoke a cigarette without feeling sick. 'Where's your maid, Melia?' he said casually. 'I ain't seen her about.'

'Day off,' Amelia said, propping her feet on the footstool so that her soles were facing the fire. 'Can't see what she wants a day off for. They never go anywhere these village gels.'

'So you'll have old Quinn to dress you tonight, I suppose.'

'No. She'll be back in time for that. I gave strict instructions.'

'Got anything planned, have you?'

'You know I have, Toby. You don't listen. Derwent is picking me up at nine. We're going up west.'

'Ah yes, I remember,' he said yawning. Now that he'd found out what he wanted to know he could pretend that the conversation was boring him. 'I wish they didn't dine so late. I'm riding over to Dorking.'

'In the dark?'

'Why not?'

'Because you haven't exactly got a good seat at the best of times.'

'I shall do well enough,' he said smugly. In fact with Melia out of the way he might do very well indeed. Especially if that servant answered the bell when he rang. He had it all planned.

Joan was surprised to be rung for so late. The servants

had all had their supper and she was helping Cook with the aspic moulds when the bell jumped and jangled.

'Thought she was out,' Cook said, looking up at the bell-board.

'So did I,' Joan said, wiping her hands and removing her kitchen apron. Miss Quinn was still with Mrs Bromwich so she would have to answer it. 'Better see what she wants. Perhaps she's come back for something.'

But when she opened the servants' door into her mistress' bedroom there was no one there.

'Yes, Miss Amelia?' she said.

'In here,' a muffled voice said from the dressing room.

Oh surely she wasn't having an attack, Joan thought, running towards the voice and wondering whether she ought to take the spare spray with her just in case. She *did* sound odd.

And she opened the interconnecting door and ran straight into Master Toby's grabbing arms. The impact took her breath away.

'Oh!' she said, trying to disengage herself. 'Master Toby. What is it?'

'You are,' he said thickly. 'You are, my booful Joanie.' He was still in his evening dress, and his face was covered in dark pink blotches, like the measles. Oh dear. Whatever was she going to do now? He oughtn't to be grabbing hold of her like that.

'Please don't!' she said stepping backwards as well as she could. 'Mrs Bromwich'ud be ever so cross.'

'My mumsy,' he said, speaking deliberately and following her step by step, 'my mumsy won't be ever so cross, as you put it, my booful Joansy-Woansy, because she won't know anything about it. Will she? She's in her own dressing room on the other side of the house with old Quinn. That's where Mumsy is. That's where she'll be for simply aeons. And I'm here with my booful.'

Perhaps he's drunk, she thought. That would account for the blotches. And she wondered how you were supposed to deal with a drunk when the drunk was one of your masters. Would she have the strength to extricate herself if she pushed against his chest? And was a servant allowed to do such a thing?

It was a great mistake, for the moment her fingers touched his flesh he grabbed them and held them so hard he crushed them bone to bone.

'Please, Master Toby,' she begged. 'You're hurting.'

'You drive me wild, you booful thing,' he said, pulling her towards him. And he certainly looked very wild. 'Can't you see what a state I'm in? Or have I got to show you? Oh it's all your fault, can't you see?'

She didn't know what to say without sounding impolite and running the risk of being dismissed for insubordination, because it wasn't her fault. She hadn't done anything. But his next words changed the situation entirely.

'I love you,' he said, panting as though he'd been running for a bus. 'That's how it is. I love you, Joany-Woany.'

What an amazing marvellous thing! Joan thought, staring at him. He loves me! The young master of this house loves me! Me! Joan Furnivall, lady's maid. 'Do you?' she said. 'Really?'

He recognized his advantage and wasted no time in following it through. 'Oh yes,' he said. 'Passionately. Course. Give us a kiss.'

She put up her face obediently. As he loved her it was the least she could do. What an amazing thing, she thought again as he pressed his hot moist lips all over her mouth. It wasn't a very nice sensation because he was dribbling so much, but as he loved her . . .

'Spiffing!' he said, when he finally stopped. 'Top hole! You are a brick! Let's do it again, eh?'

So she allowed him to do it again. And again and again, until she began to fear he would mark her collar with all that spit.

But there were footsteps approaching along the corridor. He stopped, instantly very alert, and moved away from her, putting one podgy finger to his lips to show that she wasn't to make a sound. The footsteps passed, walked on, faded in the distance.

'Phew!' he said. 'That was a close call. Not a word to anyone, mind. Promise me.'

'Yes,' she said, still stunned by the speed and improbability of it all.

'That's all right then,' he said. 'It'll be our secret, eh? A

lovers' secret. We won't let anyone else know. I'll be back.'
And he shot off through the interconnecting door, blundered through his sister's bedroom and was gone.

Does he mean me to stay here and wait for him? Joan wondered, standing alone in the drenching silence he'd left behind. It was really amazing to think how much her life had changed in the last few minutes. When she'd run up the back stairs she'd been just another servant answering a bell, now she was loved, chosen, special. It was like a romantic novel. During the last two years she and Sally had spent their rare spare moments reading lots and lots of romantic novels, where the doctor fell in love with his nurse, or the boss with his secretary or the master with his servant, but neither of them had ever imagined they would actually see such a thing happening in real life. I'll write to her tonight, she thought, thrilling with pride and pleasure because she really did have something to write about now. I shall say, 'I've got a sweetheart. What do you think of that?' Oh what a marvellous thing!

Sally's answer, which arrived nearly a week later, was rather a disappointment. 'Can't say I'd fancy him myself,' she wrote. 'He always looked a proper slob to me. But there you are, it takes all sorts. If you're happy I suppose it's alright. Only don't you let him take advantage, that's all.'

Her advice was too late. Advantage had been well and truly taken.

Fired by a combination of masculine pride, fear of discovery and perpetual lustfulness, Master Toby Bromwich had pressed on with his seduction as fast as he could. Every evening as soon as his sister was safely out of the house he stole along to her bedroom and rang the bell. And every evening as soon as Joan appeared in the dressing room he began to make love to her. On the second evening he persuaded her to let him feel her nipples, which did rather less for him that he'd expected but was pleasant enough. On the third she wouldn't undo her clothes, because she said it wasn't right, stupid girl, but he got as far as rocking against her belly for several most enjoyable seconds. On the fourth, in a sudden blaze of inspiration he brought her a present.

It was a box of Turkish Delight he'd bought in Dorking that afternoon because he rather fancied it himself.

'For me?' she said, when he produced it from his pocket. 'Oh Master Toby, how kind!'

'Told you I loved you, didn't I?' he said, much gratified by her response. And he slid two fingers down inside her blouse to see what would happen. She didn't stop him or say he shouldn't, so after a suitable interval he slid the other hand up her skirt and began to stroke the top of her leg. She didn't stop that either, although she looked sort of puzzled.

'Why don't we lie down?' he said. 'We'd be ever so much more comfortable.' If she didn't give in soon he'd be back at school, and he *did* want to do it before he went back to school.

'D'you think we ought?' she said doubtfully.

'Course,' he told her. 'We love each other, don't we?'

She agreed that they did, although she wasn't at all sure of her own feelings towards him. But she could hardly say she didn't know, could she? It would upset him too much.

'Well then,' he said, pushing her towards the edge of the bed.

She lay down reluctantly.

'Lift your skirt up,' he instructed, pushing the cheap black cotton up and out of his way. 'Then you won't get it creased.'

'Well ...' she said. 'I don't know ...'

'I do,' he said, rolling on top of her, fumbling with the buttons on his flies. Be masterful, that was the way. What had she got on? Some sort of knickers, damn things. He pulled them to one side, brushing bare flesh with his fingers. 'I do. See!' And with that one triumphant word he was inside.

I know we're not supposed to do this, Joan thought, but she couldn't think how to stop him. I know we're not supposed to. But it was as if her mind had got stuck in a groove like a gramophone needle and she couldn't think any further. She was still anxiously repeating the same opinion to herself when he gave a long groaning sigh and fell off her onto his back, with his eyes shut and a really stupid expression on his face.

She waited for a very long time feeling rather sore 'down there' and wondering what would happen next.

Finally he opened his eyes and smiled. 'I'm off to bed,' he said. 'We'll do it again tomorrow. Don't tell anyone.'

So they did. And she didn't. Not even Sally, because in the light of clear-thinking morning she felt ashamed of what they'd done and she didn't want to talk about it ever.

Nevertheless despite her shame she had established a pattern and she couldn't think of any way to stop it or change it. Master Toby came to her room every night until he left the Manor to go back to school, and after that he came home every other weekend on one pretext or another and always when Miss Amelia was at home too and she was sleeping in the dressing room. In April the entire family stayed at the Manor for Easter, so she hoped he'd keep away in case his mother found out. But he didn't. He came to the dressing room whenever he felt like it, even in the middle of the night when his sister was asleep in the room next door. And although he was always quick, she was always anxious in case someone walked in and found them or they woke Miss Amelia.

'Part of the fun,' he said, when she worried aloud. 'Don't you worry your pretty little head. Lie down. I've only got ten minutes.'

It occurred to her as he climbed laboriously on top of her that he never said he loved her nowadays. In fact he rarely said anything much and he was off out of the room the minute he'd finished. It made her feel used and dirty as well as ashamed, and that gave her a decidedly bad conscience. After all, he'd persuaded her to do it the first time by saying he loved her, so if he *didn't* love her any more, perhaps they oughtn't go on doing it. Perhaps she ought to ask him.

'Do you still love me?' she said, when he moved his face so as to dig his chin into her shoulder. He always dug his chin into her shoulder and it was really very uncomfortable.

'What?' he said vaguely, not pausing in his rhythm.

She phrased the question differently, in case she'd been too abrupt the first time. 'You do still love me, don't you?'

'Yes,' he said shortly, fitting the word to his next thrust.

90

'Course. Wouldn't be – doing – this – if I – didn't.

Her conscience was still grumbling away like an appendix underneath his incessant activity, but what else could she say? If he still loved her it had to be all right, didn't it? It was only if he didn't love her it would be wrong.

This time he spoke to her afterwards, standing beside the bed and looking down at her as he tied the belt of his dressing gown. 'You're a lucky gel to have a sweetheart like me,' he said. 'You know that, don't you? A jolly lucky gel.'

'Yes, Mr Toby,' she said, hoping it was true.

'I'll bring you a pair of stockings next time,' he offered, smoothing his hair and watching himself in the mirror. 'How would that be?'

They were the most unsuitable stockings, white silk with embroidered clocks at the heels, and a good deal too small to fit her broad feet, the sort of thing Miss Amelia would wear to a ball and that a servant could never dream of. She thanked him of course and said how pretty they were, which was true, but inwardly she was sighing at the waste, because she knew she would never be able to wear them. At Tillingbourne Manor they would proclaim the fact that she had a rich sweetheart and then sooner or later their secret would be out, at home they would be a source of derision.

'Back to the old Alma Mater tomorrow,' he said, when she'd hidden her useless present in the chest of drawers. '*Tempus fugit*, you know.'

'Yes,' she said. They were all going away the next day, Miss Amelia and her parents to London to see the British Empire Exhibition at Wembley and then to the Continent for the summer. 'I shall be back in the attic tomorrow night with the others.'

'Worse luck,' he said. 'Never mind. There's always another time, eh?'

But she wasn't sure she wanted any more 'times'. It was still pleasant to know that she was loved, if she *was* loved, but as she packed her possessions in her carpet bag ready for the move, folding his stockings in their tissue paper and hiding them under her clean aprons, she knew for certain that she didn't love him at all. In fact if the truth were told, his visitations had been so frequent and so exhausting she'd be glad to be rid of them and him.

Like her sister before her she was sending up a vague prayer for assistance, for something to happen that would sort it all out for her. She couldn't think of anything particular, but something.

CHAPTER 8

The letter arrived at breakfast time, after Grandpa had left for work. It was for Flossie and she scowled so much as she read it that both her daughters watched her with anxiety in case it was something that would bring on an attack of nerves. She read it right to the bottom of the page, paused for a second or two, breathing heavily, and then read it all over again, the fine blue paper trembling in her hand.

Then she began to shriek. 'Oh! Oh! How could she? The wicked wicked girl!'

'What's up?' Aunt Maud said, buttering bread with her usual calm.

'Look at that!' Mum said, hurling the letter across the table into the butter. 'How could she do such a thing? I don't understand it.'

Aunt Maud retrieved the letter from the butter dish, cleaned it on her apron and read it slowly, screwing up her eyes and mouth with effort. 'Oh my lor'!' she said. 'Shall you go?'

'Not got much option, have I?' Mum said. 'Whatever are we going to do?'

'Pray it's not true,' Aunt Maud said. 'That's what I shall do.'

'What a blessing Dad's not here,' Mum said.

'He'll have to know,' Aunt Maud said. 'It could affect the cottage, being tied an' all.'

'Heaven help us!' Mum cried. 'Oh Heaven help us. How could she *do* such a thing?' And she put her apron over her

93

head and began to weep, holding the folds of cloth against her eyes.

'What is it, Mum?' Peggy asked. It was too awful to see her mother crying and not to know what was the matter, especially as she suspected it was something to do with Joan. Who else could 'she' be?

Mum put the apron down at once, stopped crying and glared at her. 'Never you mind,' she said. 'It's something too shameful to talk about. Too shameful altogether. I don't know how she could have done such a thing, I really don't. You're not to say a word to anyone, either of you. I shall be out all day if I'm any judge. I'd avoid it if I could, as your aunt knows, but that's something I'm not to be allowed it seems. You can look after Baby, can't you?'

'I'm going swimming this afternoon,' Peggy pointed out.

'Oh that's all right,' Mum said. 'She can go with you.'

So she'd been lumbered with Baby all day, and Mum had gone rushing off without saying where she was going, and it all reminded her just a bit too much of that awful time when Dad was dying. She'd tried to be sensible, helping Aunt Maud with the scrubbing and feeding the pig and not saying anything, but her anxiety grew by the hour, especially when dinner-time came and Mum wasn't back.

She and Baby spent the afternoon in the swimming-pool and they were very late home because Baby dawdled back in the most aggravating way, picking wild flowers in the hedges and sitting down three times because her legs were aching. But eventually they arrived at the open kitchen door with the sun warm on their backs and the toes of their sandals white with dust, tired and thirsty and ready for tea. And what they saw and heard in the little dark room made them stop, stand absolutely still and listen with straining ears.

Mum and Aunt Maud were sitting at the table with their heads close together, talking to one another like conspirators and so deep in conversation that they didn't notice the children were there.

'So when'll it be?' Aunt Maud was saying.

'Wednesday,' Mum said. 'First thing.'

'The sooner the better. Providin' they pay.'

'Oh they'll pay!' Mum said grimly. 'Bein' it's their rotten son.'

'Let's hope it works. You never know with these things. Sometimes they don't do the trick.'

'Don't even say it, Maud.'

'How far gone is she?'

'She don't know, silly girl. Leastways she says she don't know.'

'Is she showin' yet?'

'No.'

'That's a mercy.'

And at that point Baby shuffled her feet. The conversation stopped like an electric light being switched off. Both women looked up and became artificially bright and cheerful in an instant.

'There you are!' Mum said. 'Ready for your tea, are you?'

It's something terrible, Peggy thought. She's hiding it just like she hid Dad's illness. She never told us he was dying and he was, and now she's not telling us what's the matter with Joan, so it must be something really awful. 'How's Joan?' she asked, her face taut with worry and determination. 'Did you see her?'

'She's been a bad girl and lost her job,' Mum said, still using that artificially cheerful voice. 'She's coming home on Wednesday.'

'Is she ill?'

'No, she's not,' Aunt Maud said. 'It'ud be a darn sight better for her if she were. An' that's my opinion of it.'

'Well we don't need to go into all that, do we?' Mum said, and this time her voice sounded as if she was giving Aunt Maud a warning. 'I'll make the tea.'

There was no sense in any of this. The more Peggy thought about it the less she could find. Joan was in trouble. That much seemed plain. But if she was in trouble, then being ill would make things worse not better. And if she'd gone somewhere she'd know where she'd gone. And what was it she was supposed to show? Well she won't come home on Wednesday, she thought, because Mum said something was going to happen on Wednesday, first thing, so I'll bet she's going to court. People usually went to court when they got into trouble and then they got fined or sent to prison. Poor Joan. She'll never be able to pay a fine, so I suppose they'll send her to prison. I wonder what she's done. Perhaps they put you in prison if you shout at people when you're in service. But that didn't seem probable, not really. She'd have liked to send her poor sister a letter but she knew Aunt Maud wouldn't supply the stamp in her present acid mood. It was very worrying.

However on Wednesday morning it looked as though Joan would be coming home after all, for she and Baby were woken up early so that they could take their things next door to the Matthews' house before they went to school.

'Your sister'll need the bed,' Aunt Maud said. 'It won't be for long. An' you see you behave yourselves when you're next door. I don't want complaints. Remember we're in a tied cottage and we're in enough trouble as it is.'

All day long, as the lessons droned interminably on, Peggy thought about Joan and wondered what she'd done and how she was getting on in court. When four o'clock came at last, she set off for home at once, dragging Baby by the hand, no matter how much she protested.

Mum and Aunt Maud and Grandpa were all in the kitchen but they weren't speaking to each other and there was a really terrible atmosphere. Peggy didn't dare ask if Joan was home or upstairs or anything, in case it made things worse or gave Mum an attack of the nerves.

The two girls ate their tea in an oppressive silence, and washed the dishes without a word being spoken. Then the three adults sat in their chairs and didn't look at one another. Mum was busy with her mending and Aunt Maud was reading the Bible, which was a very bad sign, for she only read the good book when she was in a bad temper. And after a further hour's endless silence Mum cleared her throat and told the girls it was time they went next door to bed.

And next door to bed they went, tiptoeing into the Matthews' cottage as though they'd been told not to make a sound.

It was a double bed but an uncomfortable one with a very lumpy mattress so it took them a long time to settle in it. They were still awake when the shouting began. It came from Aunt Maud's room on the other side of the wall and although they couldn't hear what was being said, the anger in the voices was unmistakable. It was Aunt Maud and Mum and Grandpa and they were shouting abuse at Joan, who was crying terribly, on and on and on. Now and then a word would rise out of the bedlam, sharp as a scythe, 'Slut!' 'Trollop!' 'Disgrace!' and once Grandpa's voice shouted, '... better dead!' which made Peggy shiver with a sudden terrified cold.

The row went on for ages, but at last the door was slammed and the two listeners could hear angry feet stamping down the stairs and descending voices grumbling. But Joan went on crying.

'Poor Joan!' Baby whispered.

'You stay there,' Peggy whispered back, easing herself out of the bed.

'What you going to do, our Peggy?'

'Send her a message,' Peggy whispered. With her ears strained for any sound of movement from Mrs Matthews in the kitchen below, she crept quietly across the room to the dividing wall and tapped on it with her knuckles, once, twice, three times. 'I wish they'd learnt us morse code at school.'

The sobbing stopped. Peggy tapped again. Both girls listened and waited. And then to their delight, their sister tapped an answer, faint through the plaster of the partition, once, twice, three times. It was a little triumph.

'Now we can all go to sleep,' Peggy said, when she'd crept back to bed again. 'She knows we're here an' she can knock if she needs us.'

'Are they going to send her to prison, our Peggy?'

'No,' Peggy said. Now that she'd sent her message she felt pretty sure of it. 'They're not. I 'spect we shall see her in the morning.'

But they didn't. And she didn't come down to supper in the evening either, although after Grandpa had gone off to the pub, Mum took a tray upstairs for her, which Peggy was relieved to see.

Aunt Maud was combing her hair ready for her prayer meeting. 'I'm off,' she said, when Mum came downstairs again. 'Time these children were next door.'

'I'll take 'em when I've done the dishes,' Mum said.

'I'll do the dishes if you like,' Peggy offered, feeling quite amazed at how artful she was being. 'Baby's tired. Aren't you, Baby? She ought to go to bed straight away.'

For once in her life Baby had the sense to join in the plot, and even though the yawn she gave was too enormous to be credible, Mum believed her. The minute they were out of the door Peggy took off her sandals and ran up the stairs.

Joan was in the single bed, lying on her side with the covers pulled over her shoulders. Her face was very pale and her hair hadn't been combed and there were mauve shadows under her brown eyes. 'Oh Peggy!' she said, and burst into tears.

Peggy was across the room in two barefooted strides, pushing the dangling clothing aside with both hands, and then she had her sister cuddled in her arms and was patting her back and kissing her cheeks. 'You're all right,' she said. 'You're home now. You're all right.'

'I shall never be all right again,' Joan sobbed. 'Never ever.'

'You will. You will.'

'No, no. I won't. I'm ruined. You don't know what I've done.'

'I don't *care* what you've done,' Peggy said stoutly. 'You're my sister and I love you and I think they were hateful to shout at you like that.'

'I been dismissed without a character,' Joan confessed into Peggy's shoulder.

'That just shows how hateful they were an' all.'

Joan sat up in the bed and moved her body away from Peggy's embrace so that they could look at one another. 'You won't say that when you know what I done,' she said.

'I shall.'

'You won't, Peggy.'

'Tell me an' see.'

It took a visible effort of will for Joan to say the next words and the shame on her face was painful to see. 'I let them kill my baby, Peg. I was going to have a baby. I shouldn't have been. It was wrong. Only he said he loved me. An' they sent for Mum. It was awful, Peg. Awful. An' in the end I let them kill it. How could anyone forgive me

98

for doing that?' There was no hope for her. She was ruined just like Mum said.

Why it's like the kittens, Peggy thought, affection and pity for her poor tear-stained sister rising in a flood of warmth to redden her cheeks and make her eyes blaze. 'Oh you poor thing,' she said. 'What an awful thing. Did they put it in a bucket?'

'What?' Joan said, stunned by the question. She was still aching and shocked from the brutality of yesterday morning's medical assault, the long hours of guilty pain that had torn her and the afternoon apart, the searing accusations that had left her weak and wretched all night. Oh if only she'd known all this was going to happen she'd never have let him lay a finger on her. Never. 'What?'

'In a bucket,' Peggy explained. 'Like the kittens.'

But she could see it was the wrong thing to say while the words were still on her tongue. It made poor Joan cry worse than ever.

'Never you mind,' she said, cuddling her furiously. 'You can have another baby an' I'll look after you, an' we won't let them kill *that* one, I promise.'

'Oh Peggy!' Joan said between sobs. 'You are lovely!'

'I'd better go down now,' Peggy said. 'I've got the washing-up to do. I'll knock on the wall when I'm next door.'

'Don't tell Baby what I told you, will you?'

'No,' Peggy said standing up to go. 'Course not. How long have you got to stay up here?'

'A week I think,' Joan said wearily. 'That's what Mum said anyway.'

It was a week, which was the sort of time Peggy told Baby she'd expect for a punishment.

'What's she done?' Baby asked as they walked to school on the following Wednesday.

'Shouted at someone,' Peggy lied, 'so they sent her home without a character.'

'Gosh!' Baby said in surprise, for her instincts were telling her it was something a great deal worse. 'She must have shouted jolly loud.'

'Well just don't mention it when she comes down tomorrow, that's all,' Peggy said.

'No,' Baby said earnestly. 'I won't.'

It was the last week of term. In three more days it would be the summer holidays and harvest time. And a jolly good job too, Peggy thought, for if Mum and Aunt Maud and Grandpa were all hard at work in the fields they wouldn't have the energy for shouting at Joan.

Unfortunately the corn wasn't quite ripe enough. She walked out into the fields to examine it every day and it was very slow. All that sun, she thought, squinting up at it, and it can't ripen *one* field. But at least life in the cottage was quiet now and more or less back to normal. She and Joan took it in turns to sleep on the floor the way they had before Joan went into service, and they helped Mum cook the meals and washed the dishes and scrubbed floors, and Joan worked with the rest of them, and nobody said anything much. In fact there wasn't any conversation at all, only an awful sense of brooding as though something terrible was going to happen, and that went on and on getting worse and worse until Thursday afternoon.

Mum had gone off to the pictures in Guildford as usual, Aunt Maud was visiting a neighbour on the other side of the seven acre field, and the three girls were sitting on Grandpa's little bit of grass in front of the cottage, Baby playing with her doll and Joan and Peggy mending a long tear in Aunt Maud's patchwork bedspread, when a shadow rose between them and the sun.

It was Grandpa, standing belligerently before them, mud-caked and disagreeable, his legs astride and his field hat pulled right down over his eyebrows like a helmet.

'Leave that,' he commanded brusquely. 'I got somethin' to show you.' And the words were as threatening as his appearance.

They followed him the half mile down to Tillingbourne in anxious silence. There was a blackbird singing with tremulous passion in the hawthorn hedge, and the sky was a beautiful, unclouded blue, diffusing sunshine without discrimination on placid sheep, green corn, Joan's misery and Grandpa's anger. What *was* he going to show them? Peggy worried as she followed his furious spine. It'ud be something nasty as sure as eggs were eggs.

He led them to the church, which comforted her a little, for it couldn't be too nasty, could it, if it was in a church? But they didn't go into the church, they walked round it instead, past the porch and then along the east wall until they reached the buttress that marked the division between the aisle and the chancel, and there the three girls stood in a line and waited, Joan pale-faced and drooping with fatigue, Baby close to tears, Peggy watchful and worried.

'Look at that,' Grandpa said, squinting their attention towards the wall.

They looked.

'Don't know what you're looking at though, do you?' he said, and his eyes were sharp with mockery.

Joan answered for all of them even though she felt ill. 'No,' she said, speaking quietly to deflect his anger.

'No, you don't,' he agreed. 'So I'll tell you. High time you was told. That's the wall of a cell, that is. A cell for a wicked girl.'

Now they could see that there was a shape outlined in brick in the fabric of the wall. It looked like a door that had long since been blocked in, and a very low door too, not much taller than Grandpa.

'And that,' pointing to an oblong opening in the middle of the shape, 'that's a squint.'

It looked like a letter-box, only bigger.

'They cut that,' Grandpa went on, 'so's she could see the priest taking communion. Which was all the light she had. Jest that one little hole. There weren't another openin' nowhere, not a door, not a windy, nothin', just the four bare walls of her cell. Come out to about here it did,' walking the six short feet to the edge of the buttress, 'an' that's all the space she had. Jest enough for a bed an' a few paces up an' down. Yes, that's where she was bricked up.'

Oh how terrible! Peggy thought, staring at the little space where the cell would have been. Bricked up alive. The words snagged her mind with horror, filling her imagination with terrifying images, bricks and plaster being pushed towards her eyes, crushing against her chest, inches from her unprotected head, the airless space full of

101

brick dust and falling debris, the weight of masonry an oppressive force all round her. Bricked up alive. 'Poor thing!' she said.

'Thirteen she was, when they bricked her in.' Grandpa said. 'They reckon she wanted to be a saint, put right away from temptation an' all that sort a' thing. Saint my eye. I don't reckon much to that line a' thinkin'. Nothing saintly about *that* girl, I can tell you. Oh no! *Nothing* saintly. She was a *slut*, that's what she was. A slut and she knew it. Thirteen years old, Joan Furnivall, and a slut like someone else we know. What've you got to say about that?'

Joan stood before him, her head bowed and her cheeks burning, and Peggy noticed with a rush of affectionate pity that her legs were trembling. Oh this was awful. Hadn't she been punished enough? How could she stop him?

'Can we go home now, Grandpa?' she tried. 'I don't think Joan's feeling very well.'

'No I don't suppose she is,' Grandpa said gloating over it. 'She don't deserve to feel well, and she'll feel a lot worse when she's heard what I've got to tell her. There's worse to come.'

Worse, Peggy thought weakly. How could there be? What could be worse than being bricked up alive?

'Hadn't been there more'n a year or two before she up and changed her mind,' Grandpa said. 'Which she'd got no business doing, not once she was enclosed. But she did, so you see the sort a' girl she was. And then do you know what she done? She set to with her bare hands an' she picked her way out, day by day, week by week, till she made a hole just big enough to squeeze through, and out she come and run off home to her father.'

I'd have done the same, Peggy thought, admiring the tenacity and good sense of the poor little prisoner. It filled her with relief to think of such a sensible escape. I'd have done just the same.

'Her father,' Grandpa said, gloating again, 'he weren't none too pleased to see her when they all thought she'd been settled once and for all. Her father, well he naturally thought of all the shame she'd bring down on his head, the little slut. He didn't want the bailiff coming down to see

102

him, did he? So d'you know what he done? I'll tell you what he done. He took her straight back to the priest and had her bricked up all over again. And quite right too. That's what ought to happen to all sluts, didn't it, Joan Furnivall?'

Joan licked her lips. Her eyes were bolting with distress and there was no colour in her face at all. 'What happened to her then?' she whispered.

'You may well ask,' Grandpa said, stepping towards her until his face was no more than six inches away from hers. 'She went mad, Joan Furnivall. She went mad and died.'

'Oh please,' Joan whispered. 'I didn't mean to ... I didn't know all – this – would happen. I'm not a slut, Grandpa.'

'Oh yes you are,' Grandpa said, bullying her with his face. 'You're a dirty, filthy, shameless little slut. You brought shame on this family and the bailiff down on my head an' all. If I had my way I'd ...'

But none of them ever heard what he would do because Joan slumped to the ground in a dead faint.

Then several things happened in rapid succession. Baby began to howl, Peggy dropped to her knees beside her sister and tried to lift her poor groaning head from the gravel, there was a swish of long skirts approaching along the path, and Grandpa disappeared like a rabbit into a hole.

'If you will allow me to lift her up a little, we can put her head between her knees and that will bring her round,' Reverend Beaumont said.

Peggy was limp with relief to see his good honest face looking down so kindly at them. 'She's not very well,' she said.

'No,' Reverend Beaumont said, as Joan groaned and opened her eyes. 'I can see that. It's lucky my car is in the road.' And he picked Joan up in his arms as if she were a baby and strode off with her towards the road, his cassock swinging.

Peggy and Baby followed at his heels, trotting to keep up with him, for despite his burden he was walking very quickly.

'Here it is,' he said, stopping by his car and lowering Joan into the passenger seat. 'Get in and I will take you home.'

Which he did, driving them the long way round through Gomshall and up the farm path they'd climbed on that first day, so long ago now. And when the path stopped, he parked the car neatly beside the hedge and escorted them right up to the kitchen door.

Aunt Maud opened the door.

'I return your niece to your care, Miss Potter,' he said. 'If you will allow me to advise you, I think you should put her to bed as soon as possible. She had a fainting spell in the churchyard and she still isn't at all well.'

Aunt Maud thanked him in some confusion. 'Very kind of you, Father.'

'Not at all,' the reverend gentleman said. 'Treat her gently, Miss Potter. I really do think she's been punished enough, wouldn't you say.'

Aunt Maud didn't say anything, but her face was rigid with a combination of suppressed anger and fear, because it sounded as though he knew what Joan had done and how they'd dealt with it.

'Come in,' she said grimly to her nieces, when the rector had swished back to his car. 'What your grandfather will say when he hears about this, I do not know.'

'He knows about it,' Peggy said, fighting back to protect her sister. 'He was the one took us down to the churchyard. He was the one made Joan faint.'

If she'd hoped to gain any sympathy, she was badly mistaken. 'Don't you dare say such a thing about your grandfather,' her aunt roared, red-faced with anger.

'It's true. He did.'

'You say another word,' Aunt Maud said furiously, 'an' I'll wash your mouth out with soap and water. The shame of it! I shall never hold my head up again. For the Father to know! The shame of it!'

The three girls stood awkwardly before her in the kitchen, not knowing what they were supposed to do or say, Joan ashamed, Baby afraid and Peggy burning with anger because it was all so unfair.

And grandfather kicked into the kitchen, boots first, red

in the face and breathless as though he'd been running. 'Where's your damn mother?' he roared. 'Always out galli-vantin', God damn it.' And he pushed at Baby who was the nearest to his anger. 'Get out my way, dammit.'

'Leave her alone!' Mum said, arriving home just in time to see the shove and running in through the open door to fold her precious child in her arms. 'What's she done? It's not her fault. It's *that* wretch you should be shoving about.' Glaring at Joan.

Baby burst into tears to show how hard done by she was. And then all three grown-ups began to shout at the same time and at the tops of their voices, not listening to one another.

'Sluts! Harlots!' Grandpa roared, puce in the face and stamping his feet with every word. 'I should never have taken you in. Dirty sluts, the lot of you! You deserve everything that's coming to you. You should never have been born ...'

'Nobody cares for me!' Mum shrieked. 'My nerves are in rags! Rags! How could you *do* this to me? I simply don't understand. Don't you care that you'll make me ill? For a poor widow woman to be treated so ...'

'The entire village knows, I hope you realize,' Aunt Maud shouted. 'The entire village. We shall all be ruined. I shall never hold my head up again. If the Father knows. He came here, right to my door. You're not even safe in your own home ...'

The noise of their anger was so dreadful it made Peggy's stomach shake. This is what it must be like to be in a war, she thought, stuck in the trenches with the enemy firing their guns at you and not able to run away or fight back or anything. Oh please God, make them stop.

And as if in answer to her prayer Mum and Maud both stopped shouting and now it was only Grandpa's voice ranting on. '... you and your filthy brood, Flossie Furni-vall. I'm glad you ain't a Potter no more an' that's a fact.'

'If you hadn't taken 'em all down to the village no one would've known,' Mum said bitterly. Which showed that she must have heard some of the things Maud had been saying. 'I kept 'em in, I hope you realize.'

'And now you can take 'em all out,' Grandpa said

viciously. 'That's what you can do. Take 'em all out.'

'What d'you mean?' Mum said. 'Take 'em all out where?'

'Out a' my house,' Grandpa said. 'That's where. I've had the bailiff up to see me, I'll have you know. You're to be out by the end a' next week, he sez, or I lose the cottage. That's what he sez. Be lucky if I don't lose me job an' all. You're to get out. You an' your shameful brood. Before we start the harvest. That's what he sez. Now you know.'

'But we can't,' Mum wailed, changing in an instant from open-mouthed abuse to pathetic whining. 'Where would we go? I'm just a poor widow woman. You know that. I need someone to take care of me. Where could we possibly go?'

'Should ha' thought a' that before you let that trollop loose.'

'You *must* let us stay,' she insisted. 'We shall be home-less.'

'By the end a' next week,' Grandpa said. 'That's all there is to it. I'm off out.'

'What about your supper?' Aunt Maud said.

'Give it to the pig.'

'Oh, that's nice!' Mum said, weeping. 'Walk out on us, I should. You don't care what happens to anyone, you hateful man. You don't care for me. You never did. Or poor Baby. What did she ever do? Oh! Oh! I shall be ill and it'll be all your fault.' And as her father crashed out of the front door and crunched off along the path, she blundered through the door to the stairs and stumbled up to the bedroom.

The kitchen was suddenly and horribly quiet.

'And you lot can stay in the yard,' Aunt Maud said. 'I've had enough for one day.'

They sat in the barn with Peggy's cat and talked things over. And over and over.

'Where will we go?' Joan said. 'Oh God, Peg, this is all my fault. Where will we go?'

'Wherever Mum takes us I expect,' Peggy said.

But as they were to discover in the next few fraught days their mother had opted out of the situation alto-gether.

'I can't get up,' she said to Aunt Maud next morning, lying in the tangle of the bedclothes with her eyes shut. 'I'm far too ill. I should collapse.'

Her illness didn't impress Grandpa. 'You can roll around in bed all you like, gel,' he called up the stairs to her. 'Don't make no odds to me. You're out of here next Friday. That's all there is to that.'

The weekend came and went and she was still in bed.

'If we've really go to get out when Grandpa says, where are we going to go?' Baby worried, when Monday morning brought no change.

The three girls were out in the vegetable garden, weeding, Joan and Peggy with hoes and Baby with a rather useless trowel.

'I don't know,' Joan said wearily. 'I don't know what's to become of any of us.'

The weight of a necessary decision finally settled on Peggy's shoulders. 'I'll see to it,' she told her sisters. 'I promised Dad I'd look after Mum, an' if she's ill she can't look after herself.' And Joan was too low to know what to do and Baby too young. 'You carry on here and I'll see to it.'

'What will you do?' Joan asked. 'Where will you start?'

'I shall write to Uncle Gideon in Greenwich.'

She wrote that very minute, taking pen, ink and paper up into the bedroom for a bit of privacy.

'Dear Uncle Gideon,' she said.

'We have got to get out of the cottage by the end of the week. There has been a row. Please could you find us somewhere to live in Greenwich. Mum has a pension and Joan will go to work.

'I am sorry to trouble you.

'Your ever-loving niece, Peggy Furnivall.'

Aunt Maud pulled a sour grimace when she came downstairs with the letter but handed over the address almost at once.

'Greenwich,' Peggy said as she wrote the word. 'Where is it, Aunt Maud?'

'Well bless me, don't you know that,' Aunt Maud said. 'It's in London. Right in the heart of London.'

'London!' Peggy thought with a wonderful rush of relief and hope. But what a marvellous thing! If Uncle Gideon'll only help us we can all go back to London. I'll take the poor cat.

She was aware in one part of her mind that her mother wouldn't approve, but she pushed the thought away. It was high time the poor thing was rescued from that awful Josh and if they were going to London it would be all right in the end.

'You won't get much joy from Uncle Gideon,' Aunt Maud warned as she put her address book back in the dresser. 'Keeps hisself to hisself, he do.'

But this time she was proved wrong. That Friday, on the very day they were supposed to be leaving, ten minutes after Grandpa had grumbled off to work, and just when Joan and Peggy had given up hope of answer, Uncle Gideon came down to the farm, in person and his employer's butcher's van.

'He give us a lend of it,' he said, breezing into the kitchen all red-faced and bulky and dependable. 'Good bloke our Mr Pearson. 'Lo Maudie. You kids'll have to sit on the floor. There's only the one seat next to the driver. You packed are you, Flossie? I got you a place in Paradise Row.'

Mum had drifted down the stairs wearing an old dressing-gown and a bewildered expression.

'Oh gor' blin' ol' Reilly!' he said, with exasperated affection. 'What you doin' in that rig? I promised I'd be back by three o'clock.'

Mum was gaping like a goldfish. 'Back?' she said. 'Where we going, Gideon?'

'Greenwich,' her brother said.

'Nobody told me,' Mum complained.

'Your Peggy wrote to him,' Maud said. 'Have you really got 'em somewhere, Gid?'

'Only if they look sharp,' Gideon said, 'so get your skates on, Flossie.'

The realization that her impossible problem had actually been solved lifted Flossie's spirits into a thistledown gaiety. 'I can't guarantee skates,' she said, 'but I shall have my clothes on in two shakes of a lamb's tail, you see

108

if I don't. Oh Gid, it is good of you to look after us. Can you take a trunk?'

'If it's packed in half an hour,' Gideon said, grimacing at Peggy and Joan. 'Two minutes more an' I'll go without you.'

It took three quarters of an hour to pack the trunk but it was done with such cheerfulness that it hardly seemed a minute. The china tea-set had never been unpacked and neither had the dinner service or the cutlery, so they were lifted out of the trunk still in their packing cases, dust and all, and carried off into the butcher's van straight away. Then the three children set about gathering up their belongings. Flossie had never been any good at packing, and now her inefficiency was a positive talent. She threw things into the trunk with cheerful abandon.

'It's only an old saucepan,' she cried, and 'Don't bother folding. We can iron when we're there. Poke the flat irons down the corners. That china dog can go in me spare shoes.' They were all so happy it was as if they were going on holiday. Even Joan was smiling and that really was a wonder because she cried so much these days.

While the last few things were being muddled into odd corners of the trunk and Aunt Maud was saying they'd all have to sit on the lid to get it shut, Peggy took one of Mum's old hat boxes from the cupboard under the eaves, picked up a jug half full of milk from the larder and a saucer from the dresser and sneaked off to the barn to find her cat.

It was crouched on one of the crossbeams watching the straw for mice, but when it saw Peggy it stood up at once, stretched and came leaping down.

'We're going away from here,' Peggy told it, stroking its back as it lapped the milk. 'Your next kittens are going to be Londoners and none of them are going to be drowned. It's all going to be quite different now.' And while she was talking her mind was busy working out the best way to get the cat into the box before it could realize what was happening or start fighting.

When the saucer was clean she picked the cat up in her arms the way she often did, then holding it firmly with both hands, and still murmuring, she lowered it quickly into the box. The cat was instantly alarmed and began to growl, clawing the sides of the box, and Peggy's restraining hand, in a frantic attempt to scrabble out, but Peggy held on and jammed the lid on tight just before its head could push up and out. She was panting with effort and there was a long angry red scratch on her left hand but the job was done. She tied the lid down with an old piece of rope, poked air holes in the lid with a stick and then picked up the box and strode off with it to the van, which had now been driven off the path and over the rough grass and was standing incongruously right in front of the door.

Mum and Aunt Maud and Uncle Gideon were struggling out of the cottage with the trunk, and Mum was still giggling even though Aunt Maud was cross.

'All aboard,' Uncle Gideon called out cheerfully. 'Soon be off.'

So she climbed into the van. It was dark inside and smelled of raw meat and dried blood. There was dirty sawdust on the floor and there were flies everywhere, crawling the walls and buzzing and bouncing about the ceiling.

'What've you got there?' Baby said from the shadows. She and Joan were sitting on the packing cases.

'The cat,' Peggy said, settling her swearing burden in the corner furthest from the door.

'You're not bringing a cat!' Baby said in surprise.

'Yes,' Joan said firmly, understanding and supporting at once. 'We are. And anyway it's nothing to do with you.'

'I'll tell Mum,' Baby started. 'She'll be ever so ...'

'You would, wouldn't you?' Joan said. 'You're a horrid little thing sometimes.'

'You do,' Peggy said, sitting down beside the horrid little thing and flexing her fingers menacingly to make her meaning quite plain, 'an' I'll pinch you all the way to London.'

The trunk was heaved aboard. Baby kept a wary eye on Peggy's fingers and said nothing. The doors were closed, leaving them with the flies in a horrid foetid twilight. Mum and Uncle Gideon climbed into their seats, making the van rock as though it was going to fall over sideways. The engine coughed and spluttered. Aunt Maud called goodbye. They were off.

Apart from Mum's incessant chatter, it was a quiet journey, once the cat had stopped swearing. Joan was feeling depressed and guilty and Peggy and Baby were too busy with their thoughts to want to talk much.

Baby had spent the last week trying to puzzle out the meaning of all the odd things that had been happening in their family ever since that letter arrived. She couldn't do it because nobody had explained anything to her, not even Peggy, but she'd gleaned enough from half sentences and meaning glances and innuendo to be aware that Joan's sin – and it was a sin, Grandpa had said so that awful time in the churchyard – Joan's sin had something to do with letting a man touch you – and she knew that because Aunt Maud had warned her about it.

'Don't you never let a man touch *you*, gel, never,' she'd said, sternly. 'It ain't worth it.'

And Baby had given her solemn promise. 'No, Aunt. I won't.'

And now here they all were running away from Tillingbourne because 'everybody knew'. But what did they know? That was the question nobody would answer. In fact that was a question that was so awful she couldn't even ask it. Men must be terribly dangerous to cause all this, she thought. And yet they didn't look dangerous. Grandpa was frightening when he got in a temper and shouted. And Josh wasn't very nice when he kicked the cats. But most of them looked soppy really, especially when they were dressed up for the pub. It was all very worrying. Sins you weren't supposed to commit and you didn't know what they were. Men all round you who were dangerous and you didn't know how they were going to be dangerous, so you couldn't protect yourself. Well one thing, she thought, I shan't let any of them touch me. Ever.

Over in the other corner of the van, Peggy was thinking too. She was on her way back to London at last so she should have been excited and happy, but she wasn't. She was glad they were going, of course, but what she was feeling was really no more than a vague satisfaction, like a shadow in the back of her mind. Over and above that she felt weighed down with all her newly-accepted responsibilities. It was all her doing that they were moving to

London. What if it was the wrong thing? She'd taken over the care of her mother, which she'd had to do because she'd promised Dad and there wasn't anyone else to do it. Joan couldn't help her yet because she was still so unhappy. And Baby was worse than useless. What if she couldn't manage to look after them all properly? Mum could be ever so difficult. And then there was the cat. It was stifling hot in the van and the poor thing was still tied up inside the hatbox. It could be suffocating for all she knew and yet she couldn't untie the box and let it out, because it would be frightened and it would probably run all over the place and then she'd never be able to get it back in the box again to carry it safely out of the van and into the house.

Sighing, she clung to the edge of the trunk, as the van jolted over the pot-holes and the flies buzzed angrily at being disturbed. Never trouble trouble, till trouble troubles you, she reminded herself. It's silly to worry before you have to. We'll be in London soon and then everything will be all right. I wonder how far it is?

CHAPTER 9

'I can't live here,' Flossie squealed. 'Where are we?'

The van had jolted to a halt in a short narrow street somewhere north of Greenwich Station. There wasn't a butcher's shop in sight, just a corner shop and a terrace of eight plain houses on one side of the street and a pub and a wood-yard on the other.

'Paradise Row,' her brother said, grinning at it. 'Number six's yours.'

Number six was towards the middle of the terrace. It was exactly the same as all the others, with a plain green door and one plain green-framed window on the ground floor and two identical green-framed windows on the floor above.

'But that's a house,' Flossie protested. 'I thought we was living with you an' Ethel.'

'No,' Gideon said, putting on the handbrake like the end of an argument. 'You're not. So don't even think it. Two rooms over the shop! There's barely room for us.' And he climbed out of the van.

'I can't live here,' Flossie repeated, making no attempt to follow him out. 'Not with my nerves. I shall be all on my own.'

'Oh come on, Flossie,' Gideon said, walking round to the back of the van to open the rear doors. 'It's a fair rent. There's no bugs. Nice clean house. You got the girls for company. What more d'you want? Out you get, girls. You're here.'

113

The three girls stepped out into the sunlight, blinking like owls.

We're in London now and no mistake, Peggy thought as her feet touched the cobbles, and excitement bloomed in her mind like an opening rose. She could smell it was London. All that lovely soot and smoke in the air, and horse-dung and dust and leather and old clothes, and the familiar reek of trams, hot oil and brass polish and dusty steel. There was even a faint whiff of the river somewhere nearby.

Smoke rose from the chimneys like ribbons of tattered brown gauze to drift and waver before it melted into the blue of the sky, and above the tall roof of the pub at the end of the road she could see the top of an elaborate church tower, white and outlandish as a wedding cake. But best of all was the noise of the place, the rumble and clatter of traffic, a train chuffing, woodsaws buzzing, dogs barking and lots and lots of busy London voices. Oh it was lovely!

Their arrival had gathered the usual crowd of rubbernecks, women in grubby aprons, a horde of tatty children and half a dozen mongrels, all tremulous tails, tense paws and inquisitive noses. The sooner I get this poor cat indoors away from that lot, she thought, holding the box close to her chest, the better.

Then she noticed that there was a face nodding at them from one of the upstairs windows of number six, a round amiable face with a snub nose, false teeth, small dark eyes behind a pair of round, iron-grey glasses and two rows of sausage-shaped iron-grey curls encircling a head as neat as a skull-cap.

'Mrs Geary,' Uncle Gideon explained, hauling the trunk towards the open doors. 'She's sub-lettin' to your Mum. House is hers by rights. She lives in the front bedroom.'

'D'you want a hand with that, mate?' an elderly man offered, settling his grey cloth cap back on his head after he'd wiped the sweat from his forehead with it.

'Very good of you,' Uncle Gideon said. 'Ta.'

'Needs four,' the man said, signalling to two of the boys in the crowd. 'Name of Allnutt. Two doors up. Come on lads. Lend a hand.'

114

The head above them was smiling and nodding, its double row of curls bouncing vigorously. 'Come on up,' it called. 'Where's yer ma?'

So they came on up, which was easy enough because the house was small and compact and built to a very simple plan with a scullery, a narrow hall and two rooms on the ground floor and two similar rooms above. The staircase rose precipitately through the middle of the house and parallel with the street, and having no direct light it was almost as dark as the stairs in Grandpa's cottage.

The front bedroom was the best room in th house, with two windows where the other rooms only had one, and an excellent view of the street. Besides being the best lit it was also the biggest, being over the front parlour and the hall. As soon as they stepped inside, the three girls could quite see why Mrs Geary had taken it.

It was a complete home, entire of itself, full of furniture and heavily curtained. A red baize draught excluder smothered the door, there was faded chintz at the windows, a green chenille cloth on the table and a brown chenille cover on the mantelpiece, danging a row of impoverished tassels. The grate below it was beautifully polished and had three separate hobs for kettles and irons and saucepans, and enough fire-irons for all the fires in the house. There was a chest of drawers with shelves above it on one side of the chimney and a brass bedstead on the other, there was a sideboard sitting on its haunches and sagging with unmatched china a mere six inches from a gateleg table set for tea, there were two elderly wicker chairs beneath one of the windows and a battered armchair beside the second, there was a washstand and a treadle sewing machine and a bookcase full of books and the walls were covered with prints and pictures and faded photographs.

Their new landlady was sitting in the armchair in the midst of all her possessions. 'Come in. Come in,' she said. 'Make yourselves at 'ome. I'd get up only I got these legs you see.'

The legs in question were propped up on a tapestry stool. They were wrapped in grey bandages and looked rather like two gigantic salami sausages. 'Can't get about,'

Mrs Geary explained, 'otherwise they give me gyp. Where's yer ma?'

Joan looked out of the window. 'Bringing in our china,' she said.

'Let's 'ave a look see,' Mrs Geary said, unhooking a walking stick from the back of her chair. There was a long double mirror standing between her chair and the window. 'Everything to 'and,' she said, pushing the two sides into new positions with her stick. 'Ah yes. There she is with yer uncle. You must tell 'er ter come up an' get acquainted when she's ready. D'you like me parrot?'

The room was so crowded none of them had noticed that there was a birdcage in it too. Now they couldn't take their eyes away from it, for the parrot who perched monumentally in the middle of it was a magnificent bird, huge and silver-grey with a fine red tail.

'Gosh!' Baby said with admiration. 'Does he talk?'

'Not much,' Mrs Geary admitted. 'Do yer, mate? Swears though. Swears fit ter bust.' The parrot's ability to swear had made him an indispensable companion. Mrs Geary considered herself too much the lady to descend to foul language, so the bird swore for her, taking its cue from the tone of her voice, and adapting the volume and obscenity of its utterances to suit her mood. It was an arrangement that suited them both very well indeed, the parrot because he was invariably rewarded with monkey-nuts, Mrs Geary because she'd been able to give vicarious vent to her feelings.

'It'ud warm the cockles of yer heart to hear that bird swear, I'm tellin' yer,' she said. 'Whatcher got in that 'atbox?'

'A cat,' Peggy admitted, realizing a little too late that this new landlady of theirs might not approve of cats and that perhaps she ought to have asked permission before she brought it in.

But Mrs Geary put her mind at rest straight away. 'Oooh lovely,' she said. 'Let it out quick. I must see. I love cats. Used to 'ave a tortoiseshell once.'

'What about the parrot?' Peggy hesitated.

'Lor' love yer, he won't mind,' Mrs Geary said. 'He likes company.'

So they opened the cat-box, and the cat was revealed, distressed and panting, with its fur stuck together in spiky clumps, too frightened to cry or swear. Peggy lifted it out of the box as quickly and gently as she could but it crouched to the ground in fright, and when she removed her hands it slunk across the room on its belly and hid itself behind the washstand.

'Poor thing,' Mrs Geary said. 'That's the journey done that. They don't like travellin', cats. Leave it here with me while you unpack, eh? I'll keep an eye on it. What's its name?'

Peggy hadn't thought of a name for it until that moment, but there was no doubt what it should be. 'Tabitha,' she said. 'Tabby for short.'

'It's a female then,' Mrs Geary said. 'We might get some kittens.'

'Oh yes,' Peggy said. 'I do hope so.'

Mum was calling them. 'Peggy! Joan! Where've you got to?'

'We'd better go down,' Joan said.

'Which one of you is Joan?' Mrs Geary asked, looking at them brightly.

'I am.'

'I couldn't just get you to put a match to that fire, could I, Joan dear?' Mrs Geary wheedled. 'And then if one of you could just bring me a jug a' water next time you're up I could make us all a cup a' tea. That enamel jug by the door, see. I could do with a cup, couldn't you?'

'Yes,' Joan said. 'Course.'

'I'd get it mesself, only I got these legs,' Mrs Geary explained.

So Joan lit the fire and when it had taken they all went clattering downstairs to the sparsely furnished rooms they were now renting. Flossie was in the front parlour surrounded by the contents of the trunk.

'I don't know where to begin,' she said. 'It's too bad of your uncle.'

'Where is he?' Baby asked. Unwisely.

'Gone,' Flossie said, complaining at once and bitterly. 'He couldn't even help me unpack. That's all he thinks of his sister. How am I supposed to manage with all this? I don't know where to begin.'

'I'll fill this jug,' Peggy said to Joan, 'and then we'll get cracking.'

'Everything's so dirty,' Flossie complained. 'You should see the state of the dresser.'

It took them the rest of the afternoon and a visit to the corner shop for soft soap and caustic soda to clean shelves and cupboards to her satisfaction and then to unpack. Mrs Geary banged on the ceiling to signal that the tea was ready before they were even half finished.

'What's that?' Flossie said, glancing up apprehensively. And when Peggy explained she looked even more apprehensive.

'I don't want tea,' she said. 'Not with a stranger.'

'She ain't a stranger,' Joan said. 'She's nice. You'll see.'

For the second time that afternoon Mrs Geary forestalled complaint before it could be uttered. As soon as her new tenants entered her room she swung her bandaged legs onto the floor, unhooked her stick from the back of her chair and hobbled across the rag rug to Flossie.

'Mrs Furnivall,' she said, holding out her hand in greeting. 'You don't know how glad I am to see you.'

'Oh!' Flossie said, rather nonplussed.

'The minute your brother said a widow with three girls I knew you was the ones for me,' Mrs Geary beamed. 'An' such nice girls. We've met al-a-ready. A credit to you, Mrs Furnivall. A credit. Tea's all ready. I'll bet you're gasping. I know I am.'

Somehow or other she ushered them all into position around her table as she was talking, Flossie and Joan on the wicker chairs, Peggy on the footstool, Baby on a dirty clothes basket, herself in the armchair.

'Theatricals I 'ad the last time,' she said as she poured the tea. 'Dirty beggars! They was chronic, I can tell you. An' I couldn't get down to clear up after 'em proper on account a' these legs. I'm ever so sorry. I'll bet you've had ever such a job.'

'Yes, well, it *was* dirty,' Flossie admitted. 'We've had to scrub all the shelves.' It was the first thing she'd intended to complain about.

'I knew it,' Mrs Geary said, as if she'd been vindicated. 'The dirty beggars. An' they did a moonlight. You can't trust theatricals. I *am* glad you've come, my dear. We shall get on like a house a-fire. Come on then Tabby, d'you want to get up again do yer?' For the cat, now clean and dry and quite herself again, had appeared beside the armchair and was looking up hopefully. 'She's been on my lap all the while the kettle's been boiling, dear little thing.'

'You've got a cat then?' Flossie said. 'As well as a parrot.'

Messages flashed quickly from Mrs Geary's sharp black eyes to Peggy's anxious hazel ones.

'Oh yes,' Mrs Geary said easily. 'Dear little thing. Your Peggy says she'll help look after her.'

Why, she's an ally, Peggy thought. And she drank her tea with real gratitude.

After such a start Flossie decided she might as well get on with her new landlady and the two of them embarked on a long conversation about theatricals and what mucky beggars they were and how some people didn't know how to keep their houses clean. On the second cup of tea, they turned their attention to their ailments and Mrs Geary told Flossie what awful trouble she had with her legs and, not to be outdone, Flossie replied with a graphic account of the torments she suffered with her nerves, and the parrot, responding to the querulous note in their voices, produced a sudden volley of oaths which delighted Mrs Geary and made Flossie blush.

The cat, finding Mrs Geary's legs more active than they had been earlier in the afternoon, took herself off and settled on Peggy's lap instead. And when all the tea had been drunk, and Flossie was sighing that she supposed they'd better get back to work, Mrs Geary asked Peggy whether she wouldn't mind taking the little animal downstairs into the garden to 'do her business'. And of course Peggy didn't mind at all.

The garden was little more than a backyard, since well over half the space at the rear of the house was taken up by an outhouse containing the scullery, the coalshed and an outside lavatory. There was a flowerbed of sorts although there weren't any flowers in it and the earth looked sour and black and lifeless, and a scrubby patch of trodden grass with a clothes line strung above it and three broken flower pots lying on their side, which Tabby investigated disdainfully before strolling off to sniff the earth.

You wouldn't grow many vegetables here, Peggy thought, remembering the well-kept vegetable patch behind Grandpa's cottage, and she was just stirring the dead earth with the toe of her sandal when she heard a most peculiar noise. It came from the garden next door and it sounded as though someone was sobbing or groaning. There was a tin bath lying beside the outhouse wall, so she dragged it to the fence and climbed up on it to see what was the matter.

The garden next door was full of rubbish, bits of broken ladder, old wheels, rusty tins, a mangled bicycle frame, half a mattress leaking stained horsehair and sagging springs, and standing amongst it, banging his head against the lavvy wall was a dark-haired boy about the same age as she was. He had the palms of both hands pushed against the bricks and he was groaning, 'Oh! Oh! Oh!' as though he was in pain.

'What's up?' she said. 'Are you hurt?'

He stopped groaning at once and turned his head to glare at her. His eyelids were red with weeping and all his eyelashes were stuck together like black spikes. 'Clear off!' he said.

'Well that's nice!' she said. 'I only asked.'

'Well don't,' he said. His eyes were very blue, as if crying had washed them clean.

'I thought you was hurt,' she said. What a horrid boy. He didn't have to be so rude.

'Well I'm not, so clear off.'

'You was crying enough,' she said, feeling quite cross with him.

He dashed the remaining tears from his cheeks. 'I wasn't,' he said. 'And anyway, if I was it ain't none a' your business, so you can just keep your long nose out of it.'

'Cry all you like!' she said, thoroughly cross with him now. 'See if I care.' And she got down off the bath and went to find her cat. What a horrid boy!

Fortunately there was so much to do, unpacking and cleaning and jollying Mum along and running up and down stairs with things for Mrs Geary, that she couldn't stay cross for long. It wasn't until late that night, when everything had been unpacked and put away, and they'd all had fish and chips for supper, which was a real treat, and she and Joan and Baby were squashed up together in the lumpy double bed in the back bedroom, trying to find positions that were comfortable enough to sleep in, that she remembered the boy and how rude he'd been.

'I like Mrs Geary,' Joan said. 'I wonder what the other neighbours'll be like.'

'The boy next door's horrid,' Peggy said and told her what he'd said.

'Still at least you got your cat,' Joan said. They'd found an orange box for their new pet to sleep in and now she was curled up very peacefully beside their bed, just within reach of Peggy's caressing fingers.

'There's lots a' kids in the street,' Baby said happily. 'There'll be ever such games tomorrow I'll bet. D'you think Mum'll let us play out?'

But there was no knowing what Mum would be like in the morning. They could hear her crashing about in the front parlour putting up the camp bed and grumbling to herself.

'We'll have to wait an' see,' Peggy said sleepily, stroking the cat's soft head.

The next day was the busiest and noisiest of the week for, as they soon discovered, their short street was part of the direct route to Greenwich market, so on a Saturday it was perpetually full of people either briskly on their way to market or gossiping back. Mrs Geary seemed to know them all. She sat by her open window all morning with her parrot beside her, both of them shouting down to the passers by. 'How's your Tommy? I seen 'im go along.' 'Aark! Aark!' 'Mornin' Mrs Jones!'

'You been to market yet?' she said to Peggy when the child came upstairs in answer to her knocking summons.

'No,' Peggy said. 'Not yet. We been putting the clothes away.'

'I'd cut off pretty sharpish if I was you,' Mrs Geary advised. 'The best fruit an' veg goes ever so quick. Tell yer ma not to buy any meat till closin' time. She'll get it half-price then, tell 'er. I'll come down with you tonight, if you like. Show you the ropes. Meantime if you're going that way this morning could you just be a dear an' get me a couple a' pounds a' spuds? King Edwards for preference. An' a pound a' peas, an' a bunch a' carrots. Save me poor ol' legs. Oh an' a sprig a' mint. 'E'll throw that in for free, only you got to ask for it.'

So Joan and Peggy set off to find the market, which was easy enough because all they had to do was to follow the crowd. They passed the church, which turned out to be really enormous, big enough to be a cathedral, and found themselves facing a wide crossroads where four sets of tramlines met and intermeshed, and there on the opposite side of the street was an archway made of stone with the words 'Greenwich Market' carved on the keystone. They struggled through the traffic still following the crowd, passed the pawn shop beside the arch where two racks of old coats and trousers had been wheeled out onto the pavement to attract custom, walked down a short narrow passage way between dank brick walls, and arrived.

And what a warm racketty place it was, all under cover and with so many stalls they couldn't count them, vegetable stalls piled high with potatoes and cabbages and onions, with bunches of new carrots fringing every canopy, fruit stalls heaped with redcurrants and gooseberries and neat little punnets of raspberries, stalls selling every kind of china from egg cups to chamber pots, stalls for fish and stalls for meat and one small barrow filled with eggs, raucous voices offering everything you could possibly ever want, nails and screws and ha'penny balls of string, straw hats for thruppence, bracelets and necklaces at a tanner a time, saucepans and flat irons, shoes and stockings, pens and paper, even day-old chicks, staggering and cheeping in long cardboard boxes. Oh it was a lovely place and naturally they took as long as they could to make their purchases. Particularly as Mum was in a peculiar mood.

But when they came home again, carrying the heavy shopping bag between them, Baby was playing out in the street and Mum was in the kitchen giggling and flirting her eyes at one of their neighbours.

'This is Mr Allnutt,' she said gaily. 'He's offered to put up some new shelves for us. Isn't he a darling? Oh yes you are, Mr Allnutt. An absolute darling. I won't have you deny it.'

The absolute darling was an elderly grey-haired man, busy at the kitchen table measuring planks. ''Ave 'em up in a jiffy, Mrs Furnivall,' he said. 'Don't you worry.'

'What a kind man!' Peggy said as she and Joan carried Mrs Geary's shopping upstairs for her.

But Mrs Geary made a face when they told her what he was doing. 'Oh lor'!' she said. 'I should ha' warned yer. Still, shelves ain't so bad I suppose. Don't go putting nothink on 'em, that's all. Not till you been down to number two. Wait till 'e's finished an' gone back home, then cut along. Bertie'll see you right. D'you get my King Edwards? Oh yes. They'll do a treat. Was there any change?'

It was all very mysterious, but they didn't like to question her any further when she'd obviously closed the subject. They unpacked her vegetables and put them away for her in the corner cupboard and then they went downstairs again to see how Mr Allnutt was getting on. By this time the kitchen was full of wood shavings and Mum was making him a cup of tea.

'Be lovely to have enough shelves,' she was saying. 'I shall put the saucepans up there. Set the fire will you, Joan.'

It took him all the afternoon with a pause for a bacon sandwich. Joan said she'd never seen anybody work so slowly. 'It takes him half an hour to measure a plank,' she said, as she and Peggy were washing up. 'He'll be here till midnight.'

''Specially if Mum will keep feeding him and calling him her knight in shining armour,' Peggy agreed.

But at last the job was done and the knight in shining armour gathered up his tools and departed, glowing with praise.

'Mrs Geary says not to put anything up just yet,' Joan warned as Mum bounced towards her new shelves, saucepans in hand.

'Oh what nonsense!' Mum said, plonking both saucepans down on the top shelf. 'Why ever not?' And the top shelf fell off the wall.

Both her daughters were out of the house and halfway down the road to number two before she could say a word.

'If you please,' Joan said when a small pale woman opened the door, 'Mrs Geary says could you come down to our house. Mr Allnutt's put up some shelves and ...'

She didn't need to explain any further, because a stocky young man had appeared and was already pulling a tool bag out of the hall cupboard. 'I'll come right down, lovey,' he said. 'Gone home has 'e?'

'Oh yes,' Joan assured him. 'Mrs Geary said to wait till he went home.'

'That's all right then,' he said cheerfully as they all trotted back to number six. 'He's a dear old thing, you know. That kind-hearted you wouldn't believe. Always means well. It's just he's cack-'anded, that's all. Nothink broke, was there?'

Mum was still gazing at the wreckage when they got back into the kitchen.

'I'm his son,' the second Mr Allnutt said. 'From number two. Name a' Bertie. I'm ever so sorry about all this, missus. I'll put 'em up for yer proper. We should ha' warned yer. 'E means well you know.'

'It fell down,' Mum said weakly.

'Always does,' Bertie said, getting out his screwdriver. 'Can't do a thing right. Poor old Dad. Always the same. He ain't got the hang of it. Still never mind. I'm 'ere now, missus. Soon 'ave it right, eh?' He was working as he talked, his hands deft and quick, lifting shelves, unscrewing nails, examining the state of the plaster. 'That wants fixing with a nice little wooden plug, that's what that wants.'

He was as quick as his father had been slow, briskly carving wooden plugs for every nail hole. 'There you are,' he said when he'd finished. 'That'll take the weight lovely.'

'Well,' Mum said in some confusion. 'I don't know what to say. It's ever so kind of you, Mr Allnutt.'

'Don't say nothink to the old man,' Bertie Allnutt said, smiling at her like a conspirator. ''E likes ter feel useful, you know.'

What a lovely man he is, Peggy thought, watching him

124

as he packed up his tools and walked into the hall. He must love his father ever so much to cover up for him like this. Like I loved Dad.

'See you at the ding-dong,' he said, as he stepped out into the street.

'What's a ding-dong?' both girls asked as Mum closed the door after him.

'Best part a' the week,' Mrs Geary said from half-way down the stairs. To the girls' surprise she was dressed for the street in a hat and coat and white gloves. Or almost dressed for the street for they noticed she still wore her carpet slippers. 'You jest wait an' see. Now then, you ready for this meat?'

'Are you going to the market?' Mum asked, her eyes rounded in amazement. Really this place was one surprise after another. 'Can you walk that far?'

'If I take me time, I can,' Mrs Geary said. 'One foot after another you know.'

And one foot after another she hobbled down to the town. 'Wouldn't miss me Sat'day night fer worlds,' she confided, as she and Flossie and all three girls walked through the arch and into the evening crowds. 'Now then Charlie,' she said when they reached the first butcher's stall, 'what sort a' rotten ol' cag-mag you got this evening?'

'Fer you, Mrs Geary,' the butcher said, 'nice bit a' silverside, two an' tuppence.'

Mrs Geary surveyed the silverside guardedly. 'That'll come down,' she said to Flossie, when the butcher was attending to someone else. 'We'll 'ave that for a shillin' later. 'Nother twenty minutes they'll start sellin' off. Let's go an' see the fish.'

The fishmonger she chose was offering two herrings for thruppence. 'There y'are darlin',' he sang. 'Lovely fresh 'errin'. Four a tanner.'

'Fresh!' Mrs Geary called back. 'With them eyes! Do me a favour.'

'Can't 'ave everything darlin',' the fishmonger said. 'They're lovely fish.'

'They're on the turn, that's what,' Mrs Geary said, bending down to sniff them.

'Fourpence,' the fishmonger said, slapping the fish into

a pile of newspapers. 'Shall I wrap 'em for yer?'

'Might as well,' Mrs Geary agreed. 'Someone's got ter take 'em off yer 'ands.'

'I'm a fool ter mesself,' the fishmonger complained, 'the prices I charge. Now then. Who else?'

'I'll 'ave fourpennorth,' Flossie said, entering into the spirit of the thing.

'I shall be ruined,' the fishmonger said.

Peggy was so entertained by all this that she didn't notice that there was a boy helping out at the stall. She'd been vaguely aware of two red hands getting the herring but that was all. So when the hands pushed a bundle of dirty newspaper towards her she moved out of the way instinctively.

'It's fer the cat,' a voice whispered. 'Fish 'eads. Take 'em quick, 'fore 'e sees.'

It was the boy next door.

'Ta,' she said, sliding the package into her mother's shopping bag.

'Meat!' Mrs Geary said, hobbling away.

'See you at the ding-dong,' the boy called after them.

'Who's that?' Flossie said.

'Jimmy Boxall from next door,' Mrs Geary explained. 'Poor lad.'

'He don't look particularly poor to me,' Flossie said. 'Good strong healthy-looking boy, I'd say.'

'Oh not that way,' Mrs Geary said. ''E's strong enough. Too many brains that's the trouble. Cleverest boy in the school he is. Took a scholarship to Roan's, easy as pie, so they say. Only his ol' man wouldn't let him take it. Poor kid. Cut to bits 'e was.'

'Oh,' Flossie said, losing interest. Brainy people put her at a disadvantage so she avoided them when she could.

'Wicked waste if you ask me,' Mrs Geary said. 'You got brains you oughter use 'em.'

So that's what it was all about, Peggy thought, trailing along behind them. Fancy winning a scholarship and not being able to take it. I think I'd have cried about that too. He must be clever because only very clever people went in for scholarships.

'Now for that silverside,' Mrs Geary said.

126

It was getting dark by the time they left the market and by then their baskets were full of bargains and Flossie was so pleased with herself that she invited Mrs Geary to have supper with her. 'We'll have those chops,' she said, 'seeing he was so good as to throw them in for nothing.'

'I got the mint this morning,' Mrs Geary said. 'We'll 'ave mint sauce.'

So Flossie took the frying pan down from her new shelves to fry the chops, while her daughters peeled the potatoes and shelled the peas and set them to boil, and Mrs Geary sat at the kitchen table and chopped up the mint, and they made a very good meal together. And afterwards, while Tabby was chewing the bones and Joan was washing the dirty plates and setting the saucepans to soak, Mrs Geary combed her hair ready for the ding-dong.

'Best bibs and tuckers, gels,' she said. 'They'll be starting in a minute.'

'Are *we* invited then?' Flossie said.

'Lord love yer,' Mrs Geary said, laying her comb down beside the salt cellar. 'I should 'ope so! 'Course you are. The whole bloomin' street's invited. Everyone goes to the ding-dong.'

127

CHAPTER 10

Old Mr Allnutt was the only person in the street to possess a piano. It was ancient and beer-stained and its tone was decidedly tinny but he lavished attention upon it, keeping it tuned, as well as he could, and polishing it every Saturday afternoon ready for their evening of mutual glory. Because everybody knew that without Jerry Allnutt and his joanna there wouldn't be a ding-dong, and without a ding-dong Paradise Row would hardly keep going.

The ding-dong was the highlight of the week, when work was over and working pockets were full, when the men gathered for their first leisured pint of the weekend, and the women put on their make-up and their best togs, and the kids were allowed to stay up late. Two by two, family by family, they gathered in old Jerry's front room at number four to share a pint and to sing the old familiar songs in the old familiar way. And the first person in the room was always John Cooper the pianist.

As a young man John Cooper had been a docker, proud of his strength and cockily aware that his Irish good looks could win him any girl he wanted. When the Great War began he'd volunteered in a moment of drunken patriotism and because his current lady friend was urging him on.

'Great strong feller like you,' she'd said. 'Just what Lord Kitchener wants. Soon put the fear a' God into them Huns, you will.'

But the great strong feller she sent out in 1914 came home in 1917 with both his legs blown away, and from then on he'd spent his days in a wheelchair, first in various hospitals, then with various relatives, and finally in the downstairs back room with Mr and Mrs Allnutt, who besides being his landlords, were also two devoted nurse-maids, feeding him and cleaning for him, helping him in and out of bed and his chair and the lavvy. In the afternoons and evenings Mr Allnutt wheeled him down to the Hippodrome Cinema in Nevada Street where he was employed to play the piano accompaniment to the pictures, and every Saturday Mrs Allnutt wheeled him into the front room for the sing-song. He had never had a music lesson in his life. That was a luxury reserved for the rich and the well-to-do. But he had a quick ear for a tune and during the long painful months of his convalescence he'd learned to vamp chords with his left hand on the piano in the ward, so now he could at least earn a living of sorts, and beside that, he was the darling of the Saturday street, greeted with a thump between the shoulder blades and kept well-oiled with beer all through the riot of the evening.

'There he is!' his neighbours would cry. 'Good old John. Give us a tune, John.'

And he would give them a tune. Always the same one. 'The more we are together.' What could be more suitable? 'The more we are together, together, together, the more we are together the happier we shall be.' It was the signature tune of the evening and the singers gathered, beaming and bellowing. 'Good old John!'

'Look sharp!' Mrs Geary said when the first notes struck up on that particular evening. 'We got to be there first because a' Polly.'

'Polly?' Flossie asked, dabbing powder on her nose.

'Me parrot.'

'Are you taking the parrot?'

'Course. 'E loves it. It's the company you see. Loves company. Mr Allnutt carries 'im down.'

Which Mr Allnutt did, supporting the cage carefully with both hands and talking to Mrs Geary all the way.

It's like the Pied Piper, Peggy thought, as she followed

129

them, everyone going in the same direction, following the music. He'll never fit us all in his front room.

But Mr Allnutt's front room appeared to be made of elastic. There was no furniture in it apart from two wooden benches pushed against the walls and the piano in all its glory, and as people used the open window as an extra door they managed to get in and out of the place almost at will. The old and infirm sat on the benches, the children commandeered the stairs, the young and vocal stood hip to hip wherever they could find a space, and the parrot had pride of position on top of the piano where he bounced up and down in time to the music and squawked and took bites at anything that was pushed into his cage, from scraps of food to inquisitive fingers. Beer and shandy and lemonade were slopped in over the singing heads, and from time to time delicacies appeared and were passed from hand to sweating hand, a paper bag full of brown shrimps, or a tub of cockles, or winkles, pins and all. It was picnic, party and public entertainment all rolled into one. And for the three Furnivall girls it was almost too much to take in.

Joan stuck close to Mrs Geary on that first evening, because Mrs Geary was cheerful and knowledgeable and protective, but as soon as Peggy and Baby set foot inside the room they were seized by two small girls in frilled pinafores who told them they were looking out for them because they were their next door neighbours, Lily and Pearl Boxall from number five.

'She's Lily,' the smaller of the two said, prodding her sister in the chest. 'She's nine. I'm Pearl. I shall be nine soon.'

'No you won't,' Lily said amiably. 'You got fourteen months yet. Don't exaggerate. Here, you got a cat aintcher? We seen it in the garden.'

Peggy admitted to the cat.

'Come on the stairs,' Pearl said, unabashed by her sister's criticism. 'You can sit wiv us if you like. We shall 'ave shrimps presently, when me bruvver comes. 'E always buys us shrimps.' She had blue eyes like her brother and a very open face. Peggy liked her at once.

'I shall get my frock all mucky if I sit on the stairs,' Baby complained.

'Go an' sit with Mum on the bench then,' Peggy said.

'She the youngest?' Lily asked when Baby had gone grizzling off. And when Peggy nodded, 'Yeh! Thought so. Youngest's always spoilt. The littlest O'Donavan is a horror. That's 'im over there bein' carried.'

'How old is he?' Peggy asked.

'Three,' Lily said scathingly, 'an' still bein' carried about. They live next door to you the other side, the O'Don-avans. There's ever so many of 'em. There's our Mum look, over there.'

Peggy looked to see a shabby woman in a faded brown frock standing beside the piano. She had straggly brown hair tied up in a bun and lots of lines on her face and she was holding her glass in her left hand because her right one was small and sort of withered as if it hadn't grown properly.

'Dad's up the boozer,' Lily said. 'He's always up the boozer.'

'"My ol' man!"' Pearl said excitedly, leaping from the stairs. 'Come on you two. I got to sing this.'

Peggy hadn't heard any of the songs before, but the choruses were easy to learn and soon she was joining in with everybody else and singing at the top of her voice, particularly when the words were rude. She learnt one song all through, because it was short and naughty and they sang it over and over again, dancing about in the crowded room and out of the door and into the street.

> 'Chase me Charlie, chase me Charlie,
> Lost the leg a' me drawers.
> If you find it, starch an' iron it,
> Send it back ter the boys.'

There were songs to dance to, and songs to holler, and sad songs to sit on the floor and listen to with tears in your eyes. And the shrimps were really tasty.

'Thanks ever so much,' she said, when Jim Boxall gave her a handful.

'That's all right,' he said, grandly, like a lord distri-buting largess. 'Cat like the pieces?'

'I'm keepin' 'em for her breakfast.'

131

'Don't keep 'em too long,' he warned, 'or they'll go off. I'll give you some more next week if you like.'

'Won't he mind, your fishmonger?'

'Not if 'e don't see,' he said grinning at her.

The grin made her feel so welcomed and so much at home she decided she liked him after all.

Over on the other side of the swaying crowd Flossie had found a new friend too. She wasn't really very sure whether she approved of this get-together or not. It was friendly, there was no denying that, but she had a sneaking feeling it was really a bit too common for her and her children, so when the woman sitting next to her gave a derisive sniff at the start of 'They're moving father's grave ter build a sewer' she looked round at her with understanding.

'Dreadful song,' the woman said. 'Not the sort of thing really.'

'No,' Flossie agreed.

'You're new, aren't you?' her neighbour said. 'Yes. I thought so. I didn't think I'd seen you here before. I live at the end house. Number eight, you know.' She was a very stiff woman, with a long stiff face powdered shell-pink, bright blue lids to her pale blue eyes, narrow lips enamelled red and dyed black hair marcelled into waves as hard as corrugated iron. She sat bolt upright and as straight as a board under her yellow cotton frock and she didn't look as though she approved of anything she saw.

Mr Allnutt loomed upon them with a tray and a smile. 'What can I get you ladies?' he asked. 'Mrs Roderick?'

'My usual, Mr Allnutt,' Mrs Roderick said, putting the necessary coins on the tray. 'Port and lemon if you please.'

'Same for me,' Flossie said, fishing her money from her bag and feeling glad to be making an equally ladylike choice.

'Plays lovely, don't he?' Mrs Roderick observed, tilting one ear towards the piano.

'Yes,' Flossie agreed. 'Very good.'

'Plays for the pictures,' Mrs Roderick explained. 'That's what does it.'

The pictures, Flossie thought. How lovely! 'You got a cinema here then?' she said.

132

'Two,' Mrs Roderick said proudly. 'The Hippodrome and the Empire. I go to one or the other every Thursday. All by mesself, but you got to get out now and then, haven't you?'

'I go to the pictures Thursday too,' Flossie admitted, delighted to think that the habit could continue here in Greenwich. 'Wouldn't miss it for worlds. I don't think it matters being by yourself in the cinema.'

'They got Rudolph Valentino at the Palace next week,' Mrs Roderick said. 'In *The Eagle.*'

'Oh!' Flossie breathed. 'Rudolph Valentino!'

'Such a sympathetic actor,' Mrs Roderick said.

'Oh yes!'

There was a pause while they both thought about their hero and John Cooper took a draught from his pint of bitter.

'Does Mr Roderick like the pictures?' Flossie asked, as the solo began.

'He's gone,' her neighbour said lugubriously. 'Gone long since. Took with the consumption, poor soul. Galloping consumption it was. Ever so bad he was. Well, they said at the 'orspital he was the most chronic case they'd ever seen. The most chronic case.'

'Poor man,' Flossie commiserated. 'How sad for you.'

'Yes,' Mrs Roderick said. 'It was quite a come-down, really. We had such a lovely little place when he was alive. And now I'm reduced to this. If it wasn't for my ladies I don't know how I should make out.'

'Yes,' Flossie said, trying to look intelligent although she wasn't quite sure what her new friend was talking about. 'Don't fidget, Baby dear. You'll scuff your nice sandals.'

'Can I go an' play with Marie O'Donavan?' Baby said.

Flossie smiled permission as sweetly as she could, secretly feeling very glad to be rid of her, because for all her charm Baby could be a bit of an embarrassment sometimes with some of the things she said. But then just as she got rid of one encumbrance another one came bawling into the room. Brother Gideon, red-faced and affable with drink, bellowing for his 'old friend Cooper'.

Mrs Roderick shuddered. 'That awful man!' she said. 'He don't live here you know. He's a butcher from right over the other side of town. I don't see why we have to put up with him week after week.'

Gideon had his red arms round the pianist's neck. 'How's me old mate then?' he was shouting.

'They was in the war together,' another woman explained, smiling at the embrace. 'In the trenches.'

'That's no excuse,' Mrs Roderick whispered to her new friend. 'No excuse at all. In my opinion the war has a lot to answer for. All these ex-servicemen begging in the streets. My ladies don't like it and I can't say I blame them.'

Flossie was caught between the need to preserve a diplomatic silence in order to save face, and the knowledge that sooner or later Mrs Roderick was bound to find out that she and the butcher were related. 'Your ladies?' she temporized.

'My customers, really,' Mrs Roderick explained, 'but I call them my ladies, because they're more like friends to me you see than customers. They always say so. Mrs Roderick, they say, you're the best friend a lady could ever have. So charming. I'm a corset fitter you know. Spirella corsets. Only the best, so naturally I move among an altogether better class of person in my line of country.'

'I used to live in the Tower of London when *my* husband was alive,' Flossie said, not to be outdone. 'We had a *very* good class of people there. Royalty, you know. The King and Queen were always visiting. Many's the time I've seen them arrive. Lovely people.'

'Fancy!' Mrs Roderick said, obviously impressed. 'Well then you know what I mean, my dear.'

'Yes,' Flossie said happily and she was just going to tell her new friend something more about her days in the Tower when Mrs Roderick spoke again and in a different tone of voice.

'Oh my good God!' she said, turning up her nose. 'Now look!'

By now the room was so full of people that Flossie couldn't see much more than the bouncing backs and gesticulating hands six inches in front of her face. She didn't even know where Baby had got to with that Marie, which was rather worrying, and Peggy and Joan were quite lost over by the piano. But then two of the backs turned away from one another and she caught a glimpse of a slatternly woman with uncombed brown hair, a blotchy face and a purple nose staggering into the room hauling a small huddled man behind her. Everything about him drooped, his moustache, his eyes, his lank hair, even his jacket and trousers, everything about her seemed to be falling to pieces. 'Here we are!' she called. 'Jus' in time!'

'Nonnie Brown,' Mrs Roderick said. 'She is my land-lady. Now you see what I have to put up with. Tight as a tick most a' the time, she is. Well you can see. An abomination.'

The abomination had lurched her way to the piano and seemed to be dismantling her handbag. 'I've got it in 'ere somewhere,' she called. 'Don't you worry. I'll find it.'

'What's she looking for?' Flossie asked.

'His wretched mouth organ,' Mrs Roderick sneered. 'And then he'll have to play and we'll have to listen, heaven help us all. She does this every Saturday'

'Here it is!' the woman called holding a mouth organ triumphantly aloft. 'Now we're all right. Come along, Cyril. They're all waiting.'

Cyril was shrinking into his shirt, like a tortoise retreating into its shell. 'No they're not, Nonnie,' he said. 'Really you know. They're not.'

'Quite right, mate,' his neighbours agreed. 'You give it a miss. Don't you go playin' on our account.'

But the instrument was already being pushed into Cyril's mouth.

'He can't play,' Mrs Roderick said scathingly. 'Ah, there's our port an' lemon. Ta, Mr Allnutt, you're a gentleman.'

The mouth organ was making wheezing noises to an accompaniment of catcalls and ribald remarks. 'Go on Cyril, mate. You show 'em. Why don'tcher pin it to the wall? Then you could suck it off from there.'

'Aark!' the parrot shrieked, excited by the antagonism. 'Bugger off! Bugger, bugger, bugger.'

'Is it supposed to be a tune?' Flossie asked, trying to ignore that awful bird, but embarrassed despite her efforts.

'Don't ask me,' Mrs Roderick said, sipping her port and lemon. 'He always makes that row.'

The crowd in the room began to thin as people took advantage of the lull to pop out the back or nip across to the pub for a quick one. Now Flossie could see Mrs Geary sitting stumpily at one end of the other bench with Joan squatting on the floor beside her. They were sharing a plateful of cockles and Joan was laughing and wiping her mouth with the back of her hand. The laughter and the carelessness of that gesture irritated Flossie into tetchiness, particularly after all the embarrassment she'd had to subdue. The girl had no right to be looking so happy not after the way she'd behaved. She didn't deserve it. And she won't do her frock much good sitting on this floor either, she thought, dropping her glance to check it for dirt. Then she saw what her daughter was wearing on her legs. Silk stockings! For heaven's sake! A servant dismissed without a character and she was wasting her money on expensive silk stockings. I'll get you to work on Monday, my girl, she thought crossly. High time you buckled down and got some of these silly ideas out of your head.

'I don't suppose any of your ladies are looking for a general servant by any chance,' she asked Mrs Roderick.

'Live-in or daily?' Mrs Roderick inquired.

'Oh daily.' We don't want any more living-in nonsense. She can sleep at home where I can keep an eye on her.

'Well,' Mrs Roderick said. 'As it happens I do know someone. Your girl, was it?'

Flossie nodded because speech had suddenly become inaudible. The wheezing had stopped while they were talking and the sing-song had begun again with a roaring, cynical ditty about the dreaded workhouse:

'Come inside yer silly bugger, come inside,
I thought you 'ad a bit more sense.
Working fer yer living? Take my tip:
Act a bit stupid and become a lunatic.
You get your meals quite regular
And three new suits beside:
Thirty bob a week, no wife and kids to keep.
Come inside yer silly bugger, come inside.'

Flossie paid no attention at all, either to the song or its cynicism. I'll have them both at work the minute I can, she thought, looking round the room for Peggy. They needn't think I'm going to keep them in idleness, oh dear no. That's not going to be the way of it at all. Joan can start the minute I can find a job for her and in three years time Peggy can follow her. I'm not having any more trouble from either of them.

Fortunately, as they strolled happily back to number six in the early hours of Sunday morning, with Mrs Geary still humming their goodnight song, and Mr Allnutt carrying the exhausted parrot, and all the Boxall children chattering into the house between them, neither of the girls knew that their lives had been planned for them.

'See yer next Sat'day,' Mr Allnutt said as they reached the doorstep.

'Yes please!' they said in chorus.

'Glad you come ter London then?' Mrs Geary asked as they carried the parrot upstairs.

'Oh yes!' Peggy said rapturously. 'It's the best place in the whole wide world.'

'Nice lie-in tomorrer,' Mrs Geary said.

'It's tomorrow already,' Peggy said.

'So it is,' Mrs Geary agreed. 'Nice lie-in terday then.'

The entire street had a lie-in on Sundays. Bedroom curtains stayed drawn until well after ten o'clock and then it was only the women who were up and about getting the Sunday dinner. By midday the street was savoury with the smell of roasting meat or rich stews, for even the poorest inhabitants managed some meat on a Sunday. Mrs Geary cooked hers on the hob beside her fire, and ate every last mouthful. When Peggy came upstairs in answer to her knock on the ceiling she found her sitting beside a tray full of dirty dishes.

'Be a dear,' Mrs Geary begged, 'an' ask yer ma if she wouldn't mind just rinsing these through with your things. I'd do it mesself only I got these legs. I'd be ever so grateful, tell her.'

'We shall have to watch her,' Flossie told her daughters as Joan put the landlady's dirty plate in the washing-up bowl. 'She's too crafty by half. If we don't look out we shall be looking after her, cleaning and cooking and I don't know what-all.'

'It's only a plate,' Joan said, cleaning it.

'That's how they start,' Flossie said. 'First it's a plate, an' then before you know where you are, you're doing all their work for them. Clear this table will you, Peggy.'

The next morning was wash-day and Flossie's first row with her landlady, who came downstairs before they'd finished breakfast bearing a pillow case full of dirty washing.

'I have the scullery Monday, Mrs Furnivall,' she said to Flossie, 'ter do me bits an' bobs.'

'I've just this minute lit the copper,' Flossie said, feeling she had to make a stand over this.

'Well how kind,' Mrs Geary said, hobbling towards the scullery door.

'I've just this minute lit the copper for *my* wash,' Flossie said, explaining her position as firmly and unequivocably as she could. 'For *my* wash, Mrs Geary. I always wash on a Monday.'

'Well my dear,' Mrs Geary said, speaking quite kindly, 'you'll 'ave to change that now, won't you. You got all the rest a' the week, when all's said an' done.'

'I always wash on a Monday,' Flossie repeated.

'Well there you are,' Mrs Geary said imperturbably. 'We all got ter make changes sometime or other. I'll put your soaps an' things up on this shelf, then we shan't get in a muddle.'

Flossie was seething with anger at such humiliation. She *always* washed on a Monday. All respectable women washed on a Monday. To leave it till Tuesday would be absolutely dreadful. How could this woman be so unkind? It was enough to bring on her nerves. Particularly as she couldn't say what she thought about it, being a sub-tenant. An outright row could lose them the house. Oh it was too bad! It really was! 'Get your hat and coat on,' she said crossly to Joan. 'We're going to get you a job.'

'Now?' Joan said, looking at the rasher of bacon still on her plate.

'Now! Leave that!'

138

Her years at Tillingbourne Manor had taught Joan to eat on the trot whenever it was necessary, and never to waste food. She put the rasher into her mouth whole, grabbed the remains of her bread and marge, and chewed them both quickly while she put on her hat and coat. She and Peggy managed to exchange grimaces while their mother wasn't looking at them, then there was nothing for it but to walk obediently to the front door. She went willingly enough, they all had to work, and she could hardly expect to be allowed to stay at home much longer, not after – that. And anyway, a job was only a job.

But the job her mother chose for her this time was more unpleasant than the last. By the end of that morning she was maid-of-all-work to a certain Miss Margeryson and her brother, who claimed to be 'something in the City' and was actually a poorly-paid junior clerk. They lived in penny-pinching discomfort and intense respectability on the other side of the railway tracks in a sour house in a jerry-built terrace that had been run up in a hurry by a speculator with city clerks in mind. Consequently nothing in it was quite as it should be, the chimneys smoked, the sash-frames stuck, the range was temperamental and the kitchen floor was so badly buckled it was a nightmare to clean. By the end of her first week Joan was grey with fatigue.

'I've only got one pair of hands,' she complained to Peggy on Saturday night as the two of them were getting ready for the ding-dong. 'She's on at me all the time. Polish the stair-rods, brush the curtains, pumice the door-step, do this, do that. An' then Mum wants me to wash the supper things when I get home.'

'I'll wash the supper things,' Peggy said. 'I don't mind.' She was almost as tired as her sister, because in addition to doing a lot of housework during the day, she was running up and down stairs attending to Mrs Geary.

'Ta,' Joan said gratefully. 'You're a love.'

'You going to wear your silk stockings again?' Peggy asked, leaning her head sideways so that she could brush the tangles out of her long hair.

'No,' Joan said opening the drawer to look at them. Everything had changed so much since last Saturday she didn't feel entitled to luxury any more. 'They're not suitable. Not really.'

'Why not? They was suitable last Saturday.'

'I wasn't a skivvy last Saturday,' Joan explained, buttoning her blouse. 'Silk stockings are for toffs. People who roll around all day doing nothing. Like Miss Amelia or Miss Margeryson, if she could afford 'em, which I very much doubt seein' the state of her larder. 'T anyrate they ain't for skivvies. They don't look right on skivvies.'

'They looked lovely on you,' Peggy said. 'Ever so pretty. Why shouldn't a skivvy wear silk stockings if she's got 'em?'

'You ready?' Baby called up the stairs. 'Mr Allnutt's come for Polly.'

And so their lives acquired a new London pattern, repetitive housework all through the week, an afternoon at the pictures for Flossie, an occasional visit to the wedding cake church of a Sunday whenever Flossie was feeling particularly religious, daily adventures in the little local park for Baby and her new friend Marie, shopping for bargains in the market late on a Saturday night and the ding-dong to end the week with a roar.

The Furnivalls grew accustomed to their new neighbours. They learned how to make themselves scarce when Mrs Roderick and Nonnie Brown were having one of their rows, and how to persuade Mr Grunewald in the corner shop to let them have 'tick till Friday when Mum's money comes', and they all discovered various ways to let dear old Mr Allnutt help them without recourse to any of his disastrous carpentry.

They learned that Mrs Geary's legs were bandaged because she had something called 'varicose veins' which were peculiar purple knobs and lumps that stuck out of her skin like deformed grapes, and they made rude jokes about Mrs Roderick's rich ladies and their corsets, and once, on an exciting occasion when she was safely out of the house, they took it in turns to climb on an upturned orange box and peer through the gap in her net curtains to view her formidable creations, hanging stiffly from a long rail in her front parlour, like pink tubes with laces.

140

There were bad days too, when they listened to Mr Boxall roaring at his family because he hadn't been taken on at the docks and he'd come home unemployed and belligerently drunk. Flossie said she wouldn't be a bit surprised if he wasn't knocking them about, the noise he made, and Peggy quaked to think of Lily and Pearl being knocked about. She discovered that Jim Boxall often did more work than his father, with a paper round every morning, chores to help his mother and Saturday at the market. But unlike his father he was good-tempered and predictable. He always always provided shrimps for the ding-dong and fish heads for Tabby whenever he could. And the little cat grew fat and contented, sleeping in her box beside Peggy's bed like a plump cushion.

And so August passed. It was too hot and the street was always dusty. The drains smelled worse every day and the market stalls were plagued by flies. But although Mum and Joan and Mrs Geary complained about such things, and Mrs Roderick said that life under such conditions was hardly worth living, Peggy didn't mind them at all. She was back in her native city.

CHAPTER 11

Jim Boxall had never been late to school in his life. It was a matter of pride to him. He was never late and he was never absent, except for the times when he had mumps and measles and chicken-pox and things like that, and that didn't count, because you couldn't help catching things. But on the first day of the new school year in 1925 he was the very last pupil to enter the building. The shame of having to go back to the senior boys when he should have been taking up his rightful place at Roan Grammar was so acute he couldn't bear to be seen doing it. In fact if it hadn't been for the fact that he had to look after his mother and his two younger sisters, he'd have been tempted to run away.

He'd been so happy last term when the results of the scholarship came through, walking up to the headmaster's room for the news, knowing it was good because he was going with Polly Smith and Johnny Foster, who were the other scholarship hopes, and the teachers were all beaming and nodding at them. He'd stood on the headmaster's little patch of carpet, smelling the roses on the desk, with the sun slanting in through the high window like a spotlight straight onto his face, and he'd listened to the lovely rewarding words, 'A scholarship to Roan's, Boxall. Well done! We're very proud of you', and pride had swollen in his chest until he felt twice the size. It had been the best moment of his life.

At the end of the afternoon he'd run all the way home,

142

clutching his precious letter and glowing with excitement and success. He'd been so happy he hadn't really understood his mother's muted reaction.

'Yes,' she'd said, doubtfully, 'it's ever so good, Jimmy. You're a good boy. I've always said that, ain't I?'

'Roans!' he said, seizing her round the waist and hugging her rapturously. 'I'm going to Roan's, Mum. Think a' that.'

'Is he really, Mum?' Lily said, beaming at him. 'Really an' truly?'

'Well he's got the scholarship,' Mum said, still laying the table in her awkward way, sidling from chair to chair with the plates held in her good left hand, using her weak right one like a flipper to set them on the table. She did everything slowly, hampered by the crippled shoulder that made her body tip sideways as if she was about to fall, and her expressions were slow too. A smile took ages to spread from her eyes to her mouth, and sometimes it never got there at all. But this should do it, Jim thought, putting the cruet on the table for her. This really should. After all it isn't every day of the week your son wins a scholarship.

'There was only three of us,' he said proudly. 'Me an' Polly Smith and Johnny Foster. And we all passed.'

'Will you have to wear a uniform?' Pearl wanted to know.

'Course. An' I shall learn French and Science an' take matriculation. You'll see.'

'Yes, well lovey,' his mother said, balancing the loaf against her chest before she started to cut it. 'We shall have ter see what yer Dad says.'

'Bloody lot a' nonsense!' Mr Boxall had said, rough with beer and bad temper after two days without work. 'Send it back. Roan's ain't fer the likes of us.'

'But it's a scholarship!' Jim said, fighting back despite his mother's mute appeal. 'I've won a scholarship.'

'You heard what I said. Send it back. We can't afford it. Where's my bloody tea, woman?'

'It's a scholarship to Roan's,' Jim persisted. 'The chance of a lifetime Mr Jones said. The chance to get on. To learn French and Science and History and Geography. Don't you want me to get on?'

143

'I know all about Roan's,' Mr Boxall said. 'Poncin' about in a bloody uniform that costs the bloody earth. Goin' all la-di-da on yer family. No bloody fear. You turn it down.'

'I wouldn't go la-di-da,' Jim pleaded. 'Really, Dad.'

'An' another thing,' his father went on relentlessly. 'You 'ave ter stay at Roan's till you're bloody sixteen. We'd have ter sign to it. If you think I'm going to keep you in bloody idleness till you're bloody sixteen you got another think coming.'

Mrs Boxall slid a kipper neatly onto the plate underneath her husband's beer belly. 'Nice an' hot,' she offered placatingly.

'It'ud better not have too many bones,' Mr Boxall complained, pulling his first forkful from the plumper side of the fish.

As his mother humbly slid a slice of bread and scrape beside the kipper, and Pearl and Lily retreated into the yard, Jim gathered his courage for a last stand against his father's impossible unfairness. 'It's an honour,' he said. 'There was only three of us an' I was the best. You ought to be proud of me. I passed better'n any one else.'

'You keep on,' his father said, munching the kipper, bones and all, 'an' I'll take my belt to yer. You ain't goin' an' that's final. More tea, Mavis.'

Hope and ambition congealed into a solid lump of disappointment that filled Jim's throat and made tears prick behind his eyes. He was too bitterly disappointed to be angry, and too stunned by the injustice of it to fight on or even speak.

But in those brief fraught minutes, while he stood before his father hating him with all his strength, all sorts of half-digested facts crystallized into knowledge inside his sharp young brain. He understood that his father's opposition was unreasonable and that because it was unreasonable it would never be altered. He knew that his mother's dejected expression was the outward sign of almost total defeat, and that her defeat was a combination of his father's brutality and the daily and impossible task of trying to find enough money to feed them all. And worse than both these things, he knew that his scholarship to Roan's had been the one certain way out of their poverty, that with a good education he could have found a good job and earned a good salary and looked after his mother properly. Now he would have to find some other way to do it, for it would have to be done, somehow or other, no matter what his father said. He might be defeated now but that wasn't the end of it. He wouldn't allow it to be the end of it. And with that determination in his mind, he turned and walked out of the house.

And now here he was, loitering into Randall Place School among all the other reluctant pupils, dragging his boots through the dust and wishing himself anywhere but where he was. Even when the final bell rang he didn't hurry. What was there to hurry for? Three more years of the sort of work he could do with his eyes shut, and a dead-end job at the end of it. He trailed into his new classroom hump-shouldered with dejection, reading the name over the lintel by force of habit but without any hope or interest at all. Mr Gurton.

'Just in time, Boxall,' Mr Gurton said. He was a short, sharp-featured elderly man with a narrow skull and long narrow hands and a way of darting his attention at his pupils that was rather disconcerting. 'Another second and you'd have been late and spoilt your record. Early tomorrow, eh?'

It was a surprise to Jim that a teacher in the senior boys should know anything about him. And he was even more amazed when the teacher asked him to stay behind when everyone else went into the hall for prayers.

'I've read your reports,' Mr Gurton said, shooting that penetrating look again. 'You're a very bright boy and we both know you shouldn't be here. But you are and so we've got to make the best of it. However I see no reason why you should follow the same course as all the others, and neither does the headmaster. So what we propose is this. I will give you extra maths lessons whenever I can, the sort of maths you ought to be learning at Roan's, you see, arithmetic and algebra, a little geometry later. Here's the book we shall use. You can work through that while the others are going the dull stuff. And you can do extra English and History and Geography with Mr Williams. Cheer up! There's always another chance.'

145

'Is there?' Jim asked, flatly.

'Oh yes. We send boys on at thirteen too you know. Don't lose heart.'

If my Dad won't let me go at eleven, he won't let me go at thirteen, Jim thought. But he tried to smile at Mr Gurton despite the misery of this knowledge, because the teacher was so plainly expecting it.

'That's right,' Mr Gurton said, encouraged. 'Keep your pecker up, eh. Oh and another thing. If I were you I'd join the public library. We don't have as many books in this school as I'd like. Nowhere near. There isn't the call for them. And you need to read very very widely. Oh yes, very widely indeed. Two books a week at least. I'll sign the application form for you, if you can't – um – find anyone else to do it.'

Does he know about Dad, Jim wondered. Oh God, I hope not! It would be a terrible disgrace for a teacher to know what he was like.

'We'd better cut along to prayers now,' Mr Gurton said, 'or we shall be considered part of the godless generation. We'll slip in at the back behind the top class. No one'll see us.'

So they slipped in behind the rough backs of class three just as throats were being noisily cleared for a growl through the first hymn of the morning.

To have been singled out for such very special treatment had lifted Jim's spirits. Perhaps coming back to Randall Place wasn't the end of the world after all. Perhaps there was hope. Of a different sort, but hope. 'Onward Christian soldiers!' he sang, 'Marching as to war.'

In the senior girls, on the floor below, Peggy's name was being entered in the register by her new teacher, a rather censorious-looking lady by the name of Miss Gwynne-Jones.

'And where were you born?' the teacher asked.

'If you please Miss, in the Tower of London.'

'Were you indeed? Then you'd better go and sit next to Megan Griffiths. She came from the Tower of London too. Isn't that right, Megan?'

Megan Griffiths, Peggy thought, surprise and excitement

fluttering in her chest. Could it really be Megan Griffiths? *Her* Megan, who'd been her very best friend back in the Tower. Oh, if it was, it would be too good to be true.

And it was, older and thinner, with a narrower face and work-scarred hands, but undeniably the same girl, with the same shock of dark hair and the same friendly blue eyes. Megan Griffiths. What a bit of luck!

'No talking!' Miss Gwynne-Jones instructed, as the bell summoned them to prayers. 'Sit up straight. Right you are. Class stand!'

They were very strict in the senior girls. Even whispering was frowned upon except in the needlework classes, and nobody spoke at all on the way into prayers, or on the way out. It wasn't until playtime that Peggy and Megan were finally able to talk to one another. And then they both asked exactly the same question at exactly the same time.

'What are *you* doing here?'

'Dad took a fall,' Megan explained. 'Broke his back. I think it was his back. Anyway they invalided him out the army and we had to come here. We've been here nearly a twelvemonth.'

'Poor thing!' Peggy said sympathetically, remembering the bulky soldier he'd been. 'Is it still broke?'

'No,' Megan said. 'Don't think so. He limps a bit but he can walk about an' everything. It's just he can't be a soldier. He got a job at the gasworks. Doesn't half make him pong. Tell me where you've been. You went to the country didn'tcher?'

They spent the happiest twenty minutes gossiping and reminiscing, and after an uneventful morning, they strolled out of the gates at dinner-time arm-in-arm and still talking nineteen to the dozen.

'Where d'you live?' Peggy asked.

'Here,' Megan said, turning her dark head to look at her house, 'in Randall Place. Where do you?'

'Just round the corner,' Peggy said with delight. 'Almost next door. See you 's afternoon.'

'I got lots to tell you,' Megan promised.

But as it turned out it was Peggy who had the most exciting news that afternoon.

She and Mum and Baby were eating their pudding and she'd just finished telling them about Megan and what an extraordinary thing it was to find her again here in Greenwich, when there was a knock at the front door.

'See to that,' Mum said to Peggy. 'If it's someone selling something we don't want any.'

It was the boy next door. 'I've got your cat in the lavvy,' he said. 'Can you come an' get her?'

Peggy's heart gave a lurch of alarm. 'Why?' she said. 'What's up? Is she hurt?'

'Oh no,' he said quickly, cross with himself for having startled her. 'Nothing like that. She's got kittens, that's all.'

Kittens! Fancy saying 'that's all' about kittens! 'How marvellous!' she said. 'Hang on a tick an' I'll get her box.'

'I thought you'd better take her back before my Dad comes home an' sees her,' he explained as they walked through his tacky kitchen, past his mum and his sisters and out into the rubbish in the yard. 'He don't like cats.'

'He don't like much, you ask me,' Lily said following them out. 'Can I see 'em, Peggy? Jim said I wasn't to.'

'Go back in,' Jim said. 'You know what I told you. No one's to touch 'em except Peggy. You go poking your nose in, you'll upset the mother cat an' then she won't feed them.'

Peggy was impressed by his knowledge and even more impressed to see how quickly his sister obeyed him. 'Is that true?' she asked.

'Yes,' he said. 'I read about it.'

He sounded completely sure of himself. How amazing for a boy to know about such things.

He opened the lavvy door very gently. 'They're hidden in the corner,' he whispered, 'just there, see, in among the newspapers.'

There was a pile of kindling and an untidy heap of newspapers in the corner of the lavvy. Peggy could just see the tips of Tabby's ears sticking out of the papers and the furry outline of her striped back against the grey-brown of the wood. 'She's very well hidden,' she whispered back.

'I wouldn't have seen her if I hadn't gone for the wood,' Jim said. 'How many's she got?'

148

'Haven't you looked?'

'No. I waited for you.'

There were five, three tabby, one black and one tortoise-shell, all with the same sleek round heads, the same funny little scrabbling paws, the same scrunched-up faces and tightly-shut eyes that she remembered so passionately from that first awful time. All five were sucking vigorously and Tabby herself was purring like an engine.

'If we each took hold of one end of this paper,' Jim suggested, 'we could lift them all into the box together without disturbing any of them.'

She was impressed again to think that he could be so tender. 'This is the first litter she's ever been allowed to keep,' she said, stroking Tabby's head, and as he looked interested she told him all about the way the kittens had been drowned.

He was horrified. 'How could they be so cruel?' he said. 'Poor cat! That's inhuman.'

'Yes,' Peggy agreed. 'It is. I thought so anyhow. That's why I brought her with me. Shall we lift them now?'

The transfer was surprisingly easy.

'I'll get her some fish tonight,' Jim promised, as they carried the heavy box gently through the house. 'She'll need feeding up.'

'Now can we see?' Lily demanded, standing before them arms akimbo and blue eyes determined.

So they rewarded both the girls with a quick peep before they continued on their careful way. But when they reached Peggy's front door, Jim stopped and looked thoughtful.

'What is it?' Peggy asked, because it was plainly something important.

'Could I ask you a favour? Before we go in.'

'Yes. Course. What is it?'

'Mr Gurton says I've got to do a lot of reading. I've got to join the library. Two books a week he says. The only trouble is ...'

'Yes?' she encouraged.

He hesitated for quite a long time before he spoke. 'Well it's my Dad,' he confessed at last. 'It ain't just cats he don't like. He don't think much of reading neither. Says it's sissy. And he gets in tempers sometimes.'

Yes, Peggy thought, we've heard him, but she didn't say so, because you weren't supposed to know what went on in other people's houses.

'And when he gets in a temper – well – he throws things about. Sometimes.'

'You'd like to keep the books in our house,' Peggy said, understanding. 'Oh that's all right. They can stay in my bedroom. On the chest a' drawers. No one'll throw 'em about in there.'

So the arrangement was made. Fish-heads for shelf-space. And the cats were carried through into Flossie's neat kitchen.

'What on earth have you got there?' she asked. It was a rhetorical question because she could see exactly what they'd got.

'Oh!' Baby said. 'Kittens. How smashing!'

'Hum!' Flossie disapproved. 'Well you can take them straight upstairs and give them to *her*. They're no concern of ours. I got enough to contend with without having kittens all over my kitchen. Well go on. What are you waiting for?'

I've got to tell the truth now, Peggy thought, and she wished she'd told it in the first place, aware of her mother's gathering displeasure. Jim Boxall was standing just behind her and she glanced back at him quickly, wondering what he would say if a row broke out or Mum had an attack of nerves in front of him. He was splendidly calm, looking straight at her with those fine blue eyes of his, half smiling as if he meant to encourage her.

'Well ...' she said, taking courage from him. 'It's just ... she don't belong to Mrs Geary, you see. She's my cat. I brought her with us from the farm.'

'Oh for heaven's sake!' Flossie said crossly. 'Whatever for?'

'Because they kept killing her kittens and I couldn't bear it.'

For a few seconds there was a thinking silence in the kitchen. The clock ticked, Tabby purred, the kittens made tiny squeaking noises as they suckled. And it seemed to Peggy that Jim's presence was protective, and she was glad he was there.

Finally Flossie spoke. 'If that isn't just like you, Peggy Furnivall,' she said, and there was affection in her voice as well as exasperation. 'Well you'll have to feed 'em and look after 'em, that's all. You can't expect me to do it.'

'Oh yes,' Peggy promised happily. 'I will. They won't be any trouble I promise.'

And they weren't. They were a source of daily delight.

For the next six weeks Peggy watched them, enthralled. They seemed to grow by the hour, opening dark blue eyes to look at her, learning to stagger about on those tiny ineffectual paws, becoming plumper and more fluffy as their fur thickened, and finally developing full sets of charming whiskers that stuck out above their eyes and on either side of their pretty faces like fine white cotton threads. When they started to play, hiding behind chair-legs, and leaping out to stalk imaginary prey or scuttle after screwed-up bits of newspaper, it made her warm with pleasure just to watch them. Tabby was an excellent mother too, despite all her early miseries, although feeding such a healthy family reduced her to a scraggy leanness that Peggy hadn't seen in her before.

Fortunately Jim Boxall kept her regularly supplied with fish heads and as many pieces as he could scrounge, and in return, Peggy looked after his books, receiving them into her care as soon as his father got home from work or the pub in the evening and handing them back to him every morning on the way to school. He was very useful when the time came to find homes for the kittens, for he seemed to know the family history of all the many eager applicants.

'Not there,' he would say when he was consulted. 'They had a dog once an' never fed it.' Or, 'Yes, they'll do. Their mum's ever so kind.'

By the time half-term arrived Peggy had accepted him as her principal ally, after Megan Griffiths, in the necessary childhood conspiracy against difficult adults.

'I'd like to give him a Christmas present,' she confided to Joan. 'He's been ever so good with Tabby an' everything.'

'What would you use for money?' Joan asked, ever practical.

Peggy had to admit she hadn't got any.

'Well there you are then,' Joan said. 'So you can't, can you?'

But it would have been nice just the same. 'I could have bought him a book. He's ever so fond a' books.'

'What sort a' book?' Joan asked.

'One like that,' Peggy said, nodding in the direction of Jim's latest library book.

'*Kidnapped*,' Joan read, opening it and scanning a couple of pages. 'What's he reading this for? It's about Scotland. I didn't know he was interested in Scotland.'

'He's interested in everything,' Peggy said, admiringly. 'He reads two books every week.'

'I don't know where he finds the time,' Joan said. 'It'ud take me a month a' Sundays to get through a thing like that.'

But reading was as much a pleasure to Jim Boxall as following the progress of her kittens had been to Peggy. This was partly because it gave him such a feeling of power and competence to be pitting his wits against the great writers, but mostly because he had found a mentor.

On his third visit to Greenwich library he'd been browsing among the fiction shelves, wondering what on earth he should chose, when there was an odd scraping sound behind him, and looking round he saw Mr Cooper in his wheelchair being pushed towards the shelves by one of the O'Donavan boys.

'Whoa back,' Mr Cooper said to his assistant. 'There's our Jim. Which one are you going to pick eh, Jim?'

Feeling rather foolish Jim admitted that he wasn't quite sure, yet.

'Have you read any Dickens?' Mr Cooper asked.

'Only bits of *David Copperfield* at school.'

'Try *Oliver Twist*,' Mr Cooper said. 'Make yer hair curl, that will.'

So Dickens' classic was found and chosen, and after they'd both had their books stamped, Jim offered to push his neighbour to the picture palace, since that was where he said he had to go.

'Much obliged,' Mr Cooper said and added, grinning at the young O'Donavan boy, 'you cut off home before you crack yer jaw with all that yawning.'

They talked about books all the way to the cinema, and when they parted Jim offered to wheel Mr Cooper to the library whenever he went there himself, 'which looks like being once a week if I'm to do as Mr Gurton says'.

'Take him serious,' Mr Cooper said. 'Nothink like reading. You take my tip. I've done a powerful lot a' reading since the Great War. Opened my mind, it has. Well I tell you, if I'd known everything I know now when the war started, I'd never ha' gone rushing off to join the colours. Never in a million years. Take Dickens for example. He can tell you more about poverty in five pages than all the politicians in the country could do in five years. Even if they knew about it, which I very much doubt. You read as much as you can, son.'

'There's so many books in that library, that's the trouble, Mr Cooper,' Jim said. 'They make my head spin.'

'Don't know where to start, eh?' Mr Cooper said. 'Is that it?' And when Jim nodded. 'Well then I tell you what. What say we make a bargain? If you'll push me down to the library once a week, I'll tell you what you want to know about the books. How would that be?'

So another bargain was struck. One pair of young hands to push the wheelchair in exchange for as much information as a thirty-year-old head could provide.

It was very useful information. Over the next few months Jim was introduced to tales of adventure by Robert Louis Stevenson, Raphael Sabatini, Victor Hugo and Sir Walter Scott. He read a play by George Bernard Shaw which he didn't really understand and poetry by Keats and Shelley which he didn't understand either but which sounded lovely and poetry by Wilfred Owen, which he understood very well indeed with a searing pity for the suffering of the soldiers the poet described, and he'd just borrowed a novel called *Mr Kipps* by H G Wells when something happened one morning in May that made him wonder whether you really could learn everything you needed to know from books.

CHAPTER 12

The three Furnivall sisters woke that Tuesday morning to an extraordinary silence.

'Why is everything so quiet?' Peggy said. She could hear all sorts of tiny sounds, sparrows chirping in the garden outside, the blind trilling in the chill breeze of early morning, even the trickle of water falling back into the basin where Joan was washing herself. It was like being back in the country.

'Don't know,' Joan said, bending forward to splash the soap from her face.

'There's no trains,' Baby said. 'That's what it is.' The railway station was less than a hundred yards from Paradise Row and the noise of trains chuffing and clattering was such a perpetual accompaniment to their street life they'd long since ceased to notice it. Now there was no sound of it at all, no doors banging, no feet running, no whistles shrilling, nothing.

Peggy was thinking about all the other sounds that were missing. 'There's no trams either,' she said. 'How funny! Why has everything stopped?'

Mum didn't know and hadn't noticed. 'Has it?' she said, pouring out the tea. 'Well never mind, eat your bread and butter.' She still called it butter even though they never rose to anything better than margarine these days.

'Perhaps Mrs Geary'll know,' Peggy said.

But they'd slept rather late that morning and there wasn't time to talk to Mrs Geary. So it was Megan who enlightened them on the way to school.

'It's a strike,' she said. 'Everybody's stopped work. Dad says.'

'Will there be school?' Peggy hoped. The streets were full of children all heading towards the gates, so it didn't seem likely.

'Oh yes,' Megan said. 'There'll be school. Bound to be.'

And sure enough the teachers were all there, every single one of them, and the school day wasn't changed a bit, which was rather a disappointment. But the silence continued. It was really rather eerie.

That afternoon when school was over, Jim Boxall wheeled Mr Cooper down to the library and all the other kids in Paradise Row walked through St Alphege's churchyard into Church Street to see what was happening, but nothing was. There were gangs of dockers all in their dirty work-clothes mooching about between the Mitre and the Eight Bells, smoking cigarettes and watching the road as though they were worried about what they might see in it, and down by the Empire Cinema on the corner of Bridge Street, there was another crowd, this time of tram drivers and conductors, all standing very close together and some of them reading leaflets. The children were amazed at how wide the street looked without any trams, and how important the shops seemed. But the emptiness was unnerving and it was chilly standing about.

'Is it going on long?' Megan wanted to know.

Nobody knew.

'What's it for?' Peggy asked. But none of them knew the answer to that either. So after a while as there was nothing happening and nothing to see and rain was beginning to spit down upon them, they all drifted back to Paradise Row.

Joan came home that evening laughing because Mr Margeryson had gone off to work on a bicycle. 'He didn't half look soppy!' she said. 'Ol' Miss M was ever so cross. You'd think the railway had come out on strike on purpose to upset her. She went on and on about it all day. And then the milkman came, and milk's gone up tuppence a quart. She wa'n't none too pleased about that neither. Oh it's been a day an' a half!'

The strange happenings continued. The next day as Peggy and Baby were eating their dinner there was a sudden hullabaloo from the direction of Church Street. Despite Flossie's protests the two girls ran off at once to see what it was. This time the street was full of people and bristling with anger. There was a tram in the middle of the road beleaguered by a seething mass of cloth caps and punching fists and flying stones. Most of its windows had been smashed and there was a policeman on the running board hitting out with his truncheon and roaring at the driver.

'Start up!' he was shouting. 'Start up! Run 'em down if you have to!'

What a horrid thing to say! Peggy thought, and she looked at the driver to see whether he would do as he was told. He looked very well-fed. More like a nob than a tram driver. And he was wearing beautiful clothes, kid gloves and a classy check jacket and a most expensive-looking hat. But he didn't seem to want to run people down. He was trying to inch the tram forward, and he was doing it very badly so that the long vehicle bucked on the rails and swayed quite dangerously from side to side. After a few seconds it gave such a wild lurch that the crowd leapt away from it in case it struck them, and at that it was off, humming along the rails and shedding broken glass as it went.

'Gosh!' Baby said. 'Fancy that!'

'I wonder what'll happen next,' Peggy said, looking at the shards of broken glass littering the road. 'Someone ought to sweep that up or the next horse to come along'll get its hooves cut.'

The street was full of men hot from their fight, milling about, shouting and wild-eyed, reliving their victory.

'I don't think I like this, our Peggy,' Baby said, edging backwards away from the kerb. 'Why is everyone so cross?'

'I don't know,' Peggy said, and added sensibly, 'I vote we keep out of it.'

But that was easier said than done. On Saturday morning Mum sent them both shopping as usual, and Megan went with them because she had errands to run too.

It was a dark morning, already drizzling with rain. The cobbles were slippery and the unused tramrails black with greasy moisture, so the three girls walked at the trot, eager to be out of the weather and away from the strike as quickly as they could. The shopping took longer than usual because the market was crowded and prices were up whichever stall they visited. They hunted in vain for cheaper goods and Peggy even queried the new prices, but the answer was always the same. 'It's in short supply, dearie. Can't get the stuff through, you see, on account a' this strike.'

'I shall have to leave something out,' Peggy said, when she'd bought the eggs her mother had ordered and the cheapest bag of flour and half a pound of loose sugar. 'I shan't be able to buy soft soap as well as potatoes.'

Baby agreed. 'We can put off washing for a bit,' she said, 'but you got to eat.'

Megan just had enough money to cover her purchases, but not a ha'penny left over. 'I don't know what my Mum'll say,' she worried, gazing into the emptiness of her purse.

'Better get back quick,' Peggy advised, 'In case there's another tram.'

So they picked up their shopping baskets and marched out into Church Street. And got a shock.

The street was full of armoured cars, a whole long convoy of them spinning over the wet cobbles on their solid wheels, all painted khaki and pointing their cannon at the crowds of strikers who lined the street to watch them, sullen with fury. They were escorting about a dozen lorries, grimly driven and with labels on their sides saying 'Food Only' and 'Food Supplies', and there were mounted police clopping along on either side of the column, caped against the rain, and two lorry loads of troops with rifles.

'It's like a war,' Megan said. 'That's a cannon sticking out the front a' that one.'

'They won't fire it, will they?' Baby said nervously.

The sight of the soldiers and the anger and tension all round her put Peggy into such a muddle of emotions that she couldn't answer for a moment. She was remembering her father, striding along beside the State Coach in his

157

beautiful red uniform, smiling at her as he passed, and the guardsmen at the Ceremony of the Keys, so protective and splendid, with the Yeoman Warder shouting 'God Preserve King George' and how safe she'd felt being looked after by them. This was like a nightmare. It was unreal to be watching British soldiers pointing guns at her neighbours. That wasn't what they were for, them or their guns. They were for fighting the enemy. And it was just as unreal to see the dreadful state her neighbours were in. Their faces were so dark and so distorted with rage they were almost unrecognizable. Like Grandpa Potter when he was in one of his terrible tempers. And in a deeper and more terrified level of her mind she was wondering what on earth she would do if they started firing those awful guns. Where could they hide out here in the street? Would people let them run into their shops and houses for protection?

'They won't, will they, our Peggy?' Baby persisted.

Peggy pulled her mind back from her worries to comfort her. 'No,' she said. 'Course they won't. They're British.' But looking at the angry faces all round her she knew she wasn't at all sure. 'Come on, let's get home.' I'll ask Jim about it at the ding-dong tonight, she thought. He'll be bound to know.

That evening when the grown-ups were all singing 'Dear old pals' she went to sit on the stairs beside her next-door neighbour.

'Ain't it awful this strike,' she said companionably. 'I hope they stop it soon. Did you see the soldiers this morning?'

His face darkened as if he was annoyed. 'Yes I did,' he said, 'more shame to 'em. They're traitors to their class, that's what they are.' He was quoting what Mr Cooper had said in the library, and that made him feel grown-up and knowledgeable.

It made Peggy feel rather stupid because she didn't understand what he was saying. She decided to talk about the price of food because everybody understood about that. 'Sugar's gone up a penny a pound,' she said. 'Ain't it awful?'

He scowled as though his eyebrows were being pinched.

158

'This is a strike,' he said. 'A general strike. There's jobs at stake. How can you rabbit on about sugar at a time like this? Don't you know nothing, Peggy Furnivall?'

'Not much,' she admitted humbly. 'They never tell you nothing, do they? An' there's no papers.'

He softened a little at this. After all if Mr Cooper hadn't told him about it in the library on Tuesday, he wouldn't have known much either. '*I'll* tell you then,' he said, and explained, 'It's to help the miners, you see.'

She didn't see, but she nodded at him encouragingly.

'The mine owners told the miners they'd got to work longer hours for less pay. So the miners said no, and quite right too, seeing they're on starvation wages as it is. And then the mine owners locked 'em out so's they couldn't work even if they wanted to. Imagine that, being locked out a' work and with no money coming in. So now all the other trade unions have decided to stop work an' all, to show solidarity with the miners and to let the mine owners know they've gone too far. An' that's what they've done. They've stopped everything, mines, trains, buses, trams, docks, everything. An' they won't go back to work again until the miners get a fair deal. *Now* what do you think?'

She was impressed and her face showed it. 'I never knew none a' that,' she said.

'It's the very first time there's been a general strike,' he told her and he was glowing with the pride of it. 'I think it's noble. All the poorest workers standing together for a better deal, thousands and thousands of them, losing pay, an' going without, but standing firm, d'you see, an' that's why they'll win.'

'Like an army.'

'Yes, that's right. Like an army fighting a just war.' That was Mr Cooper's phrase too and it thrilled him to be able to use it. A just war.

'Will it go on long?' she asked.

He knew the answer to that too. 'As long as it takes.'

'Well if that's what they're doing I hope they win,' she said.

At that moment Mr Allnutt came striding into the room from his kitchen bearing a most peculiar object before him on a battered tin tray. It consisted of a short plank of wood

159

with a thick cylinder of coiled wire balanced on top of it. There were lots of untidy ends of wire sticking out of the plank in front of the cylinder and two yellow wires leading from the cylinder into a pair of black headphones which looked very ugly and uncomfortable.

'There you are!' he said proudly. 'My new wireless set. Whatcher think a' that?'

'Did he call it a wire-less?' Megan said, giggling at him once he'd passed, 'But it's *all* wires. That's all it is, wires an' a bit a' wood.'

The singing petered out, as their neighbours turned to see what he'd brought. A space was made on one of the benches and the wireless was lowered reverently into position. People were coming back into the room from the street, flocking round their host, waiting excitedly for their turn to put the earphones over their ears and listen. Even Mrs Roderick was in the queue.

'If you want to know what's really going on,' Mr Allnutt said, encouraging them, 'you listen to this. No good expecting that rag a' Winston Churchill's ter tell you the truth. *British Gazette,* I ask you!'

'I know what it is,' Jim said with sudden recognition. 'It's a radio. They're broadcasting the news. That's what it is.' And he jumped up from the stairs and went to join the throng, with Megan and Peggy following dubiously after him.

They had to wait ages before the earphones were put into their hands and then what they heard was really rather a disappointment. It was a man's voice droning on about the law. 'Sir John Simon,' it said, 'speaking in the House on Thursday night made it clear that every railwayman who was on strike in disregard of his contract was personally liable to be sued in the County Court for damages, and every trade union leader was liable in damages to the uttermost farthing of his personal possessions.'

Peggy couldn't understand a word of it and relinquished the earphones to Mrs Allnutt after a few puzzled seconds.

'It's a man. Talking.' Mrs Allnutt said. 'Listen to that, Mrs Roderick.'

Mrs Roderick lowered the earphones gingerly across her

marcel waves. 'Can't hear a thing,' she said. 'Only buzzing.'

'What?' Mr Allnutt said. 'Give it here, Mrs R. Can't have that.' And holding one earphone against his right ear he listened intently. 'Must be something loose somewhere,' he diagnosed. 'Early days you know. Hang on a tick. I'll soon fix it.'

They hung on, chattering together like starlings, and for a great deal longer than a tick. A strong smell of burning drifted back to them from the kitchen and presently Mr Allnutt emerged with a soldering iron steaming in his hand. 'Keep well clear!' he called. 'Now then let's see.'

It took him such a long time to find the right wire to fix that the sing-song began again while he was at work. Three songs were sung and he still hadn't located the fault although he called out a progress report between every verse, and was cheered and applauded. Finally after much running in and out to reheat the iron, his son persuaded him to take the wire to the fire and he and his machine disappeared into the kitchen again, to his wife's considerable relief.

'He's such a worry with that awful thing,' she confided to Flossie. 'I've been worried out me wits one a' these kiddies'ud go an' get burnt.'

'Still,' Mrs Geary commiserated, 'it's nice to get a bit a' news. I've missed my *Evening Standard.*'

'Standard!' the parrot agreed. 'Star, Newstandard!'

'Well will you hark at that?' Mrs Geary said impressed. 'He's a caution! He must've heard the newsboy.'

'More than I have,' Mrs Roderick complained. 'They could have kept the papers going.'

'I wonder how long it'll be before we see a paper again,' Flossie said.

It was sooner than anyone imagined.

When Megan arrived to call for Peggy on Wednesday morning, a mere nine days after the strike began, she said her Dad had got a paper and it was all over. 'They called it off, so Dad says. Yesterday evening.'

'Thank heavens for that,' Mum said, buttoning Baby's coat. 'Now perhaps we can have a bit of bacon for a change.'

'Tomorrow?' Baby hoped.

'We'll see,' Mum said cheerfully taking her stand on the front doorstep ready to wave goodbye.

Mrs Boxall was opening her door to urge Pearl and Lily out and they could hear Jim leaping down the stairs.

'Strike's all over, Mrs Boxall,' Mum said. 'Back to normal now, eh?'

'Oh!' Mrs Boxall said, giving Pearl a little push with her good hand. 'Off you go or you'll be late.'

'Who won?' Baby wanted to know.

'The soldiers,' Megan said. 'Soldiers always win. They've got the guns.'

'It doesn't matter who won,' Mum said. 'It's over. That's the main thing.'

But Peggy was wondering what Jim would say because she could see him coming towards them along the dark hall.

When he stopped out on the pavement she could see he was biting his lips with emotion. 'It ain't true,' he said to Megan. 'They'd never give in so soon. They was winning. It can't be true.'

'Perhaps Mr Allnutt heard on the wireless,' Peggy suggested.

He was knocking on the Allnutts' door as she spoke.

Mr Cooper opened it and both children could see from his expression that the news was as grim as they feared.

'Called off last night,' he said. 'I can't understand it.'

'What went wrong?' Jim asked.

'No idea, son. You'd better go to school or you'll be late. I'll tell you dinner-time if there's anything else on the wireless.'

'It's a tragedy!' Jim said to the girls as they walked to school. 'A disaster! What'll happen to the miners now?'

That evening Mr Baldwin broadcast to the nation. He said the ending of the strike was a 'victory for common sense', and added 'our business is not to triumph over those who have failed in a mistaken attempt.'

But the newspapers triumphed just the same. The *British Gazette* ran the headline, 'Men to return forthwith. Surrender received by Premier in Downing Street.' And the *Mail* crowed, 'Surrender of the revolutionaries.'

It was a total and ugly defeat. And as they were all to

discover, after a defeat the victors take their spoils and exercise their new-won power and the losers suffer. The miners struggled on alone for nearly six months but there was no strike pay for them because the funds were dry, and in the end starvation forced them back to the pits, where they were obliged to work longer hours and for less pay, exactly as the owners had required them to do in the first place. And of course other employers were quick to follow the lead of the triumphant mine owners. Soon rates of pay were being cut in other manual jobs and even clerks, who had thought themselves above the argument and had turned out in their thousands to help break the strike, now faced the necessity of cutting their living standards as their income dropped. Although some of them were cute enough to cut someone else's living standards instead. And one of these more astute gentlemen was Mr Margeryson, Joan's employer.

Flossie was most upset.

'Are you sure you've not annoyed him?' she asked tetchily when Joan came home with her unwelcome news.

'No,' Joan said miserably. 'He says it's the strike. Everybody's got to take a ten per cent cut to pay for the strike.'

'That's all very well but what are we supposed to do?' Flossie wailed. 'It's enough to bring on my nerves. Well I can't manage with less than you give me and that's all there is to that. You'll have to make do with less in your pocket, that's all.'

'I have little enough as it is,' Joan said. 'Two an' three it was. Now it won't even be a shilling. Just as well I don't smoke.'

'Could you get another job?' Peggy wondered. 'Somewhere nicer.'

But Joan sighed most miserably. 'Not with my record,' she said. 'No one'ud have me. The only way I shall ever get away from old Miss M is if someone'll marry me. And who'll do that?'

'I'll see if Jim can get me a job in the market Saturdays,' Peggy promised, trying to comfort her.

But even Saturday jobs were hard to come by now, and try as he might Jim couldn't persuade anyone to take her on.

Meals in the Furnivall household diminished. Bread and scrape replaced bacon and eggs for breakfast and dinners were often reduced to vegetable soup or potatoes baked in their jackets. It upset Flossie to be living so poorly but it was either that or go without her weekly trip to the pictures and she knew she simply couldn't live without the pictures. She justified her decision by telling herself that her three girls had always been strong, even Baby for all her delicate start. A little hardship wouldn't hurt them, provided it didn't go on too long. They only had to hold on for a little while and Peggy would be at work. Five school terms. Why, it was hardly any time at all.

To Peggy, secretly worrying about their lack of funds and cursing the law that kept her unprofitably at school when she ought to have been earning for her family, five terms was a very long time indeed.

'I wish they'd let us leave at twelve like they did in the old days,' she said to Megan. 'Mrs Geary was at work on her twelfth birthday. She was telling me.'

But they wouldn't, so it was no use fretting about it.

The misery of that first winter after the strike was made worse by bitterly cold weather. There were storms and gales all through November and at Christmas-time it snowed, thawed and snowed again, so that the streets were full of trodden re-frozen slush, brown-smeared and litter-embedded and looking uglier by the day. All three of the Furnivall girls got chilblains and Megan caught the flu and was very ill for nearly a fortnight.

The spring was late and cold and the summer was the wettest in living memory. Tabby produced another litter, which cheered them all a little, although Peggy was glad there were only three kittens this time, because there were fewer fish pieces to feed her with now and she was as hungry as her mistress.

But the year passed eventually, and three of the five school terms were over, and now the older pupils began to leave, one by one as they reached their fourteenth birthday.

'I wish I'd been born in September,' Peggy said to Jim as they walked to school one foggy November morning.

164

'When were you?' he asked.

'August. I shall have to wait till the end of the year.' Her snub nose was quite red and the chill was making her eyes water.

'Poor you,' he said. 'I go in February.'

'Have you got a job?'

'Apprenticeship,' he said, but his face was so pinched with cold she couldn't tell whether he was happy about it or not. 'Warrenden Brothers, the marine engineers, in Deptford Creek. Better than nothing I suppose. At least I can start getting some qualifications.' The failure of the strike had made him more determined to educate himself than he'd ever been. Without qualifications a man was nothing.

'At work?' she said.

'No. At evening classes. I've signed up for English and General Science. Start January.'

'Ah.'

'It's a funny world,' he said, 'when you got to wait to leave school before you can get educated.'

And put like that she had to agree it was.

They walked on together in companionable silence, she thinking how much she wished she could start work in February too, he pondering the basic unfairness of the world and how it ought to be put to rights.

He was glad to be leaving school, and glad that he would soon be earning, but although it was better to be going to an apprenticeship instead of to a dead-end job, an apprentice's wages were very low indeed, and nothing to the sort of salary he could have commanded if he'd been allowed to take his place at the grammar school. It had been a bitter day for him when half a dozen of his class mates sat the second chance scholarship and he'd been left in the classroom. But what was the use of hoping or entering? His father would have refused that just as he'd refused the first. Now at least he would be his own man with his own wage, however small. And February was only ten weeks away.

He left school quietly, as they all did, collecting his reports from the headmaster on his last afternoon and walking away from the building without a backward

165

glance. It was a cold bleak day and the houses in Randall Place were huddled and grey like a row of little old men. But he had already started his evening classes and was enjoying them very much, and tomorrow he was beginning the next stage of his life and would be a wage-earner, and that was what was important. As he turned the corner into Paradise Row he was humming to himself with pleasure.

The next morning he was awake at half past six, and up, washed, dressed and breakfasted by seven. He was full of restless energy, eating his bread and marge on the prowl, hovering behind his mother while she cut his sandwiches and made up his lunch-box.

'Two of yer now,' she said proudly, smiling at him.

He gave her a hug. 'Everything'll be different from now on,' he said. 'Only don't you tell *him* what I'm giving you.'

Mention of her husband made Mrs Boxall wince and turn her ear towards the stairs. 'He'll be down presently,' she said, listening to the clumping sounds above their heads. 'Better get off before, eh?'

So he went off early.

It was bitterly cold out in the first light of that February morning, and the gaslight in the windows of Paradise Row was so pale it was almost colourless. He turned up his collar against the chill, tucked his lunch-box under his arm and trudged off towards Church Street, where the trams were humming and clanking and he could hear a car hooting.

The main roads were a little more lively and the gas lamps here gave a better light, buttery yellow with a blue corona. There were plenty of men on the pavements walking to work, just like he was, and several cars and delivery vans already busy among the trams. He quickened his pace, heading towards Billingsgate Street and the wharves. And found he was whistling to himself.

'Well hello!' a voice said behind him. 'Where are you off to?'

It was Johnny Foster, his old rival, lucky Johnny Foster who'd taken up his scholarship and gone to Roan's, perched on a bicycle with a newspaper sack round his shoulders, his fair hair dampened by mist and his glasses glinting in the gaslight.

'Work,' Jim explained, with just a touch of pride.

'No kidding,' Johnny said. 'You can't be. We've only just started the third year.'

Jim had almost made himself forget what a long education boys were given at Roan's. 'Yes well,' he said. 'Some of us start earlier than others.' It was no good getting upset about such things.

'Poor you,' Johnny said. 'I started German this year. Can't say I like it much, all those declensions. It's worse than French and that's saying something. Science is OK. We've got a super stinks lab.'

Jim was irritated by this conversation despite his intention to make the best of his lot. 'You're lucky,' he said.

'Yes,' Johnny agreed, 'so they keep telling us. But it takes a lot of work you know. It's not easy.'

It would have been for me, Jim thought. 'You on your paper round?' he asked trying to change the subject.

'Yes, bit of a bore, but you've got to show willing.'

He looks different, Jim thought, noticing the uniform blazer and the neat shirt and tie underneath his friend's macintosh, and he talks different. Two and a half years and they've quite changed him. He sounds like a toff. And he knew he was jealous of the change and was annoyed with himself for succumbing to such an ugly, useless emotion.

'Better be off,' he said. 'Mustn't be late on my first day.'

'Where's the job?' Johnny asked casually.

'Warrendens.'

'That dump!' Johnny said disparagingly, wiping his nose on the back of his hand. 'Poor you! Well rather you than me, that's all I can say.'

Humiliation, jealousy, anger and a searing sense of the injustice of his life suddenly boiled in Jim's chest and rose towards his throat in a treachery of tears. He had to get away, to put a distance between himself and Johnny's thoughtless success before he burst into tears. God, what a disgrace to weep in the street, and in front of Johnny Foster too. It couldn't be borne. He turned on his heel abruptly and for the first time in his life stepped out into the road without looking.

The van hit him in the arm and the chest. The blow was so sudden and unexpected it stopped his thought and his breath together. He knew he was being propelled through the air, that he was falling sideways, his arms spread like wings; he felt the shock of his landing, the force of it spreading through his body in terrifying uncontrollable waves; then darkness pressed him into the pavement.

CHAPTER 13

The arrival of a policeman in Paradise Row in the middle of a quiet Thursday morning caused a dreadful stir. Mrs Geary saw him first, naturally enough, glimpsing his dark uniform in one corner of her mirror just as she was arranging her legs more comfortably on the footstool. She swung the mirror round at once to see where he was going.

'Mrs Furnivall!' she called. 'There's a bobby in our street. Come an' see!'

Flossie was up the stairs in an instant, avid with interest. The two women watched with mounting concern as the policeman marched towards them. They were quite relieved when he knocked next door.

'Now what?' Mrs Geary said peering through the gap in her net curtains. 'D'you think it's *him*, Mrs Furnivall?'

'Nothing would surprise me where that man's concerned, Mrs Geary,' Flossie said. 'I've always said he'd get himself into trouble sooner or later. A man with that sort of temper.'

But when the policeman left and Mrs Boxall ran to their door, white-faced and shaking, to stammer out her news, they were both ashamed to have been so uncharitable.

'Jim's been knocked over,' she said. 'Hit by a van, poor kid.'

'Is he bad?' Flossie asked.

'His arm's broke, the copper said. An' something's happened to his ribs. Cracked I think he said. Oh dear. I

169

got to go up the hospital right away, an' there's the girls coming home ter dinner any minute. What if I'm not back in time, Mrs Furnivall? Oh dear, oh dear, I don't know whether I'm coming or going.'

'Poor Jim!' Mrs Geary said, hobbling down the stairs. 'What a dreadful thing! You cut along, Mrs Boxall dear. We'll look after 'em. Don't you worry.'

'But I don't know how long I shall be,' Mrs Boxall grieved. 'Oh dear, oh dear, what will his father say?'

'Take as long as you like,' Flossie said, patting her shoulder. 'They'll be all right with us, won't they, Mrs Geary?'

'You'll pop in after, and tell us how he is, won't you?' Mrs Geary said.

But Mrs Boxall wasn't back when her children came home for their dinner and by then the news was up and down the street. Lily and Pearl were most upset, and so was Peggy.

'I shall go and see him,' she said. 'Poor Jim.'

'They won't let you in,' Flossie told her. 'They don't have kids in hospitals. They like to keep it quiet.'

'I'm not a kid,' Peggy said sensibly. 'I shall be out at work in August, don't forget. They'll let me in, you'll see. They let me in to see Dad.'

'That was different,' Flossie said. 'You were next of kin. You're not next of kin now.'

'Then I shall go with Lily,' Peggy said, doggedly. 'She's next of kin. We'll go tonight. Nobody else'll go tonight I'll bet.' That wretched Mr Boxall wouldn't set foot in the place. He'd be off up the pub and Mrs Boxall would have to wait in to feed him.

'Oh,' Lily said, doubtfully, 'I don't know. I mean ... Perhaps Mum won't let us.' She didn't really want to go to the hospital at all. Hospitals were frightening places where people went when they were all covered in blood and they were going to die. She knew that even though she'd never been inside one. Besides it would mean actually having to see what had happened to Jim. It was bad enough knowing without having to look.

But for all her quiet demeanour, or perhaps because of it, Peggy's determination was implacable. At twenty-five minutes to seven that evening the two girls presented themselves at the gates of St Alphege's Hospital as visitors for Jim Boxall, Men's Surgical.

'You relations?' the porter quizzed.

'Tell him,' Peggy said, prodding Lily.

'I'm his sister,' Lily obeyed.

'Down that corridor,' the porter instructed. 'Third on the left.'

It was the first time Peggy had been inside a hospital since her Dad died, and the memory of that occasion filled her mind as she walked down the long corridor, smelling the familiar, frightening mixture of disinfectant and floor polish. Dear Dad! What a long time ago it seemed, standing beside him in that white room, promising to look after Mum, wanting to cry and knowing she mustn't. Lily clung to her hand, whimpering that 'she didn't know, she really didn't know', but the decision had been made and there was no going back on it now. She was a soldier's daughter, born in the Tower of London. And anyway the doors opened at seven.

There were small crowds of visitors waiting outside every door along the corridor, humble in their dark working clothes, and talking in whispers as though they were in church. Peggy and Lily stood at the back of their particular crowd and so they were the last to walk into the ward when the bell rang and a stern-faced sister opened the door. Then there was such a scramble as the other visitors rushed towards the beds that it took a few seconds before Peggy could see where Jim was, and then she could only be certain it *was* him because his was the only bed left unvisited.

He looked so awful that the sight of him gave her a shock despite her determination to stay calm. He was propped up in one of the beds in the middle of the ward, wearing hospital pyjamas and not moving. His left arm was encased in white plaster, there was a wide bandage all around his chest and his face was so bruised and swollen she could barely recognize it. Lily began to whimper again.

'Hush up!' Peggy hissed at her, giving her arm a shake. 'You make that noise you'll upset him.'

'He looks so awful,' Lily whispered.

171

'Smile at him,' Peggy said, and she sounded so fierce that Lily did her best to obey, stunned that her gentle neighbour was showing such unexpected force. Whoever would have thought it?

But the force was for a purpose. Peggy knew instinctively that whatever else the two of them might do or say they should be quite sure not to let Jim know how bad he was or how awful he looked. Visiting Dad had taught her that all those years ago. He'd be in pain, he was bound to be, and pain was enough to contend with without having to cope with them making a fuss.

'Hello,' she said brightly as they approached the bed. And she was pleased to hear how normal her voice sounded.

''Lo Peg,' he said, speaking thickly because his lips were swollen. He had an awful black eye, almost closed up, the left side of his face was red and purple with bruises, and when he turned his head she could see a long red cut on his chin sutured with spiky black stitches.

'Don't say nothink,' she advised. 'I'll ask questions and you can nod. I've brought your book for you, see.' Holding it up towards his good eye. 'I don't suppose you'll feel much like reading just yet, but I'll put it on your locker for when you're ready.'

He was relieved by her tact and good sense. After a day drained by shock and torn by almost perpetual pain he was too exhausted to talk. His ribs ached and his arm pulsed, even now through all the drugs they'd given him. But he managed a nod to thank her.

'Now then,' she said, when she'd made Lily sit on the side of the bed where he couldn't see her and had sat down on the more visible side herself, 'what do you need? You got hankies?'

Slight shake.

'D'you need some?'

Equally slight nod. They'd only be bits of old rag but he didn't tell her that.

'That's the way,' she approved. 'I'll bring some tomorrow. I'll make a sort a' list. Then we'll go home an' leave you to sleep, won't we, Lily? You'll feel better tomorrow. Toothbrush?'

The questions continued, gently and easily, letting him

172

take his time to rest between each one and think for as long as he liked before answering. Then she signalled to Lily and stood up to leave. And Lily almost wrecked the visit.

'Poor old you, Jim,' she said as she stood up. 'Does it hurt much?'

He shook his head, but being reminded of his pain seemed to renew it, and the effort it cost him to deny it was movingly obvious, for tears welled into his eyes and his swollen lips began to tremble.

'Course it hurts,' Peggy said lightly, turning the moment and the awkward question aside. 'You are soppy, Lily. Ain't she soppy, Jim? I don't know how she ever got to be so soppy.'

This time he nodded, eased by the teasing note in her voice, and managed to control the trembling.

He's so brave, Peggy thought. It hurts him terribly but he won't let on. And she was torn with admiring pity for him. 'We'll be back tomorrow,' she promised.

'Not me,' Lily said, as they walked off along the corridor. 'You can come if you like but you count me out. I seen enough. Don't he look awful!'

'All right then,' Peggy said easily. 'I'll come on my own.'

And did, bearing a pile of cotton rags from Mrs Geary, a copy of *Nicholas Nickleby* from Mr Cooper, and a battered toothbrush and a message from Mrs Boxall.

'Your Mum says she'll try an' get in tomorrow,' she said. 'You look a lot better.'

'Yes,' he said. 'Feel a lot better.'

'I got lots a' messages for you,' she said. She'd made it her business to gather them so as to have something to talk about. 'Mr Allnutt says would you like some writing paper. I think he wants you to write him a letter.'

This time she sat beside him for the full hour and entertained him so well that he missed her when she left.

By Saturday evening he was waiting quite eagerly for her arrival. She was his only visitor that evening and the only one he was likely to have, as he knew with resignation. Now that his mother had talked to the sister and understood that he wasn't going to die and that it was simply a matter of waiting for the plaster on his broken

173

arm to come off, his cracked ribs to mend and his cuts and bruises to heal, she was content to leave him where he was.

'Perhaps they'll feed you up a bit,' she'd said hopefully as she left the ward that afternoon. 'I'll come in if you want me for anything.'

'No,' he'd said. 'I'm all right Mum.' And he'd thought of Peggy as he spoke. Dependable Peggy, the good neighbour. *She'd* visit him.

That evening they talked about Mrs Roderick and her hideous corsets, or to be more accurate Peggy talked and Jim listened and laughed as often as he dared, for speech and laughter were both too painful to be attempted too often.

'How's Tabby?' he asked, when they'd criticized most of their neighbours.

'Missing your fish.'

'I'll be home soon, tell her,' he said.

'Will you?'

'In about a week, they say. When they've took the stitches out. An' then I'll go straight down the market and scrounge some pieces. It'll be the first thing I do.'

'She'll like that,' Peggy said. 'She missed 'em this evening.'

He suddenly realized what day it was and what else was being missed. 'You ought to be at the ding-dong,' he said, feeling remorseful because she'd foregone it on his account. Now that really *was* friendship.

'I'm going straight there when I get back, don't you worry,' she said. 'They're all waiting to hear how you are.'

She's taken responsibility for me, Jim thought, but it didn't surprise him. It seemed a perfectly natural thing for her to do.

And so the visits and the conversations continued. By Wednesday he had recovered enough to tell her about his injuries and to describe what little he could remember of the accident. On Thursday he told her about the nightmare he'd had the night before.

'I was falling through the air,' he said, 'and there was this pit full a' snakes all hissing and writhing. I can't stand snakes. Never could.'

174

'I know how you feel,' she said, and exchanging confidence for confidence, she told him about the ghost in the Tower, who 'must have been buried alive to walk like that', and the Tillingbourne anchorite, 'bricked into a tiny cell with no windows or light or anything, imagine it', and how her greatest fear was the thought of being bricked up alive like they were.

He was amazed by the story and by her confession of fear. 'Not likely to happen nowadays though,' he said, to bring them back into comfortable territory.

'No, thank heavens,' she agreed.'They was horrible in them days.'

'Changed a bit now,' he said. '*You* wouldn't want to be an anchorite, would you?'

'No,' she said. 'I would not. And I wouldn't ha' wanted to be one then neither.'

He looked at her, sitting so steadfastly beside him, and it occurred to him that until this week he'd never really looked at her before. She'd been one of his neighbours, that was all, a short brown-haired girl with the sort of bland, chubby-cheeked London face that he saw over and over again in the streets and markets, and here in the hospital too. But now he was noticing other things.

'You've got green eyes,' he said.

Such a personal observation made her blush. 'They're like my Dad's,' she said, maintaining her composure with difficulty. 'Greeny-brown with brown stripes.'

'So they are,' he said, looking at them again. 'You got a tabby cat and tabby eyes.'

And that pleased them both and the pleasure encouraged her to tell him all about her father and what a dear kind man he'd been and how much she'd loved him.

'Lucky you,' Jim said, when she stopped to draw breath. 'My old man's not ... Well you know what he's like.'

'Yes,' she admitted. 'I do.' In the curtained privacy of a hospital ward, under the buzz of other people's conversations, it was possible to say such things.

'He's rotten to the old gel sometimes,' he said. 'He don't treat her right. When I've finished my apprenticeship there's gonna be some changes I can tell you.'

175

'What will you do?' she asked.

'Give her enough money to feed us fer a start,' he said, quite fiercely. 'Then I shall get out of that house. Find her a flat with a bath and running water and an indoor lavvy.'

'Leave Paradise Row you mean?'

'Yes. Course. Wouldn't you?'

She hadn't thought about it. 'No,' she said. 'I don't think so. I like it there. It's nice. What about the ding-dong?'

'Don't you want to change things?' he asked. It didn't seem possible that anyone would go on enduring life in Paradise Row if they had a chance to escape from it.

'We had a rector in the country,' she said, remembering him, 'used to preach about making changes. Always on about it he was. He used to say, God give us the grace, or something or other, to ... what was it?... change those things that ought to be changed and endure those things that ought to be endured, and know the one from the other.'

'That's right,' he said, delighted by the quotation. 'Change things, you see. That's what we all ought to do. Why should a rich man live in luxury up Blackheath and the poor pig it in Paradise Row? Why shouldn't we all have baths and a bedroom of our own and plenty to eat?'

'I don't know,' she said. She'd always taken the prayer to mean that they were supposed to put up with things. What can't be cured must be endured, as Dad used to say. It was odd that he should interpret it so differently.

The sister was ringing her bell to mark the end of the visiting hour.

'See you tomorrow,' Peggy said, rising to go. And in an attempt to end their conversation on a lighter note. 'I'll change your library book. That's a change I *can* manage.'

'Goodbye, Peg,' he said, smiling at her gratefully. 'Thanks for coming.'

'Soon be home,' she said.

But by the time his stitches were out and his ribs were sufficiently healed to be allowed home to a riotous reception at the next Saturday night ding-dong, nine more days had passed and they had established a friendship that had become so intimate it was quite a relief to be relinquishing

176

it and returning to the light of common day. But her admiration for his endurance and courage and his gratitude for her good sense and reliability continued unabated, and long after they both thought they had forgotten them, they were still putting down stronger and stronger roots.

CHAPTER 14

There were times when Baby Furnivall found herself wondering whether it was really a good thing to be so spoilt. She knew how spoilt she was, of course. How could she be off knowing when she always got the best of everything? First in the bathtub before the kitchen fire of a Sunday evening, best cut off the joint every Sunday lunchtime, a new frock when Joan and Peggy both had theirs turned, ha'pennies for sweets, going to the pictures every school holiday with Mum and Mrs Roderick. Although to be honest that was difficult sometimes because Mrs Roderick was so sticky. Not that she could ever get Joan and Peggy to understand that. They thought it was unfair, because Mum had never taken them when they were at school. And Mum made matters worse by some of the things she said.

Take that first time, when they'd gone to see Al Jolson in *The Singing Fool*. Peggy had just started work as a housemaid at Miss Jones' over on Blackheath, and she'd come home with her hands all cracked and bleeding from the soda she had to use for cleaning, just at the very moment when she and Mum had their hats and coats on ready to go out. So it wasn't really the best of times. But Mum couldn't see that.

'We're just off,' she'd said. 'Your supper's dished up. It's on the stove.'

'Off where?' Peggy asked, rubbing her hands.

'To the pictures. It's the first talking picture. Al Jolson.'

178

'Is she going?' Peggy said, glaring at her sister.

The glare had put Mum's back up. 'And why not?' she said. 'We can afford it now.'

'Now that I'm working,' Peggy said bitterly. 'Oh don't say it. Now that I'm working.'

'If you're going to be unpleasant we shall go all the quicker,' Mum said. 'It's not nice to be jealous of your sister. You should try and control it. We all have to work, you know.'

Peggy walked across to Baby and held out her chapped hands right in front of her eyes. 'Take a look,' she ordered. 'That's what work does. That's what'll happen to *your* hands when the time comes. Take a good look.'

It was really upsetting. She didn't have to do that. There was no call to be so nasty. Fortunately Mum soon put a stop to it.

'Come along, Baby,' she said, heading for the door. 'We can't stop here listening to spiteful nonsense. Put your hat on.'

So they went off to the pictures which was ever so good and soon made her forget about Peggy's unkindness.

And Peggy was left to eat her supper in the empty kitchen with only the cat for company. Serve her right.

But there were other things too. When Mum first bought her a bed of her own she'd been ever so pleased. But she soon discovered that there was a snag to it. Once she was out of the way, Peggy and Joan lay awake at night whispering together in that great bed of theirs, and when she asked them what they were talking about, they told her she was too young and ordered her to go back to sleep, which was horrid of them because it made her feel ever so left out.

She often felt left out, if the truth were told. It was hard for her to make friends. Marie O'Donavan played with her now and then and at school she drifted from group to group, but she was always on the edge of things and never accepted by anyone, and although she took pains to be bright and cheerful and to look as pretty as she could, because she knew how important it was for a girl to look pretty, she never found herself a best friend. Joan went off to the pictures with all sorts of friends, servants like her and nannies that she met in the park, and Peggy had Megan from the Tower, and Lily next door and even Pearl now that they were all out at work, but she had no one. Even the cat didn't like her. It never sat on her lap, at least never of its own accord, and yet it jumped up to make a fuss of Peggy every time she sat down. It wasn't fair. Sometimes she felt so sorry for herself she sat down and cried.

But at other times she wondered whether being spoilt wasn't half the problem. Last year, when they were all making special New Year resolutions because 1 January was going to be 1930 and the start of a new decade, she'd decided to make a special effort not to ask for favours. And she'd done it. For a jolly long time. Nearly three months. Well, two and a half anyway. But it didn't make any difference because Mum offered her treats anyway and she couldn't refuse without looking ungrateful and running the risk of upsetting Mum or bringing on her nerves. And the new decade was just the same as the old one had been. Worse if anything. People were still being laid off work and there was never enough money. Even the banks were in trouble. There been a slump or something over in America and after that shops went bust and closed down nearly every week. Even nice ones like Cleavers where they sold hats. And now it was the second spring of the thirties, the early leavers were already off to work and she was faced with a dilemma.

In July she would have to start work too, and she was dreading it. She really couldn't bear to go into service like Joan and Peggy. They always looked tired, positively grey sometimes, and their hands were awful, red and swollen and scored with cracks and lines, awful. She'd known that without having them pushed right under her eyes. What she wanted was a nice clean job in a shop, like Amy Jennings, where she could look pretty and she wouldn't have to work until her back ached. But that wouldn't be easy. If she got herself a shop job Joan and Peggy might get cross. And they'd certainly say she was spoilt, because that's what it would look like. It was all very difficult.

In the end, of course, she did what she'd always known she would do. She begged her mother for special treatment, choosing her moment carefully when Flossie had just got home from the pictures and Joan and Peggy were still at work.

'Mum,' she said, as they were setting the table for supper. 'Must I go into service?'

'Where else would you go?' Mum said, laying out knives and forks.

Encouraged by the question Baby began to wheedle, remembering to drop her head and pout prettily and lisp a little because that always worked with Mum. 'Please don't send me into service,' she said, squeezing out a few tears. 'I couldn't bear it. I really couldn't. I shall die if you send me into service.'

'My dear child!' Flossie said, caught up by her daughter's emotion. 'What is it? Tell your old Mum. Don't keep it to yourself.'

So Baby spilled out all her hopes and fears, with considerable artifice and no restraint, stressing how frightened she was of working in a strange house on her own, and confessing that she thought she might be going to have nerves, 'just like you Mum', and finally describing the sort of job she really wanted, in rose-tinted detail.

To her relief, when Mum had listened and sympathized and wiped away her tears, she agreed to do something about it.

'Don't you worry, darling,' she said. 'I won't send you into service if you don't want to go. I couldn't do that to my darling, now could I?'

The poor child really wasn't strong enough to be a servant, as she told Mrs Roderick when they went marketing together the next morning. A position as a shop assistant would be altogether better. Mrs Roderick agreed with her, saying it was very suitable and offering to keep her ears open for possibilities. And after two weeks a possibility was found. Baby could be taken on as a shop assistant and trainee telephone operator with Dodds, the ladies' outfitter. She would only get a nominal wage of five shillings a week for the first four weeks while she was training but Flossie said they could manage that, with Joan and Peggy working. And Baby was only too happy to agree to it.

181

The only difficulty that remained was how to tell Joan and Peggy about it.

'Perhaps it would be better not to say anything 'til you start,' Flossie said. 'Just in case they get a bit shirty.'

'Oh dear,' Baby said, assuming her pathetic face. 'D'you think they will?'

'Probably,' Flossie said. 'Nasty jealous natures the pair of them. Never mind. We'll cross that bridge when we come to it, eh?'

Baby could see the sense in keeping quiet but that didn't stop her wanting to brag about it, especially when the others were nasty to her, or the weather was rotten. Like it was on that chilly May morning as she made her solitary way home from school. She was cold and lonely and she knew she'd feel ever so much better if she could do a bit of swanking.

Mrs Geary was looking out of the upstairs window. Actually standing up and leaning on the sill with her head sticking right out of the window.

'You seen your Ma?' she called.

'No,' Baby answered. 'Why?'

'I don't know what she'll say,' Mrs Geary chortled. 'Wait till you see.'

'See what?' Baby asked. But Mrs Geary had put her head back inside the window.

Intrigued by the thought that something was up, Baby quickened her pace. The front door was ajar so Mum had probably popped down to the corner shop, but Peggy was already home and it sounded as though she'd brought Megan back with her, which she often did when it was their half-day. Baby could hear them both giggling in the kitchen.

''Lo Peggy,' she called. But the words froze on her lips when she entered the kitchen for Peggy and Megan were standing in front of the mirror admiring their reflections, and they'd both had their hair bobbed. It made them look entirely different, plumper somehow and more womanly, which was only natural considering they were both seventeen. But Baby had never thought of them as young women before that moment. It quite took her breath away.

'What d'you think?' Megan asked, turning to face her.

'I done hers and she done mine. Ain't it stunning?'

Stunning was the word. They not only looked grown-up but very fashionable, with their short hair bushed out on either side of their faces and curly fringes covering their foreheads. It even made their old dresses look modern too. Or had they altered them? Now that Megan worked for a tailor she made all sorts of alterations to her clothes.

'We treated ourselves to new hats an' all,' Peggy said. 'What d'you think a' that?' And she picked a blue hat from the table and lowered it onto her head. Unlike her old cloche that covered all her hair and hid most of her face, this one had a brim that was turned back to reveal her face and her forehead and her pretty new fringe. Baby thought it was lovely and immediately wanted one herself.

'Will you cut my hair too, our Peggy?' she asked.

'No,' Peggy said, flatly. 'You're too young. Wait till you've left school and you're out at work.' It had annoyed her that Mum was allowing Baby to stay on until July. Let the horrid little thing wait. It would serve her right for being a spoilt brat.

'Oh come on, our Peggy,' Baby began to wheedle. 'It wouldn't hurt you.'

'What wouldn't hurt who?' Mum said, coming into the kitchen behind her. 'Good gracious, Peggy! What *have* you done to your hair?'

'D'you like it?' Peggy said, and there was just a hint of a challenge in the question.

'It'll take a bit of getting used to,' Mum said diplomatically. It wouldn't have done to say anything too critical with Megan standing there listening. And most of the girls were cutting their hair these days, so it was only to be expected. But really! 'Don't go getting silly that's all.'

'Can I have mine cut too?' Baby asked.

'No you can't,' Flossie said firmly, venting her ill temper on the next possible target. 'You're too young. Why isn't this table laid?'

Right, Baby thought, noticing the triumphant glances that passed between Peggy and Megan as she threw the cloth across the table. If that's the way you're going to go on, I shall tell you about my job, and then you'll be sorry.

'When I leave school ... ' she began.

183

But Mum interrupted her with a really dreadful scowl. 'Where's Joan?' she said.

'Gone up the park,' Peggy said. 'She's not coming back for dinner. She told us breakfast-time, don't you remember?'

'Again?' Mum said, carrying her shopping bag into the scullery. 'That's the third time this month. If she goes on at this rate I shall begin to think she's left home. Well I hope she has the sense to get herself something to eat that's all. All this gadding about won't do her any good. It might be spring but it's jolly cold still. Come and help me dish up this pie, Peggy. Are you staying, Megan? It's only hash but you're welcome to it. You can have Joan's share since she's took herself off.'

'When I leave school ... ' Baby tried again.

'We don't want to hear that,' Mum said firmly. 'Come and eat your dinner.' And she gave Baby another scowl, directing it at her for several seconds and with a force that showed she wasn't going to allow any argument.

Oh! Baby thought, she's going to get shirty. It's not fair. She ought to let me tell, with them having their hair cut and buying themselves hats and everything. But the scowl had to be obeyed. At least that left Joan as the principal source of irritation. Mum'll be ever so shirty with *her* when she comes home.

Her mother would have been more than shirty if she'd known exactly where her eldest daughter was at that moment. And furious if she could have seen who was accompanying her.

At twenty-one Joan had grown into a competent young woman with a mind and a will of her own, although she was very careful to keep both of them hidden from everybody except Peggy. Short rations at work and at home had kept her very skinny but being slim suited her, making her sandy hair look thicker and her brown eyes seem enormous in her long pale face. In fact, although she wasn't aware of it, she was much the best looking of the Furnivall girls.

She still worked for Miss Margeryson and her awful brother, but in the five years since they'd first hired her, they had aged considerably, and that was a great help to her. Now they were both very short-sighted and Miss

Margeryson was more than a little deaf, although she never admitted it to anyone and especially not to her servant. But it meant that she no longer saw dust on every surface and she couldn't eavesdrop on any of Joan's conversations with the tradesmen at the kitchen door. Consequently the housework didn't need to be anywhere near so thorough, and now and then it was possible for Joan to order a little extra milk, or a lamb chop, or a currant bun or two for her own consumption. All of which made life marginally easier. And there was better to come.

Just before Christmas the baker's roundsman was taken ill with bronchitis and for two days the van arrived at the door driven by the master baker who was quick and cross and not given to conversation. But on the third day a different knock heralded the arrival of a new roundsman, and this one was young and brash and had the rough good looks of a ploughboy or a miner or a sailor. He was short and stocky with broad shoulders, solid limbs and short-fingered hands, and his face was broad too, with high cheek bones and small dark eyes, and shaggy, uncombed hair tumbling over his forehead. There was something arresting about him, something bold and self-satisfied, a dark dangerous masculinity, cocky and with a hint of ruthlessness, as if he knew he would get whatever he wanted if he made a play for it. He made Joan think of the black tom-cat that came howling for Tabby.

'Good morning to you, pretty lady,' he said, giving her the eye in the most impudent way. 'What can I do fer you this morning?'

'Cottage loaf,' she said, and as he was making her feel daring, 'and a ha'penny bun.'

'Fer you or the old gel?' he asked, saucing her.

She answered in kind, grinning at him, 'None a' your business.'

'Tell you what,' he said, 'I got an iced bun here. Ought ter be a penny be rights. You can have it fer ha'penny, fer being a pretty lady.'

'You'll get the sack you go on like that,' she said, accepting the bun and the compliment.

'Wouldn't do it fer anyone though would I, darlin'?' he said.

'*I* don't know what you'd do,' she said. And there was more truth in the words than she'd intended. The dangerous quality about this young man was really most attractive.

'See yer tomorrow,' he promised, swinging his basket over his arm. And he was gone, leaving the strong smell of his new-baked bread behind him.

All through that day Joan found herself remembering him. The encounter had bucked her up. There was no denying it. To be saluted as a pretty lady was good for her self-esteem, even if he said it to all his customers and didn't really mean it.

The next day she tidied her hair and checked her appearance in the mirror before his arrival. Soon she was looking forward to his visit as the best part of her otherwise wearying day.

He was always so cheerful, even in March when the weather was miserably cold and they had four days of incessant snowfall. On the second day of it he looked so cold that she invited him into the kitchen and made him a cup of tea to thaw him out. She'd just settled Miss Margeryson in front of the fire in the parlour with a rug over her legs and a book for company, so she knew they wouldn't be discovered. And besides, she couldn't bear to see his nose so red. It quite spoilt his looks.

He was excellent company, poking fun at all the people in the street, imitating the la-di-da way they spoke and mocking the impoverished state of their kitchens.

'Load of old bats they are!' he said, holding the cup between his mittened hands. 'Stingy! My eye you wouldn't say so! Ain't got two ha'pennies fer a penny and they give 'emselves airs you'd think they was royalty. "I'll have two loaves my man." "Mind where you're putting your feet." An' then you gets round the back an' they ain't got enough grub in the kitchen to feed a sparrer. Empty jars everywhere. Makes yer sick.'

He stayed for nearly a quarter of an hour and the memory of his company spiced the rest of the day and quite made up for the chill of the house.

By the time the bad weather was over and the first warm air of spring was urging Miss Margeryson to mutter about spring cleaning, they had got into the habit of taking tea together at least once a week. But now that the old lady was on the prowl again it was a little more difficult.

'Tell yer what,' he said, one particularly pleasant morning when his usual invitation wasn't forthcoming. 'Why don't you an' me go to the pictures.'

It was a decision, not a question, but she dithered. 'I don't know,' she said.

'Why not?'

'Well, for a start I don't know your name.'

'Sid. Sid Owen. Neighbour a' yours if you did but know it.'

'Are you?'

'Thames Street,' he said, pushing his cap to the back of his head, dark eyes flashing, daring her. 'Right then. Meet you at the park gates half past one.'

'When?' she said weakly.

'Well Wednesday a' course. Your half-day.'

So she agreed. And ever since then they'd gone to the pictures every Wednesday afternoon. They'd taken the first steps towards the process known locally as 'walking out', but they kept it a secret for the time being because neither of them were at all sure how their relations would take it, she because of her shameful past, he because he was only twenty.

On that afternoon in May they were walking in Greenwich Park and he had just stolen his first kiss, grinning at her in triumph as they drew apart.

'Now you're my gel,' he said.

'Yes,' she agreed, hoping he'd kiss her again, because although it had been a rather rough kiss and he'd taken her by surprise, it had excited her.

'Don't tell no one,' he said, pulling her towards him again. 'Not yet. Keep it a secret.'

'Yes,' she said, agreeing at once because there was another kiss coming.

The Furnivall household fizzed with secrets that spring and summer, like a box of fireworks newly lit.

Even sensible Peggy had a secret. She shared it with Megan because Megan was her best friend and Megan had a similar secret but, like Joan and Sid, neither of them said anything about it at home. It was too personal and private and Peggy had an occasional suspicion that it was just a little bit silly. But it had happened, it was a fact, and one that took all their attention in the most pleasurable way, filling their minds with delicious dreams and sustaining them with anticipation through the long hours of their working day. Peggy and Megan had both fallen in love.

It had happened on the afternoon they'd cut their hair, almost as if their new appearance had propelled them into new experiences. After they'd eaten Flossie's hash, they walked down to the market together to get a few 'bits and pieces' for Mrs Geary, strolling arm in arm and chattering to one another all the way. Although it was still cold for May the sun had broken through the cloud and seemed to be shining straight down onto their heads. Megan remarked upon it.

'Quite right,' Peggy said gaily, 'So it is.' And she began to sing 'The sun has got his hat on', dancing along the pavement in tune to the words.

They were still giggling and singing as they walked into the market.

'You're in a good mood,' the egg man said.

'Yes,' Peggy said, grinning at him. And there standing right behind him was the most handsome boy she'd ever seen, tall and fair with lovely blue eyes and the faintest fluff of fair moustache on his top lip. She was instantly and very decidedly smitten as she told Megan afterwards.

'He made me go weak at the knees,' she confessed happily. 'Just like they do in the novels.'

'Gosh!' Megan said. 'Do you think you're in love?'

'I don't know,' Peggy admitted. 'Do you think he'll be there Saturday?'

He was, and even more handsome than she remembered him. This time he smiled at her, which was hardly surprising as she'd been standing by the egg stall for nearly twenty minutes hoping he'd notice her and wondering where Megan had got to. He didn't say anything, but that didn't matter, a smile was enough. In fact a smile would be enough to live on for the rest of the week because he really was the most handsome boy. Oh

188

where was Megan? She couldn't wait to tell her.

She found her friend by the china stall, gazing into the middle distance with an enraptured expression on her face. 'Isn't he just it?' she said when Peggy arrived beside her.

'Who?'

'That boy on the till.'

He looked very ordinary to Peggy, but Megan was in love too. 'He's got such lovely broad shoulders,' she said. 'And heavenly eyes.'

That night at the ding-dong while the others were singing their raucous songs the two girls compared notes. Their feelings were remarkably similar and wonderfully strong. 'We must be in love,' Megan decided. 'Ain't it grand.'

Peggy wasn't really sure that grand was the right word to describe her new emotions but they were certainly absorbing. She and Megan spent all their time and energy either preparing for their visit to the market or reliving every moment of it afterwards. The visits themselves were short, sweet and soon over. But by dint of careful detective work they discovered what their two young men were called, Peggy's beloved being Tom and Megan's Harry, and they lurked outside the market at closing time in case either of them came out alone and there was a chance to get talking. The chance was never given. Neither of the young men paid much attention to them, but that was part of their charm, and allowed the two girls to weave the most delicious fantasies about the sort of marvellous daring things that might happen if only they would. The more distant they were, the more they loved them.

The summer days passed in a swoon of dreams. They didn't even notice the flies and the smell of drains.

Until the end of the school term and Baby's first day at her new job. Then the storm broke.

'You're getting dolled up, aintcher?' Joan said when Baby was putting on her uniform in the bedroom that morning.

Baby looked shifty and went on dressing herself. Now that the moment had come when her marvellous secret was finally going to be revealed, she was too anxious to want to show off about it.

189

'Posh sort a' rig for a servant,' Joan persisted. The anger on her face was growing plainer and more menacing by the second.

Silence.

'Where *are* you going to work?' Peggy said, growing suspicious.

Silence.

'Come on, Baby,' Peggy said. 'Tell us.' There'd been altogether too much mystery about this job. Neither Mum nor Baby had ever said anything about it and now she could see how suspicious that was. 'Where are you going?'

'Dodds,' Baby admitted, and she could feel her heart sink with the word. Mum had been right to keep quiet about it. There *was* going to be a row.

'The outfitters?'

'Yes,' Baby said, adding truculently, 'Well, why not? We don't all have to be servants you know.' If they were going to be nasty she'd fight back.

'I'll tell you why not,' Joan said fiercely. 'Because it ain't fair, that's why not. Me an' Peggy work bloody hard for a living, an' you ought to work bloody hard too. Dodds!'

'What's all that row?' Mum called from downstairs. 'Breakfast is on the table. Look sharp or you'll all be late.'

'She's going to work in a shop,' Joan said, furious with accusation.

'Yes,' Flossie said. 'She is. She's got to work somewhere. Eat your bacon while it's hot.'

'D'you think that's fair?'

'Now don't start,' Flossie warned, 'unless you want to bring on my nerves. What's done is done. There's no point talking about it.' And she busied them and bustled them and refused to let any of them talk again until they were leaving the house.

So the protest was shelved. For the time being. And Baby went off to work looking smug. But that wasn't the end of it. How could it be when it was so unfair? That night when Baby went to bed still full of herself and how well she'd done on her first day, neither of her sisters would talk to her. Even when she grew deliberately tearful and complained that they were being hateful and she'd tell Mum, they still ignored her.

190

'People who behave like greedy little pigs,' Joan said pointedly, 'must expect to be cut.'

On the second night Baby cried so much when they ignored her that Peggy felt quite sorry for her. But she agreed with Joan that something had to be done and as Mum wouldn't allow either of them to talk about it, even though they both tried every morning and evening, punishing Baby with silence was the only thing they could think of to show their disapproval.

That next evening, when Mum had spent the whole of supper-time telling them that they should let bygones be bygones and wailing that they were giving her the most terrible nerves, 'keeping on about it', Peggy decided to walk down to the library with Jim Boxall. It was something she often did now that the weather was fine and she'd developed a taste for romantic novels, and on this particular evening it gave her a break from the brooding bad temper in the house. On the way back, almost on impulse, she told him about Baby's favoured treatment and asked him what he thought about it. He was always so sensible and if he said it was unfair she would know they weren't making a fuss about nothing.

His reply was practical. 'If you don't want to go on being a housemaid,' he said, 'why don't you get a job in a shop too? They don't pay well but there's plenty of work about.' Which was more than could be said for jobs in the engineering trade. There were rumours that his own firm was going bust, but he didn't tell her that, because he hadn't told anyone. It was a private worry. The sort of thing men kept to themselves.

She looked up at his reassuring face, at the familiar scar on his chin and the broken nose that always reminded her how brave he was, at his blue eyes looking at her so seriously, and she was warmed by his good sense.

'Yes,' she said, 'of course. That's what we ought to do. That would solve it, wouldn't it.' And a jolly sight better than all this rowing.

But Joan was too enmeshed in anger to agree. 'We ought to have it out,' she said. 'Why should they get away with it? If we just go quietly off and get ourselves new jobs they'll think it doesn't matter any more. They'll have won.

And I'm damned if I'm having that.'

She was so cross that Peggy gave up trying to persuade her. I'll wait a day or two and try again, she thought. It'll start to blow over in a little while.

But of course it didn't. At the end of the week when all three of them arrived home with their pay packets, the second secret was out and then there was no restraining Joan's fury.

She turned on Flossie ablaze with anger, hurling Baby's pay packet across the table. 'Five shillings!' she yelled. 'You let this spoilt brat of yours work for five shillings! What were you thinking of?'

'It's only for four weeks,' Flossie said huffily.

And Baby said, 'I'm being trained,' spitting the information into her mother's words and her sister's fury.

'Trained!' Joan said scornfully. 'I'll give you trained, see if I don't. All these years we've worked and slaved,' she said to Flossie, 'and we've never said a word about all the money you've took from us. Neither of us. Have we, Peggy? And now, just when things ought to be getting easier, you send that God-awful brat into a shop to work for nothing, and we've got to slog our guts out to keep her while she trains. Slog our guts out so that she can ponce about as a telephonist. It's bloody unfair.'

'Language!' Flossie reproved. 'You watch your mouth, my girl. You're not too old for me to wash it out with soap and water.'

Joan ignored such a pitiful diversion. 'She got this job on our backs,' she said. 'Mine and Peggy's. That's the truth and you know it.'

'Peggy,' Flossie said, appealing for help. 'Tell her to stop. Tell her it's not true.'

'It is true,' Peggy said. 'There's no point lying. You've been very unfair. Both of you. I wonder you can't see it.'

'She's too delicate for housework,' Flossie said, trying to justify herself.

'And we're not?' Joan yelled. 'We're not? Oh I can see it all now. You've never cared for us, either of us. It's always been Baby. Your precious Baby. Spoiled bloody Baby. I'd like to scratch her rotten eyes out.'

'Don't you touch me,' Baby shrieked leaping away from

192

Joan's outstretched fingers. 'Mum! Stop her! She'll do me a mischief.'

Peggy was running between them, aching to placate them, to stop this awful row before it got any worse, but she couldn't find the words to persuade them and anyway they were making such a row they weren't listening to her.

'Baby,' she begged. 'Hush! Joan, don't. Please don't. They'll hear us next door. Mum, look let's ...'

'You don't care for me!' Flossie shrieked. 'You know what a state my nerves are in. You're making me ill the lot of you.'

'Serve you right!' Joan shouted. 'You've had this coming to you for years.'

'Oh!' Flossie wailed. 'How can you say such things? Can't you see what you're doing to me, you hateful girl?'

'No,' Joan said coldly. 'I can see what *she's* doing to *us*. And it's bloody unfair.'

Flossie took two strides across the kitchen and slapped Joan hard across the face. The crack of the blow echoed like a gunshot. 'Shut up!' she shouted. 'Shut up! Shut up! I've had enough!'

'Don't you dare hit me!' Joan roared. And she dealt her mother a return blow that sent her reeling back against the dresser.

There was a split second of total silence while they all looked at one another in horror. Then Flossie opened her mouth and began to scream. She screamed without stopping and without restraint, on and on and on, in a dreadful hysterical abandonment, her face distorted and her mouth as wide as a cave. Peggy could see her uvula throbbing as she screamed.

'Mum! Please!' she begged. 'Come and sit down. I'll make you a nice cup of tea.'

'Yes Mum, please,' Baby said, shocked white by such a display. 'Don't keep on.'

They were wasting their breath. Flossie couldn't stop. She was screaming as she breathed, lost in a echoing limbo of pent-up fury and guilt and self-pity. She couldn't even see them.

None of them heard Mrs Geary hobbling down the stairs but they weren't surprised when she walked into the kitchen.

'Hysterical,' she said, speaking calmly as though finding a screaming woman in her kitchen was an everyday event. 'Make her lie down. She won't scream so easy lying down.'

But it took all three girls a very long time to coax their mother to her bed in the front parlour, and she went on screaming even when she was flat on her back.

'You'll have ter get Dr Thomas,' Mrs Geary said. 'Nip round the corner, Baby. Quick as you can.'

Baby was shaking with fright but she did as she was told. She'd never meant *this* to happen. Never. All she'd wanted was a good job and not to be a servant. Oh dear, oh dear!

CHAPTER 15

Dr Thomas was not accustomed to being called out to
Paradise Row. He knew from long experience that the
people of that district were loath to ask for medical advice,
preferring to dose themselves with patent medicines or
horrible concoctions of their own devising, so he was intrigued when a pasty-faced child appeared on his doorstep
requesting his immediate attention for a mother who had
taken a fit. It could well be something interesting, he
thought, as he picked up his bag.

It was a disappointment to discover that his patient was
nothing more than a foolish woman who'd lost her temper
and been screaming too much. She had her eyes tightly
shut, her face was swollen and blotchy and when he spoke
to her she gave a dramatic shudder and began to sob, but
her pulse was slow and steady and there was no sign of
any medical abnormality whatever.

Her three daughters stood at the foot of the bed and
watched him anxiously. When he first saw their three pale
faces grouped together against the dark green of the wallpaper he was reminded of the three graces, but he revised
his opinion on second glance because it was only the eldest
who had any looks. She was a willowy young woman with a
foxy face and sandy-coloured hair, quite charming in a
raffish sort of way. The other two were distinctly ordinary.

'Is it a brainstorm, doctor?' the middle one asked
anxiously.

'No, my dear,' he said kindly. 'It is not. Just a

195

temporary upset, that's all. Your mother will recover in an hour or two, you have my word for it.'

'Only she *does* suffer with her nerves you see,' she confided.

'I don't doubt it,' Dr Thomas said. She looked just the type. 'I will ask my dispenser to make up a sedative for her. Call round to the surgery in half an hour and he'll have it ready for you.'

'Should she stay in bed?' the pretty one asked.

'Keep her quiet for a day or two,' the doctor temporized. The poor creature probably needed a rest and if he gave his permission now, she would be allowed to take one. It was a situation he'd often encountered. 'One of you could look after her, I dare say?'

'I'm out at work all day,' the pretty one said quickly. 'I'm the breadwinner.'

'I couldn't,' the youngest said, assuming a pathetic expression that made her look half-witted. Not a prepossessing child. 'I've only just started work. This week. At Dodds the outfitters. I'm a telephonist. They wouldn't like it if I was to stop, would they?'

'What about you?' Dr Thomas asked the middle one.

She thought for a second before she agreed and the little delay annoyed the doctor. What was there to think about? You'd imagine she'd jump at the chance to get off work for a while and stay at home with her mother, especially with two sisters around to earn her keep. Some of these working-class girls simply didn't know what was good for them.

'I will send you my bill in due course,' he said, shutting his bag. It had been a waste of his time and he would charge accordingly.

'Well?' Mrs Geary said, hobbling out of the kitchen as soon as Peggy had closed the door on his departing back.

'I'm to stay in bed,' Flossie said, in a new weak voice. 'It's brain-fever, Mrs Geary. Brain-fever! Oh my poor girls! How will they manage?'

They managed because Peggy gave up her job and took over the running of the house. And very difficult it was without her earnings. Even when Baby finished her four week training and brought home a proper wage packet they were still short of money. Finding two guineas to pay the doctor was a nightmare. And Mum was so demanding, always calling her for something or other, a fresh glass of water, her pills, her nerve tonic, to be helped out to the lavvy. Sometimes it was difficult to keep even tempered, especially as she never got any respite from it.

Megan called round on what would have been their afternoon off, all prettied up and ready for their trip to the market. It was quite a shock to Peggy to realize that since the row she'd hardly given Megan a thought, and, what was worse, she'd forgotten about her handsome Tom altogether. In fact it was a few seconds before she could remember what he looked like.

'Come out for half an hour,' Megan urged. 'Just to the market an' back. You know. It'ud do you good. You look awful.'

'I can't,' Peggy said. 'Who'd look after Mum? Mrs Geary can't. Not with her legs.'

'You could leave her for half an hour, surely to goodness.'

'Well I could but what if she took another fit?'

'You ask me there ain't a lot wrong with her,' Megan said trenchantly. 'She's got a lovely colour. Better than yours.'

But Peggy didn't think it was worth the risk. So Megan went a-marketing on her own. She was back within twenty minutes, awash with tears.

'He's gone,' she sobbed. 'Oh Peggy, he's gone. His family's up an' done a bunk. The salad woman said. All in the middle of the night. Nobody knows where to. I asked an' asked an' nobody knows. Oh Peggy, Peggy, I shall never see him again.'

'He'll turn up somewhere else,' Peggy comforted. 'He's bound to try for another job.'

'No he won't,' Megan wept. 'They went out the district. The salad woman said. They owed to everybody. I shall never see him again. Never.'

Peggy sat her down in the kitchen, offered strong tea and let her enjoy a good cry. It wasn't until long after her heart-broken friend had been comforted and gone home and she was busy remaking her mother's bed for the

second time that day that she realized that she hadn't
thought to ask whether her own beloved was still working
in the market. But by then she was too tired to care. You
get over love pretty quick, she thought, stooping to tuck in
the covers. After the impact of that awful row her grand
passion seemed a trifling thing. It was rather sad, or would
have been if she'd had the time to think about it.

'Hop in,' she said to Flossie. 'That's all nice and
comfortable now.'

'You're a good girl,' Flossie said leaning forward out of
her chair to kiss her. 'I don't know what I'd do without you
an' that's a fact.'

But it was poor consolation for the ending of her first
'pash'.

For the next three weeks Peggy struggled on, doing the
housework and the shopping, cooking the meals, washing
the clothes, and waiting on her mother hand and foot. On
4 August her birthday came and went unremarked. Occasionally Baby would offer to help with the washing-up or
the ironing or the mending, but Joan was no help as all.
She was rarely in the house except to sleep and eat her
meals. She left earlier than usual in the morning and as
soon as supper was over and the dishes were done she was
off out again.

'Got a young man,' Mrs Geary said nodding sagely.
'That's what it is. You mark my words.'

But Peggy didn't think that was the explanation. There
was something hard and determined about her sister these
days that didn't fit in with a girl who was being courted.

'We'd know if it was that,' she said.

'How would you know?'

'She'd be happier.'

'Not necessarily,' Mrs Geary said, biting off her thread.
'Love's a funny business. Takes people all sorts a' ways.
Don't it, Polly?'

'Bugger, bugger,' the parrot agreed. 'Star-new-stan-
dard!'

'He's a caution,' Mrs Geary said. 'You coming to the
ding-dong termorrer?'

'If Mum's up to it.'

'She'll be all right,' Mrs Geary said. 'We can nip up an' down. Yer uncle can sit with her fer a bit. He said he'd be coming. You've missed three weeks on the trot now an' last Saturday was a corker.'

But in the event they didn't nip up and down to Flossie that Saturday evening, because Joan arrived about an hour after the singing began, arm-in-arm with a stocky young man, and once she'd gathered eveyone's attention she had an announcement to make.

'This is Sid Owen,' she said, and to Peggy's eyes her expression was hard and bold and rather alarming. 'We're going to get married.'

The news caused an immediate stir. Nonnie Brown staggered across the room, spilling half her brown ale on the way, shook Sid's hand for such a long time that they wondered when she was going to stop, and then insisted that Cyril should play the wedding march in their honour. And while it was being sucked to tunelessness, the rest of the ding-dong flocked to congratulate them.

The four O'Donavan girls were shining eyed with the wonder of it. 'Will you wear white, Joanie?' the eldest asked. 'Are you having bridesmaids?'

'Gosh!' Baby said. 'Fancy you getting married, our Joan. I'll be a bridesmaid won't I?'

Gideon was delighted. 'I love a good wedding,' he said. 'When's it going to be?'

It was all worked out, Joan told him, 'Sid's got a job as assistant baker in the Deptford branch,' she said proudly. 'Starting September. Assistant baker with two rooms over the shop.'

'Lucky you,' Lily Boxall said. 'So will it be September?'

'Third Sat'day,' Sid told her. He looked very full of himself, like a tightly-blown balloon, and he felt very full of himself too, now that he'd got his nerve back. On that amazing evening when Joan first told him she'd like to get married he hadn't known what to do or say.

They'd been up on the common, necking the way they usually did, and he was just letting his hands wander in a hopeful sort of way, when she caught hold of them and squeezed them and gave him one of her bold grins.

'D'you know what, Sid Owen,' she said, 'I think we

ought to get married.'

He was so surprised his mouth fell open and he forgot to shut it again. 'What?' he said.

'Married. You know, wedding-bells, bride and groom, confetti.'

'What you an' me?' They were much too young. They couldn't get married yet, could they?

'Why not? You've got a new job, I've got a bit put by. I'll bet you could get a couple of rooms over one of the shops, a fine baker like you.'

'Well ... ' he wondered.

'Be a cut above the rest of 'em,' she urged. 'Married man, home of your own. You think. An' I bet he'd give you a raise an' all if you was to ask for it.'

The idea took hold, a wife, a raise, a home of his own. 'Are you perposin' ter me?' he said. 'Didn't you ought ter wait for me ter perpose?'

'Go on then,' she dared him.

'Well all right,' he said. 'I suppose we might as well.' But despite the reward of her kiss it all seemed very unlikely.

He was very surprised when everything fell into place exactly the way she'd predicted, and now, standing here in the midst of their admiration, full of importance and desire and pride of ownership, he was pleased to think he'd made his decision. He'd be twenty-one in September, twenty-one and an assistant baker and a married man. Better than any of this lot, and a bloody sight better than his miserable father.

'You'll give me away, won't you Uncle Gideon,' Joan said.

'Glad to,' Gideon said. 'What's yer Ma say about it, eh? I'll bet she's tickled pink.'

'We ain't told her yet,' Joan confessed. 'Have we, Sid? We thought it'd be nice if we all went down tonight and saw her together. A sort of family party, me an' Sid an' you an' Aunt Ethel.'

'Course,' Gideon agreed, understanding what she was up to, but keeping his thoughts to himself. 'After the next song, eh? When I've finished me pint.'

None of them noticed that the only person who hadn't

rushed forward with congratulations was Peggy. She'd been sitting on the stairs when Joan came in, and the news had surprised her despite Mrs Geary's warning, so she'd stayed where she was, hidden by the shadow of the half wall. But when the next song began, which was 'Knees Up Mother Brown', naturally, to match their high spirits, she threaded her way quietly through the bouncing mob to put her arms round her sister and give her a hug.

'Hello Peg,' Joan said, hugging her back. 'He's just gone to get a drink. What d'you think?'

'Have you known him long?' Peggy said, speaking close to her sister's ear. She didn't shout because Mrs Roderick was sitting on her bench immediately behind them, listening for all she was worth, and she didn't want Mrs Roderick to know their family secrets. But the question had to be asked nevertheless. She couldn't believe that their sensible Joan would have made a decision like that in a rush. She must have thought about it.

'Since Christmas,' Joan said into her ear.

'And you kept it secret all that time.'

'Till I was sure. Yes.'

'And you're sure now?'

'Yes,' Joan said. But there was no happiness in the word. It was just a flat affirmative, spoken without feeling, dropped into the babble of the song like a pebble in a pool.

'Do you love him?' Peggy ventured when the next great roar of song gave her the necessary cover.

That was answered almost flippantly. 'He'll do.'

It wasn't very reassuring, but by now Peggy couldn't think what to ask next.

'Tell you what,' Joan said, putting her head close to her sister's ear again and speaking quietly. 'Come September I shall be my own boss, my own house, money for my keep. Think a' that. I shan't have to go to work no more, shan't have to watch Mum spending my wages on Baby, nothing like that.' And now there *was* passion in her voice and her eyes were gleaming.

'You deserve it,' Peggy said affectionately, 'after – all that – you know – in Tillingbourne.'

Sid was elbowing his way back towards them with an overflowing glass in each hand. There were other things that had to be said before he reached them.

'Don't say nothing about it to ... ' Joan began.

''Course not,' Peggy reassured. 'As if I would.'

'There y'are,' Sid said, giving them both the benefit of his daring eyes. 'One for you an' one for your pretty sister.'

To Peggy's surprise Joan changed from her serious mood into instant teasing. 'How d'you know she's my sister?' she said.'You ain't been introduced.'

'She is though, ain't she?' he answered. 'You're Peggy, aintcher? Have a beer.'

'No thanks,' Peggy said. 'It's very kind but you have it. I got mine on the stairs.'

The song and dance had bounced to a halt.

'Come along then, Joan,' Uncle Gideon said, looming upon them red-faced and glistening with sweat. 'Time fer yer Mum. Coming with us, Peggy?'

'Well ... ' Peggy said. She didn't want to witness this meeting at all but she couldn't think how to extricate herself.

'Time to cut off an' get the shrimps, Peggy,' Jim Boxall said, squeezing into the space beside her.

'Oh yes,' she said gratefully. 'I *did* promise, didn't I?' It was the first she'd heard about cutting off to get shrimps but she told the lie easily and Joan accepted it.

'See you when we all get back then,' she said as they went their separate ways from the doorstep.

The street was in semi-darkness, patched with shadow between the golden blooms of gaslight at each end of the terrace and the pulse of light and sound from Mr Allnutt's raucous front room, their flat-fronted houses reduced to monochrome by the half-light, yellow bricks grey, green paintwork black. But above the little white dome that topped the spire of St Alphege's church the sky was still pale green with light, and when Peggy looked back over her shoulder to watch the deputation jostling into number six, she found she was looking straight into a blaze of colour. The western sky was streaked with fire and burned red and orange and rich gold above the shabby dullness of the long slate roof of the terrace.

The savagery of such a sky on this particular, peculiar

evening was disturbing. Life had been so muddled since Mum took ill. That awful screaming fit had been savage too, like an explosion. It was as though it had broken them all open, wrecking the order of their nice ordinary lives, making a nonsense of what they thought they knew. She felt she'd been picking up the pieces ever since, and none of them made sense. Just at the very moment when she'd been planning to get herself a better job she had to stay at home and look after Mum. She didn't complain, of course, because someone had to do it, but it was hard just the same. And it was hard to understand all sorts of other things too. It was summer and yet there were men lurking on the street corners looking cold and depressed. Three million men on the dole according to Mrs Geary's *Daily Herald*, 'bright young things' spending more on one party than she could earn in a year, shops going bust when they were full of things people would rush to buy if they only had the money, Mum keeping to her bed when she wasn't ill, Joan marrying Sid when she didn't love him. And Sid himself.

'Penny for your thoughts,' Jim said as they walked companionably up the street towards the Mitre and the shrimp stall.

She didn't know what to say to him. She couldn't lie, not to Jim Boxall, and it would be disloyal to tell him she was thinking uncharitable thoughts about her sister's young man.

'You don't like him,' he said easily, striding along beside her.

That surprised her. 'How do you know?'

'It was written all over your face. That's why I rescued you.'

'Yes,' she said. 'Thanks.'

'What are friends for? So go on, admit it, you don't like him.'

'Well no,' she admitted, 'I don't really. Not much.'

'Why not?'

She thought for a while before she answered. 'He looks as if he's got a temper,' she said. 'As if he could hurt you if he wanted and he wouldn't care.' It was the arrogant tilt of that square head, the way he bunched his fists. Then she corrected herself. 'No, that ain't fair. I don't know nothing about him. I didn't ought to say things like that.'

'That's the sort he looks to me,' Jim said. 'We got a bloke at the works just the same. Punch you soon as look at you. Oh well, let's hope we're wrong. What does your mum think?'

'She ain't met him yet,' Peggy said. Then she realized that was no longer true and she wondered what was being said back at number six. And that stopped the conversation because, once again, she couldn't say what she was thinking without being disloyal. So she walked on in silence. One of the nice things about Jim Boxall was that you didn't have to talk if you didn't want to. I'll bet Mum has an attack of nerves, she thought, as they turned the corner together.

In fact, having been provided with an audience Flossie was taking the news quite well.

When her visitors first arrived in her sickroom, she was tossed through a succession of conflicting emotions, blushing embarrassment at being caught in bed, irritation at Joan for bringing Gideon along without warning her, anger because it was such a smack in the eye to be presented with a *fait accompli*. 'We're going to get married' indeed! The effrontery of it.

But just as she was drawing breath to say something biting, the young man made eyes at her and told her she was even prettier than her daughter, and that mollified her and helped her to keep control of herself in front of Gideon and Ethel. It was nice to be admired, and specially by such a handsome young man. It made her feel better in herself than she'd done for days. Oh much better.

Gideon was being very jolly, talking about the wedding and where it was going to be and how he'd have to give the bride away, and Joan and the young man were laughing and teasing and saying they really wanted a quiet wedding – the very idea! – so Flossie didn't need to say anything very much. But as the cheerful banter went bubbling on, it suddenly occurred to her that this news was a heaven-sent opportunity. Ever since she'd had what she called her 'little fit' she'd hidden away indoors, too ashamed to face her neighbours after making such an exhibition of herself,

204

and the longer she hid the more difficult it was to contemplate getting out and about again. Now she had an excuse.

'I can see I shall have to get better in double quick time now,' she said to Sid.

'Don't you do no such thing,' he said, feigning distress. 'I wouldn't want that on my conscience. Well I mean ter say, what'ud my mates say if they knew I'd been the cause of dragging a pretty lady out of her bed? I'd never hear the last. Into it maybe. Out of it! Never!'

'You bad boy,' she pretended to scold. 'What a thing to say to an old, married woman!'

'Never old!' he said gallantly. 'Old I won't have, not with your pretty face an' all. No, no, you stay where you are, Mrs F. We can't have you running round after us, can we, Joanie?'

'I shall get up for dinner tomorrow,' Flossie decided. 'Then we'll see how we go on.'

It was an excellent excuse, and what was even better it brought her the instant and gratifying status of a martyr.

'Such a good woman,' Mrs Roderick told their neighbours. 'She was that ill you'd never believe – brain-fever you know – oh yes, terrible – and yet here she is working all hours for this wedding and never a word of complaint. Such a good woman.'

'Well you have to make an effort, don't you,' the good woman said with modest self-deprecation. And her opinion was applauded too.

Actually apart from sending out invitations to her family and Sid's father, who seemed to be the only relation he possessed, poor boy, she wasn't doing very much. All her neighbours rallied round with offers of help. Mrs Roderick was making the bride's dress and two beautiful bridesmaids' gowns for Baby and Peggy, Mr Cooper would provide the music, and she could get lots of cheap booze from the Earl Grey. Old Mr Allnut said he'd run up a few trestle tables, and young Mr Allnut promised to check them on the quiet. 'Can't have the food collapsing on us, can we, Mrs F?', and she had so many offers of help with sandwiches and jellies she could have fed a regiment. Even Mrs O'Donavan offered, poor woman, although with all those kids of hers, and another one on the way, they all know she'd never have the time to do anything. Still, as they all said, it's the thought that counts.

There'd only been one sticky moment and that was when Mrs Roderick discovered that Gideon was giving the bride away.

'Gideon Potter?' she said in disbelief. 'That awful butcher!'

'I'm afraid so,' Flossie confessed, looking shame-faced. 'I don't see how I can avoid it. He's – um – related to them you see, so naturally . . . '

'Ah!' Mrs Roderick said. 'That accounts. I wondered why they would keep calling him uncle. It's not just a courtesy title then?'

'No,' Flossie said. 'So you see . . . '

Mrs Roderick decided to be charitable. 'Ah well,' she said, 'if he's their uncle there's not very much you can do about it. We have to stick to protocol when it comes to weddings and we can't be held responsible for the short-comings of our in-laws. I daresay there's some good in the man. He's always seemed very fond of your girls.'

'Oh yes,' Flossie agreed, much relieved to be let down so lightly. There was no need to explain exactly who Gideon was. 'He's a rough diamond but he's got a heart of gold.'

'Quite,' Mrs Roderick said.

So Gideon was accepted and now it was only Peggy who was being rather a disappointment to her. And that was because that wretched Megan Griffiths had led her astray again. She'd come giggling round to the house early one Monday morning just as Mrs Geary was filling the scullery with her washing, and off they'd both gone in those silly hats of theirs, chattering like monkeys and leaving her all on her own. And nearly two hours later they'd come giggling back to tell her that they'd both got jobs at Aimee's, the posh haberdashers in Nelson Road, and they were starting that afternoon.

'Whatever did you want to go and do that for?' she said when Megan had gone home for her dinner. 'I'd have thought there was quite enough work for you here without looking for more.'

Peggy's calm was infuriating. 'We need the money,' she

said. 'This wedding won't pay for itself.'

'We shall manage,' Flossie said. 'We always have.'

'Not if you keep inviting people,' Peggy said.

'I don't keep inviting people.'

'You do,' Peggy said firmly.

And it was true. She'd invited half the street. The quiet wedding that Joan had been hoping for was rapidly turning into an extension of the ding-dong. On the rare occasions when she spoke about it Joan said she didn't mind. If that was the way Mum wanted to go on it was all right with her, providing she didn't have to foot the bill. But the money had to come from somewhere.

All through that August Paradise Row bustled with preparation. It was unseasonably cold and wet but nobody minded. Over in Westminster all sorts of serious things were happening, but they paid no heed to them either. On 23 August the Cabinet resigned because they couldn't agree to go on paying the dole to so many unemployed, and the next day Mr Macdonald formed a National Government, and soon the papers announced the date of the General Election as 27 October.

But as Mrs Geary said to Mr Cooper, 'I can't see it matters what sort a' government we got, Labour, Conservative, Liberal, none of 'em know what ter do. If there ain't jobs, there ain't jobs.'

And Mr Cooper didn't argue with her because he was trying to tune the piano.

'Let's have our wedding first,' young Mrs Allnutt said happily. 'As far as I'm concerned the rest a' the world can go hang.'

So hats were trimmed and flowers were ordered, enough trestle tables were produced to fill Flossie's front room, and finally the dresses were made and tried on to gasps of appreciation.

And a very nice wedding it was, even if it did turn out to be a bit more expensive than Flossie anticipated. Gideon wore his brown boots, his spotted scarf and his best bowler hat, and gave the bride away with a most theatrical flourish, Ethel wept with emotion, and Mrs Geary burped, and the parrot swore so much at the wedding breakfast-cum-ding-dong that they had to cover him up with a cloth and hide him in the scullery. Joan looked very pretty in her white gown with a crown of orange blossom on her tawny hair, and her two bridesmaids were charming in pink, and whatever anyone's secret opinion of the groom might be he was certainly handsome. His father turned out to be a wizened little man who spent the whole time showing off about how well his son had got on but nobody paid much attention to him. There were far too many other things going on.

Even Grandpa Potter and Aunt Maud attended, although Peggy thought they were a nuisance, because Aunt Maud ate far too much and kept complaining she was feeling sick and Grandpa had to be watched all the time because he sat in the corner all through the ding-dong muttering darkly that 'no one would ever have married her, oh no, not if they'd known what I know.'

But what was important was that the mystical deed had been done. Joan and Sidney Owen had been pronounced man and wife in the church of St Alphege, had cut their wedding cake together and were accepted as a couple.

It wasn't until the baker's van arrived to drive them off to their two-roomed flat in Deptford, that Peggy realized how final it all was and how much she was going to miss her sister. As the little vehicle clopped round the corner and out of her sight, and Mum and Mrs Roderick were waving tearful farewells, she could feel the atmosphere changing around her. A chill wind had sprung up while they were saying goodbye and the air was decidedly wintry. Shivering she walked back into Mr Allnutt's front room.

Mr Cooper was playing their goodnight song, 'Memories, memories, dreams of love so true', and some of the guests were already standing round the piano arm-in-arm and singing softly. The room was hazy with blue cigarette smoke and their swaying bodies were wreathed in it as they wallowed in the melancholy nostalgia of the song, remembering childhoods long ago, broken love affairs, and the old old pains of loss and rejection.

The familiar sentimental words brought tears to Peggy's eyes. This won't do, she scolded herself. I ain't been left alone. I shall see her next Saturday. Being married ain't the end of the world. And it suddenly occurred to her that now Joan was married she could have another baby and this time she could keep it. Suitably comforted and quite her sensible self again she set about gathering up the empties.

Grandpa Potter was asleep in the corner with his jaw dropped and his mouth wide open, Aunt Maud was nowhere to be seen, Baby was eating something out of a crumpled paper-bag, and Mum and Mrs Roderick were head to head in the corner reminiscing about their long-dead husbands. It was all rather melancholy. But over by the window an argument had begun between Mr Brown, old Mr Allnutt, Bertie Allnutt and Mrs Geary and as that at least sounded lively she wandered over to the edge of it, intrigued by the noise they were making.

Mr Brown was holding forth about the unemployed. What a peculiar thing to be talking about at a wedding. 'The government ought to do something,' he said. 'Three million! It's a bloody scandal!' His little, seedy face was pink with passion.

'I don't see what they could do, Cyril,' Mrs Geary said. 'If there ain't work there ain't work. It's a terrible time to get married.'

'You see, what it is,' Mr Allnutt argued in his reasonable way, 'what it is it's an international problem. No one government will ever be able to solve it.'

'Don't talk to me about the government,' Bertie Allnutt said. 'They oughter be shot, the lot of 'em. Putting on dress suits and sucking up to the nobs. And they was supposed ter be Socialists.'

'That Macdonald's the worst,' Mr O'Donavan put in. 'We elected him to lead a Labour government an' what does he do? He goes an' joins the Tories.'

'They don't know how to run things in this country,' Mr Brown said scathingly. 'None of 'em. They should go over to Germany. Take a leaf out of their book. There's a chap there knows exactly what ter do. Put the nation first he says. Put people to work building roads. Get rid of all the Jewboys. They're half the trouble.'

'Is that a fact?' Mr Cooper said, mocking him.

Mr Brown bristled. 'He's got the right idea, you ask me.'

209

'Who has?' Mrs Geary said.

'This German chap, What's-'is-name. Adolf Hitler.'

'Never heard of him,' Mrs Geary said. 'Look at that, Peggy, my glass is empty.'

CHAPTER 16

Changes began at number six Paradise Row as soon as the ding-dong was over and the wedding guests had departed.

'You two girls can sleep in the double now,' Mum said, 'and that'll leave the single for me.'

Baby was annoyed. 'But that's my bed,' she protested.

'Don't be stupid,' Flossie said wearily. It had been a long day and she was drooping with fatigue. 'You don't own beds.' It would be a relief not to have to keep putting the camp bed up and down every morning and evening. 'Anyway, just think. Now we can have a proper front room for company.'

'I know all about front rooms for company,' Baby complained. 'Nobody ever goes in them.' But she had to accept the new arrangement just the same.

In the months that followed the wedding, Peggy was often rather lonely when she was at home. She missed Joan's company very much, and especially at night, for that was when they'd always talked to one another. And the mornings were made tense by Mum's nerves, which were often particularly fragile when she woke.

The newspapers were full of gloomy reports too, only in their case it was the health of the national economy that was causing concern. There were between six and seven million people living on the dole because their breadwinners were unemployed, and the editors all declared that 'something had to be done about it.' In November the newly-elected National Government took action. They introduced a 'means test' which was designed to ensure that only the most poverty-stricken families would be allowed to receive what the posh papers were calling 'State charity'.

'Fat lot a' good that'll be,' Mr Allnutt said bitterly. 'They won't make jobs appear by starving the unemployed, poor beggars. If there ain't work, there ain't work. Look at John Cooper. Now the pictures are all talking they give *him* the sack. Supposed to be progress that is. Well progress for the film stars I dare say but it ain't done much for him.'

So many people were unemployed, or like Mr Boxall only offered work on rare occasions, that Peggy felt quite guilty to be holding down a job of her own, even though it was a very poorly-paid one. But she wouldn't have it up for the world, because the time she spent behind the counter at Aimee's was the most enjoyable part of her day. The hours were long and sometimes her back ached with so much standing, and sometimes she found it hard to be patient when one of the wealthy customers was particularly pernickety, but despite all that she and Megan had a lot of fun in the shop. And most of it stemmed in one way or another from Mr MacFarlane.

The shop was owned and named by Mrs Aimee MacFarlane who was tall and determined with iron-grey hair and a will to match. But her husband was a different creature altogether. For a start he was more than a head shorter than Madame Aimee, a small, dapper, kindly man, and what was even better, a man without the slightest trace of a sense of humour. He did all the day-to-day work of running the establishment and lived in constant awe and occasional terror of his formidable wife. Consequently he was a figure of fun to his young assistants, and his appearance first thing in the morning, bouncing down the carpeted staircase in the middle of the shop beaming his greetings at them, was enough to set all five of them giggling.

'Currrtesy and efficiency, gurrrls!' he would cry in his burring Scots.

And they would all chorus back at him, 'Yes, Mr MacFarlane. Currrtesy and efficiency.'

212

He didn't seem to mind when they mimicked his accent, and he seemed impervious to all the tricks they played on him. Once they put all the drawers in the wrong places in their neat glass-fronted cabinets and he spent the rest of the morning patiently setting them to rights and worried sick in case his wife came in and caught him at it. On another occasion they blacked out Megan's front teeth with soot and had the poor man pale with anxiety on her account for the rest of the day.

They put salt in his tea and drawing pins on his chair. When the shop was closed for the night and the goods were being covered, they hid under the dust-sheets and crawled behind the counters and pretended to faint when he was passing. And their laughter bubbled and welled in the empty spaces the customers had left behind, echoing along the panelled walls and between the high mahogany counters.

'It's being so cheerful as keeps us going,' they said to one another. And the silly catch phrase set them giggling all over again.

And of course, Mr MacFarlane was the first person they rushed to tell whenever Megan fell in love, which she did with quite amazing regularity. She was an entertainment for them too, because her pashes were so short-lived and yet she claimed each one as 'the real thing' and spent her every spare moment in a dewy-eyed day-dream about her current beloved.

'Who is it this time?' their amiable employer would ask. And when he was told, he would shake his head and suck his teeth and say it was 'Extrrraordinarrry!' which delighted them all the more.

After that first brief pash for the handsome Tom, Peggy had remained heart-whole. Whenever she saw the young man nowadays she thought how insipid and silly he was and felt ashamed of herself for weaving such a stupid fantasy about his empty-headed innocence. In fact she was beginning to wonder whether the whole business of being in love wasn't simply a figment of an overheated imagination. She couldn't imagine any of the married couples in Paradise Row ever behaving like Megan. The O'Donavans were always weighed down by babies, the

Browns were a joke, Mr Boxall was a thug who terrified his wife, even Bertie Allnutt and his wife were quiet and prosaic although they seemed quite fond of one another. Sometimes when she saw a courting couple walking hand-in-hand, she wondered whether some people managed to sustain that lovely light-hearted feeling for longer than others, but it was impossible to be sure.

She would have liked to ask Joan what she thought about it, but although her sister came to visit every early closing day, love was the one thing they never talked about, and Peggy didn't like to open the subject because that might have looked like prying into her sister's private life, and she didn't want to pry.

Actually like so many girls who marry young to get away from home the new Mrs Joan Owen was preoccupied by the discovery that there was a price to pay for her freedom, and that ironically the price was a sudden and total dependence on a stranger. Sometimes it alarmed her to realize how very little she knew about Sid Owen. The teasing and daring that had attracted her to him in the first place was still in evidence but now she was seeing other and less attractive sides to his nature. It was one thing to sit in the pictures together laughing and flirting, and to kiss under the trees on the way home, safe in the languorous knowledge that they couldn't 'go any further', quite another to have to endure 'going all the way' when she wasn't really in the mood for it, and then get up at three next morning to light the stove so as to cook him breakfast before he went down to the bakehouse.

He was so particular about everything, that was the trouble, and he could go roaring off into a temper at the least little thing. The table had to be set according to his specifications, his dinner had to be ready on the stroke of twelve, with a bottle of Watney's pale ale beside his place, and woe betide her if she'd bought him some other brew. She'd made that mistake once and had the bottle hurled across the room at her, and although she'd ducked out of the way, it had broken against the wall and spattered the curtains, and that had meant hours of cleaning and scrubbing afterwards.

As the months passed she learned how to placate him,

thinking ahead so as to forestall a row. But even so she was often caught out by a temper she hadn't foreseen, and sometimes she was slapped or punched or thrown across the room. And when the spring came and she knew for certain that she was pregnant she made a mistake that could have had even more serious consequences.

She'd been so happy about her condition it hadn't occurred to her that he wouldn't welcome it too. He'd taken her to the pictures that night to see *I am a Fugitive from a Chain Gang*, which he'd enjoyed very much, and as they walked home through the buzzing streets she slipped her hand into the crook of his arm and told him the news.

'You're what?' he said.

She mistook his annoyance for surprise and told him again.

'I'm expecting,' she said happily. 'Ain't it grand?'

'No it ain't,' he said, shaking off her hand. 'What was you thinking of you stupid woman? We can't afford a baby. You'll have to get rid of it.'

She drew herself away from him, remembering the pain and humiliation of that awful abortion, the horror of killing that poor fragile baby. 'No,' she said. 'I won't.'

'You will if I say so,' he said, threatening her with his face.

Anything else, she thought, but not that. 'It's *my* body,' she said. 'You can't tell me what to do with my own body.' She was trembling with the fear of what she might provoke but she had to make a stand.

'Yes I can,' he said, still threatening. 'You're *my* wife. You belong to me. If I say you'll get rid of it, you'll get rid of it, unless you want a walloping.'

Could he make her do it? she wondered, looking sideways at his glowering expression and feeling more and more afraid of him. He was cruel enough to hit her, but did he have the right to force her to get rid of her baby? She knew enough now to realize that abortions were illegal but fear was confusing her.

'Well?' he asked, as she'd been silent for a long time.

'All right,' she said. 'But don't let's talk about it now, eh?'

He took that as agreement and instantly became his

215

charming teasing self again. 'How about some fish an' chips?' he said. 'I could just go a pennorth, couldn't you?'

She carried that conversation about in her mind for the next three weeks like a great cold stone weighing her down. She could imagine his fury if she didn't do as she was told, but she knew she couldn't do as she was told even so, and especially when the child wriggled inside her. 'Don't you worry, my darling,' she said to it. 'I won't let anyone hurt you. Ever. You're much too precious. I'll think of something.'

In the end she decided she would make a public announcement to the family. She and Sid and old Mrs Geary were invited to high tea every other Sunday now that Mum had a front room for entertaining in. So there was the ideal opportunity ready made. She persuaded her mother to invite Mr Owen to their next high tea, explaining that she'd 'got something to tell you all', and Flossie, who had a pretty good idea what that something would be, was quick to arrange it. Now it was simply a matter of choosing her words.

She waited until they'd all been served and the tea was poured and they were all enjoying Mum's meat pie and pickles, and laughing at Peggy's tale of the latest high jinks in 'Aimee's Quality Haberdashery', then she took a deep breath and began.

'Mum,' she said, 'Mr Owen, what would you say if I told you you were going to be grandparents?'

Sid sucked in his breath in an ominous whistle, and old Mr Owen made a grimace, but before either of them could say anything Peggy was on her feet, and rushing round the table to throw her arms round her sister's neck and hug her rapturously. 'Oh Joan!' she said. 'How gorgeous! I'm so happy for you. When's it going to be?'

'September,' Joan said, hugging her and beaming at Mum. And then Mum and Baby got up to hug her too.

'Wonderful news,' old Mrs Geary said, putting down her teacup and smacking her lips. 'Wonderful! Nothink like a baby to cheer you all up, that's what I always say. Warms the cockles of yer heart, don't it Mr Owen?'

After that, there wasn't very much that either of the Mr Owens could do or say, except agree.

But Joan still had to face Sid on her own when they got back to their rooms. They were such small cramped rooms that there was nowhere to hide.

It was still quite warm when they got home and the heat from the ovens below had risen into their living-room bringing a faint smell of dough with it. It was excuse enough for Joan to open the window to 'let in the air' Actually what she was doing was letting out the sound, for she'd learned from experience that Sid was less likely to have a row if he thought someone could overhear him.

'Nice to see your Dad,' she said, beginning to set the table ready for their early morning breakfast.

He sat in his chair by the fireplace and loosened his collar.

'I thought you was going to get rid of it,' he said, but he didn't look angry or cruel, he looked battered, as if someone had been hitting him.

'I took pills,' she lied, smoothing the table cloth. 'They didn't work.'

'Can't you do nothing else?' he asked, and the battered look increased, folding the skin on his cheeks and forehead into anxious furrows.

'Not now,' she said, sensing victory. 'It's too late for anything now. We shall just have to put up with it. I'll have to book the nurse soon.'

'Bloody babies,' he said, and stomped out of the room, ducking his head to avoid hitting it on the lintel, and scowling horribly.

That was the last time he mentioned the subject. It was as if he'd blotted the very idea of the baby right out of his mind. Joan booked the midwife while he was working, and knitted clothes for the baby when he wasn't in the room to see her, and gathered the things she would need for her confinement in an old orange box and hid it under the bed. And once a week on early closing day she went to Paradise Row where she and Peggy made loving plans and were entirely happy together.

'I can't wait to see it,' Peggy said over and over again. First the kittens, and what a lot of kittens Tabby had had, and now a baby for Joan. It was perfect.

'If only it didn't take such a long time,' Joan said,

217

rubbing her back. It was aching rather a lot these days and the ache was wearying. 'Your Tabby's got the right idea. All over in nine weeks, lucky thing. I'd rather be a cat when I'm carrying and that's a fact.'

Tabby carried two litters during Joan's pregnancy, and the second was born four days before Joan's baby was expected, if it could truly be called a litter, for it consisted of a single tabby tom-kitten with white paws and a very loud voice.

Jim came in to see it just before Joan was due to leave, bearing his customary offering.

'You ought to keep him,' he said, stroking the kitten. 'Your Tabby's getting old. I don't reckon she'll have many more.'

'I might at that,' Peggy said, for there was sense in his suggestion and it was a very pretty kitten. She felt curiously dispassionate, accepting that her dear old Tabby couldn't live for very much longer. 'She *is* old, ain't you Tabby?' she said, stroking the cat's head. 'She's got an old face.'

'Poh! Deary me! The stink a' them fish heads!' Joan protested.

'They're good for you,' Jim told her cheerfully. 'Nothing better for nursing mothers. I'll bring *you* some if you like, when the time comes.'

'No thanks,' Joan said. 'I'd rather have a nice bit a' cod and two penn'orth.'

'You cook the chips, I'll bring the cod,' he promised.

How easy he is about it all, Peggy thought, admiring him. He's the only man I know who ever talks about kittens and babies and that sort of thing. All the others avoid it or get embarrassed, but it never bothers him. And not for the first time she thought how lucky they were to have him as a next-door neighbour.

And then Baby came crashing in through the front door full of complaints because she'd been made to work the telephone all day and she didn't think it was fair. 'It's made my ears go all red,' she wailed. 'Look.'

'Hideous,' Jim agreed and left them to cope with her.

'Time I was off,' Joan said, easing herself out of her chair. Or Sid'ud be back from his football match before she was home and then there'd be the devil to pay.

Now that she was so near to her confinement her anxiety increased by the day. She worried that the birth might remind him how cross he'd been when she told him she was expecting. She worried that she wouldn't be able to keep the flat clean while she was lying in, and that really would annoy him. And worst of all, she worried that he wouldn't take to the baby, that he wouldn't like it, that he might even hate it.

So she was relieved when her labour started quietly and conveniently after she'd cleared the supper things and he was downstairs in the bakery. She crept down the same stairs as quietly as she could to warn her next-door neighbour, Mrs Rudney, that she'd be needing the midwife, just as they'd arranged to do all those months ago, and she stood with Mrs Rudney as her oldest boy set off on his bicycle with the message, and felt pleased that everything was going according to plan. Then she went back upstairs to set the table for breakfast and make up the bed the way the midwife had shown her. Now that the moment had come she was totally calm.

It was a long labour and a painful one, but that didn't worry her. She recognized the pain and felt that she was used to it, having suffered it that first time for nothing except misery. Now she was almost glad of it, for now there would be a live baby at the end of it all. Her own dear live baby. So she and the midwife laboured on, sweating and weary but adapting to the rhythm of the birth. And at last in the early hours of the morning the child slithered from her body into the midwife's waiting hands and she knew herself delivered and was suddenly overwhelmed by a rush of such powerful emotion that she was physically shaken by it and fell back among her pillows trembling and weeping.

'Oh my dear, dear baby,' she wept, taking the infant in her arms, 'my dear, dear baby. I've waited such an awful long time to see you.' And the baby gazed up at her with enormous dark eyes, depending on her, trusting her. 'I shall love you for ever,' she promised, kissing that dark damp head.

'A little girl,' the midwife said with great satisfaction.

'What are you going to call her?'

'Yvonne,' Joan told her. She'd chosen the name all on her own, right at the start of her pregnancy. A daughter, with the dearest little round face and fine fat rosy limbs and dark hair that was so soft it really was like silk, and those beautiful, beautiful eyes. Sid was forgotten. He no longer had any relevance. There was only this beautiful trusting baby.

The midwife left when Sid came grunting upstairs for his breakfast and by then Joan was in full command of herself and her new situation. 'Mrs Rudney'll cook for yer,' she said. 'All you got to do is ring their bell.'

'What you got then?' he said gruffly, peering at what little he could see of the baby in its swathing of shawls.

'A girl.'

'Oh. You all right? I mean, everything go all right, did it?'

'Perfect,' she said, and this time she smiled at him because he was so awkward and ill at ease. 'What sort a' night did *you* have?'

'The usual,' he said, stomping out of the room.

That evening, in answer to her postcard, Mum and Peggy and Baby came to visit the newest member of their family. And true to his promise, Jim sent a large piece of cod from the market, which Mum cooked for her while the others sat on the bed and admired the baby. Peggy was thrilled because the little thing held on to her finger and looked at her.

'She's gorgeous,' she said to Joan. 'Just look at those tiny nails. I could eat her.' And just what you deserve, my poor big sister. A beautiful perfect baby. Just what you deserve. 'We're going to keep the kitten, did I tell you? I've called him Tom. Won't she just love him when she's bigger?'

'She's looking round for food,' Joan said lovingly as the baby began to root against Peggy's supporting arm. 'I'd better have her.'

How she does love her, Peggy thought as Joan began to suckle the baby. There was no doubt at all about this love. It was as strong as the love they'd all felt for Dad. 'When

220

she's a bit bigger and it's warm enough we can take her up the park,' she said. 'She'll like that. Oh won't we have some fun together.'

And they did. Which Mrs Geary said was just as well, given the state of the world. 'It's a rough old time to be born,' she said to Flossie, 'so good luck to 'em, That's what I say.'

It *was* a rough old time and in January it got rougher. There were more people out of work than ever, the weather was freezing cold with heavy snowfall and the worst blizzard for years and Mr Brown's hero Adolf Hitler was made Chancellor of Germany. In February, when Tom had grown into a fine sleek little cat and on the very day Yvonne was five months old, there was a mysterious spectacular fire in Berlin. The Reichstag building was burnt to the ground, and not long afterwards news came through that the German Communist party had been blamed for it and many of its leading members had been arrested and sent to prison, just in time to get them out of the way before the German General Election in March.

'Very nasty,' Mr Cooper said, as the evening papers were passed round at the ding-dong. 'I don't trust that Hitler chap an inch. He's locking up the opposition, that's what he's doing, and that ain't democratic. And all them young fellers strutting about in uniforms, doing the goose-step, Hitler Youth. If we don't watch out he'll be giving 'em guns next. That was the way the last lot started.'

'The last what?' Baby asked.

'War, child,' Mr Allnutt explained patiently. 'The last war. We don't want another war.'

'Oh that!' Baby said, drifting away from them. All this talk about war was so boring. Almost as bad as the way Peggy and Joan would keep going on about Yvonne. You'd think there'd never been any other babies born in the world. No, what she really wanted was to find someone who could advise her on the best way to go blonde. She knew you had to use peroxide, but she didn't know how much and she was sure it would be tricky.

In the end she persuaded one of the girls in the shop to help her, but she didn't make a very good job of it because it came out streaky. And to make matters worse, on the very day she made the change, Mum had a letter from old Aunt Maud to say that Grandpa Potter was dead and to invite them all to the funeral.

'*You* can't go with hair like that,' Mum said. 'What would people think? It wouldn't look respectful. Whatever possessed you to do such a thing?'

'It's no good going on at me,' Baby pouted. 'It's done now. And anyway I didn't know he was going to die, did I?'

'I don't think I can go,' Joan said. 'Not with Yvonne so small and Sid wanting his dinner and everything.'

So in the end Peggy and Flossie went on their own.

It was a peculiar experience for Peggy to stand beside the grave in a churchyard that seemed to have shrunk and gaze across at a village that now looked small and lost among the fields. Mum and Aunt Maud wept a little as the coffin was lowered into the earth but Peggy felt no sorrow at all. She was remembering how spiteful Grandpa Potter had been, and thinking how little he'd ever loved any of them. But none of it mattered now, she thought, looking at the dark earth lying on the coffin, you can't hurt any of us now, and Joan has a beautiful baby to make amends for all the things you made her suffer. But then she felt ashamed of herself for being so hard-hearted, for he *was* her grandfather after all, and she made an effort to pray for him and mean it.

After the ceremony they walked back to the cottage along the same, well-remembered, muddy path while Aunt Maud told them what a fine pig they'd had last year, for all the world as if they'd never been away. 'Lovely bacon he made, an' lard! Why that pig gave so much lard you'd never credit it.'

At the cottage they drank polite tea with the neighbours and tried to swallow Aunt Maud's bone-dry sandwiches and nobody mentioned Grandpa Potter once. But just before it was time to walk down to the station for the return journey Aunt Maud took them both upstairs into her billowing bedroom, signalling with her eyes that she had something private to tell them.

'Thought you ought to know,' she said, when she'd closed the door. 'I'll be getting wed in a week or two. I

222

don't want the rest of 'em to know about it yet awhile.'

'Why Maudie!' Flossie said. 'You sly old thing, Who's the lucky man?'

'It's only old Josh up the end cottage,' Maud said flatly. 'Nothing to write home about. I shall lose the cottage you see now Dad's gone, so we thought we might as well. He could do with someone to keep house for him, now he's getting on a bit, an' I need a roof over me head. So it's a suitable sort of arrangement all round.'

Flossie kissed her quite affectionately. 'Well I wish you joy,' she said. 'It'll be quiet I dare say?'

'Just the two of us.'

'Very sensible.'

And there's another marriage without love, Peggy thought, looking at the thin, grey hair on her aunt's round head and remembering how Josh used to kick the cats about. She needs a home and he needs a housekeeper. How sad.

But she forgot about her grandfather and her aunt the minute she was back with Joan and Yvonne, for the bigger the baby grew the more absorbing company she became. It was a joy to see her smiling and babbling and crowing and clapping her pretty plump hands together. Unemployment might be as bad as ever, Mum might be touchy with nerves, all sorts of things might be wrong with the world, but this baby was living proof that there was always hope.

CHAPTER 17

That summer was extremely hot. In June the heat was pleasant. It produced a fine crop of roses in the wealthy gardens of Blackheath and allowed Joan and Peggy to take the baby to a weekly picnic in the park. But by mid-July it had become excessive. The shops sweltered and the market bred flies, and down in the crowded backyards of Paradise Row the drains and dustbins smelt so bad that the stink permeated every part of every house. The Saturday night ding-dong spilled out into the street and stayed there, and when the dancers were exhausted they sat on the pavements, resting their backs against the brick walls and fanning themselves with anything they could find for the purpose, handkerchiefs, old newspapers, even Jim Boxall's library book.

'What I would like,' Lily Boxall said one particular airless evening, 'is to go down to the seaside and sit in the sea right up to my chin. Suit me a treat that would.'

'Well why not?' Mr Allnutt said. 'We could all go down. Bank Holiday Monday. We could take a charabanc. Needn't cost the earth if we was to all club together. What d'you think?'

Once it was said they could all see what a marvellous idea it was. Providing they could afford it.

'Would kids be half-price?' Mrs O'Donavan asked with understandable anxiety.

So they clubbed together, kids half-price, and the charabanc was hired and they went to Brighton, singing all the way in their open-topped wagon as it trundled between wooded hills and the long dry Weald of brown cornfields and sun-baked meadows. And Joan and baby Yvonne came with them because they were 'family'. It was a proper treat, especially as nearly three quarters of them had never seen the sea before except at the pictures. And Brighton was a wonderland with all those little kiosks along the promenade selling shrimps and cockles and whelks and jellied eels, and pubs roaring on every corner.

'London by the sea,' Mr Allnutt said, as they climbed out of the charabanc on the high promenade. After the dust and stink of Greenwich this place was so clean and bright, with the white paint of the huge hotels gleaming behind them and the railings along the promenade as blue as the sky and two piers like something out of a fairy-tale. 'London by the sea.' He was twice the size with the pleasure of the outing and the thrill of his successful planning.

The O'Donavan kids were shrill with excitement. 'Can we go on the beach, Ma? Can we? Can we?'

So the party divided, men to the pubs and women and children to the pebbles, where they found another row of kiosks built in the arches under the promenade, where they were selling cheap tin buckets and spades, and sticks of rock and Indian toffee like pink cotton wool.

'Gaw! What a place,' Lily Boxall said. 'Look at all the people.'

The roads and pavements had been crowded enough but there were so many people on the beach they could barely see the pebbles. Every inch of space between the promenade and the edge of the sea was covered by some body or other, standing or strolling or sitting on the stones. Some were even spread out on their backs fast asleep, as though they were in bed. It was as if the entire population of London had come down to the seaside for the day.

'Let's paddle!' Pearl said, heading off towards the sea.

So the Boxalls and the Furnivalls edged themselves an inch or two of foreshore, and while Flossie, Mrs Geary, Mrs Roderick and Mrs Boxall guarded the bags, the younger ones stripped off their sandals and headed for the water.

It was luxurious, beautifully cooling after the heat of the

225

journey and lukewarm when you got used to it, like a huge salty bath that you didn't have to fill or empty. Pearl and Lily and Baby tucked their dresses in their knickers and waded out until the water was above their knees and Joan took all the baby's clothes off and let her wallow in the water in chortling nakedness. But Peggy went for a swim.

As soon as she'd been sure they were really going on this outing Peggy had treated herself to one of the new knitted swimming costumes. It was years since she'd been for a swim, not since Tillingbourne, and she knew she might have forgotten what to do, but she was determined to try, just the same.

Now, after struggling out of her clothes and into the costume inside an awkward tent made by two towels held up by Mum and Mrs Geary, she picked her way over the painful pebbles and strode out into the sea. And of course she hadn't forgotten. She could swim as well as ever. And the touch of the water, silky against her skin, brought back so many remembered pleasures, the sensation of speed as her thrusting legs propelled her through the water, the rhythmical splashing she could hear in her wake, the sight of her hands and arms flashing pearly-white against the green, the sun warming her face and shoulders when she finally stood up to catch her breath, throwing back her head and shaking her wet hair, so that water drops spun from her in a dazzling shower.

Which was how Jim Boxall saw her as he walked down the beach to join his sisters. It stopped him in his stride with an upsurge of desire that was as strong and sudden as it was unexpected. Peggy? he thought. Could that really be Peggy swimming? He'd had no idea she could swim. Nor that she could look so beautiful.

'Come an' join us,' Lily yelled at him. 'It's lovely. Ever so warm.'

So he rolled up his trousers and joined them, and got splashed for his pains so that his shirt clung to his chest and his dark hair was soon as wet as Peggy's. They paddled until Joan said Yvonne was beginning to feel cold to the touch and then they all staggered back up the pebbles to dry themselves while Peggy disappeared inside her tent to change back into her cotton dress again. And he wanted her all the time.

'I'm starving,' she said, when she emerged from the tent and she began to rub her hair vigorously with her towel.

'You would be,' Baby said, arranging herself on her towel ready to sunbathe.

'We'll get some shrimps,' Jim offered, hoping she'd accept and the others would stay where they were.

To his annoyance both his sisters took him up on his offer and Baby came too. When the shrimps had been bought and he suggested a walk along the promenade, they said they wanted to go on the pier. So off they all trooped, eating and giggling, to sample the delights of the hall of mirrors, the helter-skelter, what the butler saw and a new machine called a 'love meter' on which you could 'measure your sex appeal'. Baby spent five minutes squeaking and protesting before she would submit herself to the test and then walked off in a huff when the machine pronounced her 'harmless'.

'Let's go back on the beach,' she said. 'I'm sick of this silly pier.'

So to Jim's considerable pleasure, Baby and his sisters went giggling back to the beach and he and Peggy were able to go for the walk on their own.

They climbed the hill of an upper promenade, heading east and gradually leaving the crowds behind them, eating their shrimps as they strolled. The view from such a high vantage point was spectacular. They could see both the piers and the entire length of the promenade below them and the people on the beach were as small and dark as a swarm of ants.

But Peggy was mesmerized by the sea, spreading before them, vast and green and endless.

'I never thought it'ud be so big,' she said.

'You've seen it in the pictures,' he said. 'Must have.'

'Yes,' she agreed. 'But it's not the same.' At the pictures you saw a dark heaving mass, hardly worth looking at. But this was very different. She leaned her arms against the railings and gazed at it, trying to find words to express what she felt. It was so beautiful, all that gorgeous greeny-blue water, so still and peaceful and yet powerful too, sparkling all over with little flashes of sharp white light as though someone had sprinkled it with diamonds.

'It makes me think of a piece of Shakespeare we had to learn at school,' she said. And she tried to quote it. '"This precious stone set in a silver sea." Or something like that.'

'"This demi-paradise",' Jim said, quoting it for her. *Richard III* was one of the plays he'd studied in his first course at the evening institute.

'This fortress built by Nature for herself
Against infection and the hand of war.
This happy breed of men, this little world,
This precious stone set in a silver sea
Which serves it in the office of a wall
Or as a moat defensive to a house,
Against the envy of less happier lands,
This blessed plot, this earth, this realm, this England.'

She was most impressed by his learning, but sensible as ever, asked, 'Will it?'

'Will it what?'

'Protect us. Like a moat.'

'Don't know,' he admitted. 'I haven't thought about it, to tell the truth.' And he wasn't thinking about it then either. He was enjoying the sight of her bare arms, her bare warm rounded arms, leaning along the railing, rousing him most pleasurably for the second time that day. In fact he'd been in an almost continuous state of desire for her ever since he'd seen her swimming. It was as if she'd been transformed, as if she wasn't Peggy Furnivall his next-door neighbour, the girl he'd known nearly all his life, but some rare gorgeous creature ripening in the sun, a water-nymph or a goddess or a . . .

'I could go a cup of tea,' she said, smiling at him. 'Shrimps don't half make you thirsty.'

'We'll get one,' he said. But he didn't move.

'Good,' she said. But she didn't move either.

'There's a good film on at the Empire this week,' he said. 'Would you like to see it?'

'Who's going?' she said, still easy and lazy, looking out to sea.

'Well,' he said. 'I thought you might like to come with me.'

'Just you?' she said, looking at him quizzically. 'Are you asking me out?'

He realized he was feeling nervous, almost anxious. 'Yes,' he said. 'I am.'

She smiled at him again, surprised but pleased. If she accepted, this would be her first date. Fancy her first date turning out to be with Jim Boxall. But why not? They were both nineteen now. She'd just had her nineteenth birthday. They were old enough. And there'd be no harm in it. 'Yes,' she said. 'All right. Ta.'

He was filled with delight, as if he'd won a great prize. 'Come on,' he said seizing her hand and pulling her away from the railing. 'Race you back to the others.'

It was his third surprise of the afternoon that she beat him with yards to spare. I'm going to take her to the pictures, he thought, escorting her into the cafe. I'm actually going to take her to the pictures. If it's all right we might go every week.

But the Fates had other plans for Jim Boxall and Peggy Furnivall.

229

CHAPTER 18

On Tuesday morning when Jim Boxall went back to Warrenden Brothers after the Bank Holiday he found the workshop buzzing with anxious talk and no work being done.

'What's up?' he asked his fellow apprentice.

But the boy didn't know. 'Foreman said to wait,' he told Jim. 'Not to start or nothink, just ter wait.'

'Sounds bad,' Jim said, and foreboding clenched its fist in his belly.

It was bad. They could see that as soon as the foreman came back. He looked as though he'd shrunk and his face was grey. 'Can't wrap it up,' he said. 'The firm's going bust. There's no new orders come. This one's the last.'

'How long d'you think we got?' one of the older men asked.

'Two, three weeks,' the foreman said. 'They'll close down gradual.'

'Can't yer do nothink?'

'Fer Chrissake Percy, I can't *make* work. I only wish I could.'

They accepted his answer and his news dully. In two or three weeks they would be unemployed. They'd been half-expecting it for over a year, and talking about it for several months, but even so there was an awful finality about being told. In two or three weeks they would be on the scrap heap. It was shattering news. They set about their work that morning, listless with defeat.

At the end of the day the foreman had a quiet word with his two apprentices.

'You're young yet,' he said to the boy. 'You ain't done two years, have yer, so my advice to you would be ter try something else.'

'Like what?' the boy said dully. 'Course there's masses a' jobs round here. I don't think.'

The foreman ignored his misery and his sarcasm. What could he say to either?

'It's you I'm sorry for,' he said to Jim. 'Being so near an' all. How long you done?'

'Five years,' Jim said. Five years of grinding effort in the heat and stink, of burnt hands and cut fingers and bone-aching exhaustion, five years from the first humiliation of being greased in to the last humiliation of being sold out, five years for nothing.

'I'll see you get a good reference,' the foreman said.

'Thanks,' Jim said, being polite because the foreman was trying so hard. Not that it would help him get another apprenticeship or even another job. And if he didn't get another job he wouldn't be able to afford any more evening classes. And just when he'd started on his third course, which was Economics and really interesting.

The unfairness of it kept him numb all through the day. He worked mechanically, saying nothing. It wasn't until he was home and out in the yard sprinkling the lavvy with Keating's powder and flushing out the drains with Jeyes fluid the way he did every evening, that his rage burst through. He hurled the milky fluid into the drain with such force that it splashed up the wall. 'Bloody sodding God-awful world!' he swore.

'What's up?' Peggy's voice said from the other side of the fence.

'Lost my job,' he said briefly, looking up at her. 'Sorry about the French.'

'That's all right,' she said. 'You swear all you like. I don't mind. You got a right to swear.'

Then they both realized that their outing to the pictures might be affected, and neither of them knew what to say, he because he didn't want to call it off, she because she didn't want to embarrass him.

'These drains are awful,' she said. 'If it don't rain soon we shall be stunk out the house.'

'This time yesterday we was at the seaside,' he remembered. 'Down to earth with a vengeance today.'

'Yes,' she agreed, picking up her can of Keatings. 'If only it wasn't so hot.'

'We're still going to the pictures,' he said. It was half statement, half question and she answered it as such.

'Yes. Course. We could go Dutch if you'd like.'

The idea of asking her to pay for her own ticket appalled him. 'No we couldn't,' he said stiffly. 'I asked you, so I'll pay.'

I've upset him, she thought, recognizing hurt pride. 'All right,' she said, trying to soothe him. But when she looked over the fence he'd gone indoors.

They went to the Empire Cinema that Friday as they'd planned. It wasn't a success. When he'd asked her out, in that magical sunshine with the sea and the rest of their lives dazzling before them, he'd imagined how it would be, sitting in the darkness watching the flicker of the screen side by side. He'd thought how he'd cuddle her. He'd even hoped he might kiss her goodnight. The reality was miserably different.

They sat discreetly apart, contained within the plush arms of their seats and not speaking. In the interval he bought her an ice-cream and tried to make conversation, but apart from discussing the film there didn't seem to be much else to say. And then horror of horrors Megan Griffiths came giggling down the aisle to join them with a grinning gang of people they used to know at school.

'Hello!' she said. 'Fancy seeing you two here. I didn't know you was coming tonight, Peggy. We could've all come together if you'd said. Remember Spotty? He said not to come over, daft ha'porth, in case you was courting. There you are, Spotty, what did I tell you? They're neighbours. They're not courting, are you?'

They tried to remember Spotty and agreed that they weren't courting. And when Megan dragged the hordes back to their seats for the second half they were more embarrassed with one another than ever. By the time they'd walked home through the stifling heat of yet another airless night they were quite relieved to part company.

'Thank you for coming with me,' he said politely as she fished the front-door key through the letterbox on its string and fitted it into the lock.

'Thank you for asking me,' she said.

I shall never get to kiss her goodnight now, he thought unhappily as he pulled the string of his own door key. Damn that Megan and her stupid Spotty. And he went straight up to bed in a very bad mood.

The next two weeks were miserable. On the day the works finally closed he went down to the pub with all his workmates, got drunk for the first time in his life, and regretted it bitterly when he woke with a throbbing headache the next morning. But hungover or not he was up at the usual time and out on the street the minute he'd eaten his breakfast. Somehow or other he would find another job, no matter how badly paid or how objectionable. There were bills to be met and Mum and the girls to be looked after. He couldn't sit idle.

By the end of the week he was working part time in a local warehouse sweeping floors. The week after that he helped a local window cleaner who'd injured his shoulder in a fall and said he 'couldn't face the top floors yet awhile'. And so he continued, accepting whatever was on offer, enduring whenever there was nothing at all, and keeping out of the house so that his father wouldn't know what was happening, because he had enough to contend with without the old man making scenes. By the time September came round it was clear to him that he couldn't afford to enrol for the second year of his course in Economics, and for several days he was miserably cast down, because he'd lost his education as well as his job.

But then the weather broke at last with a day of rain, marvellous, soft, sweet-smelling rain. It was such a change after that long stinking drought that people came out of their doors and stood in the street with their faces upturned to enjoy it. Old Mrs Geary opened her window and leaned so far out of it that Pearl and Peggy were afraid she'd fall.

'No fear,' she said. 'I got a good strong instinct fer self-preservation, don't you worry. Ain't it grand, eh?'

And the parrot, who was sitting beside her at the window, agreed, with a cacophony of squawks and obscenities.

'Let's go up the park,' Pearl said. 'It'll be gorgeous up the park.'

So she and Lily and Peggy went to the park and as Jim had just come home they took him along too, to stroll under dripping trees and skip over damp earth and watch the grass recovering before their eyes.

'Just look at that,' Pearl said. 'It's all going green again. I never seen nothing as quick as that.'

It encouraged them all, this sign that nature could heal so rapidly.

'You'll get another job soon,' Peggy said to Jim, when Pearl and Lily had gone rushing off to be showered under another tree, 'you'll see. Things'll change.'

'They're changing already,' he told her, 'but all in the wrong direction. The more people there are out of work the less money there is to spend, the less money to spend the fewer goods made, fewer goods made fewer people employed to make them. It's a vicious circle.' He'd read enough about economics to understand that. 'Nothing'll change until the government starts to employ people, like they're doing in America in the Tennessee Valley. Even Herr Hitler knows that.'

'Oh don't let's talk about Herr Hitler,' Peggy said. 'Not in all this lovely rain. Things'll change here too, you'll see.'

'Only if we make them change,' he said almost fiercely. 'It's no good enduring things. You got to take action.'

Action, she thought, it's always action with him. 'Is that what you're going to do?' she asked.

'The minute I can figure out what action to take, yes. It ain't fair, Peg, grinding people down like this. There ought to be work for everyone, more and more of it, not less and less.'

She was looking at him with such pity that he had to change the subject, 'Next time we come for a walk,' he said, wiping the rain from his eyebrows because it was dripping into his eyes, 'let's leave the girls behind.'

They took a lot of walks in Greenwich Park that autumn,

sometimes on their own and sometimes with Joan and the baby. It wasn't the same as the romantic intimacy of the cinema, but at least, as they told one another with cheerful frequency, they were spared the company of Megan and the impossible Spotty, who turned out to be Miss Griffiths' latest pash, although what she saw in him neither of them could possibly imagine.

Despite his hunger for action odd jobs grew more and more difficult for Jim to find. In October he worked for ten days helping the park keeper burn the autumn leaves, in November he went back to the warehouse for a day or two, but it wasn't until January that he found a permanent job and then it was one without a future. One of the garages in Blackheath that serviced the cars of the well-to-do advertised for an odd-job boy, and as he seemed quick and willing they took him on. He was still there in April and by then he'd learned so much that the manager had increased his pay and was allowing him to strip the engines.

Now, at last, he could afford to ask Peggy out properly.

It was a great disappointment to him that she refused his offer.

'I'm ever so sorry,' she said, 'but I can't. Not just yet. Joan's going to have another baby you see. It's due in three weeks time and I'm going to look after Yvonne.'

He knew about the baby of course because he'd seen the pregnancy developing. 'Oh,' he said, controlling his expression with an effort. 'I see. Later then.'

'When it's born,' she promised.

But when it was born she spent all her spare time over in Deptford helping with the housework.

'Poor Joan,' she said. 'She's got enough to do looking after two babies without doing all the housework as well.'

Privately Jim thought she was being just a bit too unselfish, but he didn't say anything because it wasn't his business and because he suspected that she wouldn't take any notice of him if he did.

The babies were so pretty, that was the trouble, so pretty and so loving. Yvonne was twenty months old when her brother was born and just beginning to talk. She could say 'Mum-mum-mum' and 'Dadda' and 'More p'ease', and while she was staying at Paradise Row and sleeping with her aunty Peggy she said 'Weggy' as clear as clear to the delight of the entire household. She was a sturdy little girl with plump legs and a stolid way of walking. Her face was still round with her father's high wide cheekbones and her mother's decided nose and large greeny-brown eyes that were very much like Peggy's. The dark hair that had pleased Joan so much when she was born had lightened to a pale nut-brown and now it was long enough to cut into a short bob with a fringe, which Flossie said made her look a proper little girl. Naturally Peggy adored her.

And now there was another pretty baby, her brother Norman, born on the last day of May 1934, more than a pound heavier than his sister and with a very healthy appetite, dark-haired and dark-eyed and in Peggy's opinion totally delicious.

'You are lucky,' she said enviously to Joan as the baby suckled and Yvonne lay on the bed between them with her head on her mother's knees. 'To have two babies like this. I wish it was me.'

'It will be,' Joan said easily.

'I'll have to get married first,' Peggy grinned.

'You don't want to be in too much of a hurry to get married,' Joan said. 'Take your time an' choose a really good man. That's my advice. Someone to look after you, like Dad used to do.' It was the nearest she'd got to admitting that Sid wasn't the best husband alive, and she looked away from her sister when she'd finished speaking to show that she didn't intend to continue into a confession. Sid had taken this second baby quite well, all things considered. He hadn't told her to get rid of it this time, and he hadn't complained much when early morning-sickness made her slow with the housework.

In fact she was beginning to wonder whether he wasn't getting quite fond of little Yvey, bringing her little iced cakes from the bakery and mending her toys and patting her soft hair with those blunt hands of his, looking down at her with that sheepish expression he wore when he was feeling affectionate and didn't know how to put it into words. No, there was a lot of good in Sid Owen if you knew where to look for it, so she ought to be loyal.

'That'ud take a lot of doing,' Peggy said, understanding

the words and the distancing look. 'Dad was special.' And rather to her surprise she found she was thinking of Jim Boxall, sensible Jim who knew about cats and kittens and didn't mind talking about babies, Jim Boxall who looked after his mum, and cleaned the drains and the lavvy every night, Jim Boxall who had fine blue eyes and long tender eyelashes and was desperate for a job. 'Very special.' I wonder whether he'll ask me to the pictures again.

He did but not until the middle of June and by then Paradise Row had something very peculiar to talk about.

It was Mrs Geary who noticed it first.

'Come up here, Mrs Furnivall,' she called one fine Tuesday morning, when Flossie was preparing the washing downstairs in the scullery. 'Come an' see this.'

'What is it, Mrs Geary?' Flossie called back. 'I got a lot to do.'

'Foreigners, if I'm any judge,' Mrs Geary said. 'Come an' see. Only look sharp or they'll be gone.'

So Flossie came up to see.

There were two odd-looking men walking up the street towards the corner shop. They were dressed entirely in black, in long, flapping overcoats and grubby black trousers, and their hats were low crowned with a wide flat brim like a black dinner plate. Both were bearded and both looked extremely pale, but the most peculiar thing of all was the way they wore their hair, in two long thin ringlets hanging past their ears and right down onto their coats.

'Jewboys,' Mrs Geary said. 'Bet you anythink.'

The two men walked into the corner shop.

'Now watch,' Mrs Geary said.

They watched for quite a long time. But nothing happened.

'Exactly,' Mrs Geary said when Flossie remarked on it. 'Nothing does. Nothing happened last time. There was three fellers and a woman went in last Thursday and they never come out neither. Thought I was seeing things, that's why I watched 'em this time.'

'They can't have disappeared,' Flossie said leaning out of the window to get a better look. 'They're probably taking a long time because they can't speak English.'

As they watched, Mrs Roderick came out of her house and walked down the road in her straight-spined way towards the shop. 'Packet of pins,' she explained. 'I always seem to be out of pins.'

They waited until she came back again.

'Anyone else in the shop?' Mrs Geary asked casually.

'Only me,' Mrs Roderick said. 'Very slow this morning he says.'

'There you are,' Mrs Geary said triumphantly. 'What did I tell you? Something's going on. I'm going down to see what it is.'

So Flossie left the washing and they both went down.

The shop was empty just as Mrs Roderick had told them. There was only Mr Grunewald standing behind his counter among the biscuit boxes and the tins of condensed milk and the cards hung with bootlaces.

'Good morning,' he said hopefully.

'I'll take half a pound a' Bourbons,' Mrs Geary ordered. A little extravagance would put him in a good humour.

The biscuits were weighed.

'Got company have yer?' Mrs Geary said casually as the paper bag was passed across the counter. 'We seen 'em come in.'

Mr Grunewald's face fell from friendly smile to guarded anxiety in an instant. 'You won't say nothink, will you Mrs Geary. I wouldn't want the rent man to ... Not that there's anything ... if you know what I mean. They don't pay rent or nothing like that.'

'Course not,' Mrs Geary assured him. 'You know me, Mr Grunewald. You can 'ave who you like in the 'ouse. No concern a' mine. We was just wonderin' who they was.'

'They're from Germany,' Mr Grunewald explained. 'Friends of friends. They stay one night, maybe two. That's all, you got my word.'

'Visiting?' Mrs Geary probed.

Mr Grunewald swallowed hard and decided to take this lady into his confidence. He'd known ever since his first refugees arrived two weeks ago that sooner or later the street would find out. At least Mrs Geary was likely to be sympathetic. Not like that Mr Brown.

'They're refugees,' he said. 'Jews. They're on the run

238

from Germany. All Jews would run from Germany if they could. It's that man Hitler. He says Jews are to blame.'

'What for?' Flossie asked.

'What for? For everything. For the unemployed, for firms that go broke, for people being hungry, for everything. It's a bad time to be Jewish in Germany. So many Germans full of hatred. You wouldn't *believe* half the stories I hear. Jews not allowed in school, Jews not allowed to marry, Jews being spat at in the streets, Jews being beaten up by the Brownshirts, and worse to come, they say. There are laws on the way, Mrs Geary, that will let that awful Hitler put a man in prison simply for being a Jew.'

'Good God,' Mrs Geary said. 'He couldn't do that.'

'He could. He will. It's an old, old story, Mrs Geary. Jews are always the ones to be blamed when things go wrong.'

'I've seen it in the papers,' Flossie said. There was a little paragraph about a Jewish shop being daubed with paint, but she hadn't paid much attention to it, and she'd never imagined that Jews would turn up in Paradise Row as a result. 'No one'll say anything,' she promised Mr Grunewald. 'If the rent man asks, they're friends come visiting.'

'They only stay two, three nights,' Mr Grunewald said again. 'Just till my cousin in Manchester can find them somewhere.'

'Whatcher think a' that?' Mrs Geary asked as she hobbled back to number six.

'Sounds a bit far-fetched,' Flossie said, 'putting people in prison for being Jews, but then again, they'd hardly come all this way for nothing, so there must be *something* in it.'

That was the general opinion in Paradise Row, except for Cyril Brown who said Jews were all the same the world over, as far as he could see, damn liars every one, and they'd be fools to believe a word of it. 'Hitler's a fine bloke,' he said. 'He's got the right idea.'

The *Daily Mail* agreed with him. Or did he agree with the *Daily Mail*? The newspaper was full of praise for the German Chancellor. Hitler, it said, knew exactly how to cope with unemployment. He had embarked on an ambitious programme of state construction, most of it admittedly geared towards war, but beneficial for all that, building armaments' factories and a network of *autobahns* and improving the railway system so that men and arms could be carried anywhere he wished. Jews and other undesirables were being cleared away and their homes and jobs given to local Germans, and any young men still without jobs were being drafted into an 'army of labour' which would be used in a great national 'battle for work'. Everybody, the newspaper claimed, everybody had to admit that the new Chancellor had done a lot of good. When he came to power there had been four million unemployed in Germany. Now the figure was down to just over two million and it was still falling.

'Bloody fools,' Mr Cooper said, throwing the paper onto the floor in his anger. 'Can't they see what he's really doing? We shall have another war if we don't look out, and then God help us. He ought to be stopped.'

But nobody seemed to know how to stop him and as there were plenty of industrialists in England and elsewhere who certainly didn't want to, and what's more, were prepared to put their hands in their pockets to support him, nothing was done. Mr Grunewald continued to open his door to refugees who arrived in ones and twos all through the summer and the autumn and well into the New Year of 1935. Mr Brown continued to grumble about it but he didn't say anything to the rent collector. Flossie and Baby went to the pictures every week with Mrs Roderick. Peggy went on helping her sister and enjoying the company of Yvonne and baby Norman. Jim went on servicing cars and finding it more and more boring with every day that passed. And from time to time he and Peggy went to the pictures and didn't hold hands.

In short, like the rest of the English that year, they all continued in their age-old tradition of muddling through, enduring what had to be endured, and enjoying such trivial and happy events as they could. On 6 May, while Herr Hitler was planning a spectacular Olympic Games that was to be held in Berlin in a year's time, London was celebrating the Silver Jubilee of Their Majesties King

George V and Queen Mary.

The denizens of Paradise Row had a lovely time. They draped their houses with bunting and hung balloons on the streetlamps and a banner reading 'God Bless Our King and Queen' on the woodyard fence, and while the royals were in St Paul's giving thanks for a long reign, they dragged their tables and chairs out into the street and held a riotous street party. Mr Cooper played the piano and everybody sang and Mr Brown played his mouth organ and nobody listened, old Mr Allnutt ran up and down fixing wobbly table-legs with wedges of wood that fell out of place the minute his back was turned, all the women wore paper hats above their aprons, and Mrs Roderick made a creation called a charlotte russe which was much admired and tasted of strawberry blancmange with an aftertaste of tinned salmon.

But no matter how much they enjoyed themselves, they knew it was only an interlude. Later that month the *Daily Herald* broke the news that Hitler had started to draft his young men into a real army. Apparently he had announced quite openly that he had already conscripted half a million men and intended to conscript more, and what was worse, he now admitted that he was forming an air force too. It was a direct violation of the Treaty of Versailles and the most alarming news to come out of Germany to date. Now and rather late, the British Government began to respond. They started up a recruiting campaign to encourage more young men to join the Royal Air Force, asking particularly for technicians to service the new planes in their expanding force.

And one of the young men they encouraged was Jim Boxall.

He saw the advertisement in a copy of a local paper that had been left on the passenger seat of a Bentley he was cleaning and servicing. When the job was done he sat on the low garage wall in the sunshine for ten minutes' rest and a fag, and while he was smoking he read the paper through. And there was the advertisement. He was tempted by it, he had to admit it, for although the pay wasn't very good the prospects were. Two shillings a day was about the same as he was earning at the garage but

241

the promise of 'modern technical training' after more than a year in the wilderness of untrained labour was a very strong incentive indeed. He tore the advertisement out of the paper and put it in his pocket. If things got any worse, there was always the RAF.

Things got worse two weeks later.

242

CHAPTER 19

'You got the armbands?' Megan giggled. 'Give 'em here. Quick, quick.'

'Hold on a tick,' Peggy said, giggling too. 'Your hair's coming unstuck.'

The two girls had met outside the side entrance to Madame Aimee's and they were preparing the first lark-about of the morning. They'd both painted black moust-aches on their upper lips with eyebrow pencil and they'd made their fringes wet and plastered them across their foreheads in two hideous cowlicks, and now as a finishing touch they were pinning on their armbands. They'd made two out of red wrapping paper with Nazi swastikas stuck to them drawn in black ink on two circles of white card-board. All jolly authentic. It was going to be a lark and a half.

'Come on, Adolf!' Megan said, peering through the glass of the door. 'They're all there.'

They could see Mr MacFarlane and the other girls already in the shop polishing the counters and uncovering the goods.

'Forvart!' Peggy instructed and the two of them giggled through the door and goose-stepped into the shop, giving the Hitler salute all the way and shouting 'Sieg Heil! Sieg Heil! Sieg Heil!'

They were an instant, squealing success.

'Och you bad, bad girls,' Mr MacFarlane said, pretend-ing to scold, but the hoots of laughter all round him were making him smile too much for anyone to take him seriously.

Megan and Peggy sent young Susie to keep a look out for Madame Aimee at the foot of the stairs, and then they broke into the song and dance routine they'd been practising the previous evening.

'Whistle while you work,' they chirruped, singing the chorus to the seven dwarfs song from Walt Disney's new film.

> 'Adolf Hitler is a twerp
> He's quite barmy, so's his army
> Whistle while you work.'

The catchy tune soon had all the other assistants singing along, Mr MacFarlane clapped in time to the rhythm and the two youngest girls began to dance round the counters. They were making such a noise that they almost missed Susie's warning whistle. In fact they were only just back behind the counters in time before Madame Aimee appeared at the top of the stairs, fierce of face and spine. Megan and Peggy were still cowlicked and moustachioed so they had to kneel on the carpet and pretend to be picking up pins to keep their faces hidden.

'Mr MacFarlane,' Madame Aimee said icily, 'a word if you please.' And she led the poor man into her sanctum, her skirts swishing disapproval. It was, as the two girls told one another afterwards, absolutely priceless, it really was. Even though they felt a bit sorry for poor old Mr Mac being nagged behind the frosted glass. 'It will not do George. You shouldn't encourage them. They're unruly enough without you making them worse.'

'Och, my dear, girrls will be girrls. We all need a wee bit of fun from time to time. There's no harm in being cheerful.'

'If they wish to be cheerful they may do it in their own time, not the firm's. What if a customer were to see such capers?'

'With rrespect, my love,' Mr MacFarlane tried, 'the doors are not yet open this morn ... '

'High time they were,' his love informed him, 'and let me tell you, if Miss Furnivall and Miss Griffiths are not in

244

a fit state to serve then I shall dock their pay. Ten minutes for every minute lost.'

But thanks to the liberal application of Peggy's cold cream and a quick flick of Megan's hair brush. Miss Furnivall and Miss Griffiths were demure behind their counters and ready for anything, even Madame Aimee. Which made the joke better than ever.

That evening the two friends went to the pictures, reliving their song and dance act all the way to the cinema. And all the way home. And outside the Earl Grey there was Jim Boxall glumly sipping ale with a group of men who used to work at Warrenders, so they told him all about it too.

'We've had a day an' a half, ain't we, Peg,' Megan chortled. 'Start with a laugh an' you never look back. That's what I say.'

'Hitler's no laughing matter,' Jim tried to tell her. The things that were going on in Germany were far beyond a joke now.

But she thumped him in the chest and laughed at him. 'Oh get on with you, you old kill-joy!' she teased.

There was just enough truth in the taunt to sting him. He'd had a dreadful day at the garage with two belligerent customers and a difficult wheel change, and now he had so little money in his pocket he couldn't even offer them a drink.

'He's a murderer,' he insisted. 'Not a comedian. He has people shot when they don't agree with him. Or put in prison. Jews get beaten up in streets just for being Jewish, didn't you know that? I can't see anything funny about him at all.'

'Oh-er!' Megan teased. 'Who's your friend, Peg?'

Peggy was still charged with the bubbling gaiety of the day. The last thing she wanted was to stand on the corner and talk politics, even to cheer Jim Boxall. 'Come on, Megan,' she said. 'I'll walk you to your door.' And they went giggling off along the street.

'Night night,' he called, as they swung away.

'Night night, Jim,' she called back, and she darted one glance at him over her shoulder before distance and darkness smudged her features.

245

After she'd turned the corner into Randall Place he wished he could have tried to enjoy their joke a bit more and cursed himself for being such a serious fool. 'Time I was off,' he said to his mates. There was no point in hanging around waiting for her to come back. He'd only make a fool of himself if he tried to talk to her again that night.

He walked dismally along the street to the door of number five. But as he fished his key through the letter-box, he heard a rumpus going on in the kitchen that put all other thoughts out of his mind.

His father's feet were stamping along the hall towards him as he opened the door.

'What sort 'a time d'you call this?' the old man yelled, breathing drunkenly. 'Oh it's you.'

'Who did you think it was?'

'That bloody girl.'

Lily or Pearl? Jim wondered as he walked through into the kitchen. But Pearl was sitting fearfully beside the stove, holding up a skein of wool in both hands for her mother to wind into a ball.

'She'll be home presently,' Mrs Boxall tried to placate. 'She's out with Arthur Walters,' she explained to Jim. 'You know Arthur Walters.'

'Oh well, that's all right then,' Jim said, more for his father's benefit than in answer to his mother. 'She won't come to any harm there. Nice bloke.' Arthur Walters was the accounts clerk at the shop where Lily worked and he'd been escorting her to the pictures for several months now. A quiet, kind, conscientious young man.

'I won't have it,' Mr Boxall grumbled. 'Coming home all hours. I won't have it.'

'Why don't you go on up to bed and let me see to her?' Mrs Boxall said.

But Mr Boxall settled himself massively in his chair. 'I'll see to her,' he threatened.

It was really rather nerve-racking waiting for the key. When they heard it they all jumped up, but Mr Boxall was on his feet and along the hall before any of them could intervene. They followed him, crowding into the hall as he yelled abuse at Lily. 'You dirty little trollop, what sort a'

246

time d'you call this?'

'It's not late, Dad,' Lily began, 'me an' Arthur ... '

But she didn't get any further because her father suddenly lashed out at her, punching her about the head with both hands and roaring like a bull in a stall.

Then the hall was full of movement, Lily running towards the kitchen bent double to avoid the blows, Pearl catching her in her arms, Jim leaping at his father to grab at one punching fist while someone else was grabbing at the other. Arthur, was it? And somebody crying and wailing, 'Oh don't. Please don't. Don't! Don't!'

'Upstairs,' Jim shouted to Arthur. But his father braced his feet against the bottom stair and refused to budge, flailing to shake off his captors. It was several confused seconds before the two young men could drag him into the kitchen and force him into his chair.

Lily was bathing her face in the scullery with Pearl standing guard at the door.

'Now then,' Arthur Walters said, speaking reasonably but holding Mr Boxall down with both hands gripped on his shoulders. 'We must come to a decision.'

Now that his anger was spent, Mr Boxall was rapidly lapsing into lethargy, beer clouding his mind and thickening his speech. 'What's 'at?' he said, trying to turn his head so that he could see who was talking. 'What you on about?'

'I'm on about you,' Arthur said, 'hitting my girlfriend. That's what I'm on about. I'm on about you lamming into the girl I'm going to marry.'

Mr Boxall didn't seem to understand what he was saying, but everyone else did.

'Are you really?' Pearl said, instantly cheered.

'Oh I'm so glad,' Mrs Boxall said.

And Lily walked out of the kitchen and held Arthur's arm. There were several ugly red bruises growing on the side of her face and she had the start of a black eye but she was glowing with pride.

'We were going to tell you later,' Arthur said, 'but now ... Well now, I think we ought to get married just as soon as ever we can. You obviously can't stay in a house with a man like that.'

The man like that was snoring.

'Quite right,' Jim said, giving his approval. 'You get out of it, Sis. Best thing all round.'

'How will you manage?' Mrs Boxall worried. 'Have you got anywhere to live?'

'I shall talk it over with my Mum and Dad,' Arthur told her. For a quiet unobtrusive young man he was handling all this extremely well. 'We shall manage somehow. But if you think I'm going to leave my Lily to be punched about, well ...'

Then Lily threw herself into his arms and burst into tears and said he was the dearest man alive and she'd marry him tomorrow.

And Arthur told her to get her hat and coat and pack a few things because he was taking her home to his parents.

'I shall marry her as soon as ever I can,' he told Jim as Lily was kissing her mother goodbye. 'You'll sign the consent form, won't you, if the old man won't oblige?'

'Forge it, d'you mean?' Jim asked, delighted by his daring. Whoever would have thought it of quiet Arthur Walters?

But in the event no forgery was necessary, even though the wedding was arranged within a fortnight because Arthur soon found somewhere to live. His parents rented a three-storey house in Thames Street, which had been scheduled for slum clearance for several years. There was plenty of room in it even if it was always damp and often bug infested.

'You're welcome here if you like,' his mother said, when she'd heard their story. 'You could have the two top rooms, couldn't they, Percy? You'd have to cook for yourselves on the fire, but I dare say you could manage that, 'til you find something better.'

So the banns were called and Mr Boxall signed his consent as if there had never been a row. Soon he was telling the neighbours that he was all for it, and when the wedding day arrived on a warm June Saturday with Pearl and Peggy and three-year-old Yvonne as bridesmaids he spent the afternoon strutting about the street as though he'd arranged it all.

He reverted to type within ten short days, roaring at his

wife because she'd forgotten to buy his bottled beer and lashing out at Pearl for 'being in the bloody way'.

Fortunately, having talked it all over in advance with Lily and Arthur, Pearl now knew exactly what to do about it. She kissed her mother, packed her bag and left the house without a word. By the time Jim came home from the garage half an hour later, she was settled in at Thames Street in the little back room on the first floor that used to be the nursery.

'Bloody ridiculous,' Mr Boxall grumbled, when he was sober enough to understand what had happened. 'What she want to go an' do a thing like that for?'

Neither his wife nor his son enlightened him, she because she wouldn't dare, Jim because he had something more important to consider.

For several years, ever since they'd started work in fact, he and his sisters had been clubbing together to pay the rent, because their mother rarely had enough money left over at the end of the week to cover it. Now, with both girls gone it looked as though he would have to pay the entire rent himself and that was going to be an intolerable burden, besides being grossly unfair, because although he didn't mind looking after his mother he saw no reason why he should fork out for the old man as well. No, the time had come for Mum to make up her mind to leave. She could take a nice little flat, somewhere cheap that he could afford, and then he'd settle her in all nice and cosy, and he and the girls would take responsibility for her.

'There,' he said with great satisfaction when he'd found a suitable flat and explained his plans to his mother. 'What d'you think? Place of your own. No more rows. Steady money. What d'you think?'

Her response was a terrible disappointment. She went on clearing the cloth in her stooping methodical way as though what he'd just told her wasn't important. 'You're a good lad,' she said, smiling at him. 'You mean well. But I can't do it.'

'Why ever not?' he said. It hadn't occurred to him that she might refuse and the surprise of it was most unpleasant.

'I married him,' his mother tried to explain.

249

'People get divorced.'

'Not our sort, Jimmy. Divorce is for the nobs.'

'Well you could leave him then. What's to stop you?' What was the matter with her? She was being really silly. She ought to have jumped at it.

'Once you're married,' his mother tried again, 'it's sort of difficult. You can't just up sticks when times get hard.'

'Get hard?' he queried. 'I've never known 'em when they wasn't hard.'

'Well I dare say,' she said vaguely, straightening the chenille table cloth and not looking at him. 'That's how it is though. Can't say no different.'

'So you won't leave him,' he said and he sounded as exasperated as he felt. 'You won't take this flat.'

'No,' she said sadly.

'He'll knock you about.'

'Very likely.'

'Don't you care?'

'Not much good caring. You got ter put up with it.'

'I don't understand you,' he said, throwing up his hands in exasperation.

'You will in time,' she sighed. 'You're young yet. Don't let's talk no more about it, eh?'

She'd put her head to one side in the placatory gesture he knew so well, an unspoken plea for gentleness and acceptance that was so familiar he'd responded to it before he could stop himself. 'All right,' he said, 'but ... '

She put one finger on his lips. 'Shush' she begged. 'Jimmy dear, shush.'

So he shushed. But it upset him terribly and occupied his thoughts all through the following day. To have planned for this moment for so long only to have it rejected out of hand was very painful. It took him the rest of the day to come to terms with it, to grow through it until he could accept that his mother had a life of her own over which he had no power at all and that although he only dimly understood her reasons he had to let her live as she saw fit. It was a sobering day and one in which he matured from idealistic boy to thinking man.

When work was over he took his dog-eared advertisement out of his pocket and considered it, for the umpteenth time that summer. The garage job was a dead-end. There was no denying that. And he couldn't really help her much whether he stayed or went. If he did join the RAF at least the pay would provide her with occasional money for clothes and shoes. It would mean leaving his friends and Peggy Furnivall too, but after that one extraordinary day at the seaside they'd fallen back into their old neighbourly ways and he couldn't see any hope of anything better. Look at the way she was that evening outside the Earl Grey. It would also mean that he'd be joining the armed forces and preparing for war, which after all he'd heard from Mr Cooper was hardly something to be undertaken lightly. But the war was coming, everybody knew that, and when it came he would be involved in it sooner or later anyway. So why not take action now, as the posters were urging? Take action now and be ready when the time comes.

In the end he asked for an afternoon off from the garage and went up to the RAF recruiting office in Kingsway to sign on. It was a peaceful summer's day, an irony that wasn't lost on him, and he was welcomed with drawling enthusiasm.

'Just the sort of chap we're looking for,' the officer said, leaning back in his chair. 'Just fill in this form will you.'

The form was filled in and the putative airman sent home to await 'the next step', which turned out to be a routine medical examination and a written test, both of which he passed with ease. Then it was simply a matter of waiting to be 'called'.

His family took the news in predictable ways. His father ignored it, his sisters kissed him and teased him about being a hero, and his mother wept a little and said she was 'proud as Punch'.

But Peggy seemed to be rather upset by it. 'Does that mean you'll have to go away?' she asked.

''Fraid so,' he said, almost as laconically as the recruiting officer, 'unless they train airmen by correspondence course.' She looked quite cast down. Was she going to miss him, he thought, hardly daring to hope so, but hoping so just the same.

First Lily and then Pearl and now Jim, Peggy was

thinking. I shan't have any friends left in the road. But she tried to be encouraging. 'It's a good life, so they say,' she observed, keeping her voice light. 'When are you going?'

'Oh not for ages yet,' he said, hiding his disappointment. She wasn't going to miss him after all. 'All sorts of things could happen before they call me.'

The first of the expected wars broke out ten days later. On 3 October the papers were full of the news that the Italians had invaded Abyssinia. Later that week the first newsreel shots of the fighting were shown at the local cinema.

Flossie and Mrs Roderick were appalled at what they saw. And they weren't the only ones. At the ding-dong that Saturday the talk was all about dropping bombs and using gas against unarmed civilians.

'They're just a lot of blackies with spears,' Gideon said. 'Don't stand an earthly. Not against bombers.'

'No more would we, come to that,' Flossie said. 'It made my flesh creep, Gid.'

'It's the gas,' Mrs Roderick said. 'You just imagine if they was to use gas.'

'Nothing worse,' Mr Cooper agreed. 'Now d'you see why we mustn't have a war?' He was so anguished by the thought that another war might begin that he'd even persuaded one of his old comrades to push his wheelchair at the head of an anti-war rally. There'd been several in London during the last couple of months, quiet and sober and very well-attended, but still nobody was taking any notice. 'You can't say we don't know what gas does. Not after the last lot.'

Peggy was thinking about Yvonne and little Norman. 'If they dropped gas,' she said, 'what would happen to the kids?'

'Same as happened to the poor bloody infantry,' Mr Cooper said bitterly. 'They'd have their lungs burnt out and their tongues covered in sores. They'd choke to death.' He was too upset to protect his neighbours by silence. This was too important. It had to be talked about.

'Now Mussolini's started it won't be long before Hitler starts too,' Mr Allnutt said. 'He's been making enough noise about the Rhineland.' Which was horribly true, for the Führer had been making one ranting speech after another insisting that the Rhineland should be 'returned to Germany'. 'I reckon if we don't give it to him he'll send his troops in and take it anyway.'

'You were right about that Hitler,' Peggy said to Jim as the bitter talk went on. 'I reckon you'll be glad to get into the RAF.'

'Yes,' he agreed. 'I think I shall.'

CHAPTER 20

Jim Boxall never forgot his first sight of RAF Uxbridge. For someone who until then had never travelled further than a charabanc trip to Brighton, the journey had been an excitement in itself, by tram to London Bridge and then through the complications of the tube to Uxbridge, which looked an open countrified sort of place after the hemmed-in streets of Greenwich. He was in a state of such powerful and complicated emotions that every detail of the day was etched into his mind as if it were red hot.

Outside the station he found that he was one of a group of about twenty men all clutching travel warrants and smoking cheap cigarettes and trying to look as though they knew where they were going. They were too ill at ease and embarrassed to greet one another but fortunately after four or five shuffling minutes a lorry trundled up to take them on the last leg. They were herded aboard, and began to introduce themselves to one another. Jim learned that his two immediate neighbours were called Froggy and Jock but he was too excited to remember any of the others, and in any case it didn't seem any time at all before they'd arrived.

One minute they were rocking along an empty country lane between bare trees and scrubby hedges, joking to one another about the 'rotten bus service', the next they were gazing up into the white sky where a small silver biplane was descending gently and purposefully straight towards them. They could see the red, white and blue markings on its tail fin, the roundel on its side, its red nose cone, even the helmeted head of the pilot. It gave them an undeniable thrill. The RAF, Jim thought. I'm in the RAF now. There's no going back.

Then the lorry swung in through the gates and deposited them at the guard house. And the RAF engulfed them. There were men in uniform everywhere they looked, walking briskly among long rows of wooden huts, or being marched about in well-drilled columns in a central square. The noise was incessant, drill corporals yelling, boots crunching gravel, hands slapping rifles, butts thwacking ground. There was even a side-drum clicking somewhere out of sight.

They stood in line outside the guard room as a roll was called and learned to say 'Yes, Sergeant' in answer to their names. Then they were marched off to another hut and put in the charge of a corporal called Waller, who was short and dark and looked uncomfortably belligerent, which as they soon discovered was only to be expected when his nickname on the camp was Shit-house Wallah and his favourite form of punishment was latrine duty.

'This is East Camp,' he shouted at them. 'Those are your bunks, which you will keep clean, neat and tidy at all times. Now follow me.'

They spent the rest of the day being marched about and standing in queues. They queued for everything, to be given their service number and identity disks, for a medical which Jim found acutely embarrassing, to be issued with their kit which took hours, to be given their inoculations which were very painful, and at last, when they were all bewildered and exhausted they stood in yet another queue to be allowed to enter the mess hall.

Here they were ushered to a long table where they sat eight to a side and in complete silence, as though they were back at school. But the food was very welcome after such a day and when the orderlies wheeled their trolleys in from the kitchen and a meaty steam rose from the galvanized iron trays, Jim could have cheered with relief.

'Blimey! What a day!' Froggy said, when they were finally allowed back to the hut 'to get some kip'. He was an odd-looking chap with thin mouse-brown hair and bulging eyes and the widest mouth Jim had ever seen, but he'd stayed irrepressibly cheerful all through their long day and he was still grinning even then.

'A day an' a half,' Jim agreed, taking off his new boots and rubbing his heels.

'D'ye reckon there'll be anythin' left for us tay do tomorrow?' Jock said.

'Plenty,' Jim said. 'You could lay money on it.'

'I'm sick of queueing,' Froggy complained, grinning again.

And that got a chorus of agreement from every new recruit in the hut.

During the next few days they learned that the camp was so overcrowded that they would have to queue for everything. It became a normal part of their lives, like the interminable square bashing, an initiation that had to be endured before they could be considered airmen. Froggy and Jim rapidly became 'oppos'. They soon discovered that they shared the same taste in literature, had both studied history and economics and had the same dry sense of humour. And the more they talked to one another the closer friends they became.

Later that week Jim wrote four postcards, one each to his mother and his two sisters, and as a considered after-thought one to Peggy. 'We shall be square bashing for three months,' he told her. 'I shall be glad when it's over I can tell you. It's worse than the gym we had to do at school. At least we didn't have to do that in army boots. The grub's good, plenty of it and served hot. I've had a haircut that makes me look like a fugitive from a chain-gang. Give my love to the kids. Look after yourself, Love Jim.'

The sight of his familiar writing on that postcard made Peggy feel peculiarly lonely. She missed his presence next door more than she'd imagined she would. From time to time when she heard Mr Boxall shouting abuse or throwing things about, she found herself thinking of the old days when Jim hid his library books in her bedroom and brought fish for old Tabby and Tom, and it seemed to her that there was a huge empty pit yawning in the emptiness next door.

And when she came down to light the stove one bitter January morning and found her poor Tabby lying cold and dead by the hearth, with Tom sitting puzzled guard beside her, the emptiness yawned wider than ever, for Jim would have understood what a wrenching loss it was and now she had to endure it on her own.

He wrote her the most tender letter, pointing out that she'd given the old cat a good life and let her have lots of kittens and that if she hadn't rescued her from the farm she would certainly have died long ago. 'And you've got Tom, don't forget.'

Which was all true, Peggy thought, reading the letter with Tom curled companionably on her lap, but the loneliness remained.

And it continued even when he came home on leave in March, for he spent all day in Thames Street with Lily and Pearl, and in the evenings he went to the pub with Mr Cooper and Arthur Walters, and although he walked down to the market with them all on Saturday evening and was marvellous handsome company at the ding-dong, he spent most of his time talking about the camp and his new friends there, which was understandable but disappointing, or discussing the German occupation of the Rhineland which was understandable but alarming.

By the time his leave was up and she and Mrs Geary were waving him goodbye from the upstairs window she knew how much she was going to miss him this time and how much she'd valued his company before he went away. Apart from Joan, on the rare occasions when she wasn't too worried about Sid and the children, there was no one she could talk to the way she'd always talked to Jim Boxall.

The thought made her sigh.

'You'll miss him,' Mrs Geary said.

'Yes. I shall.'

'Pity you can't go with him.'

'What, join the RAF you mean?'

That wasn't what Mrs Geary meant, but the old lady had the good sense to keep her meaning to herself. There's no point saying anything now, she thought. It'll only make the poor kid miss him more than ever, and she's got

257

enough on her plate with her mother going on about her nerves all the time and that Baby flibbertigibbeting. And anyway it don't look as if the penny's dropped yet. Next time maybe.

But next time wasn't for another two months and then it was only a thirty-six hour pass between one course and the next and he was so excited by his success he couldn't stop talking about it.

He'd passed his five week course for 'Fitter's Mate' and now he was qualified to train as a flight mechanic. Froggy had failed the course, which was a great disappointment to both of them because it meant that they would have to part company, but they both knew that he would soon find something else and they'd promised to keep in touch.

'I'm posted to Henlow,' Jim said to Peggy and Flossie and Mrs Geary at that night's ding-dong. 'Report back Sunday night. Now I shall be servicing planes.' He was bristling with excitement, his dark hair thicker than they'd ever seen it, and his eyes shining.

They're exactly the same blue as his uniform, Peggy thought, admiring them, and he's so broad-shouldered now he's put on a bit of weight. And suddenly, for a brief dizzying second, she wished she could put her arms round his neck and kiss him. The feeling was so strong she was quite shaken by it. She wanted to kiss him, to stand as close to him as she could possibly get and hold him tight and kiss him. Oh dear oh dear, how awful. If she didn't watch out she'd end up being really fast, if she could feel things as quickly and strongly as that, and all for no reason. What a good job thoughts are private. She turned away and stopped looking at him so as to give herself a chance to calm down, and Baby came swishing across the room in her new crêpe de Chine blouse and hung onto his arm and fluttered her eyelashes at him in that infuriating way of hers.

'How's our handsome airman, all in his gorgeous uniform?' she said, clinging so hard she sent his arm downwards.

'Thirsty,' he said, finishing off his beer and dislodging her hand in the process. How unattractive she was with that dyed hair and that awful lisp she would put on. Not like Peggy, who was beautiful in her quiet way, even if she wasn't spangled with sunshine. And the memory of their day in Brighton washed back into his mind bringing desire with it. If only she was interested in me, he thought, but she was walking away from him, talking to Joan and Mrs Geary. And he remembered how embarrassed she'd been at the pictures that time, and that brought a familiar sinking of heart and desire.

'How's the Royal Air Force?' Mr Cooper said turning from the piano at the end of his tune.

'Posted to Henlow,' Jim said, relieved to be back on safe territory again.

That night he dreamed he was swimming in the sea with Peggy in his arms, and that they were making love under the water where no one could see them.

And that night Peggy was dreaming too, walking on a floating cloudway with her arms about a man she knew was her beloved, who was sometimes Jim, which was wonderful and easy, and sometimes a faceless, shapeless man, which was horrible and made her feel afraid. How stupid dreams are, she rebuked herself when she woke, and she got up at once to shake it out of her memory. It's no good thinking about Jim in that way. No good at all. And she thought how embarrassed he'd be if he knew about it and resolved never to tell him or anyone else.

When she said goodbye to him over the garden fence later that afternoon she managed to be perfectly calm and friendly without a trace of silliness.

'Write to me,' she said, 'and tell me how you get on.'

'I will,' he promised.

It wasn't the sort of letter to keep tied in pink ribbon.

'The U/T Flight Mechanics, that's us,' he wrote, 'are in the old station as No 5 wing and the U/T Flight Riggers are in some new huts they've put up as No 2 wing. The course will last eight months and it's thorough. They are giving us all the gen, engine-fitting, handling and servicing, working carbon and alloy steels, ferrous metals and their heat treatments, various tools, taps and dies, drills, taper pins, pitch diameters, root thread, morse taper. You name it we do it. Yesterday we stripped down a Jupiter from a Bulldog and next week we shall be stripping a Kestrel from a Hart. Look after yourself. Love, Jim.'

There you are, Peggy told herself sternly, he's not interested in me. Not in that way. I'm a friend and neighbour, that's all, and I'll have to be content with that. Still at least he didn't seem to be interested in any one else and that was some consolation, for she knew now that she would be jealous if he was. Look at the way she'd felt when Baby was being so silly trying to flirt with him. If only he hadn't gone into the RAF. Oh damn this war, she thought. I wish it would either hurry up and start or go away altogether.

It was an ambivalent wish but one that was shared by a good many people in London that summer, particularly as the news from the Continent was always so bad, and particularly as it invariably brought changes. In May Hitler's friend Mussolini announced that he had annexed Abyssinia, and in July a Spanish friend of his called General Franco led an uprising against the Spanish government. The newsreels were soon showing pictures of the uprising and horribly upsetting they were, of rifles firing and terrified civilians caught in the middle of a gun-battle with nowhere to hide.

Flossie said it stopped her heart beating she was so frightened, and certainly her trip to the cinema that week was followed by three days of constant nerves and bad temper.

'If a war comes here we shall all be killed,' she said. 'Why doesn't someone do something to stop them? What's the good of a League of Nations if they never do anything?'

A fortnight later something *was* done, although she didn't approve of that either.

In amongst the advertisements for bricklayers and plumbers and carpenters in the local newspaper was a plea for part-time workers to assemble civilian gasmasks.

This time it was Mrs O'Donavan who took up the offer, leaving her seven small children in the care of the eldest girl still at home.

'It's horrid work, so it is,' she told her neighbours, 'but you've got to make the effort, have ye not? I couldn't stand by and see the poor souls lying gassed in their beds and me doing nothing to save them. Not after all those poor Abyssinians.'

'Gas masks!' Flossie snorted. 'I never heard such nonsense. Haven't they got anything better to do with their time than frighten us all? That won't do any good. It'll only make people run away.'

Two of Mrs Roderick's wealthiest customers agreed with her. That summer they sold up their London homes and went to live in the country. Flossie said she could quite understand it, but Mrs Roderick was aggrieved.

'Such cowardice,' she said. 'I thought they were made of sterner stuff.'

'I suppose it's hard to know what they're made of,' Peggy said to Megan, when the two of them were gossiping in the shop. 'Not when they're packed inside those great stiff corsets she sells them.'

'They all look the same to me,' Megan grinned. 'Like the Chinese. I can't tell 'em apart.'

'It won't help our trade if they're all going to run away,' Peggy said.

But Madame Aimee's sales didn't drop and the next pair of runaways were the poorest couple in Paradise Row.

Peggy woke one night later that month to hear Mrs Geary hobbling about in her room next door. She got up at once to see what was the matter and found the old lady sitting by the window watching the road through her mirror.

'Shush!' she whispered when Peggy came in. 'Don't make a sound. They're doing a moonlight.'

'Who is?'

'Next door. The Boxalls. Come an' have a butcher's.'

In the pale blue light from the full moon they could see a wooden handcart propped up beside the kerb. It was loaded with old chairs and pots and pans and kettles and an assortment of badly-rolled rag rugs. Mrs Boxall was trying to push a cardboard box into the muddle.

'They're owing two weeks' rent,' Mrs Geary said. 'She was telling me. I knew this would happen once young Jim went away.'

'Why,' Peggy whispered. 'Did he pay the rent?' But she realized as she asked the question that of course he'd paid

261

it. It was just the sort of thing he would do.

The flit was over in twenty minutes for poor Mrs Boxall had very few belongings to move and Mr Boxall was frantic to be off.

'Where are they going?' Peggy asked as the two bent figures trundled their cart down the road towards the pub. 'She didn't say,' Mrs Geary whispered. 'Lily'll know. Time we was getting back to bed. It's parky sitting here. You wouldn't be a love an' just pop down an' get me some fresh water would you? I'd go mesself only these legs are giving me gyp.'

'Two rooms down by the gasworks,' Lily told them when she came visiting that Saturday. 'Nasty pokey little rooms they are. Ought to be slum clearance. I'm so cross. All these years we've kept her comfy and now see what's happened. He can't even manage the rent.'

'Your poor Mum,' Peggy commiserated. 'Is she all right?'

'She says she is,' Lily said. 'But I don't know.'

'Have you told Jim?' Peggy asked. 'He'll be upset.'

'Now that's a funny thing,' Lily said. 'I sent him a post-card straight away, 'cos that's what I thought too and he wrote me back a most peculiar letter.'

'Peculiar?' Peggy echoed. 'What was peculiar?'

'He said we was all adults now an' we all had to make our own decisions an' live our own lives.'

'That's not like Jim,' Peggy agreed, wondering at it.

'He said he'd go over and see how she was next time he gets leave and sent his love an' all that sort a' thing but ...' She looked perplexed, her blue eyes troubled.

'What'll happen to next door?' Peggy said deciding to change the subject. 'Will you an' Arthur take it?' That'ud be lovely. To have Pearl and Lily next door again and without their awful father.

'I asked him,' Lily said, 'and he says we could just about afford it, but he couldn't bear it. Not to live in the same house where Dad was always lammin' into us. He says it would remind him. You got to see his point.'

So she and Arthur and Pearl stayed where they were for the time being and Peggy's two new neighbours were a couple of elderly men who ran a small flower shop off the

High Street. They were called Mr Crosier and Mr Budleigh but were soon known to everyone by their Christian names, which were Leslie and Ernest.

Peggy wrote a full description of them to entertain Jim. 'They're a funny looking pair. Ernest is a big man and rather fat and he's got long straight white hair and he wears wrinkly jumpers and sagging trousers, and Leslie is short and ever so neat, quite dapper really, with a toothbrush moustache and an army haircut. Never a hair out of place. They're as quiet as church mice most of the time and then they suddenly break out into a screaming row and rush about the house slamming doors. Then it all goes quiet and they're back to being mice again. Leslie threw his dinner into the garden yesterday and I'm sure I could hear poor Ernest crying afterwards. They've put up net curtains and scrubbed the front step and now they're clearing all the rubbish out of the garden and planting dahlias in the flowerbeds. Imagine that.'

'I shan't know the place,' Jim wrote back.

There were other changes in the road too. Just after Leslie and Ernest moved in, the electricity board arrived to instal electricity in all the houses. Mrs Roderick didn't like it because she said electric light was bad for the eyes, but Mrs Geary and Mr Allnutt were delighted, he because he could now use an electric soldering iron, 'think of all the useful jobs I can do with that', she because she could buy one of the new wireless sets that you plugged into the mains.

In August, while Hitler was prancing about at his Olympic Games in Berlin, two more changes came to Greenwich. The clearance of the slums in Thames Street finally got underway and a block of splendid new flats began to rise in Creek Road.

And in September Mr Bertie Allnutt took a job in Slough in one of the new firms that the government had commissioned to make aircraft parts. It was much better paid than the job he'd been doing in Deptford and it gave him the chance to buy his own house like one of the nobs. After a cheerful farewell ding-dong, he and his family left Paradise Row in high spirits and a battered van. Now there was another empty house in the street and this time

263

Arthur and Lily took it on, with Pearl as their lodger to help them out with the rent.

Peggy thought it was lovely to have them back and even lovelier when Lily told her that she was expecting in the spring. 'Does Jim know?' she asked.

'Not yet,' Lily said. 'I'll tell him Christmas time. They must let him home for Christmas this year surely. Now he's got somewhere to stay.' Last Christmas he'd have been on his own in the house with Mum and Dad, and Dad was always at his most disagreeable at Christmas time, so they could all see why he wouldn't have wanted that.

But in the middle of December he wrote to both his sisters and to Peggy to tell them that he was half-way through the course and would be staying on camp until it was finished. 'I shall have some leave in the spring,' he said. 'Just think. When you next see me I shall be a fully-qualified Flight Mechanic.'

The letter made Peggy feel bleak. This would be his second Christmas away from home and he didn't seem to mind. He never said he missed – well – any of them. Not that he should. There was no reason why he should. But it would have been so nice if he had.

But his sister answered her letter cheerfully. 'When you next see *me*,' she wrote, 'I shall be a fully-qualified mother.'

'That'll bring him if nothing else does,' she said to Peggy and Pearl.

The three of them were busy in the kitchen of number two making a shepherd's pie. Peggy had been invited to supper that evening and had accepted on condition she was allowed to help with the cooking.

'Seamus O'Donavan's got a job making gasmasks with his mum,' Pearl told them. She was mincing onions and weeping copiously.

'I'd've thought they'd got enough of the things by now,' Lily said.

'We're all to have one,' Peggy said, adding milk to the mashed potatoes, 'so the paper says.'

'I wish it wouldn't,' Lily said. 'It's enough to give you the creeps all this talk of war and gasmasks and bombs and everything.'

'It makes you wonder what'll happen next,' Pearl said, wiping her eyes.

'My baby'll happen next,' Lily said, patting her belly.

But she was wrong.

That spring when the sky was pleasantly blue, the market stalls were yellow with daffodils and the gardens round the park were bold with the bloom of white and purple lilac and the long golden ringlets of laburnum, the newsreels were full of monochrome horror.

A little market town in Spain had been bombed by Franco's German aeroplanes. It was called Guernica and the day Franco had chosen for its destruction was market day when its streets would be crowded with shoppers. The newsreels showed horrific shots of men and women terribly injured, children screaming, houses blown to pieces, and bombs falling like grotesque eggs from the belly of terrible planes. 'Heinkels,' the commentator said, 'and Junkers.' The names were as ugly as the aircraft. The attack started at half past four in the afternoon, and from then on the town was bombed and machine-gunned by wave after wave of aircraft flying in every twenty minutes until a quarter to eight. There was nothing to stop them and nowhere to hide. The carnage was dreadful.

This time Flossie came home from the cinema in a state of collapse and took to her bed for the next two days, prostrated with nerves, which Mrs Roderick said was hardly to be wondered at. 'Showing such things,' she said angrily, 'in the middle of the afternoon when you're not expecting it. It ought not to be allowed.'

But Peggy was profoundly moved by what she'd seen.

'I feel I should be doing something about it,' she wrote to Jim, 'only I don't know what.'

'Cheer up,' he wrote back. 'We're developing a plane that will be more than an answer to the Heinkels, if we can get enough of them built in time.'

He had meant it to be an encouraging letter but Peggy was cast down by it. What if we can't get them built in time? she thought. And for several weeks her dreams were riven with the scream of falling bombs and the terror of children she couldn't help.

But then Lily's baby was born, a small skinny boy with

a bald head and his father's face. He was called Percy after his paternal grandfather and Lily declared him the prettiest baby alive, but Mrs Geary told Peggy privately that she thought he looked 'like a skinned rabbit, poor little beggar. Though I dare say he'll grow out of it in time. They usually do.'

Jim came home briefly for the christening and stayed at number two with his sisters, which he said was quite a treat even if young Percy did spend rather a lot of the night crying to be fed. 'But I dare say he'll grow out of it,' he said to Peggy.

There were rather a lot of things for this baby to grow out of, and his skin wasn't one of them. He remained thin and fretful for the first six months of his life, putting on weight very slowly and to the continual concern of his mother and father. But at last he was strong enough to sit up in a high chair and take mouthfuls of lightly boiled egg or a spoonful of custard. And that was such a relief to Lily that she grew quite lightheaded.

'Now he's sitting up he'll be a different child,' she promised. 'We shall have him dancing at the ding-dong in no time.'

That December the New Year ding-dong was held in the Earl Grey, because Mr Allnutt had had the flu and his wife said he was to give himself a chance to recover instead of rushing about organizing a party.

'No one'll mind,' she said. 'You'll see.'

And nobody did. Although the party had quite a different flavour. They wore paper hats and sang the old songs but their hearts weren't in it. Perhaps it was because it had been such a difficult year with the threat of war so close and so many people in the street involved in war-work in one way or another.

Mrs Roderick said she'd be jolly glad to see the back of it. '1937,' she said. 'What with one thing and another, it's been a perfectly dreadful year. Almost as bad as '36.'

'Has it?' Baby said, examining her red nail-varnish. 'I thought it was all right. Not exactly thrilling but all right. You had a coronation.'

'Oh yes,' Mrs Roderick agreed heavily. 'We had the coronation but think what we had to endure beforehand, with the Prince of Wales such a disappointment to us.'

'Oh that,' Baby said, dismissively.

'Yes, that,' Mrs Roderick told her. 'It isn't even two years since poor old King George passed away, and if you ask me it's just as well he did when you consider what's been going on ever since. The poor man must be turning in his grave. Turning in his grave.'

'Yes well ... ' Baby said, trying to get away.

But Mrs Roderick was determined to give vent to her grievance. She held on to Baby's skirt and continued with her lecture. 'To get himself mixed up with an American was bad enough,' she said, 'but a married woman, like that Mrs Simpson. Well really! And she's so ugly. You could understand it if she was a beauty. Fancy giving up the throne of England for a woman like that. I can't imagine what he sees in her. She looks as though she's been run over by a bus.'

'Yes, well ... ' Baby said again, sending frantic glances to her mother to be rescued.

'And now there's his poor brother got to be king and I'm sure I don't know how he'll make out stuttering the way he does, poor man. I think it's a scandal.'

'Yes,' Baby decided to agree. 'It is. Shall I get you another drink, Mrs Roderick? That glass looks jolly empty.'

Over by the piano Uncle Gideon was talking about the Spanish Civil War to Mr Allnutt and Mr Cooper.

'A bad business,' Mr Allnutt was saying, sympathizing with the Spanish government. 'They won't be able to hold out against Franco much longer, not with Hitler sending him planes and guns. We could've stopped that, surely to goodness.'

'It's a rehearsal,' Mr Cooper said. 'That's what it is. They're testing all those planes. Trying 'em out for the real thing when they invade Hungary or Austria or poor old Czechoslovakia.'

How boring they all are, Baby thought. I wish Jim was here. And she remembered again how jolly good-looking he was in his uniform and wondered whether he'd got himself a girl out on his RAF base. She didn't actually fancy him herself because he was more like a big brother really, but he was useful to flirt with and she didn't want someone else to have him.

Flossie was grumbling to old Mrs Allnutt that it was perfectly dreadful the way the government was going on. 'Making gasmasks,' she grumbled, 'building aeroplanes. You'd think they want a war. Why don't they go over and talk to that Hitler, that's what I want to know? Talk to him and make him stop all these awful things he's doing. That's what they ought to do. He's only a silly little man when all's said and done.'

Peggy was sitting by herself in a corner alone with her thoughts. We are all drifting, she thought, drifting nearer and nearer to a war we don't want and we can't avoid. It was futile and terrible and inevitable and it made her want to cry. Whatever 1938 had to offer, she was sure it would be difficult and painful.

CHAPTER 21

'Aye. It's serious,' Mr MacFarlane said. 'There's no way oot of that.'

The morning's copy of the *Daily Herald* lay on the counter before him. 'Czechoslovakia crisis,' it said. 'Chamberlain flies to Germany. Hitler speaks.'

'That's all we ever hear,' Megan complained. 'Hitler speaks. Hitler speaks tomorrow. Hitler speaks Wednesday. Speech by Hitler. And where is this Sizzek place anyway? I can't see why it's so important.'

'It's important, lassie, because we might have to go to war to protect it.'

'Well that's daft if you ask me,' Megan said. 'What's it got to do with us?'

'Do you think we will, Mr MacFarlane?' another girl asked. 'Go to war I mean.' There was no larking about this morning. The news was far too grave for that.

'I dearrly hope not,' Mr MacFarlane said. 'Perhaps Mr Chamberlain will make them see a wee bit sense.'

'Until all this started I'd never even heard of the place,' Megan said. 'It can't be *that* important.'

'It's half past eight, Mr MacFarlane,' Peggy pointed out. 'Madame Aimee'll be down any minute. Did we ought to open the doors?' The conversation was upsetting her because she knew in her bones that this crisis was horribly important. It was the only one that had stayed on the front page of the newspapers day after day, and it had been going on all through the summer.

'Oh aye,' Mr MacFarlane agreed, looking round nervously for his wife. 'Chop chop, girrls. And currrtesy and efficiency remember.'

It had been a glorious summer. Even now, in the middle of September and with the autumn approaching, the days were warm and easy. And yet London was a city preparing to be bombed. Every day brought changes and all of them alarming. Long ugly slit trenches were being dug in all the public parks, and brick sheds labelled 'Air Raid Shelter' were being erected on several street corners, while important buildings like banks had already been barricaded behind mounds of sandbags. And last week they'd all been issued with gasmasks, which looked and smelt quite terrifying and were the clearest and most unavoidable sign that the authorities thought that war was inevitable.

'It *is* coming, ain't it?' Peggy said to Mr MacFarlane as Megan sped to open the doors.

'Aye. I fear so, lassie. If our Prime Minister cannae prevail.'

'It makes me feel helpless,' Peggy said. 'I wish there was something I could do.'

He looked at her thoughtfully, stroking his moustache with his forefinger. 'Do you?' he said.

'Yes. I do.'

'Even if it were dangerous?'

She thought about that for a while, then she said 'Yes' again.

'You could join the ARP if you'd a mind,' he said.

'Would they have me?' Peggy asked. She'd heard of the ARP, the organization to provide Air Raid Precautions. Who hadn't in those jittery times? But it hadn't occurred to her that she might be eligible to join them. Join the ARP. Now that *was* a good idea. And just the right sort of thing for a soldier's daughter, born in the Tower.

'I could introduce you,' Mr MacFarlane offered, 'if you'd a mind. I've – ah – been a part-time warden, d'ye see, for quite a wee while now.'

It was a characteristically modest understatement. He'd been a member of the ARP for over eighteen months, as Peggy found out when she met him that evening at the

Wardens' Post on the corner of Billingsgate Street. And on his recommendation she was received with open arms and a cup of strong tea.

The post was actually somebody's front room and there were eight people already crowded into it, five men and three women. They all told her their names but she was so nervous she forgot them as soon as they were spoken, except for a small dark-haired woman who was called Joan, which was easy to remember, and the Chief Warden who was called Charlie Goodall. She was given a tin hat with W painted on the front, a whistle, a form to fill in, and an ARP respirator which was a lot bulkier than the one she had at home but smelt just the same. Then her name was added to a duty list.

'If it came to it,' the Chief Warden told her, 'we'd want you on duty for two evenings a week for about three hours. I'll take you on a tour of the local shelters after the talk. Show you the ropes. We have talks most weeks, various topics, a' course, black out, blast, gas, that sort a' thing.' He was very casual about it all, as if they were preparing for a Boy Scout outing. But that reassured her.

'Tonight's gas,' the woman called Joan told her as they drank their tea. 'You come with Mr MacFarlane, didn't you?'

'Our Mr MacFarlane's a tower of strength,' the Chief Warden said. 'Speaking of which, there's a demonstration of one of them new barrage balloons tomorrow afternoon. Anyone free to go?'

Nobody answered although he looked at them all one after another.

'Well I could,' Peggy volunteered, 'if you like. Seeing it's early closing.'

'Capital,' the Chief Warden said. 'Right. That's settled then.'

'What do you want me to do?'

'Oh just watch it. See what they're like. See what you think of 'em. That sort of thing. They've asked us to send someone along. It's a courtesy really.'

There was a rustle of interest near the door, a newcomer arriving.

'Our speaker,' the Chief Warden said and set off to welcome him.

271

Peggy followed him. 'Um – excuse me,' she said politely. 'You ain't told me where it is.'

'No more I have,' the Chief Warden laughed. 'That's me all over. Two o'clock at the Tower.'

'The Tower of London?'

'That's the place. D'you know how to get there?'

The Tower, Peggy thought, and her heart expanded with affection at the memory of it. The dear old Tower. 'Oh yes. I know how to get there.'

The pleasure of it sustained her through the first five minutes of the talk, while the speaker, who was a mild-mannered man with a slight lisp, embarked upon a list of the 'known gases used in warfare'. But when he got to phosgene and was describing its effects, the horror of what he was saying pulled her into the present with a jolt. How on earth were you supposed to cope with someone when he was frothing up his lungs? Or choking to death before your eyes? And what if it was a child?

The obscenity of it clogged her mind long after the talk was done and the chit-chat was over. It was still upsetting her as she walked home through the quiet streets from one peaceful lamp to the next, past the cheerful racket of the pubs, the shuttered shops, noticing for the first time how many drawn blinds there were, and thinking of the children sleeping peacefully behind them.

I wish Jim was home, she thought, as she turned the corner into Paradise Row. He was the one person who would understand what she was feeling.

And there he was, striding down the street towards her, clear in the light from the streetlamp on the corner, as if she'd conjured him up by wishing for him. He looked more handsome than she'd ever seen him, with his tunic unbuttoned and his tie loosened and those long legs striding in such a strong steady rhythm that the cloth of his trousers seemed to ripple as he walked. He was so at home in his uniform now, with that funny little cap set at a jaunty angle on his dark hair and his buttons gleaming as they caught the light. And he was smiling at her as they approached one another, such a warm, loving smile that it made her yearn to run and throw her arms round his neck and greet him with a kiss.

She didn't do any such thing, of course. She was far too sensible for that.

'Hello,' she said, standing still as he walked the last few steps towards her. 'I didn't know you'd got leave.'

'Ten days,' he told her. 'It's been brought forward. I've been accepted on a new course. For engine fitter.' It was obviously very important to him. He was glowing with the pride of it.

'That's good,' she said.

'Yes,' he agreed. 'It is rather. It's the engine for the new fighter planes I was telling you about. The Spitfires.'

'Oh yes,' she said, trying to remember what he'd told her.

He grinned at her. 'What's the news?'

Now it was her turn to feel proud. 'Nothing much,' she said. 'I've joined the ARP.'

Naturally, he thought. She would. 'Good for you,' he said, nodding at her. 'Is that where you've been tonight?'

'Yes,' she said. 'They've been learning us about different gases and how to recognize them by their smell. Lewisite smells of geraniums, so they say.' Telling him like this, calmly and out in the open air, lessened the evil of it a little.

But then Baby came squealing down the street to join them. 'Well hel*lo*!' she said to Jim. 'Fancy seeing you! I didn't think you'd be back for ages yet. Here, d'you know what the blighters have gone and done now? They given us all gasmasks! I ask you!'

'She won't wear hers,' Peggy said. Let him know what a fool she was being.

'I can't wear it,' Baby said. 'It suffocates me. I can't breathe in it. It wrecks my hair and it makes my mascara run and you can't see anything out of that silly eyepiece. It's perfectly horrid.'

'I should write and tell Hitler if I were you,' Jim advised. 'I'm sure he wouldn't want to make your mascara run.'

Lily was standing on her doorstep with Percy in her arms urging the little boy to wave to his uncle. He was sixteen months old now and beginning to look quite sturdy. 'Ain't you the lucky boy? Look who's come to see you.'

273

So they all went their several ways.

'See you tomorrow,' Jim called as he strode into number two.

'Where've you been?' Baby said. 'You're back jolly late.' It wasn't like Peggy to be gadding about at night. Usually she only went to the pictures with Megan and came straight home afterwards in her dull old way. Baby had been dancing at the local palais, and she still smelt strongly of sweat and Evening in Paris.

'Tell you when we're in,' Peggy said. It would be better to tell Mum and Baby at one and the same time just in case they got shirty. You never knew with either of them these days.

Fortunately Mrs Geary was still downstairs in the kitchen. The two women had been listening to 'Band Wagon' on Flossie's new radio.

'You done what?' Mum said, frowning with displeasure. 'What d'you want to go an' do a thing like that for?'

'Good fer you, gel,' Mrs Geary said, decidedly. 'You got my vote.'

'The ARP!' Flossie complained. 'You'll be out all hours, I hope you realize.'

'That's right,' Peggy said, agreeing with her, because that was one way to placate her and avoid an attack of nerves. Since that awful screaming fit she'd treated her mother's nerves with great caution. 'I shall be out tomorrow afternoon for a start.'

'Jim Boxall's home,' Baby said, changing the subject because that was another way to deal with nerves.

'Is he?' Mrs Geary said. 'Well that's nice. Tell him to come up and see me tomorrow morning, will yer, Baby? You could pop in on your way to work couldn't yer. I got something I want him ter do for me. Now then Peg, tell us where you're going tomorrow afternoon.'

It was quite a surprise to Peggy when Jim Boxall came knocking at the door the following afternoon just as she was putting on her hat and coat.

'Escort to the Tower,' he said. 'Reporting for duty.' He was smiling at her but his eyes were wary because he wasn't quite sure how she'd take it.

'Escort to the Tower?' she laughed. 'I don't need an

274

escort to the Tower. I was born there.'

'Yes, I know,' he admitted at once. 'It was Mrs Geary's idea. She thought you ought to have company.'

'Soppy ha'pporth,' she said affectionately.

The words and their tone encouraged him. 'You like her a lot, don't you?' he said as they walked out of the house together.

'Yes, I suppose I do.' She could be a bit of a pest sometimes with all the errands she wanted run, but she was an old love really.

'I can tell,' he said.

'How?'

'You called her soppy,' he explained. 'You always call people soppy when you like them. You called Lily soppy when I was in hospital that time. And when you're playing with Yvey and Norman you call them old soppies too. It's your word.'

She hadn't given it much thought until then but he was right. It was her word.

There was a chill wind blowing straight up the street. She tucked up her collar and put her head down against it. The little protective movements touched him. Sensible Peggy, he thought, sensible Peggy who knows how to endure things. If only she wasn't quite so sensible sometimes. If only she could act the way she did in his dreams.

But they were walking in the light of common day, catching a tram, sitting side by side without touching, as pure and proper as nuns.

'Least it's a bit warmer in here,' Peggy said, fishing in her pocket for her fare.

'I'll pay,' he told her. 'I'm the escort.'

As it was only tuppence she agreed. 'It'll be really funny to see the Tower again,' she said.

And it was. It gave her the oddest sensation, a mixture of affection and yearning nostalgia and regret for the passing of time. After all these years, she thought, standing on Tower Hill and looking across at the familiar buildings. How long has it been? Fifteen years? Sixteen? She'd been about eight when they left and now she was twenty-four. A lifetime. And yet there it was, just the same as she remembered it, the stone-solid walls with their dark arrow-slits peering down at the grassy bank that had once been the moat, with a village of towers and barracks and terraces behind them. The White Tower high on its mound, with those four grey domes topped by four gilded weather vanes, and the wind in the east, she noticed, the twin towers of Middle Tower and the Byward, the Bloody Tower and Traitor's Gate, Wakefield, and Lanthorn, and the Salt Tower where she'd felt the ghost. She could remember every single one.

'There it is,' Jim said, turning her by the elbow so that she was pointing in the right direction. 'There's your balloon. Over there on the ground, look.'

The balloon was a heap of crumpled silver fabric, rubberized cotton, so Jim told her, sprayed with aluminium. It looked like a deflated elephant and far too cumbersome to be capable of flight, but there were gangs of Auxiliary Air Force men labouring over the carcase with great intensity and determination, so they stayed where they were on the edge of the crowd and waited.

And the elephant expanded before their eyes, swelling and shifting, sprouting ears or flippers, swelling further and further, rounder and rounder until with a squeak of rubber on grass it took off and began to float into the air, trailing its restraining cables.

The little watching crowd gave it a cheer.

'That's the ticket,' a man near them said. 'That'll keep the buggers out. They won't be able to bomb us with them things in the air.'

Peggy glanced a question at Jim. 'How high will it go?' she said.

He was knowledgeable about that too. 'A few thousand feet,' he told her. 'Four, five, no more. If there's enough of them, they'll stop the Stukas. That's what they're designed for. To stop dive bombing.'

'But ordinary bombers'll get through?'

He gave her the truth, 'Yes.'

Then we shall be bombed, Peggy thought, the Tower and the docks, the theatres and cinemas, St Paul's and all the lovely churches that have stood here for ages, it will all be destroyed. Her dear, dear London. And the memory of the broken buildings of Guernica, the weeping women and frantic children and the ghastly, broken dead crammed her mind with horror, and she thought of Joan and the kids and old Mrs Geary and Mr Cooper in his wheelchair and dear old hamfisted Mr Allnutt always trying to help, and tears brimmed out of her eyes before she could control herself.

'Peggy?' he said. 'What's up?'

The tenderness in his voice melted the little control she had left. 'Oh,' she said, her face crumpling, 'it's all going to be destroyed and I love it so.' She was ashamed to be crying in public, making an exhibition of herself, and right outside the Tower too in the very place where she should have been at her most controlled, but she couldn't help it. All the feelings she'd been carrying about with her for so long, unspoken and unacknowledged, fear of war, love for her city, and above all her endless hopeless love for him, came welling up with her tears. Turning, she hid her face in his tunic because it was *his* tunic and the nearest available cover.

He'd never seen her cry before, and the sight of that anguished face precipitated him into instinctive action. He put one arm round her and began to rub her shoulder, comforting her as though she was a child. 'Don't cry, my little love,' he said. 'I can't bear to see you cry.'

She lifted her head with the tears streaming down her cheeks. 'Jim?' she said. Had she been hearing things or had he just called her his little love?

He was fishing a clean handkerchief from his trouser pocket. 'Dry your eyes,' he said, opening it out for her. 'I can't bear to see you cry.'

She dried her eyes obediently, while he stood with both arms encircling her, warm and close at last, so close that he could feel her breath fluttering underneath his chin. 'My little love,' he said again.

'Am I?' she said. Such an unnecessary question when he was beaming his love at her.

Now that he'd spoken he was full of unexpected confidence. 'Oh yes. Always have been. Didn't you know?'

'No,' she said. 'I didn't think you were interested. Leastways not in ... ' He was still beaming at her, encouraging her to change direction. Had she known it? 'I don't *think* I knew. I might've done.' The encircling warmth of his arms and his mouth so red and those blue eyes so tender were making it difficult to think at all.

'I think I've loved you since we was both kids,' he said.

The pleasure of standing in his arms was so intense she was almost afraid of it. And a little embarrassed too because they were in such a public place. 'People are looking,' she said. 'I don't think we ought to.'

'Let them look,' he said. He was smiling so widely his face had quite changed shape. 'Do them good. I love you. Love you, love you, love you. Do you know that? D'you know it *now*?'

'Yes,' she said, rather breathlessly. Was this really happening or was she dreaming it all? She was swimming in emotion and sensation, buoyed up, carried along.

'And you?' It was demand, entreaty and question all at once.

'Yes,' she said. 'I've loved you for as long as I can remember.' But then she glanced round her anxiously in case she'd been overheard and was relieved that the people nearest to them were making a lot of noise and looking up at the balloon.

'Let's get out of here,' he said. He needed to kiss her and hold her very close and *show* her how very much he loved her.

They went to the pictures. Neither of them paid the least attention to the images flickering on the screen for this time they were in the back row among all the other courting couples with the freedom to kiss as long and as often as they wished. By the time the lights came up for the interval they were dizzy and dishevelled and drowsy-eyed.

'We're daft,' he said, leaning back in the seat still cuddling her. 'All this time an' never saying a word.'

'Soppy,' she said. She felt quite drunk with all that kissing.

'I nearly told you that day at Brighton,' he confessed.

'I wish you had.'

'What would you've said?'

'The same.'

'Would you 've?'

'Oh yes.'

What a lot of time we've wasted, he thought, aching to kiss her again. 'Still I have now.' She was flushed and beautiful and ought to be kissed. Come on, turn the lights out.

'Oh yes, you have now.'

'And I've got ten days. Where shall we go tomorrow?'

But she never got the chance to tell him because the lights dimmed.

They spent the next ten days in a trance. Jim visited his mother and his mates from Warrenden's and took Mr Cooper to the library and went shopping with Lily and Percy, and Peggy went to work as usual, but these things were simply interludes, to be lived through as quickly as possible. The evenings were what counted, when they would walk arm-in-arm through the parks and eat fish and chips together and go to the pictures. The papers were full of the news that Mr Chamberlain had visited Herr Hitler at Berchtesgaden, 'I had a long talk with Herr Hitler. It was a frank talk, it was a friendly one', and that he was flying home to discuss the situation with His Majesty's Government, but neither of them took very much notice. The Premier could go to Berchtesgaden or Bad Godesburg or anywhere else he wished. They were on holiday from wars and crises in a love-drenched world of their own.

When that final Sunday came Peggy cooked the Sunday joint for her family and invited him to share it. So they spent the last hour of his leave sitting side by side at the Furnivall table and so obviously in love that Baby felt quite jealous of them.

'I suppose you'll marry him now,' she said, when Peggy came back from the station without him.

'We've only just started walking out,' Peggy said. But it came as quite a shock to realize that neither of them had said a word about marriage and that she hadn't even thought about it. It had been enough just to love him and to know that she was loved in return.

'Shush,' Flossie said. 'Listen to this.' She was sitting beside the radio with one ear as close to it as she could get

279

it. 'They're mobilizing the ARP. Did you know that, Peggy?'

'What?' Peggy said, walking across the kitchen to listen too. They couldn't be. That would mean they thought the war was going to start at any minute.

'I repeat,' the announcer was saying, 'all ARP personnel are to report to their nearest Post or present themselves to their Chief Warden as soon as possible.'

'Did you hear that, Peggy?' Mrs Geary called from upstairs.

'I'm on my way now,' Peggy said, putting on her hat and coat. But she still couldn't believe it was serious. Not now, when the sun was shining and Jim loved her.

Even when she'd walked down to the Post, and Mr Goodall had given her a copy of their new duty rosta and told her to consider herself 'on call' from that moment on, she still took it calmly.

On Monday evening she listened to the sound of Hitler ranting and raving at the Sports Palace in Berlin and the baying of the crowd, roaring '*Sieg Heil! Sieg Heil!*' and it all seemed stupid and childish. She was sure it would all be resolved in the end without going to war. Mr Chamberlain would see to it.

The next morning she had her first love-letter from Jim and spent the day in a glow of well-being because of it. Even when she saw the placards announcing that the Navy had been mobilized she felt no alarm. The new fighter planes were being built as fast as they could get them off the production line, Jim had said so. And in any case there simply couldn't be a war. Not really. Not if it came to it. Something could happen.

That night after work she took a tram to Deptford and went to see Joan.

Yvey and Norman were in their pyjamas drinking a late night cup of cocoa.

'Guess what,' Yvey said. 'Daddy's gone to join the army.' She was rosy-cheeked in the firelight with a six year old's gappy teeth and her straight hair neatly brushed and as glossy as a polished cob nut.

'Has he?' Peggy said in surprise.

'Territorials,' Joan explained. She seemed excited by it,

with a brooding sexuality about her that Peggy hadn't seen since she was courting. 'Him an' his pals. Went off three hours ago. What d'you think a' that?'

Peggy understood that the news should be praised and praised it.

'Daddy's going to be a soldier,' Norman said, lifting his head from his mug. He had a moustache of cocoa over his top lip which he tried to lick clean. 'He's going to have a gun, Aunty Peggy. I'm going to see it. Me an' him made a gingerbread man this afternoon.'

'An' me,' Yvonne said. 'I made one too.'

'You ate yours,' Normal disparaged. 'I'm never gonna eat mine, Aunty Peggy. I'm gonna keep it for ever and ever.'

He'd been so happy in the bakery that afternoon, down there in the floury heat with Yvey and Dad and all the other bakers. Dad had showed them how to make dough and shape bread and cut out gingerbread men and they'd stood beside him and watched, pink cheeked with heat and pleasure.

'There y'are,' he said when the little men were finally cooked, 'that's for you to remember me by when I've gone for a soldier. One fer you an' one fer Yvey. Now you can make 'em for me while I'm away, can't you Norm?' And he gave the little boy a wink as one man to another. 'What d'you say ter that?'

They'd both kissed him, the way they always did in the bakery, because somehow or other it was easier to kiss him in the bakery when he was all over flour and his face was red from the ovens.

'That's my good kids,' he'd said proudly, kissing them back. 'Now run upstairs to yer ma while I'm finishing up.'

And they'd run upstairs and here they were with the precious gingerbread man lying on a plate on the dresser.

'Couldn't wait five minutes to enlist, once they'd made their minds up to it,' Joan said. 'Hardly ate any of his supper. Rushing off. You never saw such a carry-on.' He'd looked so handsome, with that rakish daring she remembered so well, bold and bright eyed and cheeky, like he'd been when they first met. She couldn't wait for him to come home.

'There won't be a war,' Peggy said. 'Not now. Chamberlain'll stop it. You'll see.'

'They've mobilized the fleet,' Joan said. 'That's not so good. Come on you two, time you were abed.'

'I'm sure it'll be all right,' Peggy insisted as her niece and nephew kissed her goodnight.

And sure enough two days later the Premier flew back to Heston from his third meeting with Hitler, this time in a place called Munich, waving a piece of paper that he said meant 'Peace with Honour'. Hitler had promised that he had 'no further territorial claims in Europe' and that if he were allowed to 'free the Sudeten Germans' he would be content.

'Peace in our Time,' the newspaper headlines shouted with relief. And the *Daily Express* even went so far as to claim, 'Britain will not be involved in a European war this year or next year either.'

'Bloody fools!' Mr Cooper said, when he took a rest after the third rendering of the 'Lambeth Walk' that Saturday. 'The Czechs spend millions to build a line of defences against the Nazis all along their Sudeten frontier and we come along and make them give it all away. And who to? The bloody Germans. The self-same bloody Germans it was supposed to keep out. Now there's nothing to stop the bugger walking straight in and all over them. It's enough ter make you spit blood.'

'I thought you didn't want a war,' Flossie said.

'No more I do,' John Cooper told her. 'Never have. But this ain't the way to prevent it. We've sold the poor bloody Czechs right down the river.'

'Not if Mr Hitler keeps his word,' Mrs Roderick said, sipping her port and lemon.

'Hitler is a crook,' Mr Grunewald told them. 'A thug.' He knew, more than anyone in the room, how violent the Nazis were. 'Thugs don't keep their word.'

But the months went by and things stayed surprisingly quiet.

'I shan't get any leave till I've completed this course,' Jim wrote in his next letter, 'which won't be till March if I'm any judge. It's a lifetime. I haven't kissed you for twelve whole days, I hope you realize. Dear God, twelve

282

whole days and only dreams and memories to keep me going. I shall be a shred of my former self when you see me next.'

'I shall be glad to see you again even if you are only a shred,' she wrote back. 'A shred would be better than nothing. I miss you more than I can say. Very quiet here. Is this Spitfire they're testing the one you were telling me about?'

In January, while they were still yearningly apart, a Spitfire flew from London to Paris in 41 minutes and at a speed of over 400 miles an hour.

'That's our beauty,' Jim wrote. 'Ain't it grand? Now we've got two fighters faster and more manoeuvrable than anything Hitler's got or anything he's likely to get. First the Hurricane and now the Spitfire. Thank God. You should see the engine, Peg. A masterpiece of engineering. What am I saying? You should see the engine. I don't want you to see an engine. *I* want to see *you*. Still we're more than half way there now. I shall be home in March. Can't wait.'

In February the ARP began to distribute shelters for people to dig into their back gardens. They were little more than a hoop of corrugated steel but the Chief Warden said they would withstand anything short of a direct hit. Peggy would have liked to order one for her own family, but you had to have a garden big enough to contain it and the little backyards in Paradise Row were much too small. Somehow or other, during the quiet months of that winter and the growing menace of that early spring, acceptance of this war had been gradually seeping into her mind. The papers were always full of pictures of Hitler and his storm troopers, marching about in their jackboots and those ugly tin hats of theirs. And more and more people were making preparations for air raids. Madame Aimee had cleared the coal from one side of her cellar and taken down stools and deckchairs and a square of lino to stand them on, and her latest idea was to see if she could run the radio from the electric light. And at home Mum and Mrs Geary had taken everything out of the cupboard under the stairs and put it up in the attic, 'just in case'.

And two days after Jim came home on leave at last,

Hitler marched into Czechoslovakia, just as Mr Cooper had predicted. There was no opposition. How could there be? Six days later he was telling Poland he wanted Danzig and the Polish Corridor.

Now everybody in England knew it was just a matter of time.

CHAPTER 22

'Now you make good an' sure you send the kids off,' Sid Owen said, hoisting his kitbag onto his shoulder. 'The minute they're sent for, you send 'em.'

'Yes, well all right,' Joan said unwillingly.

'Never mind yes well all right,' Sid said. 'You do it. You want to go, don't yer, kids?'

Yvonne and Norman stood dubiously before him on the kitchen hearth-rug. Neither of them wanted to be 'sent off' but they couldn't say so, partly because they weren't quite sure what being 'sent off' really meant, but mostly because he was so dead set on it whatever it was. Breakfast was over and another peculiar day had begun and things had a way of happening whether or not you wanted them to. So Yvonne said, 'Yes, Dad', and tried to sound as though she meant it.

'Good gel,' he approved, buttoning his fags into the breast pocket of his tunic. 'You got yer bags packed aintcher?'

'Yes, Dad.'

'Righto then, give us a kiss. Be good kids. Do as yer mum says when I'm gone.'

'Couldn't we just wait an' see before we send them?' Joan tried. The thought of this evacuation was making her feel sick.

He wouldn't even allow the suggestion. 'Don't start that again,' he warned. 'You've give your word, so let's have no more of it. If I say they're to go, that's it, they're to go. You don't want 'em here to be bombed, do yer? OK, then. You send 'em. If I come home an' find 'em still here you'll know about it.' He glanced at the clock on the mantel-piece, ticking the tinny seconds away. 'Time I was off. Look after yourself, old girl.'

It was all unreal, Joan thought. Just when they were happy together again he'd got to go to Salisbury Plain as if he was a proper soldier. And the kids had got to be evacu-ated. It was more than she could bear to think about.

'Give us a kiss then,' he instructed, daring her with those bold dark eyes. And when she kissed him briefly, 'Gaw dearie me. Is that the best you can do?'

She kissed him again, more passionately this time, but the passion made her feel how wrong this was, all of it. Ever since he'd joined the territorials he'd been such a rewarding, insistent lover, quite his old dashing self again. They'd been really contented with one another, hardly rowing at all, and now they were going to be parted, and he'd be sent off to France, she knew it in her bones, and then what would happen to them?

'Remember what you promised,' he said, heading for the door. 'You're to send 'em. No turning back, eh?'

There's no turning back for any of us now, Joan thought bleakly as she listened to his boots descending the stairs. 'Come to the window,' she said to Yvey and Norman, 'and we'll wave him goodbye.'

It was Friday, the first day of September 1939, and the news was grim. The British and German governments had been exchanging notes for more than a week, while the German army massed all along the Polish frontier, and at dawn that morning German troops had finally carried out their long-threatened invasion. In England the army and navy were mobilized. Every window in London was hung with black-out curtains of one kind or another, and many of them had been criss-crossed with brown paper too as a precaution against flying glass, because everyone knew the air raids would start as soon as war was declared. That was always the pattern. There were gangs of council workmen in the streets busily painting white patches along the kerbs and white lines around the base of everything and anything protruding from the pavement, like trees and telephone boxes and pillar boxes, and there were sandbags heaped against the windows of every building in the High Street. Some of the local schools had been evacuated already and the rest were waiting to be called. It was a very vain hope indeed to say, 'It might not come to it.'

Yvonne and Norman's school rang the bell to announce their evacuation half an hour after their father left. And while it was still ringing, a boy on a bicycle came pedalling furiously up the High Street to augment the summons by knocking on doors.

He was in a most enjoyable and dramatic hurry, powering along the middle of the street with his body bent forward urgently over the handlebars. He barely allowed himself time to stop when he rang the doorbells. He simply stood astride the bike and knocked and rang. And at every house his doleful message was the same.

'They're going, missus! They're going!'

All along his route sash-cord windows were creaked open, anxious faces appeared to acknowledge him.

But Joan was quicker than he was. She'd sped down the stairs and opened the side door before he had time to take his finger from the bell.

'Where to?' she panted. 'Where they going?'

'New Cross Gate,' the boy called back to her, already on his way to the next shop. 'They're going missus!'

It was as though he was crying the end of the world.

'Get yer bags,' Joan said briskly. 'You got a clean hanky, Norman? There's a bar a' chocolate each. Put it in your pockets. Better go to the lavvy just to be on the safe side.'

'I don't want to go to the lavvy,' Norman protested as she pushed him towards the bathroom door. 'Can I take my gingerbread man?'

'Try,' she urged him. 'See if you can squeeze some out. Then you can take your gingerbread man. Where's yer gasmasks?'

She jollied them all along, being cheerful as much to keep her own spirits up as to help them. The street was full of mothers and children running down towards the school.

287

'Where are we going?' Norman asked as they jogged along.

'To the country,' Joan said, trying to encourage them. 'You know, where it's all fields and there are cows and sheep and chickens. You'll like that, won't you?'

'No,' the little boy said stoutly. 'I shan't. Why can't we stay here with you?'

'It won't be for long,' Joan said. 'You'll soon be back, you'll see.'

'How soon?' Yvey asked. She was very near tears, her bottom lip trembling.

'No time at all,' Joan said.

'A week?' They were very near the school gate. She could see the teachers walking about and the kids forming lines like they did to march in of a morning.

'Run in quick,' Joan said. 'Mustn't keep them waiting. Make sure you don't get parted, Yvey. You keep tight hold of Yvonne's hand won't you, Norman?' The anguish of this parting was tearing at her throat. 'Go on. Quick.'

They kissed her hurriedly and ran into the playground, and for a few seconds they were lost to sight in the crowd of small figures trotting and running to the assembly point. Then she could see them both standing in line, and one of the teachers was checking the labels they had pinned to their coats and opening their gasmask cases presumably to see that the gasmasks were inside.

'You going home, Mrs Owen?' her next-door neighbour asked.

'No fear,' she said. 'I'm going with them as far as ever I can. I'd go all the way if only they'd let me.'

It seemed a very long time before the lines were all in order and the headmaster blew his whistle for silence. From the pavement the little crowd of mums couldn't hear what he was saying to their children, but presently one of the teachers came out of the building with a banner on which a big letter T was painted. She handed it to two of the older boys at the head of the first line and after a last minute glance at her anxious pupils, she led the crocodile out of the gate.

There was no sound in the street at all except for the tread of all those little boots and shoes. Not a child spoke,

288

not even when they passed their mothers. They crossed the road meekly, clutching their luggage, with their gasmasks bumping against their legs. Some of the boys had remembered to wear their school caps and some of the girls wore berets, but most of them were bareheaded, neatly brushed and combed like Yvonne or tousle-headed like her brother. They looked very young and very small and horribly vulnerable walking obediently away in the summer sunshine.

Their mothers followed along behind them, uncertain but determined, and the crocodile straggled through the streets to New Cross Gate and up the incline to the entrance, where they had to wait while the school before them was led down to the platforms. The entrance was blocked with children and they could hear the trains steaming below them.

'Now!' the headmaster called and the crocodile shuffled forward, small pale faces looking anxiously over laden shoulders for one last glimpse of their mothers, small pale hands waving unnaturally like flowers in a storm-force wind. They crossed the entrance hall far too quickly and began the descent of the steps. Joan watched with anguish as her two little ones gradually disappeared, first their luggage, then their hunched shoulders, then their two poor little strained faces, then their pretty heads, until all she could see of them was their waving fingers, Norman's still clutching his gingerbread man. It was as though they were being torn into strips and removed from her piece by piece. And all round her mothers were keening to their children with one voice. 'Goodbye darling! Goodbye! Goodbye! Oh my darling!' Then they were gone.

Joan found that she was weeping without control, the tears brimming out of her eyes so fast that she could hardly see, and her neighbour was crying too, sobbing aloud. The two of them hung on to each other for support until another crocodile arrived and nudged them out of the way.

'Come home an' have a cup a' tea,' Joan suggested.

'I'm supposed ter be at work,' her neighbour said, but she accepted the tea just the same. 'You need company at a time like this.'

Over in Madame Aimee's High Class Haberdashery, the Chief Warden was talking seriously to Peggy and Mr MacFarlane.

'Once the balloon goes up,' he was saying, 'we shall need a lot more full-timers. I thought of you two straight away.'

'Aye, well, you could have our Peggy I dare say,' said Mr MacFarlane. 'I've no wish tae lose the girrrl, but as you say ... As to mysel', who'd keep the shop if I were to agree to 't?'

'Madame Aimee?' Charlie Goodall suggested.

'Aye well, mebbe,' Mr MacFarlane said doubtfully. 'We'll see.'

'Start tomorrow,' the Chief Warden said to Peggy. 'Eight o'clock at the flats.'

'Yes,' Peggy agreed quietly. It was only to be expected. Somebody would have to look after the black-out, and sound the alarms, and be on duty when the air raids began. But she was only giving him part of her attention, because she was thinking of Yvey and Norman and wondering where they were and how they were getting on. The Greenwich streets had been full of departing children all morning, so they must have gone.

Yvonne was sitting in the middle of a six-seater compartment that was now accommodating eleven children and a teacher. She had her coat wrapped tightly round her knees and she was thinking what an awful journey it was. Katy Burnett had eaten her sandwiches as soon as the train pulled out of the station, even though Sir said she wasn't to, and then, of course, she started sicking up. She would. Sir held her head out of the window but the sick blew back inside and went all over everything, and everybody yelled and said Yuk! and Ergh! and tried to clean themselves up with their hankies. And then Norman said he felt sick too and Sir held him out of the window and such a long way out that Yvonne was terrified a train would come along and knock his head off the way Mum had always said it would.

Being reminded of her mother was the most painful thing about the journey. While she could talk to her friends and tell Norman off and read her comic, she was more or less all right, but thinking of Mum made her want to cry. Sir tried to make them sing and they *did* sing, for quite a long time. 'Whistle while you work, Adolf Hitler is a twerp' and 'Run rabbit run', but they didn't know all the words and Sir had to keep stopping to hold people out of the window so it wasn't a success.

But at last, after hours and hours and hours the train chuffed to a halt, brakes squealing, and they were all allowed out of their stinking compartment and found themselves standing on a wooden platform right out in the country.

Sir said they were to stand in a line while the train emptied and then he'd go and see what was what. So they stood in the sunshine, clutching their luggage, and waited. Yvonne was glad that she and Norman had suitcases, because some of the kids only had brown paper parcels and they were all coming undone.

'This way,' Sir said. 'They've got us a coach.'

It was a jolly old-fashioned coach, with tiny little windows and scratchy seats and it bounced along the road as though it was made of rubber, throwing them all from side to side and jolting them into the air. But fortunately it didn't have to go far. After rattling them along between hedges it suddenly stopped alongside a wooden hut. There were two women in green uniform standing on the step and they came down at once and bustled all the kids into the hut and told them they could eat their dinner if they wanted to.

'Please Miss,' Yvonne asked, as politely as she could, 'Please, Miss, where are we?'

'You're in Sussex, my dear,' the woman said. 'Eat your sandwiches up nicely and then you'll be taken to your new homes.'

So they ate their sandwiches as nicely as they could when they were sitting on the floor, and Norman said he was thirsty, and Katy Burnett said she wanted to go to the lavvy. And they waited.

Presently people began to arrive, peering in through the door at them as if they were animals in a zoo. And after a while a woman walked into the hut, strolled about, looked them all over, and said, 'Two strong boys' as though she

291

was ordering two pounds of sugar. And two of the big boys were told to stand up and go with her. The next lady said she wanted, 'A clean little girl.' And after her five or six women came in together and there was quite a bustle of movement and leave-taking.

'You won't let me go on my own, will you Yvey?' Norman asked, his little round face puckered with anxiety.

'Course not,' Yvonne assured him, even though she had no idea how such a thing was to be done.

'These are just the ones,' Sir said coming to stand beside them. 'Yvonne is a very good needlewoman, aren't you, Yvonne?'

'Yes, sir,' Yvonne agreed, her heart thumping most unpleasantly. There was an ugly man standing with Sir and he was looking straight at her and Norman. Oh a horribly ugly man, a great fat lumpy man with a face like one of those bloodhound dogs, with a long fleshy nose and watery green eyes and great big yellow false teeth.

'This is Mr Ray,' Sir said. 'He's going to take you home.'

'Back to London?' Norman said hopefully.

Mr Ray cleared his throat by coughing in a bubbling sort of way. 'Don't be stupid,' he said to Norman. Then he turned to the lady with the list. 'I don't think I want the boy. He's a bit on the small side. 'Aven't you got another gel?'

'He'll grow,' the lady promised. 'Brother and sister you know. Less trouble. She'll look after him, won't you, um?'

Yvonne assured them both that she would, of course she would. And Norman clung to her hand and scuffed his shoes along the floor.

'Oh all right then,' Mr Ray said. 'Come on.'

So they picked up their cases and followed him, walking several paces behind him as that felt safer and seemed to be what he wanted. They went past several tatty cottages, one roofed in straw which was really amazing, and a church which seemed to be hiding behind a lot of trees and then on downhill for quite a long way until they came to a glass-fronted shop standing all by itself at a bend in the road.

292

There was nothing in the window except a white urn full of flowers standing on a shelf covered with a black-out curtain, but there was an explanatory sign above the window that said 'W Ray Undertakers and Funeral Directors.'

'Here we are,' Mr Ray said, and he led them round the side of the shop and through an open door into a very dark passageway. 'I'm back, Mother,' he called. 'Any messages?'

'No,' a voice said. 'It's been as quiet as the grave.' And then it laughed in a gloating sort of way and Mr Ray laughed too as he led them into a dark room where a long thin lady was sitting sewing a piece of bright pink satin.

If Mr Ray was bad, Mrs Ray was worse. She was tall and straight-spined and formidable, with thin grey hair, small pale eyes and a nose like a spoon. And she didn't like either of the children one little bit. They knew instinctively. And they were right, as children usually are in such circumstances.

The Rays had married late in life and had consequently avoided the nuisance of having children. They had taken over the funeral parlour from Mr Ray's father after his own demise, and were known locally as 'Rays the Dead', but in a village as small as Myrtlebury there was too little trade for them to make 'a living out of dying' as they jokingly put it. For as they frequently told one another, 'If people don't die in the natural course of events we can hardly go round killing them off to make business.' So when the government announced that people in the reception areas for evacuation would be paid eight shillings and sixpence a week for every evacuee they took into their homes, Mrs Ray saw at once that this was an excellent way to supplement their income.

'They won't eat much, Father,' she promised. 'I'll see to that. If you get us two girls they can earn their keep and help with the sewing.'

She wasn't too pleased to see that one of her proposed little girls was a five-year-old boy.

'Land sakes,' she said, setting aside the pink satin, 'What've you gone and brought us a boy for, Father? Boys are nothing but trouble. You'll have to get him changed.'

'I don't want to be changed,' Norman said, hanging on to Yve for dear life.

Mrs Ray swept across the room and whacked him round the ear. 'You speak when you're spoken to,' she said. 'Nobody asked you.'

Norman began to cry and Yvonne made faces at him to stop and shook his hand where it was hidden in the folds of her coat, because these two ugly grown-ups were cross enough without making them worse.

'Stop snivelling,' Mrs Ray ordered. 'Now you're here I suppose I'd better show you where you're to sleep. But don't go making yourselves too much at home, that's all.'

The room she showed them into was a small back bedroom furnished with a small square of carpet grown grey with age, a chipped jug and wash basin, a chamber pot and an iron bedstead on which was a very stained mattress, two pillows without pillow cases and a folded pile of dark brown blankets. There were no curtains at the window and the gaslight didn't look as though it had been lit for ages.

'Bedtime is six o'clock,' Mrs Ray said patting one of the stains on the mattress ticking. 'I shall serve supper at five sharp, not a minute before or after. If you're not back by five sharp, I shall clear the table and you'll have to go without. Breakfast at seven, this room to be cleared by eight, supper at five. You can go where you please between times just so long as you understand you're not to hang around the house. Church on Sundays of course. We've got to keep in with the church in our line of business. Is that clear?'

The two children stood stupefied before her. Neither of them had understood a word she was saying but they didn't admit it, because one whacking was enough.

'Yes, Miss,' Yvonne said, squeezing Norman's hand to encourage him to say yes too.

'Off you go then,' Mrs Ray said, pushing them towards the stairs. 'Back at five.'

So they wandered out of the house and into the lane as that was what she seemed to want them to do. It was a lovely summer's afternoon. The sky was blue and there were birds singing in all the trees.

'I'm ever so thirsty,' Norman said.

'There's a tap over there,' Yvonne noticed. 'In amongst those funny looking trees. Look Norm, they're growing apples. There's little apples all over those trees.'

So they climbed through the hedge and drank at the tap and picked one or two of the biggest apples from the trees. But they were very sour and hard to chew, and after a while they gave up trying to eat them.

'If we sleep in that room where are we s'posed to hang our clothes?' Norman asked. Mum had been most particular that they should hang up their clothes when they arrived.

'We'll keep 'em in the cases,' Yvonne decided. 'We might not be here very long.' And she offered up a silent prayer to her Maker. Please God don't let us be here very long. 'Least we can sleep together. That's good, ain't it?'

'How are we going to know when to go back for supper?' Norman worried again.

'We'll sit up here and watch the house,' Yve said sensibly. 'Perhaps she'll look out for us, like Mum does.'

But as they discovered later, there was a clock somewhere that struck the hours, so they were able to walk past that horrible urn full of flowers and into the back door on the very stroke of five.

Supper was sardines with bread and margarine which neither of them enjoyed at all. Mrs Ray stood guard over them as they ate, and immediately their plates were empty she sent them out to the lavvy and marched them into the front parlour. There was a pile of pink satin on the table and a box full of cheap cotton wool beside it.

'That's your sewing,' she said to Yvonne. 'I've pinned the seams together. All you've got to do is sew them up. Neat stitches if you please. And you,' turning to Norman, 'you can stuff the finished ones. Not too full. There's no need for extravagance.'

The two children worked for more than an hour while Mrs Ray sat on the opposite side of the table and cut out more shapes from a roll of blue satin she took from the cupboard. Nobody spoke and there was no sound in the room except the click of her scissors, the tick of the clock

and the rasp of the cotton thread as Yvonne pulled it gingerly through the satin, trying hard not to buckle the cloth
or mark it with her fingers.

But at last the clock struck seven.

'That's enough for one evening,' Mrs Ray said, removing
the cloth from Yvonne's hands and putting the lid on the
box of cotton wool. 'Bed.'

And with that she marched them upstairs to the attic. It
was already growing dark and the room smelt damp and
unwelcoming.

Neither of them got much sleep, for by then they were
so homesick that they spent most of the night in tears.

'I don't want to stay here, Yvey,' Norman whispered
over and over again. 'I want to go home.'

'So do I,' Yvonne said, crying with him. She'd been
brave all day and now she simply couldn't go on being
brave any longer. 'Oh so do I.'

Back in Deptford Joan had spent a wakeful night too,
wondering where they were and how they were and
missing them with a perpetual yearning ache in her belly
that no thoughts could ease. At daybreak she gave up
trying to sleep and got up to begin her first day without
them. Perhaps a good scrub round would make her feel
better. Housework was usually a cure for most of her
miseries. But it was no help to her that Saturday. By mid-
morning her two rooms were spotless and she was still full
of anxious energy. That afternoon she washed the curtains
and cleaned the windows and turned out the kitchen
cupboards, lining them all with fresh newspaper. But the
misery remained and next morning when she'd washed up
her solitary cup and saucer there was nothing left for her
to do. She put on her hat and coat and took a tram to
Greenwich.

Paradise Row wasn't itself either, although it took her a
little while to work out what was different about it. She
was used to the street shelter now, large though it was, a
great flat-roofed ugly brick-built box blocking the middle
of the roadway, and she'd grown accustomed to the sight
of black curtains edging the windows, because there was
black-out everywhere. No, what was new that morning

was the emptiness of the street and the awful silence. And that was because there were no kids about.

'Come on in, lovey,' Mum said as she opened the door. 'Did they go off all right?'

'Bloody war!' Joan said, breaking down as soon as the door was closed behind her. 'I don't see why we got to have our kids sent away from us just for a pack a' bloody foreigners. We should keep out of it. Bloody war!'

'You have a good cuss,' Mrs Geary advised, hobbling down the stairs towards her. 'Do you a power a' good. No good keeping it in.'

The parrot was cussing fluently above their heads. Now and at last it was possible to give full vent to her feelings and to swear and cry for as long as she needed to.

'I'll put the kettle on,' Baby offered when the worst was over. 'Nice cup a' tea.'

'That's right,' Mum said walking Joan into the kitchen. 'Nice cup a' tea, an' then you can stay to dinner, eh. They'll be all right, you'll see. I'll bet they're having the time a' their lives in the country. Think how you used to enjoy it at Tillingbourne when you was little.'

Peggy had a sudden seering recollection of the slaughter of the pig, but she shrugged it away quickly. This was no time for such thoughts. 'I'd better put on some more potatoes,' she said smiling at her sister. 'I'm on duty at two o'clock.'

'On a Sunday?' Joan said.

'It's being full-time,' Mum explained, basting the joint. 'She has to work all sorts of hours now.'

'I'm sorry I swore,' Joan said. 'It's just I miss them so. It's so quiet.'

'The O'Donavans went yesterday afternoon,' Baby said, as if that explained the lack of noise.

'What, evacuated?' Joan asked.

'Back to Ireland,' Mrs Geary told her. 'All the lot of 'em. Sold up every mortal thing they possessed so she was telling me, an' even then they only just scraped up the fares. God knows how they'll make out now!'

'So how many kids have we got left in the street now?' Joan asked.

'Only Percy,' Peggy told her. 'Lily could've gone with

him only she wouldn't leave Arthur. She said she couldn't bear for them all to be split up.'

'I know how she feels,' Joan said.

'Mr Chamberlain's speaking at eleven o'clock don't forget,' Mrs Geary said quickly, changing the subject before Joan could get upset again.

'Put the wireless on,' Flossie said to Baby, who was standing near the sideboard where the radio stood.

So they had light music while they drank their tea and washed the cups and saucers and set about peeling the vegetables. And by the time the announcer introduced the Prime Minister just before eleven fifteen they were all feeling much easier and happier. Big Ben struck the quarter and the weary reedy voice of their leader spoke to them across the air waves.

'I am speaking to you from the Cabinet Room at 10 Downing Street,' he said. 'This morning the British Ambassador in Berlin handed the German Government a final note stating that unless we heard from them by eleven o'clock that they were prepared at once to withdraw their troops from Poland a state of war would exist between us. I have to tell you now that no such undertaking has been received and that consequently this country is at war with Germany.'

'Oh God!' Baby said. 'Just when I've had my hair permed.'

'Well that's it I suppose,' Mrs Geary said. 'We can't say we didn't know it was coming.'

'Now what?' Joan said to Peggy. 'What happens next?'

What happened next was a series of public announcements. The blowing of whistles and the blaring of horns were now forbidden 'as these could be confused with air raid warnings', theatres and cinemas were to be closed down 'to minimize the chances of a large crowd being killed by a single bomb'.

'Oh lovely!' Mrs Geary said.

'Now,' the wireless went on, 'an announcement about food.'

But the announcement didn't come. There was a long silence in which they could hear papers being shuffled about and somebody whispering. Then the National

Anthem began to play. It hadn't got further than 'God save our gracious king', when the air raid sirens began to wail, rising from a low growling note into an anguished howl and then descending and rising again, and again, and again.

'Oh my dear good God,' Flossie said, jumping up. 'They're here already. Quick! What shall we do? Oh my God, whatever shall we do?'

Peggy put on her tin hat and assumed command. 'Take your coats,' she said, trying to sound calm even though she didn't feel it. 'Go straight to the shelter,' She was half-way to the door.

'Quick!'

'What about Polly?' Mrs Geary said. 'I can't leave Polly.'

'I'll bring him if there's time,' Peggy promised.

And to everyone's surprise, she did, but only after she'd shepherded all the inhabitants of the street into their damp brick fastness in the middle of the road. Mr and Mrs Grunewald came under protest and Nonnie Brown refused to enter at all unless she could bring her gin bottle with her, and John Cooper had to be carried bodily into the shelter by Mr Allnutt and Mr Brown because his wheel-chair was too wide to push through the entrance.

It was dark, dank and smelly inside, and the slatted seats were damp to the touch.

'We shall all be killed!' Flossie moaned over and over again. 'I can feel it in my bones. My nerves'll never stand this you know. I shall be a nervous wreck.'

Leslie was weeping.

'Oh do shut up,' Ernest said, frowning at him. 'You make matters worse with all that boo-hoo.'

'Shut up yourself,' Leslie said. 'You don't know how I feel.'

'Try some gin, darling,' Nonnie Brown said drunkenly, waving the bottle at him.

'Let's have a song,' Peggy suggested, trying to remember the advice she'd been given in all those ARP lectures.

'Song?' Leslie said. 'You must be joking!'

'Bloody, bloody, bloody bugger!' the parrot squawked.

'Aark! Sod that! Aark! Aark!'

'Oh Christ,' John Cooper said to Mrs Geary, almost laughing, 'that bloody bird of yours!' and then they all began to laugh, in peals of hysterical guffaws that were almost sobs. Even young Percy joined in, clinging round his mother's neck but giggling weakly. And the parrot shrieked at them all above the din.

They were making so much noise that at first they missed the rising note of the all clear.

'Blimey!' Mr Allnutt said. 'Twenty minutes. That was quick.'

They stumbled out into the summer sunshine. There was no sign of an air raid anywhere as far as they could see, no dead bodies, no bombed buildings, no smoke, only a strong smell of burning potatoes.

Leslie gave a shriek and rushed into number five. 'Now look what you've made me do,' he yelled to Ernest. 'Dinner'll be ruined I hope you realize.'

'Oh yes, of course. It's always my fault,' Ernest said following him. 'Everything's always my fault. I started this war I don't think.'

'Well really,' Mrs Roderick said with icy disapproval, 'What a way to go on. Here we all are in danger of our lives and they carry on like that. I don't know what the world's coming to. I'm glad some of us manage to control ourselves.'

The Furnivalls walked back into their house at Mrs Geary's pace.

'I wonder where they went,' Mrs Geary said. 'Must'a gone somewhere. That stands ter reason and they ain't come here.'

'Thank God for that,' Flossie said. 'We don't want 'em. My nerves couldn't stand it.'

'Now what?' Baby asked.

'Dinner first, while it's hot,' Mrs Geary said. 'Then I suppose we shall all have to wait and see.'

As she followed her family back into the house, Peggy was secretly rather pleased by the way she'd acted. It was true that they hadn't been in any real danger, but none of them had known that at the time. She'd done all the right things in the right order, despite her fear, and nobody had panicked. It was quite a feather in her cap. She didn't say anything about it, of course, because she didn't want to brag, but it was rewarding just the same.

'I shall have to get a job,' Joan said to her as they were eating dinner. 'I can't stand this waiting about, and if we're going to have air raids it'll give me something to think about.'

She started work at a local munitions factory the following morning. But they all had a lot of waiting about to do before any munitions were to be used in action.

CHAPTER 23

After such a dramatic start to the war the days that followed were rather a come-down. Instead of the much dreaded, long expected bombing, nothing happened. In fact if it hadn't been for the newspapers nobody would have known there was a war on and soon even the newspapers were calling it a phoney war. Hitler's invasion of Poland continued unchecked and there was a ship sunk somewhere out in the Atlantic, but it was all too far away to disturb the residents of Paradise Row.

However as the weeks passed they began to learn what it was going to mean to live in a 'state of emergency'. They were told to carry gasmasks with them everywhere they went, they were issued with numbers and identity cards, which didn't please Mr Brown at all, and ration books which John Cooper said was a damn good idea, because at least they'd all have fair shares if food was rationed, and they had to accept the new chore of 'doing the black-out' every dusk and dawn, and the new hazard of trying to travel about in total darkness.

Old Mr Allnutt went out to post a letter on the third dark night and got knocked off his feet by a passing cyclist he hadn't seen. He came home with a ripped jacket, a grazed face and a chipped tooth, which he endured stoically, but after that he said he'd had enough of the black-out to last a lifetime and he'd stay indoors of an evening now until the war was over. The ding-dong was cancelled 'for the time being' which made their lives extremely dull.

And they grew so accustomed to the flood of Government leaflets that were posted through their letterboxes that most went straight into the nearest drawer unread.

''Nother one a' them "Don't do this, don't do that's"' Mrs Geary would say when she saw a buff paper lying on the doormat. 'Bloody cheek. Who do they think they are?'

Peggy felt rather differently about all this information because it was issued by the Civil Defence and she knew how useful it could be. So she kept all their leaflets in a neat bundle in a shoe-box in her bedroom, just in case. And that meant that she was the person the neighbours referred to when they wanted to know what was being planned.

'Ask our Peggy,' Flossie would say proudly. 'She's our warden you know.' She'd quite forgotten how vehemently she'd opposed the ARP in the first place. Now she was all for it.

As the uneventful regimented days passed into uneventful regimented weeks and months, Peggy became steadily more useful. Without air raids to justify it, the black-out was a constant source of irritation and friction. The call 'You're showing a light!' was usually followed by a row and as the months passed the Wardens grew more and more unpopular. But Peggy seemed to be able to coax her neighbours into good behaviour without shouting at them, so it was Peggy who was sent to persuade the recalcitrant citizen.

She was issued with a uniform now that she was a full time member of the ARP and that pleased her too, for it was smart and businesslike, a dark blue battledress with 'warden' on the shoulder in gold lettering and the letters CD beneath a crown on the left breast pocket, and dark blue trousers which were warm and practical especially on night duty, even if they did scandalize Mrs Roderick. Besides, being in uniform made her feel closer to Jim, who wrote to her every other day and came home to see her whenever he had leave. In fact, taken all in all, her life was remarkably happy despite the war.

She did have one worry, that was true, but it was a private one, and her anxiety was tempered and confused by such extraordinary pleasure that it was difficult to know how to respond to any of it.

Part of the trouble was the enveloping darkness of the black-out. By the time Jim came home on his first forty-eight hour leave of the war the theatres and cinemas had been opened again so they were able to go to the pictures as usual, but their walk home was in almost total darkness and there were shop doorways every black inch of the way to tempt them to stop and kiss again. Not that they needed much temptation, especially as kissing standing up was even more pleasurable than kissing in the back row of the pictures. That night their love-making progressed by delicious and gradual degrees until they were both sore with ungratified desire.

Peggy protested each new embrace because she wasn't sure how far they ought to go. 'I'm sure we shouldn't,' she said into the muffling warmth of his tunic.

'Go on,' he urged. 'Who's to see us? You want to don't you?' And when she had to admit she did, 'Well then.'

'What if it's wrong?'

'It doesn't feel wrong does it?' he said, nuzzling into her neck.

'No,' she admitted, because it didn't. Not at the time. It was only afterwards that she wondered. And by then it was a bit late.

On his second short leave he came to collect her with an old raincoat over his arm, and that evening instead of going to the pictures they strolled into the park to walk and talk among the trees, and finally to sit on the raincoat and watch the sunset.

'This time next year we'll get married,' Jim said. 'I should've got my props by then.'

As a proposal it wasn't the most romantic thing she'd ever heard. 'Got your props?' she asked.

'I shall be an LAC.'

'Oh well as long as I know,' she laughed at him.

'I should be on five bob a day by then,' he said, 'and we shall get marriage allowance of seventeen bob a week. We could manage on that, couldn't we?'

'I expect so.'

'That's what we'll do then.'

'And where are we going to live?' she asked.

'Oh, we'll travel about,' he said easily 'Like a pair a' gippos. You get moved about a lot in the RAF. You could come with me.'

Peggy considered this briefly. It wasn't an inviting prospect. It would mean leaving her family and her friends and living out of a suitcase all the time. 'Perhaps the war'll be over by next year,' she said. 'Then they wouldn't have to move you about so much.'

'Some hopes,' he said. 'We shan't see the end a' this for a long time.'

'We might if they got on with it,' Peggy said. 'All this pussy-footing around. I don't know what they're playing at.'

'You let 'em pussy-foot as long as they like,' he said. 'The longer this phoney war goes on the better. They're delivering Spitfires and Hurricanes as fast as they can get them off the production line, but we haven't got anywhere near enough.'

It had grown dark as they talked. Now they could only see one another if they sat very close together. The grass was black, and there was no sign of the trees except for an occasional feathery outline silhouetted against the sky when the moon swam out of its cloud-cover.

'Why are we talking?' he said. 'Why don't we lie down?' And he spread the raincoat invitingly over the dead leaves.

They lay side by side and kissed one another in their private darkness. There wasn't a sound among the trees and no light except for the intermittent moon. They could have been alone in the middle of the countryside and he was holding her so tightly she could hardly breathe, his hand in the small of her back urging her closer and closer.

'Love you, love you, love you, love you,' he said, the way he always did, kissing and fondling. And then he was lying right on top of her and the pleasure of it was so acute it was making him groan.

To be urged on by such strong sensation was so tantalizing it took an effort of will for Peggy to speak. But she had to make the effort, because she wanted him so much it was making her dizzy and she knew that if she didn't stop him soon they might go too far.

305

'You got to stop,' she panted. 'Please.'

He lifted his chest and shoulders away from her, supporting himself on the palms of his hands. She could see his eyes shining in the faint moonlight and his hair falling over his forehead, and that ardent urgent expression that moved her so much. 'Why? Don't you want me to?'

'You know I want you to,' she said, and the words sounded like a groan. 'Too much. That's the trouble.'

'Well then,' he said. 'Let me.'

She wriggled out from underneath him and sat up, straightening her clothes. 'We mustn't,' she said. 'Not that. It ain't right.'

'Go on,' he said. 'There's a war on. It's different now.'

'No,' she insisted. 'It ain't. It ain't right.'

'Middle class morality,' he mocked, stroking the side of her face and pleased to see that she shivered at the pleasure of it. 'How long we got to wait then?'

'Till we're married I suppose.'

'Oh God, Peg, that won't be till next year. I've just told you. You're not going to go on saying no till next year?'

She didn't know the answer to that. Perhaps she wasn't. Perhaps she was. She'd said no for the moment and that was enough to be going on with.

'What are you scared of?' he persisted. 'I wouldn't get you pregnant.' He'd braved the barber's final embarrassing question after an unnecessary haircut and was fully prepared.

In a vague way she'd accepted that he would know what to do about that. 'No,' she said, speaking more calmly now. 'It ain't that. 'It's just – oh, I don't know – I don't think we should. It ain't right.'

He sat up too, sighing with resignation, fished his battered packet of fags out of his pocket, and shook out two cigarettes, putting them both in his mouth to light them and shielding the flame of the match carefully with both hands. When they were both alight he passed one across to her as he usually did. 'There you are, kid,' he said, lovingly. 'I take a pretty dim view of this, you know.'

She drew on the cigarette, glad that he had accepted her interruption with such good grace. 'I do love you,' she said.

306

'One day perhaps you'll show it,' he suggested, narrowing his eyes against the smoke.

He looked so handsome, narrow-eyed and firm jawed and tousled in that admirable uniform, that her heart contracted with distress at the thought of what she'd just done to him, letting him go so far and then saying no. It wasn't kind. 'I'm ever so sorry,' she said. 'It's just ... '

'I know what it is,' he said. First time nerves. He'd heard a lot of talk about it, most of it ribald. 'Come on. Time we was getting back.'

After he'd returned to Catterick at the end of his leave, kissing her goodbye at the station most ardently to show her that he loved her as much as ever, she was glad she'd said no. It was the right thing. Everybody knew that. And in these days they all had to try and behave as well as they possibly could. Everybody knew that too. The certainty that she *had* behaved well despite temptation increased her private sense of worth even further. She was sensible Peggy Furnivall who could be depended on to do the right thing no matter what. And even though she had a sneaking feeling that she was being smug, she went on feeling virtuous and pleased with herself.

It was Joan who was miserable. Despite being kept very busy in the factory by day, she missed her children painfully.

'If only they was old enough to write a proper letter,' she said to Peggy late one night at the end of October. Flossie and Baby had gone to the pictures and Peggy had just come off the day shift so they had the kitchen to themselves and plenty of time to talk. 'They send me a postcard reg'lar as clockwork, every Tuesday morning it comes, but they always say the same thing. You can't really tell how they are from that, now can you?'

The postcard she pushed across the kitchen table to her sister was neatly-written but it sounded impersonal. 'We are well. We like it in the country. Mrs Ray is looking after us alright. Love from Yvonne and Norman.'

'Yes,' Peggy said. 'I see what you mean. Don't they ever say anything else?'

'No. They don't. I reckon they write it up on the black-

L.P. - 14
307

board for 'em and they just copy it.'

'No news is good news,' Peggy offered, trying to comfort.

'It's their bein' in the country I can't stand,' Joan said. 'I'd go down an' see 'em, only Sid mightn't like it.'

'Well don't tell him,' Peggy advised. 'What the eye don't see the heart can't grieve for. He's not coming home this weekend is he? And you've got the money now you're working.'

'I asked him to go last weekend,' Joan said. 'He said it'ud upset them. Do you think it would?'

'It might,' Peggy said. 'People do say it's better just to leave them where they are.' She'd had to deliver an ARP leaflet last week saying just that.

'It's such a worry,' Joan said. 'Mrs Jones' two came back yesterday. That's twelve of 'em back now just in our street.'

'But they're the weakly ones,' Peggy said. She didn't approve of evacuees returning. What was the point in sending them into the country to be safe if they all came trooping back? 'Your two are made of sterner stuff.'

'I hope so,' Joan said. 'So you think not to visit?'

'Yes,' Peggy decided, giving her advice firmly as she always did these days. 'Leave it a bit longer and see, eh?'

'That's what Sid said,' Joan told her. 'So I suppose I'd better. If only they could write me a proper letter.'

The next morning she wrote to them both at length and lovingly, as she always did, but this time she threw out a hint in a PS 'Can you tell me a bit more about how you are, my darlings? What do you have to eat? What is your bedroom like? What are they learning you at school?'

The next Sunday postcard was more difficult for Mrs Ray to write. 'You'd better say you're getting on all right at school,' she instructed as the children sat before her at the kitchen table with their pens and their blotting paper and a bottle of blue-black ink before them. 'There's the words.'

Yvonne copied neatly while Norman waited to add his name. And as there was rather more to write and she had a little more time that evening she tried to include an honest answer to her mother in addition to the words Mrs Ray had written out for her. If she kept it hidden under a corner of the blotting paper, they could put the stamp on it quick and take it down to the pillar-box and nobody need know.

'What are you hiding there?' Mr Ray said, leaning across the table to peer at her and the postcard.

'Nothing,' she said, pulling the blotting paper even further across.

'Give it here,' he said, snatching the postcard.

Yvonne watched with alarm as her message was lifted into the air.

'What's this?' he roared when he saw what she'd written. ' "We don't like it here. We want to come home." Is that the sort of thing to write to your poor mother. You *will* upset her. What nasty children you are. I can see we shall have to teach them better manners, won't we, Mother? I'll get a little cane for them tomorrow. It's about time their behaviour was taken in hand. "We want to come home" indeed!' He was furious at such deceit, and frightened too in case their treatment of the pair got out.

'We do want to go home,' Norman said. 'We do too.'

'That,' Mrs Ray said bringing her face right down to his level to threaten him with it, 'is because you're a nasty cowardly little thing. And you ought to be ashamed of yourself to say such things.'

'A cane, Mother,' Mr Ray said. 'That's what they need. They'll be much nicer children when there's a cane in the house.'

The cane was bought the next day and hung ceremoniously on a nail beside the fireplace. It had an immediate and unforeseen effect. Norman was so frightened by it that he wet the bed.

The warm dampness spreading against her legs woke Yvonne up. 'Look what you're doing,' she whispered to her terrified brother, thumping him in the back to wake him. 'Why didn't you wake up and use the pot, you dirty boy? You'll get the stick, you see if you don't.'

'Perhaps it'll be dry by morning,' Norman hoped.

'No, it won't,' Yvonne said. 'There's too much of it, I'm sopping wet. We shall have to sleep up the other end.'

Sure enough the mattress was still wet when they woke in the morning.

'We'll cover it up with a blanket,' Yvonne decided. 'Then she won't see it.' Norman's woebegone face was making her feel sorry for him. 'Come on, we'll get off to school quick before she says anything.' Luckily it was their turn to go to school in the mornings that week.

But although Mrs Ray rarely swept their bedroom and usually only opened the door to check that the blankets had been folded according to her instructions, that morning she was alerted by the smell.

'You filthy little pigs,' she said, when the two children crept into her kitchen for their dinner. 'What's *that*, eh?' She had the cane in her hand and was pointing with it at their shameful mattress, which was propped up against a chair in front of the stove, steaming.

'We're ever so sorry,' Yvonne said. 'We didn't mean to.'

'I'll give you sorry,' Mrs Ray said grimly. 'I'll make you sorry you was ever born. Come here.'

They shuffled towards her, their hearts thumping like drums.

'We didn't mean it,' Norman tried, but she cut off his words and into his legs with the first swish of the cane.

It was a furious assault, but neither of them tried to run away from it. Where could they run? They stood where she tugged them and endured, wincing at the impact of the first blow, whimpering at the second and crying aloud by the time the last descended.

Mrs Ray hung the cane back on its hook, her face grim with satisfaction. 'Pull your socks up,' she instructed. Red weals were rising on the pale flesh of their calves and there was no need for anyone to see that.

They pulled up their socks, inching them gingerly over the stinging.

Mrs Ray turned her attention to dinner.

'If you think I'm going to waste good food on filthy little pigs that wet their beds you've got another think coming. Bread and water for you. That's all you deserve. And think yourself jolly lucky you get anything at all. You're nothing better than animals.'

The kitchen was hot with bad temper and rank with the stink of the mattress. By now Yvonne was feeling so sick it was almost impossible to chew anything, let alone dry bread. But she made a valiant effort, swallowing the first mouthful and taking a sip of water to wash it down, and presently Norman followed her example as well as he could for crying.

Their hostess stood over them until they'd forced down every harsh crumb and their plates and mugs were empty. 'Now get out into the yard the pair of you,' she said, 'and don't let me *see* you till bedtime.'

'Oh Yvey,' Norman cried when they were in the orchard and out of earshot, 'what are we going to do?'

'I don't know,' Yvonne admitted.

'Let's run away.'

'Where to?'

'Home.'

'We'd have to go on a train,' Yvonne said reasonably. 'We come on a train, so we'd have to go back on one. An' we don't know where the trains are, do we?'

That was true.

'We can't stay here,' Norman persisted. 'She'll hit us all the time now. We'll have to tell somebody we can't stay.'

'Who?'

Neither of them knew.

'We'll tell Mum,' Norman said.

'How?'

'We'll write a letter. I mean, you can write a letter an' I'll sign it.'

'They'll read it.'

That was true too.

'You won't have to wet the bed again,' Yvonne said.

'Oh I won't,' Norman said earnestly. 'I promise.'

'See it wet see it dry?'

Norman licked one finger and held it up for her inspection, wet and then wiped dry.

But of course it wasn't a promise he could possibly keep.

After that first awful day he wet the bed with terrifying frequency and they were both caned for it every time, even though he confessed that he was the one to blame.

'You're as bad as one another,' Mr Ray told them. 'Dirty little pigs the pair of you. Dirty slummy little pigs. But we won't let you get away with it, will we, Mother?'

311

There were days when Yvonne said she didn't think it could get any worse. Caned in the morning, sent to school hungry, kept out of the house in the cold of December with nothing to do when they weren't at school and nowhere to go except to prowl the lanes with the other evacuees who were kept out too. 'It's just got to get better.'

But she was wrong. Christmas was the worst day of the lot. They missed their mother most terribly then, sitting chilled and silent in the church while a strange vicar boomed above them, and mute and miserable in the Rays' dark parlour while their hosts entertained them with ghoulish tales of Christmas funerals. And back in Deptford, waking alone in her flat without them, Joan grieved too, missing them so much it made her ache all through her body. Even when she cut across to Paradise Row for Christmas dinner, she couldn't really enjoy the meal or the company for thinking of her poor lonely kids stuck out there in the country. Oh a dreadful day!

And then it was February and in February the winter began.

That first winter of the war was one of the coldest that anyone could remember. Down on the south coast the snow lay in drifts as high as a man's thigh and all along the shoreline the sea was so cold that it froze into thin grey ice-floes that heaved and shifted on the sullen water. In mid-Sussex, roads were impassable for days at a time, pipes froze solid, schools were shut, sheep had to be dug out of the snow, and the children's uncurtained bedroom window was perpetually patterned with thick ice crystals growing up across the glass like complicated white ferns. Now they had to trudge to school through heavy snow and across exhausting drifts, their bare knees stinging with cold. Before long they both had chilblains on their fingers and toes and Norman had a bright red crop all round the lobes of his ears.

And as if that weren't enough they had another problem to contend with too. When the evacuees first arrived in Myrtlebury they outnumbered the local kids by nearly two to one, so although they were deeply resented – for hadn't they invaded homes and taken over the local school for half of every blessed day, and didn't they just stink –

when resentment boiled over into pitched battles out in the fields, the intruders usually won. Now, after five months, the position had changed. So many of the Londoners had gone back home that the evacuees were fewer in number than their reluctant hosts. And the snow provided an ideal weapon. With a stone as the violent centre of every hard-packed ball, battle could be joined in earnest. And was.

The locals lay in ambush behind the drifts when school was over for the day, and if they weren't wary the 'vacuees were caught by a sudden attack, which was often quite dangerous, for when a snowball struck hard it could cut.

The first time Norman ran back to Mr Ray's house with blood streaming from a gash on his forehead, Mrs Ray was cross with him.

'Don't come running to me for sympathy,' she said. 'If you will play rough games that's what you'll have to expect. Go and clean yourself up and don't get blood all over everything.'

The second time, when both children were cut, they cleaned themselves with handfuls of snow and didn't say anything when they got back.

By now their despair was total and numbing. The longer this evacuation went on the more like a trap it felt. There was no one they could tell and nowhere they could escape and the war was still 'on'. Sir said so. And it was no good complaining about the cold because everybody in England was cold. Sir told them that too.

In Greenwich it was Peggy who found it particularly hard to keep warm.

For once in her life Flossie Furnivall approved of the bad weather. She and Mrs Roderick were convinced that the Jerries wouldn't send their bombers over in a snow-storm, and now that they'd both got their little pocket torches and a secret supply of No 8 batteries they were ready for anything. The cinemas were open every after-noon and some of the films were really lovely with dancing and singing and such pretty clothes. It quite took you out of yourself and it was cosy all sitting close together on those nice plush seats.

'If you ask me,' she said, whenever anyone complained,

'this cold can last as long as it likes.'

'If you ask me,' Peggy said, 'it can stop tomorrow. I'm sick of it.'

The warden's post at the flats had been draughty in the autumn, but now it was hung with icicles inside and out. Even with mitts and gloves on her hands her fingers were numb with cold within minutes of coming on duty. Charlie Goodall invested in a Thermos flask and provided hot coffee for the night-shift, but they were still long hours and they passed with glacier slowness.

Flossie knitted thick gloves for her and an even thicker muffler and knee-length socks to wear under her Wellingtons but the cold penetrated every single garment however thick. And to make matters worse Jim's leave was cancelled because of the weather.

'Pretty ropey here,' he wrote from Catterick. 'The oil is so cold it keeps congealing and then the engines won't start.'

Pretty ropey was an understatement. They spent the winter dealing with flat starter-motors, burst valves, and congealed oil. The wind whistled across the airfield unobstructed, and as the temperature of the aircraft metal was usually several degrees below freezing, their fingers went numb within a few minutes of starting work. And there was nothing they could do to lower the viscosity of the oil. They tried a mobile heater to warm it before they transferred it into the aircraft's tank, but unexpected scramble exercises made that method impractical. They tried canvas covers designed to fit the engines, cockpit, mainplane and tailplane, and even the propeller blades, but they weren't the solution either. When they got damp they froze nearly solid, and then it took far too long to undo the lacing and release the plane for action.

Several times a day, the propellers had to be turned by hand to break the cold seal of the oil in the cylinders, and then once they were started the engines had to be run excessively to warm up, and that caused problems too. There was never any end to it because the fighters had to be on almost perpetual stand-by.

But the one consolation in all this was that the phoney war continued. The fighters were on stand-by but the

German bombers didn't arrive.

'We've run through the rule book,' Jim wrote to Peggy, 'and now we're thrown back on our own resources. That's what happens with a combination of war and foul weather. You improvise. Most of us here are pretty brassed off what with the snow and no leave. Still it can't last for ever. I keep lighting two fags every time and then I don't know what to do with the other one. I haven't kissed you for months! Roll on the spring. The minute the thaw starts I shall be knocking on your door, to see if you've thawed out too.'

But when the thaw eventually began, it wasn't Jim who came knocking on Peggy's door, just as she'd got home from night-shift one morning, it was Sid Owen.

'Off ter France in a few days,' he explained. 'Embarkation leave, this is.' He looked very smart in his uniform but there was something odd about his expression that put Peggy on her guard. If she hadn't known what a bold man he was she'd have thought he was anxious, the way he kept wrinkling his brows and looking away from her.

'Wish you luck,' she said, wondering what he really wanted. She felt too tired to want to entertain him for long but there was nobody else to do it. Baby was at work and Mum had gone off to get the shopping

'Thing is,' he began, frowning again. 'Thing is, I got a favour to ask.'

'Yes?'

'It's my Joan you see,' he said. 'She ain't exactly in the pink nowadays. Leastways I don't think she is. Always on about the kids and whether they're all right an' that sort a think. So what I was wondering was, could you keep an eye on her for me? Just till I get back.'

'Of course,' Peggy said at once, smiling at him with the first real warmth she'd shown towards him since he married her sister. Fancy him looking after Joan like this. Perhaps she'd misjudged him all these years. 'Don't you worry about a thing. We'll all look after her.'

'Ta,' he said. 'I knew if I came an' saw you ... '

CHAPTER 24

Once she'd had her first much-thumbed letter from 'BEF in France', Joan wrote and told the kids that their father was on active service. It was a proud moment for her and she wanted them to share it. 'Your daddy is in France with the army', she wrote. 'They are going to beat Hitler and then the war will be over and you can come home.'

Yvonne read the entire letter without help and showed Norman the words where it said 'your daddy is in France with the army' so that he could decipher them too, and when they'd both read it several times they took it to school to show their teachers, walking between the wakening hedges with the precious paper clutched in Yvonne's right hand. There were primroses under the hedges and the apple trees were already putting out pink and white blossom and Daddy was going to beat Hitler. After that awful winter things were coming right again.

'You must be very proud of him,' Sir said, when Yvonne showed him the letter. 'You must write to your mother and tell her how proud you are, mustn't you. Or better still you can write a message on your Easter card. We're all going to make Easter cards this morning, when we've done our sums.'

'Are we going to post them?' Yvonne asked, seeing hope of deliverance at last.

'We're going to pack them up in a big parcel,' the teacher told her, 'and send them all to Mr Griffin back in London and he's going to deliver them for us.'

'Can I write anything I like?'

'Of course.'

So when the card was drawn and she'd coloured it neatly and Sir had folded it in two for her, she sat quietly at her desk and wrote her first uncensored message to her mother.

Joan came home from work that evening tired to the bone. They'd had a terrible day in the factory. The new explosives they were working with were so potent that they all had to wear special cream on their hands and faces for protection, but that day her skin was irritated despite the cream, and the smell in the workshop had made her feel sick all afternoon.

When she saw the envelope lying on the doormat at the foot of the stairs addressed in Yvonne's lovely round familiar handwriting she was cheered at once. She stooped to pick the letter up, moving slowly because her back was aching and opened it with her thumb as she was climbing the stairs, relishing the moment and feeling just a little closer to her distant children even though they were only linked by paper. An Easter card, she thought, dear little girl. I'll bet she's done it herself, with that yellow chick drawn so neat and everything.

She half filled the kettle and set it on the stove to boil, then she sat down at the kitchen table to read her message. The pathetic words gave her such a shock, it was like being punched in the stomach. 'Plese coem and get us,' Yvonne had written. 'We are unhappy hear. Mr and Mrs Ray are nasty. With love from Yvonne. Plese, plese coem.'

She put the card in her bag and without even stopping for the cup of tea she needed so much she set off for Greenwich.

To her anxious eyes, the kitchen at number six seemed to be full of noise and people. Jim was home on his long-awaited spring leave and he and Peggy were sitting at the kitchen table eating an early supper before she went on duty. Mrs Geary was knitting in the corner by the wireless set, and Flossie and Baby were putting on their make-up ready for a night at the pictures.

Joan plunged into her news without greeting or prelimi-

317

nary. 'They want to come home,' she said, 'I've had this awful letter. They're unhappy they say. You look. What am I going to do?'

Flossie put her lipstick on the mantelpiece and swept across to read the card. 'Poor little beggars,' she said. 'They're unhappy right enough. No mistake about that. Turn the wireless down a bit, Mrs G.'

'I knew it,' Joan mourned. 'I always said it was a mistake, only he wouldn't have it. What am I going to do?'

'Leave 'em where they are,' Peggy advised, unconsciously using the words of the ARP poster. 'They're bound to be homesick now and then, anybody would, but at least they're safe.'

'I don't know,' Joan worried, dithering beside the table.

'It's nice writing,' Baby said when she'd read the card. She felt obliged to make some contribution and didn't know what else to say.

'Oh dear oh dear,' Joan said.

'Have a cup a' tea, lovey,' Mrs Geary offered. 'There's one in the pot.'

But it was Jim who made the most pertinent remark.

'What do you want to do?' he asked.

Joan's answer was immediate and honest. 'Go straight down there an' see for myself.'

'We'll go tomorrow,' he said. 'First thing.'

'We?' Joan asked.

'I'll come with you.'

How straight and quick he is, Peggy thought. Make a decision, act on it, no messing about. Her own advice seemed negative now beside his good sense. 'I'll come too,' she said, making her own decision equally quickly and when he looked a query at her. 'It's all right. I can sleep on the train. Well, cat-nap anyway.'

'You better stay overnight,' Mum said to Joan. 'I'll make up the camp bed, then you can make an early start.'

So they went to Myrtlebury on the first train out of Greenwich the next morning. It was a cool spring day, all gold and blue and green and white, a day of budded daffodils and tender primroses and willow catkins trembling like lambs' tails under a blue sky full of white clouds billowing clean as sheets. A hopeful day, Peggy thought,

318

striding along the dusty lane towards Myrtlebury with Jim close beside her, hopeful and peaceful and miles away from air raid shelters and tin helmets and the long cold watches of the night.

But Joan carried guilt and anxiety through the Sussex lanes like a yoke across her bowed shoulders, as the familiar smells of the countryside rose to plague her, damp earth and decaying leaves, middens and muck heaps, stale straw and stagnant pools. There was a dung spreader at work in one field they passed, tossing manure into the air in dark pungent gobbets and she could hear sheep bleating pitifully somewhere out of sight.

'It's so cruel in the country,' she said as memory stuck pins in her mind. 'I should never've sent 'em, only he would have it. I always knew it was wrong. It's all very well people saying send 'em, they don't know what it's like, and I do. I always knew it was wrong.'

They let her grumble, he out of compassion for her anxiety, she because she remembered Tillingbourne.

And presently they came to the village school and the sound of children chanting tables.

Joan went straight in through the half-open door, her face eager and her feet quick now that she'd arrived at last. But she emerged minutes later to tell the others that the London children weren't there.

'Only the locals in the morning,' she said. 'Our kids come in in the afternoon.'

'Where are they now?' Peggy asked.

'In their billets, the teacher said.'

So they followed the lane a little further. It was a surprise to all three of them when they rounded the bend in the road and discovered that the address that Joan and Peggy had been writing to all these months belonged to an undertaker. And their second surprise was the sight of Mr Ray, who came to answer Joan's knock wearing his obsequious professional face, drooping with assumed sorrow.

'How can I help you, Madam?'

'I've come to see my children,' Joan said, standing belligerently on his doorstep, feet astride.

'Children?' he said, misunderstanding her. 'I don't believe we have any children in our chapel of rest at

319

present. Always such a sadness, children.'

'My children,' Joan said, scowling at his idiocy. 'Yvonne and Norman Owen. My children.'

Understanding dawned visibly. The expression changed from unctuous to guarded, and then, after a quick glance at Jim's uniformed belligerence, with equal rapidity from guarded to welcoming. 'My dear Mrs Owen, of course.'

'Where are they?' Joan said, setting her arms akimbo.

'Oh,' Mr Ray said vaguely, his watery eyes flickering, 'somewhere or other. Out at play you know. We don't proscribe them in any way. Come in, why don't you, Mrs Owen? I'll send someone out to find them.'

'We'll look for 'em,' Joan said to Jim and Peggy, 'and we'll all come back when we've found 'em.'

'Where to?' Jim asked. As a townie he was lost among all these fields.

Fortunately Joan and Peggy knew where to look. 'Water's our best bet,' Joan said. 'There's got to be a stream or a river somewhere.'

And sure enough there was a group of scruffy children paddling in a rather muddy stream just below the undertaker's house.

'Yvey?' their leader said. 'No, Miss. She ain't here.'

'Probably got the stick,' another urchin offered.

Joan's heart contracted with rage and misery. The stick. She knew it. Hadn't she always known it? 'Who gives her the stick?'

'Her foster mum.'

Oh she does, does she? Joan thought. I'll see about her. But first things first. 'Where does she go when she's had the stick?' she asked.

'Up the barn most times,' the urchin told her, pointing at a distant building covered in decaying thatch.

They ran to the barn, stumbling through the weeds and willows at the water's edge, tripping over fallen branches, leaping forward along the slippery path.

But at the barn door, Joan stopped and signalled to the others not to make a sound because she could see her children squatting among the straw. They had a jam-jar full of water set between them and Yvonne was bathing her brother's legs with a dock leaf. Even from the door and

320

in the half light of the barn Joan could see the red weals and purple bruises on their arms and legs.

There was no doubt now what had to be done. No doubt at all.

'Yvey! Norman!' she called. 'It's Mummy. I've come to take you home.'

They hurled themselves into her arms, weeping with relief, and soon all five of them were sitting on the straw cuddling and kissing and examining injuries, talking and weeping and laughing all at once.

'Take 'em to the station,' Jim said to Joan when the first flush of the reunion was over. 'Me an' Peg'll pick up their things.'

'I've got a score to settle with that old humbug and his wife,' Joan said.

'You stay with the kids,' Jim told her. 'We'll settle the score, won't we, Peggy?'

But settling scores with Mr Ray was like picking up jelly in a sieve. He oozed away from every accusation.

'All children need discipline, as I'm sure you'll agree,' he said, when he'd ushered them both into his sitting room and Jim had told him they'd seen the results of his caning.

'Discipline's one thing,' Jim said angrily. 'Brutality's another.'

'Oh come now, not brutality,' Mr Ray demurred. 'You make me sound like a Nazi.'

'We shall need their ration books,' Peggy said, practical as ever.

'Oh come now,' Mr Ray said again. 'There's no need for that. Is there, Mother?' For Mrs Ray had walked into the sitting room to see what was going on.

'The children are going home,' Peggy told them. 'If you'll get their ration books. Mrs Ray, we'll pack their bags.'

That news put both the Rays into an obvious panic. 'No, no,' Mrs Ray said, her long face twitching as she searched through a drawer in the sideboard. 'We'll pack, won't we, Father? We wouldn't dream of putting you to the trouble. Here's the ration books.'

'No trouble,' Jim said, walking straight past them and out into the corridor towards the stairs. 'Up here is it?'

'No,' Mr Ray said, following him. 'No, no. I forbid it.'

I'll bet you do, Jim thought pounding up the stairs. 'In here is it?' he asked his hand on the nearest doorknob.

'No it is not,' Mrs Ray said icily. 'That's our room. You can't do this.'

But Jim was throwing open the other two doors on the landing. Bathroom. Lumber room. Up the next flight with Peggy at his heels and the Rays puffing protestations after them. One door. That's it.

The sight and smell of that dark attic room shocked him so much that he stood where he was for a second just taking it in, stained mattress, stinking pot, naked light bulb, dirty brown blankets, no furniture, no sheets or pillow cases, just their two pathetic suitcases full of dirty clothes that the poor kids had obviously tried to keep as tidy as they could for they were all folded up. 'No wonder you didn't want us to see this,' he said to Mr Ray.

'They're very naughty children,' Mr Ray said. 'Always dirty, aren't they, Mother? We've done our best.'

'We'll pack for you,' Mrs Ray said, trying to put her body between Jim and the sight of the bed. 'You don't want to do that.'

'Hop it,' he said to her. 'Come on, Peggy. The sooner they're out a' this the better.' And he began to fling the few clothes that had been left on the bed into the nearest case. 'I've never seen such a pig heap. You ought to be ashamed of yourselves, letting kids live like this.'

Mr Ray tried to draw himself up to his full height, always a difficult thing for a stout man to do. His jowls were quivering with outrage. 'You dare to come in here,' he shouted, 'breaking in, accusing us. You don't stop to think what we've had to put up with. We took your filthy children in when nobody else would have them, let me tell you. Slum children, that's all they are. Worse than animals. More than any decent God-fearing people could stand. You ask anyone in the village.'

'Out my way,' Jim ordered as he and Peggy put the last of the smelly clothes in the cases. 'There's a jersey in the corner, Peg. And what's this?'

There was a piece of rock-hard pastry under the pillow.

'That's his gingerbread man, poor kid,' Peggy said.

'Must bring that. It's his treasure.'

'I forbid this,' Mr Ray said, and he blundered forward as though he was going to barge them both out of the room with his belly.

It was a great mistake. Jim seized him by the scruff of his neck and flung him to one side. It was such a sudden and violent movement that the older man was caught off balance and fell backwards right into the damp centre of the mattress.

'Mother!' he yelled. 'Stop them! Mother! Do something!'

But Mrs Ray was crouching by the window with her hands over her mouth.

'Look what you've done,' her husband shouted. 'I'm soaking wet. My trousers are ruined. You've got piddle all over my best trousers.'

'Think yourself bloody lucky it ain't rammed down your throat,' Jim said, closing the second case.

'I'll have the law on you.'

'No you won't,' Jim said calmly picking up the cases. 'Because if you do we'll report you to the NSPCC for assault and battery. Come on, Peggy. We're finished here.'

It was a marvellous journey home, so full of relief and happiness and excitement, it was over almost before they were aware it had begun. Jim was purring with the success of their expedition, Joan sat between her two smelly children and cuddled them all the way, and Peggy put her head on Jim's shoulder and took her cat-nap in satisfied exhaustion.

'Bath,' Joan promised happily when they all arrived at New Cross Gate. 'Clean clothes, a nice meal. What d'yer fancy?'

'Fish an' chips,' they said with one voice.

'Thanks ever so much for coming with me,' she said to Jim and Peggy.

'What are neighbours for?' Jim said, and Peggy kissed her and hugged the kids.

By now Peggy was looking very tired. 'Bed for you,' Jim said, as they climbed aboard the Greenwich train.

'You got a one-track mind,' she teased him sleepily.

'Who's fault's that?'

It was true, Peggy thought, as she settled her head on the rough cloth of his tunic and began to drift to sleep again. I was wrong about sending the kids away. She knew that now and was pained by the knowledge, because she'd been so free with her advice and Joan had taken it so trustingly. I *have* been smug, she thought, as the train rocked her soothingly against his chest. Smug and wrong. Wrong about the kids, wrong about us. And before sleep sucked her downwards she made up her mind to put things right.

'We'll have a ding-dong,' Mr Allnutt said. 'A welcome-home ding-dong. Poor little beggars. We can keep the doors shut an' nail the black-out down.'

'An' invite the Warden,' his wife said, smiling at him. A ding-dong would be lovely. Just the right thing. They hadn't had a get-together for months. Not since the war broke out. High time they started up again.

It was a riot. John Cooper said he'd never heard such a noise and the parrot was so happy it nearly choked itself trying to squawk, sing and swear at the same time. They sang 'The more we are together' and 'Knees up Mother Brown' and 'The Lambeth Walk' and Mr Brown played 'There'll always be an England' on his mouth organ and because there were so many people singing the words the tune was almost recognizable, and they 'Rolled out the Barrel' and Percy was allowed to stay up late to be with Norman and Yvonne who were the guests of honour and the heroes of the hour.

'You can 'ave whatever you like,' Mr Allnutt promised them. 'Top brick off the chimney.'

But they both said they'd rather have shrimps and Uncle Gideon said he'd cut off and get them directly.

'Be a treat to get some air,' he grinned. With the windows blacked out, the door tightly shut, and so many people singing and dancing, the heat in the little room was unbearable. 'Turn out the light. I'm going to open the door. Anyone else want ter get out?'

There was a scramble at the open door as dark figures emerged into the street, and two of them were Peggy and Jim.

324

'Where's our lovebirds off to?' Mrs Roderick's voice said out of the darkness.

'Same as you, Mrs R,' Jim said. 'Breath a' fresh air.'

'I'm off home to get me glass,' Mrs Roderick said. 'I don't like drinking out of other people's. Mind how you go. Don't forget the shelter.' It was pitch dark out in the street, and their little pocket torches only gave a pool of faint light immediately in front of their feet.

Jim and Peggy walked arm-in-arm down the inky street until they came to the boot scraper beside the front door of number two.

'Has she gone?' Jim asked, peering back for the flicker of Mrs Roderick's torch. There was no light in the street at all. 'Good,' he said, fishing the key through the letter-box. 'We've got the house to ourselves.'

And a bed to spread out on in the back room he rented from his sister, and a lock on the door to keep the world at bay.

'You had this all planned, didn't you?' she teased as he drew the lock to. They'd kissed all the way up the stairs and they were both breathless with a heady combination of desire and anticipation.

'Correction,' he said, 'I had it all hoped.'

She put her arms round his waist and kissed him lovingly. When they drew apart the question on his face was too clear to need words.

'Yes,' she said, switching out the light.

Afterwards he opened the black-out curtains and they lay side by side on his crumpled bed and smoked in lazy contentment, watching the burning tips of their two cigarettes swimming gently up and down like two red fireflies in the darkness. They could hear the ding-dong below them, the piano sounding quite clear above the babble of cheerful voices.

'OK?' he asked.

'Yes, very OK. Hunky-dory.'

'I love you so much,' he said, stroking her hair with his free hand.

'More than you did before?'

'Much much more.'

Lying like this, so warm and easy, with her head on his shoulder and his finger in her hair, she couldn't think why she'd made them both wait so long. Reason told her she ought to have waited until they were married, that she ought to feel ashamed, but she didn't, she felt wonderful, with that amazing pleasure still echoing, spreading languorous waves of well-being all through her.

'If I stay here much longer I shall go to sleep,' she said.

'Go to sleep then. I'll let you.'

'They'll miss us.'

'No they won't. Not in that crush.'

'I can't stay here all night.'

'You could. All night and every night if you wanted.'

It was a tempting idea but it had to be resisted. 'If we did *that* they'd all know. I couldn't bear anyone to know, Jim.'

'They won't,' he assured her. 'We'll be so discreet they won't know a thing. Like spies.'

'You'd make a lousy spy,' she laughed.

He pretended to be annoyed. 'I'd make a first-rate spy.'

'With your face?'

'What's wrong with my face?'

'Nothing,' she said, kissing it. 'I love it. Not very good at hiding your feelings though, is it? Even old Mrs Roderick calls us the lovebirds. God! I wouldn't want Mrs Roderick to find out. Think how *she'd* gossip.'

'No one'll find out,' he said, sitting up reluctantly. 'We'll go back to the ding-dong in a minute. When they're making a racket. They're a bit quiet just now.'

So they knocked at Mr Allnutt's door when the company were in full voice singing, 'If it wasn't for the 'ouses in between.' And just as he'd predicted, nobody paid any attention to their return. Percy was fast asleep on his father's shoulder, Joan was cuddling both her nice clean sweet-smelling children, Mrs Roderick and Flossie were on their third port and lemon, 'Well if you can't run to a bit of extravagance in wartime when can you?' and Cyril Brown was arguing with Mr Allnutt and Uncle Gideon and John Cooper.

'Another two months, that's what I give it,' he was saying. 'Two months an' it'll be all patched up an' we can get back ter normal.'

'Get away with you,' John Cooper said. 'You mean to tell me we'd stand by an' let Hitler run all over Europe?'

'Jack next door's got his call-up papers,' Gideon said. 'That don't look like the end of it to me.'

'We don't know the half of what's going on behind the scenes,' Cyril Brown persisted. 'There's peace plans all over the shop. The Pope's working on it, an' the Queen of Holland and the King a' the Belgians, an' that feller Roosevelt. Oh no! We'll patch it up. I'd lay money. We don't want ter fight the Germans. We got too much in common.'

'Like an air force and an army,' Mr Allnutt said wryly. 'You do talk out the back a' your neck sometimes, Cyril.'

'Two months,' Cyril said, nodding wisely. 'You mark my words. April May it'll all be over. You'll see headlines in the paper by May.'

Sure enough there were headlines in the paper. On 10 May the *Evening Standard* declared, 'Nazis invade Holland, Belgium, Luxembourg: many airports bombed. Allies answer call for aid. RAF planes are in action.'

The phoney war was over and the fighting was about to begin.

CHAPTER 25

The Stuka screamed towards them out of an immaculate blue sky, the shrill note of its engine rising higher and higher as it dived. At the first sound of its approach people on the crowded road had begun to scatter, now they were running pell-mell, scrambling into ditches, falling in panic, their faces distorted with fear, shouting orders, yelling and screaming, here a man pushing his children before him with both hands, there a woman with a baby clutched to her breast, old men stumbling bleary-eyed, dogs barking frantically, soldiers taking cover behind their carriers, families crouched together along the flanks of deserted cars, as the killer plane bore down upon them, its guns spitting fire.

Sid Owen had his rifle at the ready, like the rest of his platoon, but he had to concentrate to hold it steady because fear was making him shake. The plane was nearly overhead. They could see its blunt nose cone, the black crosses on those bent wings, the pilot grinning behind the glass cover of his cockpit, as his guns cut a red swathe through the mass of bodies on the road below him.

'Fire!' the sergeant yelled into the uproar. But the order was unnecessary. Most of his men were already blazing away, aiming in sheer fury at this huge obscene untouchable target.

Two bombs were falling, twisting in the air as if they were bouncing.

'Take cover!' the sergeant's voice yelled. But there

wasn't any cover. Only the trailer and the dust of the road. Sid just had time to fling himself to the ground and cover his head with his hands before the first bomb exploded, lifting the earth under his chest and filling his mouth with dust. Then the second, further away, as grit and debris fell in a stinging shower, punching his shoulders, spattering the road, crunching against the roof of a nearby car.

'Take cover!' Sid said bitterly to the boy lying beside him.

The boy was weeping. 'Fucking war!' he said. 'Fucking Stukas! Fucking Frenchies.'

'You all right, Tommy?'

'Fucking war,' Tommy wept. But he didn't seem to be bleeding.

Sid got to his feet, surprised by how stiff and tired he felt all of a sudden. The road was full of wreckage and bodies. And it was horribly quiet. Even the dogs weren't barking.

He lit himself a fag and offered one to Tommy. 'There y'are, Tommy,' he said, ''ave a drag.'

'Ta, mate,' Tommy said, taking the cigarette gratefully, his fingers trembling. He was doing his best to recover although his eyes were bloodshot and swimming with unshed tears. 'Fucking 'ell, Sid! That was close. I thought I was a goner that time.'

People were moving again, crawling out of the ditches, running to the injured, weeping with grief and shock. There was blood everywhere, pumping out of wounds, seeping into dark pools under fallen bodies, even splashed along the side of their carrier. And the keening of grief was as terrible as the scream of the Stuka. A woman rocked the blood-red body of her baby in her arms, two small children sat beside the dead body of their father, huge-eyed and silent, too stunned to speak, an old man wandered aimlessly among the wreckage picking up shoes, dogs sniffed the corpses, one of the carriers was on fire belching black smoke, a soldier was being sick, leaning against the trunk of a pollarded tree, his face greeny-grey above blood-stained khaki.

'Let's be havin' yer,' the sergeant said, appearing from behind the carrier. 'Render assistance, you two.'

'Where d'yer want us ter start?' Sid asked. How could you render assistance after a massacre?

There was an old woman struggling to right a cart that had been tossed onto its side in the middle of the road.

'Start with her,' the sergeant said. 'We can't none of us move till that cart's out the way.'

There was a medical orderly attending to the soldier and some other people trying to staunch a woman's head wounds with her shawl. Two lads were carrying the dead to the side of the road.

Tommy and Sid walked through the scattered bags and bundles to the cart. 'Leave it to us, gran,' Sid said to the woman. And she stood aside for them, meekly obedient.

'You ask me,' Tommy said as they heaved the cart onto its wheels, 'the Dutch had the best idea. Give in. Let the buggers take what they want.'

'They might want London,' Sid said.

'They could have it, as far as I'm concerned.'

'You ain't got kids, Sunshine,' Sid said. 'It's different when you got kids.'

Ever since he'd arrived in France he'd known the truth of that, in a vague unspoken sort of way. Now, standing here in the bloody aftermath of this attack, the knowledge was certainty. Jerry was cruel and ruthless, and if there was anything he could do to stop them crossing the Channel and attacking Joan and his kids he'd do it. What a bloody good job he'd signed the kids up for evacuation. They were well out of it in the country. 'It's different when you got kids.'

'Let's get moving,' the sergeant said.

'What about *them*, Sarge,' Tommy said, looking at the two dusty bodies by the side of the road.

'Never mind them,' the sergeant said. 'Can't do nothing for them, can yer? Right then. Let's be 'aving yer.'

The section began to climb aboard the carrier, and while he waited his turn Sid fished in his pocket for another fag. As he withdrew the packet it dislodged the letter he'd been writing to Joan that morning. Was it really only that morning? It seemed a lifetime.

The crumpled paper drifted down into the dust. 'BEF

France.' he'd written. 'My dearest Joan. Quiet today. Lovely weather.'

That's a laugh, he thought, reading the words as he lit his fag. No point in picking the letter up. It was out of date now. He'd write another when he got the time. If he ever got the time. As he climbed into the driver's seat he could hear heavy gunfire to the south and the occasional rattle of machine-gun fire.

'Fuckin' war,' young Tommy growled, climbing in behind him.

'Shut yer face, Tommy,' one of the other men said affably. 'Look on the bright side. Least we ain't bein' bombed for the moment.'

'Bright side!' Tommy growled again. 'Retreatin'?'

'Only tem'pry, lad,' the sergeant corrected. 'Only tem'pry. Strategic retreat. You keep yer eyes skinned fer Stukas.'

Until that morning they'd been with the rest of 131 Brigade defending the line marked by the River Escaut, part of an army, entrenched behind field-guns with their mess-tents, supplies, petrol and ammunition close at hand, apprehensive because they knew they would soon be in a scrap but feeling vaguely confident that they would win it when it came. The arrival of the German panzers was such a shock they still hadn't recovered from it, all those tanks rolling across the fields in such numbers and at such speed. They'd put up a fight, followed orders, fired endlessly, seemingly in every direction but the right one, but the tanks kept coming and everything was murderously confused. By the time they were given the order to retreat it seemed inevitable.

Since then they'd been travelling, and every single road they'd taken was more crowded than any thoroughfare they'd ever seen, choked with people and grinding with vehicles of every description, many of them in one another's way, none moving in any kind of order, most drivers keeping a fearful watch on the sky above their heads. The muddle had been loud, frantic, chaotic and continual. There were refugees everywhere, streaming along every road, in tatty processions, carrying every kind of luggage, from sacks to attaché cases, whole towns on the move, women carrying their babies in shawls, men with small children on their backs, kids pushing prams, old women limping along in their dusty black with sticks to support them, families on overloaded carts hauled by straining farm horses, and once, trudging among them, heading in the opposite direction, several straggling columns of French infantrymen, humpbacked under their heavy kit.

The platoon was moving again. Sid began to inch the carrier forward, sounding his horn and shouting, but no one got out of his way, and after struggling for about a hundred yards they were stopped by a broken-down car which had skewed sideways, and together with the crowd that had gathered to get it started again, was completely blocking the road. There was a dispatch rider hurtling through the dust towards them on his motorcycle and he had to stop too. So the sergeant jumped out of the carrier and walked across to see if he knew what was going on.

He had orders for the armoured division at Arras.

'What's happening?' the sergeant asked.

'Search me, mate. There's a rumour the Frenchies have folded up an' gone home.'

'What Frenchies?'

'Ninth army.'

'Bloody hell fire!' the sergeant said. 'On the Meuse?'

'Yup.'

'What all of 'em?'

'So they say.'

'Bloody hell fire!' the sergeant said again.

The car began to move, swung round until it was facing the right direction, and juddered off leaving a stink of petrol behind it. The dispatch rider purred away at once, driving stylishly through the debris on the road.

'Now what, Sarge?' Sid asked.

'Follow-me-leader,' the sergeant suggested. 'If we still got any leaders.'

'We got old Churchill now, don't forget,' Sid said. Winston Churchill had taken over as Prime Minister on the day after the German invasion of the Low Countries. And a bloody good job too.

'Where *are* we, Sarge?' Tommy said.

332

'How do I know?' the sergeant joked bitterly. 'Ask Hitler.'

'I wish we knew where Daddy is,' Yvonne said to her mother at breakfast-time. She'd examined his last letter carefully several times, because she could read the envelope now, although she'd given up trying to decipher the handwriting on the paper. 'When do you think you'll have another letter, Mum?'

'He's in France,' Joan told her, ignoring the question about the letter because she couldn't answer it. She hadn't heard a word from him since he'd written on 10 May, which was the day the Germans invaded Holland and all this started, and ten days ago. He could be anywhere, fighting, injured, even killed. 'He's fighting the Germans,' she said with more authority than she felt. 'Hold still while I brush your hair. How d'you manage to get such tangles in it?'

'When's he coming home?' Norman asked, looking up from his last slice of bread and jam. That was far more important than letters. Dad had said they wasn't to be in London. He'd be ever so cross if he came home and found them here, and then what would happen?

'Not yet awhile, I don't suppose,' Joan said, glancing at the anxious lines wrinkling the child's forehead and feeling she could give him that much consolation at least. 'They got a bit a' fighting to do yet.' But it was hard to imagine anyone fighting in this beautiful weather. The little patch of sky she could see through her kitchen window was a gorgeous blue and the sunlight was dappling the entire room with discs of pale bright colour, on the checks of the tablecloth, the plates on the dresser, Norman's grey shirt, his dark hair, gilding his cheek bones and the line of his jaw, touching Yvonne's hair with gold. Oh what a good job she'd got them back home. They were so much better at home. He hardly wet the bed at all now.

'Tomorrow?' Norman asked. 'Will he come home tomorrow?'

'No.'

'Next week?'

'Not for months and months,' Joan said. 'Not till the cold weather comes.' From what the papers and wireless said it didn't look as though the British army was doing very well. They'd retreated twice now, as far as she could make out, and the Germans always seemed to be advancing.

'When's that?' Norman persisted.

'Look at the state a' your neck,' Joan said. 'I thought I told you to wash behind your ears. Now don't forget Aunty Baby's coming to collect you at four o'clock and take you back to Gran's. Be good kids.'

'Will Uncle Jim be there?' Yvonne wanted to know. She liked Uncle Jim. He told them funny stories about the things that happened on his RAF camp, and all in his funny way of talking, about 'kites being pranged' and people being 'clueless' and 'clots'. It was smashing.

'No. You know he won't,' Joan said. 'He went back ages ago. Where's your coat? You'll need that come this evening.'

Mum had been very good about having the kids after school and giving them tea and everything. It was a real gift when food was rationed and in short supply. And the best of it was that she didn't seem to mind how long they stayed.

'I like having them,' she said that evening when Joan arrived in Paradise Row late and breathless and apologetic. 'They can stay as long as they like. They've been helping me get the tea.'

'I'm sorry I'm late,' Joan said. 'It's been a rush job. 'Lo Peggy. Oh dear, I am being a nuisance. Perhaps I should stop going to work.'

'You're not being a nuisance,' Flossie told her. 'So you can just stop worrying about it. And if you take my advice you'll go on earning as long as you can. Oh I know you can live on a soldier's pay. I lived on a soldier's pay for years and years. But you can't live well on it.'

That was true, Joan thought. The pay at the factory was very good. Double what she'd been earning with that horrid old Miss Margeryson. In fact she was better off now than she'd ever been, and now that the kids were home she didn't mind how horrid the work was. She'd bought new clothes for the kids this summer and new shoes and there was plenty of money for food and still some left over for a dress for herself.

'Earn while you can,' Peggy said. She was on night duty that week so she was in uniform ready to go out. 'That's one good thing coming out of this war, with so many men in the forces they've got to pay women a decent wage to do the work.'

'I'd give it all up to have Sid home and safe,' Joan said.

'He'll write soon,' Peggy said giving her a hug. 'You'll see.'

But he didn't and the news got worse by the day.

It was always the same and always bad. The Germans were advancing. They'd taken Amiens and Abbeville. They'd reached the English Channel. They were pressing on to Boulogne, surrounding Calais.

On 21 May the wireless reported optimistically that British armoured divisions had been gathered at a place called Arras, that a break through was being attempted and that fierce fighting was going on.

'Arras again,' John Cooper said. 'Poor buggers.'

And it wasn't long before they heard that the poor buggers had been defeated.

Now it was plain that a full-scale retreat was in operation. Rumours grew by the hour, all of them alarming. The British army was surrounded, cut off, defeated. A whole battalion had been massacred. The soldiers were burning their lorries and setting fire to petrol dumps. There was no hope for any of them. They were being captured in their thousands. The Fifth Column were at work all over France.

The days passed, prickly with apprehension, as people all over Britain waited for news, crowded about their wireless sets, living in abeyance from one bulletin to the next. It was as if their lives had no consequence beyond the outcome of this struggle. Joan grew gaunt with worry. It was seventeen days since the German invasion but it seemed like months. She'd had one letter from Sid in all that time, and that was a brief postcard to say that he was well, that he hadn't been injured and that he sent his love to the kids.

'He could be anywhere,' she worried to Peggy, when her sister came visiting one evening late in May. 'What are they doing? That's what I want to know.'

The news of what they were doing broke the following morning.

Calais had surrendered, the Belgian army had capitulated to the Germans just before dawn and the evacuation of the British Expeditionary Force had begun. Troops were being taken from the beaches at a place called Dunkirk. Regular bulletins would be broadcast throughout the day.

They were broadcast during the next nine momentous days as ships great and small converged on those distant beaches, and the massive rescue operation continued. Horrific tales filtered through rumour to England. The German air force was bombing and strafing at will, there was only a handful of RAF fighters there but they were working miracles, the whole of Dunkirk was ablaze.

But then other stories began too. It wasn't just the Royal Navy that was at Dunkirk. The army was being taken off the beaches by civilian ships too, a miscellaneous fleet of fishing boats and ferries, pleasure boats and steamers that had been gathered in secret at dead of night and crossed the Channel in a great armada to help with the rescue. Mrs Roderick was full of it when she came to call for Flossie for their weekly trip to the pictures.

'The Thames has been denuded,' she said. 'There's hardly a boat to be seen. Went through at midnight so Mrs Bertleman was telling me. The *Royal Sovereign*'s gone and the *Royal Daffodil* and the *Gillyflower*. It's amazing!'

'That'll do it,' Mrs Geary said. 'Island race, you see. All sailors at heart we are. That'll do it.'

''Course, they'll never get them all home,' Mrs Roderick said. 'Not with the best will in the world. They got millions of men out there.'

'If they get half of 'em out it'll be a miracle,' Flossie said. 'Are they going to broadcast any more tonight d'you think?'

'Bound to,' Mrs Geary said. 'Be on the nine o'clock news?'

'Then I think we'll give the pictures a miss,' Flossie said to Mrs Roderick. 'See what they say.'

'Quite right,' Mrs Roderick agreed. 'We'll have a game of cards. Baby'll make up a four, won't you, Baby?'

So they played cards.

'Where's your Peggy?' Mrs Roderick asked as she picked up her first hand.

'Up the Post,' Flossie said. 'On duty.'

'Jim's not home then?'

'No.'

'Where is he posted these days?'

None of them knew where Jim was.

'Didn't Peggy say?' Mrs Roderick asked.

'She don't say much these days,' Mrs Geary said, arranging her cards.

'Why should she?' Baby said rather tartly. Mrs Roderick was a jolly sight too fond of gossip. 'You don't have to be talking all the time. Jim don't say much either.'

'Strong silent type,' Mrs Roderick approved. 'It's being in the RAF I expect.'

They would all have been surprised to know that Jim Boxall had been talking non-stop since six o'clock that evening.

His squadron had been transferred that day from Catterick to Hornchurch to replace a squadron that had been in action over France during the retreat. There was a lot of repair work to do and they'd started on it as soon as they arrived.

He'd swung into his billet at the end of that first afternoon in the hangars, flung himself across his bed, lit a fag and closed his eyes with weariness when a familiar voice said, 'Jim Boxall or I'm a Dutchman,' right in his ear.

It was Froggy Ferguson. Still very recognizably Froggy Ferguson, wide of mouth, bolting-eyed, and grinning. ''Lo Frog,' Jim said. 'Fancy seeing you here. I thought I'd got shot of you back in Uxbridge.'

'You don't get shot of me so easy,' Froggy grinned.

'So what you doing here?'

'I'm a sparks.' And sure enough there were the sparks on his tunic sleeve. A qualified wireless operator and mechanic, no less. 'Come for a beer.'

It was a cheerful reunion. They hadn't seen one another since those first days in Uxbridge, nearly five years ago, so they had a lot of gossip and scandal to catch up on. Froggy seemed to know everything there was to know about their old oppos.

'Remember old Tammy Shanter? Saw him in Debden last summer. He's got a wife and two kiddies. And Jock? He's training to be an air gunner.'

And he was also very knowledgeable about the airfield and the squadron that had just gone to Catterick.

'They've been flying sorties over the beaches,' he said. 'Bloody shambles by all accounts. They've got the entire British army camped out on the sand apparently, standing in queues waiting to be taken off. All the roads into Dunkirk are jammed solid. So full of trucks they look like khaki rivers from the air, so one of our chaps was saying. Your lot are going over tomorrow.'

'Yes, I know,' Jim said. 'Will we get them all off?'

'It'll be a miracle if we do.'

But the miracle continued, as people all over Britain held their breath and said their prayers and tuned in to the BBC.

On 28 May 17,000 men were taken safely off the beaches, on 29 May it was over 47,000 and during the next two days more than 100,000 came home. Soon pictures of the returning army were filling the papers and wives were receiving letters and telegrams from the British ports.

But Joan heard nothing.

Yvey and Norman scanned the papers every day for the first sight of their father, convinced that they would see his picture sooner or later, walking up a gang-plank or waving cheerfully from the deck of a troopship, but they were always disappointed.

'He can be as cross as he likes if he'll only come home,' Norman said.

'Perhaps he'll come tomorrow,' Yvonne hoped.

But the days passed and it was 4 June and the papers were cheering that over 338,000 men were home and dry, that the last soldier had been lifted from the beachhead, the last little ship had limped to port.

And still there was no news of Sid Owen.

Joan was bleak with distress.

'It's the not knowing,' she said to Peggy. 'He could be

338

dead somewhere out there. How would I know? People say they left dead bodies all over the place. Didn't even stop to bury them.'

'It's early days yet,' Peggy tried to comfort. 'You think how many men they've brought back. It could take weeks to sort them all out. I'll do Norman's school shirt, shall I?' She'd come to supper that evening, but being Peggy she was helping out with the ironing while Joan cooked their cauliflower cheese.

'He could be wounded,' Joan said, stirring the sauce.

Peggy thought it was safe to allow that and better than thinking he was dead. 'Yes, he could,' she said. 'In a hospital somewhere waiting for someone to write a letter for him. Very likely.'

'He wasn't always the best husband alive,' Joan said. 'Had a right pair a' fists on him sometimes, to tell the truth, but I wouldn't wish this on him. Not for the world.'

'Course not,' Peggy said, removing Norman's shirt from the ironing board and folding it neatly.

'I don't think I shall ever hear,' Joan said. 'I'm beginning to give up hope.'

'You mustn't give up hope,' Peggy said. 'None of us must give up hope. We've all got to keep going.'

It was Churchill's message that evening too. As Peggy and Joan were washing their dirty plates, the House of Commons was listening soberly to the Prime Minister as he told them that the fight would continue.

'We cannot flag or fail. We shall go on to the end. We shall fight in France, we shall fight on the seas and oceans, we shall fight with growing confidence and growing strength in the air. We shall defend our island whatever the cost may be. We shall fight on the beaches, we shall fight on the landing-grounds, in the fields, in the streets, and in the hills. We shall never surrender.'

Ten days later the German army entered Paris, and two days after that the French front collapsed and Maréchal Pétain became president of France. Now it was simply a matter of time before the country was handed over to Hitler.

And on the morning after the final fall of France Joan got the letter she'd been waiting for.

She saw it on the doormat as she was taking the

children downstairs on their way to school. A small ominous-looking envelope with foreign markings on it. Oh God, not the offficial letter, she begged. Please God not that.

'Just a minute,' she said to the children, heart pounding. 'I'll just read this before we go.'

It was addressed in Sid's clumsy handwriting and had been sent through the Red Cross from a prisoner of war camp, somewhere in Germany.

'He's all right,' she said to the children, struggling to control herself because they were standing so still and looking so solemn and anxious. 'He's been wounded. Not much. A flesh wound he says. He's a prisoner. He's all right.'

And then they both tumbled into her arms to kiss her and hug her and they were all crying with relief.

'We'll have a ding-dong,' Flossie said. 'We've something to celebrate now. I'm so glad you've heard. What a relief.'

It was a curiously happy celebration. They should have been cast down by the serious state of the war or dismayed by the loss of their last ally but they weren't.

'If you ask me,' Mrs Geary said finishing her gin, 'we're a jolly sight better off without allies. All they ever do is give in all the time. Lily-livered lot.'

'Shameful,' Mr Allnutt agreed. 'At least now we all know where we are.'

'It'll be a long fight,' Leslie warned.

'Never you mind,' Ernest said. 'We're all in it together. That's what counts. Hitler needn't think we're finished because we're not. We'll show him.'

'There'll always be an England,' Mr Brown declaimed, rosy with patriotism and four pints of beer.

So naturally John Cooper played the song and they all sang it.

'There'll always be an England, and England shall be free.
If England means as much to you as England means to me.
Red, white and blue, what does it mean to you?
Surely you're proud, shout it aloud, Britons awake.
The Empire too, we can depend on you.
Freedom remains, these are the chains nothing can
    break.'

340

By the end of the evening they were in a mood of unquench-
able optimism.

'We'll show the buggers,' they said to one another as
they kissed goodnight. 'They needn't think they've got the
better of us.'

It was a mood they shared with more and more people
as June blazed into an English magnificence of peaceful
roses, honeysuckles and warm light evenings, a mood that
spread by some curious national osmosis until there was
hardly a man or woman the length and breadth of the
country who wasn't touched by it. The army was home.
The rescue at Dunkirk had been a miracle. We would fight
better on our own.

There was a cocky cheerfulness in the streets, lots of
jokes and leg-pulling, jaunty whistling and easy laughter.
It even affected the way people walked, heads up, shoulders back, with a strut and a swagger as if they were
marching to stirring music.

There was no logical reason to any of it, but the defeats
and anxieties of the last few weeks had taken most people
beyond logic or reason. This was the stubborn, illogical,
unwarranted optimism which is both the curse and the
strength of the British in adversity. They might have their
backs to the wall, they might be rationed, blacked-out,
without allies, they might not have enough planes or ships
or guns, beleaguered in their tight little island, but it never
occurred to anyone to doubt that sooner or later right
would triumph and they would win the war.

And over in America one of the leader writers of the
New York Times put words to the mood.

'So long as the English tongue survives,' he wrote, 'the
word Dunkirk will be spoken with reverence. In that
harbour ... at the end of the lost battle, the rags and blem-
ishes that had hidden the soul of democracy fell away.
There, beaten but unconquered, in shining splendour, she
faced the enemy, this shining thing in the souls of free men
which Hitler cannot command ... It is the future. It is
victory.'

CHAPTER 26

'Sometimes I think my life is just passing me by,' Baby said, pouting at her reflection in the mirror. Her latest perm hadn't been at all successful. All the waves were going the wrong way.

'No it ain't,' Megan said cheerfully. 'What are you on about?'

'I'm all by myself in this family,' Baby complained, spreading scarlet lipstick across her top lip. 'That's what I'm on about. Nobody ever thinks of me. Jim's come home on a forty-eight so of course Peggy's gone rushing off to Croydon with him. I don't count any more once he's home. Joan's got a week's holiday. A whole week. You'd think she could spend a bit of time with her sister on a week's holiday. But oh dear no. She's taken the kids off somewhere instead. She's always taking the kids off somewhere. Mum's at the pictures. Surprise surprise! Even the cat's gone out. I don't know why I bother.'

'Well I'm here now,' Megan said, ignoring the complaint. 'Where d'you want to go? Pictures? Up the palais? You say.'

They'd planned this outing at the last ding-dong when Megan was rather jolly with drink and although she'd had second thoughts about it she was keeping her promise. You had to feel sorry for Baby sometimes. She never seemed to have any friends.

'John from the paint shop was going to take me out, you know,' Baby said, powdering her nose. 'And then he came in yesterday and said he couldn't. Not a word about being sorry or anything. Just he couldn't. "Oh charming!" I said. "That's really charming." And do you know what he said then? He never meant to take me out anyway. It was just a dare. "Oh really charming!" I said.'

342

'Are you ready?' Megan asked.

'No. Not yet. Well then he said. "You're not Betty Grable you know!" I was livid ...'

'Are we *going?*' Megan asked, standing up and slinging her gasmask over her shoulder.

Baby spread another layer of lipstick across her mouth. 'So I was telling you,' she said.

'You don't need any more lipstick,' Megan said. 'You got enough on already.'

'Oh that's right,' Baby said petulantly. 'Tell me off. Criticize. I should. Everybody tells me off.'

'I wasn't telling you off,' Megan said, floundering in the sudden backwash of Baby's heavy emotions. 'I was only saying ...'

'Everybody tells me off,' Baby said, tears welling into her eyes. 'I can't do a thing right. Ever. Oh now look! You've made my mascara run.' Black streaks were falling from her wet eyelashes and meandering down her carefully rouged cheeks. 'Oh God! I look an absolute sight!' and she ran through the kitchen, pushed past Megan and clattered upstairs.

Now what? Megan thought. She is peculiar. No wonder she ain't got any friends if she goes on like this all the time.

There was a rattle at the front door as the key was pulled through the letter-box. She could hear voices. Jim's and Peggy's. Well thank heavens for that.

'Hello,' Peggy said. 'You still here? I thought you'd have gone by now. What's up?'

'Your sister is,' Megan said.

'Where is she?'

'Upstairs. In a paddy.'

'Megan's waiting for you, Baby,' Jim called up the stairs. 'Are you coming down?'

'Oh do go away,' Baby's voice replied. It sounded muffled and tearful. 'I can't bear it.'

'I'd give up if I were you,' Jim said to Megan. 'If she's piping her eye you could be here for hours. Come to Croydon with us. We're going to visit Froggy and his sister.'

'I promised to go out with her,' Megan said, looking very uncertain. They could hear Baby sobbing in the room above their heads.

343

'He's quite right,' Peggy said. 'She could go on like this for ages. She can be a real pest sometimes.'

'Are you coming down or ain't yer?' Jim called again.

'Go away!' Baby wailed.

So Megan went to Croydon with Jim and Peggy.

It was 15 August 1940 and a glorious summer afternoon. Croydon was quite perky in the sunshine with the trolley buses shining red as tulips and the glass of the shop windows glinting and dazzling between its protective lattice-work of brown paper. They took a 42 tram down North End, passing the new white frontage of Allder's department store and the age-blackened bricks of the Whitgift Hospital, in a street full of affluent shoppers. Megan was most impressed, both by the width of the street and the wealth of the shops. 'Better'n Greenwich by a long chalk'. But Peggy was thinking what a lot of uniforms there were in the streets these days, soldiers, airmen, WVS, even the occasional sailor swaggering along, bell-bottoms flapping.

'We're all at war now,' she said to Jim.

'Not today,' he said, giving her a squeeze. 'Day off today.' And his eyes said, 'love tonight.'

The unspoken message roused her most pleasurably but the pleasure trailed shame in its wake. She wanted to sleep with him, of course, of course, but it was still wrong what they were doing. They should have waited. But how could they wait? How could they marry with a war going on, and everything changed and God knows what ahead of them?

'Here we are,' Jim said.

Froggy's sister turned out to be a neat young woman in her middle thirties called Claire. She didn't look a bit like her brother, which Peggy thought privately was just as well. She had a rather wider mouth than most women and she shared Froggy's pale colouring but her eyes were small and shrewd and her head neatly shingled and she was stylishly dressed, in a trim yellow tea-gown that put her two guests at a disadvantage in their cheap skirts and home-made blouses.

But she was a good hostess and made them all very welcome, serving them a three course dinner, which they found rather disconcerting, in the modern dining room of her third floor flat, where a wire-haired terrier sat on the hearthrug like a modern statue, its sculptured legs and well-trimmed whiskers unbelievably straight and clean.

'That's my Totty,' she said. 'His kennel name is Moses Tutankhamun the Third, if you ever heard of anything so ridiculous. So I call him Totty.'

She also fed him tit-bits from her plate, and when dinner was over, they all had to take him upstairs onto the roof of the flats 'for a breath of fresh air'.

It was extraordinary up on the roof, for being a modern construction the entire area was as flat as a school playground. It had been roofed over by a dome made of thin wire mesh, presumably to prevent the playing children from falling over the edge, and there were garden seats set beside the chimneys and the water tower. They had a spectacular view south across the tree-lined streets of South Croydon and all the way to the hills and woods and green fields of Purley and Addiscombe. They could even see the north downs in the distance, humped like pale blue whales.

'Gosh!' Megan said. 'What a view!'

'Come over the other side,' Claire suggested. 'It's even better there.'

'Why didn't you tell us you was one of the idle rich?' Jim hissed at Froggy, once his sister was on the other side of the roof and out of earshot.

'Nobody asked me, Sir, she said,' Froggy grinned.

'That's torn it,' Peggy said, teasing Jim. 'What you going to do now, Mr working-class Boxall?'

'I shall give it serious thought,' Jim said. 'I take a dim view of this you know, Froggy.'

'Does he see everything in class terms?' Froggy asked Peggy, laughing at his friend.

She could see that the question had irritated Jim and she was afraid that she might have annoyed him too by calling him working-class like that, so she thought for a few seconds, trying to find something soothing to say.

'Not everything,' Jim answered for her. 'Only politics, religion, education, economics, war. Trivial things like that.'

'And marriage?' Froggy asked.

'Well of course. You'd be asking for trouble if you married out of your class.'

'He's a Puritan,' Froggy said to Peggy. 'You'll have to watch that.'

'But Peggy was watching the sky. 'What's that?' she said.

'What's what?' Jim asked looking up too. 'Hey, Froggy. Look at that!'

There was a squadron of planes flying in formation above the Anerley Hills, unfamiliar dark planes trailing white con trails. They could hear the laboured droning of their engines in the distance.

'D'you recognize them?' Froggy asked.

But before Jim could answer him the planes were recognized in a most specific way. They could hear the pounding of anti-aircraft fire and shell bursts began to open like surrealistic black roses in the blue sky beside the planes.

'They're Jerries!' Jim shouted. 'They're Jerries.'

And on a bombing raid too, forming a line ready to attack, making shallow dives one after the other as the shells burst all around them. Now there were plumes of black smoke rising from the ground after every dive and they could hear the crump of the explosions.

'Where is it?' Megan said breathlessly, running to join them and standing close to Peggy.

'Croydon Airport, I'll bet,' Froggy said. 'They're bombing the airport.'

There was something unreal about it, as if they were watching a film, only a film in natural colour instead of black and white, for now there were flames among the smoke.

And then as suddenly as it had begun, the raid was over. The planes regrouped and flew back the way they'd come, climbing into the blue, leaving their white trails behind them, as innocent as lambs' tails. And the smoke of the anti-aircraft fire dispersed too, elongating into grey wisps, and finally vanishing like the planes.

'Good God, Bertie,' Claire said to her brother. 'We've seen an air raid.'

346

In the shock of the moment none of them registered that Froggy's name was Bertie.

'Why didn't somebody sound the sirens?' Peggy asked.

As if in answer to her question the sirens began to wail.

'Bit late now,' Froggy said.

'Perhaps it's another lot,' Claire said, squinting up at the sky. 'Should we go down to the shelter, do you think?'

'If it's another lot we shall see them coming from up here,' Froggy told her. 'We'll give them a quarter of an hour and see what happens.'

So they waited in a rather eerie silence, staring out across the peaceful countryside. War had come to London at last, but none of them could take it in. That's what it's like to be bombed Peggy was thinking, planes diving and guns firing and earth thrown up hundreds of feet into the air, but it was still unreal. They're bombing airfields, Jim was reasoning, so it'll be our turn sooner or later. And the thought was still casting a chill into his mind when the all clear went.

'Let's go dancing,' he said. They needed to enjoy themselves, to feel alive and full of energy, to put as much pleasure as they could between themselves and the bombs that were going to fall. 'Where's the nearest palais, Froggy?'

So Claire telephoned her young man and told him to meet them in the Lido and they all went dancing. And a high old time they had, stumbling and giggling through waltzes and quicksteps and even attempting foxtrots for once although they didn't know the steps. But the floor was so crowded and there was such an electric excitement in the place that nobody minded what sort of dance they were doing. And at the end of the evening when they'd smooched the last waltz with the lights romantically dimmed and their faces spangled by the dazzle of the spinning chandelier, Froggy said he'd come back to Greenwich with them so that he could see Megan to her door.

'Well ta,' Megan said, 'but there's no need really. I can go with Jim and Peggy.'

'Oh reason not the need,' he said in a voice that showed he was quoting from something. 'Don't argue. I'm coming with you.'

And did.

Jim was pleased. 'Gives us more time on our own,' he said to Peggy as they stopped to kiss in the darkness. 'Cook me breakfast tomorrow?'

'Can't you cook your own breakfast yet?' she teased.

'Yes, OK. Breakfast I can manage on my own,' he said, teasing back. 'But there are other things, now our Lily's got a job.'

Lily had followed Joan's example, and after arranging for Percy to be looked after during the day by his grandmother in the new council flats round the corner, she'd taken a job in the local munitions factory. So the house was conveniently empty.

They cooked a leisurely breakfast of Peggy's potato cakes and one precious rasher of bacon each and they read the morning paper, which reported 'Germans raid airfields. 71 German planes shot down,' and then since they were still officially on holiday from this war, they went to bed, to the sharpest and most prolonged pleasure they had ever known. It was as if their unexpected preview of the battles to come had sharpened their capacity for delight.

Afterwards as they were sharing his last cigarette Peggy looked around at the little room as if she was seeing it for the first time, at his books ranged so neatly against the walls, at the gaudy stripes of all those Penguins, blue and white, and orange and white, and the green spines of the history books, at the pale curtains and the striped bedspread and the sunshine shadowing the wall with the long barred pattern of the window frames. How extraordinary that she'd never noticed that before. Nor how green the little garden was beyond the window.

'Let's go up the Park,' she said.

So they walked in Greenwich Park, arm in arm among sweet chestnut trees heavy with white blossom like carved candles, over grass more green and luscious than she'd ever seen it and speckled all over with a rich pattern of white daisies and glistening buttercups. Below them the colonnades of the Naval Hospital shone white against the blue sky and the Thames was blue too, sky-blue and olive-green, the colours shifting and changing as she watched, and shimmering with sharp points of diamond-white light.

'Do you remember that day at Brighton?' she said.

'I was thinking the same thing,' he answered, smiling as he remembered. 'As a moat defensive to a house.'

'Will it keep them out?'

'If the Channel's rough enough, and we have command of the air.'

'Which is why they were bombing airfields yesterday.'

'Yes.'

They'll bomb Hornchurch, she thought. Hornchurch and all the other airfields round about. And London. But she didn't say anything because there wasn't any need to put it into words. He knew all that as well as she did. Probably better.

He was lighting two cigarettes, concentrating on the flame of the match.

'Tabby eyes,' he said, handing hers across to her.

'Jim?'

'I've got my props.'

'I noticed.'

'We *did* say we'd get married when I was an LAC.'

'We can't though, can we,' she said, exhaling a long column of smoke. 'Not now. I couldn't leave London now, could I? Not with air raids coming.' Their surreptitious love-making still filled her with guilt, especially after-wards, but guilt was preferable to running away from her city just when she was most needed there.

He recognized the truth of what she was saying even though it upset him to hear it. 'No,' he said. 'I suppose not.' He didn't want her to stay in London. She might be injured when the Germans started bombing. She might get killed. And that thought was so terrible that it made him grit his teeth.

She saw the tell-tale movement of his jaw and under-stood it. 'We've got a job to do,' she said sensibly. 'Both of us. Me in London. You in the RAF.' It was better just to get on with it and not to think about what might happen.

But they both thought about what might happen as they kissed goodbye later that day, standing at the station with his arms round her waist, gazing at one another without words but with a new anguished intensity as if they were trying to print the memory of what they saw

349

deep deep in their minds. Just in case.

And as the train finally pulled their hands apart, they both said the same thing in the same voice. 'Take care of yourself.'

He worried about her all the way back to Hornchurch, and dreamed about her all night, but the minute he stepped into the hangars the next morning the war engulfed him to the exclusion of everything else. There had been a raid the previous afternoon and the ground crews were still picking up the pieces. The hangars were full of aircraft under repair. There was no time for the formality of greeting, just a job to be done and as quickly as they could do it.

'When do they want 'em?' Jim asked as he worked.

'Yesterday.'

'Bad show yesterday,' his oppos told him in the laconic shorthand of their RAF slang. 'Jerry had a field day. Two of our kites pranged.'

'Whose?'

The casualties were named in the same unemotional style. It was easier to say that someone you knew had 'bought it' rather than use the awful word 'killed'. But it was death just the same however you spoke of it.

They worked at speed, stripping down raddled engines, repairing bullet holes, replacing parts wrecked beyond repair, swearing as they got in one another's way. Nobody needed to tell them how urgent it was.

In mid-afternoon their own squadron was scrambled to intercept a wave of incoming raiders, and when the planes returned and the ground crews went out to service, refuel and rearm them, Jim saw for the first time what air battles could do to planes and pilots.

There were three Spitfires in his flight and the first two landed safely, both planes unharmed, both pilots laconic with triumph, but the third returned with its undercarriage shot away and had to make a crash landing. The fire tender and the ambulance raced alongside the runway to keep pace with his descent, but the ground crews could only stand by in anguished impotence and watch as the torn plane dropped on its belly, bounced, skidded, one wing ripping against the runway, crumpling like paper and

350

hissing sparks, slowed, skewed and finally stopped without bursting into flames and with the ambulance a few feet away from the nose cone. So far, so good, but they all knew they only had a few seconds to get the pilot clear and douse the plane before it became an inferno, and those few seconds were even more anguished than the landing had been. But the fire tender was beside the plane, hosing it with foam, the pilot was being hauled out of the cockpit. They'd made it.

He was very badly injured, his flying jacket wet with blood and his young face seamed with sweat and dirt and completely colourless. As the ambulance crew eased him onto their stretcher and his blood dripped onto the tarmac he opened his eyes, tried to smile and said, 'I bagged the bugger. Tell the CO.'

The heroism of his return fired the entire squadron. It amazed Jim to realize that he felt an almost paternal protectiveness for 'his' pilots now. Until the battle began he'd looked on them as men apart, admiring their flying skills, who wouldn't? but irritated by the upper-class ease of those drawling voices, and the arrogance that allowed them to swan through every regulation.

Now, as the German attack continued and more and more sorties were flown, the arrogance became something entirely admirable, a superb, understated courage that played down fear, made light of injuries, dared death. Now nothing was too good for these men or their planes. The ground crews worked unstintingly, by day and night, snatching sleep when they could, aware, tired though they were, that a mistake could cost one of their pilots his life. And the pilots flew more sorties than anyone had ever thought possible. And still the Germans came.

After a week of it, days and nights began to merge into one another. They lost count of time. There was nothing except this daily, exhausting battle in the air. Sometimes they only had thirty-five minutes to service, refuel and rearm the planes before their pilots strode out to take them up again. It was a scramble in every sense of the word.

And a scramble that was watched with admiration and anxiety by everyone in England because so much hinged on the outcome. If the RAF were defeated and the weather and the tides were right, Hitler would invade. His invasion barges were waiting on the other side of the Channel from Flushing to the Pas de Calais. So the BBC bulletins spread news of the air battles in their phlegmatic British way, and the newspapers reported 'The Battle of Britain' in admiring detail, and in London, newspaper sellers wrote their placards with perky humour as though they were reporting a cricket match. 'RAF versus Luftwaffe. Today's losses. Germany 98, England 13.'

And all over South London people watched the skies as the dog-fights roared above them, following the swirling con trails of the embattled planes as they drew paisley patterns in the summer sky, and taking shelter when the bombers were overhead. Sometimes there were as many as four alerts in a day and they heard the crump of a distant explosion and the pounding of anti-aircraft fire all around them and once a Messerschmitt roared out of the sky in flames and exploded in a garden over in Plumstead. But there were no bombs dropped in Peggy's corner of Greenwich and although she was on duty and heard plenty of stories about 'incidents' elsewhere there were no local incidents for her to attend. Sometimes as the sirens wailed their alarm she wondered how she would behave when she saw her first bomb victim, and sent up a silent prayer that she wouldn't fail. But it was the airfields that were being attacked and the airfields that were being bombed and that made her worry for Jim's safety.

Halfway through the month his squadron was moved back to Catterick, ostensibly for a period of rest, but Catterick was under fire too and they flew almost as many sorties there as they'd done in the south. They returned to Hornchurch after a fortnight almost as fatigued as they'd been when they left the place and there was more work to do than ever.

The day after their return was warm and sunny with a light, southerly breeze, a perfect day for opps, but unfortunately as perfect for the Luftwaffe as it was for the RAF. The klaxons sounded half-way through the afternoon when Jim and his team were half-way through a difficult repair.

'We'll finish it later,' the Flight Sergeant said. 'Take cover.'

There was a sandbagged trench alongside the hangar within easy running distance but the raiders were overhead before they reached it. Nine Dorniers loosening out from a V formation, the first on its bombing run fifty feet above the hangars. The gunners let fly with everything they had, but they didn't have much, Bofors, three-inch heavies, machine guns left over from the First World War. Two Hurricanes were in pursuit. They could hear the tracers, and the scream of their engines as they pulled out of a dive.

And then the first bomb exploded on the runway, shaking the ground under their feet and lifting so much earth into the air that for a few seconds they couldn't see anything at all in a darkness of dirt and dust. The second bomb hit a hangar, scattering pieces in all directions. Then there were long minutes of confusion, engines roaring, a plane screaming to earth, gunfire, explosions, the rattle of falling debris, as they crouched behind the sandbags and the attack went on, for ever and for no time at all.

And then the planes were roaring off again and they were scrambling out of the trench, legs shaking, and running to the hangars, moving like automata without any sense of being in control of their movements.

There were about ten craters on the runway, one of the hangars was completely gone, there was debris everywhere, shattered planks and bits of paper and torn pieces of corrugated iron, and over by the mess hut there were several large joints of meat scattered on the ground, wrapped in bits of air force uniform.

Jim was inside the hangar before he realized that what he'd just seen were the remains of a man. Dear God. The remains of a man scattered like joints of meat. Nausea rose into his throat and for a few seconds he stood still, swallowing and trembling. The remains of a man.

This is war, he thought. This is what war means. If they can do this to an air field they could flatten Paradise Row. They could flatten Paradise Row and kill everyone in it. And hard on that thought came resolution. We've got to beat them. No matter what any of us have to endure we've got to stop them.

CHAPTER 27

'There goes that dratted siren again,' Mrs Geary exclaimed. 'No peace for the wicked. How am I supposed to clean this cage out if they will keep sounding the sirens all the time?'

The parrot's cage was on her tea table, with its feed and waterbowls emptied and a fresh bag of sand ready beside it, but she was only half-way through scraping the dirt from the bottom of the cage.

'Better leave it,' Flossie said. 'Just in case.'

'Bloody Hitler,' Mrs Geary complained, putting the cage to rights as quickly as she could. 'Never a minute's peace. I'm sick of it, Flossie, keeping on all the time.'

'Bloody, bloody, bloody,' the parrot agreed, dancing hopefully from claw to claw.

The siren wailed eerily, up and down, up and down. It was Saturday 7 September and nearly tea-time. The battle between the Luftwaffe and the RAF had been going on for nearly a month now and the two women were so used to hearing the sirens they hardly took any notice of them. It would only be another dog-fight.

'I suppose we'd better go down to the shelter,' Flossie said. 'You know what Peggy says.' Peggy was on duty at the wardens' post at the flats but her advice was followed whether she was at home or not.

'I'll just finish this,' Mrs Geary said easily. 'We shall hear 'em if they come over.'

'I think I can hear them already,' Flossie said, and sure

354

enough the sound of labouring engines was droning into the afternoon air. She put her head out of the open window to see where they were. 'Oh my dear good God,' she said, her spine stiffening with the terror of what she saw. 'There's hundreds of them. Come down quick. They're after us.'

The sky was black with German bombers, flying up-river in relentless formation like a flock of iron birds with their fighter planes silver as midges beside them. Flossie was so frightened her throat swelled with terror, stopping her breath.

Mrs Geary caught her fear at once and began to cram the tray back into the cage, her hands clumsy. 'You will take him?' she said. 'Flossie?'

'Oh damn the parrot,' Flossie said, already on her way out of the room. 'It's us you should be thinking about. Come on! If they start bombing now we shall be blown to bits.'

'I can't leave Polly,' Mrs Geary said stubbornly, hauling the cage off the table so violently that the bird stumbled from his perch and fell against the wires squawking. 'Not if we're going to be bombed.'

'Oh for crying out loud!' Flossie said taking the cage from her in exasperation. 'Hurry, will you!'

The anti-aircraft guns over in Woolwich were firing now and the noise overhead was intense and terrifying. 'Come on!'

They slipped and stumbled down the narrow stairs and hobbled into the street, where their neighbours were all running headlong to the shelter too. Flossie caught a glimpse of Mrs Roderick's green coat as she hurtled through the entrance and she could hear Leslie's high-pitched voice shouting hysterically, but then she and Mrs Geary were in the push and scramble at the entrance and the first bombs were falling with a loud screaming whistle that sounded as though they were coming straight down on top of her and made her stomach shake with terror.

It was dark and smelly inside the shelter and it took Mr Allnutt some minutes to light the hurricane lamp.

'We're in it now,' Nonnie Brown said, as the little light spread through their darkness. 'We're in it now.' She sounded happy and excited, as if she'd arrived at some long-awaited party.

'Oh do shut up,' Leslie growled at her. 'We shall all be killed. I left Ernest in the shop with the new chrysanthemums. He'll be killed as sure as fate. We shall all be killed.'

The parrot was still squawking, its feathers dishevelled and one eye perpetually closed.

'Make it shut up,' Flossie said to Mrs Geary. 'My nerves are in shreds without that bird.'

'Come on Polly. Good boy! Nice Polly!' Mrs Geary said to the bird but the shrieks went on.

Mr and Mrs Grunewald arrived panting and pop-eyed, with all the men from the woodyard and three customers who lived round the corner.

'My boy's at work,' one woman worried. 'What'll they do at work? They ought ter let 'em home. Don'tcher think they ought to let 'em home? Oh dear, oh dear, what if something happens?'

'They'll have shelters somewhere,' Mrs Geary tried to comfort her. 'He'll be all right, you'll see.' But the woman was weeping.

Flossie became aware that John Cooper was missing. 'Where's Mr Cooper?' she said, shouting to be heard above the din outside.

Nobody knew.

'Did we ought ter go an' find him, poor man?' Mrs Allnutt said.

'No,' Flossie said at once. 'You have to stay in the shelter. They said on the leaflet.'

'We shall all be killed,' Leslie moaned. 'I was just getting his tea and now he's going to be blown to smithereens. And all those chrysanthemums fresh in this afternoon.'

'Bloody sod it,' the parrot said, opening its eye at last.

Behind the thick walls of the shelter they could hear the drone of engines and the screaming descent of bombs. And all so close. Leslie was right. They could be killed at any moment.

'Bloody bloody bloody,' the parrot said.

'If you don't stop that bloody bird,' one of the woodmen

shouted at Mrs Geary, 'I'll take it out its cage so help me and wring its bloody neck.'

'Oh the bugger!' the parrot said.

'You're not supposed to bring pets in a shelter,' another man complained. 'What if a bomb fell on us, it could bite someone.'

'You oughter put it outside,' the first man said, advancing on the parrot as though he meant to carry the cage out himself.

Alarmed by the fear and antagonism all round it, the bird clacked into a paroxysm of obscenity, using every swear word it could lay its black tongue to.

'This is too bloody much,' the first man said. 'We shall all go mad if we have to put up with this.' And he put his hand on the cage ready to lift it.

To Flossie's surprise Mrs Geary stood up at once and lifted the cage away from him. 'All right, young man,' she said. 'We know where we're not wanted don't we, Poll?' And with great dignity despite her hobbling gait, she carried the cage out of the shelter.

'Mrs Geary!' Flossie cried. 'Don't go out there. You'll get killed.' But the old lady had already gone. Oh this was awful! 'You shouldn't have said that to her,' she rebuked the man.

'An' you can shut your face an' all,' he growled at her. 'Shelters ain't fer pets.'

For a few seconds Flossie drew on her power to try and find an answer to him but then a stick of bombs began to fall somewhere horribly close by. They could hear each one whistling down, one, two, three, four. The smell of fear in their dank shelter was overpowering, and now that the parrot was gone they could hear every sound much more clearly. Five, six.

Mrs Roderick was weeping quietly into a handkerchief. 'I wish your Peggy was here,' she sobbed to Flossie.

'She'll make her rounds presently,' Flossie remembered with relief. Peggy visited all the shelters in her area whenever there was a raid. 'She'll be here presently. She knows how bad my nerves are when the sirens go. We shall be all right when Peggy comes,' she told the shelterers.

But Peggy was already at her first incident.

357

When the yellow alert came through she'd been in the wardens' post with Mr MacFarlane and Charlie Goodall and four other local wardens. They'd just brewed a pot of tea, and Charlie reckoned they'd have time for a quick cup between the yellow alert and the red, if it came. The speed and violence of the attack was a surprise to them too.

'They're after the docks,' Mr Goodall said as they stood in the doorway and looked up at the armada in the sky. 'God help the poor buggers in the East End.'

The barrage balloons bobbed above them, shining silver in the afternoon sun, and above the balloons the bombers were being harried by RAF fighters that roared through the formation spitting tracer fire, but the Germans pressed on with their attack, the front rank circling ready to make a bombing run. To Peggy's mesmerized eyes, the movement of their manoeuvre looked oddly beautiful in that peaceful blue sky. This was the moment she'd been trained for, the moment she'd been expecting and dreading and yet now that it had finally come she felt detached from it. Even when the first bomb fell, twisting and turning in the air before her eyes she couldn't believe it was happening. The explosions and the shock waves and the clouds of dust spuming into the sky were all unreal.

'Come on,' Charlie Goodall said, checking the strap of his tin hat. And then they were on their bicycles and pedalling unsteadily through the street towards their first incident.

I mustn't let them down, Peggy thought, pedalling mechanically and trying to steel herself for the ordeal ahead of her, not when I was born in the Tower and I'm a soldier's daughter. And the words that the Reverend Beaumont used to say all those years ago in Tillingbourne, came into her mind unbidden as a blessing. 'Lord give us the strength to endure those things that have to be endured.' And she said the words to herself praying ardently, 'Lord give me the strength. Please.' And after that she felt a little hope, a little warm hope that she would be able to endure, that she would manage somehow, despite her fear. And they propped their bikes against a wall and walked into the dust cloud.

There were mounds of bricks under her feet, bricks and

broken planks and shards of glass, so that she slipped and stumbled as she climbed, and as her eyes grew accustomed to the sting of the dust she saw a body lying, limbs askew, among the wreckage, a trousered body with its head turned away from her, thick hair matted with blood and brick dust, one white hand smeared with what looked like brown grease. She knew at once that whoever he was he was dead, there was something so broken and discarded about him. But she went across to make sure, because that was her job and now that she was here she had to do it.

There was still some warmth in the wrist she took gently between finger and thumb but no pulse at all. How could there be when half his face had been cut away by flying glass? She looked at the horror that had been his head, taking a mental note of it so that she could write her report afterwards, and she felt vaguely pleased that she could do all this without being sick. Then, working slowly as though she had all the time in the world, she straightened his limbs, closed his remaining eye, and pulling a torn curtain out from among the planks, covered him up in a neat bundle, folding the edges of the cloth around his body as though she was tucking him up in bed.

Then she was sick.

The rescue teams were climbing about on top of the wreckage. One house had been blown to bits and its neighbour was sliced in half. It was eerily quiet. There were no screams, no cries for help, only Mr MacFarlane's voice reed thin in the dust calling, 'Over here, Mr Goodall. Over here.'

Peggy scrambled towards him. 'There's a wee lass down there under a table or something,' he said, and now they could see that he was holding up a large piece of brickwork in both hands, straining to stop it from falling back into the pile.

'Get a lever under,' a man's voice said.

'You're all right, lassie,' Mr MacFarlane soothed. 'We'll soon have ye oot. Dinna fash yersel'.'

It took the rescue teams such a long time for them to lift the wreckage from the table, even though there were dozens of eager hands working at speed. When the last lump was lifted away and the table was revealed at the bottom of the hole they'd made, Peggy could see that it was cracked in two but the child huddled underneath it was alive. Mute with shock, covered in brick dust, her clothes shredded, but alive.

The only trouble was that she wouldn't or couldn't crawl out. She seemed to be frozen where she was, sitting crouched under the tilted table, her eyes staring.

'Someone'll have to go down and get her,' Mr Goodall said. 'Someone small. You'll do, Peggy.'

And so it was Peggy who was lowered into the hole on a rope to lift the child from her prison. 'Can you put your arms round my neck, lovey?' she asked as she crawled under the table. And the child did her best to obey.

'That's my darling,' Peggy encouraged, dragging her clear. 'I've got you. Peggy's got you. You're all right.'

It was rather upsetting that as soon as they'd been been hauled out of the hole the child began to cry, clinging about Peggy's neck and howling in anguish, her face distorted. 'I want my mummy. I want my mummy.'

'You're all right, lovey. You're all right,' Peggy said over and over again, chafing the child's cold limbs as she carried her to the waiting ambulance. 'We've got you out, see. You're all right.'

'Shock,' a nurse explained, enveloping the little girl in a red blanket. 'Is there anyone else?'

There must be, Peggy thought, but until that moment she hadn't thought of any others. She hadn't even considered how terrifying it would be to be lowered into a hole in the ground, where they could both have been buried alive. All her emotions and energies had been caught up in the rescue of this child. Now her mind started to function again and she realized the danger they were all facing and her legs began to tremble.

'We'll wait five minutes,' the driver said.

Mr Goodall was organizing a team on the far side of the ruin, and she could see Mr MacFarlane lying on the bricks with his ear to the mess, listening. So she controlled her stupid legs and went to join them.

'There's someone groaning,' Mr MacFarlane said as he stood up. 'If we could just get this ceiling lifted.'

The lifting gear arrived, more rubble was shifted and the woman was finally located, smeared with dirt and streaked with blood, unconscious but still alive.

'Two,' Mr MacFarlane said with satisfaction. 'How long did that take us, Charlie?'

It was nearly two hours, which surprised them all. Nearly two hours and the raid still going on all round them. But as the ambulance team were strapping the woman onto a stretcher, the all-clear sounded and after a few minutes people started to emerge from their shelters. Soon an anxious group of neighbours had gathered on the remains of the pavement.

Mr Goodall was still searching the wreckage where the kitchen had been. 'Easy, lads,' he warned, as the rapid removal of a piece of broken timber brought a landslide of bricks and plaster tumbling. 'Listen again, Mr Mac. Go and talk to the neighbours, Peggy. See if you can find out who's supposed to be at home.'

The neighbours were too shocked to have much idea. 'Being it's Saturday,' one woman explained, 'they could be anywhere. Old Man Terry'll be at Catford. I can tell you that. Up the Greyhounds.'

Peggy wrote down what little they could tell her and turned to climb back over the bricks to Mr Goodall. Directly in front of her, rising above the shattered roofs was an immense cloud, thick, grey-white and billowing. At first she thought the weather had changed but then she realized she was looking at the smoke from a fire and she was stupefied by the size of it. It was the biggest fire she'd ever seen and very close, just over the river. Now that her mind was functioning again she remembered hearing fire-engines racing past them all the time they'd been rescuing the little girl.

'It'll be the docks, Miss,' a man in a cloth cap told her. 'Rotten bleeders!'

'They've set fire to the docks,' she told Mr Goodall when she'd climbed back to his perch on the brick pile.

'I know,' he said shortly. 'Cop hold a' this.'

They worked on at the site until the rescue teams were satisfied that no one remained under the rubble, and by that time the smoke cloud had grown so big they couldn't see the top of it. It stretched for miles on either side of the river and now they could see red and yellow flames licking up into the base of it.

'They'll be back tonight with a marker like that to aim for,' Mr Goodall said. 'Cut off home, have something to eat, get some kip. We shall all be needed tonight.'

So Peggy went home, to a street frantic with rumour, a mother prostrate with nerves and no sign of Mrs Geary or her parrot.

'Oh Peggy, whatever are we going to do?' Baby said. 'She could have been blown to bits. We've been in the cellar all afternoon at work and when we came out and saw the fire ...'

'Have you asked the neighbours?' Peggy said taking off her tin hat.

'No. I came straight home as soon as they let us out. We had to stay in the cellar for ages. There were firebombs in the road and Mr Jones said ...'

'Put the potatoes on,' Peggy said, wearily, 'and I'll go and find her.' She was dog-tired and riven with pity, the face of that injured woman still filling her mind, but family was family. They had to be cared for too.

Mrs Geary was in the kitchen at number four, she and Polly and Mr Cooper, and she was so drunk she couldn't stand up.

'Lil' drink,' she explained, trying to focus her eyes. 'Keep 'a pecker up.'

'The Chief Warden says there'll be another raid tonight,' Peggy told Mr Cooper. 'Will you take her to the shelter?'

'Can't go to the shelter no more,' Mrs Geary said. 'Won't take me parrot, so bugger 'em. That's what I say.'

'We'll stay here, won't we mate?' Mr Cooper said, patting Mrs Geary's limp hand.

Peggy was too tired to argue with them. 'Well go under the stairs then,' she advised. 'It's going to be a rough night.'

It was rougher than any of them could possibly have imagined.

As soon as she'd eaten Baby's badly-cooked chop, Peggy fell asleep in her chair with her poor cat purring

362

with relief on her lap, but tired though she was she went back to the wardens' post when they sounded the siren. She wasn't supposed to be on duty until the morning but she felt she ought to help. And besides, she wanted to be out in the open air, up and out and with something to do, not cramped in a shelter, waiting and not knowing.

The docks were still burning, dear God, and the smoke cloud was now thousands of feet high, more black than grey and full of red sparks. But far far worse than the smoke was the sight and sound of the fire beneath it, which roared into the sky in a massive wall of flames, red, lurid, seething and infinitely terrible, and stretching as far as she could see. All that fuss about black-out, she thought, and now London itself had become one great burning torch to guide the bombers to their target. How could they miss? She could hear timber crackling and roaring over in the Surrey Docks as she cycled down to the post, and she could smell it too, like some overpowering bonfire. There were so many smells, burning rubber, burning leather, burning paper and mixed among them, a sweet treacly smell that was probably burning sugar. What a wicked waste!

'It's all the way from Beckton gasworks to Bermondsey,' Mr Goodall told her when she arrived at the post. 'Ten miles long. There's ships on fire in the Millwall Docks. Never seen nothing like it. They've got fire engines from all over London. Ten miles from end to end.'

Then it must be in Deptford too, Peggy thought, her heart shrinking, it must be where Joan and the kids are. But there wasn't time to think any further because the ack-ack started up and they could hear the bombers approaching in the darkness beyond the fire and presently one of the wardens came running in to the post with news of a clutch of incendiaries down by the river.

'Stirrup pumps,' Mr Goodall said. And they were off.

It felt horribly exposed out there in the streets with no sandbags to protect them and only their tin hats between them and the shrapnel that was now falling in white-hot fragments into the road. If a bomb falls what shall we do? she wondered. There was nowhere to take cover except doorways and precious few of them, for as she now realized, most of the houses in their area had no front gardens and no porches.

And as if to show her what they would do, she heard the descending swoosh of a falling bomb at that moment. They were all flat on their faces in the road in an instant and they stayed there until the explosion had roared into the air around them and the shock waves had rippled the road beneath them and the debris had finished falling.

'Where was it?' Mr MacFarlane said as they got up again, dusting themselves down and adjusting their helmets.

It had been quite a long way away. And yet it had sounded so close. 'You stay here and deal with those,' Mr Goodall said. 'I'll go and see what's what.'

There were six small blue fires burning like fireworks in the middle of the road just ahead of them.

'Sandbag 'em,' Mr Goodall said, jerking his head towards the usual pile of sandbags sagging in front of the entrance to a street shelter. Then he ran off in the direction of the bomb.

It was quick and easy to douse the fires, to Peggy's relief, because the cobbles hadn't allowed them to take hold and the bags smothered them completely, but the next part of the operation wasn't easy at all. An incendiary had fallen through the roof of an empty three-storey house nearby. They could see yellow flames licking out between the roof tiles, and by the time they'd broken in and run up six flights of stairs, the attic was well alight, the flames raw and alarming in the cramped darkness of that little sloping room. Peggy was filled with panic at the sight. They must put it out, and quickly too, before the Germans saw it and used it as a target for another bomb.

'I'll work the pump,' she said to Mr MacFarlane, 'you get the water. Only hurry.' In their slopping run up the stairs more than half the water in her bucket had been spilled.

It was very hard work. The plunger in the stirrup pump had to be pushed up and down at an exhausting speed. After the fourth bucket Peggy's arms were aching and she was completely out of breath, and what was worse, the fire seemed as strong as ever despite all the water they'd thrown on it. Fortunately two more pumps arrived just as she and Mr MacFarlane were giving up hope and between them they finally managed to get their 'incident' under control. There was a gaping hole in the roof, the timbers were burnt black, they were all soaking wet and covered in smuts, but the fire was beaten.

Now that the flames were gone there was no light in the attic except for the red glow from the patch of sky they could see through the roof and the small white beams of their inadequate torches.

'Och, Peggy Furnivall,' Mr MacFarlane said swinging his torch towards her, 'you look like a nigger minstrel.'

Peggy took off her tin helmet and wiped the dirt and sweat from her forehead. Her face felt as though it had been covered in hot oil. 'Now what?' she said.

'Back to the post, mebbe?'

It was quite a relief to be inside in the familiar order of their familiar headquarters, back to where life was normal, or as near normal as it could be with the noise of the raid still going on above them.

'I wonder where Mr Goodall got to,' Peggy said. And where *that* bomb fell. And who was hurt.

They had time for a quick wash, a mug of tea and a cigarette before Mr Goodall came back and settled down to write his report of their two incidents. But he had no time to tell them about *his* incident because even before he'd started his mug of tea there was a rattling clatter like somebody dropping a tray full of tins out of the sky. It turned out to be another basket of incendiary bombs, scattered over an even wider area and with even more fires. But this time they knew what they were doing. They were beginning to learn how to tackle a fire, working in from the edges, dampening steadily. There was less panic and more order. And in a peculiar way they were even getting used to the raid itself. Having so much to do kept your mind off the horrors.

Even when they were called to a fire in a tenement crowded with people, they managed to cope, working in two teams, one to evacuate the tenants to a nearby church hall, the others to fight the fire until the AFS arrived. But as they ran from the tenement to the church hall shepherding half a dozen terrified children before them, 'Quick! Quick! Never mind your shoe. Leave it', Peggy heard a new sound that made the hair rise on the nape of her neck.

Gunfire? Surely not. And yet the rattle was unmistakable. Had they come up the river with their damned invasion barges?

'It's the Royal Arsenal,' one of the firemen told her, shouting above the din. 'Terrible it is. Out a' control they reckon. We been there hours. I never seen nothing like it. They got fireboats out on the river with shells all bursting round 'em. Like a battle.'

It isn't *like* a battle, Peggy thought grimly. It *is* a battle. And we're the troops. The citizen army, that's who we are. And if Hitler thinks he can grind us down he's got another think coming. Anger against the wanton destruction of her city had been rising in her all day and all night. Now she recognized it for what it was and welcomed it, because it was strong and passionate and damped down her fear. Damn him, she thought furiously. He needn't think he can beat us.

CHAPTER 28

On that first awful night of the blitz the bombers stayed overhead until dawn. When the all-clear finally sounded Peggy was so tired she hardly knew what she was doing. She walked home to Paradise Row through the smoke and dust like an old woman, her back bent, her eyes bloodshot, covered in filth from her tin hat to her boots, and fearful of what she would find. And there was Paradise Row, still dark because there was so little daylight filtering through the smoke, but miraculously intact, not a door off its hinges, not a window broken, not a brick out of place. She stumbled in through the door limp with fatigue and relief.

Flossie was sprawled in her chair beside the kitchen fire wearing the martyred expression that showed she was in the middle of an attack of nerves. But when she opened her eyes and saw the state that Peggy was in, she was so shocked she sat up at once, nerves forgotten.

'Good God alive, girl,' she said. 'What *have* you been doing?'

Peggy was too tired to tell her. She flopped into the nearest chair and closed her eyes.

'Put the kettle on,' Flossie said to Baby. 'We'll make a cup of tea and then we'll get that boiler lit. You need a bath.'

'Where's my poor Tom?' Peggy said.

'Under the stairs,' Baby told her, filling the kettle as well as she could with such a limited flow of water coming from the tap. 'Hiding. He's been there all night. Wouldn't come out for us. He might if you called him.'

But it wasn't until the tin bath had been carried in from the garden and set before the fire with a clothes-horse draped with towels to serve as a screen, and Flossie had washed her daughter as if she was a little girl and helped her into a clean nightgown, that the terrified cat answered her call.

'Take him up to bed with you,' Flossie said. 'He'll be company. We'll have dinner late today. I'll give you a shout when it's ready.'

So Peggy and Tom went to bed, and Peggy was asleep before her head was settled on the pillow.

'I'm tired too,' Baby pouted, when Flossie came downstairs again.

'Not like that you're not,' her mother said, quite sternly. 'I don't know what they think they've been doing to her. You get and peel those potatoes.'

The dinner was nearly cooked when Joan and the children arrived in Paradise Row. They'd walked best part of the way because the roads were in such a mess.

'There's all bricks and planks and bits of houses everywhere,' Yvonne told her grandmother. 'We had to climb over it.'

Norman was clutching his trophy from the night, a large jagged piece of shrapnel. 'There's bits all over everywhere,' he said importantly, 'an' you have to watch your step for broken glass.' He'd learnt that from his trek, if nothing else. 'I brought my gingerbread man.'

'What a night!' Joan said. 'It was terrible up our way. The printing ink factory burned right down. You know, Gilbey's printing ink. You should ha' smelled it. There's nothing left of it this morning. And the Delta Metal works is still smouldering and they got the Royal Arsenal. It's a wonder we weren't all killed. I dread to think what Sid would say if he knew. He still thinks they're in the country.'

'Ain't you told him yet?' Baby said.

'What the eye don't see the heart can't grieve over,' Flossie said. 'Much better not to tell him. Where's the good upsetting the poor man? He's got enough to contend with in a prison camp.'

'Where's Peggy?' Joan asked.

'Sleeping it off,' Flossie said, making a warning grimace to show that she shouldn't be disturbed. 'She was up all night. Come home like a ghost at eight o'clock. I've put her straight to bed.'

'Did you go to the shelter?' Joan asked.

'Yes, we did,' Baby said, 'and I wish we hadn't. It was absolutely foul. The hurricane lamp kept going out. You can't imagine how foul it is listening to bombs falling on you in the pitch dark.'

'The bombs didn't fall on *you* though, did they?' Joan said. 'You ain't even lost any windows. You should see ours.'

'We stayed downstairs in the bakery office all night,' Yvonne told them, full of the importance of it. 'We stayed in the office while they baked the bread. All night. Mr Rudney said he was buggered if he was going to let Hitler stop the bread.' She was delighted to be able to report such open swearing.

'Language,' Joan rebuked mildly.

'That's what he said, Mum. I heard him.'

'Well maybe you did, but *you* mustn't say it. Where's Mrs Geary?'

'Upstairs,' Flossie said, making her most disapproving face. 'She's got a hangover. And serve her jolly well right.'

'Good heavens!' Joan said, preparing herself to enjoy a scandalous tale.

And someone rang at the doorbell.

'It's open!' Flossie called, expecting one of the neighbours. 'Push.'

But the woman at the door was a stranger wearing the green uniform of a member of the WVS.

'You don't happen to know where I could find the warden, do you?' she asked. She spoke in the plummy tones of the upper class although her face looked pleasant enough.

'The warden,' Flossie said, irritated by the woman's voice and protecting her young with determination, 'is upstairs asleep. She's been up twenty-four hours and twenty-four hours is enough.'

'Quite,' the woman said. 'I wouldn't worry her only they

369

told me at the post that she would be the one to know.'

'Know what?' Flossie said, still belligerent.

'Where I could find the key to number seven. There is no record of the tenants leaving the property but it does appear to be empty.'

Flossie walked out of the door into the street. 'It'll be on the string I dare say,' she said. 'That's where they always left it and they went off so quick I'll bet it's still there. Why do you want it?'

'I have seventeen bombed-out families to house before nightfall,' the woman said. 'That is an empty house, I believe. It is all quite in order, I assure you. I have authority from the owner.'

Flossie pulled the key through the letter box of number seven. 'There you are,' she said. 'What did I tell you? They went all of a sudden you see. Number three's empty too. It's for short lets. We have people in and out all the time but there's no one in it now. Have you got that on your list?'

'Very good of you,' the woman said. 'This is a terrible business. We all have to pull together in times like these.'

'Who's that?' Mrs Geary said hobbling down the stairs as the woman walked down to number three.

'She's a sort of housing officer, I think,' Flossie said. ''T any rate, we're to have a bombed-out family next door.'

'Well I hope they don't bring any bugs with 'em, that's all,' Mrs Geary said. 'We had a charity family put in when I was a nipper. Crawling alive they was. Hello, Joanie.'

The family moved in while Mrs Geary and the Furnivalls were eating their dinner, two dishevelled sisters and their seven children and a very old man who was called Gramps.

They'd come from the East End and they were still stunned from the horrors of the night they'd just endured. 'There's nothink left of our street,' one of the women told Flossie. 'One bleedin' bomb an' the 'ole bleedin' lot fell over. Like a pack a' bleedin' cards they was. Jerry built see. No substance to 'em.'

'Well you're all right here,' Flossie said. 'Nothing fell on us.'

'Like a pack a' bleedin' cards,' the woman said. 'We got

370

nothink but the clothes on our backs. That an' the beddin' the WVS give us.'

'Never mind,' Flossie said. 'People'll rally round. You'll see. I got a couple a' chairs an' a spare teapot you could have. That'ud be something.'

Peggy was sitting by the fire with the cat on her lap, writing a letter to Jim, just to assure him that she was safe and well. Later she would write at length and tell him everything about the raid but for the moment a short note would have to suffice. 'What are they like?' she asked when her mother came in for the teapot.

Flossie decided to be charitable. 'All right I suppose,' she said. 'I'm lending them a teapot and some chairs. They've lost everything. They're in ever such a mess, but I dare say they'll look better when they've had a wash. Only I hope they'll do it before they come in our shelter. It was smelly enough in there last night. Perhaps I ought to lend them a basin.'

'We shan't have any more raids, shall we?' Baby asked, aghast at the idea.

'Yes,' Peggy said shortly. 'We shall.'

'How many?'

'I don't know. Ask Hitler.'

'You're telling me lies,' Baby pouted. 'I don't think he'll bomb us again. He couldn't be so beastly.'

But of course she was wrong. From then on the bombers arrived every single night, week after week, month after month. For the first fortnight there were short daylight raids too, but it was the blitz by night that did the most damage.

Nevertheless in the days after that first long raid, Londoners began to settle to their new existence. Fire watchers were appointed to keep a look-out for incendiaries, because they knew now that you had to douse those vicious little bombs as soon as you could after they fell. Rescue teams were organized, using unemployed building workers whose knowledge of the construction of their local houses gave them the edge when it came to estimating where survivors might be found. And after the rescue teams, gangs of salvage workers to remove what they could from the shops and stores that were damaged beyond

371

repair. And after the salvage workers, demolition teams to pull down walls that were standing but dangerous and to clear the roads.

Shops that had only had their windows blown out, boarded up the holes, hung defiant messages on the boards and opened the next day. The first ones merely said 'Business as usual' but as the days and the raids passed the messages grew more witty. 'More open than usual' some shops said, and the wrecked police station hung a sign on its now remaining door which said, 'Be good – we're still open!' A barber wrote a long message to his customers 'We've had our close shave – come in and get yours' and in one dress shop where there was no glass left in the window at all and the models stood tipsily askew in dresses that had been ripped to shreds, the owner expressed his feelings in a single word, written in letters three feet tall. 'BLAST'.

There was a crazy gaiety about the place, a reckless determination. Life went on regardless of the mess and the lack of sleep. The trams ran as soon as the roads were cleared and their rails had been unbuckled, newspapers came out every morning no matter what sort of battering Fleet Street had taken the night before, Parliament sat, the Courts were at work, the police directed the traffic round wreckage that was being cleared and past streets that were closed because of unexploded bombs, typists sat in the streets in tin hats and typed their letters al fresco when their offices were mere piles of bricks.

One reason for the new mood was that those who had no stomach for the fight and the money to rent a house away from it, had packed up at once and left. 'And good riddance to 'em,' Mrs Geary growled. 'We don't want their sort here.' Many had their cats and dogs destroyed before they went. On Monday there were queues outside all the RSPCA clinics. 'What a callous thing to do,' Peggy said, stroking Tom. 'You'll take your chance with me, won't you, Tomkins?'

But the Londoners who remained were a different breed. The raids had begun, officialdom had been caught napping, so now they would make their own arrangements and look after themselves. Some went trekking every night to sleep in the nearest piece of open country and return in time for work every morning. Greenwich Park was soon full of trekkers and so was Hampstead Heath. In the East End they stormed the tube stations and despite official disapproval forced an entrance to an obvious underground shelter. For many it was the only real home they would know all through the blitz, cold, damp, poorly-ventilated and without any sanitary arrangements at all except for a bucket or the tunnel, it was still better than facing the bombs above ground. And among the families that camped out in the underground were Flossie's next-door neighbours.

'Can't stay 'ere, love,' the elder of the two sisters explained to Flossie, when she handed back the teapot and the chairs. 'It's not we ain't grateful, because we are. You've been ever so good to us, all of yer, giving us a lend a' things an' everything. It's just it don't seem nat'ral down 'ere. It's too much in the open if you know what I mean. An' that shelter a' yours is bleedin' chronic.'

That was Mrs Geary's opinion too. She'd left her poor parrot at home and sat out the second night among her neighbours, but what with the noise of the raid and lack of sleep and anxiety about the bird, next morning she decided she'd had enough.

'I shall sleep downstairs while this goes on,' she announced. 'In the front room. We'll get a shutter ter go over the window to stop the glass. Polly can go in the cupboard under the stairs. He'll be safe enough there. Look how your cat goes under the stairs. Instinct, y' see. They always know the best sort a' places, animals.'

Flossie was none too pleased to have her front room requisitioned in this high handed way and for a few days relations between the two women were decidedly cool. But then the local papers let drop a little item of news about a street shelter sustaining a 'direct hit, with many casualties.' Paradise Row was horribly alarmed.

'Many casualties,' Mr Cooper said sitting outside his house in the September sunshine with the newspaper across his knees. 'That means they were all killed, poor buggers.'

'Stands ter reason they'd be killed,' Mrs Allnutt agreed.

373

'If that roof was ter come down on yer, you'd all be squashed flat. Wouldn't stand an earthly.'

'Well that's it!' Baby said when she brought the news back to number six. 'If that's what's going to happen I'd rather be in my own bed when it does. At least I could get a bit a' sleep on me own bed. I can't stand much more of this sitting up all night. It's giving me bags under me eyes. Why don't we sleep downstairs like Mrs Geary?'

So they turned both the downstairs rooms into dormitories, and Mrs Geary got Mr Allnutt to make two wooden shutters for the windows, which were a surprisingly good fit, and although it was cramped and uncomfortable at least there was a lavvy out the back and they could make tea when they felt like it and the long vigil of the night raids seemed less scary in the comfort of the kitchen.

To Peggy out on the streets in the thick of it all, the raids were always full of danger and horror. No matter how many times she saw an injured person eased from the wreckage she never grew accustomed to it. And death was worse. She learned various tricks to allay her fear, keeping busy being quite the best of them, but the sight and smell of sudden death, particularly this sudden undeserved awful death, tore her to pieces every time.

Sometimes when the raid was over in the early morning and they were still technically on duty she and Mr MacFarlane would climb up to the top floor of the flats and look out over the city just to reassure themselves that it was still there. There was a vibrant quality about those early mornings, an extraordinary exhilaration, a sense of pure joy to be alive. Because they *were* still alive despite everything, and the bombers had gone, and the barrage balloons were shining pink and silver in the sunrise, and there was white frost sparkling on the pavements below them, and London, dear old dependable London, was still there, spread out before them like some huge patient prehistoric beast, tattered and wounded but still alive and much much too big to kill.

But there were other times when she felt so low after a long night among the injured that she had to retreat to the empty bedroom upstairs as soon as she got home and sit in her old chair by the window to weep out her distress, usually into Tom's tabby fur, because whenever she was home the little cat followed her about all over the house.

'It's a nightmare,' she wrote to Jim. 'So many people killed. So many dreadful injuries. There was a kid last night with both legs gone. Couldn't have been more than thirteen. What sort of a life will he have now? He'll be like poor Mr Cooper. And a man with half his face cut away by flying glass. And a woman with her chest caved in and blood pouring out of her mouth. Oh dear, I'm sorry to burden you with all this when you've got enough on your plate, but I can't talk to Mum or Baby about it. They're both so nervy these days. Mum's drinking Sanatogen by the bucket load.'

'Much good may it do her,' Jim wrote back. 'Personally I've always thought it was pretty poisonous muck but there's no accounting for taste. Burden all you like, my lovely Tabby eyes. I wish I could get home to see you but you know what it's like. Last chance for Hitler to invade is around the end of the month. If he misses the tide, and he can't beat Fighter Command (and he *can't* beat Fighter Command, we're much too good for him) we shall be safe till the spring and perhaps they'll give me a spot of leave, and about time too!'

But there was no leave and no respite for any of them yet. The battle in the air continued with increasing ferocity as the Luftwaffe redoubled their efforts to ground the British planes and leave the skies clear for the invasion. And the newspapers reported the scores day by day, 'Luftwaffe 62 – RAF 13', 'Germans lose 73 planes – 28 of our aircraft are missing – 14 pilots safe', until the long daylight raid on 15 September.

CHAPTER 29

It was a misty dawn, the grass sharp with dew, the trees shrouded and silent like the waiting planes, the light in the eastern sky echoing the colour of the smoke ribboning from a hundred early morning cigarettes as the airfield yawned to life. Breakfast was cooking. Ground crews were called. Pilots woke in their uncomfortable huts beside dispersal sheds all round the perimeter. A misty dawn.

Jim woke immediately as he always did, and got up immediately too, walking out of the grumbling fug of the hut into the freshness of open air, observing automatically that it bid fair to be a fine clear day and good flying weather. The mist was just beginning to clear, lifting like a stage gauze to reveal the rich peaceful colours of wet grass and autumn leaves, and as it rose the birds began to sing. It was so quiet outside the hut he could hear every single note of the chorus. Extraordinary to be listening to such joyful sounds on a day when there was bound to be a battle in the air. Extraordinary to be standing there, miles from home, miles from Peggy, waiting for the battle to begin.

Still, he thought, grinding out his cigarette against the wall, at least we're ready for 'em now. The squadron was at full strength, his flight was in tip-top condition, it was better odds.

Two of his oppos came yawning out of the hut, with their hair standing on end and their eyes still narrowed with sleep.

'What d'you think?' one asked him.

'We're in for a busy day,' he answered.

By eight o'clock, when they were breakfasted and ready for action, the sky was as blue as summer and there was a covering of low white cumulus cloud. At nine the buzz went round that the first German planes had been sighted over the coast. Jim's ground crew were impatient to get started so the planes were soon checked and fuelled and armed, but then nothing much happened, although the atmosphere crackled with tension. Their pilots sat around outside the hut waiting, the phones crackled occasional messages, cards were played, pipes were smoked, the dogs retreated into the shadow.

When the call finally came to scramble it was as if they'd all been sitting on springs. The flight was in the air in minutes, heading south towards the Thames and the fields of Kent.

From that moment on there was so much happening that none of them had any time for anything else except the job in hand. Occasionally one of the crew would look up to where the battle was weaving white paisley patterns against the blue sky, at the red sparks of distant machine-gun fire, at Dorniers little more than black dots at the head of their long con trails, flying in formation, lozenge, square, arrowhead, but breaking under attack from plunging Hurricanes and Spitfires, at black smoke billowing from a stricken plane as it howled downwards, at the roar and wreckage of explosions. But for most of the time their attention was fully occupied with their own planes and their pilots. Flights went up at regular intervals and flights returned, their own three safe and ecstatic with victory.

'How many, sir?' Jim asked the first of his pilots to return.

'Two. Possible third. Jock got one. Bloody good show.'

The news of the battle filtered through to the ground crews. There were 300 Dorniers in the attack with a full complement of escorting Messerschmitts, and the RAF was causing havoc in their close packed formations. By midday the returning flights were claiming that Jerry had turned tail, by twelve thirty the skies were clear and the first attack was over.

There was just time for the pilots to be debriefed, eat and catch a quick nap while their planes were checked, repaired, refuelled and rearmed. At two o'clock the Dorniers returned and battle was resumed. This second attack seemed to be both quicker and longer than the first, because by then they were all so keyed up that time, energies and actions had all extended beyond their normal bounds. Tales of amazing gunfights began to spread and were relished between flights; Goering had thrown everything he had into this fight, two planes from their squadron were down but only one of the pilots had bought it, the other had been seen ditching in the Channel, the Germans had lost sixty aircraft, seventy, ninety, over a hundred. Now they watched the sky whenever they could because they knew that this battle was bigger than any they'd seen to date. And at the end of the afternoon when the remaining Dorniers droned back towards the Channel, they were all sure that they had been part of a decisive victory.

Just how decisive was revealed by the nine o'clock news that night which reported that 185 German aircraft had been shot down, and that two battles had been won that day, one by Fighter and the other, less publicized, by Bomber Command, who had been attacking the German invasion fleet for weeks and now knew, at last, that it couldn't be used that year. Whatever happened in the weeks ahead the Germans couldn't invade until the spring. The weather, the tides and the RAF were all against them.

Next morning the newspapers were all full of praise for 'the gallant victors of this decisive battle'. '185 shot down,' the headlines blazed, 'Greatest day for RAF'. But it was Winston Churchill, broadcasting to the nation, who said what everyone was thinking, his famous voice growling across the air, gravelly and indomitable, his words so splendid that no one who heard them would ever forget them.

'The gratitude of every home in our Island,' he said, 'in our Empire, and indeed throughout the world, except in the abodes of the guilty, goes out to the British airmen, who, undaunted by odds, unwearied in their constant challenge and mortal danger, are turning the tide of world war by their prowess and by their devotion. Never in the field of human conflict was so much owed by so many to so few.'

'Quite right too,' Jim wrote to Peggy, 'but don't imagine it's over. They'll go on attacking us and they'll go on bombing London and the other provincial cities, we've only stopped the invasion. Still at least things will ease a little now. You never know I might get a thirty-six hour pass.'

He came home on just such a pass three weeks later.

As soon as she knew he was coming Peggy asked the Chief Warden if she could have a thirty-six hour pass from her duties too.

'Don't see any reason why not,' Mr Goodall said. 'We're well staffed at present and now they've stopped their daylight raids we're not quite so hard pressed. God knows you've earned it. Just don't go off and get married just yet awhile that's all. I couldn't afford to lose you now, not even to the RAF.'

'I won't do that,' Peggy assured him. 'I promise.' But oh it would be good to be with Jim again.

She was shocked to see how much he had changed. He looked older and tougher, with lines on his face that hadn't been there the last time she saw him, his nose more obviously broken and worry lines etched across his forehead and between those dark eyebrows. But she was so proud of him. So very proud. Her airman in his admirable uniform. And he made love to her more tenderly than he'd ever done.

'My lovely Tabby eyes,' he said. 'I've missed you so much.'

She turned in his arms to look into his eyes. 'I can't believe you're here,' she said. 'It feels like years since we was last in this bed. I can't believe it's true.'

'Have I got to show you it is?' he laughed at her. 'All over again?'

'No,' she said. 'Not yet. Unless you want to.'

But he was already lighting their two cigarettes.

'We're so delicate,' she said, running her fingers along

his forearm. 'Human beings I mean. You can tear our flesh open with a little thing like a matchstick we're so delicate and yet we go and invent bombs. It don't make sense.'

'No gloomy thoughts,' he said pretending to scold. 'We ain't got time to waste being morbid. What shall we do tomorrow?'

'This?' she suggested.

'As well as this.'

'What say we go dancing? I ain't been dancing for an age. Not since that day in Croydon.'

'That reminds me,' he said. 'Froggy came down with me this time. Staying with his sister. We could make a four-some.'

'A foursome?'

'You an' me an' Froggy an' Megan.'

'Is that still going on?'

'Seems to be. He writes to her every week.'

'Imagine,' she said, surprised by the news. 'It can't be love. He ain't her type. But I'm glad she sees him. Well all right then. Make it a foursome.'

So the next afternoon they took a tram and a bus to Croydon to call on Froggy and all four of them went dancing. Peggy was impressed to see how easy Froggy and Megan were with one another and began to wonder whether there might not be something in it after all. And when the dance was over, she and Jim spent their last two hours at the pictures, cuddled together in the back row. It was really very miserable to have to say goodbye after such a happy time. She was quite dispirited on the way to the station, although she tried not to show it.

'Flower to cheer the pretty lady,' Jim said, imitating the flower sellers' husky street cry, and turning she saw that he was picking a tall pink weed from the bomb site beside them.

'Wear it to remember me by,' he said, sliding the stem into her buttonhole.

'Thirty-six hours is such a short time,' she said, as he put his arms round her.

'I'll be back,' he promised. 'Soon as ever I can. Give us a kiss.'

380

She was still wearing the weed when she got home after seeing him off. Mum had just popped down to the shops according to Mrs Geary who was happily installed in the best armchair with Tom on her lap.

Baby was arranging her hair in front of the mirror. 'What on earth's that in your coat?' she said, turning up her nose at it. 'It looks like a weed.'

' 'Tis a weed,' Mrs Geary told her. 'That's the fireweed.'

'It's growing everywhere,' Peggy said. 'On all the bomb sites. Some places are quite pink with it. Jim picked it for me. I think it's pretty.' The little pink flowers with their purple sepals were delicate against the rough cloth of her coat.

'We used to call it London Pride when I was a girl,' Mrs Geary remembered.

'What a perfect name,' Peggy said, thinking how appropriate it was. 'London Pride and here it is growing on all the bomb sites.' I shall write and tell him what a perfect gift it is.

There were lots of other Londoners who knew the name of the weed too and soon the splendid irony of its appearance was being celebrated in pubs all over the city. And just before Jim was due home on his second thirty-six hour pass, Noel Coward broadcast a new song he'd written in its honour.

Flossie and Mrs Geary were most impressed. 'Never thought much a' the man up to now,' Mrs Geary confessed. 'It's that awful la-di-da voice of his. Puts you off. But he's bang to rights about this, an' no mistake.'

'London Pride,' the gentleman sang in his odd clipped drawl,

'has been handed down to us,
London Pride is a flower that's free.
London Pride means our own dear town to us,
And our pride it forever shall be.

Every blitz our resistance stiffening
From the Ritz to the Anchor and Crown.
Nothing ever can break or hide
The pride of London town.'

'Perfect,' Flossie said with tears in her eyes.

The wireless was a great comfort to them during the blitz. They listened to the news religiously every night and morning because you could depend on the BBC to tell you the truth no matter what it was. But there were all sorts of other wonderful programmes too. Gracie Fields singing so beautifully. And Vera Lynn. J B Priestley with his postscripts after the nine o'clock news on Sunday, *In Town Tonight* on Saturday and *Hi Gang* and *Henry Hall's Guest Night* and *Sandy Macpherson at the Cinema Organ*. They even gave household hints, which Mrs Roderick said ought to be called 'How to cook meals with no food.'

'How we shall make out with Christmas coming I do not know,' she said. An even when supplies of currants and sultanas and dried fruit suddenly appeared in Mr Grunewald's shop she was not appeased. 'It won't be the same,' she said darkly. 'It won't be the same at all.'

And it was true. It was hard to imagine Christmas among the bombs.

'But I suppose we'd better make an effort,' Flossie said, 'for the kiddies anyway. They must've had a pretty rotten time last year down with those nasty old gravediggers.' She always referred to the Rays as gravediggers. Undertakers sounded altogether too respectable for such unpleasant characters. 'I'll see if I can get a little chicken. You'd like that wouldn't you, kids?'

'We'll go halves,' Joan offered at once. 'Hang the expense eh, Mum?'

'We could have Lily and Percy and all of them for tea,' Flossie said. 'Do him good to have a day with other kiddies, poor little man. Is Jim getting leave?'

'I doubt it,' Peggy said, yearning to see him again.

'Oh well,' Flossie said busily, 'if he does one more won't make any odds. I wish I could have made a proper cake, like in the old days.'

'What day is Christmas?' Baby wanted to know.

'Wednesday,' Flossie told her. 'Why?'

'So Boxing Day's Thursday. We shan't get to the pictures that week then, shall we?'

'No,' Flossie said, 'I suppose we won't. Never mind. We'll go Sunday.'

'I don't like Sunday pictures,' Baby complained. 'They're all oldies.'

'Some of those old pictures are jolly good,' her mother said easily. 'I like them.'

'Well I don't,' Baby said pouting.

'I wonder if we shall have a raid Christmas Day,' Mrs Geary said, diverting them before Baby could get nasty.

'Oh I do hope not,' Flossie said. 'They ought to stop over Christmas, surely to goodness.'

'Nasty lot them Jerries,' Mrs Geary said darkly. 'Wouldn't put it past 'em to come over.'

But they didn't come over, at least not on Christmas Day, and the Furnivall family had a well-deserved and peaceful feast, with a cake of sorts, even if it wasn't iced, and a pudding that was really quite good, and even four handmade table decorations, that Yvonne and Norman had coloured in at school, Father Christmas, a reindeer, a lop-sided snowman and Winston Churchill in a purple siren suit, cigar and all.

Jim didn't get leave but that was hardly to be expected and Peggy knew he would be home again in the new year. Meantime she had a letter in her pocket, a cat on her lap, a good meal in her belly, and no air raid. And that, after a hundred and nine night raids, was luxury enough.

CHAPTER 30

Flossie Furnivall had bought clothes for all her family that
Christmas, pretty blouses for the three girls, trousers for
Norman and a nice warm skirt for Yvonne, and on a
sudden impulse she had treated herself to a new pair of
shoes. Her old ones were worn into such a state that the
cobbler said he simply couldn't patch them up any longer.
So she'd splashed out and bought herself a lovely new pair,
brown brogues with a broad-patterned tongue and bold
patterning all round the sides.

'Very nice,' Mrs Roderick said when she came to call
that Sunday night. 'And a new hat too. I gather you had a
good Christmas. You are the swell.'

'Present from my Peggy,' Flossie said happily, adjusting
the hat on her newly-brushed hair. 'How do I look?' It was
a red hat and her lipstick matched it exactly.

'Good enough for Buckingham Palace,' Mrs Roderick
said, as Baby came flouncing out of the kitchen, blonde
locks swinging. 'Is she coming?'

'No *she's* not,' Baby said crossly. She'd painted her lips
in a scarlet cupid's bow that didn't quite match the true
lines of her mouth and as a result she was fixed in a
perpetual pout. 'You know I don't like old pictures.' And
she flounced up the stairs.

'She's in such a mood,' Flossie confided, as she and Mrs
Roderick walked out into the cold air of the afternoon.
'You just don't know how to please her sometimes.'

'Personally I wouldn't even try,' Mrs Roderick said,

sniffing, partly with derision and partly because the cold was making her nose sting. 'But there you are, she's your daughter not mine. Quick! Look! There's our tram.'

They hadn't allowed very much time to get to the cinema, so to see a tram approaching right on cue was a piece of luck. But their luck ran out on the journey because there was a hole in the road and some repair work going on, so the tram had to stop before it reached the cinema, and that left them with more than a quarter of a mile to walk. Consequently they arrived when the B picture had already begun.

'Let's go and have a cup of tea somewhere and go in when the big picture starts,' Flossie suggested. 'I don't like seeing the end before the beginning.'

But Mrs Roderick wouldn't hear of it. 'I can't hang about in the cold,' she said. 'Not at my age. I should catch the rheumatism. Let's go in. At least it's warm inside.'

'Oh ...' Flossie dithered, wondering whether she could plead nerves as a reason for tea. It was very difficult to plead nerves with Mrs Roderick because she was so forceful. In the end she decided to agree. 'Oh all right then. But I shall keep my eyes closed.'

But of course she couldn't keep them closed for long and certainly not for more than half an hour, the sound of those syrupy voices and all that lovely swirly romantic music was too enticing. Soon she was lost in the romantic world that she needed so much these days and that sustained her so well, war and rationing and bombing all forgotten, as the peerless heroine danced in the strong arms of her suave hero between urns tastefully arranged with the flowers of all seasons under a sky full of summer clouds scudding past in a storm-force wind that wouldn't damage anything. Smashing!

In the interval she and Mrs Roderick treated themselves to a packet of Du Maurier cigarettes.

'You need a treat now and then to buck you up,' Mrs Roderick said, as she always did.

And Flossie agreed, smoking like a film star, as she always did.

In fact, until the notice came up on the screen to tell them that there was an air raid on, it was a most enjoyable outing. But at that point it went wrong.

'Well I'm off home,' Mrs Roderick said. 'This is where we came in anyway.'

'Oh don't go yet,' Flossie whispered back, not taking her eyes from the screen. 'This is the best bit. See it to the end.'

'I have seen it,' Mrs Roderick said. 'I told you. This is where we came in.'

People in the rows behind them began to shush her. It was bad enough to have their enjoyment interrupted by the notice without this woman making a noise.

'I'm off,' Mrs Roderick said. 'You coming or not?'

'No, no,' Flossie whispered, still absorbed. 'Must see this bit. She was patting her handbag with the pleasure of it.

So Mrs Roderick left her to it. 'I'll call for you shopping tomorrow,' she said. And went.

Flossie didn't notice her going. The heroine was drifting about the screen in a lovely floating négligé squirting perfume all over herself in a lovely languid way as if she had all the time and money in the world. What a life!

In the wardens' post Peggy and Mr MacFarlane had been playing cards. They'd been on duty at the post since eight o'clock that morning and the time had hung rather heavily once the routine chores were done. But as soon as they were given the red alert everything speeded up. Within minutes a messenger boy arrived on a bicycle to tell them that there were incendiaries at Christies Wharf. They sent two wardens down in case they were needed, and the wardens sent the messenger back almost at once to say that there was nobody to evacuate but that they'd found a serious problem. The wharf was locked up for the weekend, there were no fire watchers on duty there, and the incendiaries had already taken hold. When the AFS arrived the fire was out of control and soon the entire wharf was ablaze, the two hundred telegraph poles it contained going up like a bonfire in a roar of red and yellow flame that could be clearly seen outside the post, with sparks shooting like red stars hundreds of feet into the darkness.

'I hope Joan's all right,' Peggy said. 'And the kids. I

don't like it when they start on the warehouses. There's a lot a' warehouses round her way.'

'Och they'll be away under cover,' Mr MacFarlane said, wiping his eyes because the smoke was making them water. 'Your sister's a sensible girl.'

Actually Joan and the children were being well looked after. When the raid began they were in the house next door with Mr and Mrs Rudney. And as soon as Mr Rudney heard the noise of the bombers, he decided that this was going to be 'a big one' and took them all down to the cellar.

'They're after something special tonight,' he said. 'You mark my words.'

'Just so long as it ain't us,' his wife said, following him down the wooden stairs into the coal-damp darkness under the house. 'You got the torches?'

What they were after was the City of London, left empty and unattended, like Christies warehouse, because it was a Sunday and the Sunday after Christmas what's more. And they were after it at a particularly vulnerable time, when there was plenty of cloud to give them cover, and when the tide on the Thames was exceptionally low. Within the first hour of the raid they dropped over three thousand incendiary bombs on the heart of the City and because there was no one to give the alarm, the fires took hold secretly and then spread and raged. By seven o'clock there were so many fires out of control that the sky was blood red with reflected light and outside the wardens' post it was so bright that Peggy and Mr MacFarlane could read notices and newspapers as if it were daytime.

The wardens who'd gone down to Christies Wharf had seen it all. They came back full of awed excitement.

'There's fires everywhere you look. It's even worse than the docks was that time. Look at that sky!'

They looked at the awesome red of the sky for a very long time, feeling helpless and angry and yet acknowledging a shameful crawling excitement at the drama of what they were witnessing. This was no longer a series of fires, it was one enormous blaze and it stretched as far as they could see, the flames growing higher and denser as they watched. It was as if the whole of the city was on fire.

As if Hell itself had come to their city.

Other wardens arrived to report back at the post, and the stories they brought with them were horrific. Every building in London was on fire on both sides of the Thames all the way from Moorgate and the Barbican right down to the South Bank. St Paul's was ringed with flame, the cobbles in the streets were burning, the tram rails were melting, and as a final heart-stopping horror, the firemen had run out of water, and the fire-boats on the Thames couldn't get near enough to the riverbank to help because the tide was so low.

By now the light from the inferno was so very bright it was like being on a stage under red floodlights.

'We're off duty in ten minutes,' Mr MacFarlane said to Peggy. 'Should we stay on a wee bitty longer, d'ye think?'

But she never got a chance to answer him because at that moment their messenger came cycling back to the post, his face gilded by the firelight, his eyes bulging, breathless with the news that there'd been a terrible incident in Blackwall Lane.

'Parachute mine hit them big flats at the corner a' the Woolwich Road,' he gasped. 'You know the ones. Them big four storey ones. Knocked flat. There's dead bodies everywhere. Blew out all the winders in the hospital, St Alphege's, you know. An' there's about ten shops gone. An' the cinema.'

Peggy felt her blood running cold in her veins. 'The Granada?' she asked.

'Yeh! That's the one. There's dead bodies all over the place.'

'What's up, lassie?' Mr MacFarlane asked, his earnest face all concern.

'My mum was up the Granada this afternoon.'

'When did it happen?' Mr MacFarlane asked the boy.

'Quarter ter seven.'

'Would she still be there at that time?'

'She might be.'

'Then you must go straight there and see,' Mr MacFarlane decided. 'Leave the post to me. The night team will all be along shortly. No, no, not a word. Off you go.'

So she went, cycling through the deserted streets with

the sky glowing red as nightmare above her and the roar of the fire throbbing like the terror of her own heart. But being Peggy she tried to be sensible. She'd go home first. After all Mum could have gone home long before the mine fell. She could be sitting in the kitchen at that very moment as right as rain, and wouldn't they laugh about it then.

But number six was unlit and empty, and her mother wasn't in the shelter either, although Mrs Roderick was, and she was very surprised to hear that Flossie hadn't come home.

'I knew she'd get caught in the raid,' she said. 'Would stop to see the end of the picture, you see. I hope she's all right.'

'So do I,' Peggy said, grimly. But she went on being sensible, taking the time to write a note to Baby and Mrs Geary, to tell them that she'd 'gone to an incident in the Woolwich Road' and propping it against the clock on the mantelpiece where they'd certainly see it in that awful bright light. Then she set off on her journey again, worrying and arguing with herself all the way.

The boy could have got hold of the wrong end of the stick. It might be just an ordinary HE not a parachute mine. And even if it was, Mum could be taking shelter somewhere nearby. Never trouble trouble till trouble troubles you. But no matter what she tried to tell herself, fear and anxiety howled in her mind all the way, and when she got to the Woolwich Road she knew at once that they were both justified.

The junction was full of debris. A whole row of shops seemed to have crumbled to pieces and fallen into the road, and where the flats had been there was a pile of rubble as high as a house. The rescue teams were still working in the ruins, there were several covered corpses lying where the pavements should have been and the whole scene was stained by the awful light from the fire, as if everything and everybody there was covered in blood. Oh dear God, Peggy thought, dear dear God!

She got off her bicycle and stood where she was until her heart was beating more normally and her stomach had stopped shaking. Most of the people she could see were

rescue workers or wardens, and after a few seconds she
realized that the warden standing on the broken steps of
the cinema was a man she knew, so she propped her
bicycle against a wall that was still standing and went
across to ask him if he knew anything about the casualties.

'Very bad,' he said. 'We've had ten dead and ever so
many injured.'

'Any names?'

'Someone you know, is it?' he asked, sensing the anxiety
she was holding in check.

'My mum.'

'I'd cut across to St Alphege's if I was you,' he advised,
turning his head towards the hospital behind him. 'That's
where they was all taken, being it's so near. Though mind
you they've took a pasting an' all tonight.'

So Peggy climbed over the wreckage and walked
towards the hospital. In the lurid light she could see that
most of the windows in the front of the building had been
blown out and when she got through the gate and into
casualty she found that none of the electric lights were
working. But there was a nurse on duty at reception with a
candle and a list of admissions, and to Peggy's relief her
mother's name wasn't among them.

'But I'd check the ward if I was you,' the nurse advised.
'We've had quite a few brought in unconscious.'

'Yes,' Peggy said, swallowing back her distress. 'I will.
Thank you.'

'I've got some clothing here you might like to see,' the
nurse said. 'Not very much I'm afraid. A hat, shoes,
gloves, handbags, that sort of thing. One of the wardens
brought it over. It might help.'

'Yes,' Peggy said again, her mouth dry.

'Come through into the office,' the nurse said, picking
up her candle.

The collection was spread out over a bench, lost and
pathetic, like items in a jumble sale. And her mother's new
red hat was right in the middle.

'Then she must be here,' the nurse said, after reading
the label on the hat. 'It was found on the cinema steps. I
am sorry. Can you find your own way to the wards?
They're all in surgical.'

It seemed such a long walk to the wards, down corridors flickering with red light and echoing to the shouts and crashes from the continuing rescue. Never trouble trouble till trouble troubles you. Lord, give us strength to endure that which has to be endured. Please God don't let her be dead.

The first ward she came to was still shuttered and very dark. There were nurses moving among the beds, candles in hand, and somebody was groaning in that low, terrible, instinctive way that Peggy now knew meant a pain beyond endurance.

'Yes,' the Sister said, appearing beside her, angel-faced in the candle-light.

'I'm looking for my mother.'

'Of course. Would you care to follow me.'

They walked slowly from bed to bed, carrying their little blue edged light before them. Flossie was in the fourth bed.

Peggy was so relieved that her legs gave way under her and she had to sit down quickly on the bedside chair or she would have fallen over.

'She's all right,' she said. 'Oh thank God!'

'She's just come down from theatre,' the Sister told her, 'but she's as well as can be expected in the circumstances.'

Peggy looked at the cradle over her mother's legs and nodded to show that she understood, but she was so stunned with relief she missed the warning tone in the Sister's voice.

'Could I stay with her till she comes round?' Peggy asked.

'It could be quite a long time.'

'I don't mind. I'm not on duty till eight tomorrow morning.'

So she sat by the bed in the groaning darkness and waited. At a little after ten o'clock the all-clear sounded, and around midnight the ward lights came on again to an audible sigh of relief from the nurses. And as if the light was a signal Flossie stirred and opened her eyes.

'That you, Peg?' she said thickly. 'Where am I, gel?'

'In hospital,' Peggy said. 'You're all right.'

'Thought I was at the pictures,' Flossie said. And slept again.

The second time she woke she sipped a little water and complained that the light was hurting her eyes. The third time was at six o'clock and by then Peggy was beginning to think she ought to go home.

'You been here all night?' Flossie said.

'Yes.'

'I've been here all night then.'

'Yes.'

'I'll get up presently and fix that stove,' Flossie said. 'It's ever so cold in here. Fancy being here all night. What is the world coming to? I'll have a little nap and then I'll get up.'

'I'll come in and see you tonight,' Peggy promised, as Flossie closed her eyes.

'Um.'

It was cold and slightly foggy out in the street and the red light was still casting an eerie patina over the bomb site. But the bodies were gone and so were the rescue teams and the street was silent and empty.

Her bicycle was still where she'd left it the night before, so she pedalled wearily home. Now she realized that her neck was aching and her feet were sore and her eyes were smarting with smoke and unshed tears. So as there was no one to see her she cried all the way home.

Baby was still fast asleep in her bed on the kitchen floor and she stirred and grumbled when Peggy came in.

'What's a' time?'

'Quarter to seven,' Peggy said. 'Get up, Baby, I've got something to tell you.'

'Tell away,' Baby said easily, staying where she was.

'Mum's in hospital.'

Baby woke up at once and sat up in a fury. 'She ain't,' she said. 'You ain't to say such things.' But now she remembered that Mum hadn't been in the house when she got in last night. 'She was down the road with Mrs Roderick, wasn't she? Well then, how can she be in hospital?'

'Don't be a fool,' Peggy said. She was too tired to cope with one of Baby's tantrums. 'She is. She's been hurt.' Now that she was home she realized that she hadn't asked anyone about her mother's injuries. 'Her legs are hurt. I told her we'd go in and see her tonight.'

'She can't be hurt,' Baby insisted. 'If she's hurt who's going to look after the kids? Joan'll be here with them in half an hour, I hope you realize.'

Peggy had forgotten all about the practical details she'd have to attend to now. 'We'll think of something,' she said. 'Just get up, will you? I'd like to get these beds cleared before they come.'

'And who'll get the shopping?' Baby went on. '*I* can't, I hope you realize. Not when I'm at work all day. I shan't be able to do anything.'

And she didn't. Of course. It was Mrs Geary who looked after the kids all day and Joan and Peggy who queued at the shops in their lunch hour. And that evening it was Joan and Peggy who went to the hospital because Baby said she couldn't possibly go, not when there was a raid on.

Flossie was wide awake and complaining. Her face was deathly pale and there were two bright spots of unnatural redness in the centre of her cheeks, but her speech was clear and she could focus her eyes and she looked much more like herself than she'd done the night before.

'I've got the most awful pain in my legs,' she said, when they'd kissed her and settled into chairs beside her bed. 'They won't give me anything for it. I do think it's mean. Go and see if you can persuade 'em, Peg, eh? They'll do it for you.'

'I'll see the Sister,' Peggy promised. 'In a minute. How d'you feel apart from that?'

'They won't tell me where my shoes are either,' Flossie said. 'I had my new shoes on. I remember particularly. They say they don't know. What a lot a' nonsense! They must have took 'em off before they put me to bed. I don't want 'em lost. Good money they cost me.'

They let her talk for the half hour that was left of visiting time and then they went down to see the Sister.

'She's got rather a lot of pain in her legs,' Peggy said, tentative and polite, but hopeful. 'Could you give her something for it?'

The Sister looked at them carefully before she answered, which was rather disconcerting. 'If there were anything we could give her to stop this pain, we would,' she said. 'But the truth is, there isn't anything. The truth is ... it's a phantom pain you see. It wouldn't matter what we gave her, she'd feel it just the same. The truth is ...'

The two sisters looked at her questioningly. 'A phantom pain?' Peggy prompted.

'Her legs were blown off in the explosion,' the Sister said. 'I *am* sorry to have to tell you. The left leg is gone below the knee, the right went six inches below the hip socket.'

Peggy felt sick and stupid with shock. 'But she's feeling pain in them,' she said. 'There must be some mistake.'

'They often do,' the Sister said sadly. 'We don't know why it is, but we see it over and over again. There's no mistake, I'm afraid. What I'm telling you is true. She is feeling pain in limbs that aren't there any more.'

The two sisters left the hospital that night in a very bad state.

'Poor Mum,' Joan said, 'how will she manage?'

'We'll have to manage for her I expect,' Peggy said. 'The first thing is to get her over the operation and well enough to come home.'

'She looked awful,' Joan said.

'Never mind,' Peggy tried to comfort. 'Perhaps she'll be better tomorrow.'

'Are we going to tell Baby how bad she is?' Joan asked.

Peggy considered it. 'Not just yet,' she decided. 'You know what she's like. We don't want her going hysterical and upsetting the kids. Time enough when Mum's back home. We'll be more used to it ourselves by then.'

The next evening Baby suddenly decided she ought to visit her mother too, so all three of them went to the hospital. Flossie looked a great deal worse. She slept through most of the visiting hour and groaned in her sleep.

'I can't see the point if she's going to sleep all the time,' Baby grumbled. 'Why didn't you tell me she was like this?'

'Just shut up,' Joan said, frowning at her. 'Can't you see how ill she is? She's ever so bad. Worse than you know.'

Baby decided to ignore that remark. It was altogether too painful. 'Hospitals make me nervy,' she complained.

'You make us sick.'

'I shan't come again if you're horrid.'

It upset Peggy to hear them quarrelling. And as her

394

mother was still deeply asleep she went off to find the Ward Sister and see what she had to say. It wasn't encouraging.

'Yes,' the Sister agreed, 'she is a bit worse today, I'm afraid. But you must remember she sustained very serious injuries and we are doing all we can.'

The next night Joan had to stay at home with the kids because Mrs Rudney was out at work, and Baby said she'd had enough of hospitals for one week and what was the point anyway, so Peggy went alone. Her mother was awake but she seemed feeble and small as if she was shrinking and fading.

'I've been lying here thinking about your father,' she said. 'He was a good man, you know, and I wasn't always as kind to him as I should've been.'

Peggy decided to ignore the confession and concentrate on the praise. 'He was a very good man,' she said. 'A dear.'

'I couldn't help it, you know,' her mother said, reaching for her hand. 'It was my blessed nerves. I've always suffered terribly with my nerves.'

'I brought you some flowers,' Peggy said, taking her hand and giving it a little squeeze. 'I put them in the vase, see? Ain't they pretty?'

But Flossie didn't look at the flowers. 'If anything was to happen to me,' she said, 'you know, you would look after Baby wouldn't you?'

'Nothing's going to happen to you, Mum,' Peggy said, swallowing her tears. 'You're going to be all right.'

'She's always been delicate,' Flossie went on. 'Even as a little thing. I used to have to boil the milk for her. She couldn't take it cold, you know. Upset her poor little stomach. Nerves, you see. She's nervy. Like me. Always took after me, much more than the other two.' Her voice was getting softer and slower, drifting away. 'You will look after her, won't you?'

'Yes, all right, I promise,' Peggy said.

'Good,' her mother said. 'I shall go to sleep now. You can go home if you like.'

But Peggy sat out the hour and afterwards she was glad she had. For when she presented herself at the ward at eight o'clock the next evening the bed was empty.

CHAPTER 31

There were things that had to be done. She knew it, but she couldn't think what they were or where she was supposed to do them. She was overwhelmed by fatigue, as if she were walking about at the bottom of the sea, dragging an enormous anchor behind her, wading with ponderous slowness through an obscurity of heavy waters, where faces ebbed away in mid sentence and voices went echoing in long distorted reverberations like tangled weed.

The doctor was talking to her, occasional words wriggling into her ears like minnows, in – slick slick – and out again without leaving a trace of their meaning behind. 'Septicaemia,' he said, 'very serious injuries' 'so very sorry', and she could hear her own voice agreeing with him, 'Yes – Yes,' as she wondered why the light was so green.

Afterwards she supposed she must have done all the things that had to be done, for her mother's body was returned to the house and an undertaker arrived who seemed to know what he was doing, and there was a pile of letters ready for the post and addressed in her hand-writing. But she passed the days in a stupor, numb with exhaustion and grief, accepting Baby's howling incomprehension and Joan's frozen-faced sorrow with equal calm. Even the air raids were distanced. She could hear them going on overhead as she lay wakeful in her bed in the kitchen, but they meant very little to her, and nor, even more oddly, did the knowledge that she ought to have been on duty at the wardens' post. Mr Goodall had told her not to come in until the end of the week and she'd obeyed without question or thought, as though it didn't matter.

It wasn't until the day before the funeral that her senses returned to her in a flood of grief so severe that she had to put her face in her hands to prevent herself from crying aloud. She was standing in Leslie and Ernest's florist shop waiting to see the wreaths, breathing in the woody scent of the chrysanthemums and thinking how pretty flowers were when they were massed in vases one above the other, and it suddenly struck her that her mother would never see flowers like that ever again. The tears were rolling from her eyes before she could control them.

'Oh!' she wept, as Leslie leapt towards her. 'Oh dear. I'm so sorry.'

'Now don't you worry, my dear,' the old man said, leading her gently to a chair. 'The most natural thing in the world.'

'I promised Dad I'd look after her,' she sobbed. 'I gave him my solemn word. And now she's dead. I couldn't stop her going to the pictures, you see. If I'd known I'd have stopped her. I would. I would. If I'd known. And all them others. That poor man with half his face gone and the woman with her chest smashed in and the boy with no legs. So many, all covered up. Full of life one minute, blown to bits the next. Oh it's awful. Why can't we stop it? We ought to stop it.' Grief was making her incoherent, the words tumbling into one another. 'So many good people dead. I can't bear it.'

Ernest's round face loomed into focus, more wrinkled than ever in his anxiety, that long white hair of his falling towards her. 'You must come home with us at once,' he said. 'She must, mustn't she, Leslie? You need looking after my dear, that's what it is. You've carried too many burdens for far too long. We'll shut the shop. I'll put the notice up.'

They dried her tears and waited until the first rush of her grief was over and then they led her home, one on either side, holding her tenderly by the elbows as though she might fall if they weren't there to prevent it. Which in her present state might well have been the case.

Once they were in Paradise Row they took her into their house, wrapped her in a blanket like a swaddled baby and sat her in a chair with a glass of brandy to sip while they busied themselves, lighting the stove, arranging flowers, setting the table. It was soothing in the kitchen, everything was so neat and so richly coloured. They'd got green flock wallpaper on the walls so it was really more like a dining room than the all-purpose workshop she lived in next door. The table was oak and there were four upholstered chairs to match and a really rather splendid oak dresser crammed with brightly coloured china, and flowers everywhere she looked, printed on the curtains, embroidered on cushions piled on an oak settle, linked petal to petal in a border strip underneath the picture rail, and standing alive and sweet-smelling in vases and jardinières all over the room.

'Now you come and sit up to the table,' Ernest said. 'You can keep that blanket round your legs. It won't hurt. Would you care for some more brandy?'

'Oh no thank you,' she said, covering the top of the glass in case it was given despite her. 'You'll make me tipsy.'

'And a jolly good job too,' Leslie said. 'Does you good to be tipsy now and then. We always take a little nip when we're feeling low, don't we, Ernest? Best thing in the world, brandy. You drink it up.'

Ernest was removing a stewpot from the stove and dividing the contents between three soup plates. It smelled and looked delicious.

'Not for me,' Peggy said quickly. 'Thanks all the same, but that's your rations. I can't eat your rations.'

Ernest clicked his teeth. 'There's plenty,' he said. 'We've eked it out nicely. We've all got a nice big chunk of bread to go with it. You just eat it up, my dear, and stop fretting.'

She looked from one kind eager face to the other, beaming at her, willing her to accept. 'Well if you're sure,' she said. And was whisked into her place at the table immediately.

It was an excellent meal and she felt better by the mouthful. And there was a second course too, a steamed pudding with raspberry jam, which Leslie said was his speciality. 'You must eat every last scrap or I shall take

398

offence,' he said, dividing it neatly into three.

So she ate every last scrap.

'We ought to have some more brandy, don't you think?' Leslie suggested when their plates were clean. 'Finish with a flourish.'

But the flourish at the end of this meal was even better than brandy. There was a knock at the door and when Ernest went to open it he came back into the room with Jim Boxall.

At the sight of him, Peggy wept again, but now there was a familiar chest to cry against and longed-for arms to hold her and comfort her. 'Oh Jim,' she said, 'I *am* so glad to see you. How did you get here?'

'Thirty-six hours compassionate.'

They sat on the settle together while he cuddled her with one arm and dried her tears with his handkerchief, and the two old men hovered about them, murmuring and approving, and telling Jim about the landmine and her bravery in little snatches and snippets of conversation. 'Terrible tragedy – twelve killed, you know – no lights at the hospital – nor windows either – no lights no windows, imagine – they had to operate by candlelight – this dear girl's been so brave – too brave – looking after everybody the way she does.'

'That's my Peggy,' he told them. 'She'd carry the world on her shoulders every minute of the day an' night if I didn't peel it off now an' then.'

'You ought to get married,' Ernest said. 'I can't think why you don't.'

'I got to look after Mum,' Peggy tried to explain. 'I mean, I had to look after her,' feeling bleak because she was speaking in the past. 'And there's the ARP.'

'Never mind the ARP,' Jim said practically, warning the two old men with a quick glance over the top of Peggy's head that this wasn't the time to be talking of weddings. 'You got everything arranged for the funeral? Do you know who's coming?'

'I got a list somewhere,' she said, trying to remember where she'd put it.

'Leave it to me,' he said. 'You just come home and show me where it is.'

'What a blessing you're back,' Ernest said. 'I don't know how she'd have managed all on her own. I really don't.'

By now Peggy's sobs had subsided. Jim wiped her face with his handkerchief as the two old men looked on tenderly. 'OK to go next door?' he asked, and when she nodded, 'That's my girl.'

She kissed her two rescuers goodbye. 'Thanks for everything,' she said. 'It was ever so good of you.'

'Yes,' Jim said. 'Thanks for looking after her.' He'd never thought much of these two peculiar men if the truth were told but now he was reassessing his opinion.

'What are friends for?' Leslie said, flushing with pleasure.

'If there's anything else you need,' Ernest added, 'you just give us a call.'

But there was nothing else Peggy needed now that Jim was home. His arrival made everything possible again. She remembered all the things she had to do the moment she stepped inside her own front door. She told him about the wreaths she'd ordered, she knew the time of the ceremony, she felt that she could sustain it all now, the nightmare had begun to recede.

And the next morning when people began to arrive she was steady and composed, standing beside Jim to welcome her subdued guests, Uncle Gideon and Ethel looking ill at ease in black, Aunt Maud and Josh looking old and bent and as grey as dust, Mrs Roderick weeping, the Allnutts pale and patient, John Cooper blowing his nose, Mr MacFarlane protective, Joan stern and her children baffled, Baby sniffing behind a spotted veil.

The service was mercifully brief. Too many bomb victims were being buried that day and there was no time for a long oration at the graveside, which was just as well because it was bleak and cold out there among the headstones. And when it was over and the mourning party had nibbled Peggy's sandwiches and drunk tea from her assorted cups, Jim began to suggest them towards the door. Maud and Josh had a train to catch, Mrs Roderick was escorted home by the Allnutts and Mr Cooper, Gideon and Ethel seemed only too glad to be gone. Soon only Mrs

Geary, Mr MacFarlane, Jim, the two children and the three sisters were left in the kitchen.

'I'll away now,' Mr MacFarlane said, taking his tin hat from the hook in the hall. 'God bless you, my dear.'

'Tell Mr Goodall I'll be down to see him tonight,' Peggy said.

'No, no,' Mr MacFarlane said. 'There's no rush.' And he kissed her before he left. 'You just bide here a wee while longer.'

'I'll give you a hand with those plates and cups,' Joan offered when he'd gone. 'Then we'll make tracks.' She was busy and practical and seemed quite herself again, getting on with her life as she got on with the housework, putting death and funerals behind her.

Peggy didn't have the energy to get out of her chair. That awful numbing fatigue was engulfing her again. Seeing Joan recover so quickly had made it worse. She watched as the kitchen was set to rights and Yvonne and Norman were bundled into their coats and Balaclava helmets.

'That's it then,' Joan said, 'we'll be off. Come on, kids.'

'We'll walk you to the station,' Jim said, looking at Peggy. 'Breath a' fresh air'ud do us good.'

Despite her lack of energy, or perhaps because of it, Peggy obeyed him like a child. They all walked down to the station, huddled against the cold and not talking. The hoardings were covered with posters giving advice and instructions, 'Be wise – keep mum', 'Make do and mend', 'Careless talk costs lives', 'Dig for victory', 'We want your kitchen waste', 'Beat fire bomb Fritz'.

'Funny that,' Peggy said.

'What?' Joan asked.

'The hoardings. I must have seen them every day for years but I've never noticed them before.' She was in a most peculiar state, noticing things that weren't important and paying no attention to the things that mattered. It was almost as if she'd become somebody else.

'Forever telling us what to do,' Joan said, dismissing the hoardings with a glance. 'Gets on my wick. As if we ain't got enough to contend with. Tatta, Jim. Tatta, Peg. See you Sunday. Give your Aunty Peggy a kiss, kids.'

Jim and Peggy stood on the platform and watched their train rattle away, its criss-crossed windows patterning its progress like some overgrown caterpillar, its roof dark grey with dust.

Peggy sighed. 'Everything's so shabby,' she said. She was noticing that too.

'Time for a quick one,' Jim decided. 'You don't have to go back yet awhile.' And he walked her across to the Station Arms and ordered a couple of pints.

It was warm and crowded in the pub and the smell of spilled beer, sweat and tobacco smoke was reassuring even if it didn't comfort her.

'Your neighbours were right, you know,' Jim said, wiping the froth from his mouth on the back of his hand.

'Which ones?' Peggy asked without much interest. 'About what?'

'The two old fellers where we used to live. About us getting married.'

'Oh them.' She couldn't drum up any interest in them or the subject. He was talking about marriage and yet here she was sitting in a heap too tired to be interested. Oh dear.

'Them,' he said, watching her.

She drank her beer wearily, saying nothing. There was no vitality in her at all and the sight of her forlorn face roused him to a determined protectiveness. 'I'll tell you what we're going to do,' he said. 'First we'll finish our beer, and then we'll go down the registry office and we'll call the banns and get married.'

'What? Now?' What was he saying? How could they get married?

'No,' he said, unperturbed. 'Not today. In four weeks' time. I've got ten days' leave at the end a' the month, remember? One to get married on, eight days honeymoon, day to get back. Piece a' cake! I shall probably be a corporal come the summer. We could live on a corporal's pay as easy as pie. So that's what we'll do. You've been looking after people quite long enough. Now I'm going to look after you.'

Surprise and pleasure tempted her out of her lethargy at last. 'Well it would be lovely,' she said, smiling at him, such a slow gentle smile that it made him ache to put his arms round her and start protecting her there and then. To be looked after, she thought, to leave the blitz behind and drop all her responsibilities and just go off somewhere quiet and peaceful all on her own with him. Oh, it *would* be lovely. 'I don't know though.'

'What don't you know?'

'It's just ...' she said, her brow puckered with the effort to find the right way to tell him all this. 'Oh I don't know ... If it wasn't for the war and us not having any money, I'd've married you long ago. But you know that anyway. It's just ... Well I can't walk away from it all now. Not with the raids still going on and everything. It wouldn't be right, would it?'

The publican was roaring with laughter behind the bar, and the sound annoyed Jim, making him brusque.

'Yes,' he said firmly. 'It would be right. Absolutely right. You need looking after. I need to look after you. So that's what we'll do.' It was a statement, a decision, there was no doubt left in him at all.

She began to worry. 'But where would we live?' she said. 'How would we manage? There's invitations to send. Weddings take ever such a lot a' work. Oh dear! It's too soon after ...'

'We'll marry first,' he said, wearing his most stubborn expression, 'and sort all that out afterwards.'

'But what about Baby? How will she manage the rent if she's all on her own? I promised Mum ...'

'Baby earns a darn sight more than you do,' he said. 'You don't have to worry about Baby. Do her good to look after herself. She's a lot tougher than you think.'

'Oh dear,' she worried again. 'I don't see how we can.'

'I do,' he said. 'Just leave it to me.'

She was too tired, too stunned and, beneath her fatigue, too pleased to argue any further. If that was what was going to happen, she thought, it would happen. Perhaps it was meant to.

So they went to the registry office, and she watched while he applied for a licence, filled in forms and booked their wedding. In half an hour the whole thing was signed and settled.

'Now,' he said, 'we'll go shopping and get the ring, and then I shall have to be getting back. You got three weeks to buy yourself a dress and that's all you've got to worry about. An' a hat from old Madame Aimee's perhaps. Joan'll see to everything else.'

The next three weeks spun past in a confusion of activity. As he'd predicted, Joan and Mrs Geary threw themselves into wedding preparations, delighted to have a reason for celebration, organizing a sing-song, ordering booze, even baking a sponge cake with two precious eggs and tremendous enthusiasm. Mr Allnutt set up trestle tables which actually remained upright if a trifle precarious, Mrs Roderick recovered from her grief and re-trimmed her best hat, Uncle Gideon arrived with a canteen of cutlery as a wedding present, and Tom slunk away to the empty bedroom upstairs where he curled himself up on top of the chest of drawers, scowling with displeasure.

And then it was their wedding day and they were standing side by side in a registry office so full of people that there wasn't room to turn around, repeating their promises after the registrar while their guests sneezed and coughed and blew their noses and burst into a bedlam of congratulation the minute the little ceremony was over.

'Just what we all needed,' Mrs Geary said, handing round refreshments at the ding-dong afterwards. 'We've all had a darn sight too much grief just lately, what with one thing an' another. Ain't that right, Gideon?'

'Flossie would've approved a' this,' he agreed, taking the proffered sandwich. 'I can tell you that. They're a lovely couple. Me an' Ethel was just saying so.'

'Best thing all round,' Ethel agreed. 'She'd only ha' moped, poor girl, if she'd stayed at home by herself. This'll take her mind off it.'

It had actually taken her mind off everything, and so effectively that it wasn't until she was at Victoria station later that afternoon and struggling through the usual crowds of kit-bagged servicemen, that Peggy realized that she was married.

'Mrs Peggy Boxall,' she said, turning the ring on her finger.

'Suits you.'

'Where are we going, Jim?'

'It's a secret,' he said beaming at her.

She didn't try to guess where it was. Let it be a surprise. Honeymoons were supposed to be secret, weren't they?

The train was packed, as trains always were. They had to stand in the corridor side by side and hemmed in with kitbags as they rattled past bomb sites and wrecked buildings and long patient queues of muffled women shuffling in the rain. Then they were chuffing through muddy fields, past stained cattle and grubby sheep grazing stolidly in the darkening air, but it wasn't until they burst from a tunnel to find themselves facing a hillside smothered in houses that she began to suspect where they were. A large seaside town somewhere on the south coast.

'Is it Brighton?' she asked.

'Course,' he said. Where else would they go?

It was a Brighton much changed from the light-hearted resort they'd enjoyed when they were both nineteen. This was Brighton at war, full of servicemen and women, bristling with defences, with a vast rough iron-grey sea to protect it. There were concrete anti-tank blocks and rolls of barbed wire all along the beach, the kiosks were shut and shuttered, and the façades of all those once-smart hotels were chipped and weather stained and badly in need of paint. But in an odd sort of way it seemed proper that it should be so run down. It was part of the war, the outward sign of struggle and endurance.

'Dear old Brighton,' Peggy said, and to Jim's relief, despite the sleet and the grey skies, her face looked warmer.

They spent most of their precious eight days alone together in a small room just off the Lanes. Once she had been given Jim's ration coupons, the landlady took them under her protection, mothering them with fires and the best meals she could produce given 'this dratted rationing', but otherwise leaving them discreetly alone, assuming that they were in the customary state of most of her honeymooners. But in fact they made love rarely, because Peggy was still numb with mourning and Jim was too aware of her feelings to urge her, and even then the first time, tender and gentle though it was, reduced her to weeping.

'Oh dear,' she cried, sobbing against his chest. 'What a way to go on. Oh dear oh dear. On our honeymoon an' all. I *am* sorry.'

'Cry all you like,' he soothed. 'It ain't a honeymoon. We had that years ago. Remember? All I done now is make an honest woman of you.'

The little joke made her smile, a weak smile and tear-washed, but a smile nevertheless. 'I never thought we'd get married like this,' she said.

'No more did I,' he admitted. 'That's the war for you. Not sorry, are you?'

'Oh no, no,' she said, kissing him at once to prove it. 'I'd never be sorry. Never ever.'

'That's all right then,' he said, reaching for their cigarettes. 'One last fag an' then we'll get some sleep, eh?'

They lay together snug under the covers, and smoked and talked. Despite death and grief and wartime miseries, this leave was still something to enjoy, a time set apart with no duties and no queueing and their meals cooked for them, a rare chance to sleep late every morning and go out dancing or to the pictures every night, but the real luxury was having time to talk. There were so many things to talk about, the war, of course, and the RAF and the blitz, Flossie and the awful days after her death, his mother and how impossible it was to look after her, and finally and most rewardingly, the sort of life they would live together after the war.

They were still talking on their last afternoon, when they walked uphill to the station through the darkening streets. There was a raid on, and somewhere over the Channel they could hear the engines of a Dornier and its pursuing Hurricane heading out to sea, but they were still absorbed in planning their future.

'No kids yet,' he agreed. 'You're right. We'd both be worried out of our wits having babies in all this.'

'When the war's over,' she said, snuggling against his arm. 'Oh Jim, I wish we wasn't going back. We've hardly had any time at all.' It felt so warm and right and normal here beside him. 'I wish you didn't have to go back to camp. I wish we could stay together all the time, an' live together properly, like people used to do before the war.' These days and nights spent entirely in his company had made her acutely aware of what they were missing.

'I'll find us a place to live somewhere near the camp,' he promised, 'an' then we can. It'll be the first thing I do when I get back.'

'Promise?'

'See it wet, see it dry,' he said, licking a finger the way he'd done when they were kids, holding it up for her to see, wiping it dry on his tunic. But even as he spoke he knew it would be virtually impossible.

'Soppy thing,' she said lovingly as they walked into the station.

This time they got seats, and this time as the darkness was inky black against their criss-crossed windows, they looked at one another in the dim blue light all the way to Victoria, and they talked. And over and over again they promised one another that they would find a place to live 'near the camp', that they would soon be together 'all the time', that they were married now and they would 'always be together', as if promising could make it so. And the iron miles clicked away beneath their feet, nearer and nearer to the city that would pull them apart.

CHAPTER 32

Joan and the kids had spent the afternoon in Paradise Row sitting round the fire with Baby and Mrs Geary, waiting for Peggy and Jim to come home. The kids had been playing draughts, Joan had been darning socks as well as she could with the cat on her lap, Baby had been painting her nails and Mrs Geary had been knitting a jersey with a complicated cable pattern which involved considerable lip-chewing and counting aloud. They were all annoyed when the sirens went.

'I thought we'd finished with daylight raids,' Joan complained as she put up the shutters. 'Go and sit under the stairs, you two.'

There were three camp stools in the cupboard under the stairs, so Norman and Yvonne did as they were told, taking the draught board with them.

'It won't be long,' Mrs Geary said. 'One thing about a daylight raid, it's soon over. Knit one, slip one, pass the slipped stitch – over.'

It wasn't a long raid, nor a particularly noisy one. There was a lot of ack-ack but they could only hear one or two planes and although there were several explosions they were all far enough away not to be alarming. And after half an hour and several dropped stitches, the all clear went.

'I don't think we'll stay to see Peggy back after all,' Joan said, gathering the children's coats and scarves. 'Not now the raids have started. We'll cut off home while the

408

going's good. Give 'em my love. Tell 'em I'll see 'em tomorrow dinner time.'

Once they were gone, Baby fussed and fidgeted and complained.

'Peggy ought to be back by now, surely to goodness,' she said to Mrs Geary. 'Where d'you think they are? I don't know why they had to go off on a honeymoon with a war on. I know I wouldn't.'

'Nobody asked yer,' Mrs Geary observed, 'unless I've missed something.'

Baby decided to ignore that. 'If it wasn't for this stupid black-out,' she said, 'I could look out the window an' see them coming.'

'Watched pot never boils,' Mrs Geary said, concentrating on her knitting.

'That's a stupid thing to say,' Baby said crossly. 'It has to sooner or later. Stands to reason.'

'Why don't you put one on an' see,' Mrs Geary suggested.

'One on what?'

'One kettle,' the old lady explained patiently, 'on the gas. See if it'll boil. If it does we can have a cup a' tea. I don't know about you but I could just go a nice cup a' tea.'

So the kettle was grudgingly filled, but just as Baby was grumbling round the kitchen complaining that she couldn't find the tapers, Jim and Peggy came tumbling into the hall, dropped their cases by the hatstand and romped into the back room on a wash of unfamiliar scents and smells, soot from their travel, sea salt on their clothes, garlic from their landlady's cooking. They looked well-fed and cheerful and very much a couple. Baby was instantly jealous of them.

'An' about time too,' she said.

'She means, "welcome home",' Mrs Geary grinned, setting her knitting aside to kiss them. 'No need to ask how you got on. Where d'you go?'

They settled by the fire and told her about Brighton, while Baby stood with a taper in her hand looking sour.

'Sounds a treat,' Mrs Geary said when they'd finished. 'Now what?'

'Jim's going to find us a nice little flat near the camp,'

409

Peggy said. 'Soon as he gets back there. Ain't that right, Jim?' Their fantasy was still warm in her mind, sustaining her.

'Soon as I can,' Jim said, backing her up. It might be possible. You never knew. Damn it, he'd make it possible.

Baby's jealousy spilled over into ill-humour. How was she supposed to manage if Peggy was going to live near the camp? Who'd do the shopping? Since Mum died she'd felt more and more vulnerable. There was no one to protect her now and with Jim married into the family things could be jolly difficult. It was all very nice flirting with him when he'd only been the boy next door but he'd gone and changed everything now. 'This sink's been stopped up for four days I'd have you know,' she said.

'So why didn't you fix it?' Jim asked.

'It ain't up to me to fix it,' Baby pouted. 'I ain't a plumber.'

'And Peggy is, I suppose,' he said. 'You really are the laziest little toe-rag alive.'

'Oh lovely!' Baby bristled. 'That's right. Call me names. I should. Just because you married our Peggy that don't give you the right to . . .'

There was someone scrabbling at the door, pulling the key through the letter box. The little unexpected sound alerted them all, stopping the row, making Mrs Geary set her knitting aside.

Peggy was on her feet at once and half-way across the room. 'Hush!' she ordered. 'Something's up.' As she reached the hall they could hear Joan's voice and the kids crying.

'Joan,' Peggy said. 'Whatever is it?'

'We been bombed,' Joan said as she stepped into the hall. She was ashen faced with shock and her eyes were red-rimmed. 'Got back to find the shop in half, our flat an' all. We're bombed out. We come straight back here. Oh Peg!'

Death flexed cold fingers in their warm house for the second time that month. The honeymoon was over, the quarrel seen for the petty thing it was, war had returned and with it the awful searing memory of their mother's death, the evenings in the hospital, that numbing funeral.

Norman was sobbing so much he was almost choking. 'They bombed my gingerbread man,' he wept. 'My gingerbread man.'

'Well at least it wasn't you,' Peggy said, stooping to put an arm round his quaking shoulders.

'Me an' Dad,' the little boy sobbed, 'me an' Dad made the gingerbread man.' It was all he had left to remember his father by and now it was gone. 'Me an' Dad.'

'When he comes home I'll bet you he'll make another one the first thing he does,' Peggy comforted.

'We could a' been killed,' Joan wept, hanging on to Yvonne's hand as Peggy led them all into the back room, 'all the lot of us. If we'd been there we'd a' been blown to bits.' Jim was already setting chairs for them beside the fire, and to her credit Baby had lit the gas at last. 'We could a' been killed.'

'Well thank God you wasn't,' Peggy said, chafing her sister's cold hands, gentling Yvonne and Norman into the chairs, setting their feet on the fender to warm them. 'Just as well you was here.'

Baby was standing in the kitchen door with the teapot in her hands. She was avid for details. 'How awful!' she said. 'Was it all blown up? Everything?'

Peggy made a warning grimace at her in case it wasn't the right time to ask questions, but Joan spilled into talk at once. 'Everything,' she said, sitting by the fire. 'Bomb must a' cut it in half. There's half the kitchen just hanging there up in the air, all my pots and pans, china on the dresser all broken to bits. You never saw such a mess. An' the kids' clothes all over the shop, torn to shreds. We brought what there was. It's out the front in the pram. The WVS said we was to go to the refuge but I said, "No jolly fear. We'll go to me sister's." I couldn't be doing with the refuge. You get all sorts up there. Oh God, Peggy, what are we going to do?'

'Stay here with us if Mrs Geary doesn't mind,' Peggy said at once. 'I'll look after you.'

'Why not?' Mrs Geary. 'The more the merrier, that's what I say.'

'There you are then,' Peggy said to the kids. 'You'll be all right here. We don't get bombed in Paradise Row.'

'Really?' Norman asked, looking up at her. In the warmth of the fire and her good sense he'd stopped crying and was beginning to recover. But there were still doubts. 'Gran did though, didn't she?'

'Poor Gran,' she said. 'Yes, she did. Not here though. Not in Paradise Row. I don't reckon old Hitler knows where we are down here.' Oh poor dear Mum! It was an awful way to go.

'Where d'you leave your stuff?' Jim said to Joan. He'd sensed the return of Peggy's grief and needed to turn their attention to practical things.

'Out the front,' Joan said. 'I told you. There ain't much. Just a few bits and bobs really.'

Her old pram was standing outside the door, packed with oddments of linen and clothing, Norman's teddy bear, bent saucepans, cushions, a bundle of family photographs, and tied across the top of it all, a chest of drawers, miraculously undamaged. It was so heavy it needed their combined efforts to wheel it into the hall where it stood incongruously against the yellow anaglypta.

'Was there anything else?' Jim asked.

'No,' Joan said sadly. 'Only this.'

'I'd go back tomorrow if I was you,' he advised, 'in case you've missed things. You have to lay claim to your own stuff pretty quick before someone else gets their hands on it.'

'They wouldn't, would they?' Peggy asked.

'Not much, they wouldn't,' he said. 'There's plenty a' tea leaves around. The war ain't converted 'em, it's just given 'em more scope.' That's right, he thought, talk about thieves and looters. That's better than dwelling on grief.

'Did you get your ration books?' Peggy asked as they walked back to the fire. There were such a lot of things to be attended to when you were bombed out.

'In me bag,' Joan said. 'I always keep 'em with me, just in case.'

'She's got her head screwed on, our Joanie,' Mrs Geary approved, patting Joan's hand because she looked as though she was going to cry again. Despite Jim's intervention, memories and grief were still washing all about them, unspoken but all the more potent for that.

'I'm starving,' Norman said in his matter-of-fact way. His eyes were quite dry now and there was a little more colour in his face.

'Time for supper then,' Peggy said, glad of his rescue. 'What say we get some fish an' chips?'

'I couldn't eat anything,' Joan said. 'I'd be sick. It made my stomach shake seeing it all cut to bits like that.'

'I could, Aunty Peggy,' Norman said quickly. 'You could an' all, couldn't you, Yvey?'

And although Yvonne was still quiet and pale, she agreed that she was hungry.

'That's settled then,' Mrs Geary said. 'You could pop in to the off licence fer some beer, couldn't you, Peggy? And a bottle a' Tizer for the kids. My treat. I'd go mesself only these legs are giving me proper gyp tonight.'

It was a ramshackle meal, eaten out of the newspaper in the time-honoured way with pickled onions and lots of salt and vinegar. Joan picked at a few chips and told her bomb story over and over again until she'd made sense of it, and the rest of them ate every last crumb and even licked their fingers afterwards. Then Peggy began to organize them for the night.

'Time you kids was in bed,' she said to the children. 'I'll clear up all this paper and then we'll nip upstairs and get the camp-beds down. Better look sharp or we shall have the sirens going in a minute.' She was a warden again, back home in London, doing the job she'd done all through the war. 'We'll put them under the stairs,' she said to Joan. 'There'll just be room.'

Joan was worrying again. 'We got no night things or nothing,' she mourned.

'There's all Mum's things in the chest a' drawers,' Peggy remembered. 'Sheets and clothes and underwear and everything.' She hadn't had the time or the heart to attend to them. 'You could use some of them for the time being. Save 'em going to waste.'

'What *would* she have thought of all this?' Joan sighed.

'Just as well she can't see it, you ask me,' Mrs Geary said. 'I'll tell you one thing though. She'd be glad to see you make use of her things. She kept 'em lovely. Always so particular she was. You use 'em, gel.'

413

So Flossie's sheets were taken from the cupboard and Joan found one of her nightgowns for Yvonne and an old blouse for Norman to wear as a night shirt, which made them all laugh because he looked so comical trailing about in it.

The sirens went as they were making up the beds, but by then their panic and tears were all forgotten, calmed by routine. There was such a comfort in housework and its familiar sensations, Peggy thought, and particularly in a raid, a sheet smoothing under her hands, the automatic neatness of a well-tucked corner, a whacked coal shooting sparks up the chimney to hang like red stars among the soot, the kettle whistling, tea falling fragrant into the cup, the rattle of their spoons and saucers echoed by the rattle of the trams in Church Street, small, comforting signs that life was going on despite the bombs.

'We'll play cards,' she said as the noise of the raid got worse. 'Take our minds off it.'

Watching her as she put up the card table and dealt the first hand, Jim was torn between pride and irritation. She coped with grief so well now, and her calm was admirable and catching. The kids were actually settling to sleep as though they were sure of safety, the cat was purring, Mrs Geary was unconcernedly drinking tea out of her saucer, even Joan was easing into a better state, and all these things were a direct result of that patient, stubborn courage of hers. But he knew with equal certainty that the self-same doggedness, the self-same sense of responsibility had already moved her away from him and their marriage and all the things they'd been planning together on the way home. And that was painful.

He stayed with them for as long as he could, but the raid was still going on when he had to leave. Peggy walked out into the hall to say goodbye. They stood in the jumble of luggage like a couple of refugees.

'Goodbye, Tabby eyes,' he said, kissing her. 'Write to me.'

'Every day,' she promised, kissing him back.

'You'll be all right?'

'I'll be all right.'

It made him ache to kiss goodbye. Her lips were soft

and warm and her skin still smelt of the sea. 'Oh God!' he said. 'This is awful. I can't leave you.'

'Go now,' she urged, pushing him gently towards the door. 'You don't want to miss your train.'

But that was just what he *did* want. Why did the war have to come crashing in to pull them apart just when they were so happy together? This God-awful sodding war.

He travelled back to Hornchurch in a turmoil of conflicting emotions, love, anger, remembered happiness, pride that he'd rescued her from her misery dampened by annoyance that she was back in London and facing danger again, barely satisfied desire growling beneath a most rewardingly gratified compassion.

It was a difficult journey with wreckage on the line halting his train, the Underground running slowly, and the raid going on noisily above it all. It took him so long that he only just got back to camp in time and by then he was so tired and frustrated that sleep was impossible.

He lay in his uncomfortable bed at one end of the hut, listening to the snores and grunts and farts of his companions, and was miserably lonely. Tomorrow, he promised himself, as he turned from side to side for the twentieth time, tomorrow I shall find a flat. He *had* to, because he couldn't bear for them to live apart. Not now. Not after being together night and day for nearly a fortnight.

He didn't, of course, although he stormed into Hornchurch the minute he was off duty and scanned the notice boards at every newsagent he could find. There was nothing in the *Exchange and Mart* either, but he comforted himself that at least he'd made a start.

'Nothing yet,' he reported to Peggy when he wrote to her that evening. 'Still, it's early days. I shall keep on trying. I miss you so much. All the time day and night. Especially night.'

The next day he took the Underground to Upminster and tried there. And was disappointed again.

'No, sir,' one newsagent told him. 'You won't find nothing here, and what there is you officers have took. We got a housing shortage.'

And another was quite scathing. 'Little flat?' he said. 'Do me a favour! There's a war on!'

But Jim continued his search, growing more and more dogged as his hope diminished. There must be something somewhere. One little room, that's all he wanted. But the longer he searched the more he knew in his bones that it was impossible. He'd known it all along. The camp was full of airmen mooching about in the evenings because they were parted from their wives and they all earned the same money as he did and they'd all rent rooms if there were rooms to rent. It was demoralizing.

He kept his true opinions hidden from Peggy, of course, because there was no point in them both being miserable. 'Nothing yet but you never know, something might turn up tomorrow.'

But after three weeks of it he was morose with loneliness and disappointment.

It was just as well that Froggy Ferguson was on the camp, for Froggy was his usual cheerful self and full of high spirits.

'Seen this?' he said at breakfast one morning.

'What?' Jim asked.

Froggy pushed a rather battered magazine across the table towards him. It was a copy of the *Picture Post*, with a cover showing six plump toddlers sitting one behind the other on a slide, and a headline offering 'A Plan for Britain'.

'No,' Jim said, glancing at it. He'd been too busy to read anything, except the *Exchange and Mart*, and now he was too brassed off. But he made an effort to be interested. 'Good, is it?' The *Picture Post* usually was.

'A1,' Froggy said. 'Just up your street. You ought to read it.'

Jim took the paper, without very much interest, but he didn't look at it again until late that evening after a long day in the hangars, and by then he was so tired he thought he would just flick through it before he went to sleep. But it turned out be such an absorbing issue that he was still reading it at lights out, and he read on eagerly the next morning, picking up where he'd been obliged to leave off, returning to it at odd moments during the day, digesting it piecemeal, one article at a time, eating the printed word like a man long starved of words and ideas. For what words they were. And what ideas. It even took his mind off his miseries.

The entire magazine had been given over to a consideration of the sort of world that could and should be built when the war was over. It was heady stuff. There was an article on work, that argued that there should be jobs for everyone and that the banks should be controlled by the state; there was one called 'Social Security' that urged a minimum wage for all working men and allowances for children and special forms of help from public assistance for people who were off work through no fault of their own because they were sick or unemployed; there were articles on town planning, home design, the use of the land, even leisure, written by none other than J B Priestley; and best of the lot, a marvellous piece called 'Health for All' that was written by Julian Huxley, who made it meticulously clear that if we wanted a healthy nation the first thing we had to do was to ensure that everybody in it was properly fed, and that when that was done the next thing was to establish a National Health Service into which every worker would pay week by week while they were fit and earning, like a sort of insurance, and which would then allow anyone to be given the medical treatment they needed free at the time they needed it.

By supper-time Jim felt as if he had been introduced to another world. A world full of people who thought as he did. It was just what he needed, a vision of utopia, an unequivocal call for a better, fairer society, and beneath it all the understanding that this was what they were all fighting for.

That night he wrote a long letter to Peggy telling her all about it. It made a pleasant change from reporting failure. 'Get a copy,' he instructed, 'and see if you don't agree with it. It's exactly what I've been thinking all my life. Pass it on to old John Cooper when you've finished with it, with my regards. He'll love it. Oh Peggy, it will be such a brave new world when all this is over, a world we can be proud to live in, and we are the ones who will build it. Think of that.'

It took Peggy a great deal longer to read the magazine than it had taken Jim but that was because she had so little spare time. She'd gone back to the wardens' post on the night after Joan was bombed out, and been welcomed with such obvious relief and pleasure that she felt quite proud of herself. They were such a good team and they worked so well together, no matter how difficult things were. And things were very difficult in those wintry days.

Ever since she'd been bombed out Joan had suffered from terrible nightmares. Baby stuffed ear-plugs in her ears and slept through everything, air raids, weeping, people crashing about in the dark, even the sirens, but Peggy and the kids were woken every time. And if the nights were usually disturbed the days were always over-burdened, with running the house, endless queues for shopping and never ending worries about meals and rationing.

Joan tried to help her when she could but little sleep and long hours at the factory left her so exhausted by the end of the day that she was slow and clumsy. And Baby resolutely refused to set her hand to any housework at all. And Jim still hadn't found them anywhere to live.

'I shall be glad when this war is over and we can start to build this brave new world,' she wrote to Jim. 'It sounds wonderful.' But it all seemed a long way away, especially in her present state of exhaustion. 'Perhaps things will be better in the spring. We might have found a flat by then.'

But he knew, as she did not, that the spring and calmer seas would bring a renewed danger of invasion and that Fighter Command was preparing itself for the next onslaught. In that miserable winter of 1941 their brave new world was a consolation but a very distant one. And although he wangled several thirty-six hour passes and cut across London to see her, feeding at her house and sleeping together, oh so happily, in his room at number two, he still couldn't find them a home of their own.

CHAPTER 33

'There's nothing to look forward to,' Sid Owen complained. 'This fucking war'll go on for ever.'

'Can't see no end to it,' Tommy agreed. 'Fucking war.'

'Look as if you're doing something,' their sergeant advised. 'Fritz the mitts is on this morning.'

The platoon was planting potatoes in a bleak German field on a cold March morning and their particular guard was renowned for his short temper.

Sid bent to his task again. His face was pinched with cold and captivity and his hands were caked with mud, the nails chipped and cracked and black-rimmed. He looked down at them ruefully, very different hands to the ones he'd used so cleanly and with such pride in the bakery. And now the bakery was gone too, blitzed and gone. It was all horribly depressing.

'We've been here ten months,' Tommy said. 'Ten fucking months. What are they playing at back home? Why don't they invade France and send the buggers packing?'

Sid looked across the damp fields to the foreign rooftops miles away between the hills. 'If we knew where we was, we could make a run for it,' he said.

'And get shot down?' the sergeant reminded him. 'Not bloody likely. 'Sides, how far d'you think you'd get in that rig? Have a bit a' common.'

'We could strangle Jerry an' nick his uniform,' Sid suggested.

The prisoners all round them began to join in the game.
'Garrotte a guard.'
'Fix old Fritz.'
'We could live off the land.'
'Travel by night, hole up during the day.'
'Get to the Channel. Nick a boat.'

They'd had the same conversation innumerable times since they arrived in the camp and they all knew it was an impossible fantasy. Yet they returned to it again and again, because it fed them with the hope they needed to keep going and because it reminded them that one day they would be free men again.

'And what d'you think you'd live on, you great daft Arabs?' the sergeant asked.

'Our wits, Sarge?' Tommy offered, wiping his forehead with his sleeve.

'Since when you ever had any wits?' the sergeant mocked. 'Gaw dearie me. You try living on your wits ol' son, that'ud be the quickest way to the firing squad. No, no. All we got ter do is stick it out. Hang on. Tide'll turn in the end you'll see.'

But it didn't seem to be turning at the moment. It all seemed to be running Hitler's way, as the Camp Commandant was gloatingly happy to tell them, at length, in broken English, and at every available opportunity.

They heard that London had been bombed flat, that Coventry, Plymouth, Glasgow, Bristol, Birmingham, Southampton had been reduced to rubble, that the German armies were invincible wherever they went, that because the 'poor fool English' had decided to escort their merchant vessels to England in convoy they were being picked off and torpedoed one by one. 'Sitting ducks you understand' and that 'as a consequence' the populace was starving. 'You vill soon be beaten to submission,' he said. 'You vill see.'

'Submission my arse,' Sid would growl when each diatribe was over. But it was demoralizing just the same. Particularly as they had no other source of information.

'Wonder what my ol' girl's doing,' he said to Tommy as they stooped to the potatoes again. 'I've almost forgotten what she looks like, it's been so long.'

'I dunno,' Tommy said. 'Not planting spuds, that's for certain.'

Sid would have been surprised and annoyed if he'd known. She was taking delivery of a Morrison shelter, which was the newest idea in air raid protection and had been designed for people who had no room for an Anderson shelter in their garden. This one was an indoor shelter, a huge reinforced box like a cross between a double bed and a cage, and she'd ordered it to protect the kids. She and Peggy had arranged a day off work to receive it, which was just as well because it was an enormous thing, almost too big to squeeze into the house, even in its dismantled state.

It took the combined sweat and effort of four people, Joan, Peggy and both delivery men, to manoeuvre it into the kitchen and bolt it together, and when the job was finished it filled the room.

'Bli' me!' Mrs Geary said when she saw it. 'Where's the kitchen gone?'

'We'll put a cloth over it and use it as a table,' Peggy said. Their old gate-leg table was pushed against the window, diminished to a shelf.

Baby was appalled. 'For heaven's sake!' she said. 'We ain't got room to swing a cat.'

'Can't say I've ever wanted to,' Peggy teased her, stroking Tom's tabby head.

But the kids were thrilled.

'It's like a little house,' Yvonne said, crawling into it at once. 'Ever so cosy.'

'Better than the cupboard?' Joan grinned at them.

'Heaps!' Norman said, settling onto the mattress. 'Ain't it big! I bet we could all sleep in here. Like sardines.'

And he was right. There was room for all of them to lie down side by side and sleep in security if not exactly in comfort, so when the raids were bad and the bombers were overhead, the entire household, cat and all, squeezed into their protective cage until the danger was past.

Jim was at Catterick and he wasn't pleased to hear what they'd been doing either.

When he knew he was being posted there he'd been rather pleased about it, because although it would mean

421

that he couldn't get home to Peggy on a thirty-six hour pass, a new place might give him the chance of a flat somewhere. He'd spent every spare moment on his first four days scanning the local papers and tramping the streets. But his search was as futile in Catterick as it had been in Hornchuch and for the same reasons.

'A little flat, two rooms, bed-sit, anything would do,' he'd asked, over and over again.

But the answer was always the same. 'Sorry. No. Don't know of any. Your officers take what little there is, you see.'

One newsagent promised to let him know if anything came up, but by now he had very little hope. When her letter arrived describing the shelter he received it as another disappointment. It made him aware that she was steadily adapting to their life apart and that he was beginning to accept that it was very unlikely that they would ever be able to live together properly. But he tried to see the sense of what she was doing and wrote back as approvingly as he could.

'Just as well you've got it with the spring coming, just in case AH has another bash at invasion. At least we're better prepared this time. The new Spitfire Mark V is fitted with two cannon and a superb engine. Once we get that it'll be a match for anything. Chin up! The blitz can't go on for ever. I'll get a place for us sooner or later, you'll see.'

But the bombers were still getting through and although they didn't arrive every night, especially when the weather was bad, there was a dusty weariness about London that winter, an exhausted dogged resignation. They'd been under attack for six months now and as far as *they* could see the blitz *could* go on for ever. Food was short and getting shorter. In March the meat ration was reduced to 1/10d a week and the butter ration was down to a mere 4 ounces.

But at least the Furnivall/Geary household felt safer in its new shelter. And when spring came there was no invasion, although in April the Luftwaffe made two such ferocious attacks on London that they were soon being referred to as 'the Wednesday' and 'the Saturday'. All the front windows in Paradise Row were blown out and part of Mrs Roderick's roof caved in. But there was no invasion. And then it was May and fine weather and rumours began to spread that the invasion barges had been removed from the Channel ports. Strong sunshine striped their dusty roofs with colour, broken glass suddenly gleamed rainbows, the bomb sites were bright with weeds and there were no raids for a week, for ten days, for a fortnight.

'Where's Jerry?' Londoners asked each other. 'Where's 'e got to?'

'Perhaps he's given up,' Mr Allnutt hoped.

'And about bloody time too,' John Cooper said.

But then, just as they were all beginning to relax, Megan came to call with some rather upsetting news.

'My Dad's going back in the army,' she told Peggy. 'Company sergeant-major to train the new recruits. He's got married quarters so Mum's going with him, she says.'

'What'll you do?' Peggy asked, feeling the pang of parting even before she heard her friend's answer.

'Dunno,' Megan said. 'I could get a room somewhere, I dare say. I wouldn't like to leave London. Not now.'

'Cross yer bridges when you come to 'em,' Mrs Geary advised. 'When's he going?'

'End a' July,' Megan said. 'Not long.'

'Oh well,' Mrs Geary said. 'Lots could happen before the end of July.'

And lots did, although finding a room for an airman to rent anywhere near an RAF station was still totally and miserably impossible. On 2 June clothes were rationed, on 10 June Norman was sent home from school with chicken-pox, and two days later Yvonne joined him in their sticky cage with her own uncomfortable crop of spots. As there were no more raids and the weather was extremely hot, Peggy and Joan set up two beds for them in Mrs Geary's old room upstairs, where it was marginally cooler, and where they would have a great deal more space in which to suffer.

And when the illness reached the itchy and irritable stage Mrs Geary hobbled upstairs with the wireless to keep them entertained. From then on the three of them spent most afternoons listening in to *Workers Playtime* and Vera Lynn and *Sandy Macpherson at the Cinema Organ*. And at the end of the month their little box brought them a piece of extraordinary news.

Peggy was on night duty and had just come home from a long shopping expedition. She'd queued at the butchers, the bakers and the grocers and now her back ached and all she wanted was a nice long sit-down.

Mrs Geary was watching out for her in her double mirror.

'Guess what!' she said leaning out of the window and calling down. 'Hitler's gone the other way. It's just been on the wireless.'

'Gone the other way from what?' Peggy said, putting down her basket.

'Why the other way from us,' Mrs Geary said leaning on the window-sill. 'He's invaded Russia.'

'Never!' Mr Allnutt said, stepping out of his front door to join in the conversation. 'What's he gone and done a thing like that for?'

'He's got a lot a' Germans to feed,' Mr Cooper said from his perch outside number four. 'He's after the Ukraine. That's what he's after. All that corn they grow in the Ukraine.'

'I don't reckon he's all there,' Mrs Geary said. 'I wouldn't want ter take on the Russians. Not if it was me.'

But Peggy was seeing the implication of the news. 'Then that's why he's stopped bombing us,' she said. 'He was getting ready to go an' bomb them, poor devils.' Perhaps the blitz really was over, thank God. If he'd turned on the Russians he wouldn't go on bombing London. She felt quite limp with the relief of it. It was marvellous news! It almost made her believe that Jim would find them somewhere to live.

'You heard the wireless, Mrs Roderick?' Mrs Geary called. 'Hitler's gone the other way.'

It was a swift and brutal campaign, a summer *blitzkrieg* first powering through the Baltic states and Poland and then swarming into Russia itself. There were rumours of entire Russian armies being cut off and captured, reports of 'stiff fighting', maps showing the long arrows of the German advance. It was like the conquest of Holland and Belgium and France all over again only on a grander scale.

In England the Government were soon organizing 'Tanks for Russia' schemes and munition workers were being urged to put in Sunday overtime 'for our Russian allies'. And Fighter Command went over to the offensive, with the result that Jim and Froggy were told that their Squadron were being posted to Merston in Sussex at the end of July. They were to take delivery of brand new Spitfires, and fly sorties over the Channel and the French coast.

Jim was relieved to be nearer London and Froggy said he thought it was wizard.

'Merston,' he said to Jim. 'Good show! I've always wanted to go there.'

'Never heard of it,' Jim said. 'What's so special about Merston?'

'You wait,' Froggy grinned, his wide mouth stretching right across his face. 'You just wait.'

And as he'd obviously made up his mind not to say anything more the subject was dropped.

They arrived in Merston on a bright summer day at the end of July and as far as Jim could see there was nothing remarkable about the place at all. It was simply a bare airfield with the usual hangars and huts set in the middle of the usual flat fields where the corn was already ripening in dust dry earth and the sky was a hard dazzling blue and filled the usual ninety per cent of the landscape. There was an ancient pub at the end of one runway which the pilots commandeered and rechristened 'The Old Wicker Chair' because they spent their time sitting on just such chairs out in the pub garden. But apart from that it was just the same as all the other airfields they'd used, a functional space in the countryside bristling with fighters.

'Ready?' Froggy said, appearing in the door of the hut as soon as he came off shift. He was wearing a silk scarf and looked very full of himself.

'What for?' Jim said, rather wearily. He'd been working hard and could have done with a bit of a kip.

'Come on,' Froggy said. He was dancing on his toes in

his eagerness to be off.

So Jim went with him. Out of the camp, into the narrow lane between brambles and nettles, past the farmhouse, past the pub, over a scuffed intersection of lanes and pathways, past a village school where the children were playing some sort of skipping game, 'Charlie Chaplin went to France and taught the ladies how to dance', and on along an overgrown pathway between overhanging trees and bushes grown so thick it was almost impossible to squeeze between them.

'It'ud better be worth it,' Jim complained as a branch whipped back from Froggy's eager passage and hit him across the side of the face.

'There!' Froggy said. 'What d'you think of that?'

They were standing in front of a small flint cottage, which had obviously not been lived in for a very long time. The paintwork had originally been green but now it was so faded it was almost white and in the more exposed places it was beginning to flake away from the wood, the windows were grey with grime, the letter-box red with rust, and the cottage garden was growing a luxuriant crop of hip-high weeds.

Jim grimaced. 'Not a lot,' he admitted.

'You wait ...' Froggy said. He'd got a key in his hand, and was struggling to turn it in the lock. 'Till you see inside.'

'How did you get the key?' Jim asked.

But Froggy didn't enlighten him. 'Come on,' he said.

It was mustily damp inside the cottage and there was white mildew on the backs of the four windsor chairs set neatly round a table in the little living room, and patches of ironmould on the cushions that were piled neatly on a faded put-u-up. There were curtains at the windows, but they were full of dust and hung dispiritedly, and the window sills were decorated by several dead blue-bottles lying on their backs with their legs tangled above them.

'Belongs to my aunt,' Froggy said, adding unnecessarily, 'hasn't lived in for years. Not since the war started. Come upstairs.'

They explored all three rooms of the little house, living room, kitchen and the bedroom upstairs, and shouldered the back door open to stand in the sunshine in a little back garden beside an outdoor lavvy with a long wooden seat.

'What d'you think?' Froggy asked again.

'Ought to be lived in,' Jim said, trying to keep his voice steady although his mind was spinning with hope, vibrating like an aircraft ready for take-off. Was it for rent? Could he afford it? Dare he even ask?

'I think it's wizard,' Froggy said. 'Just the place for a love nest. Course we'd have to clean it up, spot of paint, elbow grease, that sort of thing, but can't you just see it? Right out the way, all on your own, just the two of you. Whizzo!'

Jim's hopes leapt into the air. It was just the place. He could see it all. He and Peggy sitting beside that fireplace, planning all the things they'd do when the war was over and they could build a new world. And their new world could start right here. He could soon get it cleaned up, paint it, put up new wallpaper, lime wash the lavvy. It would be like a new place. A new place for a new life. 'But it's your aunt's,' he said. 'Would she let it?'

'She would if I asked her,' Froggy said with great satisfaction. 'She sent me the key straight away. What d'you think?'

'Ask her,' Jim said. 'You're right. It's a wizard idea.'

'I'll write tonight,' Froggy said, shutting the back door.

And so will I, Jim thought. So will I. I'll tell Peggy I've got some good news but I won't say what it is, not with a thirty-six coming up. He couldn't wait to see her face when he told her. What a bit of luck! His heart was racing just to think of it. 'Thanks for letting me see it, Froggy,' he said. 'You're a brick.'

'So what d'you think?' Megan asked seriously. 'Shall we take this cottage?'

The kitchen at number six was luscious with the scent of roses. There were two full jars of them standing at each end of the dresser, scarlet and rose pink and butter yellow, breathing out sweetness into the late afternoon. They'd been delivered by a breathless Ernest just after the postman had given Peggy a letter from Jim promising their arrival and telling her that he'd be home that afternoon and that he had some smashing news for her. She'd been quite touched to be given such a treat.

'It sounds terrific,' she said, putting flour in her mixing bowl. Jim should be home any minute now, but she'd just got time to make a few jam tarts for tea. 'Home of your own, right near the airfield. I'd jump at it if I was you. What's the rent like?'

'Well that's the best bit,' Megan said, 'she says we can have it for free. Think a' that! Froggy's a pet of hers apparently.'

Her brown eyes were round with the wonder of all this sudden good fortune. 'He wants us to get married straight away. It's making my head spin, Peg.'

Peggy was rubbing the fat into the flour. 'How smashing!' she said. 'Fancy old Froggy proposing. When's the great day?'

'Well . . .' Megan dithered.

'Well what?' Peggy said.

'Nothing really,' Megan said. 'Except . . .'

'Do you love him?' Peggy asked, looking her friend straight in the eyes and being Peggy coming straight to the point. 'You're not *in love*. I know that. But do you love him?'

'That's the trouble,' Megan admitted. 'I ain't sure. Leastways, not all the time. Sometimes I think I do. He's ever so kind, and he makes me laugh, and he's – sort of – well protective really. But then sometimes I wonder if it ain't because he loves me so much that I get – sort of – carried along – if you know what I mean. It'ud be smashing to have a place of me own, I don't deny, specially with Mum and Dad going off any day now. Well you see how it is, dontcher?'

Peggy added water to her pastry, stirring it with her fingers. 'Is it because he's ugly?' she said.

Megan glared to the defence of her lover at once. 'He ain't ugly,' she said. 'He's no oil painting. I'll give you that. But he ain't ugly. He's got a lovely smile.'

'You'll marry him,' Peggy said, grinning at her. 'I don't know why you're worrying about it.'

'You think so?'

'I know so, you soppy thing. I think it's smashing.'

Trust Peggy to know the truth of it, Megan thought.

She's always so sure of everything, dear old Peg. 'You'll be my bridesmaid,' she said, 'or matron-of-honour, or whatever it is?' It was more a statement than a question, they were both so sure of the answer.

'Course. When?'

'Six weeks, he says. He's in ever such a rush.'

This must've been what Jim was going to tell me about, Peggy thought. It's really rather romantic, a whirlwind wedding and a cottage in the country.

'What a bit of luck to find somewhere to live,' she said. 'Me an' Jim have been hunting for ages.' Six whole months and no nearer to finding anywhere now than they'd been at the beginning. But there was no jealousy in her. Some people got homes, some didn't. That was the way things were. There was a war on.

The tarts were cooked, the table set, and the kids home from school fed and out again before Jim finally arrived.

'Guess what!' he said as he threw his kitbag down beside the hat stand. He was bristling with excitement, his eyes shining, dark hair bushy. So handsome.

'I've heard,' Peggy said, kissing him. 'Megan just told me. A cottage in the country. Ain't they the lucky ones?'

They? he thought. And his excitement began to ebb away. They?

'Are you going to be best man?' Peggy went on, leading him into the back room. 'I'll bet you are. I'm to be matron-of-honour. Did Froggy tell you?'

'Are they getting married?' he said, following her. He was leaden-footed with this sudden awful disappointment. Froggy and Megan. Of course. Why hadn't he realized it? How could he have been so stupid? But why hadn't Froggy told him? Oh Christ, Frog, you could've said. I've spent four days living in hopes and all for nothing.

'Well of course they're getting married. Ain't it grand?'

No, no, no, he thought, as they walked into the room. It ain't. It's bloody awful, and the worst of it was that he couldn't tell her.

Megan was looking up at him, her face bright with happiness.

'Congratulations,' he said, making a palpable effort to smile.

'You must come an' stay with us,' Megan said. 'Froggy says he's going to get it all painted up lovely. I'm going down next weekend to see. Froggy says ...'

Her voice bubbled on, but although Jim heard the words they meant nothing to him. I've lost out again, he thought, and he knew he was angry and jealous, burning with the injustice of it all, in exactly the same way as he'd burned when he turned down the scholarship, lost his job, couldn't persuade his mother to leave the old man. It was bloody unfair. Why should Froggy have somewhere to live just because his aunt had money? It shouldn't be simply a matter of money. Everyone should have the right to a decent home. Everyone. There'll have to be some changes when this war's over, he thought. We can't go on living like this.

'We can all get leave together,' Megan was planning, 'an' then you can come and stay with us. We've got a put-u-up. Won't it be fun!'

CHAPTER 34

The first leave that the Fergusons and the Boxalls spent together in Vine Cottage was fraught with unspoken emotion.

Froggy was in exceptionally high spirits. It hadn't taken him long to discover that marriage suited him down to the ground. Life at Vine Cottage was absolutely wizard, good food, lots of sex, cuddles every morning. Whizzo! And to cap everything he and Jim had been promoted to corporals.

'We'll give a special dinner to celebrate,' he said to Megan.

So they did and although he didn't notice it, Megan found it rather difficult. She and Froggy didn't seem to speak the same language when it came to meals. For a start he had dinner at half past seven in the evening, which she found most peculiar, and he was ever so particular about the way it was served. She'd taken pains to arrange the table beautifully to please him, with a vase of September roses in the centre and table napkins beside each plate and knives and forks and spoons set out properly just like the toffs. The trouble was the food was really ordinary, being vegetable hot-pot followed by apple fritters, so she was brittle with anxiety about it.

Froggy had pushed the table up against the window for that first dinner so that they could look out at the garden while they ate.

'I'm going to grow carrots and onions and potatoes,' she

said, entertaining her guests just a little too brightly, 'and tomatoes and celery if I can manage it.'

How she's changed, Peggy thought, admiring her plump cheeks and the sheen of her dark hair and wondering why she was so anxious, especially when she was running the house so well. I never thought I'd live to see a domesticated Megan, all this cooking and so houseproud and talking about gardening. Perhaps it's because she's in love. Because she was in love, fairly glowing with it every time she looked at old Froggy. Which was quite amazing after all the things she'd said. And Froggy had changed too. He was still the same cheerful Froggy she'd known for so long, but he'd put on quite a bit of weight. It was a great improvement. A rounder face made him look – well – less froggy.

Megan ate her apple fritters and continued to worry. Yesterday she'd sneaked a medical book out of the library in Chichester. She'd read it because she was afraid that she and Froggy might be overdoing things. The book wasn't exactly explicit, but as far as she could make out they seemed to be all right, seeing they were newly-weds, but it worried her just the same. Being married was jolly difficult. 'Froggy wants me to plant runner beans,' she said, glancing at her husband who was signalling his real desires to her with one of his 'all-over' looks. 'I expect I shall give him what he wants, shan't I, Froggy? Sooner or later.'

'You usually do,' her husband said happily. 'What do you think of the cottage?' he asked his guests.

'Very nice,' Jim said shortly and then seeing his friend's face fall, 'You've transformed it.'

'Yes,' Froggy agreed, 'we have.' It was scrubbed clean and newly painted and there wasn't a sign of cobweb or mildew or ironmould anywhere. It smelled of soft soap and starch and wax polish, there were clean curtains at the windows and clean covers on the cushions. 'Whizzo, eh?'

Jim looked away. He'd been feeling shamefully jealous all through the meal, and it upset him to be jealous of his old friend and Megan. It was despicable, petty and shabby and despicable. He ought to be able to rise above it. And yet everywhere he looked he was reminded of the plans *he'd* made for this cottage, the hopes *he'd* entertained, the dreams *he'd* dreamed. If only he'd been the one with the rich aunt instead of Froggy.

Poor Jim, Peggy thought, watching him, I wonder why he's so unhappy. That little leaping movement in his jaw always gave him away. What was upsetting him? She'd have to see if she could tease him out of it, whatever it was. Not now, of course, later when they were alone.

She lifted her head to say something to Megan. And heard the first returning Spitfire.

Jim and Froggy were out of the room in an instant, heading for the newly-dug vegetable patch where they could get a clear view of the evening sky.

'Where are they going?' Peggy asked, surprised by their speed.

'To watch the squadron back in,' Megan explained, finishing her last fritter. 'They can't settle to anything 'til the squadron's in. We lost a Spitfire yesterday and it was one of theirs. It was awful. It upsets them ever so much when that happens.'

Of course, Peggy thought. That's what he's miserable about. I should have worked that out for myself. 'They're all in it together, that's what it is,' she said, 'like we are in London.' A community of suffering was something she understood very well.

The sleek planes followed one another onto the runway, their engines still running sweetly, smooth and strong and dependable. 'Nothing nicer than the sound of a Spitfire,' Peggy said.

And they'd all come home this time, as the two women could see from the relief on their husbands' faces.

'More coffee?' Megan offered, hoping it hadn't gone cold while they were out of the house.

'I'd rather go for a walk,' Jim said. 'I could do with a bit of fresh air.' And he signalled to Peggy with a quick imploring glance.

'Good idea,' Peggy said, understanding him. 'I could do with a walk too.' They hadn't had a minute to themselves since she arrived.

So they left the newly weds in the cottage and strolled along Froggy's neatly-cleared pathway together in the

433

greening dusk, arm in arm.

'I'm glad they all got back,' she said. 'The Spitfires I mean.'

'Yes. It's a bad show when they ...'

'I know,' she said, squeezing his arm. 'At least they all got back tonight.'

They walked on in silence and he was still obviously unhappy. Perhaps it wasn't the Spitfires.

'I wish we could get cracking and end this lousy war,' he said presently.

'We will.'

'Can't see any signs of it yet,' he said and he gave such a profound sigh that she looked up at him questioningly. 'There's no rooms, Peg,' he confessed. 'No flats. No bed-sits. Nothing. I've been all over the shop looking.'

So that's what it is, she thought, and she tried to comfort him. 'Never mind.'

The attempt failed. 'I do mind,' he said miserably. 'It drives me up the wall. I'd do anything to get us a place of our own and we've got about as much chance as a cat in hell.'

She stood still and, putting her arms about his neck, kissed him with an almost autumnal tenderness. 'Dear, dear Jim,' she said.

He drew back from her, gazing down at her, his blue eyes suddenly angry. 'Don't,' he said.

She was surprised by his sudden change of mood. 'Don't what?' she said. 'Don't you want me to kiss you?'

'Not like that,' he said angrily. 'I'm not a bloody invalid. Like this.' And he made a grab at her and kissed her with such a combination of fury and frustrated passion that she could hardly breathe. Desire was triggered in both of them and at once, hot and strong and uncontrollable. When he finally lifted his mouth from hers they were panting and quite incapable of speech or reason. There were only kisses and more kisses, flesh hot for caresses, and their aching, tormenting imperative need for love. They stumbled back-wards through the bushes, fell against trees to kiss and caress, tumbled into rustling piles of beech leaves, driven on and on. Peggy had just enough of her wits left to wonder if they could be seen, and that thought provoked

434

shame and a crawling anxiety strong enough to inhibit her
desire and deny her the final pleasure she wanted so
much. But Jim was lost, his face strained and unfamiliar
in the throes of sensations too strong to be inhibited by
anything. It was only when their passion was spent and
they lay side by side in the leaves catching their breath
that he realized how public they were being, how shamefully he'd been behaving. It was the sort of thing the camp
loud-mouths were always bragging about, the way they
went on with their good-time girls. And now he'd dragged
his lovely Peggy down to their level.

'This God-awful bloody war,' he said. 'Oh Peggy, I'm
sorry. I shouldn't have.'

She was lighting two cigarettes for them, sitting on the
beech leaves, concentrating on the flame, her face calm,
looking entirely composed and herself. 'Have a fag,' she
said, holding his out to him. 'It's all right. Really.' Her
back was aching with unsatisfied desire but she had to
comfort him, he looked so woebegone.

'I should've waited,' he mourned. 'Only a few hours and
we could have been in bed. Oh Christ, I couldn't even wait
a few hours. I shouldn't have treated you like that.'

'It's all right,' she said again, drawing the smoke into
her mouth, glad of its bitterness on her tongue.

They smoked together sitting on the ground. And were
comforted a little as the dusk descended upon them in
gentle tides of lilac shadow.

'What's up?' she said. 'It's not just the war, is it? Or not
getting a flat.'

'No.'

'Then what is it?'

'I thought we was going to live in Vine Cottage,' he said.
'You an' me. Not Froggy and Megan.' And having begun,
he told her the whole story.

It was painful to expose this petty, shameful side of his
nature, to talk of jealousy and his childish need for fair-
ness in a world which was plainly and fundamentally
unfair, but she listened to him calmly and showed no sign
of being upset or appalled, so he stumbled on, confessing
everything.

'So there you are,' he said ruefully when he'd finished.

'Now you know the sort of bloke you've married. Not very pretty, is it?'

'I love you so much,' she said. 'More than I ever have. I think you're the best man that ever lived, to tell me all that.' Her eyes were brown in the half light and meltingly tender. 'To be so honest.'

He lay beside her among the beech leaves and put his head in her lap. 'I don't deserve you,' he said. He was still shamed by his confession. 'I'm not much cop.'

'Oh yes you are,' she said, stroking his hair. 'You're brave and patient and loving. You're a very good man. We've all got faults.'

'You haven't,' he said.

'Yes I have. Look at the way I went on when Mum died. I was useless. If you hadn't been there I don't know how I'd've made out. And I can be pretty horrid to Baby when I like. Oh yes, I've got lots of faults.'

'Confession's good for the soul, they say,' he said smiling up at her. There was a peculiar nakedness about this conversation. Lying there in her warm lap with the beech leaves harsh under his hands he felt he could tell her anything, absolutely anything at all.

'We know one another so well,' she said, taking the last pull on her cigarette.

A sharp breeze had sprung up while they were talking, chill enough to make them both shiver. He was aware of it even in his thick tunic and she only had a woolly cardigan.

'We ought to get back,' he said nipping out his fag-end between finger and thumb. 'They'll be wondering where we are.'

They dawdled back to the cottage with their arms about each other, loath to relinquish this new heightened intimacy they'd found, this lovely trust and tenderness. It was quite a disappointment to reach the gate.

'About our flat,' Peggy said as they stood together not wanting to go in. 'I don't mind, you know.'

'I do,' he said ruefully.

'Well you mustn't. If there ain't any flats there ain't any flats. You'd have found one by now if there had been. I've known that for ages.'

'It wasn't for want of trying.'

436

'I know. Never mind. We can go on as we are, can't we? We're all right as we are. There's lots of people like us. We're no worse than any of the others, now are we?'

It was a relief to him to have these things said.

'I shall go on trying,' he promised, kissing her.

'I know,' she said. 'And we've got this leave now, and a put-u-up of our own even if it *is* Froggy's.'

Which made them both laugh. And laughing they walked through the gate.

So it was a happy leave after all, and by the end of it even Megan had relaxed and was beginning to lark about. In fact the last meal they had before Peggy went back to Greenwich was as easy as tea in Paradise Row.

But then they had to say goodbye to one another. Peggy had timed her journey so that she could travel in daylight and get back to the wardens' post for her eight o'clock duty. But it was miserable to part, and when she kissed Jim goodbye at Chichester station she was quite envious of Megan and wished she could have stayed on at the cottage too, even in that awful put-u-up.

It was a wish she remembered two hours later when she turned the corner into Paradise Row and stepped straight into a dramatic row between Mrs Roderick and Mrs Nonnie Brown. They were out in the street brawling like tinkers and Nonnie Brown was pulling Mrs Roderick's hair.

'Peggy!' Mrs Roderick called, standing stiff as a board under the assault, 'tell her. I didn't leave your mother to die, did I?'

'No, course not,' Peggy said, glancing up at the faces happily enjoying the spectacle from every open window. Well I'm home now, with a vengeance, she thought.

Nonnie aimed a kick at her opponent's shins while she was looking away and off guard. 'Walked off an' left 'er,' she shrieked. '*We* know. Give herself la-di-da airs an' she walked off an' left 'er.' She smelled strongly of sweat and gin and her blouse had come unbuttoned to reveal a wide expanse of scarlet neck and a crumpled chimmy streaked with brown stains.

'Where's Mr Brown?' Peggy called to Mr Allnutt, who

was watching from his doorstep.

'Down the Earl Grey,' Mr Allnutt said happily. 'Shot off the minute they started. Couldn't see him fer dust.'

'Go and get him,' Peggy ordered, for the two fighters were still snarling at one another even if they weren't lashing out. 'Your husband's coming, Mrs Brown,' she said. 'You stay there and he'll take you home. I'll just get Mrs Roderick inside and see to that eye. You stay there.'

'Bleedin' cow!' Nonnie said, swinging a punch at her neighbour. Fortunately it was so wild that it didn't connect with anyone, but the impetus of it pulled her right off her feet so that she fell face downwards in the gutter. And lay there, muttering to the September dust while her neighbours cheered and laughed and Peggy led the weeping Mrs Roderick into number six.

'I never left her,' she wept. 'I told her to come with me. I did truly. I wouldn't have left her. You know that, don't you?'

'You got a nasty cut under that eye,' Peggy said. 'I'll put some iodine on it. Don't take no notice of that Mrs Brown. It's the drink talking most of the time. I know you didn't leave her. We all know you didn't leave her.'

'I was very fond of her,' Mrs Roderick said. 'You know that. Just because I'm a bit behind with the rent, there's no call for that sort of behaviour.'

'Are you?' Peggy said. 'Hold your face quite still.'

'Well I am a bit,' Mrs Roderick admitted, wincing as the iodine bit into her cuts. 'I've lost a lot of customers, that's the trouble. People don't buy corsets like they used to. Not now. They reckon they can go without now there's a war on. Oh dear I don't know why I'm telling you all this.'

'I'd start up a new line of business if I was you,' Peggy said calmly. 'You're ever so good with your needle and there's lots of kids round here grown out of their clothes. Why don't you set up in business remodelling 'em, turning 'em over, you know, new clothes for old.'

'New clothes for old, eh?' Mrs Roderick said, considering the idea. 'Do you think I could?'

'Course. You're just the one. There that's done. I'll make a quick cup of tea. Then I shall have to be getting up to the Post.'

'You're a good girl, Peggy,' Mrs Roderick said, smiling at her as well as she could for her cuts. 'I don't know what we'd do without you.'

After the intensity of that leave the words jarred. This is the life I've got to lead, Peggy thought ruefully, the life I've chosen, and although she was still proud that they all depended on her and glad that she was so useful, she knew she'd made a hard choice. But she was a soldier's daughter, wasn't she? And born in the Tower of London. So how could she do anything else?

'Oh yes,' Mrs Roderick repeated. 'I don't know what we'd do without you.'

It was a sentiment that was repeated many times in Paradise Row that winter, for the rations diminished and the raids continued intermittently and the news grew worse and worse. She was such a comfort was Peggy Boxall, such a dependable comfort, always there when you needed her. And they needed her a lot in those dark cold days.

The papers reported that the Russians were having a very hard time of it. On 9 September, when Jim was home for thirty-six hours, the Germans started a long and terrible siege of the city of Leningrad and ten days later the city of Kiev was captured. By the beginning of October, when the thirty-six hour pass Jim was hoping for had suddenly been cancelled, the German armies were advancing on Moscow. Peggy was honest enough to admit to herself that she didn't know what upset her most, the bad news of the war or not seeing Jim when she missed him so much.

Mr Cooper followed the news with outraged compassion. 'Poor devils,' he said. 'Imagine it. Be like having bloody Germans all round London. Think how we'd feel.'

But the women of Paradise Row were more concerned with all the British ships that were being sunk out in the Atlantic. There were so many merchant ships lost that the papers didn't even name then, and the old *Ark Royal* was sunk in November and the *Prince of Wales* and the *Repulse* a month later. There was hardly a woman in the street who didn't know of someone who'd been killed at sea. And such heavy losses meant that food was in very short supply, and queues were longer and more wearying than ever. It wasn't long before the government introduced a new style of rationing by points.

It caused consternation in Paradise Row.

'I shall never work it out,' Mrs Roderick said. 'The other was all right. You just got your ration whatever it was. Even if it wasn't much. But this is awful. How are you supposed to know what you're entitled to? Four points for this, six points for that. I ask you. I shall never work it out. Never. What did they want to go and make it so complicated for? Why couldn't we have had rations instead? And just when I've got myself a nice little job with the kiddies' clothes and I thought everything was going to work out.'

'Ask our Peggy,' Mrs Geary said. 'She'll tell yer. She's ever so good with it. I just give her my ration book and she does it all for me. I'd do it mesself only I got these legs. Play me up somethink chronic in this weather they do.'

It was wickedly cold, as though the weather was conspiring with the Germans to make them all as uncomfortable as it could. On the day Arthur received his call-up papers and a travel warrant to Salisbury the sky was pewter grey with the threat of snow.

He came down to number six to say goodbye to Peggy and Joan that evening, his face peaked with cold and anxiety. 'Keep an eye on my Lily for me, will you, Peg?' he asked. 'She's bound to be a bit low.'

'We'll ask her up here the minute you've gone,' Peggy promised. 'We can listen to the wireless before I go to the Post and then she can stay with Joan for a while. It won't hurt your Percy to sit up.'

'You're a brick,' Arthur said, as he kissed her goodbye. 'I don't know what we'd do without you.'

'Quite right,' Mrs Geary said. 'Salt of the earth she is.'

But it was salt that Jim Boxall had to learn to live without as the winter worsened, for the extreme cold meant more work for electricians and mechanics and the long leave he was hoping for was cancelled until the weather improved.

'Things must start looking up soon,' he wrote to Peggy. 'Or warming up at the very least. I ain't kissed you for such a long time I'm beginning to forget how it feels. This winter's been going on for ever.'

And things did warm up, although not in the way he'd been thinking of when he wrote. On 7 December the news suddenly broke that the Japanese had attacked the American fleet at a place called Pearl Harbor. It was a surprise attack carried out without a formal declaration of war and it sank the best part of the Pacific fleet with appalling loss of life.

'Japs, you see,' Mrs Geary said, scowling at the newspaper. 'Nasty treacherous little things, Japs. Well they'd have to be wouldn't they to be on the same side as that Hitler. They'll live to regret it and serve 'em jolly well right.'

'I think it's a good thing in a way,' Joan said. 'At least it's brought the Yanks into the war. They can't go on dragging their feet now, can they?'

'Perhaps they'll come over here,' Baby said. 'Do you think they'll bring any make-up?' The shortage of lipstick and mascara was a continual annoyance to her, particularly as Joan and Peggy didn't seem to understand how important it was.

But the weeks passed and Jim still didn't get any leave and the Americans didn't come to Britain.

'Too cold for 'em probably,' Mrs Geary said. 'They're used to lots a' sunshine out in that Texas place. I seen it at the pictures. Still never mind, they'll probably give them Japs a trouncing first.'

But if the newspapers were to be believed it was the Japs who were trouncing everybody else. They seemed to be as good at winning battles as the Germans. They took Hong Kong on Christmas Day, Borneo in January, Singapore in February. There was no end to their success. Nor to the Germans'. In January the British newspapers began to write about a German general called Rommel who'd landed in North Africa to help the Italians in their fight against the British 8th Army and was defeating the British tanks in one battle after another.

It was horribly demoralizing, particularly as the weather was colder than ever, with two inches of snow falling on 1 February and twenty-two per cent of frost recorded in London.

'As if we haven't got enough on our plates without this,' Mrs Allnutt said, tottering down to the market with a walking stick to support her over the uneven lumps of trodden snow. 'I can't feel my feet, Peggy.'

'No more can I,' Peggy said cheerfully. 'Hang on to my arm. Have you heard about Megan?' She'd had a letter from her that morning and was itching to spread the good news.

'No,' Mrs Allnutt said obligingly.

'She's expecting. Ain't it grand?'

'Smashing. When?'

'June, she says. I had a letter this morning.'

'When's your Jim coming home?' Mrs Allnutt said, sliding on. 'We ain't seen him fer ages. He's all right, is he?'

'He's very busy,' Peggy explained. 'They all are. It's the cold. It makes a lot of extra work with everything freezing up you see. Ice is bad for the engines.'

'It's bad for the feet an' all,' Mrs Allnutt said. 'I don't know how we put up with it.'

'It's being so cheerful as keeps us going,' Peggy said, quoting a catch phrase from a character called Mona Lot in Tommy Handley's radio show *ITMA*, and that made them both laugh and warmed them sufficiently to get them over the next frozen ridge of snow and up into the High Street where the trams kept the roads clear.

And then just to cap everything the government announced that they were raising the draft age for men to fifty-one and that they had decided to start calling up unmarried women.

Baby was horrified. 'They can't do that,' she said. 'I can't go in the army, I'd have to wear uniform. Imagine it. I'd look a freak.'

'You'll have to go if you get called up,' Joan said, with some satisfaction. 'Do you good. Make a man of you.'

'And you can just shut up,' Baby said, scowling at her. 'What am I going to do, our Peg?'

'You could go in the WAAF,' Peggy said, 'if you don't fancy the ATS.'

'Or join the Civil Defence like Peggy,' Joan said. 'You'd like that. Out all hours with the raids on.'

'I think you're both being foul,' Baby said and flounced

442

out of the house, blonde hair swinging.

But at last it was March and although several eighteen-year-old women in the neighbourhood had already received their call-up papers, Baby was still at large, the snow had finally gone and Jim was allowed home for ten precious days. Mr Allnutt decided they would have a ding-dong to celebrate and to cheer poor Lily up because she'd been very low since Arthur went into the army. It was the first ding-dong they'd had for a very long time and they were all looking forward to it, even though Mrs Roderick and Nonnie Brown would both be present and they still weren't on speaking terms.

'Still,' Mrs Allnutt said to Peggy, 'we can sit 'em one at each end of the room. There's always ways an' means. Is Mrs Geary bringing Polly? If the worst comes to the worst we'll get him swearing and he can drown 'em out.'

But it wasn't Nonnie or Mrs Roderick who caused a stir at the party. It was John Cooper and he did it quite inadvertently by arriving with a copy of the *Evening Standard* and the news that the RAF had bombed a German city called Lübeck. The centre of the city had been completely flattened.

Cyril Brown seized the paper and waved it in triumph. 'And about bloody time too!' he said. 'Serve the buggers right. They've had it coming to 'em.'

Joan wasn't so sure. 'Was it an army base?' she said. 'Something to do with the army or the navy or something?'

'It was a picturesque city,' John Cooper said, reading from the paper. 'A medieval town it says, a port. It had a timber built medieval centre.'

'What's it matter?' Cyril said. 'They've asked for it and now they're getting it. I'm sick of hearing how we can take it all the time. It's about time we started dishing it out for a change.'

Peggy was appalled. 'We're bombing women and children,' she said. 'That's what we're doing. It's dreadful.' And she looked across the room to where Joan and Lily were dancing with Norman and Yvey and little Percy.

'And what d'you think they been doing all this time?' Cyril shouted at her.

'Two wrongs don't make a right,' Peggy told her doggedly. 'We ought to be behaving better than them. Not worse.'

And suddenly she was overcome with weariness, tired of the war and the cold and the long hours queueing, of being married and having to live apart, of the shabby, shoddy endlessness of it all, and she knew she was perilously close to tears and ducked her head to gain control of herself. And Jim, alerted at once, took her by the elbow and began to steer her out of the room and away from trouble.

'Come on,' he said, 'You need a break from that lot. Bit a' peace and quiet.'

It was very quiet out in the street with just enough moonlight to show them the way and the air smelling of soot and coalfires.

She followed him into number two and up the dark stairs to the room that was now 'theirs'. They pulled the black-out curtains and lit their little bedside light, listening to the piano twanging below them. Then they comforted one another by making love, very gently and tenderly.

'This war's making us all cruel,' she said as he lit their two cigarettes.

'Not you,' he said tenderly, lying back among the pillows to admire her. 'You've got more love in you than anyone I've ever met.'

'It is though, it's making us cruel. Mrs Roderick and Mrs Brown fighting in the street, and people gloating. Just think what Cyril was saying. Serve 'em right. Women and children.'

'For some people, yes, I suppose it is. We've had too much bad news. That's what it is. We need a victory.'

'Yes,' she said seriously. 'We do. But not by bombing women and children.'

'Something to lift our spirits,' he said, flicking ash from his cigarette. A victory, or if not an out-and-out victory a success, a little hope, some joy.

But where could such things be found in a world at war?

444

CHAPTER 35

Baby was standing on the pavement outside the entrance to the market when the first Americans came jazzing into town. It was an electrifying experience. She was so used to the discipline of the British troops stationed around Greenwich that she hardly noticed them. Well there wasn't very much to notice, was there? They all marched together with such dull precision that the tramp of their boots sounded like a single pair of feet, all caps set at the same angle, all arms swinging to the same rhythm, nothing remarkable about that. These soldiers were another breed altogether.

For a start they were preceded by the jazziest military band she'd ever heard. It set her feet tapping at once. And then, when the troops appeared round the corner they were all black, every single one of them, and they weren't marching at all. They were leaping about and jumping in the air, and marching backwards and sideways and all sorts, chewing and grinning. Soon people on the pavements began to cheer them and to clap in time to the rhythm, and they waved and grinned, showing very white teeth. It was like a carnival.

'They're smashing,' she said to Joan and Peggy and Mrs Geary when they were eating their Woolton pie that evening. 'Where d'you think they're stationed?'

'I wonder you didn't follow 'em and find out,' Mrs Geary said rather acidly.

'I'll bet they're smashing dancers,' Baby said, unabashed

445

by her sarcasm. 'I shall go to the Palais on Saturday and see.'

And she did, returning home very late indeed with her hair tousled and her shoes covered in dust to report that she'd danced every single dance and she'd never had such a smashing time in her life.

'They're ever so comical,' she said. 'There was only white ones there tonight. They're called GIs and they call you Honey and Sugar and funny things like that, and they've got the most peculiar names, Hank and Marvin and Sergeant Buzzywitzy or something, imagine, and they give you gum and sweets. I think they're smashing.'

'She wants ter watch out,' Mrs Geary warned, 'or one of 'em'll give her a bit more than gum. Specially the way she goes on with that hair.' She'd never approved of peroxide blondes. Fast, the lot of 'em.

But Baby was hell-bent on a life of pleasure. And despite her dumb blonde appearance she was shrewd enough to work out how to get it without having to pay the traditional price. And she knew exactly what the traditional price was. There were no secrets now about poor Joan's disgrace, only the memory of how awful it had been, and the residual fear that men were bestial and brutal and had to be kept in check for your own protection and never allowed to touch you anywhere they shouldn't. So what you did was flirt and tease and make eyes, which got you gum and candies and doughnuts and plenty of dancing partners, but always arrange beforehand to go home in a crowd.

Sometimes despite her careful plans the crowd broke up into snogging couples as soon as they left the dance hall and then things could get a bit difficult, but she usually found that she could deal with most over-amorous Yanks providing she stopped their hands wandering the minute they started. In fact it was often better to make a speech as soon as they showed signs of wanting to do anything more than just kiss her. It was really quite a good speech. She said she wasn't a good-time girl, and she was only trying to make them feel at home in a foreign country, and she did hope they hadn't got the wrong idea about her, and if they still pressed on regardless she cried a few pathetic tears and told them she was an orphan. And that usually worked a treat.

She was shrewd enough to have taken action to avoid the call-up too. By dint of listening and questioning she found out that some people were in what was called reserved occupations, and that some firms could keep a few of their most valuable staff out of the forces for six months at a time by making a special plea for them. So she put herself out to become one of Dodds' most valuable employees, taking over the book-keeping from Mr Trotkins when he went away to the army and doing it in addition to her job on the telephones. She'd had to tell quite a few lies to get the extra job, well not lies exactly, sort of half-truths, about how good she'd always been at arithmetic, and how easy she'd always found it. Actually adding up columns of figures was jolly hard work and took her much longer than she pretended, but it was worth it. Anything was better than going in the army. Of course what with dancing all hours and working all hours she didn't have the energy for any housework or shopping or anything like that. But luckily Peggy understood and did all that sort of thing for her. Good old Peg. She didn't seem to mind how much extra work she did. And all that nonsense about finding a flat and living with Jim near the base seemed to have died the death. Thank heavens. Things were much better as they were, with Jim coming home on leave now and then and Peggy free to look after the house.

In the summer, when London was swarming with Yanks, she teased her sisters to go up West with her and the kids and see the new arrivals for themselves.

'Look at all them lovely uniforms,' she said to Yvonne. 'It's lovely cloth. Ever so soft. Better'n that horrible rough stuff our fellers wear.'

Joan grimaced but said nothing.

'Ain't they fat!' Yvonne said as two plump GIs strolled past, their sleeves straining with well-fed flesh.

'You should see what they eat,' Baby said. 'I never seen so much food. They make smashing doughnuts. They're ever so expensive but it don't worry them. They earn so much you'd never believe it.'

447

'How much?' Norman wanted to know. Now that he was eight he was very aware of money.

'Ever such a lot,' Baby told him happily. 'Three times as much as our fellers.'

'Overpaid, oversexed and over here,' Peggy whispered to Joan, quoting the current jibe against all these wealthy invaders.

'They don't bother to pay our troops good money,' Joan said sourly. 'They're only cannon fodder, poor beggars.'

'What's cannon fodder, Mum?' Norman asked.

'Men like yer Dad,' Joan told him. 'Proper soldiers. The ones that do the fighting and get killed and captured and put in prisoner a' war camps instead a' poncing about London all the time, showing off.'

'Well that's nice!' Baby said, bristling. 'What a thing to tell the kid. They're our allies. Don't you take no notice, Norm. Yanks are nice. Least they bring a bit a' colour to the old place.'

Peggy was looking at the Londoners going about their business stolidly and unobtrusively among the new arrivals and she couldn't help noticing that the Americans' smart uniforms and innocent baby faces were making their hosts look shabby and war-worn. She was so used to old clothes and skinny children and faces grey with fatigue that until that moment she'd hardly noticed them, but now she was aware that Londoners had been worn down and washed out by this war that they'd been fighting for so long on their own, and she felt a fierce passionate pride for their endurance and courage.

But Joan was frowning. 'Time we was getting back,' Peggy said, to forestall a row. 'What say we have faggots for supper?'

So domestic peace was restored. At least for the time being.

Baby's behaviour rankled Joan a great deal that summer. 'She's so bloody bone idle,' she said to Peggy the next Sunday morning as they were preparing the vegetables for Sunday dinner. 'Half past eleven and she's still abed, selfish little pig. She'll need to get up and lend a hand next week if you're off to Merston.'

'Perhaps I'd better not go,' Peggy said, looking worried.

'You go, mate,' her sister advised, tossing a peeled potato into the saucepan so violently that the water splashed all over the draining board. 'You've earned a rest. I'll see to *her*.'

'Oh dear,' Peggy said, but then they both laughed, because Baby was asking for it really.

And she was looking forward to her visit ever so much. Ten days in Vine Cottage again with Jim and Megan and Froggy. The two men had both got leave and they'd planned all sorts of outings.

Froggy had even wangled a car. Trust Froggy. He and Jim and a very rotund Megan were all sitting in it waiting for her when her train arrived at Chichester station.

'Trip round the town,' Froggy said, as she climbed into what remained of the back seat. 'Market Cross, cathedral, cinema, all round the city walls.'

'Chauffeur-driven too,' Jim said, beaming at her.

They had tea at an old-fashioned tea house, which Peggy said she really needed, and they went to the pictures, which Megan said was jolly uncomfortable because she didn't fit into the seats, and after that they went to a pub, which was full of airmen and where they all sang 'Roll out the Barrel' and 'There'll always be an England' and several rather more scurrilous ditties, and at closing time they went rattling off through the black country lanes and arrived back at Vine Cottage, giggling and merry. It was like a holiday.

'And so it should be,' Jim said. 'We've earned it.'

The next day was sunny and peaceful and they spent it sitting in the garden. They had their dinner out there, and the two men did the washing up afterwards, and at tea-time Megan lowered herself to her knees in her vegetable patch and uprooted four handfuls of radishes for them to eat with brown bread and butter, no less.

'We are spoilt,' Peggy said, smiling at her. It was lovely to see her so much easier in this marriage.

'D'you like 'em?' Megan asked, pleased with her produce.

'Smashing.'

'She'll get indigestion sure as fate,' Froggy said. 'Always does these days when she eats radishes.'

449

And sure enough just before Jim and Peggy went out for the evening, Megan began to make grimaces and complain about feeling uncomfortable.

'I warned you,' Froggy said, pretending irritation and exuding concern. 'Where's your Rennies?' And he shot off into the kitchen to see if he could find them.

'It's giving me proper belly-ache,' Megan said. 'I shall have to lie down if it gets any worse.'

'Well lie down then,' Peggy said.

'I don't like to,' Megan said, making another grimace.

'Why not?'

'Well, not with you two staying. You can't go lying down when you got company.'

'We're not company, you soppy thing,' Peggy said, hugging her. 'We're Jim and Peggy, remember? You lie down all you like. Anyway we're going out.'

She and Jim went back to the pub for another raucous evening, and this time they travelled by bicycle, with Peggy balanced on the crossbar.

When they came out into the street at closing-time it was pitch dark. So they pushed the bike and walked back side by side, and what with the darkness and frequent stops for kisses it took them a very long time to make their short journey.

'Shush,' Peggy whispered when they reached the hedge. 'Don't make a noise, I'll bet they're in bed.'

But when they reached the front door there was a strange bicycle propped against the wall. So it looked as though somebody else had come to visit them.

Froggy was sitting on the put-u-up smoking and looking very ill-at-ease, and there was no sign of the visitor or Megan. But before Peggy could open her mouth to ask what was happening, the answer mewed above their heads, in the small unmistakable cry of the new born. Froggy threw his cigarette onto the lino and ran.

'Oh!' Peggy said with delight. 'D'you think they'll let me see it?'

'What now?' Jim said. 'When it's just been born?'

'Course. Why not? I'd love to see it. Wouldn't you?'

'Not now,' he said, aghast at the idea. 'Not now. Not when it's just ... No I wouldn't.'

How funny men are about birth, Peggy thought. They face death all the time nowadays and yet here he is shying away from a new baby. And then it occurred to her that she hadn't seen a new-born baby since Norman was born, and she found her heart throbbing with excitement at the prospect.

But she had to wait for nearly an hour before the midwife left and Froggy came crashing into the room to tell her she could come up if she wanted to. He was pink-eyed with emotion and babbling incoherently. 'A daughter,' he said as they climbed the stairs. 'She's so little. A beautiful little ... Oh a marvellous ... A gorgeous wizard little ...'

The baby lay in the crook of Megan's arm, swathed in a knitted shawl, damp and pink and peaceful and exactly like her mother, with the same dark curly hair, the same wide-spaced eyes, even the same shaped mouth. Only her funny snub nose was different. A most delectable baby and just the sight of her made Peggy warm with pleasure.

A new life, she thought, a new life after all the deaths and the terror of the raids and all those poor devils hauled out of the wreckage shocked and bleeding and helpless, a new perfect life. And she suddenly remembered the grass growing before their eyes in Greenwich park when the rain ended that long drought, oh such a long time ago, and how she and Jim had walked under the trees with the rain fresh on their faces marvelling at the wonder of it. New life reasserting itself just when they'd resigned themselves to parched earth for ever. And tears of pure joy sprang into her eyes and rolled down her cheeks.

'I'm ever so sorry,' Megan said smiling at her in the most beautifully relaxed way. 'I was going to give you such a nice holiday too. Bad timing.'

'Oh no!' Peggy said swooping across the room to kiss her. 'Perfect timing. I couldn't ask for anything better. What are you going to call her?'

'Winifred,' Megan said kissing the baby's dark head. 'After Froggy's mother and old Churchill you see. Winnie for short.'

'Winnie,' Peggy approved. 'She's a beauty, Megan.'

And Winnie for short opened her dark blue eyes and

looked at them for a long stunning second before she slept again, and at that they both wept and kissed one another and admired the baby over and over again and were rapturously happy. New life. Oh what could be better in the midst of war?

Peggy spent the next eight days looking after mother and child. Jim was persuaded upstairs to see the baby after the midwife's visit at the end of the second afternoon and he was plainly delighted with her, because he and Froggy spent a long time hitting one another on the back and pretending to box one another, until Megan protested that they were setting the poor little thing a very bad example, at which they settled down in the two basket chairs and embarked on a discussion of the sort of education system Great Britain should introduce after the war. Megan went to sleep in the middle of it, but Peggy listened to every word.

'Every single child should have the chance of a full education,' Jim said earnestly. 'A grammar school education. The best you can get. And at the state's expense, with grants for poor kids. Why should you be debarred from an education because your old man can't pay? That's barbarous. Your Winnie should go to a grammar school whether you're rich or poor.'

'You ought to speak at our next current affairs meeting,' Froggy said. 'You'd go down a treat.'

'I might at that,' Jim said. 'I been thinking about it.'

'What is it?' Peggy asked.

'A sort of debating society, I suppose you'd call it,' Jim told her. 'Discussing the sort of society we want when the war's over. ABCA send us pamphlets about it and the officers set it up.'

'Who's ABCA when they're at home?'

'Army Bureau of Current Affairs,' Froggy explained. 'Morale boosters.'

'Then you should,' Peggy said. 'You'd be just the one for it. When's the next meeting?'

Jim was yawning. 'Tomorrow evening,' he said. 'And, before you start, they've got a speaker.'

'Are you going?' she asked.

'No, we're on leave.'

'I think you should,' she urged. 'It sounds just the thing.'

'Wouldn't you mind?'

'No, course not. I'll stay with Megan and the baby. You go. You'd enjoy it.'

So after some deliberation the two men went to their meeting.

They returned in a state of high excitement, rushing up the stairs to the bedroom, throwing themselves into the chairs, their faces flushed, bright-eyed and glowing.

'Guess what,' Froggy said, throwing his cap in the air. 'Jim was the speaker.'

'Gosh!' Megan said. 'Why?'

'The real speaker didn't turn up,' Jim said. 'Ill or something. I sort of stepped into the breach.' He was still amazed at his daring, remembering the breath-stopping moment when he'd looked down at the ranks of faces turned toward him and realized that they were all waiting to hear what he was going to say. What *he* was going to say. Imagine it.

'Gosh!' Megan said again. 'How did it go?'

'Rather well,' Jim admitted, looking massively proud of himself.

It had actually gone down much better than 'rather well'. He hadn't had any really clear idea what he was going to say when he stood up and made his offer, but the topic was education, and the officer who introduced him had spoken in the drawling tones of the public school, and that provided just enough resentment to stiffen his resolve and show him where he ought to start.

'I come from Paradise Row in Greenwich,' he said. 'We got a big school just round the corner, where they teach you the three R's and send you out in the world to be factory hands and skivvies. Up on the heath there are public schools where the rich send their kids to learn Latin and matriculate and be sent to universities. And just up the road there's a grammar school called Roan's, where ordinary kids can go if they pass the scholarship and their old man's got enough money to afford the uniform. They take thirty boys from Greenwich every year. They used to tell us it was the thirty brainiest boys. But I can tell you

453

different. It ain't the thirty brainiest, it's the thirty brainiest who can afford it.'

They were looking at him eagerly, agreeing with him.

'And another thing,' he said. 'If they can take thirty brainy children, why not thirty-five, or forty, or sixty? Who decides which brainy children go to grammar school and which don't? Where do they draw the line? And if it comes to it, why should they draw a line at all? Nobody draws a line for the rich kids. They get the best of everything whether they're brainy or not. But for poor kids it's like the pigs going to market in the nursery rhyme. This clever kid gets an education, this clever kid gets none.'

He was warm with nerves and enthusiasm, and his heart was still beating like a drum, but his audience were with him. He could feel it. Their support rose towards him through the fug of cigarette smoke.

'So what d'you think we ought to do about it?' one man asked.

'I'll tell you,' he said. And did, outlining all the plans he read about in the *Picture Post* and adding a few of his own for good measure. 'We need a new type of school,' he said, 'a new kind of education system. That's what we need.'

'He'll end up a politician,' Froggy said to Peggy, when they'd relived the entire meeting for her benefit. 'You see if I'm not right. They were cheering him come the finish and stamping on the floor.'

'I knew it,' Peggy said with delight. 'I knew you'd do it.'

'And he'll do it again,' Froggy said. 'Won't you, Jim? Now you've started.'

By the end of that leave Jim had been booked up for three more sessions, and had plainly and happily embarked on a career as a public speaker. He said he was really bucked and Peggy was so proud of him she felt twice the size.

After such an eventful holiday it was an awful comedown when their leave finished and Megan's mum arrived to take over the job of looking after Megan and the baby. This time it was especially sad to pack her bag ready to be driven to the station.

'But you'll come back, won't you?' Megan said, pretty among the pillows.

'Whenever I can,' Peggy promised. 'I got to keep an eye on Winnie, ain't I, and see how Jim's getting on with this ABCA business. I shan't be able to keep away.'

But although neither of them knew it then, her next journey was to be a very long one, for in August the squadron was posted to Harlech in north Wales.

After a full year of married life Froggy was distraught to be leaving Megan and the baby, and swore he didn't know how any of them would make out. But Corporal Jim Boxall, public speaker, knew exactly.

'Thirty-six hours are useless,' he wrote to Peggy, 'so I shall wangle a fortnight by running two leaves together and then I'll book a room in a pub for us. Hang the expense. We've earned it. I don't intend to live for months and months without you. I love you too much. Anyway it's time we started to live like the nobs. The first of the changes, eh? If I'm going to talk about them I ought to start living them.'

After such a forceful invitation how could she refuse? So it was all arranged and she took a fortnight's leave and travelled to Wales to join him. It was like journeying to a foreign country, all these great hills and porters calling out the rolling unfamiliar names of the stations.

It was just as well that Jim was there to meet her, for Llanbedr didn't sound a bit like the way it was written.

They walked along a street bounded on one side by a fast-flowing grey river and on the other by a terrace of grey stone cottages each with two gables and a neat tiled porch before the door. The women they passed nodded and smiled and it was amazingly quiet after the noise of London. They could hear Peggy's train puffing away from them across the bay.

'It's all under water at high tide except the road and the railway,' Jim said. 'We're staying by the crossroads. That pub down there. See? Down those steps.'

It was an idyllic leave, the first time they'd been entirely on their own together since their honeymoon. They walked in the wild hills and ate together in the pub, really rather well considering the state of food supplies, and they talked. They decided where they would live – in London of course – and how they would educate their children – in one of Jim's new schools of course – and what jobs they would do in peacetime. 'Something a bit better than a garage hand,' Jim said. 'I've had men's lives depending on my work ever since the Battle of Britain. I shan't settle for anything less important than that.' And at night they cuddled together in a huge tumbling feather-bed and loved and slept as they pleased with no raids or duties to prevent them. Every night for twelve nights. Peggy said she felt like a proper old married woman again.

'Very proper,' he said. 'How could you be anything else, when you're married to me?'

It was their last morning and they were still lazing in bed. The sun had been up for hours and was already strong, casting patterns of brightened colour across the counterpane of their rumpled bed and edging Jim's contented profile with shining white light.

'You've got a halo all round your face,' Peggy said, tracing the bright flesh with her fingers, down the lumpy ridge of his broken nose, over his lips, that looked so hard and felt so soft, down that stubborn jutting chin, loving every inch.

'Saint Jim,' he grinned at her, catching her fingers and kissing them.

'Not after all the things you've just been doing,' she laughed back.

'And you haven't?' he teased.

He was sending such love towards her from those dark-lashed eyes that she felt quite weak to see it. 'Three more hours,' she said, glancing at her watch and trying to be practical. 'What shall we do this morning?'

'As if you didn't know,' he said gathering her towards him.

Oh a perfect, perfect leave. And they even managed to extend it for a few more precious minutes because he travelled back with her as far as Harlech. As they kissed goodbye through the carriage window, they were so easy with love and sunshine that they felt as though they were only parting for the day, like a married couple setting off for work in the morning to be reunited at night.

It wasn't until the train had pulled out of the station and she found herself alone in the compartment with seven strangers that Peggy felt the misery of their parting, and then partly because she had to keep it hidden and partly because it was such a sharp contrast to the happiness she'd been feeling for nearly a fortnight, it stayed with her all the way back to Greenwich.

If only Hitler hadn't been born, she thought. If only there hadn't been a war. We could have settled down in Paradise Row like Arthur and Lily. I might even have had kids, like Megan and Froggy. But it was no good thinking like that, she scolded herself, trying to be sensible. There *was* a war and they all had to fight it. But she missed him achingly, this new famous Jim, and she thought of him all the way home, no matter how hard she tried to think of other things.

CHAPTER 36

'I've had such a funny letter from Sid,' Joan said, taking it from her handbag and holding it out for her sister to see. 'He wants some more snaps of the kids he says, because – what was it? – "I'm missing out. Yvonne nearly eleven. She was seven when I went away. I am missing out on all this. And Norm such a little lad. There will have to be some changes when this war is over and I come home again. A better life for you and me and the kids. We been talking about it, me and the lads. There will have to be some changes." What d'you think of that?'

'He's quite right,' Peggy said. 'There will. That's what Jim says too.' She'd just come home after an eight-hour duty and she was tired and grubby and needed a wash and a nice long sleep, but she made an effort to answer because she knew how much Sid's letters meant to poor Joan.

'It's the first time he's ever wrote home like this,' Joan said, caught between being puzzled and pleased. 'It's good he's thinking about the war ending. Least that's more cheerful than going on about how bad the food is all the time. But I can't think what's got into him, talking about changes. What do you think he means, changes? What d'you think he wants to change?'

'They might be changes for the better,' Peggy said, putting on the kettle for some hot water.

'D'you think so?'

'Oh yes,' Peggy said. 'There's gonna be a great change for the better once this is over, you'll see. Stands to reason.

When you've been bombed and shot at and seen your friends and relations killed it changes you. We ain't so meek nowadays. War's made us tough. If there was a general strike tomorrow we'd win it this time. Oh yes, there'll be changes. You won't see us going back to unemployment, and kids without shoes and half starved, an' "yes sir, no sir, three bags full sir", not after all we've been through.'

'I never knew you felt so strongly about it,' Joan said, quite surprised by her sister's vehemence.

'Just because I don't say much don't mean I don't think,' Peggy said.

'But what about this letter?' Joan said, looking at it again. 'What about Sid? Sometimes I don't think I shall know him when he does come home.'

'Cross that bridge when you come to it,' Peggy advised. 'Remember what Dad used to say? Never trouble trouble till trouble troubles you. Where's Baby? Need I ask.'

'Up the Palais,' Joan said making her disapproving grimace. 'I shall be glad when they send these Yanks off to do a bit of fighting.'

'Perhaps they have a closed season and don't fight in the autumn,' Peggy said.

It was September 1942 and the fourth year of the war. Jim and Froggy were promoted to sergeants but still in Harlech, Megan and Winnie were still on their own in Vine Cottage, Peggy was still on her own in Greenwich but things were happening all around them, some of them momentous. Yvonne had gone up to the Senior Girls at the beginning of the month and was very pleased with herself, and Pearl had got her 'call-up' papers and decided to join the Land Army, and at the end of the month Arthur came home on leave with the news that he reckoned he was going to be sent to Africa.

Lily wasn't pleased to hear it. 'It won't do him any good out in a desert with all that sand,' she said to Peggy, when his leave was over and he'd gone back. 'He can't stand the heat, you know. Never could. It brings him out in a rash.'

'I expect they'll look after him,' Peggy said. 'They're bound to take doctors.'

'Oh Christ, Peg,' Lily said, her face crumpling into tears. 'What if he's shot? There's terrible fighting going on out there. What if he's shot?'

'He ain't gone yet,' Peggy tried to comfort. 'They mightn't send him. He could have got it wrong.'

But he hadn't. The Allied armies were on the move at last, going over to the offensive, preparing for invasion. Although none of them knew it then, he was to be part of an operation code-named 'Torch' which was designed to crush Rommel's renowned panzer divisions between two Allied armies, British and American, working together for the very first time.

That winter was dominated by two massive battles, one in Russia, round the great city of Stalingrad, and the other in Egypt round a small town called El Alamein. Paradise Row followed the fortunes of both with breathless attention, tuning in to the nine o'clock news every night for the latest bulletin, hoping almost against hope for the victory they all wanted and needed so much.

The war in the desert seemed to have been going on for ever, with the British troops advancing and retreating over the same barren land until the names of Mersa Metruh and Sidi Barrani and Tobruk were as familiar as Bisto and Sunlight soap. But in August a new general had been sent out to put an end to retreats. His name was Bernard Montgomery and before long he was spectacularly successful.

Battle began on 24 October. 'Great tank battle in desert' the papers said, and it was clear from the tone of the wireless announcers that something decisive was going on. Peggy and Joan and Mrs Geary listened to every bulletin and even Baby took an interest. And on 5 November good news came at last.

'Rommel routed,' the *Daily Mirror* cheered. 'Huns fleeing in disorder'. And they quoted the official communiqué from the British Headquarters in Cairo. 'The Axis forces in the Western Desert, after twelve days and nights of ceaseless attacks by our land and air forces, are now in full retreat.' The Allies had a victory.

Three days later Operation Torch began and British and American troops were successfully landed on the

460

coast between Casablanca and Algiers, and Private Arthur Walters was among them.

Lily was so worried she lost weight visibly. And naturally the campaign was followed avidly by everybody in Paradise Row. Despite their concern for 'young Arthur' it was marvellous to watch the Jerries being steadily pushed back on both fronts, nipped between the two armies. Soon pictures of burnt-out German tanks began to appear in the papers and comforting shots of captured German troops looking exhausted and dispirited with their hands in the air.

'Serve 'em right,' Mrs Geary said with great satisfaction. 'Give 'em a taste of their own medicine. See how they like it.'

'Bugger, bugger, bugger,' the parrot agreed, dancing happily.

Good news bred more good news, as if spirits were being lifted wherever anyone was fighting the Nazis. At the end of November, on the very day that Lily received her first letter from Arthur saying that he'd seen action and was perfectly all right, the BBC broadcast the news that the Russian winter had begun.

'Now we shall see some changes in Stalingrad,' John Cooper said. 'Russia's best ally, the winter. It did for Napoleon and now it'll do for Hitler.'

And sure enough the next bulletin told them that the Germans were suffering from the effects of the extreme cold, and on Christmas Eve the Russians in Stalingrad launched what the papers called 'a massive counterattack'.

'What a Christmas present if them ol' Russkies could send the beggars packing like we done in the desert,' Mrs Geary said. 'Now we are looking up.'

And they continued to look up, as the mood of hope and optimism steadily grew.

Over in Harlech, Sergeant Jim Boxall was optimistic too. While his squadron was carrying out regular sweeps of the Irish Sea on the look-out for any U-boats or Focke-Wulf Condors heading off to attack the British convoys, he was servicing their precious planes and continuing his career as a public speaker.

At meeting after meeting he outlined his vision, describing a world where no one need be afraid of falling ill, where arts would flourish, where all children would be given the very best education, where the mines, electricity companies, gas companies, docks and railways would be run as the great public services they ought to be instead of being milked for the private profit of the greedy rich.

When the meetings were officially over, groups of enthusiastic supporters followed him to the NAAFI to continue the debate, talking on into greater and more compassionate detail, about allowances for children, medical centres for families, a state wage for mothers so that the great social act of raising a family didn't reduce parents to poverty. It was exhilarating and positive. Oh they were on the move now and no mistake.

'I shall be home in the New Year,' he wrote to Peggy that Christmas. 'It's very cold here, real brass monkey weather, so I'll come to you this time. I've got such a lot to tell you.'

It wasn't a successful leave despite all their new-found optimism.

For a start all three Furnivall sisters had heavy head colds. Peggy was red-nosed and shivery for most of his ten precious days, and to make matters worse when he went to visit his mother he found that she'd had bronchitis and wasn't at all well either.

'I ought to get back to work,' she told him anxiously. 'I been off nearly a fortnight.'

He understood her anxiety at once. 'Is it the rent?'

'Well yes,' she admitted. There was no point in pretending. Not to Jim. 'My wages take care of it as a general rule, you see.'

He did see. 'I'll take care of it this time,' he said. 'If you promise to stay indoors until you're quite well and you don't let the old man get his paws on it.'

'You're a dear boy,' his mother said gratefully. 'It's two weeks. I hide it in the teapot. He don't think a' looking there.'

So two weeks' rent was hidden in the teapot, and then he went out with her ration books and bought a week's rations to keep her going.

'I've spent my entire leave visiting the sick,' he said to Lily, grinning at her in mock complaint.

'Better luck next time,' she said without very much sympathy. 'At least you get leave. My poor Arthur's still stuck in that awful Africa.'

Two days later a local tragedy made him ashamed to have been complaining. It was a shock to everyone in South London, an awful reminder that the war was still being fought on their own doorsteps and certainly wasn't over, not by a long way.

At lunch time on 20 January, when the barrage balloons were down for repair, a lone Focke Wulf roared up Sangley Road in Catford with nothing to prevent it, machine gunning the people below it.

Fourteen people were injured and six killed, including a young mother and her eleven-week-old son. Then as if that weren't bad enough, the plane circled and flew on a bombing run over Sandhurst Road. The pilot had one 1,000 pound bomb and he dropped it on the local school.

It was a direct hit, straight through the side of the building into the dining hall on the ground floor, where the children were gathered for their midday meal. It was fused to explode in just under one minute so as to give the pilot time to get clear, and that short pause was enough to allow about thirty children to scramble through the ground floor windows and run for their lives across the playground. But the kids in the hall had no escape.

Six teachers and thirty-eight children were killed and more than sixty others were seriously injured. The grief and carnage at the site were so terrible that for once reporting restrictions were lifted so that everybody could know the full extent of the tragedy.

'This wicked, wicked war,' John Cooper said when he read the news.

And Peggy cried at the thought of all those young lives gone. 'Oh Jim,' she wept. 'How many more kids have got to be killed? How much longer is this going on?'

But at least, as he told her through her tears, there was hope now that the terrible business could be ended. 'We are getting there. Believe me.'

'But so slowly,' she said.

At the beginning of February the German Sixth Army surrendered to the defenders of Stalingrad and the long dreadful siege was over. In March Rommel left Africa in disgrace, with the Allied armies there completely victorious. Despite bombs and grief and unnecessary deaths there *was* light at the end of this war-black tunnel. The residents of Paradise Row had a ding-dong to celebrate.

And as always Winston Churchill put the general optimistic feeling into memorable words.

'This is not the end,' he said. 'It is not even the beginning of the end. But it is, perhaps, the end of the beginning.'

Now there was a scent of victory in the air. Everyone was looking forward to the day when the Allied armies would invade Europe and begin to drive the Germans out of all the countries they'd occupied and back behind their own frontiers again. The newspapers were constantly talking about it. 'Second Front' they shouted. 'Stalin urges Second Front now.' 'Preparations for Second Front steam ahead.' 'Is this the year of the Second Front?'

And it certainly looked as though it would be for London was full of troops, gathering for the invasion, British, American, Canadian, Australian, Free French, Poles. Mr Allnutt said it was a regular League of Nations.

The civilian population of London went on enduring things in their usual dogged way. There were very few of them now whose homes hadn't been damaged to a greater or lesser degree and rations were shorter than ever but at least the raids were over and it was possible to get a good night's sleep. In six Paradise Row the kids still slept in the Morrison shelter every night because they said they liked it, and Mrs Geary stayed in the front parlour because she said the stairs were beyond her, but except when Jim was home on leave, Joan and Peggy and Baby slept upstairs, all in the same room, like old times. The RAF and the American Army Air Force had virtual command of the air now and German planes were rarely seen, except for the occasional loner attempting a reconnaissance flight. So there was very little danger. It was just a matter of waiting.

In June Jim's squadron returned to Sussex, and the four friends spent a long leave together in Vine Cottage being entertained by little Winnie who was a year old and crawling into everything. Froggy had been posted to a new station over in the east of the county, but he'd bought himself a little Morris so that he could get home as often as possible.

'It's ever so busy here,' Megan said to Peggy. 'They're changing everything ready for the war in Europe. Jim says they won't start until they're good and ready. But I hope it's soon. Everyone is so keyed up about it.'

It started on 10 July with a sea-borne landing, not in Normandy as Joan and Peggy were secretly hoping, but in Sicily, and once again Arthur was part of the invading army.

Now there was another campaign to follow and another reason for Lily to worry. Yvonne and Norman pinned a large map of Italy on the kitchen wall and plotted the progress of the Allied army day by day. And young Percy came in sometimes to see what they'd done, because his Daddy was one of the soldiers at the front.

'Do you think he'll bring me back a bit of a tank when he comes home?' he asked Yvonne.

'I 'spect so,' Yvonne said. 'Write an' tell him you want a bit.'

'I don't think I could write all that much,' Percy said. 'How do you write "tank"? Is it like "cat"?'

'No,' Norman said. 'It's got an A in it though.'

That wasn't much comfort to the anxious scribe.

'Draw him an aeroplane,' Yvonne suggested, 'an' I'll write what you want underneath. I'll show you how to do a Flying Fortress.' The big American bombers had just arrived and she was most impressed by them.

'Never mind flying fortresses,' Joan said, 'it's time for your tea.'

'Aunty Peggy's not back yet,' Norman pointed out in his solemn way. 'We can't start our tea without Aunty Peggy.'

They couldn't go to bed without Aunty Peggy either.

'Where's she gone?' Yvonne asked.

'She's gone out with Uncle Jim,' Joan explained.

'They've gone dancing. You'll see her in the morning.'

'We'd better,' Norman growled. 'She's to come straight in here. You tell her.'

'Lie down and go to sleep and then I will,' Joan promised. 'You got your torches and yer whistle, aintcher?'

'Course,' Yvonne said, settling onto her pillow.

Neither of then noticed that Baby was out of the house too. But then Baby didn't kiss them goodnight and read them stories. And Baby had left the house very early that evening while they were having their tea, because she was going to the Lyceum in the Strand.

CHAPTER 37

Of all the dance halls in London, the Lyceum was decidedly Baby's favourite. She went there as often as she
could afford it and particularly on a Saturday night, when
it was packed with GIs and very loud and lively. The
bands were American too, big bands like Glen Miller's, in
smart uniforms, with brass players who all stood up to
blaze away and drummers who threw themselves about in
the most exciting way with sweat flicking off their foreheads like rain and with their hands moving so fast you
could only see a blur. And as if that wasn't exciting enough
the GIs were such smashing dancers, especially when
they did the jitterbug, jumping and stamping and twirling
you with one hand, round and round, or lifting you bodily,
legs flying, to swing you over their hips or toss you from
one hip to the other. It was the most exhilarating thing
she'd ever experienced.

The Lyceum was such a civilized place. It had been
built as a theatre before they turned it into a dance hall.
So at the end of the dance floor there was a slope where
the orchestra pit had been and there was still a stage
where the band played and a circle and boxes where you
could sit and look down on the dancers instead of standing
by the wall where everybody could see when you hadn't
got a partner. Not that Baby often found herself in that
position, for she was a good dancer with a marked sense of
rhythm, light on her feet and quite prepared to be reck-

less, renowned as one of the Brits who knew how to 'cut a rug'.

But sometimes a peculiar sadness would catch her out just when she was enjoying herself most and she would stand by the side of the dance floor lost in thoughts she couldn't control, remembering Mum and how happy she'd been as a kid, envying the courting couples smooching on the dance floor, wishing she could be loved by someone too, anyone would do.

That night she drifted into sad thoughts almost as soon as she arrived beside the dance floor. The lights were lowered and they were playing 'We'll meet again' and everybody was singing the words which were horribly sad when you knew you wouldn't meet again. And a voice spoke at her shoulder.

'Would you care to dance with a guy with two left feet?'

'What?' she said, turning.

He was a very ordinary-looking American with one of those bland faces they had, all round and snub nosed, and he was wearing a pair of their peculiar specs which didn't do much for him, but he repeated his request with such a funny earnest expression on his face that she said 'Yes' and allowed him to lead her onto the floor.

He couldn't dance for toffee nuts and she told him so when the music stopped playing.

It didn't upset him or put him off in the least. 'Gee!' he said. 'If that ain't the cutest thing! Can't dance for toffee nuts.'

'Well no more you can,' she said.

And that made him laugh too. 'Would you like a drink?' he offered. 'Or some candy? For a peace offering.'

'Yes,' she said. 'I'm starving hungry.'

'We'll get a pass out,' he said, 'and I'll feed you.'

So they got two tickets to let them in and out of the dance hall and he took her off to Doughnut Dugout and fed her.

Despite his two left feet and his unpromising appearance he was good company and she stayed with him most of the evening. His name was Gary Svenson, Sergeant Gary Svenson, and he came from Wisconsin.

'So what you doing over here?' she asked, because GIs

always liked to tell you what they were doing.

He was with the US Amphibious Unit in Deptford.

'Fancy that,' she said. 'I live in Greenwich.'

His eyes lit up at that so she decided to change the subject. 'And what's an Amphibian Unit when it's at home? I thought amphibians was frogs.'

'Landing craft,' he explained. 'For beach landings. Let's dance.'

'Yes,' she said. 'Let's cut a rug.'

They cut several rugs that evening and at the end of the dance she allowed him to escort her home, and was delighted because he was such a gentleman. He took her right to her door and didn't even try to kiss her. Imagine that. All he said was 'Same time next week?' So she agreed.

From then on they went dancing every week. And after four or five weeks he asked her to the 'movies' and they sat in the back row and he didn't even try his luck then. She was most impressed and liked him more than ever. If it was a courtship it was an amazingly delicate one, and made a nice change from all those other Yanks she'd had to fight off in dark alleys.

One night at the end of June he surprised her by suddenly asking a question she wasn't expecting.

'You go off into a dream sometimes, honey,' he said. 'Where do you go?'

'I don't,' she said.

But he persisted in that funny quiet way of his. 'Sure you do,' he said. 'We all do. You were off in a dream when I first saw you. Standing in the dance hall.'

She remembered as he spoke. 'Oh yes. I was.'

'So what was the dream?'

'I was thinking about my mum,' she said. 'She was killed in an air raid. That's what I was thinking about.' And it's something you'll never understand, she was thinking quite crossly. You ain't been bombed. But his next words were an even bigger surprise.

'I reckoned that was what it was,' he said. 'You had the feeling about you, honey. A sort of aura.'

It was as if he knew what she'd been feeling that night and her face was full of inquiry as she turned to look at him.

469

'I lost my best buddy in Africa,' he answered her. 'Blown up. Right in front of me. I know precisely what you were feeling.'

'Oh Gary!' She kissed his cheek, instinctively and gently, like Mum used to do to her when she was little and sad.

As he moved his head equally gently and met her lips in a kiss full on the mouth, a lover's kiss, tender and unalarming, but a lover's kiss for all that.

'Oh honey!' he said. 'You're my girl. I knew you would be from that first moment.'

I suppose we're courting, she thought, as he kissed her again. And it pleased her that she didn't mind and that she felt safe with him.

In fact as the days passed and they continued to go out with each other and there was no alarm and no unpleasantness, it pleased her more and more to think that there was a man in her life now, especially when Joan was writing one of her interminable letters to Sid or when Jim came home on a thirty-six and Peggy spent every minute of it with him.

The kids were still absorbed with the war in Italy. During July they stuck little flags all round the coast of Sicily to mark the progress of the British and American troops, and in the middle of August, when the island surrendered, they painted it red from one end to the other and stuck a Union Jack in the middle of it. Percy's father sent letters home nearly every week, so as it was the holidays he came in every day either to show them a letter or to see what they were doing.

It annoyed them that things got even more exciting once they were back at school in September, because they had to wait until the end of the day to adorn their map. But Aunty Peggy suggested that they should pin bits of newspaper up beside it with the latest headlines, and offered to collect good ones for them, and that restored their good humour.

Soon the entire wall was hung with information. 'Palermo falls', 'Mussolini resigns', 'Badoglio Prime Minister'. Uncle Jim said it looked like an Ops Room when he came home on one of his long leaves in the middle of the month.

And what was lovely about it was that the news was always good. 'Invasion of Italy' the headlines said on 4 September, and five days later, 'Italy surrenders – official'.

'One down and two to go,' Mrs Geary said cheerfully as they pinned the paper to the wall.

But it wasn't quite as easy as that.

The next headlines were all about the Germans moving into northern Italy and taking Rome, and as the weather got colder the campaign was bogged down in mud and mountains, and days went by without any news of a victory.

'Why ain't we advancing no more?' Yvonne asked her mother.

'Don't ask me,' Joan said. 'I'm not a general.'

Aunty Baby said she didn't know either, but that was no surprise to either of them because Aunty Baby never knew anything and anyway she was always out with that funny-looking American of hers.

'We'll ask Aunty Peggy,' Norman decided, when November began and the armies still didn't seem to be getting anywhere.

But for once Aunty Peggy's answer was no help to them. 'Poor devils,' she said. 'Wars are awful. I shall be jolly glad when this one's over.'

'There ain't any victories no more,' Yvonne said.

'No,' Peggy agreed. 'They have to fight ever such a long time for a victory. You just think of them fighting out there in the rain, and all them Russians at Kiev all this time, and the Americans fighting the Japanese. It's going on all over the world. There's never any end to it.'

She looked so woebegone and worried that Yvonne took action at once to cheer her up. 'Go and put the kettle on,' she said to her brother. 'Aunty Peggy wants a cup a' tea.'

And a very good cup it was. But it couldn't soothe Peggy's worries although, naturally, she pretended it had.

The trouble was that the ARP News, the paper that brought all the latest information to ARP personnel, had just reported something so alarming that she didn't want to believe it. The Germans, they said, were threatening reprisals against Great Britain by means of a secret

471

weapon more deadly and destructive than the most powerful high-explosive bomb. 'There is the possibility,' they warned, 'that we shall soon have to face a period not unlike that encountered in the heaviest blitzes. We would do well to prepare ourselves.'

Not long after this initial warning other snippets of news about a German secret weapon began to appear in the national newspapers. The *Daily Express* carried a report from Stockholm that hundreds of 'pilotless planes' were being built, and the *Daily Telegraph* spoke of 'evidence of a secret weapon, crewless, radio-controlled and loaded with explosives' and added that the building sites of these new robot planes were currently being bombed.

'What do you think?' Peggy asked Jim when he came home on one of his short leaves at the beginning of December.

'All very likely,' he said. 'But not to worry. We shall be invading in the spring, bound to be, and if they have got robot planes the launching sites will be one of the first places we shall liberate.'

'Well I hope so,' she said. 'We've had enough without robots.'

'Hang on till the spring,' he advised, carefully lowering his cap onto the hair he'd just been combing. 'Now are we going to the flicks or not?'

'Never trouble trouble,' she said, smiling at him. He was quite right. It might never happen.

Preparations for the invasion of France went ahead all through that winter. A new Allied Expeditionary Air Force was formed specifically for the invasion and the RAF 2nd Tactical Air Force took over the bulk of Fighter Command and became part of the new force. There was constant activity in the south of England as convoys of army vehicles all brightly marked with the circle and star of the new Liberation Army, clogged the roads. And military manoeuvres took place on every acre of open heathland.

Froggy's squadron was equipped with Typhoons whose job was to be shooting up enemy vehicles and tanks and Jim's was sent on sweeps of the Channel. And in December Bomber Command, urged to it by Air Marshall 'Bomber' Harris, began a series of raids on Berlin.

Nonnie Brown and Cyril were delighted and spent most of the Christmas ding-dong lauding Bomber Harris to the skies. But Peggy felt they were making a mistake.

'If we bomb their capital city and they really have got a secret weapon,' she said to Joan, 'don't you think they'll be more likely to use it?'

'I hope to God they don't,' Joan said. 'There's no way a' knowing though is there?'

'Not till they drop the things,' Mrs Geary said cheerfully. 'Is anyone going out for more stout?'

But although no one in Paradise Row knew it at the time, the secret weapons weren't ready, so it wasn't a robot plane that attacked London at the end of that January. Retaliation was by more conventional means. On the night of 22 January the sirens went at eleven o'clock and the bombers stayed overhead until five in the morning. On 29 January, they returned again, this time when Peggy was on duty. And then during the first two weeks of February London was raided every night. It was, as people were soon saying, a regular 'little blitz', and although it wasn't as devastating as the blitz itself had been, because the raids were shorter and the bombers fewer in number, it came as a nasty shock just the same because the Germans were using a new type of bomb. It was called a firepot and consisted of a canister containing over two hundred incendiary bombs that were released a layer at a time during its fall, so as to produce a cascade of bombs that would cover a very wide area.

For the first week Peggy was on night duty and so she saw the descending shower of fire bombs at uncomfortably close quarters. It took as many stirrup pumps as they could muster to deal with so many potential fires in the two minutes it took them all to land and explode and their descent was noisy and very frightening.

But at least there were more searchlights now, panning across the sky with their huge white beams, and the anti-aircraft units put up such a barrage that the sky was full of colour like a firework display, with flares hanging in lurid clusters and tracer shells scrawling high red parabolas across the darkness. And for all their fury the raids were soon over.

At six Paradise Row the children slept in the shelter, the windows were boarded up as soon as the sirens went, and Joan and Baby and Peggy brought their mattresses downstairs again.

'Just like old times, eh?' Joan said as she made cocoa for the three of them, standing in the kitchen with one ear cocked for the squeal of a falling bomb.

'Damn Germans,' Baby said. She was sitting on her mattress putting her hair in curlers. Her face was greased with night cream and she was concentrating furiously, scowling so hard that little gobbets of cream were squeezed between her eyebrows.

'Oh my giddy aunt, look at you,' Joan said, coming back into the room with three mugs on a tray. 'If your Yank could see you now.'

'Well he can't,' Baby said, taking a mug. 'Ta.'

'Just as well,' Joan said. 'What's on the wireless, Peg?'

Peggy was consulting the *Radio Times*. A broadcast was a good idea. It would take their minds off the raid. She was still on stand-by and quite likely to be called out again so she couldn't go to bed for several hours yet.

'No don't let's,' Baby said.

'Why not?' Joan asked her, putting out her hand for the magazine.

'Well ...' Baby said, looking at them thoughtfully. 'The thing is ... The thing is I've got something to tell you. Well not exactly tell you, I mean. The thing is ...'

'Spit it out,' Joan said. 'It's that Yank, ain't it?'

'Well yes,' Baby admitted. 'He's asked me to marry him.'

'Good God!' Joan said.

'Well you needn't sound so surprised,' Baby objected, pouting. 'I ain't that bad a catch. He says I'm beautiful. The cutest girl he's ever seen, he says.'

'He ain't seen you in curlers,' Joan pointed out.

They'll fight in a minute, Peggy thought, and she intervened at once to prevent it. 'Do you want to marry him?' she asked.

'Yes,' Baby said. 'I do. It's about time I was married. Everybody else is.'

'Everybody else ain't,' Peggy said, rather tetchily,

474

because she was tired and it was such a silly reason to get married.

'Well you and Joan are,' Baby said, unabashed. 'So why not me?'

'You don't love him though, do you?' Joan said.

'I don't know,' Baby said, carelessly. 'I like him. He's not like all the others, always grabbing at you and trying to touch you where they shouldn't and getting all hot and sticky and everything. Anyway I think all this love business is overrated. How do people know when they're in love? Tell me that. I think they're making it all up half the time.'

'You know when you love someone,' Peggy said, 'because you put them first without thinking about it. You ought to know that, Baby. It's what Dad done with us.'

'Quite right,' Joan said. 'That's what I do with my kids. It's just what I do.' How wise Peggy was sometimes. 'I must've been following Dad without knowing it.'

'You wouldn't get very far going on like that these days,' Baby said, rolling up her next lock of hair. 'Not with men anyway.'

'Like what?' Peggy said.

'Not thinking. Doing things without thinking.'

'You don't have to think,' Joan explained. 'You just act natural. It's an instinct.'

'I always think about things first,' Baby said. 'Always. I couldn't just do things without thinking about it first. *That* wouldn't be natural to me. Besides, what if I was to end up pregnant?'

'You'll end up pregnant if you get married,' Joan reminded her. 'Most of us do.'

'It's all right if you're married though, ain't it?' Baby said, bitingly. 'It's when you ain't there's trouble. And that's what comes a' doing things without thinking. Asking for trouble.'

'Don't you dare start on about that,' Joan said. 'I've had enough to put up with on that score without you starting.'

'Let bygones,' Peggy intervened quickly. 'Are you going to marry this Gary of yours?'

'What do you think, our Peggy?' Baby asked. 'Should I?'

For the first time in her life Peggy gave advice that wasn't entirely unselfish. 'Yes,' she said. 'I think you should, all things considered. I think he'd make a very good husband for you.' And inside her head she was happily planning. With Baby off my hands I could leave Joan and the kids more often and go off and stay with Jim. I might even run to a hotel somewhere. That would be a real treat. 'When does he want it to be?'

'Well we ain't fixed a date,' Baby admitted. 'We was just talking about it.'

'I'd fix a date pretty quick if I was you,' Joan advised. 'There's ever so many weddings these days. If you don't get organized you won't find a church to take you.'

'Oh there's no rush,' Baby said lightly. 'We'll think about it come the spring I expect. Anyway we couldn't have a wedding with all this bombing going on, could we?'

The all-clear began to growl up into the reassurance of its long steady note.

'Well it's not going on now, thank heavens,' Peggy said. 'I'm for some shut-eye. You can tell us what you decide when you've decided.'

The little blitz was over by the middle of February. And at the end of the month when Jim came home on a thirty-six hour pass before being posted to Tangmere, Baby and Gary appeared at number six late one Saturday evening, hand in hand like children, to announce that they were going to get married in May.

'We've been to church,' Baby said. 'An' we've seen the vicar. It's the first Saturday in May.' She was glowing with excitement, clinging to Gary's blunt hand. 'Just the family. And everyone at Dodds of course.' It would do them good to see her triumph. 'You'll come won't you, Jim?'

'If I can get leave,' Jim said. 'There's quite a lot going on these days you know.'

Gary gave him a conspiratorial smile. 'You can say that again, Bud,' he said.

'He's going on manoeuvres in April,' Baby explained. 'That's why we've chosen May.'

'It's non-stop manoeuvres nowadays,' Joan said. 'It'll be this year, won't it?'

476

'Looks like it,' Jim said laconically. 'This calls for a celebration. Let's have a ding-dong.'

'What, now?' Baby said, her eyes round with delight.

'Now.'

'But it's ever so late.'

'No it's not,' he said. 'It's just the right time.' Just the right time, he thought looking at his patient Peggy. It would do her good not to be looking after Baby all the time.

His posting to Tangmere was very short-lived. In March, while Peggy and Joan were sending out invitations to the wedding, he was sent to Friston, and wrote home to Peggy to tell her that the squadron now had new Spitfire X11's with the most magnificent Rolls-Royce Griffon engines, and that he couldn't wait for his next long leave. In April he was posted to Devon, and by then it was plain that the invasion was imminent.

'I shan't be back for the wedding after all,' he wrote to Peggy. 'But I dare say Baby will be able to get spliced without my presence. I hope it all goes well. Write and tell me about it when it's over and done.'

CHAPTER 38

Even though she went on telling everyone she was only going to have a quiet wedding, Baby invited all her workmates to attend and all her neighbours in Paradise Row, even Nonnie Brown and that awful Cyril, which Joan said was downright unnecessary. Then she went off on a shopping spree and spent all her remaining clothing coupons on a length of expensive white satin for a 'proper' wedding dress and commissioned Mrs Roderick to make it for her.

There was hardly a moment when she wasn't busily planning something or other, buttonholes and bouquets from Ernest and Leslie, how to eke out the extra rations for the wedding breakfast, what Uncle Gideon would be wearing, because he had to look his best when he was giving her away, a bridesmaid's dress for Yvonne and special flowers for her hair, a pageboy's outfit for Norman which the little boy resolutely refused to try on, declaring it made him look 'a proper sissy', even what tunes she wanted Mr Cooper to play at the wedding ding-dong.

'It's a wonder she ain't got a ribbon for the parrot,' Mrs Geary said.

'I'd keep quiet about it if I was you,' Mr Allnutt advised. 'You might give her ideas.'

'The only thing she ain't ordered up is the weather,' Joan said. 'And she'd do that if she could.'

'Well I hope it keeps fine for her,' Mr Allnutt said. 'It is her day when all's said and done.'

Gary sent her a letter every day, saying how much he was looking forward to their wedding and how much he loved her, and she wrote back to him saying the same things almost word for word, because she wasn't very good at writing letters. And April passed from showers to storms.

'Oh look at that rain,' she complained, as a torrent lashed against the windows. 'It'ud better not rain on my wedding day, that's all.'

'Write and tell the Met Office,' Joan advised. But Baby was already on her way out of the kitchen to pick up the mail.

Towards the end of April Gary wrote to say that his manoeuvres were due to start 'tomorrow or soon after' and that he wouldn't be able to write for a day or two but that he and his best man would see her at St Alphege's Church at eleven hundred hours on 6 May. 'Don't be late,' he urged, 'or I shall be nervous.'

She took his instructions most seriously and wrote out a schedule of events for the wedding day. 'Rise at 7.30 a.m. Breakfast 8.00 a.m. Pageboy and bridesmaid dressed by 10.00 a.m.'

'She'll be lucky,' Norman snorted when he saw his instructions. 'If she thinks I'm sitting about in that outfit all day she's got another think coming.'

'You'll do as you're told, and stop arguing,' Joan said.

But he contrived to be out of the house running errands for Mrs Geary until nearly a quarter past ten on the wedding morning, while the bride was alternately dressing and yelling for him down the well of the stairs.

'I'll swing for him if he ain't back directly,' she shrieked.

'Here's yer uncle come,' Mrs Geary said from her seat beside the mirror. 'My eye, you do look a swell, Mr Potter,' as Gideon, who was wearing his old brown suit and a new pork pie hat that didn't quite fit him, preened into the house.

After his arrival events began to go as planned. Yvonne was sent to tease Norman out of the corner shop and bring him back to be coaxed into the hated suit, and at five minutes to eleven precisely the bride made her appearance in the doorway resplendent in her white satin with a

479

bouquet of cream roses held to her bosom.

The bridal procession was very grand and noisy, as well it might be when the entire street was taking part. They marched down the middle of the road in a self-conscious, chattering parade, past the Earl Grey and up the passageway to the church. And in the south entrance they were met by the verger, who was lurking rather anxiously to tell them that the groom hadn't arrived.

Baby was put out but decided to be gracious. 'The guests can go in,' she said, 'and we'll take a turn round the church.' Let people see what a lovely bride she was. There was no harm in that.

So she and Uncle Gideon and her pretty bridesmaid and her scowling page walked all round the church, along Straightsmouth Street and up the alley and back through the High Street collecting admiring stares all the way. But the groom still hadn't arrived.

'One more turn,' Baby said. 'He'll have come by then.'

So they took another turn, this time walking at a snail's pace and causing quite a bit of comment, especially among the shoppers who'd witnessed their first appearance. But there was still no groom.

'Perhaps you would care to wait in the vestry,' the verger suggested. 'These things do happen. Wartime, you know.'

So they waited in the vestry. And waited. And waited.

By now it was a quarter to twelve and the congregation was audibly restive.

'Where's he got to?' Baby said. The skirt of her lovely dress was all creased at the back where she'd sat down and her patience was beginning to crease too. 'All that carry-on about me not keeping him waiting and now this.' She looked very disagreeable. 'Stand still Norman, you're scuffing all your shoes.'

'I've only got two,' Norman pointed out, with the devastating logic of the ten-year-old.

But she wasn't amused.

Finally when the clocks had all struck midday, the curate appeared to say that he was most frightfully sorry but the next wedding party had arrived and as they were due in the church at twelve o'clock he really would have to

480

ask her to make way for them.

'But I ain't been married,' she protested, flushed with anger and humiliation.

'Yes, yes, I know,' he said sadly. 'But we can hardly marry you without a groom, can we?'

'I shall stay here,' she said. 'I shall stay here until he arrives.'

'You may stay if you wish, of course,' he said, 'but your party have already gone back to your house.'

The walk back home was the longest and most humiliating return of her life. She kept her head up and her eyes straight in front of her gazing at nothing, but her cheeks were scarlet and she was panting with distress, and when she got back to the house and had to step inside where all her guests were waiting for her, fury and shame rose in her like a hot tide. She was trapped, marked, rejected. How could this be happening to her? There was nowhere to go, nowhere to hide and they were all looking at her, laughing at her, mocking her. She put back her head and began to scream. And once unleashed the scream went on and on, higher and higher, while her guests fell back before her, shocked and deafened.

'Just like her mother,' Mrs Geary said to the astonished assembly, as Joan and Peggy leapt towards her and half-led half-dragged her through the throng and upstairs into the relative privacy of her bedroom.

'Don't,' Peggy begged. 'Oh don't, Baby please. You'll make yourself ill.'

But her sister threw herself across the bed and went on screaming.

'Leave her be,' Joan advised in a whisper. 'I reckon she'll get over it better if she's on her own. It can't be much fun to be seen in a state like that, poor thing. Let's go down and explain to the others.'

'How can we explain?' Peggy said. 'What are we gonna say?'

'Say he's been delayed,' Joan advised. 'Train not running or something.'

But the guests were already listening to another explanation, which the sisters heard as they went down the stairs.

481

'Jilted,' Nonnie Brown was saying with great satisfaction. ''S the same the whole world over. Can't face it when it comes to it, none of them, and off they goes. Men! Wouldn't give you tuppence for 'em. Leave you in the lurch soon as look at yer. 'S always the same. Cyril was the same. Weren't yer, mate?'

Cyril looked very surprised at this and so did his neighbours.

'We might as well eat the food,' Peggy said, bringing in a plate of sandwiches from the kitchen. 'It'll only go to waste else, even if he turns up tomorrow.'

'Quite right,' Gideon said, stepping in to help her. 'Long past my dinner-time. Whatcher got? I'll have a bloater paste.'

So they fed their guests and poured them beer and lemonade shandies and brown ale for Gideon and a nice port and lemon for Mrs Roderick, and the first embarrassment was eased away. Mr Allnutt said what a shame it all was, and Mrs Allnutt told them she was sure there was an explanation for it. 'Something to do with the war,' she said. 'Bound to be. Trains not running or broken down or something. He'll turn up tomorrow like Peggy says, you'll see. Poor boy. It ain't just Baby. It's as bad for him really.'

And although they didn't all believe in her excuses, most of the guests agreed with her if only for politeness' sake. At one o'clock the party from Dodds took their leave, saying how sorry they were and how much they hoped it would all turn out for the best, and once they'd gone the neighbours left *en masse*, shuffling out in renewed embarrassment, not knowing what to say. Gideon and Ethel were the last to leave, urging Joan to keep them posted.

'Anything we can do, you know where we are,' he said.

'Thanks,' Peggy said. But what could any of them do? They'd have to wait for the explanation, the same as Baby.

Joan began to gather up the dirty glasses. Now that the guests were gone they could hear Baby sobbing in the room above their heads.

'What are we going to do with her?' Peggy wondered, glancing up at the ceiling.

'Leave her be,' Mrs Geary said. 'She'll get over it. She'll

probably get a letter tomorrow explaining it all.'

But Joan wasn't sure. 'It makes me think of Mum and the way she went on that time,' she said.

'If she ain't better by tomorrow,' Peggy decided, 'we'll get the doctor to her.'

'The letter'll do the trick,' Mrs Geary said.

But no letter came and Baby was still weeping two days later. By then Joan insisted that a doctor was necessary.

She came late that afternoon, a brisk young woman with a weary smile and no time to spare. She took Baby's temperature, which was normal, and her pulse which was normal, and looked down her throat, which she pronounced 'normal for a woman who's been crying too much'.

'There's nothing much the matter with you except hurt pride,' she said. 'You should get up and get on with your life. That's my advice.'

'Shouldn't she have some medicine?' Peggy asked as the doctor began to walk downstairs.

'No,' the doctor said without looking back. 'If she starts screaming again, slap her. And now if you'll pardon me I've got some real patients to attend to.'

'What a perfectly beastly doctor!' Baby wailed. 'Can't she see my heart's been broke? Oh how could he do this to me? That's what I can't understand. If he was here I'd give him such a piece of my mind. And he hasn't even written to me. He might have written. Oh, if I knew where he was ...'

But Sergeant Gary Svenson was beyond her reach and her anger. Operation Tiger, the manoeuvre he'd told her about, had gone very badly wrong. Thirty miles out to sea, at half past one in the morning, the American landing craft and their two escorting destroyers had met up with a flotilla of German E-boats, which they hadn't expected and weren't prepared for. In the ensuing battle hundreds of Americans were killed. At the very moment when Baby was walking so unhappily back from the church, Gary Svenson's bullet-ridden body was being washed ashore. It was found at a place called Slapton Sands and, like all the other casualties of the incident, it was never reported. With the invasion so close too many other lives were at risk to let such a devastating secret out to the press.

But what was good for national morale was devastating to Baby. Despite the doctor's diagnosis she continued to suffer. She stayed in her room for the next ten days, with the blinds drawn and only the wireless for company, her hair uncombed and her face puffy with tears and pallid for lack of make-up. Mrs Geary said she had too good an appetite to be really ill, because she ate everything that Peggy brought up to her, but her woebegone appearance roused her sister's tender compassion.

'I feel so sorry for her,' she said, 'being jilted. And I'm sure she was jilted otherwise he'd have written. That doctor was heartless. I think she's ill with her nerves. Like Mum.'

But on the second Friday morning Baby had a visitor who improved her health quite dramatically. It was Mr Dodds, no less, and Mr Dodds had a question for his employee.

'We need to know how we stand,' he said, when he'd waited for Baby to make herself presentable and had been ushered into the sick room, '*vis-à-vis* your reserved occupation. If you're not well enough to return to work on Monday we may have to make some other arrangements. For Miss Doris perhaps.'

Baby made up her mind at once. 'I'm ever so much better, Mr Dodds,' she said. 'It was a shock you see, but I'm ever so much better. In fact I was thinking of coming in tomorrow, knowing what a rush Saturday is, only my sisters said I shouldn't.'

'Monday would be soon enough,' Mr Dodds said. 'It's just we had to know, you understand.'

'Of course,' Baby said giving him her sweetest smile. 'It's ever so good of you to come round.'

She went back to work the next morning, looking pale and withdrawn and wearing her oldest cardigan to ensure that people would feel sorry for her.

From then on she went to work as usual every day, but at home she took to her bed as soon as she'd eaten her supper, declaring that her nerves were 'in shreds', and she didn't emerge from her room until after she'd been served breakfast there in the morning. At the weekend she stayed in bed from Saturday evening till Monday morning, listening to her wireless and playing patience, with her hair in curlers and her face covered in cold cream and a bottle of Sanatogen ostentatiously at her elbow.

'And how long's this going on?' Joan said to Peggy crossly, when a month had passed and she was still playing the invalid.

'Don't you be cross an' all,' Peggy begged. 'It's hard enough dealing with her.'

'Have you told Jim what she's doing?'

'No,' Peggy admitted. She didn't like to, because she had a feeling he'd been rather less than sympathetic. Everyone was being so horrid about poor Baby. She couldn't help having nerves.

'Well you should,' Joan said.

'Give her time,' Peggy said.

'I know what I'd give her,' Joan said trenchantly. 'That doctor was right if you ask me.'

CHAPTER 39

It was one o'clock on Tuesday 6 June 1944, and like
everyone else in Britain, Peggy and Joan and Mrs Geary
were listening to the wireless. John Snagge was reading the
news with his usual splendid calm, and on that afternoon
his calm was even more admirable than usual for this
bulletin was the one they'd all been waiting years to hear.
'Under the command of General Eisenhower,' he said,
'Allied naval forces supported by strong air forces began
landing Allied armies this morning on the northern coast of
France.'

'It's started,' Joan said. 'Thank God for that. It's
started at last.'

'An' about time too,' Mrs Geary said.

But Peggy was thinking of all the men who must have
died during the morning while she'd been shopping and
doing the washing and on call, not aware of what was
happening. She could see them falling, hear their groans
and cries, imagine their injuries. 'Poor devils,' she said.
And she thought of Froggy who'd be going over as soon as
there was a landing strip, and of Jim, who'd be going too
with the Second Tactical Air Force. 'Poor devils.'

She wasn't supposed to know about any of these things,
of course. There were posters everywhere warning of the
danger of careless talk, and letters had been rigorously
censored for months. Even Irish workmen had their mail
opened, according to Mr Cooper, because there were
plenty of Germans in the South of Ireland primed to listen

to gossip. And during the last few months there'd been plenty to gossip about for it was plain to everybody that preparations for the invasion were reaching a climax.

The last time she'd been down to Vine Cottage Peggy had been impressed by the long queues of tanks and armoured vehicles that she'd seen standing nose to tail in every country lane, bulky under their camouflage netting, massively waiting. She was used to the sight and sound of squadrons of American Flying Fortresses passing overhead on their way to bomb the Germans but in recent weeks they'd been roaring past every hour of the day and night and the roads had been choked with military convoys going to and fro in every direction in the most confusing way but with every vehicle clearly marked by the new bold sign of the Combined Armies of Liberation, a simple white star inside a white ring. There was such tension everywhere, such bristling non-stop activity. She and Joan had told one another only yesterday that they couldn't see how any of it could be kept secret no matter how hard anyone tried.

But now D-Day had arrived and they learned with surprise that the greatest secret of all had been kept from almost everybody, and that was the location of the landings. By skilful misinformation the Germans had been persuaded to expect this invasion in the Pas de Calais, and had sent the bulk of their panzer divisions there in readiness. And now the Combined Armies of Liberation were in France at last, on the beaches of Normandy, where they were least expected. And the final battle had begun.

'Good luck to 'em,' Joan said. 'It all depends on them now.'

That evening the newspapers trumpeted the good news. 'Landings Succeed.' 'Beachheads wider and deeper.' 'Nazi defences gunned into silence.'

But among the reports from the front Peggy noticed one small paragraph warning about the likelihood of reprisal raids on London and hinting that Hitler had a secret weapon that he might use at any time. And being Peggy she remembered all the rumours about robot bombs and took it seriously.

'We're not out of the wood yet,' she said to Mr MacFarlane that evening, 'are we?'

'No lassie,' he agreed. 'Not by a long chalk.'

Froggy Ferguson was sent to France five days after the invasion. They'd been on stand-by since D-Day plus two and it was all such a rush he only just had time for a quick dash to Merston to say goodbye to Megan and little Winnie, who was out in the garden happily making mud-pies when he arrived.

'Look after yourself,' he said, being brisk about it because it would have been a poor show to break down or weep or anything.

'You've got to come back, Froggy,' Megan said, blinking back her tears. 'I'm not sure 'cos I've only missed a month, but that's not like me, you know, so I think I'm expecting again.'

Emotion caught him by the throat despite himself. Another child, just when he was going to France.

'Good show,' he said, gulping. 'You'll look after yourself, won't you. Take the orange juice. That sort of thing. And look after little Winnie.'

'Oh Froggy,' Megan said flinging her arms round his neck. 'Please don't get killed. I love you so much.'

'Me too,' he said holding her close, his face strained and pale. 'Promise me you'll look after yourself.' I can't bear to leave you. You mean everything to me.

'Yes, yes, yes. I promise.' Say you love me, Froggy. Say it. I couldn't bear you to go without saying you loved me.

'I'll be thinking of you,' he said. He was half-way into the driver's seat as if he was eager to be off. Which in a peculiar sort of way he was. The sooner they got stuck into this war and finished it for good and all, the better. And yet going meant leaving her. And leaving her meant he might never see her again.

'Oh God, Megan, I do love you so,' he said. And started the car.

The long battle continued as the invading armies struggled to get off the beachheads and capture the hinterland, and Froggy's Typhoons were in the thick of it from the moment they arrived. But it wasn't until 12 June that news broke that the American Airborne Division had captured a town. It was a place called Carenton, and its capture meant that the Allies were on their way to the port of Cherbourg. That night when Peggy and Mr MacFarlane came on duty Mr Goodall had all three evening papers ready for them to read all about it.

There was so much to talk about that at the end of their shift they were still discussing the progress of the campaign, standing outside the Post and watching the sky, not that they expected to see anything in it, but out of force of habit.

Mr MacFarlane was the first to hear the engine. 'Yon plane's in trouble,' he said.

'What is it?' Peggy said, for she didn't recognize the sound of the engine. 'Ours or theirs?'

It was making a very peculiar noise whatever it was. A terrible rattling and clattering.

'There it is,' Mr Goodall said. 'It's on fire.'

There was a burning plane heading towards them from the south-east. They could see red flames spurting out of it into the dark sky. But to their amazement it was flying straight. Straight and fast, about 400 mph according to Mr MacFarlane, and very low. Much too low for an enemy aircraft.

They watched as it rattled overhead and flew on towards the river. To Peggy's eyes there was something alien about it, something dark and sinister and unnerving.

'I don't think that's a plane at all,' she said. 'On fire and flying straight?'

And the engine suddenly cut out. There was a long pause and then a very loud explosion, much louder and longer than any ordinary high explosive bomb, more like the sound of an exploding bomber fully loaded.

Next day the newspapers reported that a German aircraft had been shot down in the East End. But the wardens were told the truth about it. They had seen the first of Hitler's vengeance weapons, the flying bomb he called V1.

'God help us all,' Mr MacFarlane said, when he'd read the bulletin. 'Have we no' had sufficient?'

But it appeared not. For three days there was no further

sign of the robot planes, but then the attack began in earnest, and they were launched against London one after the other.

They looked even more sinister by daylight than they had at night, flying at such speed with flames trailing behind them, black and quick and mindlessly cruel. And as everyone in London soon became aware, the damage they did was much much worse than that of an ordinary bomb. The explosion shattered windows a quarter of a mile away such was the force of the blast. People were blown into the air and hurled against walls and furniture. Some were stabbed by spears of flying glass or injured by the rubble that was flung in every direction, and those directly under the impact of the warhead were literally blown to pieces.

After attending her first horrific incident Peggy came home to tell Joan that she must send the kids out of harm's way the minute she could.

'Megan would have them, I'll bet,' she said. 'They'd be company for her and Winnie now Froggy's gone. Why don't we write to Megan?'

For once Joan didn't argue. She'd seen the immediate results of a robot bomb on her way home from work that afternoon, and one of the mangled corpses still lying in the road was a child no bigger than Norman.

So two days later the kids packed their bags and were evacuated to Merston. This time, once they'd been reassured that they weren't going back to that Mr Ray, and that their mother was coming with them all the way, and that she'd come down and visit them every Sunday, honour bright, they went happily enough. And Megan made them very welcome and settled them in with carrot cake and cocoa and showed them their two little camp-beds next to the cot upstairs and told them they could take it in turns to sleep in the double bed with her if they liked.

It was a great relief to Joan and Peggy to have them settled out of harm's way, because by then the flying bombs were coming over virtually all the time, sometimes with little more than a quarter of an hour between one and the next. The old air raid alarm system was very little use in such circumstances, and there wasn't much point in taking shelter, because, as Mrs Geary pointed out, 'if you did that you'd be in the shelter all day long and most of the night an' all'. So most Londoners went about their business as usual, except that they kept one ear cocked for the sound of that dreadful engine, and when it got too close they edged towards the nearest cover, ready to fling themselves to the ground or under a table or into a doorway the minute it cut out, for once that happened they only had twelve seconds to protect themselves. But it's exhausting to live on your nerves all the time, and after five years of war and a limited, monotonous diet, very few people had the reserves to cope with it. They did their best to reduce the terror of the bombs by giving them rude names and calling them buzz-bombs or doodle-bugs, but they were whistling in the dark and they knew it.

After a few weeks, Joan and Peggy were ragged with tension and fatigue. There'd been so many dreadful incidents. The United Glass works in Anchor and Hope Lane, the RAF balloon site at Riverway, Merryweather's in Greenwich High Road, where they made fire engines, Highbridge Wharf in Eastney Street, where a 250 ton floating dock was sunk. There was no end to the death and destruction and no matter how many terrible injuries Peggy saw she never got hardened to it. And in the dreadful seconds between the engine cut out and the explosion she was always afraid, convinced as she flung herself to the ground along with everyone else that the bomb was coming straight at *her*.

Only Baby seemed able to cope, and she did it by continuing to play the invalid. While she was at work she listened for the doodle-bugs and took cover when they fell the same as everybody else, but at home she refused to acknowledge their existence. She went straight up to bed the minute she'd had her supper and stayed there until it was time to go to work in the morning. She slept with earplugs in her ears and cold cream on her face and saw nothing wrong in allowing Peggy to wait on her hand and foot.

'My nerves were bad enough before all this,' she explained to her sisters. 'Now, well what with the wedding and now these buzz-bombs it's a wonder I can get to work. You don't know what I'm suffering.'

'I know what Peggy's suffering,' Joan said angrily to Mrs Geary. 'She ought to make the nasty little pest get up and do her share of the housework, instead of taking meals up to her the way she does.'

'No good us saying anything,' Mrs Geary said. 'Your Peg'll have to think that out for herself. She can be jolly stubborn when she likes.'

Actually Peggy's stubbornness was partly due to fatigue. She simply didn't have the energy to urge Baby into better behaviour, particularly as she knew that any argument was likely to lead to a bout of hysterical weeping. It was easier just to wait on her.

'She'll come round,' she said wearily, when Joan broached the subject. 'Don't let's talk about it now.'

But Joan was aggrieved and wanted to talk about it. And the more she couldn't mention it at home the more she discussed it elsewhere. She told Megan about it every Sunday, and at the end of July, when Jim came to Vine Cottage for half an hour to see how Froggy's two girls were getting on, she decided to tell him. He hadn't had any leave since the doodle-bugs began and he was eager for news.

'You know Baby's took to her bed since the wedding, dontcher?' she said. 'Has Peggy told you?'

'She's done what?' Jim said, his face strained with disbelief.

'Took to her bed,' Joan repeated. 'She's hardly ever out of it when she's at home. Says she's got nerves, if you ever heard the like. What's she got to have nerves about? She should try working in munitions with them damn things coming over all the time, or being a warden.'

'And what does Peggy say?'

'Well you know Peggy. She puts up with it. Breakfast in bed. Lying in till midday Sundays. You ask me she wants a good clip round her ear 'ole. She gets more like Mum by the day, painting her face, dyeing her hair, primping in the mirror. It makes me sick.'

The news had made Jim look serious. 'OK,' he said. 'So what d'you want me to do about it?'

But Joan didn't know what she wanted. She wasn't even sure whether she wanted anything at all. It was enough to have a willing ear to complain to. 'We've got enough on our plates,' she grumbled on, 'all of us, without her making herself an invalid.'

'I tell you what I think,' Megan said, wading into the conversation. She was sitting in the window keeping an eye on the three kids playing in the garden. 'I think you ought to rent a little flat somewhere, just for the two of you, an' take her right out of it and leave Baby to get on with it.'

The superb naivety of it made Jim's eyes start out of his head. For a brief second, looking round at her cottage, the cottage he'd wanted so much, he was tempted to tell her all about it, but then he controlled himself and tried to answer calmly. It would upset her terribly if she was to know all that.

'I been flat-hunting ever since we got married,' he said. 'If I could've taken her out of it I would've done. Long ago. There ain't a flat to be had. Nowhere. Not for love nor money. I've tried and tried.'

'Oh dear!' Megan said, aware that she'd put her foot in it and embarrassed by her clumsiness. 'I am sorry, Jim. I didn't know.'

He shrugged the subject away. 'How could you? Well anyway ... Just one of those things.' Then he turned to Joan who was still frowning at her tea cup. 'I'll talk to her about this Baby business next time I'm on leave,' he promised. 'Now I'd better cut back to camp or I shall get put in Jankers for going AWOL. They're getting very tight now we're on stand-by.'

Actually he'd already got three days' leave so as to get up to Greenwich for Peggy's birthday on Thursday. He'd bought her a present and was rather pleased with it. It was a bright headscarf and he'd got it without coupons from a street corner spiv. Before Joan spoke to him he'd been intending to write to her that evening to tell her he was coming. Now he decided against it. If Baby was really exploiting her the way Joan said, it might be better to walk in unannounced and catch her at it.

After he'd gone, and while Joan was saying goodbye to Yve and Norman, Megan sat by the window thinking over

493

what he'd said. Until that afternoon she'd assumed that he and Peggy were happy living from leave to leave. Now she realized what a lot they'd endured. It must have been really miserable to have been married all this time and never have anywhere to live. Poor old Peggy. Poor old Jim. If I could do anything about it, she thought, I would. I wonder whether they'd like to stay with us for a few days. Probably not. That put-u-up was jolly uncomfortable and they wouldn't get much time on their own with three kids running about the place. But if there was anything she *could* do, she'd jolly well do it. Poor things.

The next day she let Yve and Norman stay off school for a treat because they were feeling homesick, and after dinner she took all three children into Chichester. There wasn't anything much to buy in any of the shops except the rations, but it was nice to walk on pavements for a change instead of cinder paths and to hear the nice familiar rattle of cars and carts all round them instead of tractors, and besides, it gave her a chance to meet up with some of her friends. She'd lived in Merston for such a long time now that she'd made a lot of friends, mostly women of her own age with babies or toddlers, so she rarely went into Chichester without finding someone to chat to.

That afternoon was no exception. Down by the market cross in the middle of the town she met up with the dairy-man's wife, a friendly young woman called Jenny.

The two of them stood in the shelter of the cross and exchanged gossip for a happy half hour, while their assorted children eyed one another and wondered how long they were going to be kept waiting.

'It's nice to have a chat now and then,' Megan said as she prepared to move on.

'You ought to live in Chichester,' Jenny said. 'Then we could chat every day.'

'Couldn't though, could I?' Megan said, making conversation.

'Why not?'

'There ain't any places to let.'

'Well now that's where you're wrong,' was the surprising reply. 'There's a house up for rent this very morning as ever is. I seen it on my way down. Some RAF type had it apparently and he's off to France. You could have that if you wanted.'

Megan was instantly very interested indeed. But this was heaven sent. Meant to be. 'Tell me where it is,' she said. 'Who's got it? What's the rent? Everything.'

'Well blow me down,' Jenny said. 'Are you going to take it then?'

'No,' Megan told her. 'Not me. A very dear friend of mine.'

So after a most satisfactory visit to an estate agents where she laid claim to the house and begged a sheet of paper and pen and ink to write to Jim, she took the first country bus out of town and lugged her three grumbling children to the guardhouse at RAF Merston.

There, by laying on the charm with a trowel, she persuaded one of the guards to get her letter delivered to Sergeant Jim Boxall.

'He'll probably be in the hangars,' she said. 'Or I could tell you his flight if you like.'

'You ain't supposed to know that,' the guard rebuked, flirting with her. 'Classified that is.'

'If you get it down to him double quick I won't tell Hitler,' she said. 'I promise.'

So it was sent down double quick and Megan took the children home at last. 'We'll have a special tea,' she said. 'We've earned it.'

'Why, Aunty Megan?' Norman asked. 'What have we done?'

'We've done miracles,' Megan told him. 'That's what we've done. Miracles.'

Jim had spent the day in the hangars working on an obstinate repair. He was covered in grease when the guard delivered Megan's note so he smudged the paper with black finger prints simply by pulling it out of the envelope. But when he saw what she'd written he threw the little note into the air whooping with triumph. A house at last! A house of his own here in Chichester! It was too good to be true.

'How long we got till we're off duty?' he said to the nearest airman, looking at the clock.

'About twenty minutes, Sarge.'

'Where's me bike? I'm off into Chichester.'

Excitement sped him into town. A home of his own. Just wait till he told Peggy. And such a home too, as he discovered when he'd paid the first week's rent and had walked round to see it, just outside the city walls and right in the centre of a quiet terrace facing a green. What could be better?

He couldn't wait to get to London and tell her the news. Good old Megan! he thought. What a friend she was!

That night he wrapped his present into the smallest brown paper parcel he could contrive and tucked it in his tunic pocket, ready to set off as soon as he came off duty the next afternoon. Then he walked down to Vine Cottage to see Megan and thank her.

It was one of the most cheerful evenings he'd spent for a long while, and by the time he finally went back to camp he was in a state of such excitement that sleep was impossible. In a matter of hours he would be with Peggy telling her about their very first home. In three days they could be living in it. She could travel back with him at the end of his leave and they could spend every spare moment together until he got sent to France. Megan was right. It was a Godsend, coming like this, just at the right time, when he needed her more than he'd ever done in his life. He lay in the darkness listening to the sleepers all around him and planning his campaign. He wouldn't tell her straight away. No, he'd keep it and savour it. First he'd give her the scarf and wish her happy birthday and then he'd take her to the pictures and when the lights went down he'd give her a big kiss and then he'd tell her.

But like so many human plans it didn't work out that way.

For a start it was pouring with rain when he arrived that evening, the drops falling so steadily that he was soaked in the short walk from the station to Paradise Row. As he stood on the pavement waiting for her to open the door, the rain trickled from his hair and ran down his face.

'Oh!' she said, blushing with pleasure at the sight of him. 'Why didn't you say you was coming? I'm on duty in twenty minutes.'

He kissed her, but briefly because he was so wet and

496

followed her into the kitchen shaking the rain from his cap. It was a disappointment that she was going on duty but it couldn't be helped. He'd take her to the pictures tomorrow and give her the scarf now. Or maybe he'd tell her the news now before he gave her the scarf. But then he saw the tray.

It was lying on the top of the Morrison shelter table neatly laid out for one with a tray cloth, a cruet set, a cup of tea and a steaming Welsh rarebit. The sight of it made him feel suddenly and extremely angry. Joan was right. She *was* being used by that selfish sister of theirs. No, he wouldn't tell her about the house yet, he'd deal with this Baby business first and get it over with.

'That your supper?' he said.

She blushed again, this time with embarrassment. 'Well no,' she admitted. 'It's for Baby. I was just going to take it up to her. Her nerves are ever so bad.'

'So that's still going on, is it?' he said, looking at her so fiercely that she quailed before him. 'Joan told me about it. She's got you on the run good and proper.'

'No,' she said, feeling she ought to defend her sister. 'She ain't. It ain't her fault, Jim. Think what she's been through.'

'Been through!' he said angrily. 'She got stood up, that's all. And probably no more than she deserved, spoilt little brat. Put that right down!' as Peggy picked up the tray. 'If she wants to eat she can come downstairs and sit up to the table like everyone else.'

'She's ever so bad, Jim. Really.'

'She's ever so selfish,' he corrected, taking the tray out of her hands and putting it back on the shelter, 'and you're making her worse.'

'That Welsh rarebit'll get cold.'

'Let it.'

'I said I'd be up with it directly.'

'You won't.'

He was standing between her and the door, looking taller than usual and extremely handsome, his eyes very blue in the fading light of the evening. 'This has gone on long enough,' he said, 'and now it's got to stop.'

She was so tired. 'I must look after her,' she said. 'She's delicate.'

497

Her fatigue made him feel angrier than ever. She was all eyes and there was no colour in her face at all. 'I tell you what I think,' he said. 'I think you should pack your bags now and come back to Sussex with me and stay with me until I go to France.'

'How could I do that?' she said wearily, 'I've got to go on duty.'

'Bugger going on duty,' he said happily. 'We've got a house.'

To his immense disappointment she was too weary to respond. 'What?' she said.

'A house,' he said, his face blazing. 'We've got a house.'

'Where?'

'In Chichester. It's smashing. I paid the rent on it yesterday.'

'Oh,' she said, and the word was so flat it made his heart sink to hear it.

'So you'll pack, won't you,' he urged. 'You could send a message to the Post. They'd understand.'

'No,' she said, still speaking in that flat, exhausted voice. 'I couldn't do that. They depend on me.'

'So do I.'

'Not like that, Jim.'

'Oh come on, Peggy,' he said trying to persuade her. 'Don't be a clot. OK. Go on duty just for tonight. You can come with me tomorrow. That's reasonable.'

'I can't. You know I can't.'

'Why not?'

'Not with the buzz-bombs. I can't walk off. Not now. Not after all this time.'

'Oh for crying out loud, why not? Other people do.'

'Not me,' she said stubbornly.

'Why not?'

She knew why not in the more instinctive part of her mind but she was too weary to be able to explain. It was a matter of pride. She'd spent so long under fire she couldn't desert now. Not now right at the very end. 'It's only for a few more weeks,' she said. 'Mr Mac reckons.'

'In a few more weeks I shall be in France.'

'Oh don't say that.'

'In France. Come on, Peg, don't be such a fool.'

498

'I ain't a fool,' she said, with weary pride. 'I'm a Londoner. I was born in the Tower. I can't run away, don't you see?'

'There are other Londoners. Someone'ud take your place.'

'I can't. What if we was to all think like that? Oh what's the good of talking about it?' It was making him so cross and she had to say no.

'I'll tell you what's the good,' he said, his rage growing. 'We're what's good. We're what's important. Love is important. It's the most important thing in the world. Oh come on, Peg, we've wasted enough time on other people. We ought to think of one another for a change.'

'I do think of you,' she pleaded. 'I do, honestly. All the time.'

'You don't,' he said. 'You think of Joan and Baby and being a warden. Everybody else but us.' He knew he was being unfair to her but rage was carrying him along like a torrent. 'We count too. You and me. Or don't you care that I love you?'

Her voice was so small it was almost a whisper. 'You know I do.'

'Then show it. Come away with me now. Stay with me until I go to France. It might be the last chance we have to be together. We might be killed, either of us. You might be bombed. I could be killed in France. We're in the middle of a war, for Christ's sake. Stop being so bloody noble and think of yourself for a change.'

He was pacing the room in his agitation, fists clenched, scowling.

'I can't,' she said. 'Besides ...'

'Besides what?'

'Nothing,' she said withdrawing at once. 'I've got responsibilities, that's all.'

'What responsibilities? The kids are in the country. You can't say you've got to look after them.'

'There's Joan. I promised Sid I'd look after Joan.'

'Joan's a grown woman. She can look after herself.'

'Well maybe she can, but Baby ...'

'Bloody Baby,' he said exasperated beyond endurance. 'I suppose you've promised to look after her too.'

'Yes,' she admitted huskily. 'I promised Mum.'

His fury was making him look so handsome, that dark hair bristling and his shoulders so square and his eyes as blue as the sea that day in Brighton.

'Seems to me,' he said bitterly, 'I'm the only person alive you ain't promised anything to. But then I don't count.'

'You do.'

'Then come away with me.'

They were standing toe to toe like boxers, and he was panting with fury. 'This has gone on too bloody long,' he said. 'Now you got to make your mind up one way or the other. Either you say you'll come with me now or by God I'll walk out straight back to Merston and I'll go off to France and I'll never see you again and that'll be the end of it.'

Her lips were so pale they were almost white. 'You don't mean it,' she said.

He didn't mean it, but he'd boxed himself into a corner. Now it was a matter of pride to stand by what he'd said. 'Yes,' he told her. 'I do. So make your choice.'

'I ain't got a choice,' she said, husky with unshed tears.

'You have,' he insisted, 'but you're such a bloody fool you're making the wrong one. You should choose me. I love you. I thought you loved me.'

'I can't leave the Post. Not now.'

'And that bloody Baby.'

'Oh please don't let's quarrel,' she begged.

'That bloody sodding Baby!' he said, and he turned on his heel and pounded out of the room and up the stairs, his rage too extreme to be contained any longer.

Baby was lying comfortably against a mound of pillows listening to the wireless and eating a bar of chocolate.

'Oh,' she said. 'You can't come in here. I'm in bed.'

'Get up,' he said. 'There's nothing the matter with you.'

'I've got nerves,' she said pulling the bedclothes up under her chin. 'My nerves are dreadful. I been through a tragedy.'

'Tragedy my eye,' he said. 'You been jilted, that's all. And that's not a tragedy. A tragedy's being burnt alive in a tank, or shot out the sky. A tragedy's innocent kids blown to bits, unarmed refugees machine-gunned. Don't talk to me about tragedy. You don't know the half of it.'

'I've got nerves,' she tried again.

'You've got five seconds,' he said. 'That's what you've got. Five seconds and if you're not out that bed and getting dressed I shall take all the bedclothes and throw them out the window. You've played this game quite long enough. Now it's over. Five seconds.'

How magnificent he is, she thought, seeing him with the new vision of excited outrage. 'All right,' she said. 'But you'll have to leave the room. I can't very well dress in front of you, can I.'

'Up!' he said, reaching for the quilt. 'Out!'

She got out of bed at once, and stood before him shivering in her nightgown.

'Now get dressed,' he said, 'and go downstairs and help your sister. There's nothing the matter with you. See?'

And he was gone, banging the door behind him.

The outburst had calmed him. He walked down the stairs feeling much more reasonable. Now he could talk to Peggy properly without anger getting in the way.

But the room was empty. There was only a note propped whitely against the clock. 'Had to go,' it said. 'On duty. Love Peggy.'

'Bloody sodding duty!' he said, and stormed out of the house.

Upstairs in the bedroom Baby heard the door bang and clutched her hands to her bosom. How amazing that old Jim should turn out to be so handsome and attractive. Why, he was just like Rhett Butler. I'll get dressed, she decided, and tidy this room up a bit. If he comes back tomorrow I must look my best for him. She drifted across to her mirror and sat before it contemplating her reflection. I've let myself go, she thought. Her roots were really quite black. First thing tomorrow when it was light she'd touch them up. There was enough peroxide in the cupboard. Oh he was just like Rhett Butler.

CHAPTER 40

It was a hideous night. To have started it by quarrelling with Jim was so awful that Peggy couldn't bear to think about it. She was still shaky when she reached the Post and still trying to understand how on earth it could have happened. He couldn't have meant what he said. They hadn't broken up. They couldn't have. Not after all this time. And yet he'd said it. He'd looked as if he meant it. Oh God, she thought, if he really meant it what am I going to do? It was just as well Mr MacFarlane had changed shifts and wasn't on duty with her. She'd have hated him to see the state she was in.

She made herself a cup of strong tea and smoked two cigarettes to calm herself and then the others arrived and she had work to do and that helped her recover. And not long after that they heard their first V1s, and within the hour they were called out to their first incident, and the first led straight to the second, for the two local doodle-bugs that night fell within two hundred yards and a quarter of an hour of one another.

The first demolished a line of lock-up shops, all empty except for the last one where the rescue team discovered a tramp pinned by the legs under a huge chunk of fallen wall. Peggy sat by his head and talked to him while they dug him out. He was fully conscious and said he couldn't feel any pain but it took a very long time to lift the wall and the minute he was free he went pallid with shock, groaned into unconsciousness and was dead before the ambulance team could ease him onto the stretcher.

And then as if that weren't bad enough they heard the next doodle-bug approaching, looked up to see its fiery tail a few hundred feet above them just as the engine cut out, and only just had time to fling themselves to the ground before the explosion lifted them into the air, broken bricks and all.

This time the target was a four storey tenement and the rescue was long, difficult and terrible. It took both rescue teams and all the equipment they could muster. Six people had been killed outright and they took another fifteen from the wreckage, some of them horribly injured.

By the time the last body had been removed the sky was pale green, they could hear the first trams running in the High Street, and there was enough daylight to reveal the full, ugly extent of the damage. Peggy was torn with pity and so tired that her bones ached.

Even a cup of strong sweet tea back at the Post didn't revive her, and when Mr MacFarlane came on duty, fifteen minutes early as usual, he took one look at her face and ordered her home at once.

'My dear girrl,' he said, when she protested that she hadn't finished her stint. 'You go strraight back this minute. I'll not tek no for an answer, the state of ye.'

So she stumbled home.

Lily was on the doorstep waiting for Joan to come to work, with Percy standing patiently beside her.

'You look all in,' she said as Peggy walked towards her. 'What a night, eh? We heard 'em come down. Did you go to both of 'em?'

Peggy nodded. 'There you are, Joan,' Lily called into the house. 'She *was* there. What did I tell you?'

Joan emerged from the kitchen, her hair tied up in her workaday scarf. 'Lo, Peg,' she said. 'I'd get to bed if I was you. You look rotten.'

'I'll wait till Baby's gone,' Peggy said. There was no point in trying to sleep with Baby crashing about the bedroom.

'She's doing her roots,' Joan said grimacing. 'And our Mrs Geary's been out all night. Went off to see the Allnutts and Mr Cooper just after the nine o'clock news and never came home.'

'Dirty old stop-out,' Lily laughed. 'Come on then, Joan. You ready? If we don't look sharp I shan't have time to get my Percy to the flats.' Now that the school holidays had begun her Mum looked after Percy during the day.

'Look after yourselves,' Peggy said, giving her automatic warning, tired and miserable though she was.

'And you,' Joan said, and the two women walked away along the street with Percy small and trusting between them.

The kitchen was quiet and peaceful after the struggles of the night. I'll just sit down for a few minutes, Peggy thought, and then I'll boil up a kettle and have a bit of a wash and by that time Baby will've gone and I can get to bed. I'll think about the row later when I've got more energy to face it.

It was bliss to take off her tin hat and hang up her tunic and sit down quietly on her own in the chair beside the window. Or not entirely on her own, because Tom came sidling out of the kitchen to leap up on her lap the minute she'd settled and Polly was biting his toes in his cage in the cupboard under the stairs. The cupboard door was wide open, presumably to give the poor thing some air. But it was being quiet for once and the cat was soothing company across her knees.

'I'll give you some milk presently,' she said to him, stroking his soft fur as she closed her eyes. She could hear the clock ticking and Baby humming to herself in the room above her head, and there was a strong smell of honeysuckle drifting through the window. Leslie's honeysuckle that he'd trained over the fence. Oh the lovely easy peace of it.

She heard the doodle-bug when it was still a long way away, that hateful rattling engine clear above the sound of the trams and the distant chuff of a train. 'Baby!' she called. 'There's one coming.'

'Be down in a minute,' Baby called back. 'I'm nearly finished.'

'Leave it,' Peggy called as the doodle-bug got closer. 'Do it later. It's coming our way.' The noise was very loud now and getting louder.

504

'Two more bits,' Baby called. 'I can't leave it half done. I shall look a freak.'

And the engine cut out.

Peggy just had time to grab the cat and fling herself into the shelter. She was pulling the wire mesh behind her, hitting her foot in her haste, when there was a roar that filled her ears and blotted out the room and lasted for ever and ever. The floor was heaving like a surf wave under her straddled legs and there was a pulsing darkness all round her and the air was so full of dust that she had to struggle for breath. Her mouth was full of it and there were bits of grit on her tongue. She hung on to the mattress with both hands to steady herself, but it was no good, she was toppling sideways as though she was being pushed by some powerful invisible force. And as she fell she turned her head towards the mesh and saw bricks and chunks of plaster falling towards her, hurtling and tumbling in appalling slow motion, growing bigger and bigger the nearer they fell. Buried alive, she thought, and the terror of it pulled her down into darkness, still choking and struggling.

When she came to, the darkness was total and so was the silence, and for a few bewildered seconds she thought she was in the Tower. The Salt Tower, wasn't it? Yes it must be because it's so dark. The Salt Tower, and there's a ghost on the stairs and the Bullough twins have run off with the torch.

She was so afraid of the ghost. It was there waiting for her. Waiting to push her in the back as she ran down the stairs. Oh if only Dad was in here! It would be all right if Dad was with her.

There was water dripping somewhere. A tap dripping. She could hear it quite clearly and it puzzled her because she couldn't understand why there should be water dripping in the Tower. And a smell of gas too. No, not Dad, she thought. Dad's dead. He's been dead ages. It was Jim she wanted. Dear, dear Jim. Her own dear dependable Jim. And then she remembered that she wasn't going to see him again and she yearned for him with a terrible aching sensation in her belly that was stronger than her fear.

505

And at that moment, with a palpable jerk in her brain, like a jigsaw piece clicking into position, she knew where she was and why she was afraid. I've been bombed, she thought. I'm in the shelter under the house. I've been buried alive. Buried alive, dear God! And the horror returned again in that dreadful darkness, making her shake. Buried alive like the anchorite in Tillingbourne all that time ago, when Grandpa Potter was so cruel. And she remembered that the anchorite had dug herself out with her bare hands, and wondered whether it would be possible to dig her way out of this. But there was no strength in her arms. She couldn't even raise one hand from the floor. And that made her feel more afraid than ever.

She lay in the terrible darkness breathing in dust and dirt as her heart juddered like a broken engine and her legs began to shake. I'm going into shock she thought, recognizing the signs as her mouth trembled and her belly shook. And she knew there were things you had to do when people went into shock but she couldn't remember what they were. Not that she could have done any of them even if she had remembered, trapped in the darkness. Still at least I'm alive, she told herself, trying to be sensible. I ain't been killed. Now what have I got to do? What do you have to do when you've been bombed? She ought to know that. And she tried to push her brain to remember. But her brain was stuck fast in fear and wouldn't function, no matter how hard she tried.

Please God help me, she prayed frantically. Please God. I can't bear this. And the old prayer from Tillingbourne came automatically into her mind. Give me the strength to endure what has to be endured.

There was a movement beside her in the darkness and a faint rasping sound like panting. She put out her hand instinctively towards the sound and touched fur. Tom, she thought. And alive too, for the fur was warm. Then she remembered the torches and the whistle and knew that they were kept under the pillow and felt about in the darkness to find them, relieved to discover that she could move her right hand even if the left one was still heavy and useless. There were sharp pieces of brick under her fingers, rubbish of all kinds littering the bed clothes. Mind

506

out in case there's glass. Fumbling to right and left she felt the edge of the pillow and, pushing her fingers underneath it, found a torch. And it was working. Thank God.

In the little beam of light she could see debris all round her. There was a lot of dust and several pieces of plaster and brick that were much too big to have been blown through the mesh, so there must be a hole in the shelter somewhere. She played the torch over the roof above her head and saw that it was crushed down and sloping sideways and had been gashed open at one end. And she realized that she was lucky to be alive and wondered whether she'd been hurt and hadn't noticed yet. Lots of injured people didn't feel the pain of their injuries until quite a long time after the incident, as she knew better than most. But no, her arms and legs were intact and so were her hands and feet, although her shirt was torn and she could feel dampness on one shoulder and there was a smell of blood coming from somewhere. But then the smell of blood was always strong after a direct hit. You smelt it everywhere.

Tom's eyes glinted in the darkness, red as rubies, and she put the torch down so that she could see him without alarming him, and reached out her fingers to stroke him. There was dark blood streaked across the fur on his back, so that could be what she was smelling, but *his* limbs were all intact too, and after a few minutes he crawled towards her, crouched on his belly, and crept into her lap.

It was a great comfort to feel him there. 'You're all right, Tom,' she said and was horrified by how croaky her voice sounded. She realized that her mouth was still full of dust and grit and she tried to spit it out without frightening the poor cat. 'They'll get us out soon,' she said to comfort them both.

Then she remembered that Baby had been upstairs doing her hair.

'Baby!' she croaked. 'You all right? Baby? Say if you are.'

But there was no answering call and no sign of any movement among the debris even though she scanned it several times with her torch. And after all that effort she didn't have the energy to call again for quite a long time.

She must have hidden away somewhere, she comforted herself. If I've survived, and old Tom, then she'll probably have got through as well. But she wished she'd answer. 'Baby! Baby! Where are you?'

Then she must have fainted away or fallen asleep for the next thing she was aware of was a loud scraping noise and a choking sensation, the air gritty with dust, and total darkness again. Had she turned out the torch? And where was it? But she hadn't got the energy to search. She knew she ought to shout for help, but she hadn't got the energy for that either. She felt ill and weak.

Am I dying? she wondered. Is this what it feels like when you're dying? Oh Jim, she thought as tears oozed out of her eyes, please come and get me out. She wanted to be in his arms, held tight and safe. But they'd had a row, hadn't they? He'd said she was to choose. She remembered that. And she'd chosen to go on looking after Joan and Baby. How could she have been so silly? Where was Joan? she wondered. She couldn't remember. Had she gone to work? I ought to call to Baby again she thought, but she couldn't make her voice work. She could only think of Jim and that awful row. Choose between us, he'd said. Come away with me, he'd said. Now. She remembered it clearly. And he'd been right. She should have chosen him. She should have gone away with him there and then. Oh how much she wished she had.

Dear God, she prayed, please let me get out of here and I'll go with him wherever he wants. Tomorrow. Today. Right away. Just let me see him again, just once, please dear God. It would be terrible to end with a quarrel. And such a stupid quarrel too. Because she knew now that he'd been right in all the things he'd said. Their love for one another *was* the most important thing. He was more important to her than anyone else in the world. Oh please dear God, let me get out and see him again.

508

CHAPTER 41

When Jim Boxall stormed out of the house that evening he was in such a fury he hardly knew what he was doing or where he was going. It was still raining, in a heavy pervasive shower, and already growing unpleasantly dark as if the sky was angry too. For sheer unmitigated bloody pigheadedness! To refuse their house, their first, very own house, after all these years, and just when he was going to France. How could she be so bloody stupid? He crashed into the High Street, his face dark with fury. And there was a pub. It was just what he needed. A good strong Scotch. A good strong double Scotch.

He made his entrance so precipitately that he didn't see Ernest and Leslie who were sitting in a corner talking to John Cooper, but they saw him and came across at once to lead him back to their table.

'Didn't know you were on leave,' Ernest said. 'Not embarkation, is it?'

He controlled himself with an effort and tried to speak lightly. 'You don't get embarkation leave in this war,' he said. 'You just get sent.' And he drank his whisky quickly.

'How's it going over there?' John Cooper asked. 'Does anyone know?'

'According to plan, so they say.' It was still an effort even to be civil. What a state to be in!

'Terrible battle at Caen,' Leslie said.

'Yes. It was.' The whisky was warm in his throat, melting his anger at last.

509

They plied him with more whisky and they talked war and invasion, peace and politics, and presently they were joined by a sailor and his three friends, one of whom was an old hand from Warrenden Brothers and remembered Jim being there 'in the old days'. There was a piano playing in the snug and some raucous singing by rough London voices. 'Dear ol' pals, jolly ol' pals'. Yes, he thought as the whisky fuddled his rage, this was what he needed.

The first explosion made him jump. 'Good God!' he said, as the glasses rattled and dust leapt into the air. 'What was that?'

'One a' them doodle-bugs,' John Cooper said, shifting in his wheelchair as if the reverberation had made him uncomfortable. 'Noisy beggars.'

The second sent several men out into the street to see where it had fallen.

'Looks like Blackheath way,' one said as they returned.

What with the whisky and his anger it didn't occur to Jim that Peggy might be attending either of them. And when his old friends from Warrenden's remarked that it was 'getting a bit hot round here' and suggested moving on to somewhere else, he said goodbye to John Cooper and the two old fellers and went with them, drunkenly affable.

They spent the rest of the night in an amiable pub-crawl that took them further and further north and west. By chucking out time they were in Thames Street and Jim was decidedly unsteady on his feet.

'My ol' woman lives round here,' he said, peering into the darkness.

'Stay the night with her then, I should,' one of his new friends advised.

So he went knocking on his mother's door.

She was already in bed, but she came down pointing a timid torch to see who it was and pulled him into the house at once for fear of showing a light.

'Yer Dad's asleep,' she warned as they climbed the stairs to her rooms. 'Best not to wake him.'

'Can I stay the night?'

'Looks as if you'd better,' she said. 'There's only the floor, mind.'

510

'Pillow and a blanket,' he said, 'an' that'll be dandy.'

He slept almost as soon as he'd wrapped himself in the blanket, exhausted by emotion and drink. And he didn't wake until well after eight o'clock the next morning, with a mouth as dry as old leather and a throbbing headache.

There was no sign of his father except for an empty mug and a greasy plate on the table. His mother was riddling the fire. 'You had a skinful last night, didn'tcher?' she said mildly. 'Yer Dad said to leave yer.'

'Got any aspirin?'

She tossed him the little bottle from the mantelpiece, and he caught it and took two tablets as the events of the previous night rushed back into his mind, the row, Peggy's pathetic face, Baby in her frowsy bed, Peggy's pathetic face, the pub crawl, Peggy's pathetic face.

'How's Peggy?' his mother said, sitting back on her heels.

'Fine,' he lied, hoping the aspirin would take effect soon. 'She's fine. It's her birthday tomorrow. I've brought her a present.' And he'd forgotten all about it, shouting at her like that. In the light of that calm morning he was ashamed of the way he'd behaved, all that shouting and going off on a pub crawl and getting drunk. And it wasn't her fault. She was only being herself, trying to do her best, the way she always did. It was that lazy sister of hers. She was the trouble, rolling around in bed all the time. And that thought made him grin rather ruefully, for wasn't he rolling around too and late in the morning? Eight o'clock and still not up.

'Is that the time?' he said, glancing at the clock on the mantelpiece. 'I got to be off.'

'There's tea in the pot,' his mother said.

He was out of the house a quarter of an hour later, and caught a tram by running for it as it moved off. He couldn't wait to get back to Paradise Row and make it up. It was all too bloody silly for words, rowing like that after all these years. They'd live in the house sooner or later. He shouldn't have sprung it on her when she was tired. He hadn't given her a chance to think. And he ought to have gone down to the Post and put things right yesterday evening instead of getting plastered. Well never mind, he'd go straight to number six and give her the present and make up with her now.

When he turned the corner into Paradise Row he was whistling happily. The shock of what he saw froze the sound on his lips.

'Christ!' he said aloud. 'Oh Christ!' Trying to take it in with his brain stunned and none of his senses functioning properly. The street cordoned off, the woodyard gone, and the fence. A crater where the shelter had been. The terrace wrecked. Two houses gone? Three? Whose were they? Was it number six? Impossible to see in the smoke and filth and clouds of dust. 'Oh Christ!'

There was an elderly policeman on guard by the cordon. 'Not down here if you please, sir,' he said, looming out of the dust.

'I live here,' Jim said, stepping over the tape.

The man's expression changed at once. 'Ah well if that's the case, sir, perhaps you wouldn't mind just seeing the warden. Over there by the rescue truck.'

Jim hadn't noticed the rescue truck, nor the two ambulances standing by at the other end of the road. And even now as he walked towards them they seemed unreal, because this couldn't be happening. She couldn't be bombed. Not Peggy. Oh dear Christ not Peggy! Why weren't they digging? They ought to be digging her out. What was the matter with them all? Why were they just standing about? Didn't they realize she was in the house? Well if they wouldn't do anything, he would. He ran onto the wreckage and began to pull away the bricks with his bare hands, frantic with distress, fear screaming in his head. 'Peggy!' he called. 'Peg!'

Someone was beside him, holding him by the arms, and Mr MacFarlane's voice was soothing, 'It's all right, son. It's all right. Everything's all under control.'

'It's number six,' he said, eyes staring wildly. 'Don't you understand? It's number six. Peggy's house.'

'Aye. We know,' Mr MacFarlane said 'They'd a Morrison there. She could be in the Morrison. They'll be digging it oot just as soon as ever they can. They've a chimney to bring down first, d'ye see?' And he turned

512

Jim's body so that he could see the demolition teams and the leaning stack of the chimney lowering over the wreckage.

The Morrison, Jim thought, but that made him remember the tray and their dreadful row. 'Have you heard her?' he asked, trying to calm himself. 'Do you know she's there?'

'No. Not yet. If you'll just come down, eh?'

'We should be digging,' Jim insisted, still wild with shock and grief. 'Don't you understand? My Peggy's under that lot. We should be digging her out.'

'Aye,' Mr Mac said gently. 'We will. Just as soon as ever we can, but they've to get the chimney down first and they cannae bring the chimney down if we're in the way of it.'

He was so sensible and so calm that Jim saw the sense of it, even through his panic, and allowed himself to be led back to the road. The first shock was beginning to ease. It was possible to think. 'When did it happen?' he asked. 'What about Joan and Lily? Had they gone to work?' They ought to have gone to work. With any luck ...

'Number two's still standing,' Mr MacFarlane said. 'We're pretty sure your sister and Joan went off to work before it happened. We saw the wee lad in the flats. He was – eh – looking oot the windy just beforehand. We've sent a message to the factory just tae be sure.'

But Peggy, Jim grieved. Where was Peggy? Oh God don't let her be dead. Hurry up with that bloody chimney he urged the demolition team, for Christ's sake. Don't just stand there.

Someone was pushing open the door to number eight and an odd grey figure was staggering into the road, calling as she came, 'I'm all right. I'm perfectly all right.' Mrs Roderick, covered in dust from head to foot, but still magnificently upright in her supporting corset. 'I'm all right.'

A nurse sped across the rubble to wrap her in a blanket and Mr MacFarlane headed towards her too. 'You're fine,' he encouraged. 'You're right fine. Could you bear to answer a few wee questions?'

'Yes, yes,' Mrs Roderick said, standing in her blanket like a dusty squaw. 'I told you. I'm perfectly all right. Hello, Jim.'

513

'Did Mr Brown go off to work this morn?'

'Six o'clock,' Mrs Roderick said. 'Regular as clockwork. Nonnie popped out to the shops just before.' And then without any warning her face crumpled into tears and she began to howl.

'Go with the nurse,' Mr MacFarlane said, patting her shoulder. 'You'll be fine with the nurse.'

'I'm perfectly all right,' Mrs Roderick howled as she was led to the ambulance. 'Perfectly all right. I ought to stay and help. People have been bombed.'

Mr MacFarlane was writing in his notebook. Actually standing in the rubble, writing, as though he was book-keeping or something. The sight of such mundane clerical activity in such a terrible setting drove Jim to fury again. 'Can't that wait?' he said. 'Where's the bloody rescue teams? I thought they were supposed to be the first in action.'

Mr Mac put his book away. 'They're working in the shop,' he said. 'There were people in the ...'

But Jim was already half-way down the road. The shop, of course. She could have popped down to the shop. That's where she'll be. And the shop was still standing, barely damaged. There was even some glass left in the windows.

They were carrying a stretcher out with the first casualty as he reached the door. It was Mr Grunewald, pale and bandaged, with his wife grimed and blood-stained but walking beside him holding his hand.

'How many?' Jim asked the stretcher bearer.

'Five,' the man said, not varying his pace or looking back.

'Any deaths?'

'No.'

The third victim was carried out. A woman he'd never seen before. Then a man walking unsteadily and holding a blood-soaked pad to his forehead. Five. Five. Who's the fifth?

It was Mrs Geary, hobbling and cross, without her glasses, and with a lump as big as a hen's egg rising on her forehead. 'Who's that?' she said peering at him as he approached.

A nurse followed her out of the shop. 'Let's just get you

to the ambulance, dear,' she said.

'Bugger off,' the old lady growled. 'I ain't going in no ambulance and that's flat. The bugger's bombed my house. You just get me a chair. That's all I want. My legs are giving me gyp.'

There was a line of chairs standing outside the Earl Grey.

'Let her sit down,' Jim said to the nurse. 'She's a stubborn old thing. It won't hurt her to wait a little, will it?'

'She ought to be checked over,' the nurse dithered. 'But I suppose it could wait. She's not as bad as some of the others.'

'I ain't deaf neither,' Mrs Geary said. 'There's three gels in my house I'd have you know, young woman. You don't move me till I know what's happened to them. And that's flat. You got a blanket? I'm perishing cold.'

There was a sighing sound in the air above them. 'Steady!' a voice called. 'Easy as she goes. 'Nother inch, Charlie. Easy! Easy!' And the broken chimney stack roared into rubble that filled the backyards.

'Now we shall get them out,' Jim said to Mrs Geary as he ran to join the rescue. 'Joan's all right.'

The rescue teams were quick and very well-organized. Within seconds they had two rescues going at once, one above the ruins of number six, looking for Peggy and Baby, and the other, with less hope, where number four had been, searching for the Allnutts and Mr Cooper. It was laborious work, shifting the rubble and handing it back piece by piece into the street along a willing human chain, but it was done with impressive speed. And naturally Jim was one of the first in the chain, relieved to be taking action at last. Anything rather than that awful standing about, waiting.

As he worked the church clock struck the hour. Could it really be only nine o'clock? It felt much later. Then he was aware that Leslie was working beside him, neat and dapper as ever even with his hands covered in brick dust.

'It's Peggy, isn't it?' the old man said. 'We heard it, of course, and then one of our customers told us, so we came straight back. A dreadful business.'

'Is Ernest here too?' Jim panted, stopping for a second

to wipe the sweat out of his eyes.

'Two down,' Leslie said. And sure enough there he was, working with the best, his long white hair stained red with dust. 'Don't worry,' Leslie said. 'They're ever so good. They'll get her out.'

But will she still be alive, Jim thought, under the weight of all this?

'Hush!' someone called. And they all stood quite still and looked up hopefully. One of the rescuers was lying face down on the rubble listening.

The silence lasted for a very long time and Jim was quite shocked to hear the trams rattling in the High Street. It was dreadful to think that life was going on just a few yards away as though nothing was the matter.

'Over here,' Mr Goodall called into the hush. 'Over here.'

Jim followed the others, breathless with hope. But it wasn't Peggy. It was John Cooper's wheelchair, squashed and ominously bloodstained.

'Oh God!' Leslie said at his shoulder. 'Poor man.'

Mr Goodall was following the blood trail through the wreckage, as the rescuers cleared the way. None of them really had much hope of finding their old friend alive, but even so the sight of his body, crushed and bloodied among the bricks, was an appalling shock.

'He'll not have known much about it,' Ernest said, 'if that's any consolation.' But it wasn't. It didn't even numb the pain.

'Our first death,' Leslie said sadly.

But Mr Goodall corrected him. 'Fifth,' he said. 'They were all killed in the woodyard, and Mrs Brown was the first one we found when we came in. She was on her way home from the shop. We found her basket, poor woman.'

'Then pray God it's the last,' Ernest said.

'Amen to that,' Jim said grimly, thinking of Peggy.

'If Mr Cooper is ...' Leslie said delicately, trying to prepare them all for worse to come, 'I doubt if we shall see the Allnutts again.'

Jim straightened his back and looked away from the group round Mr Cooper's body, struggling not to weep. Dear old Cooper, who'd been such a help to him down in the library, who'd never made a fuss about anything, stuck in that awful wheelchair, playing the piano and watching them all dance. And there was Mr Allnutt walking up the road, large as life, with his work-box in his hand.

At first Jim thought he was seeing things, that it was shock playing tricks on him, but then Ernest looked up and saw him too, and then all three of them were tumbling down the rubble to grab him by the hand. 'Mr Allnutt! You're alive. Thank God.'

'Just popped round the corner to fix some shelves for Mrs Jones,' Mr Allnutt said. 'It threw us about a bit I can tell you. What a bit a' luck the wife's away.'

'Away?' Ernest asked.

'Gone down to Slough to see young Bertie. Went seven o'clock. What a bit a' luck.'

They led him down the road to sit beside Mrs Geary. Best not to tell him about John Cooper. Not yet anyway. Let him get over the shock a bit first.

'Not much left is there, mate?' Mrs Geary said cheerfully. 'They got the girls out yet?'

But that horror was still to come. Ten minutes later the rescue team came upon a woman's arm, stiff and white and without any sign of life.

'I wouldn't go up there yet,' Leslie advised. 'Not just yet.' But Jim was already leaping over the rubble.

There was no way of knowing whose arm it was. Not Peggy's. Please don't let it be Peggy's. But if it wasn't Peggy's it would have to be somebody else's. And it sickened him to think that he was wishing somebody else dead in order to keep her alive. But even so, please don't let it be Peggy's.

There was somebody calling him from the street. Lily, was it? Lily and Joan standing together still in their aprons and headscarves, their upturned faces pale and anxious. 'Have they found someone?'

'Yes,' he called back. 'Don't come up.'

They were more obedient than he'd been, and stood where they were, watching and waiting.

'You'll tell us, Jim?'

'Yes, yes.' He was irritable with anxiety and fear. They

were being so slow, uncovering the body so gently. Please don't let it be her.

It was Baby, her neck broken, her blonde hair bright among the dust, and the remains of the peroxide bottle still clutched in her hand.

Jim climbed down to tell Joan and Lily. Oddly none of them wept. They stood together, clinging to one another as though they were drowning, but they didn't weep. It was as if the horror had anaesthetized them.

'Oh poor Baby!' Lily said over and over again.

And Joan said, 'Now it's only Peggy.'

'Yes,' he said, his heart leaden in his chest.

'We'll help,' Lily said. 'Tell us what we've got to do.'

Leslie and Ernest were standing side by side in the rubble. Ernest was trying to mop the sweat from his forehead with a handkerchief that was now more brick dust than cloth.

'We ought to tell Mrs Geary,' Leslie said, looking down to where the old lady was still sitting, wrapped in her blanket, waiting.

'We're standing on our house,' Ernest said sadly, looking at the piles of brick and debris under his feet. 'There's a bit of your jardinière over there. Oh God, that poor kid, to die so young.'

'I'll tell her,' Leslie decided. 'You have a breather.' And he climbed down the rubble, neat and deft as a cat.

But when he reached the wall of the Earl Grey and Mrs Geary was peering myopically towards him he couldn't think what to say. Her face looked peculiarly naked without her glasses, naked and vulnerable and lost.

'Leslie, is it?' she said.

'Yes.'

'You've found someone.'

'Yes, I'm afraid so. It's Baby.'

'Dead?' the old lady said flatly.

'Yes.'

'That bleedin' Hitler,' she said fiercely. 'He ought ter be hung drawn and quartered for this.'

'Quite right,' Mr Allnutt said, patting her hand. 'So he should. An' that's what we'll do to him, an' all, once we've caught the bugger.'

518

Leslie stood before them uncomfortably, wondering whether he ought to tell Mr Allnutt about Mr Cooper now, but before he could come to any decision, there was a noise behind him and turning he saw that Ernest was scrambling over the wreckage towards them. He had a dark object held against his chest and as he got nearer Leslie and Mr Allnutt could see that it was the parrot's cage, squashed and dented and with a dust-covered bundle of feathers lying at the bottom of it like a discarded mop.

'What's that?' Mrs Geary said, as he handed it to her, and then, as she managed to focus her eyes, 'Oh Gawd! It's my poor old Polly. It's my poor bird. That bleedin' Hitler's killed my Polly.'

And the bundle of feathers stirred, turned its head and opened one round yellow eye to glare at her balefully.

'Star-news-standard,' it croaked. 'Aark!'

'Well would you believe it!' Mrs Geary said in wonder and relief. 'You good old boy. See that, Mr Allnutt? He's lived through it. He ain't dead after all. There you are you see, you can survive. There's hope for our Peggy. You go right on back you two,' she said to Leslie and Ernest, 'and you get her out this very minute. Oh, what a good old boy you are, Polly!'

'We'll do what we can,' Ernest assured her, but he spoke without hope. When they found the poor girl she would be – well – like Baby. How could it be otherwise in such destruction?

Mr MacFarlane was calling from the wreckage. He was almost hidden by a pile of bricks but his face was pink with excitement. 'We've found the shelter,' he said. 'Over here.'

There was a rush towards him as Leslie and Ernest and Mr Allnutt ran from the Earl Grey and Jim and Joan and Lily climbed up from the street. They could see a pit in the rubble and down at the bottom of it was the top of the Morrison shelter. Was there hope? Was it possible?

'Quiet everybody!' Mr Goodall said as they crashed towards him. And when he'd got silence, 'You call her, Jim.'

And Jim called, leaning over into the little crater so as to

519

put his face as close to the roof of the shelter as he could. 'Peggy! Peggy! Are you there? Peggy!'

But there was no answer. Not a sound.

'Try again,' Mr Goodall said.

'Peggy! Peg! Say something! Peg!' He was groaning with the agony of no reply. 'Peggy, please!'

Joan was beside him, leaning into the pit. 'Someone get me a stick,' she said. 'Perhaps she's too weak to call. Come on, quick, some of yer. A stick, a pole, something to bang with.'

She was handed a piece of guttering. 'Now,' she said. 'Keep quiet.'

And she leant into the pit and knocked on the roof of the shelter, once, twice, three times, the way they'd signalled to one another through the bedroom walls all those years ago in Tillingbourne.

There was no answer.

'Knock again,' Jim said.

She knocked again, once, twice, three times. And they listened again, holding their breath, hoping against hope.

And a small faint knocking answered them. Once, twice, three times.

'She's there!' Jim whooped. 'She's there.'

'Get down out of it quick then,' Mr Goodall said. 'The sooner we get her out the better.' She'd been buried for far too long, and time and oxygen were running out.

The three of them stood in the street and watched as the rescue teams hauled away the last obstructions, clearing part of a wall, more and more bricks, and finally revealing a section of the roof, which lay aslant the shelter, crushing one corner. Lifting equipment was hauled into position as they watched, praying and hoping.

'Once that's out the way we shall see where she is,' Mr MacFarlane promised them. 'Wait a wee while.'

It was for ever, standing in the dust, not daring to hope, hardly daring to breathe, as the rescue teams hauled and dug. Please don't let her be dead. Let it be her who was knocking.

One of the men was waving. 'Now,' Mr MacFarlane said. And he led the way across the rubble.

As Jim climbed he could see that the edge of the

Morrison was jutting up from underneath the bricks. It was buckled but intact.

'Is she there?' he begged, falling onto his knees among the broken bricks, peering down into the hole they'd made.

There was something in the shelter. He could see a shape, a torn shirt, part of an arm, and the roughened fur of a tabby cat lying under the arm. 'Peggy!' he called. 'Peggy! Are you there?'

They were jacking up the top of the shelter. 'Peggy! Peggy!' Lifting out the cat, which hung between its rescuer's hands, damp and swearing.

'Let me go down,' he begged. 'Please let me get her out.' Whatever state she was in, dead or alive, he had to be the one to get her out.

They made way for him, glancing at the leader of the rescue team for his agreement. And so he was lowered into the shelter.

She was lying on her side as if she was asleep, and there was blood streaking her shoulder and congealed on her hands. 'Peggy,' he said, and he put out his hand fearfully to touch her face. And her face was warm.

'She's alive,' he called. 'She's still alive. Thank God.' And warmth flooded his own face and spread into his chest and down his arms. She was alive.

She opened her eyes and looked at him, exactly as she'd done so many times early in the morning waking to a new day. 'Jim?' she said. 'Oh Jim. Is it you?'

He was lifting her up, holding her in his arms like a baby. Her left arm was hanging limply and her shoulder was out of alignment so something was broken. But she was alive. She would heal. Hands reached into the hole to help them both out. And then he was carrying her into the light of day and the good fresh air.

'I'll come with you,' she said weakly. 'To the house. I should've said. You were right.'

'Hush, hush,' he soothed, kissing her dusty hair. 'It doesn't matter.' Nothing mattered now that she was alive. That was the important thing. 'Oh Peg, I love you so much.'

She leant her head against his chest as he climbed carefully down the rubble towards the waiting ambulance. 'I'll come to the house,' she said, 'I mean it. I should've said so yesterday. I love you more than anything.'

'I know,' he said. And he did know. They both knew. The bomb had stripped them of every emotion except love. 'Save your strength, my little love,' he said. 'First we'll get you over this. Then we'll go to the house. I promise. We'll go as soon as ever we can. Everything'll be all right. You'll see. We've got a new world to build.'